To the Citizens of South Salem

with best wishes

Dick Davidson
and
Helen Davidson

Prelude, A Novel
&
The 1854 Diary of Adeline Elizabeth Hoe

Daguerreotype of the young Adeline Elizabeth Hoe. *(© Peter E. Randall.)*

Prelude, A Novel

By Helen Taylor Davidson

&

The 1854 Diary of Adeline Elizabeth Hoe

Edited by Richard Davidson and Helen Taylor Davidson

Peter E. Randall Publisher
Portsmouth, New Hampshire
2013

Copyright © 2012 by Helen Taylor Davidson
All Rights Reserved

Produced by
Peter E. Randall Publisher
Box 4726
Portsmouth, NH 03802
www.perpublisher.com

ISBN: 978-1-931807-80-7
Library of Congress Control Number: 2012950926

For more information visit: http://perpublisher.com/per158.html

Book design by Ed Stevens, www.edstevensdesign.com

CONTENTS

Preface vii

Acknowledgements. ix

Prelude, A Novel 1

Foreword to the Diary 201

The 1854 Diary of Adeline Elizabeth Hoe 203

Diary Endnotes. 257

Selected Bibliography. 285

Author's Biography. 286

A page of Adeline Elizabeth Hoe's diary in her ornate, nineteenth-century hand. (© Peter E. Randall.)

PREFACE

I never knew my father's mother, Grace Lawrence Taylor, who was a concert pianist and who died in 1940, six years before I was born. As the last living of the six children of Adeline Elizabeth Hoe Lawrence, Grandmother Taylor inherited her mother's diary and entrusted it to my mother, Edith Howard Taylor. Forty years later she passed the heirloom on to me. A worn volume containing 120 pages of fine script, written by Great-Grandmother Addie in 1854, it lay stowed in a desk while my husband and I taught school and raised our children.

Upon retiring, we moved back to New Hampshire into the house where I grew up and that Grandmother Taylor and her sister had built as maiden ladies in 1896. Then under the spell of family history, we examined the journal which we became inspired to transcribe and annotate. Each day brought a puzzling reference to solve, an unintelligible word to master, or a name to identify as we delved into Addie's daily life.

When we finished our task, questions still nagged to be answered, even though we had sorted out her feathery penmanship and researched the period. I began to imagine a subtext for Great-Grandmother's entries and repaired to the parlor to write *Prelude*. I sat down to write near where Addie's volumes of dance music reside in Grandmother's music cabinet and across the room from the grand piano where her Steinway sat over a hundred years ago.

Writing the novel became a way to envision the relationships that appeared enigmatic in the diary, the scope and meaning of which Adeline treats with reserve and modesty. For example, what assumptions underlay her remark at the end of her uncle's wedding day? "Thomas and Mary were very cool," she wrote. Certainly she did not mean "cool" as "trendy" or "flashy" in modern parlance. She expressed restraint, self-control, and perhaps a quiet assurance, values often discredited today. Imagining a way into her thoughts through fiction allowed me a path into the mind and heart of a young girl living before the Civil War, someone whose treasuring of experience allows history to come alive.

Helen Taylor Davidson
Plainfield, New Hampshire
March 16, 2012

ACKNOWLEDGEMENTS

We are very grateful to many, many people. To all of you who somehow understood how much fulfillment we found in reading Adeline's journal—the force of her brave and cheerful voice, the window her journal opened to views of family and history—your kind enthusiasm was sustaining, and we thank you.

To Peter Hoe Burling, Adeline's great-grandson, thank you for your interest and the many helpful insights and suggestions.

David Fairbanks Taylor, another great grandson—you are encyclopedic on family history, and your fundamental impulse is always to share and help. You too, Susan.

Our gratitude to Samantha Davidson Green, fierce and skilled pilot, who somehow managed to fit into your demanding days the task of being our chauffeur and guide out to Setauket.

And to all our other children, who so enthusiastically cheered us on.

We are grateful to George Martin, scholar, biographer, and now our friend. You helped us early on with wise counsel, and your book on CCB informed and inspired us.

Thank you to Dr. William Ayres, chief curator of the Long Island Museum in Stony Brook, and to your colleague and assistant, Christa Zaros.

We are grateful to Sarah Stewart Taylor (Adeline's great-great-granddaughter) for enthusiasm and good advice, not to mention her assistance in unclasping the mystery of Limherr's breast pin.

Finally, reverent gratitude to Adeline's daughter, Grace Lawrence Taylor, for keeping and protecting the journal, and then entrusting it to her daughter-in-law, Edith Howard Taylor, for care and safe keeping until it was time to pass it on to Helen Taylor Davidson and the rest of the marvelous circle of family and friends.

Prelude, A Novel

CHAPTER ONE

In the gathering darkness of a May evening, the blowing mist from the Delaware obscured the sign outside the Blue Anchor, an inn established by Quakers in the early days of Philadelphia. "Stay hidden," said the driver, Joe Stewart, in muffled tones, directing his warning to a canvas-covered lump in the rear of the wagon. He peered up and down Dock Street to get his bearings, secured the horse's reins, and made his way inside the tavern.

The dim interior contained a host of men conversing over mugs of ale, some at the bar, some on high-backed settles by the open fireplaces at either end of the tavern, and some gathered at the rough tables scattered about the cavernous room. Some, the young driver knew, were friends, that is, Friends, or Quakers. Amid the motley mix, others were not, and some might be foes.

Edging his way through the crowd of men ending their day in lively conversation, Joe approached the bar. Those working behind the oak slab were men he knew he could trust. In Philadelphia, barkeeps were Quakers.

"Is this where I might find Elihu Pierce?" he asked an old man with grizzled whiskers and a huge strawberry birthmark that engulfed his forehead and right cheek. Without turning, the aged man continued to draw ale from a cask and made no answer. When he turned to face him, again and more loudly Joe repeated his question. It was clear that the man was nearly deaf.

"Aye, Elihu is bringing new beer into the cellar. I believe he'll likely return straightaway," he responded testily, and then he returned to his task.

Joe removed his wet and dripping top hat, and slid onto a barstool. He realized, dressed as he was in greatcoat and top hat, he differed noticeably from the dockworkers and farmhands enjoying their pints. The tobacco smoke from men cradling clay pipes, combined with the wood smoke from the fireplaces, created a stifling haze. He hoped the Quaker would not be long. He did not want to draw any more attention to himself, to answer questions, or to have to fabricate a reason for his presence.

Alone in the parlor Addie finished dusting the piano and pulled the heavy velvet drapes aside. The wide expanse of Broadway before her afforded little to hold her attention. The 5 a.m. cars had passed through, wheels and harnesses creaking as the huge cart horses pulled the loads of servants and working men to their places of employment.

It was a scant five days before the whole house would be stored for the summer. Furniture would be removed to the attic, carpets beaten, and light fixtures stored. School was over for the year; no more Latin, French, or mathematics; and piano lessons were suspended until fall. Her older sister was through with school, "finished for good," while Addie was not quite varnished. She needed another layer of learning.

At eighteen, she would be ready for the dash to find a suitable mate and then marry, as her father and stepmother would expect of her. All of these details of her life as a seventeen-year-old in 1854 in New York City meant little to her on this morning. She fed her baby half-sister's pet canary. Carefully she carried the cage to the kitchen where the cook, Tilda, was preparing tea. They each were absorbed in the routine and barely greeted one another. After adding water and seeds to the tiny receptacles in the cage, Addie retreated to the front room to wait for the rest of the family to appear for breakfast.

The street was noisier now with carriages hasting past and drovers herding their livestock downtown. Addie sat down at the desk near the window. Taking pen and ink from the drawer, she set about to write to her friend Retta in Cream Ridge. In happy anticipation, she wrote of her pleasure at being invited to the Stewarts', where there was always a stream of visitors and lively conversation. She paused, wondering how long her family might stay in the brownstone on Broadway. Ma, her stepmother, was expecting again. Already there were two baby girls: Annie, two years old, and Mary, an infant. Father would not want to give up his billiard room on the third floor for bedrooms. No, there might be the need to move soon. In any case, Addie could not wait to travel to New Jersey and several other summer destinations. Making plans to travel without parents would be a novel experience. June couldn't arrive fast enough.

Sealing the letter, she placed it on a plate in the foyer. As she returned to the parlor, both her father and sister Emilie appeared, ready for the day. Soon after breakfast, her father would leave for the printing press factory, where he would remain until the late evening. When the family carriage arrived with Uncle Robert inside, the carriage driver rang for Father. After hearty halloos, they were off for Broome Street.

Emilie and Addie both donned aprons after clearing the table and spent an hour cleaning their closets, carrying winter clothing first to sun in the yard and then to be stored in the armoire in the garret. The tedious job, up and down the stairs, went quickly as the girls discussed their upcoming trips. Later they sewed in the parlor. There was a pile of mending to do, and since childhood they had always worked at projects creating embroidery or sewing a garment. This particular morning Emilie read aloud *Katherine Ashton* while Addie completed a petticoat.

CHAPTER ONE

The young women were the older daughters of Richard March Hoe, whose wife died when they were ages six and eight. After two years as a widower, he married Mary Say Corbin from Philadelphia, a physician's daughter only seventeen years older than Emilie.

"When do you expect we should go to sit for the daguerrean?" Addie inquired, snipping a thread.

"Ma made the appointment for next Tuesday, the day before we leave for Setauket."

"Let's ask Ellen to help arrange our hair on Monday. I need curls to give my face some character, don't you think?"

"Bah, your face is your face, but it won't hurt to look our best. A daguerreotype, after all, is as good as a painted portrait."

"We shall see."

"Good morning, girls."

"Ma, it's nearly noon. Are you well?"

"It was a terrible night. Mary would not nurse and cried. I never slept." Their stepmother, lovely under ordinary circumstances, looked haggard with dark circles under her eyes. Her thick brown hair was hastily caught up in a chignon with several locks escaping. She wore a blue woolen dressing gown, loosely tied.

Addie rose from the couch and volunteered to head upstairs to take over Mary's care.

"No, you're very kind, but she's finally drifted off to sleep. Today I plan to find a wet nurse. Perhaps Tilda or Ellen knows of someone."

From down the street, voices of vendors distracted the girls from their tasks. Suddenly Emilie remembered that her favorite teacher, Miss Clarke, would be coming to tea.

"Addie, come with me to Limherr's, will you? I need to pick up the breast pin I had them make of my hair for Miss Clarke. How I shall miss her now that I'm all through school. I'm glad you have another year there so you can tell me how she is."

Looking out at the street, Addie noted several cars waiting at the carriage stop nearby, while the horses nibbled at the tree branches near the curb.

"We'll have to hurry."

Taking off their aprons, grabbing their reticules and bonnets, the young women dashed to the kitchen to tell Ma where they were going and then rushed out the door.

One of the horse-drawn cars had left, but one remained, not half full. Breathing rapidly and still fastening their bonnets, the girls began to climb on. Then Emilie looked in and noted the sign on the side, "Colored People Only." Faces gazed out at them, some soberly, a few smiling.

"Let's walk," Addie suggested. "It's only three blocks."

Skirting debris and horse buns at the side of the street, they held their long dresses at ankle height and found their way to the store. Emilie examined the finished breast pin, fashioned of gold and woven with strands of her own hair. Deeming it perfect, she paid the dapper young clerk. Meanwhile, Addie looked about the shop and admired the elegant, custom-made jewelry in glass cases.

The May sunshine made the return trip warm. Emilie hoped to present her gift immediately and to deliver it herself to her friend. Addie urged her to wait and reminded her there was much to be done at home. They rode back in a car and arrived to find Joe Stewart on the front steps.

Joe was Father's good friend, yes, and he was more than a billiard player, although he often spent the evening at their house with cue in hand. Joe was a buyer and merchant tailor at A. T. Stewart's Store downtown. He traveled often, but when in town he spent time with the Hoe family. Ten years older than Addie, Joe was a loyal confidant of both girls.

"How are the young ladies this fine afternoon?"

"We are well." Emilie unlocked the front door for him and he held it wide for both girls to pass.

"And the family?"

"Annie is fussy, and Mary, as you know, has the measles."

"That's a shame. Is your father in?"

"It's not likely," Addie said. "Have you eaten?"

"Yes, and you?"

"No, come join us for tea."

The girls removed their bonnets. Joe stretched his legs and loosened his cravat as he sank onto the sofa. Of medium height and with dark hair and eyes, he was handsome, self-effacing, and at home anywhere.

"Now, tell me if there is anything I can do to help. Your father mentioned he had a meeting about the telegraph and asked me to attend with him, but it won't happen until this evening."

"We are packing up the house. Painters will come next week. Roux and his men have been engaged for the redecoration. Let me see; you could help us take up the stair rods and roll up the carpet."

"Gladly," he replied.

They embarked on the task, beginning on the attic stairs. As Addie and Emilie removed the stair rods, Joe slowly loosened the carpet, pulled the runners down the staircases, and rolled them up, readying them to be taken to the back yard and beaten later. The girls stowed the heavy rods in the garret.

"Now, about the tea?" he reminded them.

CHAPTER ONE

In the dining room over shortbread and tea, the girls voiced their eagerness to visit Joe's sisters across the Hudson in Cream Ridge. What should they expect, what should they bring, who would be there? In addition to seeing Retta, Lydia, Charlie, and the elder Stewarts, they planned to travel on to Delaware City to visit Joe's older sister, Ann Reybold.

"How will we get to Delaware City?"

"Major Reybold," he said mysteriously.

"What do you mean? Who is he? Does he own a ketch or a schooner?" He so aroused their curiosity that their cheeks flushed with excitement.

"You will find that the *Major Reybold* is a steamboat named for Ann's father-in-law. It will take you from Philadelphia to Delaware City."

"Will you be there?" Addie asked.

"Part of the time."

Recalling a forgotten appointment, Joe drew his pocket watch from his vest. He rose and, making a hasty farewell, he left, promising to return later.

The girls filled the time until supper imagining the weeks ahead. They moved the furniture and, with Ellen's help, rolled up the carpets on the first floor. There were still the linens to be packed away and dishes and silverware to stow. The renovations required that all their possessions be out of the way.

"Did you look in on Ma? She must be resting. Neither she nor Mary nor Annie have made a peep."

Just then, Ma appeared on the landing, fully dressed and ready to go out. Although it was spring and a very warm afternoon, she was wearing her cape. Addie called up to her, "Where are you going?"

"To find a wet nurse."

"Oh no, you mustn't go by yourself. Father will find someone. You'll wear yourself out. Wait until he comes home, please."

In the morning Father would rush off to the factory, rarely taking time to comb his hair, and then, in the evenings, after a supper that often had to be re-heated or served cold, he either relaxed with friends at billiards or was off to a meeting of one of several organizations. One of them was the American Telegraph Society. If he stayed late, looking out for the printing press apprentices who remained at the factory at the end of the day, Father likely would share with them a meal that the company provided before their evening classes.

Joe returned at seven o'clock and, finding that Father still had not come home, he invited Emilie and Addie to join him for ice cream. The stroll to the café was pleasant, with the sun setting in the west and flights of pigeons silhouetted against the fading orange sky and seeking refuge for the night. They sat outside at tables to which identically clad waitresses brought their order.

Joe seemed preoccupied, Addie reflected, probably disappointed that Father was not available for their customary game of billiards.

"I won't see you again until I see you in Cream Ridge," he began. "I have some work in Philadelphia in the interim."

"We understand, don't we, Addie?" Emilie reassured him. Traveling by the cars, a ferry, and railroad would mean keeping alert, but the two young women were confident, anticipating the journey.

"Will we see you race while we are with Retta?"

"I hope there will be time for that. I understand there is a new filly with promise that my brother has been training."

Cooler after having enjoyed the novelty of strawberry ice cream at the end of a very warm spring day, the girls thanked Joe for his kindness, and they all proceeded to 309 Broadway.

Father was at home at last after a long day and held little Annie in his arms as he gathered his wits in the parlor. He greeted Joe cheerfully and, although it was nearly eight o'clock, he was ready to head for the telegraph meeting.

"While dining with Ma," he said, "I agreed to find a wet nurse, since her efforts proved fruitless earlier today. Girls, we must all give her help." He looked at their kind, eager faces and added, "But, of course, I know you have and you will."

Father was handsome in a robust, tousled way, with a cleft in his chin, merry blue eyes, and graying brown hair. He found time to question the older girls about their lives and treated them as gems in his crown.

CHAPTER TWO

Ellen came upstairs early Monday morning to wash Addie's hair and tie her locks in rags to produce sausage curls, which were all the fashion among New York's young ladies. First, she poured warm water from a ewer into a basin, and, while Addie bent over it, Ellen repeatedly soaked her long auburn hair and rubbed in scented soap. After a final rinse in cider vinegar and a brushing out, Addie's hair hung lank about her face. Then she sat quietly as the slender housemaid with skillful, work-reddened hands turned her head into a wet rag mop of knots. Aged by worry beyond her twenty-five years, Ellen lived in Williamsburgh, across the East River. As she worked, Ellen answered Addie's inquiries about her family and told Addie about her struggle to make her children behave, a task doubly difficult because her baby was ill. Her life since coming to America had not been easy. Arranging hair was a pleasant respite from her two jobs as mother and housemaid.

Addie had always felt compassion for Ellen and tried to lighten her burden when she could. The housework at 309 Broadway was shared by the servants, Ellen and Tilda, as well as Addie, Emilie, and their stepmother. Cooking, tending the babies, sewing, and cleaning filled each day; and then there were beds to make, linens to wash, fires to tend, and clothes to iron and mend—tasks were unending.

Nevertheless, Addie found time for playing the piano. She felt grateful that Father encouraged her and had bought her a fine Nunns and Clark square piano. Not a day passed that she or Emilie did not play or try out a new dance step when housework was done. They tried them all: waltzes, quadrilles, galops, mazurkas, and polkas. When Father came home, it was easy to know where he was, because he whistled. Whether arias or themes from symphonies, if the tune was catchy or beautiful, they knew he would whistle it into life.

The Hoe girls attended school, when in session, just two blocks away on Broadway. Miss Clarke, the headmistress, taught French, literature, and Latin; while Mr. Williams taught mathematics, not Addie's favorite subject, and history. Miss Wingate taught piano, penmanship, and drawing.

By late afternoon, Addie's hair was dry, and she ventured forth from her room to ask Ellen to comb it out, as she had done for Emilie. The ringlets hung evenly on each side of her face, with a center part. She looked in the hall mirror, and, although she still found herself plain, she appreciated Ellen's efforts and looked forward to going to Martin Lawrence's. How would she keep the curls overnight so as to be presentable for the daguerrean?

Addie was skeptical from the moment she heard about daguerreotypes. Would they replace painted portraits? The examples that she had seen in the homes of friends, when they went calling, were small brown and black representations of faces. Mrs. Condit was very proud of theirs and the fact that her children behaved tolerably during the process. Sarah Kenney reported that the daguerrean's parlors were exquisite and more than made up for the tedium of the picture-taking itself. "Of course," she added, "Matthew Brady is superior to a hundred other daguerreans."

When the girls had finally agreed on which dress to wear for the session at Mr. Martin Lawrence's, they rode there by omnibus after carefully tying their bonnets so as not to disarrange their hair. Ushered to the top floor to the operating room, as the daguerrean's studio was called, they met Mr. Lawrence, a huge man with a black moustache. He bid them to sit in a velvet chair. "Stay very still, my dears," he urged them in a sinuous, cajoling voice. Then he retreated to the camera several feet away and sequestered himself under a black cloth. A glaring lantern illuminated Addie's face. An eternity passed while she stared at the great, black lump of camera and operator. The picture-taking made her feel uncomfortable and naked. An itch developed over her right eye, yet she dared not move. Four minutes passed, five, it seemed. At last, Mr. Lawrence emerged and announced that she might relax. It was finished. When the chemical developing was complete, the girls would be able to view themselves.

They returned home somewhat disillusioned after their grand expectations of the visit to the daguerrean's studio and by the reality of sitting stock still, not allowed to move a muscle. Ellen eagerly asked about how it had all gone and laughed when Addie said they now knew how it felt to be a statue.

In the remaining days before the Hoe girls' summer jaunts, the house became less and less livable. The parlor made an excellent dance hall since the only object remaining in it was the piano. Afternoons Addie and Emilie devoted to calling on friends they would not see again for several months: the Westervelts, the Condits, and the Bowens. There was the hazy, hot afternoon Miss Clarke came for tea. They were forced to entertain her in the kitchen. Emilie greeted her effusively at the front door, taking her parasol and bonnet. With their schoolmistress were the Kenney girls, Sarah and Julia, contemporaries of Addie and Emilie. Conversation flowed, although the sponge cake had sunk and the milk for the tea was sour.

Addie was aware of the bond Emilie formed at school with Miss Clarke, a model of correctness and elegant poise, who spoke beautifully and was raised in London. It was she who recommended *Katherine Ashton*, Miss Sewell's novel about an English girls' school and with a moral tone generally admired. Addie preferred Dickens' stories herself.

Although she was only ten years their senior, Miss Clarke could never be "Evelina" to them, although that was her given name. She spoke soberly about social issues and reminded the girls to refrain from idle gossip and endeavor to study. When Emilie produced her gift of the breast pin, Miss Clarke, a tall woman with erect posture and beautiful in a dignified, statuesque way, responded with a blush of surprise. Emilie, ever the demonstrative sort and earnest to a fault, declared, "Miss Clarke, you are the perfect lady, and I shall always cherish the years I have spent in your school."

One would have thought so perfect a lady would have been accustomed to such adulation, but Miss Clarke seemed genuinely surprised and touched, and as she rose to leave, she smiled and took Emilie's hand. The Kenneys and Addie were an audience that responded following Emilie's presentation of her gift with a flood of chatter about the holidays; all of the younger girls well aware that September would draw them back to school before they knew it.

During the final evening at the brownstone on Broadway, cousins Theodore and Henry came to visit, and while Addie played songs at the piano, Emilie and the boys sang. Since they would see Henry in New Jersey in July, they pressed him to tell about his plans while they would be visiting the Stewarts. Cousin Robbie joined them before the evening was over.

The next day, Father and Ma packed their and the baby girls' luggage for their trip to Philadelphia to coincide with the older girls' holidays. Annie's measles were over, and it was decided that the wet nurse for Mary would bring her own baby to travel with the family.

The empty house awaited the workmen from Roux to redecorate, undoubtedly a good thing. But for Addie its vacant, bare windows foretold bigger changes to come for the family of the ever-striving and successful maker of printing presses. The street was changing. Citizens were moving north. Shops and businesses sprang up overnight. The Gothic building next door was almost the only place that was not a tradesman's shop. For Addie, it was a pleasure to visit A. T. Stewart's Department Store and wander through the displays of kid gloves from Spain, fox fur coats from Russia, and French laces.

CHAPTER THREE

"Where did you take them?" Elihu Pierce asked when Joe and his contact met outside the Blue Anchor in the alley. Somber and deliberate, the barkeep confessed he had been so heartsick that he had left the tavern without a by-your-leave. "I went home to my family when Willa brought word that my wife was about to deliver. You must have come after I left."

"No matter. I had to think of something, so I took them to the boarding house where my brother and I stay when we have business in the city. It meant that the parents had to quiet the little ones lest the landlady raise questions I could not answer. Early the next day, the man from Erie arrived, as you had planned. When the slave family and I returned to the Blue Anchor, the fellow was outside, humming a tune. He pointed to the back of the wagon and told me he was headed for Erie."

The devout and conscientious Quaker Elihu only briefly registered relief. "Nevertheless, you took a chance, since you didn't know that man at all. He might have been the wrong man, someone who had overheard my arranging your connection. We can't be too careful."

Apart from the crowd off Dock Street, the men spoke quietly and then walked toward the waterfront. Joe looked out across the Delaware and observed a steamboat approaching from New Jersey and the attendant flurry of activity as travelers and dock workers prepared for the boat to come alongside the wharf. Elihu and he listened to the wail of the whistle.

"I'm aware of the danger. When next we meet, I'll make certain that you and I speak face to face before I turn over anybody to anyone."

Having been reassured, Elihu faced Joe. The older man gravely shook his hand, turned, and walked back into the Blue Anchor. Joe pondered the mechanics of conveying dark-skinned travelers. How could he perform his clandestine task better? How might he and other conductors reduce the risks of meeting money-hungry slave hunters?

Once across the East River, Emilie and Addie bade farewell to Father's coachman, who had accompanied them on the ferryboat. They made their way through the crowd of early morning travelers and found an omnibus headed for the railroad depot. Clutching their valises in one hand and gathering their voluminous skirts with the other, they reminded one another to have the fare in hand for the ride to Setauket.

The steam locomotive hissed outside the depot as Addie and Emilie mounted the sole passenger car headed east out of Brooklyn. After taking their tickets, the conductor informed them they had a wide choice of seats and that front seats were often preferred. When Addie asked why the front seats were best, the conductor, a brisk fellow with a handlebar moustache, replied, "The least cinders."

Before school ended, Maria Seabury, Addie's school friend, had invited both sisters to visit her family for a week in June on the north shore of Long Island in Stony Brook and Setauket. Unlike Addie and Emilie, who walked a few blocks on Broadway from home to Miss Clarke's, Maria boarded with her uncle Samuel each term in the city and returned home only for vacation. The Hoe girls wondered how it would be to live among painters—not house painters, but artists. All of Maria's uncles were artists, Addie had heard. Maria told her that her uncle William Mount had indeed once painted her portrait when she was twelve. He asked her to feign being asleep, which was tedious because she had not been in the least sleepy. Addie surmised that that would be more tiresome than sitting for the daguerrean.

As the whistle blew to warn passengers of the train's imminent departure, three more people entered the car and gave tickets to the conductor: an elderly gentleman with a cane and two young Negro women, who, like the girls, carried bags as though on holiday. The old man sat just behind Addie, and the women found seats in the middle of the car. Both were well dressed and wore agreeable expressions. Soon the train lurched forward and they were off.

Looking out of the open window, the girls watched the countryside change from Brooklyn's growing metropolis with businesses and warehouses to the verdant fields to the east on Long Island with its orchards and farms where men were haying and cows dotted the rolling hills. They longed to catch glimpses of the sea, but the railway lay inland.

Emilie wondered what sorts of social gatherings there would be and if she had brought the right dresses for the occasion. The dressmaker, Mary Robbins, had spent a week at 309 Broadway assisted by Ellen in making summer dresses for both girls in time for the trip.

Addie expected the situation to be similar to what would happen in South Salem, where they visited their grandparents. They would be invited to tea and attend church services, and they might sometimes dine with neighbors. She hoped there might be dancing, which they enjoyed with cousins and friends.

When the train stopped at various towns during the six-hour ride, the passengers, with the exception of the elderly gentleman, rose to stretch their legs and smooth their gowns. Addie nodded to one of the Negro women, whom she felt she had seen somewhere, perhaps walking on Broadway.

Finally in mid-afternoon, the train puffed into Stony Brook Station. Maria's father, Charles Seabury, was there to meet the girls and amiably offered a hand with their bags. The ride by open carriage on the dusty, rutted roads to their home meant both Addie and Emilie were tired when they arrived. Maria ran from the house to greet them, giving them each an embrace. Both of her parents kindly urged them to rest before tea. Maria, her long, dark hair hanging free, appeared healthy and cheerful, already benefiting from the summer sunshine. She treated the girls always as sisters, invited them to arise early the next day for a walk, and told them of her favorite haunts that they must visit. Her mother, Ruth Mount Seabury, sister of the painters, hoped they would play the piano. Addie asked if they might meet the Nunns sisters, whom Maria often had mentioned, and see their father's piano factory, where the Hoes' piano originated. There were so many plans for so few days.

Early the next morning at dawn, Maria nudged each of her visitors and whispered, "Let's take a walk in the fields." Addie, still stiff from the long train and carriage trip, stretched and opened her eyes. The sun was only peeping over the eastern hills without a cloud anywhere. She arose and dressed for an introduction to the new locale; Emilie chose to sleep longer.

The grass was wet with dew and the birds sang all around them unfamiliar songs. Although employed by the piano factory not far from home, Maria's father also tended his farm. In the barn behind the rambling farmhouse, he kept several cows, a few sheep, chickens, a prize boar, and three sows. Already he was letting the cows drink at the water tub before milking. Maria took Addie to see the lambs in the field nearby.

As the sun rose higher and they continued beyond the farmstead, sudden views of Long Island Sound made each turn in the path more exciting. Maria took her to an ancient graveyard on their property. Wildflowers bloomed among the stones, many of them covered with moss and lichen. Pushing a spray of daisies aside, Maria drew Addie's attention to a brown stone with a very long inscription. At the top was a fiddle carved in it. Together they read the inspiring tribute to one of Maria's grandmother's slaves, who had been a marvelous fiddler.

"Did you know this man?"

"No, note the date he died: 1816, long before I was born. But I wanted you to know how he was and is still thought of here. He established a tradition of fiddle-playing, as you shall hear."

The peace in that place and the obvious esteem in which the slave was held reminded Addie of something Father had said when she and Emilie had asked permission to travel to Maria's. "No more respect for human dignity and an

CHAPTER THREE

individual's worth will you find than with the Hawkins, Mounts, and Seaburys." Their slaves had been free for years before New York abolished slavery in 1828.

Maria and Addie climbed a stone wall and on the other side was a sandy path leading down to the bay. They strolled along the strand and were amused by the sandpipers skittering along before them. White egrets waded in the marshes, and gulls soared and screamed, surveying the shore for a meal.

Over breakfast, Addie exclaimed over all she had witnessed so far, regaling Emilie, the sleepyhead, whose dress was not soaked with dew, but who vowed to walk later. Afterward all three girls busied themselves with sewing in the Seaburys' parlor and discussed meeting the families in the neighborhood.

Before the day was out, they visited the piano factory. The Hoes marveled at the magnificent array of beautiful woods used in building a Nunns and Clark piano. They met a craftsman named Steinway, who showed them the painstaking work involved in building the mechanism and described the vast effort to make each piano as beautiful in appearance as in tone.

The next day, Maria woke the girls early again. She retraced with them the route of the previous day, new to Emilie but no less interesting to Addie, and all of them were enlivened by the salt air and pleasant weather.

On the return to the Seaburys', Maria led the visitors to her Uncle William's studio, a barn with a north-facing skylight. She knocked at the wide door, warning them quietly, "We never know if William is in or out." And after a considerable pause, the huge barn door slid slowly open. The handsome William Sidney Mount, clearly not expecting company, stood before them, tall, with uncombed black hair. They were struck by his blue eyes, abstracted at first, then brightening in recognition of his niece. He proffered his hand to her two friends. Shyly self-aware, they gave him theirs.

"So, the saucy school maids have come for a visit." He stepped back as he spoke, inviting them in with a sweep of his hand. "Come see the statesman Daniel Webster. Do you know him, ladies? I have been struggling to make a picture of him as he was when he was alive, that is, a man of the people. Alas, I think I have made him look a tyrant. What do you think?"

After a pause, Addie spoke up in awe. "I think you have made a very fair likeness of the statesman, from what I have seen of him in the papers."

"Ah, but what you have probably seen are caricatures that exaggerate qualities a man has. They cannot do justice to the totality of the person."

Addie was silent. Emilie asked what else was he painting or planning to paint. He answered, cryptically, he couldn't be sure. Maria knew that sort of answer meant their visit had been long enough. It was time for a retreat.

Chagrined at her obtuse remark, Addie despaired that she had ventured a judgment so rashly. Neither Maria nor Emilie seemed in the least affected by their impromptu visit as they chattered about the new day's adventure.

There was a plan to drive east from Stony Brook to the village of Setauket, where the Mounts and Hawkins had made their home for generations. The girls asked Mr. Seabury if he would transport them. Maria wanted her visitors to meet her friends on the peninsula called "Old Fields." Carrie Strong, the Dominics, the Hamiltons, and the Morands—there were many people Maria had not seen since the beginning of the term, and she wanted the girls to meet them.

When Mr. Seabury went to harness the horse, he found the carriage was missing, possibly stolen, and he was obliged to take them in a farm wagon without springs, which gave them a bumpy ride. While they rode, he explained some of the history of Setauket, which had been the scene of intrigue during the revolution. Maria's grandparents on her mother's side kept a tavern pivotal to the gathering of information about the movements of the British. Addie and Emilie laughed to learn that the signal to the revolutionaries that the British were planning a move was for the barmaid to hang her laundry on the line. Depending on how it was arranged the Yankee generals could tell how to proceed. A spy ring gathered intelligence among British officers in New York City and traveled to Setauket in order to inform the rebels across the sound in Connecticut.

When the wagon reached Setauket village, Maria's father bid them farewell as he left them with Mrs. Nunns and her daughters, Sarah and Ellen, for the day and promised to return for them before tea and chore time. Addie found the Nunns both very pleasant young ladies and Emilie hoped they would see them often during their stay.

Maria suggested a stroll to Old Fields. After enjoying a picnic lunch, they walked to call on several homes. The day passed quickly and, although not all of those on whom they called were at home, the Hoe girls were gratified to be acquainted with Maria's circle of friends. They especially responded to the magnificent views of the sound, where the wind whipped up whitecaps under a sky of blue.

The next day was Sunday. Maria and the girls joined the rest of the Seabury family for the service at the Episcopal church in Setauket. In the afternoon, while rearranging her four-poster bed, Maria dropped one corner on her toe. It made her yowl like a cat, but she did not spend the afternoon complaining. Instead she suggested, since the weather had turned rainy and overcast, that while she and Emilie sewed, Addie might play the piano.

When Addie chose Chopin's somber Prelude in E Minor, appropriate for the mood that day, Ma Mount, Maria's aunt, brought out her violin and bow and doubled the melody beautifully. Addie wondered if the Negro man commemorated on the gravestone had been her teacher.

CHAPTER FOUR

Later in the evening, Addie wrote to Ma of their wanderings by the shore, meeting Mr. Mount and many of Maria's friends, and of the piano factory. The long walks were doing both sisters a world of good, she was sure. She noted that the sermon at the church in Setauket had been about abolition, a topic reaching even to the rural villages of Long Island.

When the hot June sun dried the grass the next day, and no more puddles dotted the roads, Maria and her schoolmates each took a novel to the woods to read. In the distance, Mr. Seabury's farmhands, a Negro and two young white men, cut the grass with scythes, each walking slowly behind the next, a swath's width away. The rhythm of their mowing was a hypnotic slow dance that lay flat the waist-high hay. Emilie asked Maria if she had ever been allowed to use a scythe or if she ever wanted to try it. She responded wryly that had she asked them, the men would have laughed, but if Emilie wanted to ask, perhaps they would allow it. "It takes skill to master mowing," Maria remarked curtly, and then she returned to *A Tale of Two Cities*.

Emilie was silent but continued to watch the haymakers. Addie lifted her eyes from the third of Cooper's *The Leatherstocking Tales* and suggested they wait to cut hay until they were obliged to help at their grandparents' farm later in the summer. "Until then, why not enjoy the holiday?" Emilie nodded, leaned back against a maple tree, and resumed reading *The Lamplighter*. The haymakers continued their paces, seemingly oblivious to the three young women whose white dimity dresses were spread wide about them at the edge of the woods.

Later in the afternoon, on the return from their respite by the field, the girls passed the Seabury barn and heard fiddle music. It was a toe-tapping jig, not at all Chopin. Coming around the corner, they spied the scythe men. One played the tune on the fiddle, while the others stepped lively in time on the barn floor. Not wanting to interrupt them, the three girls retreated and listened outside, hoping the music would go on. Then, realizing they were late for tea, they reluctantly drew away and returned to the house.

That evening the girls themselves danced polkas and waltzed while either Addie played the piano or Ma Mount played the fiddle. Maria's younger cousins and siblings joined in. The parlor curtains shook and the lampshades vibrated to the rhythms of young dancing feet.

CHAPTER FOUR

The final day at Stony Brook arrived. The sky threatened rain, yet after a day helping Maria's mother with ironing and returning the house to order after the previous evening's revels, the girls set out for a walk. Again they visited William Mount's studio and found him finishing a painting of a beautiful white lily. It was a rare thing, Maria said, as they admired the solitary, pristine flower contrasted against a somber olive background, that he should paint a still life. He made no explanation for his choice of subject, but instead he drew them aside to view some engravings. Addie wanted to ask him about them and why he preferred painting people, but, remembering her embarrassment over her glib remarks on their previous visit, she stayed silent. He sensed her reticence and pointedly asked, "Miss Hoe, have you enjoyed Stony Brook and Setauket?"

"Very much, sir."

"I hope you and Emilie will return."

"Thank you. I hope we will be welcome again," she said, looking at Maria, who smiled and gave her the glance signaling it was time to depart.

Addie turned to Mr. Mount as he pushed aside the heavy door and she ventured, "We are grateful that you allowed our interruptions of your work."

"The pleasure has been mine. Perhaps you will come to see some of my paintings in the city."

Departing by the grassy path, Maria gave her visitors an account of her uncle's will-o-the-wisp life: his never staying long in one place and seeking inspiration everywhere—from the sea, from the saloons in the city, and from the hayfields in the country. His brother Henry, who had died more than ten years before, was a painter of still lifes, while Shepherd and William tended to paint portraits. William painted scenes with people in them telling a story.

Addie and Emilie hoped they could see more of his work. When they reached the farmhouse, Maria showed them the portrait Uncle William had painted of her at twelve. Addie thought it a blissful picture. The painting hung in the dark front hall, so Maria lit a candle and held it close for the girls to see it better. Maria lay back on a dark couch, serenely at rest. The gown she wore was a soft shade of orange. Emilie remarked that it must be exciting to live among painters. Maria replied, "It is both exciting and daunting, because it is not an easy or dependable way to make a living."

CHAPTER FOUR

Addie considered her answer a moment, recalling their father's long days at R. Hoe and Company, his never-ending pursuit of a better-running printing press, and his search for a grade of steel good enough for the circular saw blade he patented. Whenever she or Emilie had voiced disappointment that he and Uncles Peter and Robert could not join them and their cousins for some lark, their stepmother would remind them of the importance of the work their father did and the cooperation it required.

Painting was a private passion individually pursued, lonely and often unremunerated enough for a living, even for a successful artist.

The humid air and resultant showers kept the sisters at Maria's all afternoon. They made use of the hours sewing, while Maria read *The Lamplighter* aloud. Later the Hoe sisters prepared their belongings for the next day's travels back to the city. Addie did not look forward to camping out in the empty house on Broadway with neither pleasing views nor bracing salt air.

Before nightfall Maria suggested one more walk by the shore and, despite the uncertain weather, they set out. As they approached the seashore and skirted a hedge of fragrant wild roses, they heard strains of music coming from the bay. Looking out, they saw a sailboat on which fiddlers and a bass violist played. There was also some sort of rhythm instrument. When they reached the beach, the boat came ashore and its occupants invited them aboard. One of the fiddlers, who was Edward, Maria's cousin, introduced them all around.

Immediately Addie recognized the two young women who rode the train with them to Setauket. The taller of the two stopped playing the violin long enough to be introduced as Elizabeth, whose friend Maude was not playing but simply enjoying the occasion. Mr. Mount was another of the fiddlers, revealing a different side of his artistic nature. A handsome Negro wearing a slouch hat, either Elizabeth's beau or a relative perhaps, was Horatio, who played what he called "the bones." He gave two of the carved whale bones to Emilie to examine. Taking her hand, he rose from his seat, invited her to sit down, and said, reaching behind her, "Allow me to show you." He placed each of the curved bones between her fingers. As the slippery bones fell to the deck, she said in a resigned tone, "I'm afraid my fingers are too feeble."

"You only need to try," he chuckled as he retrieved them and showed her how the movement of the bones by the middle three fingers against his palm made the sound.

"And practice, practice, practice," she responded, "as my piano teacher is always telling me."

"'Play, play, play' is what I prefer to say," jibed Mr. Mount. "Therein lies the pleasure."

When she was unable to coordinate them to create a sound, she gave the bones back to Horatio, who skillfully positioned them between his fingers and his palms and set the rhythm clicking for another lively piece. The strings players joined in, and, since it was a song the girls knew well, they sang along. Thus ensued a delightful musical interlude until the taut sails brought the boat across the bay. The sky was clear now, and a stiff breeze had come up. The final piece was a lilting sea chantey reminiscent of the whaling days in Setauket that Maria and her father had described during the girls' stay. As the sun was setting, a few pink clouds scudded along the horizon.

It was difficult to say goodbye the next day after what had been a delightful week. The entire Seabury family assembled on the porch. Maria's mother Ruth reminded them not to forget their novel or their sewing basket. Maria's younger brother and sister gave them warm embraces. Charles, Maria, and her older brother, Thomas, accompanied the girls to the depot. On the way, William Sidney Mount joined them. He carried his fiddle case and an enormous portfolio to the wagon. As he stowed them in the rear, he apologized for taking up too much space. Maria whispered to Addie that he had invented his own fiddle.

After more farewells at the train, Emilie, Addie, and Mr. Mount were on their way. He sat opposite them across the aisle and opened a notebook. Addie wasted no time. She asked him as the train picked up speed: "Maria said you invented your fiddle. Aren't violins made in a conventional way?"

Mr. Mount, his pencil poised to write, stopped regarding his notebook and answered, "I did invent mine. All violins are newly invented and the musical quality depends on what kind of wood one uses, the dimensions of the instrument, how thick the wood is, the shape of the peg box, and many other details." He began to jot something in his book.

"You appear to be writing music," Addie continued. "Are you inventing that, too?"

"I am writing a piece that actually imitates the trip we are taking on the train from start to finish."

"How I hope to hear you play it one day," she said. She turned to Emilie to report what she had heard, leaving Mr. Mount to his creative activity. The young ladies stared out at the escaping countryside and discussed little but how they would like to come back to Stony Brook and Setauket.

Suddenly the train lurched to a screaming, hissing halt. There was a pause until the conductor, who had hurried forward, returned from the front of the train to say that the engine had hit a cow on the track. While they waited for the poor cow to be removed and the engine to be repaired, they watched Mr. Mount continue his musical composition and, each girl finding her novel, commenced to read.

At one point Mr. Mount left his seat. The train again had stopped temporarily, and two men took his vacant seat next to the girls. They had been

CHAPTER FOUR

drinking, and in an Irish brogue boisterously attempted to engage Emilie and Addie in conversation. The young ladies ignored the strangers until the end of the trip. As they gathered their belongings, Mr. Mount found his way back to their seats and took both of their bags along with his own. Rising unsteadily, the Irishmen shouldered him aside and, tipping their hats to Emilie and Addie, made their way to the end of the car.

Mr. Mount apologized, "I'm sorry to have abandoned you. I wanted to listen to the final slowing down of the train, and I stood by the rail behind the engine."

Cousin Henry was there to greet them on the platform when at last the train arrived. He told them he had begun to be impatient when the train was late, and so they related the details of the accident and the delay. He asked if they received his letter. Did they have a pleasant week? Henry seemed to be flushed and shaky. Addie worried that he might be having another attack of the fever that he contracted on one of his trips down South. His business had taken him to Charleston and Natchez. Addie and Emilie thanked him for coming to meet them and accompanying them home.

The team of cart horses started north from the slip, pulling the omnibus toward home on Broadway. New York City seemed noisier and dirtier than she remembered. Refuse and horse dung were piled helter-skelter. Hawkers lined the street. Steam engines laboring in the factories puffed their ugly black smoke into the hot, gray sky, making a continuous din and noxious atmosphere.

Addie was relieved that it would only be a few days until they set out again. In the meantime, they would make do at home and see how the renovations had progressed.

CHAPTER FIVE

"What were you thinking, bringing the family here? There is barely room for us. Who slept on the floor? What did you give them to eat?"

Joe was packing to return from Philadelphia to New York City. He folded his good suit carefully while not answering his brother Charlie, just arrived from home in Cream Ridge. Joe brushed a shine on his leather riding boots and packed them in his bag, since he hoped to ride a horse in a race the next week.

"Did you finish your work for A. T. Stewart?"

"Well, yes, of course. Ordering material for the store didn't take long. That's easy compared with what happens on the side, as you well know." He left off packing long enough to recount the details of his latest venture transporting a family of escaping slaves.

"And if the contact you made at the Blue Anchor had been a slave catcher, your goose would have been cooked, and the poor family would be back in chains." Usually light-hearted, Charlie shook his head gravely at his brother's foolhardiness, barging ahead without a clear signal from Elihu.

Joe fixed his brother with a steely look. "What is the alternative? Yes, I take chances. But when a Negro family escapes the cotton fields to freedom…"

Charlie cut him off and held up his hand as if to appease his older brother. "Oh, granted, I know it's right. I only mean you've got to act carefully next time. Let Elihu be in charge."

"Do you truly agree with me, that risking our lives is the only way we can stop slavery? Fugitive Slave Act, or no Fugitive Slave Act?"

Charlie had always gone along with his brother's advice and schemes. There was the time, when they were in their teens, when they had climbed onto the railroad bridge to jump into the creek on a boiling hot July day. Joe led the way to the middle of the bridge, to the point where they could dive safely into the deepest part of the stream. Before they could reach it, a steam train came puffing into view. They jumped off the bridge safely just in the nick of time. As the cinders from the engine's smoke stack fizzled around them in the water, the boys swam for the shore, Charlie recalled, his pulse racing at the memory of that day.

Since Charlie seemed far away, Joe repeated his question. "Well, do you go along with me? Remember the summer we spent in Delaware? You can't have forgotten the beating one of Tony's neighbors gave that Negro boy our age—his nose bleeding, welts rising on his back."

Upon reaching home, a new maid, Bridget, Ellen's younger sister, greeted the girls and took their bags. She was glad for some company, as she was thoroughly tired of watching over the empty house with the residents away and workingmen coming and going, in and out.

"How was the country? You won't believe the changes," she volunteered, hanging up the young ladies' bonnets, "but there is no way to keep things tidy."

Addie and Emilie walked upstairs. They marveled at the newly painted billiard room and, on the second floor, their bedrooms, freshly painted and papered in pale pink roses.

While they were upstairs, the doorbell rang, and Bridget announced that a young man, a Mr. Mount, had come to see them. As they descended the stairs, Addie was mystified, since she would hardly have called Mr. Mount "young." He was older than Father, and also they had bid him farewell at the depot. However, pacing in the front parlor was William Shepherd Mount, two years younger than Addie and a quiet presence in Setauket while the Hoes were visiting. He told them he was in the city to help his uncle frame pictures, and he asked if he might see the house. The girls gave him a tour. He remarked on the excellent paneling in the billiard room.

Handsome like his uncle, who was his namesake, young William was stockier. He became more gregarious and was full of questions. He was curious about the girls' plans. At a lull in the conversation, he suddenly became aware that the girls might be exhausted from their day's travels and, with no place to sit down in the parlor, he took his leave, saying he hoped to see them again.

Later cousins Emmie Ely and Theodore came by to ask about their trip and join the girls in the kitchen for a modest supper that Bridget prepared for them. Father, Ma, and the babies were still away. Bread and cheese and tea were a sufficiency, all agreed. Joe Stewart came by and offered to bring ice cream, but the girls, very fatigued, begged him to come back the next day. And so the evening ended with the girls staying in the stuffy, third-floor guest room where the only beds remained.

Joe arrived late the next morning, cheerful and hoping the Hoe girls were preparing for their trip to Cream Ridge, New Jersey, across the Hudson. Indeed, Addie and Emilie, after rising early to beat the heat that later would make the house insufferable, and having washed and ironed their clothes, eagerly told him about their recent trip, the events still fresh in their minds. Addie recounted the visits to Mr. Mount's studio, described the richness in the colors of his oil paintings, and told of the violin he had invented. She asked Joe, who himself drew true likenesses whenever he found time, if he ever had seen any of Mr. Mount's work. He nodded and promised to take her to a gallery where there were several Mounts.

"Was there time for music? Was there a piano?" he wanted to know.

In a chorus the two girls answered, "Yes, indeed." They told of the fiddling. Emilie told of the farm hands jigging it up in the barn while they themselves hid out of sight.

"Ma Mount plays the violin, as do most of the younger children and William, the artist. The piano at the Seaburys' is never silent."

"But," Addie continued, "the high point of the week came on the final evening when we went with Maria on a walk near the bay. A sailboat floated in the distance, and we could hear music coming from it, beautiful instrumental music. The boat came ashore, and we were invited to come aboard. Several young Mounts, two Negro women, a fine violist Elizabeth and her friend Maude, both of whom we encountered on the train to Setauket, all played, including a young Negro man who showed Emilie how to play the bones."

"I was a poor player of the bones," Emilie interjected. "It looked easy when Horatio played them."

All the while Joe listened with interest, and then he remarked, "You tell of a harmonious atmosphere. Would that that were the case everywhere."

Addie studied his face. It was as if a cloud descended all of a sudden, and he looked away. What made that happen? she wondered.

Emilie changed the subject from the past to the future. She asked, "Would you tell us the details of the route to your family's house?"

There ensued Joe's well-thought-out plan for the trip to Cream Ridge, involving various modes of transportation.

"The sooner you leave the city, the better."

"What makes it urgent?" Addie wanted to know.

"Cholera is taking its toll in greater numbers with every passing day. There is talk that Mayor Westervelt plans to set up special hospitals for the victims if the epidemic doesn't abate. And there's little hope of that with the summer heat increasing each day."

Perhaps the cloud over Joe was caused by the fear of disease, Addie supposed. Even if they escaped to the quiet streets of rural New Jersey, he would have to continue to work in the city. She hoped he could spend time away with them.

"Enough grim reflection." Joe rose and invited them to go for ice cream. "I hope you are recovered from your travels enough for that."

The last days in the city were lonely, because soon after Joe went away and the house was empty. Neither Emilie nor Addie was inclined to venture out, given the threat of cholera to their health; moreover, the weather included two violent thunderstorms and a pervasive humidity.

CHAPTER FIVE

The heat of July struck them as they disembarked from the ferry and made by carriage for the train to Hightstown, New Jersey, where John Stewart, Joe's oldest brother, was waiting for them. The Stewarts lived in a large, rambling house on a tree-lined street in Cream Ridge. Retta was waiting to meet them. Margaretta Stewart, just Addie's age, rarely saw her friend, although her brothers Joe and Charlie were often in the Hoes' Broadway home.

The girls spent the first hour looking at one another, noting the manner in which their counterparts dressed, and discussing likes, dislikes, and recent activities. Addie was disappointed that Charlie, closer to their age, was in Delaware. The oldest sister, Ann, married to a Mr. Reybold, lived in Delaware City, a place the girls would visit and where Charlie's business took him. At home were Joe's parents and his sisters Retta and Lottie. Joe himself, unpredictable and reticent, was not at home, either.

The days unfolded with plenty of chatter among the girls, with sewing, music, and dancing in the evening. Retta and the girls waltzed while either Emilie or Addie played the piano. Finally, Charlie appeared one evening and set about to tease the girls. Addie found him more dashing than Joe, who, though always kind and solicitous of them, often seemed preoccupied and lately more so than ever. Charlie was broader and taller than Joe, and when he danced, his handsome face flushed red. While he danced with her, Addie enjoyed the sweeping wide circles they made, his left hand holding hers and the hem of her gown high, his right hand squarely and firmly at her waist.

"Have you and my sisters exhausted every subject, or are there still volumes to discuss?" he asked in his habitually humorous way.

"Sometimes we stop for breath."

"That is good news. I thought I had stayed away long enough for you to solve the problems of the world."

"There's never a chance of that."

Emilie, pianist of the hour, brought the waltz to a resounding close, the final chord *fortissimo*. The parlor, larger than the Hoes', allowed plenty of room for dancing, and Mother Stewart had allowed the children to roll up the carpet almost every evening for that purpose.

They all escaped the hot room to the front porch and sat on the steps to cool themselves. The air was fragrant with the scent of wild rose on a trellis nearby.

"What took you to Delaware?" Emilie inquired of Charlie.

"Matters of shipping. The family peach orchards are part of what I do."

"Do you pick peaches?" Addie asked.

He laughed, "No, we have help for that. I must see that we have markets ready for the ripe peaches when they come; how and where to ship them. My job is just…peachy."

The four girls groaned or laughed, depending on their appreciation of Charlie's wit.

Joe appeared out of the darkness, after having stabled the horses. Retta told Addie he was returning from Hightstown, where his brother John had met him. Joe was an excellent horseman and often raced on Saturdays at a track in West Flushing. Addie looked forward to seeing him ride the filly he had mentioned to her earlier.

The assembled dancers greeted Joe. It seemed to Addie that Charlie adopted a different demeanor with his older brother. He drew away from the girls to meet Joe on the path and said some words they could not hear. Joe responded in a like manner. They both joined the ladies soberly. Charlie spoke, ending the evening's fun, "Joe and I must rise early tomorrow. Have a good night, girls." And with that, the two young men disappeared into the house.

When the young women went into the house, Emilie remarked on the dramatic way that Joe's arrival affected Charlie. Addie and she wondered why, but did not press Lottie or Retta for the reason. Their father, a hearty, blustery man with a fair complexion like Charlie's, but with hair now white, emerged from the library where he had been talking with the two brothers. Joe and Charlie were disappearing up the stairs. Mr. Stewart wished the girls a good night, adding, "It will be hot, I fear, but may you have some rest."

The night was indeed very steamy, and the girls twisted in their nightgowns. By the middle of the night, they lay in pools of sweat. Addie's sleep was fitful, fraught with troubled dreams. Since she shared Retta's bed, the two of them tried to avoid one another as they tossed and turned.

All the girls awoke lame and out of sorts, especially Emilie, who complained of sore feet. "I feel as lame as an old woman," Addie remarked over breakfast. She dared ask Mrs. Stewart where Charlie and Joe were going. Their mother answered only, "On an errand." Her tone and brevity made Addie sense that she had been nosy and impertinent.

After straightening their room, the girls, moving slowly, unrolled the carpet from the previous evening's dance, repositioned the furniture and commenced to sew and visit. Lottie invited them to attend prayer meeting with her and her mother later in the day at the Baptist church nearby. Emilie agreed to go along, while Addie decided to remain at the house. As they conversed, the brothers appeared.

"What adventures today, ladies?" Charlie asked, as he sat down among them. Joe lounged by the fireplace and leaned against the mantelpiece.

Addie retorted, "What adventures have you already had?"

The young men glanced at one another. Joe finally answered, "We had to make a delivery that took us to Hightstown." Charlie retrieved a newspaper from his vest and read aloud a story about the latest additions to P. T.

Barnum's museum in the city and a tale of a man rescuing a girl on a runaway horse. Diverted, the ladies listened intently.

After dinner, when their mother, Lottie, Retta, and Emilie prepared to go to prayer meeting, Joe addressed Addie in the parlor. "Would you like to come see the quarter horse Charlie and John have been touting for months?"

Addie smiled and, placing her needle in a pincushion, she joined him in the hallway. She thought Father would have enjoyed a look at the horse and of how Joe would handle the filly. They walked behind the Stewart house, beyond the stable to a wide, grassy, fenced track. While Joe returned to the stable, Addie stood at attention outside the ring. She was apprehensive and knew a young, unbroken filly might pose difficulties, even though she knew Joe was an able rider. "Good luck," she called, as he left her.

Soon, Joe appeared with a lovely chestnut that was saddled, bridled, and side-stepping with excitement. He spoke in low tones and led the animal through an opening in the fence. Reins in his left hand, he mounted, kept his head low over her mane, and, still muttering, he nudged her forward with his knees. She started, ears alert, and then, rearing once, bolted forward with Joe bent low above her, his back nearly paralleling hers. They were off, and the horse ran a good ten minutes round and round. "How will he ever stop her?" Addie wondered. Eventually, however, her galloping subsided to a trot and, sweat evident on her neck, she acquiesced to Joe's pulling the reins tight and dismounting. He continued to lead her around the ring several more times as she made an occasional whinny, as though wondering what was going to happen next.

Addie admired the gentle command Joe exhibited and his self-assurance. Finally, he led the well-exercised horse back to the stable and invited Addie to trail along. She watched over the edge of the stall as he removed the saddle and rubbed the horse down with a tattered cloth and stiff bristled brush. Only occasionally did the filly lift a foot, causing him to step away with agility.

"You are an expert," Addie blurted out.

The horse's ears went back at the sound of her voice.

"I'm hardly that," Joe spoke, still in a calm, even voice. "I've ridden horses here since I was four and raced since I was twelve."

"Tell me where you were this morning."

"Why do you want to know?"

"There must be a reason for Charlie's mien to change completely when you and he are together."

"You see a good deal, don't you?" he replied, again parrying her question with another of his own. He removed the saddle and bridle, hanging them carefully in the tack room after he had secured the gate of the filly's stall.

Walking through the stable past many other stalls, Addie realized there was a large part of Joe's life she knew little about. She saw him in the city, dashing in to see Father, or taking her and Emilie for ice cream, or heading for the store where he supervised the merchant tailor department. Here in Cream Ridge, he was someone new to her.

They came out of the barn into the steamy July heat and bright sunshine and walked slowly back to the house. Joe paused and invited Addie to sit with him in the shade of a massive, spreading oak in the back yard. As they were approaching the tree, the servant who usually groomed the horses and worked in the stable appeared. He begged Joe's pardon for interrupting and asked if King's Grace needed tending. Joe told him he himself had taken care of her, and that she was in her stall ready for water and hay. The Negro man departed, nodding to Joe and Addie.

"'King's Grace,' what an elegant name for her," Addie remarked.

"The filly's sire was King Leo. My father hopes I'll race her in the fall."

"I should enjoy seeing that," Addie said, although that was unlikely, as she would be in school then. "Are you coming with us to Delaware City?"

Joe wiped his sweaty brow with his handkerchief and answered that he would be there for the trip down. Addie then determined to press him about his mystifying evasions.

"What will take you away from your sisters before we return? Why can't you stay the week?"

"Addie, I have business that is dangerous and requires absolute secrecy." He glanced soberly at her and then looked across the field spreading beyond the farm buildings, his face inscrutable.

She turned to stare in the direction he was looking. More puzzled than ever, she tried to imagine what business he implied beyond trading in cloth. He traveled here and there. His could not be an evil purpose. There was no malice in Joe, she knew from observing his devotion to her family and his close friendship with Father, who was an impeccable judge of character.

The silence between them grew deafening while the late afternoon sunlight passing through the oak leaves dappled the lawn and set Addie's deep auburn hair ablaze. Joe turned back to observe her, silent and lost in thought.

"Whatever it is," Addie said, looking into his dark eyes then directed toward her, "I will not betray your trust."

He took her hand and smiled. "I thank you for that. These are times of crisis. When I travel, I see injustice and cannot help but desire to set things right."

"Is that necessary? Do you mean through legal means?"

"Not exactly."

His hints left her more at sea than ever.

"Have you seen inequality in the city?" he asked her.

"If you mean poverty, yes. Ma and Emilie went to visit Ellen's family in Williamsburgh and returned telling of the nakedness of the children and the dirt and squalor in their tenement. "

"What about Negroes?"

"There are not slaves in New York City and have not been for many years, am I correct?"

"That is right, but have you thought about what happens in the South?"

"I have not been there. In Setauket, there's a sort of harmony between blacks and whites. They work side by side in the fields, dance together afterward, and play music delightfully together."

"Would that that were the case in Maryland and Delaware," Joe uttered with a sigh.

Just then they heard a commotion in the front yard. As the carriage turned into the drive, the Stewarts' retriever began to bark, heralding the ladies' return from the prayer meeting. Joe and Addie, reentering the house through the back door, met the new arrivals. Cousin Henry Seymour also arrived, dismounting from his horse and greeting the ladies in the yard.

Of all of Addie's cousins, who were many, Henry was her favorite and the one to whom she was closest. His parents lived in Bloomfield, not far from Cream Ridge, and his father was a Presbyterian minister who ran a boys' academy. Unlike the Stewarts, whose roots were in business, the Seymours favored learning and a life in the church.

For Henry there was an expectation that he too would follow in the Reverend's footsteps. Yet he was fascinated by the world his uncle Richard inhabited: his inventions, his involvement in the industrial world, and his sagacity in business. The Hoe factory employed hundreds of men and sold printing presses used by all the great newspapers in America and abroad. It remained to be seen whether Henry would be able to counter his father's wishes for him—to be a preacher or a teacher—and to find his place in industry. Addie's father, a manufacturer of saws as well as presses, often encouraged Henry to imagine a related industry and plumbed his mind as they discussed the difficulties the company faced in obtaining suitable steel and other materials. Henry realized the possibilities the future held for him and often in his letters to Addie expressed his ambition, as well as his insights about people.

To the sizable gathering in the parlor, Mrs. Stewart announced they would have a late supper and then disappeared to consult the cook. Joe and Henry discussed the events described in the *Tribune*, which the latter had brought from the city. Addie learned that Horace, a small boy of six and the son of the Hoe Company's lawyer, had died. Cholera claims another victim, she thought, one of the many afflicted in the steamy, crowded city. The parlor fell silent. Emilie shyly asked if the paper held any good news. Henry glanced in vain over the front page and turned to the inside pages.

"Ah, the suspension bridge at Niagara is proceeding, and by fall Mr. Roebling expects the lower carriage level will be ready for travelers," Henry read aloud. "Will that do?" he asked Emilie.

"Oh, do you think you will go there, Emilie and Addie?" Lottie asked. "It's a very long trip."

"Aunt Thirza has a desire to go to the resort near there to experience the water cure," Addie related. "Her rheumatism has been the bane of her life for several years. As for crossing the bridge, even if it is ready for travelers, I doubt our Aunt will venture across. I would enjoy the sight of the falls and, as long as I don't have to be in the first carriage, I might venture going across."

According to habit Addie rose early the next morning, which promised to be another hot, hazy day. Taking the pitcher from the commode, she quietly opened the bedroom door and descended to the kitchen to draw water for her ablutions. At the landing, she stopped to look out the window facing the barns and fields. In the mist she could make out a wagon with a team of horses harnessed to it. The rear of the wagon was loaded and covered in canvas but gave no clue as to what the load contained. Soon Joe appeared and climbed into the driver's seat. Shaking the reins, he urged the team forward. They disappeared around the side of the house, and she saw them no more.

Reconstructing the conversation from the day before in her mind, Addie knew Joe was involved in some venture that involved danger. She dared not press anyone but him for more information lest she betray his trust in her. She recalled the reverend's sermon at Setauket. He warned that the steam was building in the South because slaves demanded their freedom. He had prayed for peace and mentioned a resistance to chains and bondage, which could not persist forever. The Seaburys left the church debating the prospects for the future and worrying, in spite of the good relations among the races in their community. Could Joe be involved in disobeying the laws that protected the planters' rights?

Her sister and their hostesses, Retta and Lottie, were stirring. Addie forced herself to appear nonchalant as she replaced the pitcher of water on the commode and greeted the other girls. They dressed, arranged their hair, and prepared for the trip to Delaware City. After a breakfast of fresh mulberries and cream, they sat around the dining table asking Mother Stewart about their destination and something about Delaware City.

"Our family originally settled in Delaware. There are more Stewarts in Delaware and Maryland than there are fleas on a dog, and many Gregorys,

CHAPTER FIVE

too, who are my family," she added. "There's even a Joseph Stewart Canal. The Stewarts are all related, most are from Scotland. Not all are kissing cousins these days. Some have very different ideas about how to treat others." She paused. "In any case, you girls will be visiting my daughter Ann, and you will see nothing but kindness."

At that moment they heard horses' hooves and the jangle of harness as a wagon proceeded around the house. Shortly after, Joe appeared, removing his hat and hoping for breakfast. After washing up, he reappeared. Not a word was spoken about his early departure by either his mother or sisters. If they were aware of his doings, Addie had no way of knowing. He ate hungrily while the girls asked his mother to tell them more about whom and what they might expect at Ann's in Delaware City.

"You might meet Miss Fannie Morgan, who boards there and teaches piano lessons. Surely Ann will see that you drive out to the canal and to the peach orchards."

"Oh, Charlie mentioned the orchards. Will the fruit be ripe?" Emilie asked.

"Perhaps, but not likely. August is the best time for Delaware peaches. We'll see that you have some later."

Refreshed by the meal, Joe looked over at Addie and smiled. She hoped no one could see her blushing from her neck to her cheeks as she smiled back. It was an effort to concentrate on the second cup of tea Retta offered her.

Instead of the wagon Joe had driven at dawn, a carriage awaited Retta, Emilie, and Addie in the front yard, and Joe helped them load their bags in the back. Then he drove them to Bordentown. There they boarded the cars to the dock and thence went to Philadelphia on the next leg of the journey, a ferry ride on the *Richard Stockton*.

When they arrived in the city, they spent an hour seeking a certain servant whom Joe needed to meet. The streets were crowded and very hot. The girls wished they had parasols. Finally, it was Addie who spied the Negro man Joe said would be wearing a slouch hat and overalls. He stood at an entrance to an alley and appeared frightened, glancing warily from side to side. After a brief conversation, Joe directed him to stay in the city and gave him the address of a rooming house. The girls crossed the street and studied the storefront of an apothecary shop. Addie's curiosity and imagining made her unable to focus on the window display. She strained to hear the rest of the men's exchange, but could not.

"What was that about?" Emilie asked as Joe rejoined them.

"The fellow is new to the city. I gave him directions."

Addie suspected there was more to their meeting than Joe was letting on, but she asked no questions herself. They continued along the street, stopped for some refreshing ice water in a shop, and at last arrived at the dock. They were to board the *Major Reybold*, the steamship that would take them to Delaware City, but learned it would not depart for another hour. As they wearily waited on benches Joe located for them, they were surprised to see Charlie coming into view.

"I thought I would never get here in time. The cars were slow in Bordentown. The horses must feel as logy as we do in this heat. What, you ladies aren't dancing a jig here on the dock? You are about to take a voyage on the *Major Reybold*. Cheer up!"

It raised the girls' wilted spirits to spar with Charlie, whose flushed countenance belied his delight in accosting his sister and her friends about their appearance.

Joe took Charlie aside, and the two of them walked back toward the street. As they conversed, Charlie's face assumed seriousness.

The three-hour sail on the *Major Reybold* was smooth and pleasant, although when they arrived at the *Major*'s wharf in Delaware City, Addie found she had a headache due either to the motion of the boat or the fumes from the smokestack. They had been traveling since 7 a.m., after all.

Anthony Reybold, Joe's and Charlie's brother-in-law, was there to meet them. He was a great tall man with a shock of curly brown hair. He scooped up all their bags and deposited them handily in the rear of the coach, all the while inquiring after Mrs. Stewart and the rest of the family. He was every bit the opposite of Joe, who was dark, quiet, and shorter.

There was another seven-mile ride through the Delaware countryside, with Charlie riding up front with his brother-in-law Tony. They rode through farm country, the fields spreading into the distance, planted with all manner of crops and tended by slaves. Some of them waved as the carriage passed by, while others toiled on, cultivating or carrying loads of produce on their shoulders; men, women and children. Tony called back to tell the visitors which village they were entering or leaving and which crops were in season—beans or watermelon or berries. Addie studied Joe's face and pondered his secret life as he observed the plantation. When he caught her staring, he looked at her only for a second, and then he asked Charlie how long he would be with them. Joe said that, as for himself, he could stay only overnight and must then return to the city.

Finally, the carriage turned onto a curving private drive that bordered a pond, and they approached the Reybolds', a magnificent house with a porch surrounding it. With gratitude to have arrived at last, Addie took Joe's hand as she climbed down from the carriage. "You look worn out, but I'm sure Ann will take good care of you," he said. She thanked him and joined the others on the porch.

CHAPTER FIVE

Ann Reybold clearly resembled Joe. She was very beautiful, with kind brown eyes, and had anticipated how long their day must have been. She invited them into the cool front hall that seemed two stories high and led them up a circular staircase to their room. "We'll dine at seven, but you are welcome to tea beforehand if you would like."

Little Maggie, her four-year old, trailed along and, gazing up at Addie with big brown eyes, wanted to know if she knew any songs. Addie replied that after supper she could perhaps come up with something.

All of the girls chose to rest after they unpacked. Addie and Emilie decided to write letters. Addie described her day to her cousin Emmie Ely, while Emilie wrote to their stepmother. Retta napped.

After resting and changing out of their dusty, rumpled clothes, each of the girls prepared for dinner by washing in warm water that a young black servant girl brought them. Then they put on their best summer gowns, even though they knew they would be damp again immediately in the oppressive heat that would persist even after sunset. Retta remarked that their home in Cream Ridge was not as elegant as Ann's, but there was always an evening breeze from the forest on the hill.

"Perhaps a storm will end the heat wave," Addie responded hopefully, while re-arranging her lank hair.

Next to each of the girls' places at supper, Ann had thoughtfully placed a bamboo fan, and she encouraged the girls to use them. The good meal of fresh Chesapeake crab legs raised everyone's spirits. Afterward, Addie found the grand piano in the parlor and, taking Maggie in her lap, played nursery songs and sang to her the tunes her natural mother had sung to her as a child. Then Ann cajoled Maggie, amid noisy protestations, to go upstairs to bed.

As the evening wore on, Addie continued to play the piano, but when three young men arrived, she gave over the piano to her sister Emilie. Realizing that the three were engaged in a discussion of politics with Joe in the front hall, Addie and Retta began to dance together in the parlor, yet despite their lively activity, the visitors did not join in. When the girls stopped dancing and passed through the wide front hall to cool themselves on the piazza, the young men, who were neighbors of the Reybolds, were asking Joe whether he thought President Pierce would uphold slavery. Addie could not make out Joe's response. She, Emilie, and Retta, passing by, continued outside where the air was now more pleasant, though it remained close and humid.

Retta almost hissed her reaction to the domination of politics over dancing. "It seems the folks around here can think of nothing but politics and what might be brewing in Washington. Emilie, I think they are very rude."

"Why, because they aren't giving us the time of day?"

"I did not expect them to dance, but they might be civil," she whispered.

Just then, Charlie quietly appeared out of the dark and joined them. He had been walking with Tony, while they smoked cigars and discussed a horse they wanted Joe to ride the next day.

"I heard the music and supposed you were awaiting my grand entrance on the dance floor," he said in his usual, courtly, teasing manner.

Addie suddenly realized how tired she was and begged Charlie to delay his dancing until the next soirée. "Can we wait until another evening? It has been a very long day."

Charlie feigned abject disappointment, but then pulled from his pocket a sack of molasses candy and offered it all around. They spent the remainder of the evening enjoying the sweets and talking about nothing. Meanwhile, the three visitors departed into the night with hardly a farewell.

Joe joined the others on the porch. His only reference to the three visitors or their discussion was the terse remark, "They are staunch planters." Soon the young people reentered the house and, thanking Ann and Tony for their hospitality, retired for the night.

CHAPTER SIX

Addie woke suddenly in the early morning, finding someone staring at her at very close range. Little Maggie, with her chin resting on the edge of the bed, was watching Addie and hoping she would awaken and come downstairs. Despite feeling groggy after another hot, humid night, Addie roused and slid quietly out of bed so as not to wake Retta and Emilie. She took Maggie's hand, first placing her index finger to her lips, and walked with her downstairs. They descended, still in their nightgowns and bare feet, and said not a word. When they reached the bottom of the porch steps, Maggie whispered, "Come see my rabbit. He's got the longest ears you've ever seen!" She tugged at Addie's hand.

She whispered back, "It's too early to disturb the animals in the barn, don't you think? And besides, we're in our nightgowns."

"But my rabbit is in his hutch, just behind the house. Won't you come?"

Just then, out of the early morning mist appeared Joe, dressed for riding, approaching the house. He must have risen in the dark, Addie guessed, though she wondered why. She realized how she must look with her hair hanging loose and wearing only a nightdress, and she did not know what to say. She need not have worried, for Maggie jumped up, threw her arms around Joe's legs with delight, and exclaimed, "Uncle Joe, where are you going?"

"Hush, hush," he replied. "Folks are still sleeping. What are you doing up so early?"

"I want to show Addie my rabbit."

"Couldn't it wait until after breakfast?"

"Then it will be hot, and nobody will want to do anything!"

"That's true; that's why I got up early. I want to ride your father's new horse before I leave for Philadelphia. How about I fetch the rabbit, and you can show him to Addie here on the porch?"

Maggie, with a will of her own, frowned, but finally agreed to his suggestion. When Joe returned with the lop-eared rabbit in his arms, they sat on the steps, Joe holding the creature while Addie gently petted its silky brown fur. Maggie told how she had received it for Christmas; wasn't it perfectly soft? Did she want to hold it? Did Addie have any pets? When Maggie had the answers to her questions and felt Addie had admired the rabbit sufficiently,

Joe returned it to its hutch, and the little girl and Addie rose to get dressed. Maggie went inside and scurried upstairs.

Addie paused when she realized she knew no more about Joe's plans. He entered the hall. She turned at the foot of the stairs and thanked him quietly for helping her out. He came to her and whispered back, "It is rare that I can see two lovely girls in their night gowns at this hour." He reached out and pushed a lock of her auburn hair aside, the better to see her eyes.

She asked, "What will you do in Philadelphia?"

"There is some of my brother's business to attend to, but I will see you in Cream Ridge when you return there."

Understanding no more of what Joe actually did outside New York, Addie felt she met a brick wall whenever she broached the subject of his comings and goings. Perplexed, she shook her head, but he only looked back at her "poker faced," as Father would say, then turned and departed into the lifting mists.

Later at breakfast, after the entire house had come to life, Tony Reybold suggested they ride into Delaware City, visit some of their friends, and see the family peach orchard on the way. Miss Fannie Morgan, a woman perhaps in her early thirties, who boarded with the Reybolds, appeared at the breakfast table. She taught piano and needed to meet with her students in Delaware City. It was decided that Addie, Emilie, and Retta would join her for the excursion.

Addie was not prepared for the vast extent of the Reybolds' peach orchard. The road to town led through what seemed like miles of orchard. The green trees, standing in rows like soldiers, were laden with unripe fruit. Slaves were at work here and there, gathering peaches that had prematurely fallen, or they were cutting the grass under the trees. Tony explained how his father, Major Reybold, had been inspired to experiment with planting peaches and had found the Delaware climate ideal for them. The ripe peaches were shipped out of the *Major*'s wharf all up and down the mid-Atlantic coast. Addie and her sister looked on in awe. Everything about the Reybolds was huge, from the size of the man Tony himself to the plantation the family owned.

"There must be thousands of trees," Emilie said.

"Actually, there are close to a hundred thousand," Tony responded with considerable pride.

"No wonder you have a steamboat to deliver the peaches," Addie remarked. "Where do your slaves live? I have not seen any quarters for them."

"Actually, we freed our slaves and they work for us for pay. They live in a village on the far west end of the orchard. The neighbors in the vicinity are not pleased with what we have done. The three young fellows who came last night are from plantations nearby, and they don't like the example we have set."

CHAPTER SIX

Addie wondered what Joe had said to the three young men the previous evening. She realized that whatever was going on, Joe's position on slavery played a part. One day she would persuade him to explain it to her.

Delaware City was a city only in name. Coming from the teeming world of New York City, Addie found the narrow streets and quaint houses they saw upon arriving in the seaside town definitely provincial but charming all the same.

The carriage drew up before a Mr. King's home, where Miss Fannie Morgan would teach the children piano and stay over for lessons with other pupils in town. The girls all wished her a pleasant time, and the carriage proceeded to the street that bordered the docks. The visitors strolled the cobblestone street at Tony's invitation and gazed at Chesapeake Bay.

It was cooler by the shore. Boats that traversed the Chesapeake and Delaware Canal docked to deliver their wares from the South, while others unloaded from northern or other ports. Addie wondered which men were slaves and which were free among those carrying heavy loads off or onto the boats.

Retta had told Emilie and Addie about the Summit Bridge over the Canal. She urged Tony to take them to see this canal, a feat that took many years to dig. He took them first to a tavern next to the bridge, where they got out of the carriage and walked down the bank beneath the bridge, which descended at least ninety feet. At one point, Addie tripped and feared tumbling down into the water, but Tony caught her hand and they all made their way back to the tavern. After some refreshing lemonade, they returned to the Reybolds'.

All three girls were content to spend the rest of the day sewing in the parlor. Maggie and her mother sat with them, while Ann showed her daughter how to cross-stitch. Addie recalled her sampler, begun when she was only a bit older than Maggie and which she finished with the help of her stepmother.

Since the next day would be the Fourth of July, Ann suggested that would be a fine time for a picnic. She proposed that they ride out to the shore. However, the next day was so oppressively hot that the plan was abandoned; instead, the women sewed and the girls washed their clothes.

The next day was Sunday and they went in to Delaware City to St. George's Episcopal Church. The main floor of the sanctuary consisted of a mass of pews reserved for white people below and a balcony in the back where the Negroes were obliged to sit. Addie recalled that in New York City the Negroes had their own churches.

On both levels, the women fanned themselves while the minister gave a lengthy sermon about the parable of the Prodigal Son. His prayers were especially long, too, and Maggie fell asleep leaning on her father's shoulder. A few wasps flew down from the ceiling above the chancel and swooped menacingly close to the preacher's head. It did not deter him from his nest of ideas. Those in the congregation who noticed the wasps found the incident diverting.

After greeting the minister in the back of the church after they filed out, some parishioners gathered on the steps. Tony, among them, made a droll remark about the prodigal wasps come home to torment the preacher. Addie listened and pretended not to hear. Maggie complained that she was hungry until Ann Reybold poked her gregarious husband in the ribs with her fan and they made their way to the carriage.

On the way home Ann explained to Addie, Emilie, and Retta that their usual minister was away "recruiting himself," so there had to be a replacement that Sunday. The only pastor available was a retired gentleman long out of practice. "And long out of touch, if you ask me," Tony was quick to add, "but let's be thankful for the wasps who helped keep us awake." After two hours of sitting, the girls were inclined to agree.

One of Tony's brothers, Barney Reybold, met them on the road. From his horse, which responded in lively fashion to the mare pulling his brother's carriage, Barney invited them to a party the next evening. Looking to Ann, who in turn glanced inquiringly at the young ladies, Tony read affirmation in the smiles all around and accepted hastily before one horse or the other bolted. "See you at six, then," Barney called, urging his horse to a trot in the opposite direction.

Since Charlie Stewart had disappeared when Joe left for Philadelphia, Addie assumed he was involved in whatever Joe's business might be. It was therefore a pleasant surprise when Charlie arrived at noon the next day.

"I'm glad I started early," he said as he removed his hat and wiped his brow with his handkerchief. "Thunder clouds loomed the whole way. By nightfall I predict a storm or two."

The ladies informed him of the evening's plans, and he agreed to attend the party with them. "A night of conversation and dancing, I hope," Charlie added. "And a chance for the young ladies to exhibit their talents and finery."

Indeed, the three young women took him seriously and set about to present a pretty picture of themselves in the social scene in Delaware. Ann helped them as they washed their hair and ironed the best gowns they had brought. She sent the Negro maid into the garden to pick roses for their hair. Maggie hoped that she could go to Uncle Barney's, but no, her mother told her, she would stay with Naney.

Just after tea, despite distant rumbles of thunder to the north, Tony, Ann, Charlie, and the female visitors climbed into the chaise and rode the three miles to Barney Reybold's plantation, Verdant Hill. In the direction of Philadelphia, occasional flashes of lightning lit up the sky.

CHAPTER SIX

"I hope this is wise, Tony," Ann fretted. Then she added, turning to the girls, "Only a year ago, lightning struck the barn and burned it down, and some of the Negroes' homes as well."

The girls shifted uneasily, adjusting their bonnets and wondering how much farther they had to go to reach Verdant Hill. The wind picked up and, although the fresh breeze cooled their faces, announced the storm. Soon huge drops of rain began to fall. At the sound of thunder, the horses whinnied in discontent.

"We're nearly there. Gideon, give the horses their heads," Tony shouted above the thunder.

Soon the estate loomed before them, ablaze with welcoming lights. A Negro man leaped down from the front steps with two open parasols ready to shelter the guests, while another Negro grabbed the bridles of the horses. The ladies alit as quickly as their attire would allow, and underneath the parasols they skipped the few yards to the porch.

To Addie, Barney Reybold seemed a giant, even taller and more burly than Tony. When they had seen him astride a horse, it had not been apparent how imposing he was. He filled the doorway, which must have been more than seven feet high. Next to him stood Mrs. Reybold, taller than either Addie or Emilie but at least a foot shorter than her husband. She was slender and statuesque in a yellow silk gown.

Despite resembling Goliath of Gath, Barney was most cordial, inquiring about the ride over and their health. He bid a Negro woman take their bonnets and wraps. Tony introduced the girls to his relatives as "Richard March Hoe's belles, Emilie and Addie."

"Ah! The amazing inventor!" Barney nodded to them and turned to Charlie and Retta. "We have not seen you, Retta, for a long time. And Charlie, you will enjoy the fiddlers tonight, both up from Baltimore for the occasion."

From the foyer, the guests passed into the hall, similar in scope to that at River View, Tony's plantation. Yet it was not merely a parlor, but a vast, elegant room lined with chairs at intervals and floor-to-ceiling windows that looked out onto the lawn, which was occasionally illuminated by flashes of lightning. Positioned by each of the doors was a black servant dressed in livery, ready, Addie supposed, to perform the least task. There were many sconces with candles in them along the wall, casting a warm glow. Guests arranged themselves in groups of three or four. Mrs. Reybold led Addie, Emilie, and Retta to a pair of young men not far from the entrance. She introduced them as Albert and Silas Stewart. They nodded in recognition when Addie said they had already met, for they were two of the fellows who had spent the evening talking with Joe the previous week.

"Oh, I see," said Mrs. Reybold. She deftly withdrew to see to her other guests. The two gentlemen looked at each other, embarrassed, recalling the evening spent talking politics. Silas, the less shy of the two, recovered his composure and sense of courtesy enough to speak.

"We were remiss, I fear," he admitted, "to leave without a word."

"No doubt you had important matters on your mind," Addie responded.

"In fact, we disagree with Joe Stewart. He is no relation to us, by the way." Silas began to open up. "He would have us go the way of your friend Tony, opposing slavery. We were raised to the way of life that allows order between the white and black races. The superior intelligence and wisdom of the white man ensures the well-being of the black man, and the black man owes him labor in return. It is a simple relationship." As he spoke, he lowered his voice, preferring that his audience not be the Negroes in livery but only the pair of ladies from New York City needing to be set straight.

"You are going to hear a great deal more about slavery since the Kansas-Nebraska Act passed in Congress," Albert stated with a tone of finality. He looked away from the group.

"What *is* this act you mentioned?" Addie asked, even though her sister seemed annoyed and was glancing about the room for more benign conversation.

"Kansas-Nebraska will allow Kansas Territory to remain open for slavery, but Nebraska to be free," Silas explained. "The Act passed in May."

"I see. Do you think there will be slavery forever?" she asked, nodding toward a servant who offered her a glass of punch. The Negro boy looked her way briefly, his face impassive.

"Yes," Silas stated emphatically, ignoring the presence of the servant.

Albert revealed a hint of uncertainty in his silence. Then, realizing the icy atmosphere, he spoke. "Silas, let's abandon the topic."

"You're right. Politics does not belong here this evening."

Addie felt better informed, but aware of a new tension she had not recognized in social relations thus far.

Presently another servant appeared in the doorway and announced, "Dinner is served." The guests, numbering perhaps twenty, began to move toward the doors of the adjoining dining room. When all had found their places, Mr. Reybold proposed a toast, raising his wine glass, "To our guests from New York City, a hearty welcome!" at which Addie and Emilie smiled and blushed.

The meal's three courses consisted of a salad of greens, roasted ham and turkey, and Mrs. Reybold's favorite: trifle. Conversation revolved around the weather. Both of the Mr. Reybolds hoped the storm's wind would not damage the peach and pear crops. Although the thunder and lightning had subsided, the rain still pelted the dining room windows, and drafts caused by the wind made the tapers in the candelabra flicker and gout.

CHAPTER SIX

There was no more talk of slavery. The fiddlers were tuning their instruments. After the compliments paid the cook for the exquisite dessert, the diners returned to the hall for dancing. Addie anticipated the joy of a quadrille and began to tap her toe to the first strains of music. She felt also some apprehension, never having had the pleasure of a full complement of dancers. This would not be dancing in the parlor with Retta, yet she wondered if anyone would invite her to the floor.

She need not have worried. A squat, plump young man, whose tie looked extremely uncomfortable, came to Addie's side, introduced himself, and invited her to dance. She nodded, and he led her to the set, where the gentlemen and ladies were assembling. She did not catch his name amid the din of music and voices.

Each of the eight couples faced one another and bowed or curtsied. Forward and back, forward and back, the dance began. The only occasion to join hands came when the pair at the top of the set promenaded down the middle. For that Addie was grateful. Indeed, the fiddle music was lively and filled her with the pleasure she always found in dancing. Thanking her for the dance, her rotund partner retreated to the other end of the hall, where refreshments were sure to be served.

She stood observing that neither Silas nor Albert had joined the dancing. Soon Charlie, whose partner had been Emilie in the quadrille, approached her.

"May I have the pleasure of the next dance, Miss Adeline?"

"Certainly."

"Unless you and your new friend have an understanding."

"Oh poff, Charlie, I don't even know his name. I could not hear when he said it."

A waltz began, an arrangement from a Rossini opera that Addie knew, and while they danced, Charlie whirled her about in his customary, exuberant way.

In the middle of the evening, while the fiddlers ate their supper and the dancers took a very welcome rest, Miss Fanny Morgan, the piano teacher, sat down to play the piano. She remained silent a moment, allowing for the hubbub around her to subside, then, after an arpeggio or two to test the instrument, she set about to play Beethoven's *Für Elise* with authority. There was considerable appreciation from the audience standing or sitting around the piano, and they applauded generously at the conclusion. She followed with a sentimental piece that someone whispered was by Stephen Foster, a composer of whom Addie was ignorant.

The idea that a woman might be a professional musician intrigued Addie. Women were opera singers, she knew, but a woman teaching music and performing in concert, that was novel. She wondered if the Reybolds reimbursed Miss Morgan for her playing that evening. Surely the fiddlers, both men, were engaged in a professional capacity. Miss Morgan dressed frugally and only in her playing exhibited any emotion at all, closing her eyes at a particularly *rubato* section of the second piece. Addie played for pleasure and to accompany the family in singing or dancing, as did her sister. To her father, with a song ever on his lips, music was a complement to life, but it could not constitute one's sole occupation. For Addie, practicing was a means to a delightful end.

Before the fiddlers resumed, guests wandered into the hall and onto the piazza. Addie learned the name of the rotund gentleman when he found her looking out into the darkness. She was startled, for which he begged her pardon, and upon recovering, she said, "I was not able to hear your name before we danced, Sir."

"Beauregard Wise."

"Do you live in Delaware City?"

"No, I am a trader and traveler."

"What are your wares?"

"Various commodities."

The way he spoke in vaguest terms made Addie uncomfortable. She determined to extract herself from proximity to him as soon as she could. He, however, was not about to allow that.

"What brings you to the Reybolds?"

"Do you mean Anthony's, or here?"

"Oh, I know, Barney would want all the fine young women at his party. I mean, what is your connection to the Reybold family?"

Hesitating, Addie thought, why should he interrogate me? Something in his tone suggested wheedling. What knowledge could I have that he might want? At last she responded, "My father and the Reybolds have a business connection that dates from many years ago." She chose not to give a history of their connection with the Stewarts of Cream Ridge or Joe's friendship with the Hoe family.

The fiddle music gave her an excuse to end the conversation. Beauregard Wise stepped aside, and Addie followed the other guests into the hall for the final dances of the evening.

CHAPTER SEVEN

On the way home around midnight, the party saw light in the direction of Philadelphia. Ann Reybold commented, "There must be a great fire." The following morning, Joe arrived and reported that, indeed, a vast fire had swallowed a city block in Philadelphia. Over breakfast he described the conflagration.

"There was a fierce storm, and from a police officer I learned that lightning struck near Peale's Chinese Museum. Nothing is left of that building and several others. Many artifacts were lost."

"We could see a great light in the sky as we drove home last evening," Tony told him. "Despite the fact that Benjamin Franklin promoted fire brigades, more advanced steps need to be taken to fight fires in Philadelphia, and everywhere, for that matter."

"My father believes steel building frames might be an answer," Emilie spoke, having heard the same discussion many times in New York where wooden buildings often succumbed to fire.

"That might slow the destruction and give the firemen time to make a difference. When we lost the barn to lightning," Tony said woefully, "there was nothing we could have done either to prevent it or stop it once the barn was struck." He seemed to relive the event as he frowned and gripped his coffee cup with both hands.

Sensing that enough had been said of a melancholy nature, Addie turned to Maggie, who dawdled over a bowl of oatmeal.

"And what do you plan to do today, Miss Maggie?"

Looking up at Addie in surprise, she thought a moment and asked, "Will you play some songs for me?"

Her mother interjected, "The Hoe girls and Retta are leaving today. They must pack and may be very busy, Maggie."

Ignoring Ann's cautioning words, Addie agreed to teach Maggie another tune she remembered had been her favorite. Miss Morgan might not approve of this sort of music, Addie thought, noting the older woman's sour expression as she consumed her food. Although we are all tired after the party, she concluded, Maggie deserves a song.

Emilie and Retta told Joe about the soirée he had missed the previous evening. He voiced regret and hoped they all had satisfied their craving for dancing. Addie rose and took Maggie's hand once she had asked to be excused. Before they headed toward the piano, Joe asked Maggie, "How's that rabbit of yours?"

She answered, "Yesterday he ate five radishes."

Joe rose, nodded to Mrs. Reybold, and followed Addie out of the room. In the parlor Maggie climbed up on the piano bench. While Addie played and sang "Flow Gently, Sweet Afton," Joe stood behind them, listening to the lilting English air. Her light, high soprano suited the tune well. At the end of the first verse, the one she knew best, she stopped.

"I love that song!" Maggie exclaimed. "Please play it again."

"I will play it very slowly, and you can repeat each line after me, alright?"

After completing the first verse, Maggie's interest flagged. She slid off the bench and tripped away to a new activity. As she lowered the lid over the piano keys and was sliding the bench under the piano, Addie discovered Joe, who had remained throughout the lesson silently standing behind them. It was not uncharacteristic of him to observe quietly whatever transpired in the household when he dropped by. What caused her to redden on this occasion was the realization that he had seen her attempting to teach someone. "Oh, it's you! You stayed."

"I'm sorry if my staying to listen disturbs you," he began. "I wanted to ask you alone about last night."

"What might I tell you?"

"Emilie mentioned the fiddling and Miss Morgan's concert. You must have enjoyed yourself."

"Oh yes, it was by and large very pleasant."

"'By and large'?"

"If you must know, the first dance was a quadrille and a fellow—fat and unsavory somehow—asked me to be his partner. Later, on the piazza, I learned his name, Beauregard Wise."

"He is familiar to me."

"In what connection?"

"Well, go on. What happened next?"

"He began to ask questions about why we were visiting and what our connection with the Reybolds was. I received the impression that he wanted information. Luckily then, the music resumed, and I escaped to the hall. After that, I did not see him again. He had an oily manner I did not like."

"Ah yes, I can understand. You were certainly within your rights not to spend more time with him."

"Who is he? He said he was in trade, 'in various commodities.' What are they?"

"He is a slave hunter, paid by slave owners to find Negroes and bring them back."

CHAPTER SEVEN

"How do you know that?"

"Not everyone who attends parties in these parts thinks as my family and I do."

Addie had to be satisfied for the time being with his answer.

Apologizing for interrupting them, Ann Reybold entered the parlor and asked Addie if she and the others would look for a female servant for Miss Morgan when they went to Philadelphia. It was time to pack and already Emilie and Retta were upstairs making preparation to leave. En route to Cream Ridge, Joe and Tony would accompany them. The maid, if one could be found, would return with Tony.

Emilie reminded Addie to hurry. Their bags were open on the beds. Addie found her valises and set about to find all her belongings.

"Don't forget your dancing shoes you left on the porch to dry last evening. And the bonnets on the stair railing." Emilie's tone, as she assumed the role her stepmother played in looking out for her younger sister, contained some irritation. Normally Addie would have explained why she had been detained. She ignored her sister, however, and dashed down to collect the shoes and bonnets. She remembered also the reticule and sewing basket she had left in the foyer. She hurriedly folded all of her dresses and underclothes, and packed them along with *The Last of the Mohicans*, the novel she had not finished reading,

The traveling party was assembling when at last Addie descended the stairs with her two bags. Maggie ran across the front hall to embrace her. Tearfully she begged her not to go. Addie knelt down and, looking into the child's eyes, promised to send her the other verses of "Flow Gently, Sweet Afton." Somewhat comforted, Maggie let her new friend go and returned to bury her face in her mother's skirt.

"Please come again," Ann graciously urged in response to profuse thanks from all three young ladies.

Tony and Joe hoisted all the bags on top of the carriage. The air had changed and the trip promised to be pleasant. Indeed, the return voyage from Delaware City was lovely, with a light breeze ruffling the waves and sunshine dappling the water.

Upon disembarking in Philadelphia, the men again helped with the bags, depositing them at the ferry station for the next leg of the journey. Then the entire group walked away from the docks to the street where servants were likely to be procured. Addie knew that Philadelphia was a free city as far as Negroes were concerned, yet she knew that if slave catchers sighted errant slaves, they were legally permitted to apprehend them and take them away. A group of young men and women congregated near an open market that purveyed fruits, vegetables and all manner of livestock. There were white as well as black people hoping for employment. Addie thought it must be a delicate matter whom to approach. Her father usually hired their servants, often Irish people newly arrived in New York, who were recommended by their employees at the factory.

Tony beckoned to a young black woman who was perhaps Addie's age or a little younger. She came off the curb to meet the group. She answered his questions, said her name, Tally Monson, and that she had no children or husband. Addie, Emilie, and Retta listened carefully, and when Tony turned to them for their approval, they all agreed she presented a good appearance. Never having been called upon to make discriminations about choosing servants, Addie felt awkward.

Tony then told the girl she would be employed for wages by Miss Morgan, and would live at their plantation. The black young woman looked with some apprehension at each of their faces.

"Should you find fault with conditions for working," Tony continued, "you will be free to return to Philadelphia." Tally Monson seemed startled at his words. Observing her more closely, Addie could see scars on her ankles below the hem of her muslin dress, a garment that must have fitted her at a much earlier age.

Having taken in all that Mr. Reybold said, the young woman nodded, retrieved a cloth bag from the alley and followed him to the dock. Addie and Emilie bid Tony Reybold farewell, and expressed hope that he, Ann, and Maggie would visit them on Broadway.

The *Richard Stockton* ferried them back to New Jersey across the Delaware. Charlie Stewart met them at Bordentown in the carriage and, at the end of the final leg of the journey, they reached Cream Ridge after dark. Addie saved the letters from cousins Henry and Emmie Ely that had arrived in their absence for reading the next day. She, Retta, and Emilie were tired and, despite Charlie's attempts to draw them into the parlor for conversation, they went to bed immediately.

Upon arising, the newly arrived ladies were all very lame and stiff from the carriage and boat rides and from traipsing about Philadelphia the day before. Addie learned from his letter that Henry would be arriving the next day and that his ague still tormented him. Emmie Ely reported on her family's health and wished the Hoe girls would hurry back since life had become dull at home.

At breakfast, realizing that Mrs. Stewart did not seem well, Addie was glad that they and Retta had returned to be of help to her. They urged her to rest. She refused to comply until they first described all that had happened in Delaware City. Thus they spent the day together in quiet conversation, catching up on sewing and sharing their news.

Late in the day, Addie revived from fatigue and accepted Joe's invitation to take a walk to Fillmore, a part of the town where there was an old forge. He intimated that the neighborhood was especially beautiful and that she should like it very much.

"Is it very far?"

"No, and there will be no need to hurry."

She accepted after assuring herself that Mrs. Stewart would not mind their absence. Joe waited outside while she changed into comfortable shoes for walking. Emilie and Retta could not imagine how Addie could entertain walking after the exertions of the previous day.

Once out of sight of the Stewarts' house, she and Joe walked in silence for a quarter mile on the country lane. Huge oaks and maples, branches thick with foliage, bowed to them on either side. At one point the road forked and descended steeply into a shady dell.

"Tell me the history of Fillmore," Addie began.

"The early settlers used to call this 'Varmintown.' Can you suspect why?"

"No, tell me."

"There were many wild animals in those days—foxes, wolves, fishers, coon—all considered vermin."

Addie shuddered and moved closer to Joe.

"Don't worry. There aren't many of those kinds of animals left since the land was cleared. The forge I'll show you was built over a hundred years ago by an early settler, Mordecai Lincon."

They crossed over a brook at that point on a wooden bridge. Below them the stream, enlivened by the recent storms, rushed around great rocks in an incessant roar. Away from the stream, Joe turned to her and they both stopped. Addie searched his face expectantly.

"It is time I explain what I have been about lately."

"Do you mean the times you have disappeared?"

"Yes." He turned back to the lane and as they walked, more slowly than before, he related his story. "As you know, we are all in a dispute now about slavery."

"Yes."

"We in Delaware and New Jersey are particularly divided. You saw the split between Barney and Tony, no doubt. When Tony Reybold met Ann, he began to realize, much influenced by her devout aversion to slavery, that times must change. He decided to set his laborers free several years ago. To that Barney is opposed and, on that issue, he and Tony do not speak."

"It is to their credit that they remain close in most respects," Addie remarked.

"I agree. For my part, I follow my family's thinking and perhaps have influenced them. I help escaping slaves reach freedom, and that means avoiding slave catchers like that despicable Beauregard Wise. It means slipping away to gather information in odd places, places that have to be ever-changing as each Negro must be hidden and invisible. Do you understand?"

"It must be dangerous. Oh Joe, you must be careful, both for those you help and for your own safety."

"Indeed, but the brutality of slavery is a bigger ill than any of us north of Delaware understands." He stopped and pushed aside branches to reveal a slash in the bark of an oak. "Here we turn."

They moved beyond the marked tree to a narrow path winding down toward the roar of the stream. A quaint, low building, surely the forge, lay before them, surrounded by undergrowth. Joe entered the gaping door where in former times a smithy fashioned horseshoes and nails for the settlers. Above the sound of rushing water Joe called, "Will and Sam." Addie stood frozen in the doorway.

From beneath the floor a few boards began to move, whereupon Joe bent to grasp the edge of a heavy trap door that gave when he pulled on it. Up from the floor appeared two Negro heads. So as not to startle them, Addie drew back.

"Sam, Will, I'm here to tell you that tomorrow early I'll come to the end of the path and we'll head for Philadelphia. Do you still have enough to eat?"

They replied yes, they did, and thanked him, shouting over the deafening roar of the stream nearby.

"All right. See you then." Replacing the trap door, Joe retreated to the outside. In an unusual expression of intimacy, Joe took Addie's hand and assisted her as they walked through the deep grass surrounding the forge and up the steep lane. As she walked a half step behind him, her mind flooded with questions. How did the men get to their hiding place? Where did they come from? Where could they be safe? How did Joe know what to do with them? She imagined the slave-catcher Wise hunting them down like a bloodhound. Fear for Joe and the black men made her grip his hand and pull him to a stop on the empty road away from the rushing brook.

"Wait."

He turned, as he read her thoughts. "I know what you're worrying about and wondering. First of all, I have already helped ten Negroes on their way north. Will and Sam are younger brothers of a woman who has guided perhaps hundreds to Canada and other places up north. Will and Sam aren't their real names, but they need to travel incognito as much as possible, to avoid connection with the plantation from which they escaped in Maryland. Now I must ask you to keep my secret, their secret."

"Does your family know what you do?"

"Yes, my parents help by supplying food and the wagon I need to transport them. Our neighbors do not know. There are sympathizers surely in Mother's church, but no one talks openly about what is happening underground."

"Why the forge and not your own house to hide them in?"

"Mordecai Lincon's forge has been vacant for years, but it is solidly built. When we were boys, Charlie and I used to play there, and we discovered the trap door by accident. Old Mordecai must have used it to store his charcoal or tools. The forge is just one of many such hideouts along the Underground Railroad."

The evening was fast approaching as they climbed a steep incline, and the light through the foliage dimmed.

"I admire your courage to help these men. Does my father know?"

"He might suspect."

"I will not talk about it unless he mentions it. Although Emilie and I are inseparable most of the time, I will keep your secret—even from her, and Ma."

"Once I have returned to New York, discovery of my activities is less perilous or likely. But until all Negroes are declared free, what we are doing will be risky."

Addie and Joe walked the rest of the way no longer hand in hand, but she, no less agitated by the significance of all she now knew, felt bound to this taciturn Joe Stewart, putting his life on the line for unfortunate people. And he pondered the next steps in his plan for rescuing the young men.

CHAPTER EIGHT

As Joe and Addie mounted the steps to the piazza, they heard laughter. Charlie, Emilie, Retta, and younger sister Lottie were engaged in revelry. They entered the parlor in the midst of a mock argument between Charlie and Retta.

"Which tippet shall I wear today, the red, the blue, the black, the green, or the purple?" Charlie squeaked in a falsetto imitation of Retta while she hotly denied any such vanity. But he persisted. She glared while the others giggled in amusement.

"You cannot deny that in Delaware City you were dismayed not to find the perfect lace for your gown, and you complained to have left your pearl brooch at home. And there was lots of 'Oh Emilie, are my bangs straight?' and 'Addie, is my petticoat showing?'"

"Nonsense!" Retta, though generous-hearted and a most self-effacing young lady, finally had had enough and swatted Charlie's arm with her fan. Addie wondered if his persistence in teasing her was a diversionary tactic to assure that there were no questions about her and Joe's walk to Fillmore. Of course, Charlie was fully aware that the two young men at the forge needed to be cared for.

When the melee subsided, Joe inquired how their mother was feeling. Retta said she had retired still unwell after another fainting spell that day. Their father appeared and reported he was expecting the doctor from Bordentown at any time. Addie wondered what Mrs. Stewart's affliction might be and if it was rooted in her worries about her sons' involvement in transporting escaping slaves.

"Let's watch the sunset from the piazza," Charlie suggested, after glancing out the window at the rosy, dying light. Arranging themselves along the porch railing, the young people marveled at the beautiful shades of the sky, from red to violet, as the stars came out. Charlie produced a fresh sack of molasses candy, which they all shared. Retta announced that she hoped to go riding the next day, and asked if Joe would come with her.

"I will later in the day. Perhaps I'll saddle the chestnut filly."

Emilie turned to Addie and asked, "Would you show me Fillmore tomorrow?" Addie assented. She knew that by the time they got up, performed their morning ablutions, dressed, ate breakfast, and donned their bonnets,

CHAPTER EIGHT

Joe would be long gone with the wagon, the two Negroes stowed under a canvas and headed for Philadelphia.

Despite the various diversions the Stewart and Hoe children planned, they knew that Mother Stewart's condition might supersede any or all of their entertainments. Later that night, long after Addie and the others had retired, she heard the hoof beats of a horse coming to a halt, announcing the doctor's arrival at the house.

The next morning, Addie rose very early, according to her custom, and put on a shawl. She ventured into the hallway as the doctor and Mr. Stewart descended the stairs. She listened at the top of the stairs while Mr. Stewart questioned him.

"Do you think she will improve?"

"We have no guarantee," the doctor began in a gravelly, weary voice. "I suspect hers is a disorder of nerves. Give her this preparation once a day. It is my strong recommendation, however, that she will be best served by walking some each day. Fresh air and exercise are the best elixir. I shall return next week to examine her again."

"Thank you for coming out and for staying to watch over my Ann. Will you stay to breakfast?"

"I don't mind if I do."

"Come this way." Mr. Stewart led the elderly doctor to a chair in the parlor and then he headed to the kitchen to advise the servants that an extra place needed to be set for breakfast. Addie reentered the bedroom, quickly and quietly dressed in a simple gown, and came downstairs. She went to the kitchen straightaway and offered to help with breakfast. The servant, a girl younger than sixteen, seemed flustered not to have Mrs. Stewart's guidance and to have an extra mouth to feed. Addie volunteered to set the table and pick the blackberries the servant had planned to pick before inheriting the entire breakfast detail.

With a basket and directions to the blackberry patch, Addie went outside. The mists were dispersing as the sun rose. She could make out that the wagon that normally sat next to the stable was gone. Joe was already on his mission. She stepped carefully through the dewy grass and spied the patch of berries beyond the oak tree where she and Joe had sat the day he displayed his mastery of horses. The robins in the trees around her protested the invasion of their territory as she began to pick. In no time, the basket was full, and Addie's fingers were stained with purple juice from the very ripe berries.

Over a breakfast of porridge, fresh blackberries, and hot tea, the family and guests discussed how the poor woman fared upstairs. Doctor Willis, in a dark rumpled suit, listened and nodded, and occasionally wiped his double chin with a napkin. Mr. Stewart asked all the children to assist in any way they could imagine. Would the girls accompany her on short walks?

When they had nearly finished, the doctor changed the subject to the Kansas-Nebraska Act and the slavery question. Addie gathered that he knew about the Stewarts' objections to slavery. He reported that he had a patient in Bordentown who had seen a slave hunter along the county road begging information. A *frisson* of fear passed through Addie when she heard his news, for she suspected that Joe might be traveling that road, but she continued to finish the last of the blackberries and cream in her bowl. Neither did the Stewarts stop eating their meal, although a solemn glance passed between Charlie and his father. At length the well-fed doctor smacked his lips, declared the breakfast the best he had ever eaten, and was off.

Addie, Emilie, and the Stewart girls sewed much of the day and made themselves available to the ailing Mrs. Stewart, who remained in bed awaiting the beneficial effects of the medicaments the doctor left her. Only late in the day did Emilie prevail upon Addie to walk to Fillmore. Retta saddled her horse, meanwhile, and rode in the direction of Bordentown.

The weather was unpredictable and humid, with clouds overhead possibly portending a shower.

What sorts of attractions did you visit in Fillmore? Is it a village? Emilie wondered.

Addie responded as they set out with the historical details about the district, but she carefully avoided the current purposes to which their destination was put. Without Joe along, the woods surrounding the girls as they descended the hill toward the stream seemed forbidding in part because the cloudiness of the day made it extremely gloomy. When Addie related the old name, "Varmintown," her sister hoped they would not meet any vermin. When they reached the bridge, Emilie spent a few minutes gazing at the scene of tumbling water and rocks below. They pressed on.

Knowing that Joe was likely to be in Philadelphia by then, Addie saw no harm in proceeding to the forge. By the time they reached the path leading from the lane to the forge, it began to rain.

"Shall we go back?" Addie shouted over the sound of the rushing brook. "Can you see the old building?"

"Yes, let's go look inside."

Although Addie felt uncomfortable about what they might find, she and her sister proceeded through the overgrown grass and approached the forge. When they peered inside the dim interior, there was nothing out of order; the trap door was undetectable in the floor without a sign anyone had been there. Addie was relieved.

CHAPTER EIGHT

Emilie was unimpressed and wanted to abandon the dingy place. As they hurriedly retraced their steps to the road, the rain began to fall heavily. There was not much said as they kept to the verges in the shelter of the trees. At length they reached the top of the steep hill.

"Why did we decide to take a walk?" Emilie asked in exasperation, the rain soaking her bonnet. They trudged on. "Was your walk with Joe your chance to be alone with him?"

Addie, hard pressed to come up with an answer, would not and could not tell either how committed Joe was to helping slaves or how she felt about him. She cast about in her mind for something to satisfy her sister, her lifelong and closest confidante.

"If you mean, do we have an understanding; that is not the case. He is my, our, good friend. That is all."

"You'll tell me if that state of affairs should change, won't you?"

"Of course," Addie answered, hoping that there would be no more questions of that nature. At seventeen, she had not dared consider Joe's attention to her as anything more than a kindly concern and mutual interest in another's welfare, a brotherly friendship. She was flattered that Joe trusted her with his dangerous secret, but she dared not think he was more devoted to her than anyone else in his life.

When they were nearly at the Stewarts' house, Retta rode her horse alongside them. Like Emilie and Addie, she was drenched with rain. The three ladies looked at one another and began to laugh at their bedraggled condition.

"Hurry inside," Retta called to them as she urged her horse to a trot. "I'll join you as soon as I take Dolly to the stable."

Emilie and Addie shed their sodden, muddy shoes on the porch and hurried into the house while Mr. Stewart held the door open for them.

"Was it a pleasant stroll you had?" he asked with a hint of the irony that was typical of his son Charlie.

Fruit doesn't fall far from the tree, Addie thought, removing her dripping bonnet.

"Perhaps we will heed the clouds next time," Emilie responded en route to the stairs with Addie close behind.

"A sprinkle of rain never hurt anyone," he called cheerily, but they were already in the upstairs bedroom changing every item of their clothing. Entering the hall, Retta headed upstairs too.

When the Hoe ladies and Retta had dried their hair and dressed, they joined the elder Stewarts for some excellent, hot tea. Mrs. Stewart, appearing much revived, was eating and drinking. She expressed worry, however, that the girls might all take a chill. They reassured her the weather, though wet, was mild.

"Have you seen anything of Joe?" the older woman asked, a new veil of concern descending upon her. Her husband told her not to worry and to enjoy her tea.

"Joe is safe; have faith, Ann."

"Where is he that we should worry about him?" Emilie asked in her frank manner.

Neither caring to deceive nor disclose, Mr. Stewart rose from his chair and went to the window. First slowly surveying the road beyond the front yard, he took his time to answer. Addie waited for him to speak, holding her breath in anticipation of his reply.

"He went to Philadelphia on business this morning and may not return until tomorrow. Charlie went along. They'll take care of themselves." His tone was casual and matter-of-fact.

In one sense, Addie was relieved by the ambiguity in his words, but she knew why Mrs. Stewart suffered from what Dr. Willis called "nerves." Moreover, she guessed Emilie would ask Retta later all the questions Addie herself had asked Joe about his comings and goings.

Indeed, later that evening after they retired to their bedroom for the night, Emilie accosted Retta with questions, while Addie penned a letter at the writing desk to their stepmother. The two young women, sitting cross-legged in their night dresses atop the comforter on the bed, were each reading a novel when Emilie put hers down and turned to Retta.

"What is Joe's business?"

Retta did not put down her book but seemed to continue to read, only saying, "You know, he is a commercial merchant."

"What does he buy or sell?"

"He supplies materials to tailors. Didn't you know that?" Retta spoke in a blasé offhand tone, as though the subject were dull as dirt, and returned to her book. Addie admired the cool way she obscured the double life Joe was leading. Her answer and manner seemed to satisfy Emilie's curiosity. They all lost themselves in their bedtime occupations with no more discussion.

Addie wrote Ma her account of visiting Philadelphia, her stepmother's home city. She described the ease with which Mr. Reybold found the servant Tally Monson among a host of ragged people seeking employment and how his search certainly differed from finding a servant in New York City. She wrote of the walk to the stream in the rain with Emilie; she told of Mrs. Stewart's fainting spells and subsequent recovery. Throughout the letter, she resisted mentioning the Stewarts' role in opposing slavery.

CHAPTER NINE

Seated next to his brother, Charlie dozed as the wagon lurched over the roads to Bordentown, where they would meet the ferryboat to Philadelphia. He roused enough to know Joe had pulled the horses to a stop and had descended to pay the fare. Not a sound came from beneath the tarpaulin in the rear. No doubt Will and Sam slept.

The two Stewart brothers watched the sun rise over the Delaware during the ferry ride. So far, they had met only a few early morning travelers; the first appeared to be a farmer with a wagonload of new hay proceeding slowly toward the city to supply a hostler's stable. Another man guided an ox-drawn cart loaded with cans of milk and baskets of eggs, very likely packed with care by a housewife on a New Jersey homestead. They had passed them with a hasty wave and hello.

Philadelphia was waking up when the ferry docked. Shopkeepers were opening doors. A woman leaned from a second story window threatening to empty a chamber pot onto their wagon. Joe urged the horses forward, and they proceeded to the Blue Anchor. When the wagon came to a halt, both Joe and Charlie stretched and yawned, their stomachs growling.

"I'll find Elihu. You stay here."

Charlie nodded and twisted about on the wagon seat to survey the street to see how much attention passers-by paid them.

The inn was open but empty when Joe stepped inside. Elihu was alone, mopping the previous night's spilled ale and orts from the tavern floor. Joe was glad they could speak freely. Elihu looked up, smiled, and put his mop back in the pail of murky water. "Safe journey, Joseph?"

"Yes, and I am ready for your directions."

They sat, each on a stool, while the Quaker asked if the two former slaves could stay at the Stewarts' rented rooms. He explained that his usual safe hiding place was the object of suspicion. Joe was surprised and he voiced his fear that his landlady might object.

"I sent around a spy, my son, that is, who found her amenable to letting the Negroes stay at your rooms. She even agreed to feed them."

Joe reflected a moment, weighing the prospects of the escaped slaves inhabiting his rooms. Would there be danger? He did not know all the boarders. The Negroes would have to take Stewart as their last name while they awaited their next move.

At last assenting to what Elihu had previously objected, Joe and Charlie drove the wagon to the rear of their lodgings and ushered the two stiff and hungry young men up the back stairs of the boarding house to their rooms. They instructed them that they were now Will and Sam "Stewart." They would be safe until a conductor came to fetch them. The landlady would see that they could eat and sleep undisturbed in her care. Will and Sam considered what Joe told them and nodded, though not without apprehension. "We thank you," they chimed together and offered their hands to Joe and Charlie. Both pairs of brothers knew they might never meet again once a conductor for the next portion of their escape north contacted them through the Quaker tavern keeper.

Cousin Henry Seymour arrived the next day with a *New York Times* in hand, full of articles about the worsening cholera epidemic in the city, with lists of the afflicted and dead. Henry's arrival reminded Addie and Emilie that their pleasant trip was nearly over. He would accompany them home from Cream Ridge. Addie was glad to see her favorite cousin.

Mrs. Stewart, in much better spirits, invited the girls to attend the Baptist church with her later in the day. Addie realized the dress she planned to wear, the black one with jet buttons, was no longer clean. It was a good thing they would be going home, she thought. Her entire wardrobe was in need of cleaning and pressing.

Henry sat on the porch with Addie as she mended a gown that was cleaner than the black but needed hemming. His health seemed better, no more chills and fever. That meant, he said, he would be traveling again. He asked, "Where are Joe and Charlie?" The son of her father's older sister Mary, Henry was, next to Emilie, Addie's closest family friend. Yet she knew Joe's secret life had to remain her secret, too.

"They are in Philadelphia on business."

"Joe seems to have as much business in Philadelphia as he has in New York these days," Henry concluded. "Did he race while you were here?"

"I hope he returns so you can see him ride." She kept her eyes on her needle and thread.

Henry and she were interrupted by the sound of horses' hooves on the road. Around the corner the team and wagon appeared, with Joe holding the reins and Charlie at his side. Henry hastened down the steps to greet them. Addie stayed behind on the porch, grateful that she did not have to reveal to Henry how moved she felt to see Joe and Charlie come into view. Her eyes

CHAPTER NINE

welled with tears to know they were home and safe. The young men rode the wagon to the stable to unharness the horses.

Lying on a chair next to her was the newspaper that Henry had brought. Addie laid down her sewing and took up the *Times*, leafing through for articles she missed. One that caught her eye explained the Fugitive Slave Act. The author lamented the burden that catching slaves placed upon the government and therefore on all citizens. Another article referred to abolitionists as "radical" and "mad." Was it so mad to want human beings to be free? Addie pondered the issues raised. Realizing that returning slaves to their owners was law throughout the country, not just in their states of origin, she saw that Joe's transporting Will and Sam made him subject to arrest anywhere.

"A penny for your thoughts."

Her brow furrowed. Addie raised her eyes from what she was reading. Henry stood before her, having accompanied the Stewarts from the barn to the back door. Joe and Charlie were finding something to eat in the kitchen.

"What are you reading? It must be serious. You look a thousand miles away."

She did not smile. "Do you think that abolitionists are mad?"

"Ah, that is a very serious question."

"I know, but what do you think, Henry, really?"

"My travels take me to the South, where slavery is a way of life and is crucial to the livelihood of planters. Have you seen the vast fields of cotton they own?"

"You know I haven't, Henry. But you have not answered my question. Are those against slavery mad?" She took up her sewing again, listening for his answer.

"In trade there is still harmony among the states, and I hope it stays that way." Addie looked up at him and studied his gentle face. He would take the route of least resistance in life, eager for peaceful intercourse with everyone. His work selling presses for Father took him among citizens of the North and the South.

"In Boston there is certainly fervor about rights for all, as there was from the beginning of the Republic. In Natchez, it is agriculture that causes men to cling to the need for slaves."

She respected his diplomatic stance, but she wondered how Tally Monson, with the scars of manacles on her legs, would benefit from his even-handed pose.

"So freedom is only for white people?"

"For the time being, yes. Perhaps in a few years that will change. As more machines are invented, they will take over the work of slaves."

Addie smiled, appreciating his optimism about machines. Father shared that faith, which underpinned his work with printing presses. He believed that as more people could read and receive the truth about the world, the better and more humane society would become. She imagined machines doing everything: baking bread, sewing her hem, even washing clothes.

"Soon you'll have us all sitting about with time on our hands."

"There will always be work. Wouldn't you like an easier life?"

"Slaves make it easier for white people who'd have no desire for these changes you predict. How much nicer to have someone out in the field, while you can sit peacefully on the veranda."

Emilie appeared in the doorway. "Oh Addie, there you are, and Henry. Retta and I are ready to leave for church. Are you?"

"I lost track of the hour. There, I finished the hem." Bidding Henry goodbye after he bowed out of the prayer meeting, Addie hastened upstairs to change.

The women departed, arriving a little late for the service in the small wooden church with the cemetery behind it, not far from the Stewarts'. It surprised Addie to see it completely filled. They were obliged to sit in the rear near an open window. The preacher led the prayers, and they sang revivalist hymns unfamiliar to either of the Hoe sisters, who usually attended an Episcopal church in New York. Mosquitoes annoyed Addie, and she tried to swat them in the least obtrusive manner. The minister's final prayer was for peace and tranquility to reign, God willing, in the disputing states. Mention of the conflict resounded in Addie's mind and heart.

On the carriage ride home, the women all sputtered about the insects and the bites they each received by the window. Mrs. Stewart, after her illness, was comforted to visit with her friends among the large congregation. Addie was silent most of the way, both because she felt responsible for making them late to church, and because she was anticipating how to ask Joe about his trip gracefully.

CHAPTER TEN

The motion of the train soothed Addie and Emilie as soon as it pulled out of the Hightstown Station heading in the direction of New York City. Emilie leaned her head against the velvet headrest and fell asleep. Addie watched the verdant hills and dales of New Jersey as they passed by.

The final day at Cream Ridge had been hectic. Ben Cox, a neighbor and friend of Charlie's and Joe's, had invited the two brothers to ride to Bordentown. The girls washed and ironed their clothes. Ben's father and two other gentlemen came to visit in the evening. When the company left, Lottie, Lydia, Retta, and the Hoe girls were able to play music and dance. Knowing they would not see the Stewarts for an indefinite time saddened all the young women. Mr. Stewart offered to drive the Hoe girls to the station early the next morning. They retired early therefore, after packing their bags. Addie's hopes to talk with Joe Stewart were in vain, since he did not reappear in the evening.

At length, after reviewing the past week's events and hypnotized by the rhythm of the train's wheels, she too succumbed to a nap.

Awakened by the train whistle, both girls roused and searched for their bonnets and reticules. They descended the few steps from the car and waited next to the baggage car for the porter to find their luggage. Due to the length of their stay, it consisted of several valises large in size. Emilie told the porter they needed to reach the ferry. Just as he began to respond, Addie felt someone take her hand. It was Charlie. Turning completely, she saw Joe, who stood next to him, both of them winded and smiling. Joe interrupted the porter, to tell the man to pile the bags on the platform. He and his brother, enjoying the surprised look on the girls' faces, told them they had ridden over the evening before. Ben Cox had taken their horses back home with him to Cream Ridge.

Addie, Emilie, Charlie, and Joe, with their abundant baggage, made their way to the ferry, and before the afternoon was out, they were all at 309 Broadway. The lone servant, Bridget, opened the door to them. Except for her, the house was as empty as a crypt. The young men carried in all the bags from the stoop. Addie was very grateful for their cheerful company.

As they approached home, the city seemed more noisy and afflicted with bad air than ever. Although stuffy, the towering brownstone was a sanctuary from the rotting piles of garbage and horse dung on the streets and the coal smoke from the factories. The Hoe family and their friends might escape for the summer, but working men at R. Hoe and Company toiled on. Addie reflected on them and thought of poor Horace, expiring in the infernal city. She and Emilie, much privileged, could unpack their things, temporarily, after their pleasant trip, and could anticipate another departure, for South Salem, soon.

Joe and Charlie were sitting on the stairs when the young ladies came down after sorting out their belongings.

"What will it be, ice cream down the street or tea here at home?" Charlie seemed determined to keep the girls' spirits elevated.

"Come into the kitchen, and let's see what we can find," said Addie, gladly responding to his suggestions. Their voices echoed in the empty hallway.

Bridget knew of their arrival, having been warned by Ma a few days before, and she brought to the table bread, cheese, and fresh cherries, the latter "New from upstate," she announced. The four young people ate hungrily, famished from traveling.

Afterward, Joe suggested, "What do you say we play a game of billiards?"

Emilie looked doubtful since Addie and she knew that was not their territory when Father was home. "We don't know how, if you really want to know," Addie answered.

Charlie laughed. "You mean you never venture upstairs to that inner sanctum of cigars and brandy?" He and Joe were well aware of Father Hoe's habit of escaping upstairs with friends or business folk for billiards. It had not occurred to them that his teenage daughters had not joined him once in a while. The Stewart sisters were a party to every amusement at home, where they were almost as likely to race a horse around the ring as he and Joe were.

Since, due to the renovations, the light fixtures were still absent in much of the house, Emilie and Addie lit lanterns, which they carried upstairs to the billiard room. The lanterns cast eerie shadows and barely illuminated the table. Joe and Charlie took two cues, rubbed the tips with chalk, and set up the balls on the felt-clad billiard table. The young ladies watched carefully as the brothers began the game. Joe was much the better player, able to concentrate his energy in each swift movement and sink his quarry in the pocket. Charlie explained what he was doing with each stroke. Addie wondered whether demonstration or explanation was the better way to teach the game.

After Joe won the match, he gave his cue to Addie while Charlie gave his to Emilie. With much laughter and explicit direction from the young men, the girls spent a jolly evening. After several disappointing shots, Emilie observed that their dresses did not allow freedom of movement and perhaps gowns needed to be designed so that a girl could excel at billiards.

"Let's see if we can find some refreshments downstairs," Charlie suggested. He went with Emilie to locate Bridget and see what they might find in the kitchen that wasn't brandy.

"At last," sighed Addie. Joe returned their cues to the rack along the wall. Near the door they sat down next to each other on the only two chairs in the room. "Since the day we visited the forge in Varmintown, where did you go, and did the young men reach Philadelphia safely?"

"I'm sorry to have worried you. Yes, we made it to the boarding house, where I keep a room. Now, assuming the names Will and Sam Stewart, they can stay there until they meet the next conductor on their journey farther north." Joe studied Addie's anxious face as she dwelt upon his every word. "Please forgive me for burdening you with these particulars. I ought not to do so."

"No, I'm glad you trust me. When Doctor Willis mentioned that a slave catcher was in the county, while you were gone in the wagon, I dared not think what someone like Beauregard Wise might do. Not knowing is unbearable."

Joe took her hand and held it gently until they heard voices on the stairs; then he squeezed her hand and rose to open the door.

Carrying a tray of cups, saucers, and a teapot, Bridget entered the billiard room, followed by Emilie and Charlie, each with a plateful of cake and biscuits. They spread a cloth on Father's precious game table and gathered around it while Emilie poured the tea. Although it was nearly midnight, they lingered about the table.

"Surely brother Joe and I can stretch out on the table for the night." Charlie made the suggestion in his usual, teasing mock-seriousness. The girls knew Joe's rooms, not far from Broadway, were where the young men were headed, and they paid him no heed.

"It is very late, and I have work to do in the morning." Joe, ignoring his brother's remark, piled the dishes on the tray, whereupon Addie opened the door for him. They trooped down to the kitchen and stood around in the hallway reluctant to part. None of them expected to rest much in the hot city. It had been a very long day. Joe and Charlie, promising to come by the next day, finally said good night. Addie watched them cross the still-noisy street, and she closed the heavy front door, throwing the lock.

The next morning, the haze above the neighboring buildings made Addie suspect another very steamy day was beginning when she looked out the window of the spare room on the third floor. Clammy with perspiration, she doused herself well with water from the ewer on the commode. Then she dressed in a thin dimity dress to be as comfortable as possible for working. Soon afterward, Emilie awoke and did the same. The house had been virtually unlived in for weeks, and although Bridget was there to help, she had been absent until the girls arrived. Together they swept the rooms of debris and dust from the renovation. They washed the clothes from the stay in New Jersey and hung them on the rear porch. By late morning they had accomplished a good many tasks.

Aunt Thirza, who lived next door, interrupted them at noon. The wife of their uncle Robert Hoe, she and her family were often at hand, in and out of 309 Broadway. Addie and Emilie both were delighted to see her, and they happily accepted her invitation to dinner. They gathered news of the family, of who was away, who was ill. They felt especially close to Thirza because she had known their mother well and had gone to school with her in South Salem. Her dry sense of humor and laconic speech salted any conversation in which she took part. Though her hair was white, she was still a beauty, with gray eyes and fine features.

"So, you are back from the wilds of New Jersey. Did you dance holes in your shoes with the Stewarts? When did you return?"

The girls took turns regaling her with tales of Delaware City, the Reybolds' domain, and life in Cream Ridge.

"Didn't I see light in the billiard room last night?"

The young ladies looked at each other. They began to answer at the same time.

"Whoa, ladies, one at a time."

Addie set about to tell Thirza about the joke Joe and Charlie Stewart played on them, turning up at the depot. Emilie volunteered that she and Addie had attempted to play billiards, but weren't very good yet.

"What became of the young men? Perhaps they will join us for dinner."

As though summoned by the substance of the conversation, Charlie and Joe returned, knocking on the front door. Bridget admitted them and announced their arrival.

Aunt Thirza understood there was already a strong connection between the Stewart boys and her brother-in-law. She could guess, too, that there might be other reasons for them to drop in than billiards with Addie's and Emilie's father. The young men greeted her with a polite nod as they entered the parlor.

CHAPTER ELEVEN

"Will you join us for dinner this evening, gentlemen?" Thirza addressed Joe, the older of the two brothers.

"I would like that very much; however, Henry and I must go to Bloomfield this afternoon," Joe began, shifting his gaze to Addie. "We will not likely return for several days."

Addie lost her smile at that news, as though suddenly a shadow had obscured the sun. At his glance, she lowered her eyes to the empty fireplace.

"What of you, Charlie?" Thirza continued, not one to be put off. "Will you join us?"

"I shall be honored to come," Charlie answered. He was always ready for a social event. "In the morning I must leave for Philadelphia at seven, but if you do not mind my leaving early, I shall look forward to coming."

With no chairs yet in the front parlor, the visit soon ended. Aunt Thirza, Joe, and Charlie departed without ceremony. Emilie took notice of Addie's and her own frazzled appearance after the morning's exertions. "What must they have thought of our appearance?"

"Who? Aunt Thirza? She has seen us in our nightgowns many times."

"Of course not, I mean Joe and Charlie. What must they think that we are, with dust and grime in our hair, and cobwebs on our dresses?"

"I suppose they know there is plenty of work to be done."

Bridget entered the room, once the front door was closed, and brought Addie a note from the factory. It was a telegraph message from Father saying he was returning from Philadelphia the next day.

"Heavens, Father will expect the house to be in order when he comes." Addie knew they needed strong backs and many hands to help them rearrange the furniture stored in the attic.

"Let's send a message to the factory for help," Emilie suggested. "There isn't much time before closing for someone to assemble the team of workmen we need."

"Mr. Bowen will know what to do," Addie said, and located pen and paper. She dashed off a note to be delivered straightaway to the factory superintendent. Before the middle of the afternoon, seven men arrived. The young women directed the laying of the carpets, the placing of the furniture, and installation of the light fixtures. Normally Ma would have attended to these tasks, but she and the babies were already in South Salem at Grandma's. By evening the job was done.

Addie and Emilie spent the next morning with Bridget's help bringing the linens out of storage and making beds. The work went speedily, and they were pleasantly surprised to have another visit from Charlie. Violent storms had brought relief from the terrible heat of the previous day, but rain continued to fall. When he arrived, he stamped the mud from his feet at the door and shook rain from his umbrella.

"Good day," Emilie welcomed him in, and took his hat and umbrella. "Where did you come from? You were to leave today."

"The rain forced me to delay my trip. May I come in?"

"Of course."

Charlie praised the women for the dramatic transformation of the house from an empty shell to a home once again.

"Don't flatter us. It was seven men from the factory. Three hours later they had reassembled everything. When Ma returns, there'll no doubt be changes."

"Do you really expect your family to stay here?"

Emilie looked startled. "What do you mean?"

"Your father told Joe he imagines having a farm one day, north of the city. He wants to start a dairy with Jersey cows. You ladies could learn to be milkmaids."

The growth of the city around 309 Broadway made his suspicion about a move north plausible, Addie knew. She hoped that it would not happen for years. The ease of travel to her favorite destinations—A. T. Stewart's Store, Limherr's Jewelry, musical performances at Castle Garden—and the proximity to her school and friends made their present home ideal in her eyes.

Supper at Uncle Robert's, just next door, had been delightful, with all her cousins in attendance. Charlie Stewart's bantering with cousins Robbie and Arthur made excellent entertainment, while dancing after dinner made Addie and Emilie forget how tired they had been from the day's exertions.

Addie resisted the idea of any change in their life. Looking down at her apron and frock, rumpled and soiled, she suddenly laughed out loud. "You are perfectly right, Charlie. I already look like a milkmaid. All I need is a bucket and stool."

"And a cow," Charlie interjected.

"When we leave for South Salem," she went on, "I shall ask Uncle Thomas to give me lessons in the cow barn."

"Nonsense. I will stay here in the city with Uncle Robert and Aunt Thirza if any of that happens." Emilie had no interest in what she considered vain imaginings. "Besides, Father will need to stay close to the factory, as he always has."

"Ladies, I am sorry to have caused a row. How about some tea?"

After they ate luncheon together, Charlie left, the rain having stopped. The house seemed as empty as it had been with no carpets or chairs. The specter of changes they could not prevent in their lives returned. They had adjusted well when Father married Ma eleven years before. Ma was not their own mother, but she was kind, took charge of them with firmness, and wanted the best for each girl. They lacked nothing. Yet alterations to the pattern of their lives reawakened the painful grief and uncertainty that afflicted them when their mother died.

As the clouds began to lift, it pleased Addie to retreat upstairs to write to the Stewarts. She looked out from her writing desk onto the scene below. The streets were pocked with puddles in the midst of filthy mud. Horses struggled through, pulling carts. City life resumed, and people moved about. She wrote a polite note of thanks to Mrs. Stewart and expressed hope that her health would continue to improve. She included greetings for Retta, Lydia, and Lottie. As she was about to seal her letter, Emilie entered and asked to include her note of thanks in the same envelope before Addie posted it. The disruption of harmony between the sisters passed.

"Whatever changes might come, they will not happen for years," Addie concluded, to reassure Emilie and herself.

"I know, Charlie always knows a way to rile someone up, doesn't he?" Weary from the housework of the morning, Emilie stretched out, resting her elbows on the bed, her chin in her hands.

"Let's ask Father more about his plans when he arrives."

"I would venture to say it is a dream he has, but Ma could not stand the farming life. If we should marry, none of his plans will concern us anyway."

Addie did not share Emilie's certainty, since marriage seemed a long way off to her. She started a new letter. Choosing her words carefully, she wrote to Joe. Her connection with him, she reflected with pen poised in her hand, was not like any other in her life. It was friendship. She could depend on that. She wrote about the dinner he had missed the night before, the dancing, and the dramatic changes he could expect when he next visited their house. Before she finished, there were voices coming from below; the front door slammed. She hastily closed, "Your devoted friend, Addie," and sealed the envelope. She shook her sister, who had fallen asleep, and they hurried downstairs.

They found Father removing his shoes in the foyer and whistling a tune. When he saw them, he dropped a shoe, smiled, and hugged them both at once. His graying hair in its usual tangle and his blue eyes asparkle to see them, he held each one at an arm's length.

"I swear you have both grown more beautiful just since June. Tell me about yourselves. Have you neglected your music in your rambles far and wide?"

Addie and Emilie urged him to come see the house, transformed as it was by the painters. They led him through the parlor and dining room, eager to hear his reactions to the decorating and their rearrangements. He admired Ma's choice of paint that brightened the front hall and the way the amber horsehair couch looked against the wood-blocked wallpaper Monsieur Roux had recommended for the parlor. "Most satisfactory!" he proclaimed.

Then he prevailed upon them to sit down and give an account of themselves. Addie realized, looking at his kindly, intelligent face, how much she had missed him, the solidity of his presence. Before she sat down, she found Bridget and asked her to make tea. When she returned to the parlor, Emilie was describing their stays in Setauket and Cream Ridge.

"So you think I should have Mount paint my portrait? I should rather have him paint you girls, or Ma." He turned to Addie, who had recalled the dashing Mr. Mount and the picture of Maria asleep in her peach gown. She colored to think of him painting her or Emilie.

Addie described to him the musicians they encountered with Maria. He related that in Philadelphia he had heard music performed in the streets any time of day or night, played by Negroes. "Jolly tunes," he called them.

"Do you think the law will allow them to stay free in Philadelphia?" Addie saw a way to explore her father's feelings about slavery.

"I suppose you refer to the Fugitive Slave Act."

"Yes, doesn't it mean slaves must go back to their owners, no matter what state they escape to?"

"I expect it does," was his only answer.

Emilie began to shift in her chair, as though she had other things to do, other subjects to explore. "Do you think slavery will end?" Addie persisted.

"It may end eventually, as Adams and others expected, but perhaps not in my lifetime. You know New York abolished slavery before 1830."

Bridget arrived with the tea and said Emmie Ely was in the front hall. Emilie dashed out to welcome their cousin. Remaining in the parlor, Addie asked her father another question. "Charlie Stewart, who always makes jokes, said that you planned to have a farm. Was he telling the truth?"

"When last we played billiards, we talked about farming, yes. It has been my dream to find land and raise dairy cows. He was not fooling you this time."

"Soon?"

"Not soon. You are in school. The babies are small. In another five years perhaps."

Addie could reassure Emilie later. Her sister and Emmie Ely, the daughter of Father's sister Emmeline, were chatting animatedly as they entered the parlor. The conversation shifted to life in New York and Brooklyn, where the Elys lived. Emmie, taller than either of the Hoe sisters but with hair and complexion like Addie's, had heard that the famous musician Jullien was coming from Europe to New York with his orchestra later in the year, and she hoped they might go together. Father described a marvelous violin concert he attended while in Philadelphia.

"What else did you do there?" Addie's curiosity about the city where Joe transported the two young men led her to ask Father more questions than she usually would. He turned toward her, mildly surprised and pleased at her interest.

"The *Ledger* is contemplating purchasing a new press, and I went to meet with Mr. Swain and his board of officers to discuss how their press should be built. Other publishers reached me for similar talks, and I also called on a steel manufacturer there."

"Joe Stewart visits Philadelphia often."

"So I have heard."

Addie studied his face to see if he knew why. "What does he do there?"

"I believe he is a buyer for the tailoring department at A. T. Stewart's."

Father turned the conversation in a new direction. "What of the older Stewarts? Are they well?" His old friend and collaborator in the business, Charles Stewart, had produced in his foundry for many years the iron that was used for building Hoe printing presses.

"Mrs. Stewart has not been well; she fainted several times and required a doctor while we were visiting," Addie reported. "She was better when we left."

"Retta went with us to the Reybolds' in Delaware City," Emilie informed him. "Joe and Charlie were there off and on."

"That is their habit," Father commented. Addie could see that whatever he knew, it was not to be parlor conversation. Then he rose and reminded them that in the morning they must pack for South Salem.

CHAPTER TWELVE

"Will you be joining us in South Salem, Emmie?" Father asked.
"If Mother allows me to come, I will."
Emilie expressed delight at the prospect of having her cousin join them in the country. "Oh Emmie, what a grand time we will have! We can ride most every day, and—"

"*If* Mother can arrange a place for me to stay," Emmie spoke doubtfully.

In South Salem, north of the stifling city, the Hoes usually made an appearance during the summer when they would stay with Grandma and Grandpa Gilbert, parents of Addie's and Emilie's departed mother, their father's first wife, Lucy Gilbert Hoe. The girls did not presume that there would be room for a cousin on Father's side for the six weeks they would stay at the farmhouse.

"I will broach the subject with Ma, who might suggest a place when we arrive," Father said as he put his arm around Emmie when they bid her farewell.

The three young women spent many hours together in the city, one or the other of them making the ferry ride back and forth to Brooklyn. Mrs. Ely, Father's next older sister, and her husband Giles always made room for Addie and Emilie at their table, as did Aunt Thirza and Uncle Robert Hoe. Addie knew Emmie, with her love of fun and adventure, would add spice to the spare entertainments in South Salem.

Sorting and packing, washing and ironing muslins, the next day meant imagining how many dresses and petticoats and other items would be needed for the rest of the summer. Father could travel light, since his work would bring him back to the city each Monday and he could stay at home. No doubt the billiard room would see good use then. The girls each packed a trunk, in view of the long sojourn in South Salem.

A four-and-a-half-hour journey north, South Salem was home to many of Addie's and Emilie's relations. Grandfather Robert Hoe came alone to America from England in 1801, an able carpenter who helped build a bridge near South Salem at Cross River. There he met his wife. Later, they moved to the city, where he began the business of building printing presses with his brother-in-law, Matthew Smith. From times before the revolution, the Smiths, Gilberts, Meads, and several other relations, most from Connecticut, bought and settled land obtained from the Van Cortlandts, who were Dutch owners of vast tracts of land on the border with New York. Going back to South Salem meant returning to Father's and their dead mother's roots.

"Don't forget to pack some music," Father reminded the sisters. Although the Gilberts did not own a piano, he knew the Lawrences and Howes, neighbors nearby, did, and there was bound to be an evening or two for playing the piano and dancing.

By late afternoon they loaded the carriage, rode to the train depot, and at sunset met Uncle Thomas in Cross River. They rode in a wagon, hearing the news from Thomas, alternating with Father's whistling the rest of the way.

Addie was always overcome with feeling at seeing her grandparents Gilbert. Their kindly good faces reflected, in combination, the fast-retreating memories of her mother. The accents, tone of voice of Grandpa, the smile and hairline of Grandma, brought back, however fleetingly, Lucy Gilbert. Was it the same for Father? He and Ma, their stepmother, were so devoted to one another, yet did he feel grief and longing over again when he returned home to South Salem?

The elderly couple must have heard the carriage approaching, for they were on the porch ready to greet them. Grandma embraced the sisters, and Grandpa shook hands with Father. When Ma appeared soon after in the doorway, Father opened the door completely and took her hand, then embraced her without a word. She had been putting the little girls to bed, no doubt.

Most remarkable to Addie when they entered the huge, candlelit farmhouse, was the warmth between their stepmother and Grandma Gilbert. Around the oval table in the dining room, the two women together cheerfully served the meal. They circled with plates of ham and roast beef, fresh beans from the garden, bread that was Grandma's pride, and raspberry pie for dessert. Father had many questions about the little girls, Mary and Annie, who had changed without a doubt since last he saw them a few weeks before. Addie expected them to be much bigger but would have to wait until the next day to find out.

The Gilbert farm, surrounded by sturdy stone walls built by Grandpa Gilbert's father and brothers, sat at the northeast corner of two roads, one that traveled to North Salem and the other east to Lake Waccabuc. Only Uncle Thomas remained unmarried of Addie's mother's generation, the youngest of the children. It was hard to imagine why. He was good looking and seemed a capable farmer, if one could judge from his conversation with Father. He reported the first crop of hay was in the barn, that more than fifty of the spring lambs were thriving, and he and a neighbor were sawing up firewood for themselves and the village schoolhouse. At supper, he sat quietly, taking in the description that Emilie gave of the plantation of peaches they had seen in Delaware City, acre upon acre of trees tended by Negroes. Knowing that horses were a favorite topic, Addie herself told of the Stewarts' beautiful chestnut filly destined for the racetrack.

Conversation shifted to who was ill and who had died, an ever-present preoccupation, it seemed. Ma hoped Annie would sleep through the night, as she seemed feverish. A relative Addie barely knew, Minerva, was poorly, Grandma said. Agues attributed to the excessive heat, a neighbor with consumption, another with rheumatism, all received the family's consideration. Finally Grandma looked at Grandpa, who had begun to doze, and she, with Ma's and the Hoe girls' aid, cleared the table.

It was late when Thomas and Father toted the girls' trunks upstairs. The two girls gratefully made ready for bed. The day had been long. The song of a whippoorwill came to them from the dense woods behind the barn as they drifted off to sleep. The call seemed to Addie to ask a disturbing question—Whip poor Will?—ending as it did on a higher note than it began, but at the same time, heard from a distance, its repetition soothed.

CHAPTER THIRTEEN

In the huge cutting room on the upper floor of A. T. Stewart's vast department store, Joe directed four delivery men where to deposit the heavy bolts of cloth he had sent from Philadelphia to New York City. It was ten days since he had chosen the material from wholesale houses. The tailors, who either operated new sewing machines, sewed by hand, measured customers, or cut the fabric, were anxious to proceed with their work now that the supply of material had come.

"*Ich habe…,*" a bespectacled tailor began.

"English, please, Wilhelm." Joe made every effort to correct members of the staff, many of whom were newly arrived from Europe.

"I have…*geben*…given your name to Herr Milton. *Dieses mann* come to sell cloth."

"Where is he?"

"In *der* lobby."

"Thank you." Joe straightened his tie and brushed his hand through his hair. Descending the stairs to the front of the store, he spied a gentleman pacing, top hat in hand, before the glass doors.

"Mr. Milton?" he called to the stranger as he wove his way through the customers entering the popular Manhattan store. He offered his hand. "My name is Joseph Stewart—no relation to Mr. A. T. Stewart. I understand you wish to see a buyer for our store."

"Yes." Dressed in a woolen suit although it was summer and very steamy, the middle-aged man with graying hair and moustache introduced himself. "I am Alvin Milton, from Oxford, Maine. I am here to tell you about our woolen mill." He mopped his brow with his pocket handkerchief.

"Please come, have a glass of lemonade with me," said Joe.

At first the visitor hesitated, but soon he agreed to join him at a café nearby. While listening to what he had to say, Joe took from his pocket a notebook in which he wrote the salient facts and figures about this new source of cloth.

While they conferred, Joe glanced toward the door. Entering the café from the street was a well-dressed Negro woman Joe recognized. He attempted to keep his mind and ears open to Mr. Milton's pitch. However, she kept looking his way. He suddenly remembered she was the daughter of tailor William Jennings, the abolitionist. Joe had made a point of avoiding any suspicion about his other life by steering clear of Negroes near the store. Was she a conductor? Was she about to pass on to him word about a new mission?

Quickly he extracted his watch from his vest and, checking the time, interrupted the salesman. "I am sorry, Mr. Milton, I must return to report to the store manager. Thank you for your description of what Milton Mills produces. We will consider your prices, and perhaps you will kindly send me some samples?"

The gentleman looked startled, but agreed, and hastily drained the rest of his lemonade. They both rose to leave. Joe paid at the counter, assiduously avoiding Miss Jennings, who paused as though waiting for someone near the door.

Later in the day, when he had a moment to think, Joe chided himself that he had treated Elizabeth Jennings as though she were invisible. Did she know that he was a conductor, and that he was forced to be discreet at every turn? He longed to let down his façade and relax. Only with Addie, whom he admired and whose life seemed blissfully uncomplicated by either the uncertainty that surrounded his every movement or the tension that his daily work imposed, could he allow himself that luxury. Racing a horse in Flushing or New Jersey was a break from his double life. On a fast horse there was an exhilaration that relieved the watchfulness that kept him on edge. Even better, time with Addie brought a delightful respite that sustained him on the long wagon trips he took alone protecting a human cargo who relied on him for safety and sustenance.

"Ah, it's Addie, the early riser as usual." Grandma was already stirring the coals in the range, when Addie appeared and slid into the chair nearby.

"Good morning, Grandma. I hope I'm not interrupting your routine. I was wondering if you could teach me cooking."

"I suppose what with school and a regular cook at home, you don't have much opportunity for that," said Grandma as she placed sticks of wood in the firebox.

"Mrs. Reybold in Delaware City makes excellent desserts and bread, even though they have a cook. I should be happy just to make biscuits like hers, so high and delicious. Can you show me how?"

"Biscuits?" Grandma laughed, then continued, "I might have suspected that you'd want to make an English trifle or a Washington cake. But if it is biscuits you want to make, we can, and since it is early, there is time now to do it. Before we start, will you please pump the kettles full of water? I'll bring the biscuit ingredients from the pantry, and you'll find an apron hanging behind the door."

While the kettles for coffee and washing up began to simmer, and the oven temperature rose in the stove, Grandma stirred flour, salt, and pearlash—"to make the biscuits rise"—some lard, and sour milk all together in a large bowl. She explained to Addie that working quickly was her own secret to making light biscuits. On the maple breadboard Grandpa had made for her when they were first married, Grandma sprinkled some flour.

"Now, you turn out the dough onto the flour and knead it, oh, nine or ten times."

"With both hands?"

"Yes." And she demonstrated kneading the air, "like so."

Although Addie's fingers were not as deft from experience and became sticky, she managed to knead and roll out the dough with the rolling pin that she remembered Grandma had allowed her to play with when she was little.

"Was Mother a good cook?" Addie could not recall much about her mother's talents.

"Lucy learned growing up, and she was capable in the kitchen," Grandma commented as she handed Addie the biscuit cutter. "Now, try to cut the biscuits as close together as you can, so as not to handle the extra dough too much."

When the biscuits were baking in the hot oven, Grandma sent her to the cellar for some butter and honey. Their ancestor had included in the foundation, when building the farmhouse, an icy spring. From a crock immersed in the cold water, Addie scooped enough butter for breakfast onto a saucer. Then she found a jar of last summer's clover honey on a shelf and brought the condiments up the narrow stairs to the kitchen.

"Hurry, grab a hot pad. The biscuits must be done. Be careful opening the oven," Grandma cautioned, and handed her a sturdy cotton pad to protect her hand. Addie asked how without looking Grandma knew the baking was done. "The fragrance from the biscuits will tell you when they're done."

The biscuits were perhaps not as lofty as Mrs. Reybold's had been, but they were golden brown and tempting. Would they please the family just beginning to stir upstairs?

"Will my nose learn to cook as well as yours?" Addie wondered aloud.

Grandma smiled and replied, "I cannot imagine cooking or taking care of a family and household without a sense of smell."

Just then Uncle Thomas entered the kitchen by the back door. He carried a brimming pail of fresh milk. Behind him was Father, who must have risen early to assist Thomas and Peter, the farmhand, in the barn. While Thomas poured the milk into an enormous wide pan that Grandma had set on the table, Father pumped some water onto his hands in the slate sink and washed and dried them with a towel. In South Salem, Father entered into farm life with gusto, shoveling out the cows' stalls, harnessing horses, and helping with haying. Addie realized that his plans for a farm were not at all a passing fancy.

"Addie, what brings you downstairs so early?" Father asked.

"Grandma permitted me to bake biscuits. You see, I'd like to learn to cook."

Father nodded and turned to Grandma. "How does the new stove suit you?"

"The proof will be in Addie's biscuits," she said. "The old Oberlin was fine, but, thanks to you, dear Richard, I can bake three or four pies and cook several dishes all at once, why, a whole Sunday dinner with the new model you gave us. Besides, it kept the kitchen very tolerably warm last winter."

He opened the door for Thomas, who carried the pan of milk carefully into the pantry for the cream to rise.

Addie marveled that her father, whose work kept him long hours at the factory, and dealing with publishers, politicians, and men who made machines, some in faraway countries, could still find time to buy a cooking stove for his first wife's parents.

Suddenly, Addie was aware of baby Mary's cries upstairs. Father left Grandma and Addie to finish the breakfast preparations. He hurried to see how the baby had weathered the night. "Little Mary kept us up," he said as he left.

"Have Annie and Mary been well this summer?" Addie asked, while she found the cutlery and plates and began to set the table.

"You may find them unwell today, but they have been having a fine time until now."

Ma and Father brought into the dining room each of the two babies, Annie, the two-year old with arms happily encircling her father's neck, while the infant Mary appeared listless lying in Ma's arms. Addie went to Annie, who squealed in delight to see her big sister. Father leaned over, and she hopped to the floor to embrace her half-sister. Ma smiled wanly and sat down at the table with the baby. Emilie entered and seeing Ma's tired face, she was very sorry to hear of Mary's ailment, which appeared to be a fever and cough. She sat beside Ma and stroked the baby's cheek.

"Biscuits! Grandma, did you make these especially for us?" Emilie asked when Addie brought the biscuits piled high in a basket to the table.

"No, your sister made them." Grandma sat down between the two sisters, but not for long, for Grandpa called her from upstairs, needing her help getting dressed. The wet nurse, Hulda, who had come with Ma from the city, took the feverish baby in her arms and retreated to the kitchen. Father said grace, brief and to the point. "Oh Lord, for what we are about to receive we are truly thankful."

By the time the family had consumed every biscuit, along with the butter and honey, and drunk their tea or coffee, there was no doubt that Addie had made a good start in learning to cook.

Days in South Salem were different. It was possible for Addie and Emilie to ride any of several horses most anytime, as long as Uncle Thomas or a farm hand was available to saddle and bridle them. There were jaunts by carriage to New Canaan or Ridgefield to visit relatives whom Grandma wanted them to know. One day, with cousin Jane Howe, a second or third cousin, actually, there was a journey to Wilton to shop. The country roads afforded lovely views of the hills and Long Island Sound. Addie knew she would not always spend vacations at the Gilberts', but the more she saw of the world, the squalor, noise, and foul air of the city, the more she treasured the times in South Salem.

On Sundays, Addie enjoyed the church services at Mr. Lindley's Presbyterian church on the other side of Lake Waccabuc. He gave inspiring sermons and, hearing him, she perceived he had a vision for humanity unlike many ministers'. He urged compassion for all mankind, not only white men. He saw a future in which Indians, Negroes, and white men lived in harmony.

When Addie asked Grandma about the minister's views, as they worked in the kitchen, she answered that she held him in high esteem. "Reverend Lindley is a fine man. I expect he will not remain here forever, since it is the rare preacher who does stay in one place for a long time. The world has not caught up with him."

"Do you think him strange to have the vision he has?"

Grandma, who was blacking the stove, paused and looked out the kitchen window. "No, but making men treat one another as they would be treated takes more than vision."

"What do you think stops men from getting along?"

"Vanity and greed might account for a lot of the trouble. How are those apples coming along?" She looked over Addie's shoulder at the apples she was peeling for pies. "No pips with the slices now."

Discussions with Grandma were another part of the summer that Addie appreciated. Life at home in New York City was often hectic with activity—people coming and going, Father's friends and colleagues, neighbors and schoolmates, entertainments. Hours with her grandparents were quieter. They recalled the sweep of the long history of their lives. Grandpa told stories after dinner about the revolution and what the first settlers had to do to prepare the land for farming. Grandma was always working, but at the same time she shared her wisdom in the course of her tasks. Addie wondered how they stood on the issue of slavery, the pot that simmered in Delaware and New Jersey. It seemed less relevant in South Salem, where a Negro was a rare sight.

Uncle Thomas invited the two sisters to accompany him to prayer meeting one hot Sunday evening. Reverend Lindley led the gathering, which consisted of a good many Meads and Gilberts, mostly Addie's relatives from the clans who resided in the vicinity. They spied the postmaster, Cyrus Lawrence, in a pew at the front of the sanctuary with his wife and daughter Mary, whose blonde hair and especially fine lace collar attracted the attention of the Hoe girls. They sat in a pew directly behind the Lawrences. Uncle Thomas blushed when Mary turned to look at them, then smiled and nodded. Addie and Emilie each noted the exchange with considerable interest. Perhaps Uncle Thomas, who was nearly thirty, would not remain a bachelor for long.

While Emilie sewed in the front parlor one morning, Addie read aloud another chapter of *Katherine Ashton*. In plodding prose, Miss Sewell's novel set a high premium on good works and portrayed a heroine with the highest moral values. Addie wondered if they would ever finish the book, since many interruptions, the result of the girls' travels, meant reminding each other again and again what had happened in the story. Addie was relieved when Grandma entered with a letter to her, and she could lay down the novel.

"Cousin Henry's coming for a visit," Addie related after scanning the letter.

"Ah, news from the city," Emilie responded. "I wonder if he says anything about Emmie Ely coming here."

"He is coming himself when he returns from Bloomfield," Addie said, glancing up from the letter.

"Is he well?"

"He does not say. We shall soon see him, and we can judge for ourselves."

In the letter, Henry wrote that he missed the company of the girls. The house at 309 Broadway seemed terribly empty when he stopped by for a game of billiards with Father. He added that Joe had gone to Delaware City and when he returned he promised to bring a surprise for them. Addie was mystified. Had he gone to rescue more slaves from the South? Was the surprise something innocuous and pleasing? Obviously Joe wanted Henry to pique her curiosity.

She read the entire letter to Emilie and Grandma, who then rose from the sofa. "I shall go remind Imogene," she said, heading to the kitchen, "to make up a bed for Henry before Friday. Will you girls go to the washerwoman's with me later?"

"Gladly, Grandma," Emilie replied. "We'll carry the baskets to the carriage. May we stop at Uncle Solomon's store when we return?"

Addie picked up Miss Sewell's novel once again. "Now, let me see, where were we?"

The days melted into one another. Addie learned to make a fairly acceptable apple pie; her crust did not flake as desirably as Grandma's, but the consensus of the eaters was positive, and the pie disappeared quickly. Her attempt at oatmeal bread was less successful, for she left out the salt.

"Since there is an abundance of excellent cream," Addie suggested to Grandma one day, "might we make some ice cream?"

Grandma looked doubtful. "We'd need a churn, or some contraption, to make it, which we do not own."

Addie would solve the mystery of how to make ice cream. "In the city, there are shops that sell the most wonderful ice cream. Aunt Thirza knows

CHAPTER THIRTEEN

how. I can ask her." They would need ice, she knew. The ice house next to the woodshed contained blocks of ice cut from the lake and buried in sawdust the previous winter. When he arrives, Henry also might know the science of ice cream, Addie thought.

When finally Henry arrived, he brought the surprise Joe had promised, a bushel of magnificent, ripe Delaware peaches. Addie and Emilie rushed to embrace him in delight when, having ridden with Uncle Thomas from the depot, he burst upon them in the parlor. He appeared to be very well indeed, and admitted as much when Addie pressed him about his health.

"What is the news from the infernal city?" Grandpa wanted to know, shaking Henry's hand.

"The cholera is like the plague this summer. I brought a newspaper, which you are welcome to read, Mr. Gilbert." Opening his satchel, Henry handed him the *New York Times*, adding, "Here's the new penny paper." The elderly man perched his pince-nez on his nose and, after thanking Henry, returned to his rocker with paper in hand.

"Have you eaten?" Grandma asked. When Henry admitted leaving New York so early that he had not eaten all day, she waved him into the dining room, sat him down, and urged Addie to bring him some cider, bread, and cheese. As he was eating, Addie and Emilie pressed him to tell them if cousin Emmie Ely was coming up, what about Uncle Robert and Aunt Thirza, and would cousins Arthur and Theodore join them soon? What were Father's plans for the telegraph company? How were his parents in Bloomfield? What was Joe Stewart up to?

"Wait!" Henry interjected, hardly having a chance to answer a single question.

"Let's let him eat." Addie realized there would be time for answers. It was possible in South Salem to forget the vibrant, pulse-quickening nature of the city. Thousands of different faces on the street from all over the world could stimulate or, at times, weary or disgust a person, yet she would never deny wanting to partake of its variety.

Henry drained the last of the hard cider from his glass, and seemed to take forever to dab at the corners of his mouth with his napkin before addressing their many queries. He straightened his tie, directed into place the unruly lock of hair that always fell across his eyes, and cleared his throat. With exaggerated deliberation, he folded his napkin and laid it next to his empty plate. Guessing his enjoyment of the drama of having all four eyes, alight with expectation, trained upon him, both girls burst out laughing.

The more he stroked his chin, further stalling and testing their patience, the more they giggled. "Ahem, let me see. Where should I begin?"

Finally, Addie abandoned the thought that he would relate anything serious to them, for the moment at least. "Henry, what do you know about making ice cream?" Addie suspected a new avenue of discourse might get him talking. Besides, she truly wanted to know.

"There is a new machine, a hand-cranked churn, that makes excellent ice cream. I have seen one at A. T. Stewart's. There is a cedar bucket with a metal canister that fits within it." He launched enthusiastically into a full description of the workings of the ice cream churn.

"You need rock salt to mix with the ice to keep the temperature below freezing, you see? Ice melts at thirty-two degrees, and you place the mixture of salty ice around the canister in which you pour the cream and sugar and perhaps some eggs. The salted ice takes the heat out of the cream." He warmed to the icy subject. "On top of the canister is a cover that is attached to a hand crank that makes the canister spin while the bucket stays put. Do you see?" He looked from one girl to the other.

"Do you propose making ice cream yourself?" Emilie was surprised by her sister's interest.

"Perhaps not this summer." Addie was deflated to learn the complexity of the machine and process. "Seeing all the cream Grandma skims from the milk had made me want to try."

Ma, holding baby Mary with one arm and Annie by the hand, joined them. When she entered the room, Henry stood and said he was glad to see the little girls, much changed since he had last seen them in New York. Mary, recovered from her illness, diagnosed by the local doctor as scarlet fever, shyly smiled at Henry, while Annie begged him for the sweets he used to bring her. Ma expressed interest in his news. When she asked about Joe, he was vague. Had Joe come to New York? Was Joe keeping Father company?

Henry seemed reluctant to talk about him, answering only, "I don't know much about him."

That puzzled Addie since Henry, in his letter, had told of Joe's surprise gift, which turned out to be peaches. Henry, usually very straightforward, presented a studious lack of interest in Joe. Were they at odds? Had they argued about abolition? By contrast, Henry's answers about his family's health, his recent travels to Bloomfield, and the progress of the American Telegraph Company, he gave readily and completely.

CHAPTER FOURTEEN

There was a tapping on the bedroom door early the next morning. A light sleeper, Addie arose quickly and, throwing a shawl around her shoulders, she opened the door a crack.

"What are you up to?" she whispered, when she saw Henry, completely dressed and wearing boots.

"Come riding with me," he replied. "It's a perfect morning."

She closed the door, tiptoed to retrieve her riding habit from the armoire, and dressed quietly so as not to awaken Emilie, who was not partial to early morning adventures.

The midsummer dew on the grass dampened Addie's boots as she crossed the yard and joined Henry at the barn. Although it was almost chilly, the morning promised to become another hot day by noon. The sun's first rays lit with gold the trees surrounding the barn. They entered the dark stable. With Peter the farmhand's help, Henry had already saddled Paul, a tall, spirited horse, and was cinching the sidesaddle for Addie's mount. Her horse, Kate, was a docile bay of medium size that whinnied a greeting as Henry passed the bridle over her ears and led her out of the stall. Peter held the other horse's bridle while Henry, reins in one hand, helped Addie into the saddle. She rearranged her skirts and took the reins.

"Thank you for waking me," she said, once they were out of the barnyard and had found a walking pace that allowed easy conversation. They followed a path that eventually would skirt Lake Waccabuc. Birds sang in the trees around them.

"Can there be anything better than this," Henry exclaimed. "The air, the light, the woods."

"I agree. You must crave the country when you are at the office or in the factory." Addie recalled the stuffy office where Henry spent his days when he was not peddling printing equipment or helping her Father, where the steam engines operated incessantly and the coal smoke hid the sun.

"I did not mean to lie to you about Joe," he said, suddenly changing the subject. "I had not seen him when I wrote. He had come from Delaware and left a note at my boarding house that said he was leaving the peaches and would I please deliver them to you. That was all."

"I see." The path became bright with morning sun as it widened near the lake. Startled by the eerie cry of a loon nearby, the horses began to trot. Conversation lapsed between the cousins until Paul and Kate returned to a peaceful gait. The lake was tranquil, with enormous boulders bordering the glassy expanse. Above it, the mists of morning were rising into the pale blue sky. The mountain opposite was perfectly reflected in the water.

Addie felt at ease with Henry. Playmates from childhood, they had always found common interests. He enjoyed music, they had similar tastes in books, and they had learned to ride together. She wondered where his life would take him.

"Henry, where do you imagine you will be in ten years," she asked, "in business or the church?"

"I expect I will be in business. Father and I talked at home in Bloomfield about where I am headed. It is less of an argument now. Although his school makes him and Mother happy, seeing boys headed off in the right direction, neither the church nor teaching interests me anymore. The world of industry is as exciting as anything can be. Patents in our time multiply every day. A factory for useful things can be profitable." He drew up the reins, and his horse paused, as did hers.

He faced her. "Addie, do you think I am letting my father down?"

Looking into his worried face, she sought to find the right words. "I think a man must pursue what interests and excites him. Ask my father. He'd be the first to tell you to follow your heart."

"I value your opinion. Thank you for it." He patted Paul on the neck and flexed his knees to urge the horse forward. They continued along the path. Above the lake a hawk circled, its sharp eyes watching for signs of prey. Its presence caused the songbirds to hush their singing. Making a sudden, lethal dive, the bird swooped near the center of the lake and sent a spray of water into the air. Addie and Henry watched it fly off, bearing a silvery shape in its beak.

The choices of an occupation for a man were many, Addie thought. For a woman, marriage and children were the likeliest career. There was also teaching, a respectable alternative best exemplified in her life by Miss Clarke. Where will I be in ten years? she thought. "Whatever the future might hold, I hope friends and family will be at the core of my life always," she asserted as they began the final mile of the trail.

"Oh, Addie, those are what I should want for you, and you must think I am a selfish fellow not to ask about your expectations."

"I think no such thing. We are fortunate, my sister and I. We have more than most young women, and the benefits of schooling. Our parents afford us freedom to travel and see something of the country." She urged Kate to a trot; Henry's Paul matched the pace.

"Have you read *Oliver Twist*? I hope not, for I have brought it for you."

CHAPTER FOURTEEN

"Capital! Dickens is grand, and it will be great fun not to have to wait for each serial installment to enjoy it."

The Gilbert farm came into view. Uncle Thomas was turning out the cows, the milking done, and Peter, a robust boy of thirteen, toted a bucket of slops to the pigs. They greeted the horseback riders and, holding the bridles, helped them each to dismount.

"How was your ride?" Thomas asked as he and Addie walked to the house. Chores done, he carried the pail of warm milk. Meanwhile, Henry and Peter unsaddled the horses.

Addie described to her uncle the loon's eerie cry on the lake and how the hawk dove for a fish. "The beauty of Waccabuc is very fine," she said.

"Addie, will you join me for prayer meeting again Sunday evening?"

"I should be glad to go," she smiled, suspecting in all likelihood that Mary Lawrence, too, would be planning to attend. Uncle Thomas shifted the heavy bucket to his left hand and opened the kitchen door for Addie. She saw that what she and Emilie had considered extreme shyness in Thomas was actually a most gentlemanly character.

Later that day, when they were sewing in the parlor, Henry brought the girls the novel he had purchased for them, and then, bidding them farewell, he returned to the city. They were delighted with his gift. Addie vowed to finish the last chapters of Miss Sewell's book that day. While Emilie and Grandma sewed, Addie resumed reading to them the tale of the lonely young girl in the British school.

The warm afternoon and the lazy sound of the August crickets caused her to skip a word here and there, and she dozed, the early morning ride also taking its toll. Emilie, exasperated, put down the pillow slip she was embroidering and poked her in the ribs.

Addie roused. "Where was I?" She stared in confusion at the fine print.

"I have a suggestion, if you don't mind," Grandma spoke. "Why not put away this book and begin the one you were excited to receive? We are partial to Dickens ourselves, aren't we, Mr. Gilbert?"

Grandpa, who, like Addie, was also under the spell of the hot summer afternoon, answered, "What? Who?"

"We're partial to Dickens," she repeated loudly.

"Oh yes! Very partial," he echoed.

Laying aside *Katherine Ashton*, Addie took up the new volume, *Oliver Twist*, and opened to the first chapter. In the succeeding days, they followed the travails of another English waif. Grandpa managed to stay awake while Addie or Emilie read aloud, themselves well-entertained by Dickens' wit and vivid characters.

There were visits during the following week. The Misses Keeler and Reynolds, neighbors of the Gilberts, came for tea. Nettie Keeler was about to be married and told of her plans to shop for a gown in New Canaan. The Reynolds girls, Mary and Viola, related the details of the demise of their grandmother, afflicted for years with rheumatism. Grandma announced that she and the Hoe girls would be traveling to see poor Minerva. Emilie and Addie assiduously sipped their tea, both surprised to learn her intention, and both felt apprehensive about visiting this unknown, yet deathly ill person. They kept their composure and did not object among the visitors.

Cousin Jane Howe came for tea the same afternoon, and invited the ladies to enjoy her piano whenever they wished. Addie, happy to accept her open invitation, related that they had brought music from the city but had had no opportunity to play. It was agreed that there would be music the following week if Ma and Grandma could spare them for an evening.

"I should like to come along and hear what my granddaughters have learnt at school," Grandma added.

"Of course, by all means," said Jane, whose kind manner and gentle voice charmed Addie right away. She was one "who spread oil upon the waters," Grandma had said. She was barely five feet tall, and her waist was no bigger around than a saucer.

"Perhaps you have brought tunes for dancing?" Jane asked.

"Oh yes, many," Emilie answered. Ma could see no objection to music and would come herself if the babies were in good health. It was decided the party would be the next Friday evening.

Having no opportunity to practice their music thus far in South Salem, Addie and Emilie walked the next day to Jane's to try out the piano, which sounded in very good tune. They each played a half hour of waltzes, études, and galops, and Jane suggested they return any time that week to play. The piano sat in the parlor, which was small, perhaps too small for dancing, the girls sadly concluded.

"Dancing might not be proper here," Emilie commented. "What is fine in Delaware City might be unseemly among Grandma's relatives, coming from Connecticut as they do."

"I had never thought of that," Addie reflected. They asked Jane.

She laughed and said, "Times have changed. Although Grandma's people did come from New England, they are not prissy folk. If there is a fiddler, they enjoy a jig as well as people elsewhere. When the surveyors and statesmen have concluded what is Connecticut and where the border with New York lies, we can decide how much dancing is allowed."

"What do you mean?" Addie asked.

"There has been a dispute for almost two hundred years over where the lines between Ridgefield and Salem should be drawn. As for the dancing, that was meant as a joke."

CHAPTER FOURTEEN

The young ladies nodded, smiled, and were relieved that dancing was possible in South Salem.

A routine developed over the week. As soon as Addie and Emilie arose, they assisted Grandma in the kitchen, minded the babies for Ma, and finished the ironing or sewing; then they tied on their bonnets and walked to Jane's to practice the piano.

They realized their hair, grown long over the summer, was in need of attention, and, using sewing scissors, they trimmed one another's locks. Imogene, from Cross River, who helped Grandma, agreed to arrange their hair for their concert. The sisters would wear their Sunday dresses, they decided. Their piano repertoire would be divided among a single classical piece for each, a few ballads so that guests might sing, and selected dances.

The day of the party Addie baked her version of the spice cake Grandma often made for tea, with no omissions this time. It rose high in the oven, its fragrance wafting through the farmhouse. Annie begged to lick the bowl, but Ma allowed only a brief taste, not wanting her anywhere near the piping hot stove. When the cake had cooled, Addie placed it in a basket to take to Jane's that evening.

Ma gave instructions to the wet nurse to tell Father where they were, should he arrive after they left for the party. Uncle Thomas brought up the carriage, since the walk was too far for Grandma in her good shoes.

Addie and Emilie were accustomed to impromptu performances casually woven into the fabric of life. Friends came to dine or for tea, or the family—aunts, uncles and cousins included—gathered of an evening at home. At the Stewarts' or Reybolds', there had been no serious practice before they played. The event at Jane Howe's was different, not unlike the recitals their piano teacher required. Butterflies in her stomach, Addie pinned on her best cameo and dabbed a curl in place. While they rode the quarter mile to Jane's, she rehearsed in her mind the fingering for the étude she was to play.

There were several carriages in the yard when they arrived. Addie and Emilie looked surprised, and they questioned Jane when they entered the front hall. She took their bonnets and the cake basket Addie carried.

"These are the folks who want to hear Lucy Gilbert Hoe's daughters play the piano. Don't worry; they are your friends. This is not Castle Garden."

Hardly reassured, the two nodded and walked blushing to the two chairs placed near the piano. The parlor was nearly packed. Jane had arranged every chair in her house, and she brought in a bench from the back stoop as well, to accommodate the guests.

Emilie began the program with a minuet from *Don Giovanni* and executed the trills prettily, Addie thought. There was applause. Addie gathered her wits and arranged herself on the piano bench. She began to play a Heller étude, one of which she was fond and certain. Half way through, the door of the parlor opened, and in came Father with Joe Stewart just behind him. Addie, who had learned her piece by heart, lost her poise at the interruption and was obliged to start over. She swallowed as she heard the door close. During the pause, she dared not glance in the direction of the two men standing with no empty chair in sight.

The étude went flawlessly this time, and again there was applause for the other of Lucy Hoe's daughters. Addie turned to see Father and Joe smiling and clapping enthusiastically.

Emilie played two songs for all to sing, and Father stepped forward to add his melodious tenor to the voices joining in. Addie played "Flow Gently, Sweet Afton" and sang along herself, no longer gripped by the jitters she felt at first. Last of all, Emilie and she played a waltz for four hands which set several toes tapping. With the room crowded with chairs, she could not imagine how they would dance. It seemed the evening had become strictly a concert, rather than a prelude to dancing as the girls had hoped.

When the piece ended, Addie turned to find Mr. Howe, with Father's and Joe's help, removing the chairs, while the assemblage stood and milled about. Perhaps there would be a new chapter to the evening.

Jane invited everyone into the dining room for refreshments. Uncle Solomon Mead, the elderly storekeeper, among several others, came up to Emilie and Addie and praised the performance. "We don't often have an evening of music around here. You ladies are accomplished indeed. Lucy would have been proud, bless her soul." His wife at his side nodded in agreement.

The girls each felt embarrassed, but were pleased to hear his kind words. Father embraced each daughter, and Ma beamed, adding simply, "Bravo, for both of you." Others she did not know smiled and nodded in appreciation as they passed into the dining room. Addie looked for Joe, who appeared at last beside her.

The guests turned their attention to the candlelit table or, rather, the groaning board, well laden not only with Addie's spice cake but also an assortment of other tempting desserts. "Jane, you have outdone yourself!" "You must have been baking night and day." "How *did* you have time to prepare this sumptuous repast?" Voices chimed about Jane, and she encouraged everyone to partake.

Addie and Joe helped themselves to a plate of refreshments to share, and, each with a cup of punch, they repaired to the front steps. They hardly said a word until they sat down together in the cool evening air. Joe's arrival had so surprised her she still could not believe he was actually there.

"I'm sorry to have interrupted your lovely piece," he began. "I remember your saying that was one of your favorites when you played it at home."

"It was off-putting to hear the door open, but when I saw you and Father, it made playing easier. What I felt beforehand—that is another story. How are you? We are all grateful for the peaches Henry delivered."

"So you received them."

"It told me you were again in Delaware. Am I correct?"

"Yes, I was. This last trip, my cargo," he paused, glancing warily about them to assure they were alone, "was a mother and child. They are now safely in Philadelphia, staying with someone until they can move north."

"Were there any difficulties this time?"

He paused, ate a bite of cake and drained his cup, as though considering how much Addie ought to hear.

"The wait at the wharf in Delaware City was long. The sun was scorching hot that day. I feared the child, only a baby, really, might expire hidden in the wagon. Besides, as I was taking them a bottle of water and lifting the canvas to pass it to the woman, who should pause by the horses but Beauregard Wise. I recognized him from the description you gave at the Reybolds'—short, swarthy and fat, leering about at all the wagons ready to board the boat."

"What did you do?"

"I opened the bottle and drank some of the water and placed it on the seat. Mr. Wise watched my every move and then passed on to the next team and wagon."

"What about the baby?"

"Once on the boat, I was able to give the mother the bottle, and from there we went on safely to the city."

"Ever since I read the full account in the paper of the Fugitive Slave Act and realized what it could mean for you, I have not stopped thinking of the danger you face. Yet I know what you are doing is right."

"When and if you write to me, make sure you do not mention anything about slave catching. I cannot be certain my mail isn't opened before I receive it." An owl hooted insistently in the trees nearby.

"Even in New York?"

"Mr. Jennings—you've heard me speak of him?"

"Yes, you said he bought his kinfolk out of slavery years ago."

"He did, and that means any of us who deal with him, as I do in the tailoring business, are suspect since slaves are contraband and heading for Canada."

"I see. I will be careful when I write to you."

CHAPTER FIFTEEN

Father joined Joe and Addie on the steps. The guests, having finished eating, entered the parlor, and Emilie returned to the piano. She played von Flotow's "'Tis the Last Rose of Summer," one of the arrangements Father had given his daughters for Christmas. Its melancholy sentiment reminded Addie that soon they would return to New York. She realized the summer was passing quickly, even though it was still July.

"Now if you both come inside, there might be some dancing. Our country neighbors are shy and need someone to demonstrate the sets." Father's irrepressible good humor drew the couple out of their conversation and back into the bright sitting room. He and Ma prevailed upon Emilie to play a waltz, and, as soon as it began, her parents were the first to whirl about the parlor. Soon other couples joined them.

Joe and Addie stood on the fringe of the group, still absorbed in thought and one another. He took her hand and held it fast. When Emilie rose from the keyboard, she spied Addie across the room and prevailed upon her to play so that she might dance. Reluctantly Addie agreed and Joe unclasped his hand from hers. When she commenced to play a polka, Uncle Thomas, with Emilie's instruction, gave the lively dance a try.

When it was time to go, the guests thanked Jane for hosting the party and in turn she thanked the Hoe girls for providing the music. All bid her and Mr. Howe a warm farewell.

Although it was nearly midnight, Addie and Joe refused the carriage ride to the Gilberts'. Instead, they chose to walk the short distance together in the moonlight. They reached the porch, where the fragrance of Grandma's roses climbing the railing surrounded them. Joe turned and kissed her, or did she kiss him?

When she mounted the stairs and joined Emilie undressing in the bedroom, Addie's mind was far away. She slowly removed her shoes and bonnet. As she brushed her long hair, her sister wasted no time questioning her about the evening. "Are you and Joe plighted?"

"I dare not say anything of the kind. He trusts me. I trust him. He and I are friends."

CHAPTER FIFTEEN

"You know he's a most unsettled man, always darting about from one place to another."

"Let's not put the cart before the horse. We are fond of each other. That's all."

"That may be so, but it seemed tonight that he was setting his sights on you." Emilie's final shot silenced Addie for the night, and she climbed into the double bed with no more talk.

The moonlight streamed into their bedroom above the porch. The roses' scent that filled the night air would create an association in Addie that far outlasted the evening. She could not fall asleep right away for thinking of that one kiss and Joe's hand holding hers. Was he asleep? He stayed with Uncle Thomas when he came to visit. She wondered if he could sleep any better than she.

For Addie to rise at seven o'clock was very late and most unusual. Emilie still slept. The sounds of the barn—cows lowing, rooster crowing, and lambs bleating—made the events of the previous evening seem like a dream. She joined Grandma downstairs in the kitchen. Thomas was pouring the fresh milk from a pail into a pan. He glanced Addie's way. She wondered what Joe might have said of her to him. She smiled at her own presumption, knowing how silent each of the men tended to be.

"How is Miss Lawrence?" she made bold to ask Thomas. "She was not at the party."

"I asked myself the same question, but perhaps she was ill." He rinsed the empty pail after pumping water into the sink.

Grandma set Addie to the task of putting dried beans to soak for the next day's supper. Then Addie volunteered to pick cucumbers for the pickles they aimed to make later.

The garden was Grandpa's domain now that the heavy labor on the farm was beyond him. He planted the vegetables for the family after Thomas and the team of horses plowed the ground in the spring. On his knees, the old man weeded the seedlings and later hoed the crops. Getting the job done before the sun was high, he was already among the cabbages, stripping off dead leaves, when Addie asked where to find the cucumber patch. He pointed her to a tangle of vines on the edge of the garden. In no time Addie's basket was full, and she toted the abundant green fruit back to the house.

She suddenly felt the effects of not having slept much the night before when she finally placed the heavy basket on the back stoop. Opening the door for her, Grandma noted her scarlet, flushed face, and sent her to sit down in the parlor until breakfast. Taking her advice and sitting upright on the sofa, she closed her eyes and soon fell asleep. Fully dressed and with her head tilted at an awkward angle, she dreamt a disturbing dream of a child pursued by a dangerous animal, an amorphous something, and she awoke herself with her own cry of alarm.

Disoriented, she looked about her. The sound of Grandma's closing up the woodstove and the rest of the family waking up reassured her. Father, whistling the tune from the minuet Emilie had played the night before, came down the stairs and into the parlor.

"Addie, what a pleasant surprise. Have you been here all night?"

Recovering her presence of mind, she arose from the sofa and straightened her apron. "Hardly. Grandma sent me to pick vegetables and, not having slept much last night, I sat down to rest."

"I understand. You and your sister must be tired after performing for the party. In any case, would you want to go horseback riding later? As we came up yesterday, Joe mentioned that he would like to take a ride. What do you think? I'll ask Thomas which mounts he can spare this morning." Somewhat rested she nodded in assent.

It was decided that after breakfast they would ride—Father, Joe, and Addie. At the stable, they discovered that Kate, the horse Addie preferred to ride, was pulling Emilie and Ma and the babies in the carriage, taking them to Ridgefield. That meant that, given the spirited nature of the remaining horses, Paul would be hers to ride. She recalled that Henry had managed him without difficulty, and she took the reins, especially confident since Joe would be following behind her.

Their route was not the path around Lake Waccabuc. Father led them out the wide road to North Salem. He rode a young gelding that Thomas claimed had only recently been broken to the saddle. Father's faith in his ability to control a horse was considerable. He started out with Titus well reined in. Joe rode behind Addie. His mount was the tall mare Nell. Thomas trusted Joe to handle her, powerful and flighty though she was.

The day was sunny, and a cool breeze blew out of the west. Excited, the three horses began at a rapid walk. Father suggested they all canter, once the three horses had broken into a trot. Paul, Addie's horse, must have sensed their ride was some sort of competition. He began to speed up, trying to run neck and neck with Titus. Soon, despite Addie's pulling tighter on the reins, Paul had passed Father's gelding and was racing far ahead of Titus. Her hair coming unpinned and flying, Addie clung to the pommel of her saddle as Paul plunged forward. Now he was galloping, far outstripping Titus. In her terror Addie heard a horse pulling near, and she prayed that Paul would not toss her onto the rock wall that lined the dirt road.

Finally, she dared look at the horse now abreast of hers. Joe, with his head low on his horse's neck, switched his reins to his right hand, and, with his

CHAPTER FIFTEEN

taller horse galloping alongside, he snatched Paul's reins that were swinging slack on his lathering neck. He spoke calmly yet commandingly to both horses, "Here, here, here," and gradually they slowed to a walk.

Addie, her auburn hair hanging in disarray and her scarf untied, pursed her lips to hide the tears that threatened to overtake her. She and Joe continued along in silence.

When he caught up with them, Father laughed in his accustomed jollity at the sight of his daughter racing off. "Why you looked like John Gilpin on his famous ride," he exclaimed.

Addie knew the comic poem well but did not see the least bit of humor in her wild ride, not for the moment anyway. Joe, holding Paul's reins, led him behind Nell back to the stable while Father decided to continue to North Salem.

Sweeping her auburn hair out of her eyes and taking a deep breath, Addie slowly regained her composure while they rode sedately the mile back to the farm. Joe waited several minutes before speaking. Addie was grateful for his silence and for his skill in coming to her aid. Only the week before, two girls had been thrown from their horses in South Salem. One of them was stunned when her head struck a rock, and the other was badly bruised.

When at last she spoke, her voice came as a croak. "Thank you." That was all she could think to say, still feeling humiliated and drained.

Joe turned around in the saddle and smiled disarmingly. "You're welcome."

"Back so soon?" Thomas greeted them at the stable door. While helping Addie down from Paul, Joe paused and looked up at her to see what report she chose to give of the experience.

She caught his eye and gave the hint of a smile. "Paul wanted to race Titus, and I happened to be on his back," she replied. Then Joe put both hands around her waist and, as she lifted her skirts clear of the pommel of the side saddle, she slid to the ground. "Thank you again," she said.

"And what of Richard?"

"He's gone on to North Salem," Joe answered as they led the horses into the barn.

Addie was relieved when she entered the house to find that no one was there to see her. Upstairs in her room, she took her time changing her clothes, washing her face and rearranging her hair, and then she sat down to write a note to her cousin Emmie Ely. By then somewhat composed, she recalled Grandma's plans to make pickles and descended to the kitchen.

Just as Grandma was about to ask Addie about her morning, Father returned from North Salem and entered the kitchen door slapping his crop against his thigh and hanging it on a hook by the door.

"Ah, so it's Miss Gilpin I see." He sought to continue his joke.

Grandma looked from father to daughter. "What do you mean?"

Addie sat at the table slicing cucumbers into a crock.

"Father, it wasn't in the least funny. I might have been killed." She fixed him with a steady, sober gaze. "I have never been so frightened in my life."

Father, not an unsympathetic man, sat down next to her and took a cucumber slice from the crock and ate it. She ignored him.

"I'm sorry," he said contritely. "Are you all right? You have no bruises?"

"That's true, but it was a nightmare I never want to have again."

Grandma exclaimed, "Matthew, Mark, Luke and John! What happened?"

Father was quiet as Addie gave her account of her wild ride on Paul. She gave the details that expressed how disheveled and terrified she felt. She did not tell Grandma the worst part, which was Father's laughter. In any case, now he knew how she felt.

"Be careful cutting those cucumbers!" Grandma cautioned. Addie realized that she had nearly filled the crock, so vigorously had she attacked the basketful while telling her story.

"Excuse the interruption. I heard your voices out here. The house otherwise seemed empty. I hope I'm not intruding." Joe entered the kitchen diffidently.

"Of course not," Father said, as he stood and gave Joe his chair. "We've heard a reprise of the morning's ride, and I stand guilty of taking the episode far too lightly. A quiet afternoon followed by Mother Gilbert's excellent tea is in order." With that Father retreated, no doubt to enjoy a cigar on the porch.

Joe observed Addie, her task with vegetables near its end. At length, with the basket empty, she looked up and, with her anger spent, she met his gaze and smiled. Grandma instructed her about the next steps in making pickles, while Joe listened and Addie measured salt and pumped the necessary water.

"Enough about that ride." Joe wanted to put her terror and angry feelings behind them. "Thomas tells me you are going to prayer meeting with him Sunday evening. May I come along?"

"I should like that very much." Addie rose to take the crock to the cellar, where the salt and water would soak into the cucumbers. Joe, however, took charge of the heavy vessel, and Addie led him down the steep stairs to the dim cellar. He placed the crock on a low shelf, and Addie covered it with a cloth.

Before they climbed the stairs, Joe looked around the cavernous room. Addie wondered what interested him about it, for it did not strike her as a place for holding hands. He noted the spring bubbling from the rocky floor, with a bucket of cream chilling in it, and the huge brick arch under the chimney.

"Your forefathers were clever to enclose the spring for their use. The arch reminds me of a medieval castle keep, so solid and symmetrical it is." Finally, his investigation complete, he took her hand and helped her up the stairs.

CHAPTER FIFTEEN

Lame from the previous day's horseback ride, Addie spent Sunday sewing with Emilie and Grandma. Her little half sister Annie played at their feet with a cloth doll Father had brought her from the city. Baby Mary, cheerful and well, sat in Ma's lap until Father brought around the carriage so that he, Ma, and the little girls might ride around Lake Waccabuc to enjoy the cooler summer's day.

"Addie, let's hear more of *Oliver Twist*," Grandma urged.

Putting down her mending, Addie took the volume down from the mantelpiece and found where they had left off. She read several chapters to a rapt audience bent over their sewing. The villain Fagin put Addie in mind of the slave catcher, exploiting slaves for gain much as Fagin forced poor orphan boys to pick pockets in the streets of London. At length, when Addie looked up from the novel, she found her audience had increased. Joe and Grandpa had entered the parlor silently and listened from chairs near the door.

Uncle Thomas finally brought the afternoon entertainment to a close, reminding them of prayer meeting, and didn't they want their tea beforehand? For taciturn Thomas to speak up in front of the entire assemblage seemed an uncommon audacity. They all knew why the young bachelor had suddenly come forward, however. Mary Lawrence would likely attend the prayer meeting, and he did not want to miss a chance to see her. Addie closed the novel. The women hastened to make tea.

With Kate harnessed to the carriage, Joe held the reins, waiting for the three women and Thomas. Addie straightened Thomas's tie and admired how handsome he looked, his light brown hair combed and wearing his Sunday best, a significant change from his usual attire. Grandma and the Hoe girls climbed into the carriage while Thomas sat up front with Joe.

At the church, the lighted candles in sconces along the walls gave a warmth and intimacy to the austere interior. The family, as was their custom, entered the pew behind the Lawrences'. This time, however, Mary sat at the end nearest the aisle. She moved closer to her father as soon as she saw Thomas, who slid into the pew next to her. The pair smiled at each other but did not speak. Her blonde wavy hair hung long down her back, not entirely hidden by her calico bonnet. Their reserved uncle and Mary were becoming increasingly attracted to one another. Would they marry? To Addie it only seemed a matter of time. Joe cleared his throat, and Addie realized he, having returned from the carriage shed behind the church, stood in the aisle next to her. She gladly made room for him.

Pastor Lindley looked out on the congregation and began the service reading from *Psalms*. Addie was struck by the passage, "We are strangely and wonderfully made." Imagining wedding bells pealing for her uncle, she concluded that feelings for the self-effacing man sitting beside her, who had kissed her, were a strange and wonderful dream, not realizable, at least not yet. In the meantime, she thought, as she sat in the quietness of the evening service, she would pray for Joe's safety. His commitment to saving others placed him outside the straightforward simple life of marriage and a family of his own. Until he abandoned that dangerous work, she would have to resign herself to a vicarious appreciation of Thomas's and Mary's happiness. Despite her conclusions, she opened her eyes to find Joe looking not unkindly at her. She responded by placing her hand on his.

Early the next morning Father and Joe left for the city, first riding horses to the depot. The farmhand was dispatched to go with them on Kate and to bring back their two mounts from the station. The two would ride the cars to Manhattan. Before they left, Joe found Addie clearing the breakfast table. "Write to me," he implored.

To which Addie responded as quietly as she could without whispering, "You know I will," and, adding even more quietly still, "I will be careful."

CHAPTER SIXTEEN

There was no denying Grandma their company when later in the week she prevailed upon Addie and Emilie to travel to New Canaan. She was determined that they visit Minerva Hoyt. "It will be none too soon. I am afraid she will be gone very soon, if the reports my cousin gave me are true."

The ominous disease the relative was suffering from might be consumption, some relatives thought. But perhaps it was some other lingering malady. In any case, Grandma had lined up the capable barn hand Peter to drive them. The trip involved a beautiful ride, she cajoled, and there would be other stops they would make that would be more pleasing to young ladies. Emilie objected when she was alone with Addie, and later even volunteered to stay home. "I will gladly help Ma with the babies while you go."

"Suit yourself," Grandma snapped.

Ma intervened. "Wait, your grandmother would like your company, Emilie." She added that she did not need help that day, so it was settled, and the three women would go.

The day dawned clear and cool, the sun bright. The ride took them east by Lake Waccabuc, which was ruffled by white caps from a stiff breeze, then over Smith Ridge where sheep, cattle and horses grazed behind the unending stone walls. At the highest point on the ridge was the first stop. The view toward Long Island Sound was a sweep of green fields rolling down to an infinite stretch of blue water. Emilie's resistance to the trip dissipated as she and Addie both marveled at the wonderful aspect of the countryside before them. Peter jumped down, tied Kate's reins to a granite post, and helped the ladies from the carriage.

Grandma led the way to the door of a very old farmhouse. There was a wellsweep in the front yard and tiny eyebrow windows under the eaves of the house.

"We won't stay long," Grandma whispered, "but your mother would have wanted you to meet her cousin, my brother's daughter."

The Hoe girls glanced at each other, trying not to show their dread. Grandma rapped on the front door with her cane. At length, the door opened slowly, revealing a very thin woman with graying dark hair, who actually looked older than their grandmother. Her eyes were sunken with black circles under them. She took a moment to realize who Grandma was, and then endeavored to smile and welcomed them inside. It was Minerva herself, who lived alone "but for the kindness of neighbors," she said, when Grandma asked who cared for her. Addie noted her soiled dress and labored breathing, and sensed the depth of her lonely plight.

They entered the spare parlor with its very few furnishings and sat down on the sofa while Minerva slowly lowered herself into a worn rocker. She began to cough and took up a cloth from the table next to her to cover her mouth. Grandma shifted uneasily. "Has the doctor come by recently?" When her paroxysm of coughing subsided, and she returned the crumpled cloth to the table, she replied, "Yes, he comes once a week, but he says there is little he can do." She spoke very slowly.

Grandma sent Addie out to the carriage to fetch the basket of food they had brought. It was a relief to go outside the sorry house into the sunshine even for the short time it took to retrieve the pie and jar of soup Grandma had kindly prepared. She placed the basket in Minerva's primitive kitchen with only a fireplace for cooking.

When they had said goodbye, urging the sick woman not to trouble herself showing them to the door, they walked in silence to the carriage. Emilie was the first to speak. "Grandma, I am sorry I dragged my feet about coming along. I don't know why."

Grandma said nothing. Addie turned to Grandma, who had tears on her cheeks and was ransacking her bag for a handkerchief. They all knew why Emilie resisted this journey and why Grandma was determined to make it. Addie felt her mother's presence in her grandmother's sadness and her sister's lively defiance—both evidence of the loss of Lucy long ago.

Immersed in their responses to Minerva's deplorable state, all three women sat in the carriage for several minutes before they realized their driver was nowhere in sight. Addie climbed down, calling his name but not so loudly as to disturb Minerva. She walked behind the house to the overgrown backyard. "Peter, Peter, where are you?"

From a weathered shed with a brick chimney engulfed by rangy lilac bushes, Peter finally emerged carrying a massive pair of tongs. Addie ordered him to put them back at once.

"But these are perfect for the welding Thomas is doing."

"Nonsense. Take them back inside." Addie began to scold him but realized she had better save her words for the road. Sheepishly Peter followed her back to the carriage.

Once they were on their way, Grandma explained to her companions, Peter included, that Minerva's father had been a blacksmith. That accounted for the tongs and the nature of the shed. Addie asked who would inherit Minerva's property. Grandma said she did not know, but there was an uncle still alive who would likely take charge. She would write him a letter when they returned home. The sober reality of death and its implications weighed upon the visitors young and old.

It was a relief to ride on in the sunlit afternoon. They took tea at an inn when they arrived in the village of New Canaan, which was replete with shops. Peter joined them at the table and kept his silence. They consumed only half of the fruit cakes set before them and three cups of tea with sugar.

Emilie was impatient to visit shops. When they finished tea and sauntered into the street, Grandma gave Peter orders that he was to stay with the horse and carriage. In the dry goods store, Emilie encountered Miss Keeler, who was choosing material for her bridal gown. As they chatted amiably, Addie admired the laces for sale and bought a blue satin hair ribbon for little Annie. Grandma left the girls enjoying the shop's wares while she chose to sit on a bench outside and observe the life in the street, a diversion not to be savored in South Salem.

On the way home, they stopped at Uncle Solomon's general store. He welcomed them and asked after Grandpa, for whom Grandma requested a sack of his favorite horehound lozenges. Uncle Solomon also asked after the Colonel, that is, Addie's father, a title Mr. Hoe acquired as a younger man when he was a member of the local New York militia. "Has he returned to the city? What of Mrs. Hoe? Does she stay the entire summer?"

Grandma would not be distracted by Uncle Solomon's tendency to gossip. "Do you have new potatoes?" she asked.

The Hoe girls wandered about the store, marvelous in that it contained anything and everything. There was not a shop in the city or New Canaan like it. Barrels of beans, crackers, and flour; jars of sweets; tack for horses; herbs and spices; crocks of vinegar and pickles; overalls and hats—all were packed into the huge room with shelves reaching the ceiling. Addie wondered how Uncle Solomon could retrieve the items on the top shelves, even though he was a very tall man.

A stove at one end sat in the midst of the barrels of produce farmers brought in to trade for staples. Among them Solomon found the new potatoes. Examining them carefully and filling a sack, Grandma said, "Our potatoes will not be ready until September. I need a pound of raisins, fifty pounds of flour, and a quart of molasses."

Uncle Solomon filled her order while continuing to press Emilie and Addie for other bits of news. "Is your Uncle Thomas sparking with Mary Lawrence? They seem very cozy at prayer meeting."

Addie looked at Emilie, not knowing how to respond to his nosiness, and tried to seem absorbed in the display of leather boots. Emilie, on the verge of giggling at the quaint terms Solomon used, contrived a saucy answer. "Uncle Solomon, when Thomas and Mary decide to marry, you'll be the first person they will tell, I am sure."

Grandma ignored the exchange. Peter, examining the jars of sweets, suppressed his amusement behind his hat. Addie raised her eyebrows at her sister's impertinence, but she noted that henceforth Uncle Solomon paid serious attention to weighing Grandma's new potatoes, and there was no more prying. Peter carried the purchases to the carriage, and when the ladies were settled behind him, he urged Kate forward and they were home before dark.

CHAPTER SEVENTEEN

Keeping her promise, Addie sat down one afternoon near the end of July to write to Joe. She gave an account of their journey into Connecticut. She told of Emilie's and Grandpa's bouts with quinsy, and she described Annie climbing the apple tree and Thomas rescuing her with the ladder. She was careful not to allude to anything about Joe's clandestine efforts. It seemed strange not to know exactly where he might be, even though she was writing a letter to his New York address. He could be anywhere along the mid-Atlantic coast. She made bold to close her letter, "Affectionately, Addie."

The arrival of Emmie Ely, Father's niece, their cousin from Brooklyn, provided the sisters with many opportunities for entertainment. She stayed with a neighbor, Mrs. Boutin, not far away, and brought with her news of Uncle Robert and Aunt Thirza and of Theodore and Robbie, the cousins they had not seen for a month. She told of concerts in Castle Garden and tantalized them with the news that the famed opera singer Madame Grisi, who was in America on tour, would be performing soon in New York. Addie and Emilie shared the doubt that they could attend any of her concerts, since they would not return to the city until September. In any case, they conspired to visit Niagara, where many of Emmie's friends were traveling in the summer, both to see Roebling's nearly completed bridge to Canada and to take in the magnificent falls.

Grandma made no objection to one or the other of the girls staying the night with Emmie where she boarded. Adding to the pleasure of the vacation, Henry returned to spend a few days.

Then one Monday, when the mail came, there was a letter to Addie from Joe. She opened it with great anticipation after the lapse of several weeks since his brief visit. She eyed his tiny, precise handwriting of her name, and she noted he addressed the envelope to Adeline Elizabeth Hoe in "Lewisboro," the new name for South Salem recently adopted when a Mr. Lewis became the town's benefactor. "Lewisboro" seemed artificial to Addie's grandparents, and Father would always consider the village he knew to be "South Salem."

Gingerly, Addie slit the envelope open with Grandpa's letter opener, and she found not only a letter but also a sketch and a newspaper clipping. She studied the pen and ink drawing Joe had made of a young Negro woman wearing a bonnet. Wondering what it meant, she read the letter. Joe, in his reticent manner, had written only a few lines. He asked after her health and hoped her sister and grandparents were well. He said the city was as hot and dirty as ever and that his work kept him occupied, but that he missed her.

She unfolded the newspaper article from the *Tribune* and read it through several times, struck by what it recorded. In subsequent days, the account became nearly an obsession with her. Addie imagined the scene again and again:

> Peering over the edge of his high desk, the police sergeant eyed the latest miscreant flanked by two duty officers. She was a black woman, about twenty-five, with a torn dress and bruised face, with a flattened bonnet clasped in her hands. He called her name, "Elizabeth Jennings."
>
> As she stepped forward, the Sergeant could see that she limped. "What is your report, officers?"
>
> "This woman," began the taller of the two men, "tried to ride on a car reserved for white people on a Sunday afternoon."
>
> "Did you spend the night in jail, Ma'am?"
>
> "Yes," she said in a clear voice with a strong sibilant *s* at the end.
>
> "Why did you try to ride an omnibus that was plainly for white folks?"
>
> "I was in a hurry to get to church. I am the organist and I had to be there."
>
> "How can you account for your appearance?"
>
> "The conductor pushed Miss Adams, my companion, off the car, and I would not step down. The car was only half full, and I had to get to church. The driver pushed me off the car and knocked me to the ground, smashed my bonnet and beat me. These officers brought me to the jail." She stepped back, took a deep breath, looking to either side, and then proudly stared through the sergeant's desk.

Addie recalled how she and Emilie themselves encountered the omnibus "For Blacks Only" earlier in the summer. Joe's sketch reminded Addie of the lovely black woman she and Emilie met on the train to Setauket in June. They had seen her again on the sloop in the bay that delightful evening when she, Emilie, and Maria heard music on the water and were invited onto the boat where the musicians, black and white, played unfamiliar, lyrical tunes accented by the jaunty rhythms of the bones.

She kept Joe's letter, the drawing, and the clipping upstairs, safely stowed in her satchel.

Addie looked around her at the roomy farmhouse that had been her grandparents' all their lives, its fourteen rooms more than adequate for the

CHAPTER SEVENTEEN

hordes of family who arrived each summer and on vacation. Could *it* accommodate former slaves en route to safety in Canada?

Later that day, she descended to the cellar to retrieve salt pork for the beans they would prepare on Saturday. In the cool dark space with the only light from one small window, she examined the root cellar at one end, the brick arch that supported the chimney which created a room lined with narrow shelves for preserves. The only entrance to the outside was a steep set of stone cellar stairs leading into the woodshed. A person could sleep on a cot in the root cellar, and escape through the shed at night. She would get up her courage to talk with Grandma soon.

The next day, after breakfast and a pleasant ride on horseback with Cousin Henry, Addie sat down to write to Joe. She expressed her sadness over the cruel treatment of Miss Jennings, and hinted for him to tell her how she might help. She only alluded to her imaginings in the cellar and the possibility of the farmhouse as a stop on the Underground Railroad. Whenever she wrote to Joe, she changed the names of anyone involved in his other life, on the chance that if her letter were to be intercepted by the wrong people, someone from the South might be in danger, as well as Joe himself. Slave catchers could be anywhere, even in South Salem.

CHAPTER EIGHTEEN

Often preoccupied, Addie considered how she would approach Grandma about hiding a Negro. How receptive would she be in view of the danger involved? What would Thomas and Grandpa say? An escape from New York City meant coming all the way by wagon to South Salem, which would involve ferries and traveling the old road. The railroad would be too risky. She did not know how hiding on a train would be possible, since depots were prime places to be seen by persons searching for slaves. For her own part, she could see that Father, Ma, and Emilie might have to know of her idea eventually. At odd times, she fell into imagining schemes. During the night, when she and Emilie had gone to bed, she would lie awake weighing the strategies that might work.

Finally, on an August afternoon when she and Grandma were ironing, Addie decided to broach the subject of hiding slaves. "Grandma, what do you think about slavery?" She lifted the heavy flatiron from the stove and placed it carefully on the wrinkled linen tablecloth.

"You know perfectly well how I feel. Two years ago we read *Uncle Tom's Cabin*. Mrs. Lindley, the Reverend's wife, lent us a copy, and Grandpa and I took turns reading it aloud. The Negro Tom was a noble fellow, but that Simon Legree was a cruel monster. Slavery tears families apart. The sooner it's ended, the better."

"When we went to Delaware City, Emilie and I saw whole families of slaves working in a peach orchard, even little children. Then, later, in Philadelphia, we saw a young Negro woman who was waiting to be hired. Her ankles bore scars of chains. Have you heard of the Underground Railroad?"

"Let me see. It isn't a railroad with rails and tracks. Isn't it the means to transport Negroes north? The need for it arose a few years ago when that Fugitive Slave Act passed. Helping slaves to Canada is a way to get around returning them to the South."

Grandma knew a good deal more than Addie suspected about slavery, which made her want to read *Uncle Tom's Cabin* herself. As they sprinkled water on the pillowcases and re-heated the flatiron, Addie dared ask, as delicately as she could, "Grandma, would you and Grandpa hide a Negro here on the farm?"

The older woman stopped folding a bed sheet and looked into Addie's guileless young face. She turned to the window that faced the vegetable garden, where Grandpa was tearing up bean vines and placing them methodically in

CHAPTER EIGHTEEN

a wheelbarrow. "You ask that question as though you know something about the Underground Railroad. Have you heard of conductors?"

Addie nodded and went on ironing, vowing to herself that she would not give away Joe as one of them.

"I thought about that, too, until Mr. Keeler described what some abolitionists in Vermont are doing, digging tunnels under their houses to sneak Negroes from one place to another. That sounded like a lot more work than two elderly people could take on."

"I see." Addie carried a stack of linens upstairs to put away, and she reflected that Grandma was far more amenable to helping the abolitionists' cause than one would ever have suspected.

When he arrived from the city, Henry Seymour was glad to learn the entire family enjoyed *Oliver Twist*, and during his stay he joined them to hear either Addie or Emilie read it aloud. Sewing and mending always occupied a good part of each day. Reading or conversation made the tasks pass quickly. As the women worked, Henry related how treacherous the city had become, with cholera spreading each day. He reminded them how blessed they were to be in the country. "Mayor Westervelt has authorized setting up more hospitals expressly to deal with the growing numbers of victims of the disease."

"Do you fear for yourself, Henry?" Emilie asked.

"I get out to Bloomfield as much as possible and avoid the tenement districts."

Addie wondered how Ellen, their maid who lived in Williamsburgh, was faring, and she asked Henry if he had seen her at 309 Broadway. He promised to ask about her when he returned to New York.

While cholera seemed an affliction of the streets of the city, there were sicknesses like Annie's bout with croup that frightened her mother and sisters. She could barely breathe one night, and the doctor seemed to take forever to come. The terror among the family over her condition gave way to relief when she breathed easily the next morning. The doctor arrived to find her sleeping peacefully.

Addie longed for Joe Stewart to return. Father had come for several sojourns before Joe finally arrived with him in mid-August. Letters between Joe and Addie had been not without feeling, but because of the constraint of laboring not to mention Joe's secret life, they seemed bland. Addie related daily activities on the farm. Joe told of traveling to various clients in the purchase or sale of tailoring fabrics and supplies.

Heralding the arrival of the two men, little Annie squealed with glee to hear Father approaching on horseback and whistling "Yankee Doodle." When he saw his third daughter on the porch, he beckoned to her and scooped her up. They rode the final yards to the stable with her ensconced happily before him on the saddle.

Emerging from the stand of pines at the corner of the yard, Joe brought up the rear, and it was all Addie could do to keep herself from shouting with as much excitement as her little sister when she saw his dark shape silhouetted in the day's last light. Near the house, he paused and tipped his hat before heading to the stable. Addie beamed, unable to hide her gladness, then waved and anticipated his presence beside her.

With a shawl pulled tight around her shoulders, Addie sat alone on the porch steps, the almost autumnal bite in the air notwithstanding. After what seemed like enough time to unsaddle a horse ten times over, Father, with Annie in his arms, and Joe, carrying his own and his friend's bags, finally returned to the porch.

"Addie, what's keeping you outside?" Father inquired. "The air is chill. How are you?"

"I am very well," she answered.

"Oh, Papa, your pocket has something in it!" Annie proclaimed, and pressed his chest pocket eager for a treat or a surprise of the kind he often brought from the city.

"Wait until I open the door and we go inside, little one," Father said as he swept into the hallway, where Ma and the rest of the family awaited them.

Joe stayed behind with Addie on the porch, long enough for them to embrace, both hoping for more time to speak freely, yet delighted to be reunited.

Emilie opened the front door and called from inside, "Addie, where are you?"

"She's greeting Joe, I think," Father intimated, as he took his eldest daughter's arm.

"Oh, I see," Emilie said as they joined the family in the parlor. Father customarily told of the week's doings either at the factory or in his various enterprises around the city. Refreshments were usual. Sometimes Grandma brought out a pie or cake to celebrate Father's safe return, or a plate of supper if he had not eaten.

Joe and Addie entered the parlor in the middle of Father's account of the latest advances of the American Telegraph Company. "There is talk among the board of directors about a trans-Atlantic telegraph."

"Before that happens," Ma remarked, "I hope the telegraph can connect the city and South Salem so that we can know when you are coming. Then your supper can be hot."

"Surely that will come about. Already, the telegraph connection between the office and the factory makes communicating much easier and faster. It is only a matter of time before the telegraph will affect life in many other ways than in industry. You wait."

CHAPTER EIGHTEEN

Ma rose from the sofa and, carrying little Mary, bade Annie hug her father goodnight. Carrying the mechanical dog Father had brought her, Annie went around the room giving everyone a hug and then ran after her mother.

Grandma and Grandpa began to yawn, and soon retired for the night. Uncle Thomas was out visiting Mary Lawrence for the evening. Emilie asked Father if Uncle Robert and Aunt Thirza planned to join them, and he responded, indeed, any day soon, they would arrive. They talked of the Elys and how grand it was to have cousin Emmie Ely nearby. Addie listened, wondering if Joe and Charlie had risked delivering Negroes since his last visit. She was miles away when Father spoke her name.

"Addie, what music have you been playing?"

She realized she had not, nor had Emilie, walked to Jane's to play the piano for weeks. Admitting their neglect of the piano, she apologized, and Father only responded, "Soon enough you'll be back at school to exercise your rusty fingers."

"No more school for me," Emilie said with a contented sigh.

Joe had remained quiet, sitting near the window in shadow. Addie wondered if and when they *ever* would be able to talk. She was impatient to tell him of her discussion with Grandma and the prospect of using the Gilberts' cellar as a way station on the Underground Railroad.

CHAPTER NINETEEN

The next day Joe offered to help Father and Thomas gather the hay that lay drying in the field behind the barn. Raking the sweet hay in neat piles in the August morning appealed to Father, and he enjoyed the uncommon chance to work in sunshine and fresh air. When noontime came, Addie volunteered to take them water and something to eat. Joe plied his wide, wooden rake on the far side of the field. After Father and Thomas had drunk water to their satisfaction from the jug she carried, she continued across the meadow. Joe stopped as she came near and greeted her warmly. Laying down his rake, he wiped his face with his handkerchief and took the jug from her. After a long draught, he took up his rake, mounded the hay into an especially large pile, and invited her to sit a moment upon it.

Although the sun was hot at noon, a breeze swept across the open field, cooling them and ruffling her hair. Addie watched Father and Thomas resume their raking. She knew her moments with Joe were rare and precious.

"So," he began, "you have much to say, am I right? Whatever it is, I can tell you've been dying to say it."

"Am I that easy to read?"

"You were tapping your foot all evening and barely said a word."

"And you?"

"I admit I have wanted to know your thoughts." He turned to study her face flushed from the sun.

"Not long ago Grandma and I talked about abolition. She shares our ideas about ending slavery. She even said she knew of the Underground Railroad and had considered hiding Negroes somehow, but tunnels were too much for her and Grandpa to embark upon. That said, what do you think about the cellar of their house as a hiding place? You saw it yourself."

"Why Addie, I am surprised."

"Why should you be surprised? You have given me a view into your dangerous life, and I have seen what slavery means. We are 'strangely and wonderfully made,' as Reverend Lindley read from *Psalms*. Aren't Negroes just as wonderfully made?"

"I can see you have been taking the issue to heart."

"Do you think you could hide slaves here in South Salem?" She went on, excited to discuss her ideas at last. "Can their route north take them this way?"

CHAPTER NINETEEN

Joe leaned back, putting his hands behind his head, and watched swallows swooping and soaring over the field to catch insects escaping from the newly raked hay. Addie waited expectantly for his reaction to her question.

"I doubt that I could be a conductor of persons to South Salem."

"Why?" Addie asked, a dark cloud of disappointment descending upon her.

"Your idea is good and plausible. It is a matter of *my* connection to *your* family. I come here openly to visit, not frequently, but often enough to create suspicion if I were to come with a loaded wagon and without your father. No, though *I* might not come here, another conductor might be able to use the space you suggest. We must be very careful."

"I understand now."

"Does your grandmother realize that I am involved in transporting slaves?"

"No," Addie hastened to make that clear. "I have not mentioned you and what you do to *anyone* in regard to your other life."

He offered her the jug of water, and she drank from it.

"About the sketch and article you sent," she continued, "was the young woman you drew Miss Jennings?"

"Yes, I have seen her in her father's tailoring shop and elsewhere in Manhattan. Did you think she was the same Negro woman you met in Setauket?"

"Your sketch certainly bore a fine resemblance to that person. The article affected me greatly, and I can almost recount it verbatim if you asked. What has happened to her since?"

"There's talk in the tailoring district that she will have a very fine lawyer to defend her, Chester Arthur. We can only hope that she will receive some solace after her cruel treatment on the omnibus." He turned, observed Addie's profile, and was moved by the serious concern for him evident in her steady gaze and her unwavering interest in his cause and to the dangers it involved. He rose and took her hand. "Come; without your bonnet, you'll be sunburned." After helping her to her feet, he picked up the rake to go on working.

Addie collected the jug and, with many thoughts flooding her mind, retraced her steps across the meadow, skirting the fragrant hay stacks and waving to Father and Thomas as she passed.

Aiding slaves was not simple. Making slave owners understand all men, women, and children are human beings on one earth might take years in America, Addie realized. Her impatience to get on with abolishing slavery sometimes made the goal seem unachievable. It was comforting to know there were steady, committed people like Joe working toward it.

Later that afternoon, while Emilie and Addie were cutting out collars on the dining table, Emmie, their cousin, arrived to give them exciting news. Mary Lawrence was to marry their Uncle Thomas in October. The girls put down their scissors and begged Emmie to tell how she knew, since their uncle had said nothing to the family about their plans. Emmie admitted it was secondhand knowledge that she gained from overhearing Mary's father Cyrus Lawrence as he talked with Mrs. Boutin, the neighbor with whom Emmie stayed.

"It is not surprising we would be the last to know, given how quiet Thomas tends to be," Emilie remarked.

"He has been spending many evenings at the Lawrences' lately," Addie said. She went on aligning the selvages of a length of cotton cloth on the table, and, after pinning on the pattern, she commenced to cut two collars.

Emmie sat and watched from across the table. "What about you, Addie? Your sister tells me you spend every spare moment with Joe Stewart."

Addie continued to snip carefully through the layers of cloth. "Our families have been friends for many years," she replied, concentrating upon her work. "Cousin, don't usher me down the aisle so quickly."

Emilie was not about to let the subject drop. "You and Joe chatted on the porch when he arrived with Father. I would almost say that you looked agitated when you and he entered the parlor that evening. Is there something you need to tell us?"

Making no explanation, Addie simply looked up at her sister's inquiring face and said, "How many collars do you think we should cut out? There is plenty of cloth to make more."

Rebuffed, and silenced for the moment, Emilie abandoned her inquiry and asked Emmie if she might like some delicious pears. The two cousins repaired to the kitchen while Addie cut several more collars.

Although disappointed, Addie understood why Joe could not be the conductor of slaves passing through South Salem. He would draw attention among the local people, who might not be like the neighbors in Cream Ridge, where many shared his family's stance toward slavery. In fact, Father, if he knew, might be much opposed to Joe's travels on behalf of slaves. The sales of Hoe printing presses took Father and his agents to Baltimore and other points in the South. His father-in-law, Doctor Corbin, although he resided in Philadelphia, was raised on a plantation in Virginia.

The realization that Joe would arrange for another conductor to bring Negroes to the Gilberts' to be hidden came as a relief to Addie. She need not tell Grandma that Joe himself was a conductor, only that he would pass on word of their willingness to conceal persons at the farm. She mulled over the opportunities when she might discuss the issue again with Grandma.

Emilie and Cousin Emmie brought Addie a dish of sliced pears and invited her to join them on the front porch. There they talked of going to Ridgefield to shop. Emmie invited them to stay the night with her at Mrs. Boutin's, and they could all three travel to town together the next day. Addie thanked Emmie for including her, but remembered that Grandma planned to show her how to dry apples. Was that too lame an excuse? Addie hoped it would do.

CHAPTER NINETEEN

Her sister eyed her suspiciously but concluded Joe would have returned to the city with Father by then. Addie was actually obsessed with learning to cook, something Emilie regarded as best left to the hired help or their grandmother.

Before tea time, Addie walked with her younger sister Annie to the apple orchard beyond the field now shorn and empty of hay. With a sturdy ash basket on her hip and Annie by the hand, Addie passed the stable where Thomas was giving forks full of hay to the horses and cows.

"Thomas," Addie called out, "We have heard your news. When is the wedding?"

The shy bachelor glanced out the barn door and, turning bright red from his neck to his forehead, he replied, "October," and continued conveying hay from the mow to the animals.

"That is wonderful! Mary is a beautiful young lady."

Tugging at her hand, her little sister asked, "Who is Mary? That's my baby sister's name!"

Addie laughed and squeezed her little hand. "Uncle Thomas will be marrying lovely Mary Lawrence in October."

"Can I go? Where will it be?"

"I hope so," Addie replied. "We will find out all about his plans, I'm sure."

Under the apple trees laden with ripe fruit Addie picked up the best drops. Two-year old Annie climbed to a low branch and threw down the reddest apples within easy reach. When she attempted to climb to a higher branch, Addie lifted her down despite her noisy protests. The basket, mounded with apples, was very heavy; too heavy, Addie realized, for her to carry alone. They left it under a tree, and on their return to the house they stopped again at the barn.

"Thomas," she called out, expecting him still to be at work, but he had finished for the evening.

"Hello, what brings you here?" Joe asked. He was coming out of a horse stall and carrying a saddle and bridle. Addie shut the gate of the stall behind him. "I've been riding Paul once more before we leave in the morning. He's a horse needing plenty of exercise, as you no doubt recall."

"Only too well," she answered. "Would you help us? Annie and I have been apple picking, but we cannot carry the basket it is so full."

"I'll get it for you." He picked up Annie, put her on his shoulders, and they walked together in the late afternoon sunshine across the wide field to the orchard, where he gently placed Annie on her own feet and shouldered the brimming basket.

"Tomorrow we're going to prepare apples for drying, Grandma and I." She said nothing about what they might discuss besides apples, knowing that little pitchers have big ears. They walked on in some haste, realizing how late they would be for tea.

CHAPTER TWENTY

Father and Joe rode off early the next day for the depot in the chilly morning mist. Later, Emmie Ely and Emilie Hoe left in the carriage as they had planned, with Peter driving Kate, headed for Ridgefield. Little sister Annie played on the porch with her dolls spread about, while Ma sewed close by and listened for baby Mary napping upstairs. Grandpa and Thomas gathered squashes in the garden.

Addie dawdled in her room after making the beds and helping Imogene collect the dirty linen to take to the washerwoman. The prospect of confronting Grandma about hiding slaves caused her second thoughts in the bright light of the Monday morning. It was one thing to imagine a great and dangerous undertaking, but it was another to expect grandparents in their sixties to carry it out. Who was she, a seventeen-year old school girl, to expect them to entertain her scheme? In any case, she had asked how to dry apples, and Grandma was no doubt in the kitchen waiting to show her how.

First they sorted the apples Addie had collected, placing the different varieties in piles.

"Dutchess apples are no good for drying," Grandma began, as she held one up for Addie to distinguish. "They are grand for sauce and pies, and we enjoy them in late summer."

She held up a large golden apple with a rosy tinge and smiled in satisfaction.

"What is that one called?"

"Maiden's Blush. When we cut them up, you'll see the reason why. The flesh is firm and will stay white even when it's dry. Aunt Mary Seymour gave your father a cutting from their tree in New Jersey, and he brought it to Grandpa, who grafted it onto one of the old apple trees in the orchard. In the last twenty years, Maiden's Blush has thrived, as you can see."

Addie sorted the Maiden's Blush apples from the rest and brought the choice variety into the kitchen. The women washed them, peeled and sliced them, dipped them briefly in brine, and spread them on boards that Uncle Thomas had mounted on posts in the back yard. "The hot sun will dry them, but we'll have to put them in the shed, should it rain."

When the apple slices lay in neat rows on the boards with cheesecloth spread over them, to discourage the birds and bees, the two women sat down on the back steps to rest.

CHAPTER TWENTY

"Have you always dried apples this way?"

"This is how my mother taught me. Now I've heard in Pennsylvania they string them to hang in the attic, but the mice would get into them, don't you think?"

"Perhaps."

It was now or never. Addie needed to ask a different question. "Would you hide escaped slaves here on the farm in the cellar?"

"It's Joe Stewart, isn't it?"

Addie's face turned as pink as the Maiden's Blush apples. "What do you mean?"

"He is telling you about rescuing slaves. How else would you get an idea like that?"

Addie was crestfallen. What could she say? Grandma, drawing upon years of experience, read her expression. "Let's sort it all out. You are fond of Joe. He favors abolishing slavery."

Addie was at a loss for words. Dreading this interview, she saw, was not unjustified. Grandma saw the situation with the unerring clarity and practicality with which she saw frozen lambs during the early spring lambing when she brought them into the house to the warming oven, sometimes succeeding in bringing them to life, sometimes not. She had lived through the death of a daughter, wars, disease, and any number of things during her long life.

There was a long pause before Addie responded. "You see it all, Grandma." She felt tears welling up. For the first time, the trust Joe placed in her seemed violated, even though she had not said anything to give him away.

"Hold your tears." Grandma put her arm around her. "I see nothing wrong in either of the truths I've stated. To put a Negro in the cellar while the poor wretch makes his or her way to Canada and freedom is well worth doing. Joe is plainly a good man, quite a bit older than you, but all the same a worthy man. I watched him with you and Annie crossing the field last evening. He is kind. Come in the kitchen now. We have some cleaning up to do."

Saying no more, they scraped the apple peels and cores into a bucket for the pigs and reserved some to make vinegar. They scrubbed the table and utensils.

"Run down cellar, if you please, and bring up some mother from one of last year's jugs of vinegar that is nearly empty."

Addie looked vaguely frightened and puzzled.

"Ha!" Grandma smiled and reassured her. "'Mother' is the culture we'll use to start new vinegar working, like yeast. With some sugar, water, mother, the peelings, and time, we'll have plenty of good vinegar for another year. You'll find mother is slimy stuff, but go ahead and pour some into a bowl and bring it upstairs."

Addie's confidence returned as she set about another new adventure in cookery. By noon, there were apples arrayed in the sun to dry and a crock of new vinegar well underway. Nothing was wasted, she saw. Instead of feeling diminished by Grandma's insights, she felt expanded, as though her thoughts no longer existed in the solitary vacuum of her mind.

There were still many questions that Addie wished to ask her grandmother, but she wanted to write Joe first, more than anything to ask when he might return. While she and Ma conversed in the parlor in the afternoon about baby Mary's rash, likely caused by the heat, they heard feet stamping up the porch steps. Addie dashed to the front hall to find cousins Theodore and Robbie Hoe followed by Uncle Robert and Aunt Thirza, at last arriving from the city.

"Hello, hello," the young men called until they found Addie and each gave her a generous hug. Ma joined them, and Uncle Robert asked if they were all well. Grandma, hearing the ruckus, inquired if they might stay to tea.

Uncle Robert's family stayed at a house he had bought in South Salem expressly for vacationing near Lake Waccabuc. In addition to having their own children, he and Thirza were adoptive parents of the children of his deceased sister Elizabeth and brother-in-law Enoch Mead. Since the Hoe brothers owned a carriage together and lived in close proximity, they rarely were separated for long. Theodore and Robbie were like brothers to Addie and her sister, and all were nearly the same age. Their arrival brought a new social dimension to the Hoe girls' summer. Cousin Emmie and Emilie returned from their jaunt to Ridgefield to find the farmhouse bursting with conversation and activity. Little Annie and baby Mary found their way into the arms of each of the relatives. Teatime lasted until it was nearly dark.

"Wait until you see what we brought," Theodore exclaimed to Addie. He rushed out to the carriage and brought back three curious, decorated boxes. He took one, lifted the lid, and wound a key on the side. The tinkly notes of a waltz filled the parlor, inviting the young people to dance. The other two music boxes played a schottische and a galop, both very popular dances. For the remainder of the evening the Gilberts' parlor became a dance floor, once Grandma allowed them to move the furniture and roll up the carpet.

Grandpa Josiah invited Aunt Thirza and Uncle Robert to escape the parlor, after they had watched the energetic dancing awhile. "Friends, might we retire to the library, where I can hear better what you have to say?"

With the introduction of the mechanical wonders, the lack of a piano or fiddle did not mean they were prevented from dancing. Also, the music boxes were marvelously portable and could provide accompaniment at any of the places Theodore and Robbie might visit. The novelty delighted the young

CHAPTER TWENTY

women. Addie, however, reflected that by their vacation's end, they should all be very tired of the three tunes the boxes played.

Before the Robert Hoe family departed, Robbie asked Addie and Emilie to go riding the next day. Uncle Robert asked Emmie Ely to ride with them to Mrs. Boutin's in the Hoe carriage.

Emilie had yet to tell Addie about their day in town. Before they settled down for the night, Emilie brought from a sack a lovely new bonnet, maroon shantung trimmed with moss green grosgrain ribbon. It really seemed extravagantly fine to Addie.

"Wouldn't you have preferred to come with us?" Emilie asked as she rewrapped the bonnet in tissue paper and laid it carefully in a bureau drawer. "We had a lunch at the inn and ate prawns."

"There will be other times," Addie answered. She reviewed the day's events and her conversations with Grandma. "Apple-drying and making vinegar were interesting, and Grandma teaches well."

"You'll have to show me sometime. When we helped her make pies, I found the slicing of apples tedious. It stains one's fingers."

"Ah, you might be right. Without things to talk about, tasks would be dull. Did you meet any new people on your trip?"

"The Misses Keeler and Reynolds were walking in Ridgefield, and we exchanged pleasantries. We saw some very fine carriages at the inn while we...," Emilie went on reciting the day's adventures, while Addie drifted off to sleep.

CHAPTER TWENTY-ONE

The rooster crowing, the cows lowing as they ambled from the barn into the pasture, and the clanking of pails as Thomas watered and fed the sheep and pigs, all reminded Addie when she awoke that the bucolic summer was near an end. Soon to awaken her in the morning would be street vendors hawking their wares from booths along Broadway, policemen blowing whistles at vagrants, and the hooves of hundreds of horses clopping past their house.

While Emilie slept, Addie wrote a letter to Retta, telling of their piano concert and trip to New Canaan, and inviting her to come see them in the city when they returned home. Before she wrote to Joe, she pondered how to tell him Grandma's insights. Would she mention the inkling Grandma had about the feelings between herself and Joe? How would she convey the positive response the older woman had to hosting a slave? Taking pen in hand, she looked out upon the serene blue of the mountain above Lake Waccabuc, and she began to write, knowing that the morning solitude would not last:

> Dear Joe,
>
> The farm continues to be the lovely scene you left, even though the string of sunny days means it is too dry.
>
> Apples have kept us busy. I have learnt to make vinegar, and to dry apples using the basketful you kindly carried for me. Uncle Robert and Aunt Thirza have arrived with my cousins. They are excited to go riding. Emilie and I will join them later. No doubt they will put in canoes on the lake before long.
>
> Grandma and I have conversed about many things. She shares our views on central matters and is most hospitable. She is amenable to having visitors in addition to our family.
>
> When will you return? I hope it will be soon.
>
> Ever yours,
>
> Adeline

Was "visitors" vague enough? Was "ever yours" an admission of too much feeling? The ink was wet, and she watched as it began to lose its shine. With no more hesitation, she turned over the sheet of paper onto the blotter

CHAPTER TWENTY-ONE

beneath and then folded it quickly. No changes, no crossings out—the letter would have to stand.

The following weeks became a blur while the teenage cousins imagined all sorts of gatherings and outings. There was, of course, horseback riding with Robbie on the bridle trails interlacing the woods and fields of South Salem. Theodore collected all manner of rocks and butterflies and, together with his cousins, pored over his booty in the evening with a magnifying glass. There were hikes to pick blackberries on the hillsides amid enormous granite boulders, strewn generously by the glacier thousands of years ago. When it rained, the boys joined Addie and Emilie to hear new chapters of *Oliver Twist* read aloud by one or the other of the girls while they sewed. Only when the lake was perfectly smooth and no breeze blew would Addie consent to join the boys in the canoe.

Except for the blackberry pie that she made of the quarts of berries they had picked, Addie left the kitchen and cookery to Grandma and Imogene during the whirlwind of activities and excursions the young fellows initiated. The countryside became a vast playground for them and, liberated as they were from the confines of New York, Addie saw she and Emilie needed no other entertainment once the Hoe and Mead boys arrived.

Joe looked back over the previous week. On Sunday there was one expedition to carry a Negro to a safe house. Early on Monday he had assayed the condition of the newsboys' accommodations, as Mr. Hoe had requested. Were the boys who sold the penny papers getting enough to eat at the building, only recently established, where they could have a meal and a place to lay their heads? Were the adults in charge advising them responsibly to save what they earned? After his visit, Joe assured Addie's father the enterprise was off to a sound start.

The work at A. T. Stewart's store never let up. He anticipated a Saturday free of duties so that he might make use of his riding boots that lay in his rooms on Bleecker Street. The *Tribune* had announced a race to take place at one p.m. in West Flushing. If he arrived at the track early enough, his father's old friend, who was a trainer, might seat him for a race as he had done many times for him in the past. It had been months since he had made time to jockey.

Horse-racing was a childish pastime, a kind of vanity, a remnant of growing up in carefree days. "Now I'm a man, I should put aside childish things," he thought, as he guiltily pulled the boots from the closet. He dusted them off, all the same, and assembled what he needed.

A loud knock on the door jarred him from his thought. As he dropped his riding crop, he called, "Who is it?"

On the other side of the door, a low voice, in halting tones, barely audible, croaked, "It's Sam. Remember me?"

Joe pushed aside his riding apparel and hurried to open the door. Admitting Sam and checking up and down the hall for who might have seen the young black man, Joe ushered him in quickly. He noted the anguish in his tone and face, thin and drawn. "What brings you here to New York? I thought you and your brother would be in Canada by now."

"Will is there already...probably. See, I got sick, and he had to leave me behind. The conductor told me to find you here."

Joe rubbed his hand across his forehead. His plans to ride in the race evaporated as he pondered what had to happen next. "Are you well enough to travel now? Have you eaten?"

"Well...no...but I am well enough to travel." Sam seemed a shadow of the hale young man who stayed at Mordecai Lincon's forge earlier in the summer.

It was settled. Joe would need to transport Sam after dark, and after they had a decent meal. Joe returned the riding boots and other gear to the closet, and he turned his mind to helping Sam on his way.

Watching Uncle Thomas go about his farm chores, as she held little Mary in her lap on the porch, Addie saw that the rhythm of life held peace and contentment for him and her grandparents. Their ways, so different from the japes and escapes of her cousins, held for her a timeless charm she hoped would never dissipate. She determined to spend time with Thomas. Besides, she wanted to learn something of his and Mary Lawrence's plans.

After breakfast Theodore and Robbie appeared in the yard to remind the girls about going to see P. T. Barnum's elephant that was being pastured for the summer in a village not far away. "We have the carriage for the day," Robbie exulted. "Get your bonnets, Addie and Emilie; it will be great fun. Theodore has a bag of peanuts to feed the pachyderm!"

Emilie agreed to join them and made ready to go, asking the boys about the need to bring a lunch. Somewhat allured by the plan, Addie nevertheless decided to stay at the farm.

"Please stop for Emmie Ely. I'm sure she'll want to go," Addie suggested. She was glad to know the elephant was grazing in a field. Seeing it pull a vast wagon on Broadway had disturbed her. Surely in India elephants were beasts of burden, but in New York City they were out of their element, oddities subject to all manner of unnatural treatment. How would it be to live thousands of miles from home, all alone, far from the country one was used to?

"Addie, you're missing an exciting day," Theodore called, once Emilie was settled in the carriage. "Are you sure you aren't coming?"

CHAPTER TWENTY-ONE

"I'm sure. Have a wonderful day."

Finding Uncle Thomas was not easy. Grandma told Addie he had mentioned needing to repair a wall somewhere on the farm. Putting on sturdy shoes and a bonnet, she set out to follow the stone walls to find him. The walls, built a hundred years before of field stone, encircled many plots of land that were designed to accommodate the needs and purposes of the farm. Some enclosures were small, for pigs perhaps; others were larger, for lambing ewes to be separate from the rest of the flock. Very large fields were for hay or for grazing. The latter required great attention from the farmer to keep the walls secure, lest the animals escape. All these particulars Addie learned from Uncle Thomas once she located him on the far side of the sheep pasture. He was rolling the stones that had strayed, disturbed by gravity or the weather, and he used a heavy crowbar for leverage to get them in place.

He was surprised to see Addie. "Why, hello," he said as he straightened from his task. He leaned the crowbar against the wall. "What brings you way out here?"

"Grandma said you were mending a stone wall, but she did not know where."

"You look thirsty." He reached behind the wall and retrieved a jug of water, and, offering it first to her, he then took a long drink himself. They moved a few steps out of the morning sunshine into the shade of a maple tree.

"How did you know to fix this wall?"

"Three sheep got out and ended up in the brook behind the Howes'. It took half the afternoon to find them, until I walked this wall."

Thomas was more voluble than she had ever heard him to be. He described the system of walls, pointing out the different heights and types of stone used to build them. She saw in him the strength a man must have to be a farmer, with his thick neck and broad back. His large, capable hands could handle a cart horse or deliver a lamb. He was handsome, with sandy hair bleached by the sun and a fair complexion that turned red when a beam of attention was turned upon him. Curiously, he was completely at ease in their conversation about the farm.

"When in October will you and Mary be married?" she ventured to ask.

He turned to her, and indeed the blush began to color his face, but he continued with resolve. "October eleventh is the day."

"Will it take place at the church?"

"I think Mary will be telling you more about how she wants it to be." He would leave the details of this most social occasion to Mary, Addie realized, as she walked through the pasture back to the house.

After taking Ma and the two youngest girls in the carriage to visit Aunt Thirza and Uncle Robert, Peter stopped at the post office and brought back two letters for Addie and one for Emilie. He skipped up the back porch steps and handed Addie hers and, at her instruction, he took Emilie's to the hall table. Since the trip to New Canaan, the boy stepped carefully around Grandma and Addie, who were then cutting up apples for apple butter. He eyed the visiting cousins' canoe paddles on the porch with interest. As he returned to the carriage, he wondered if they might teach him to use them.

"Thank you for the letters, Peter," Addie called to him.

He waved and shook the reins. Kate stepped forward. Suddenly he pulled the reins taut. He had a message for Grandma and the Hoe girls. "I nearly forgot." He blurted out what he was supposed to tell them. "Mary Lawrence was at the post office and hoped she might come by to see you this afternoon. If it isn't all right, or if it is, I'm to let her know." Grandma gave Addie a wry smile and called back to Peter, who was chagrined that he nearly forgot the message from the lovely young woman Thomas intended to marry, "Thank you for the message, Peter, and yes, we shall be glad to have Mary come this afternoon."

Turning the carriage again toward the post office, Peter was off, not exactly unhappy to postpone shoveling out the horse stalls, and in fact eager to encounter Mary Lawrence again.

When the pot was full of cut-up apples, Addie and Ma together carried the huge cast iron kettle to the woodstove and slowly lifted it onto the back burner, where it would simmer for days once Grandma added spices and sugar.

"We must be sure Thomas or Josiah keeps elm wood in the stove over the next few days," Grandma stated as she stirred the kettle.

"Why is that?" Addie wondered.

"It is the slow-burning hardwood that will keep coals in the stove all night to cook the apple butter while we're asleep."

The women devoted the afternoon to preparing for Mary Lawrence's visit. Addie swept the porch and hall, and dusted the parlor while Ma dressed Annie and Mary in their best gowns and Grandma baked a sponge cake to accompany the tea. There was no time to open the letters Peter brought. She laid them on the bureau and quickly changed from her old linsey-woolsey dress to the white dimity frock she had saved during the summer thus far for best.

Once the girls were ready and Ma had herself dressed for the occasion, they joined Grandma in the parlor. While they waited, they picked up their sewing. At their feet, baby Mary crawled on the carpet, and Annie played with her dolls and bits of cloth Addie gave her. Thomas and Grandpa made themselves scarce. Both of them knew they were not essential to settling the finer points of wedding preparation.

CHAPTER TWENTY-ONE

Finally a carriage drew up in the front yard. Addie and Emilie went to the front door to welcome Miss Lawrence, who greeted them beaming as she descended from the carriage, helped down by her youngest brother Edward.

When they were settled in the parlor, Imogene brought the tea and cake. Conversation revolved around the health of the families and doings of their neighbors. Generally, the dry weather of the recent weeks, they concluded, had been conducive to fewer maladies.

After a polite silence, Mary shyly addressed the expectant audience. "As you may know, Thomas and I are to be married, and I have come to ask you, Addie, to be a bridesmaid for our wedding. I'm sorry Emilie is not here, for I wanted to ask her as well." She turned her blue eyes beseechingly to Addie, who looked at first surprised.

"With pleasure," she replied with alacrity, "and I have no doubt that Emilie will consent too."

"We are to be married October eleventh. It is a Wednesday, and I hope the date will allow you both to come. I know you will be in school. The reason for that date is that Thomas has asked my brothers to serve as groomsmen and both Cyrus and DeWitt will be going south at the end of that week,"

"I see," Addie responded. She had not met either of Mary's brothers, although she had heard they were aspiring businessmen. "I cannot foresee a problem. Emilie is finished with daily school lessons, although she does continue to study music and French. What do you think, Ma?"

"Your uncle's wedding is certainly an event you must honor with your presence, Addie, and I am sure your father will agree. We will warn Miss Clarke about the wedding in advance."

"Then it's settled, Addie. If you can come up from the city the previous day, you can help me dress on the morning of the ceremony, which will be early, at nine a.m. at our house."

"Will you and Mrs. Lawrence make your gown?" Grandma asked.

Mary nodded with enthusiasm, her blonde curls bouncing, and answered, "Yes, I have the material, and with less than two months until the wedding, we shall be busy. Addie, I hope that you and Emilie will wear gowns that you already own. You always dress beautifully."

"Thank you for the compliment, both for asking us to stand up with you and for your kind words about our dress."

Although Mary Lawrence had grown up in rural South Salem, she spoke as graciously as their instructress at school, Miss Clarke. Addie could see why, beyond her physical attractiveness, Uncle Thomas had gravitated toward her. She wondered if they would move to a new home.

Ma had similar thoughts. "Will you live here?" she asked, as she picked up baby Mary, who was about to crawl onto the hearth.

"Yes," she responded, turning to Grandmother Gilbert, who chimed in, "Yes, Josiah and I will gladly welcome you. Thomas has already talked with us, and it is the best plan."

She did not expand upon the reasons, but Addie knew her older uncles John and Benajah had families and farms of their own. The Gilberts' farm would be Thomas's when her grandparents were gone. He already was in charge of the farming operation.

"There will be other matters to settle, I'm sure," Mary Lawrence said, as she rose from the sofa, "but I shall write you when you return to New York City, whatever the details might be. Thank you, Mrs. Gilbert, for the refreshments."

The three generations of women each gave Miss Lawrence a warm embrace, and the little girls waved vigorously, calling "Bye, bye" to their visitor as she left.

It was well after teatime, but still Emilie and the cousins had not returned. Addie hoped they had not been trampled by Mr. Barnum's elephant. She went upstairs and took from the bureau the letters she saved to read in quiet.

Retta Stewart had written of her mother's nervous condition and its recurrence in early August. Joe had been in Cream Ridge off and on. Addie supposed those statements might well be related. She knew Mrs. Stewart, well aware of Joe's exploits rescuing slaves, must worry about him whenever he set out, whether for Baltimore, Philadelphia, or New York.

Retta wrote, too, of attending a soirée and dancing until past midnight: "We rode home in the moonless night, all of us depending on the horses' finding the way." Addie wondered who "all of us" might have been. No doubt Charlie Stewart, partial to dancing, was one of the party. Retta closed by encouraging Addie to come soon to Cream Ridge.

The other letter was from Henry, who wrote in happy anticipation of her return to the city. He had had a bout with the ague but assured her he had recovered. A visit by Jullien and his orchestra from Europe was imminent, he wrote, and when the Hoe girls were back in the city, they would all go to their concert. Henry's brother Edward Seymour was heading for Yale in September, much to their parents' pleasure. Joe and he had talked of how they missed her. She read the last sentence over several times, finding in it the resonance of Joe's feelings, as well as those of her favorite cousin.

CHAPTER TWENTY-TWO

"What do you think of the Lawrence brothers, Grandma?" Addie asked the next day. They were moving the boards laden with apples into the shed, because thunderheads were forming in the west. "Are they farmers, like Thomas?"

"Yes, they have farmed since their father became postmaster. Cyrus and DeWitt, however, have ambitions, and younger brother Edward may well end up taking over the farm."

Addie had observed the older brothers in church. They sat aloof, or seemingly so, their eyes on the pastor or the hymnal. Somewhat older than Addie or Emilie, they shared Mary Lawrence's fair complexion; Cyrus's and DeWitt's hair, however, was sand, while their sister's was gold.

Protecting the precious dried fruit, Addie stooped to brush away leaves blowing into the shed in advance of the storm.

"Emilie was delighted to learn of Mary's inviting us to be bridesmaids. She sat down immediately to write her a note of acceptance, even though it was very late when she and our cousins returned last evening. The pasture for the elephant was much farther away than the boys realized."

"I suspected their journey was going to be one of their longer larks," Grandma remarked.

Just as the first raindrops began to fall and the dull rumbling thunder sounded a warning, Addie closed the shed door and dashed into the house, following Grandma into the kitchen.

Now, Addie thought, with the prospect of a rainy day before them, playing the piano would suit her very well. She looked forward to going home to Broadway and the square piano in the parlor, where she amused herself whether sight-reading a new piece or practicing scales. She hoped that wherever Joe might be that he was safe, and she looked forward to seeing more of him soon.

Drawn by the fragrance of simmering apple butter, Ma, the little girls, their nurse, and Emilie joined Addie and Grandma in the warm kitchen.

Emilie described the Barnum elephant and its most amazing trunk. "Robbie offered it peanuts, and with delicacy the animal took them in its trunk and placed them in its mouth. The trunk must have been four feet in length, and it could stretch to be longer. Imagine, a nose that can, like a hand, perform useful operations."

Laughing, Grandma, who was stirring the apple butter, agreed. "I might use a third hand once in a while."

"Does the elephant perform farm work?"

"The man taking care of it told us that it was a novelty now, but it had been brought to America to work. It eats a tremendous amount of hay and needs a huge stable."

Emilie asked, "Can you imagine Thomas would be much inclined to buy an elephant?" Then both girls imagined the droll scene of their serious, quiet Uncle Thomas tending an elephant.

"First, let's see how he succeeds with a wife," Grandma remarked. Everyone laughed.

During the final week before returning to the city, the Hoe women retrieved what garments had been sent to the washerwoman, ironed them, and packed them, along with their other possessions, in the trunk and other luggage they had brought in July. Cousin Jane Howe came to tea once more and wished all the ladies well.

Mary Lawrence and her father stopped one evening to discuss wedding arrangements with Thomas, whose demeanor face-to-face with his intended was solicitous and gentlemanly. Addie was aware of the couple's absence from the parlor while Mr. Lawrence, Ma, and Grandma conversed. When the two returned, they held hands and glanced fondly at one another. Their obvious affinity, straightforward and simple, was wonderful to behold. Whenever she found the right mate, Addie thought, she hoped her romance would be as seemingly uncomplicated in its expression and design as Thomas's and Mary's.

On the last weekend the family would spend in South Salem, Father and Joe came from the city. They encountered the glorious weather that late August sometimes can bring, the crisp cool nights and days of cloudless azure skies and bright sunshine eliciting the first shades of fall in the occasional orange leaf. When Saturday dawned another such glorious day, Father suggested hiking up Mount Waccabuc.

Little Annie clapped her hands with delight at breakfast when he made the proposal. "May I come too?"

"Yes, but if you get tired…"

"Joe will carry me," she exclaimed, turning to him. "Won't you?"

Father smiled across the table at his friend.

"Only if you get very tired," Joe answered, trying to maintain a stern expression.

"Will we take a picnic?" Emilie asked.

CHAPTER TWENTY-TWO

"It is a good long walk if we want to reach the top. A picnic would make sense," Father said.

Addie and Emilie cut bread and cheese and packed a basket according to Grandma's instructions. Before ten o'clock the party set out, with little Annie on Father's shoulders, Addie carrying the basket, Emilie bearing a blanket to sit upon, and Joe in charge of the new telescope Father had brought to view the countryside from the mountaintop.

While Emilie regaled Father with the account of her trip to see the elephant, Joe fell in step with Addie. "How good it is to be with you again. What have you been doing if the trip to see the elephant could not beguile you?"

Her serious brown eyes fixed upon him, she responded, "One day when my sister and cousin Emmie left for Ridgefield, I had the chance to talk to Grandma alone."

"What was the outcome, which you alluded to in your letter?"

"She divined somehow that my mention of harboring slaves at the farmhouse was connected with you and abolition." Addie hesitated and turned again to face Joe. As they paused in the middle of the trail, a blue jay in a nearby pine tree flew ahead of them, shrieking in alarm. "I did not say anything about your being a conductor yourself, but Grandma immediately saw through my question."

"She suspects I put you up to this scheme of hiding slaves. Well, she has every right to think so."

"Oh, she is not averse to abolition or hiding Negroes. She shares my and your opinions about slavery, and she would gladly help. But, how can it happen?"

"What about Thomas and Josiah? Your grandpa may not exactly share her ideas."

"Oh, Grandpa is against slavery too. But with Thomas marrying Mary Lawrence in October…"

"He is actually engaged?" Joe and Uncle Thomas, although not well acquainted with one another, were the same age, and both of them took life seriously. In their very different worlds, they were responsible and dedicated.

"The date of the wedding is October eleventh, and I am to be a bridesmaid."

Joe was silent. He switched the telescope to his other hand and took Addie's hand. As the trail wound ever higher, they walked more carefully, picking their steps around the increasing number of boulders in the path. Father, Annie and Emilie were nowhere in sight, but they must have reached the top, Addie surmised. The only sound was a sighing wind in the pines on either side of them.

"Let me carry the basket," Joe offered. "It's heavier than this telescope."

"We'll trade," Addie said.

"No, I'll carry both," he insisted.

She was grateful to surrender the basket since the climb meant holding her skirt well above her boots to negotiate the rocky terrain.

"Do not worry about how to hide slaves," he assured her. "I will talk to your grandmother myself."

There were indeed obstacles to her and Joe's plans for sequestering slaves at the farm, but she had been around both of her grandparents enough to remember their oft-stated principle, "Where there is a will, there is a way."

"I will be in New York for good until the wedding," she said aloud.

"Yes, and I will be there most of the time, too, and we will have more time together."

"But there will be no way for me to be of assistance if you and the Gilberts agree to take on this enterprise."

"It was your inspiration to see that the farm cellar is an ideal hiding place, and I thank you for that. Whatever takes place in the future is out of your hands."

Addie took heart, but still doubted that all the people involved in the scheme would support it.

Up ahead, they could hear voices and, skirting an enormous boulder taller than a man, they found Father, Annie, and Emilie resting on a circle of stones. Lake Waccabuc stretched out below, gleaming in the midday sun.

"How lovely!" Addie exhaled in awe, while Joe handed Father the telescope. Adjusting the narrower end of the instrument until he could obtain a clear view of the distant hills, Father allowed Annie a peek. It took patience and a long explanation to induce her to use one eye to focus, but at last she squealed, "I see cows!" and begrudgingly gave the telescope back to her father. "And I'm hungry."

Emilie and Addie arranged the picnic on the blanket spread upon a granite outcropping. Father asked Joe about his recent travels while they ate and surveyed the landscape of eastern Westchester County, golden and green fields and lush dark forests spreading in patchwork below. While enjoying the satisfying view, Addie listened attentively.

"Have you visited Philadelphia lately?" Father wanted to know.

"I was there two weeks ago. The heat was stifling, but that's nothing new to you. Mainly I was negotiating orders for woolen cloth for the fall trade, since Mr. Jennings, among other tailors, was eager for better prices than they paid last year."

"What has been done about the rubble from the fire that destroyed the museum in July?"

"The rubble remains, but soon, no doubt, you'll find new buildings. There are plenty of hands eager for work."

CHAPTER TWENTY-TWO

"Yes, there is no dearth of workers in New York either, with steamboats arriving almost daily with hundreds of hungry, unemployed people from Europe."

Addie found no hint that her father connected himself with Joe in any way but as a friend, the son of his business associate and old friend Charles Stewart, whose foundry provided the iron R. Hoe Company used in making presses and saws.

"The Children's Aid Society may be a noble enterprise," Father went on, "sending waifs to farms on the frontier, but I like to see young men learning a trade and know they can succeed with education and at least one square meal a day to boot. Who knows what the situation might be among those farmers with the land not yielding much, food scarce, and nary a doctor for sickness?"

Little Annie began to tire of sitting still and made circles around the picnickers while she collected pebbles.

"I suppose you may be right," Joe responded. "The need for children to grow and prosper is dire, both in New York and Philadelphia, especially when cholera is rampant, along with consumption and other diseases brought from abroad. Slavery is another complication."

"Might not children become slaves of the farm families?" Her father brought up something Addie had not considered.

Joe looked out over the mountainside, considering an answer. "It seems to me there is a collision between slaveholders and settlers already erupting, now that the Kansas-Nebraska Act has passed. Slavery must be outlawed, don't you agree?"

"Yes, that might solve both problems. If slavery were unlawful everywhere in the country, Negroes and children would have a chance in life. The young fellows we employ are making their way, and they value learning, given half a chance to find out what that means." Father trained his telescope on the Catskills in the distance. Then he offered it to the others to have a look.

Emilie and Addie had not entered into the conversation, but instead they kept an eye on Annie and began to pack up the picnic basket. They all arose and stretched, stiff from sitting on the ground. Emilie shook crumbs from the blanket before folding it. Addie wrapped Annie's collection of pebbles in her handkerchief to take to Ma. They descended, refreshed by their lunch, while relaxing at the height of land and sharing lofty thoughts. Descending, Annie did not need shoulders to carry her until the final few yards of the excursion.

CHAPTER TWENTY-THREE

Not until Sunday afternoon did Addie have an opportunity to talk to Joe alone. They sat in the parlor. The rest of the Hoes left for a carriage ride, which would be their last until they returned later in the fall. Grandpa and Grandma dozed in their rockers, enjoying a "post-prandial snooze," as Grandpa called it. Thomas was visiting Reverend Lindley with Mary Lawrence to discuss the wedding service. Addie imagined the couple would cherish their time alone together on the return trip from the parsonage. She was trying to concentrate on sewing a straight seam when Joe, who had been reading a newspaper on the sofa, rose and, unspeaking, crossed the room to her.

"Come," he whispered, not wanting to waken her grandparents. She put aside her needle, thread, and the pillowslip she was mending. They passed through the hallway and into the late afternoon sunshine flooding the porch. After they sat down on the steps where he had kissed her in the moonlight some weeks before, he took her hand.

She spoke first as they looked across the lawn she had helped Thomas rake the previous week. "I shall miss South Salem. Please do come by often in New York. Sometimes I feel a fish out of water after life on the farm."

"That I can understand. We shall have to devise entertainments. Don't forget the pleasures of strolling for ice cream, the plays and concerts." Even as he spoke, he knew his time for such occasions with her would be rare given his two lives.

"I know you are right, and you always kindly invite me and Emilie to partake of many special diversions. Here there is a different but no less interesting life."

"Yes, I understand. Your roots are here, just as mine are in Cream Ridge. The older I get, the more I realize that instead of pangs of homesickness when I leave, I feel gratitude for those sound, loving roots."

"The city seems constantly changing," she went on, "new buildings rising and falling, expanding; whereas here, things stay the same, of course altering somewhat through the seasons, but remaining recognizable and ever beautiful. Do I make any sense?"

"Of course, and man-made things, while exciting perhaps, even beautiful and new, can be overwhelming, and when they are neglected, they become incredibly ugly."

CHAPTER TWENTY-THREE

Addie was grateful for his friendship, a constant whether in the city or the country. "What news do you have of Miss Jennings?"

"She is proceeding with her case against the omnibus company, with Chester Arthur's legal help. Her father is encouraged, but the city is aboil with strong feeling, despite the fact that slavery was abolished in New York before you or I were born."

"May I meet her sometime?"

"I can ask her father."

"He is a tailor, you have said."

"And an accomplished man. Did you know he had a patent for a process he invented to clean such clothing as suits, any fine fabrics that might be damaged by water and soap?" He paused and lowered his voice. "He's also buying his sisters and brothers out of slavery."

"Your sketch of Elizabeth Jennings was very fine. If I ever again have the opportunity to see Mr. Mount, the portrait painter, I shall ask him to paint Miss Jennings for all to see."

"Splendid idea!" Joe responded. "I wonder where her portrait might hang and be seen by the public, and what could come of it."

"I don't know. In any event, if she wins her case, I hope she won't be forgotten. When we get back to Broadway, I look forward to following news of her in the *Tribune*. Surely Mr. Greeley won't let interest in her die."

"Such stories keep the newsboys busy."

"Have you talked with my grandparents yet?"

"Remember," he spoke firmly, searching her face, "You are not to worry or say a word about that from now on."

Addie became very quiet and cast her gaze at the floor. The only sounds were the cows mooing as they milled about the gate, ready to come from the pasture to be milked, and soon they would hear the clanking of pails as Peter began the chores in the barn. Joe's expression softened.

She hung her head. "I'm sorry. I shall say no more about it."

He pulled her to him and gently held her in his arms, resting her head on his shoulder. There might have been more to that intimate moment had they not heard Grandma urging Grandpa awake to join Thomas at the barn and collect the eggs. Father, Ma and the rest of the Hoes would return soon.

"I will see if I can arrange a meeting between you and Elizabeth Jennings in the city. But don't get your hopes high. She may refuse."

Facing each other, they smiled. He took both of her hands and helped her to her feet, and together they went into the house.

CHAPTER TWENTY-FOUR

New York City. Although the worst heat of the summer was past and fall was imminent, September did not fulfill Addie's expectations for a temperate homecoming. Dust rose in clouds from the horses' hooves until the carriage reached the point on Broadway where cobblestones began. Men working at the side of the street mopped their brows as they rested from shoveling horse buns into a wagon. A miasma of murky smoke and dust hung in the air, making it difficult to breathe and obscuring the vivid blue sky the Hoes had left behind in South Salem. Addie worried for Annie, often prone to congestion.

"This weather can't last. It was more oppressive last week," Father commented as they drew near 309 Broadway. His optimism usually transformed dark to light. However, for Addie, who had been away for much of the previous three months, the city loomed in disagreeable patterns of want and crowdedness. The Crystal Palace and A. T. Stewart's marvelous store attracted her and Emilie, yes, but both were enclaves that allowed one to overlook the barefoot children, ill-clad and seemingly without oversight, on every corner. They and their families, if they had one, came from Ireland, England, France, Germany, and she did not know how many other countries.

When the carriage finally came to a halt, Addie looked down to see a cluster of newsboys hawking stacks of morning papers on the stoop of Irving House nearby. Father, the first to step onto the street, produced a coin from his pocket and hailed one of the young fellows, who hurried over to sell him a *Tribune*.

As the women and children climbed out of the carriage, the driver handed down the luggage to Father and Joe. The hubbub of entering the much-altered house made Addie forget the state of the city, at least for the moment. Inside the entire house had received fresh paint, not just the upper floors. Addie and her sisters dropped their bonnets and belongings at the front door and walked through each room. The pleasing colors Ma had chosen in the spring transformed the house. Father had purchased several new items of furniture. Among them were new chairs to complement the newly wall-papered front hall and an ornate walnut settee for the parlor. Ahead of Emilie and Addie rushed little sister Annie, excited to return home after a hiatus that to a three-year old seemed like years. She climbed

CHAPTER TWENTY-FOUR

onto the new settee and rubbed the smooth satin upholstery. Then she slid down to see if Tilda would be in the kitchen and might have a treat for her.

Joe found Addie in the kitchen and bid her farewell. She and Ma thanked him for his assistance on the trip home. Addie followed him to the hall, where Father stood absorbed in the newspaper. He realized his friend was departing and, putting down the newspaper, he asked, "What of the lodge for newsboys? Have you heard how it's proceeding?"

"Indeed. Several boys have begun to depend upon it, not just for a meal but to have a roof over their head too."

"It is a capital idea and one that answers a great need, I think. Let me know if my brothers and I can be of help."

"I will." Joe smiled at Addie. "I will see you again soon, no doubt. Good-bye." He went out after shaking Father's hand.

Father returned to reading the newspaper, and Addie looked over his shoulder to scan the bold headlines. Was there anything about Miss Jennings's case? Her eyes wandered to the table in the foyer and the plate on which letters commonly awaited their recipients. Examining them, she looked to see if any were for her.

There was a letter addressed to Father from Miss Clarke, no doubt relating to the tuition for school. There was one for Emilie and one for Addie herself. She was delighted to find hers was from Maria Seabury, from whom she had heard nothing for many weeks. Seeking out the new sofa, Addie sat down to learn what had transpired in Setauket since she and Emilie visited.

Maria wrote of a clamming expedition with her cousins and uncle to a favorite spot farther east on Long Island, followed by an evening of singing. Remembering the banjo harmonies and the rhythms of the bones, Addie imagined the jolly scene by the bay. Maria looked forward to seeing the Hoe girls in the city and asked how Addie looked forward to geometry. She paused to recollect their shared dislike of things mathematical. Father had only laughed when she groaned over algebra and complained how tedious she found it to be. Ma suggested that geometry might make drawing patterns for her sewing projects easier, an idea Addie regarded doubtfully.

Settling into life at 309 Broadway meant washing and sorting summer clothes and retrieving their winter clothing from the attic to air on the back porch. There were trips to the stationer's for materials for school: pens, ink, nibs, and paper.

One morning, Emilie and Addie sallied forth for a look at the latest inventory of dresses at A. T. Stewart's. By chance they met Joe Stewart there. He was discussing fabrics with several members of the tailoring department, three men in shirtsleeves and vests, who stood in a semi-circle while Joe addressed them. One of them, with a European accent Addie could not place, was asking something about woolen tweeds. When Joe realized the young women were nearby, he excused himself and came to greet them straightaway. "What brings you here, Ladies?"

"We have come to see what is new."

"You ought to find plenty to satisfy your curiosity. The new parasols from Dijon might interest you." Addie and Emilie glanced at each other amused, realizing they were seeing Joe in mercantile mode.

"Please don't let us disturb you," Emilie said, taking Addie's elbow and backing away. "Where would we find the parasols?"

"On the second floor, in front by the stairs." He turned back to the tailors.

"Thank you," Addie called over her shoulder.

"You're welcome. Good day." Nodding to the three men, he resumed their conference. A. T. Stewart's was truly a marvelous place, one of a kind in America, as the newspaper advertisements claimed. Women strolled through the aisles either alone or in pairs. Silk garments from Japan, in all the colors to tempt the eye, lay before them. Displayed attractively in an endless array, gowns in the latest French design cascaded from dress forms. An eager shop boy, not much older than Addie, saw the girls pause before a length of Battenburg lace and rushed to tout its virtues and tell its price. Since they aimed more to look than to buy, they listened politely but told him they preferred to see the parasols. He meekly bowed, pointed them to the stairs, and then retreated behind the counter.

"Mr. Stewart has his own manufactories in several foreign countries," Emilie commented as they ascended to the second floor. "Imagine Scottish ladies knitting our sweaters, French people making our undergarments and gowns, and Kashmir goats thousands of miles away providing the softest wool for Ma's scarf." The girls finally came upon the parasols. Addie admired the delicate handles, some carved of ivory, and the wide variety of elegant lace trimming the edges. There was even a black parasol with an ebony handle and wide, black grosgrain trim, for mourning, she assumed. Despite the luxury and availability of ready-made dresses in the store, Addie knew they would have their own dressmaker come to measure the womenfolk at home when they needed new gowns. In the store, she and Emilie had seen signs for dressing rooms beyond the clothing displays. The idea of undressing in a public place, even though enclosed in a private room, was repugnant to both girls. No, they were happy to have Mrs. Robbins make their dresses.

"What shall we wear for Thomas's and Mary's wedding?" Addie asked. They had left the parasol display and were passing through the ornate glass-and-marble entrance onto the street.

"Since they are both quiet and serious people, I think our brown challis will do quite nicely," Emilie responded. "Don't you agree?"

CHAPTER TWENTY-FOUR

"And I will finish the new collars I began in South Salem, one for you and one for me."

Emilie pulled her handkerchief from her reticule and held it to her nose while they passed a large deposit of horse manure awaiting the dung wagon. Two men, one black and one white, scraped the section of the street in front of the store. They kindly stepped aside to let the girls pass and then returned to their toil.

"Let's see what is new from the music publishers," Addie suggested, wondering what polkas or mazurkas or other sorts of music might have been printed since the summer began. At the street corner, after passing through the shade of many awnings and studying displays in the windows of shops, they turned west and soon arrived at Meyer's, a shop with sheet music to sell. Finding a new schottische available and a waltz for four hands, Addie bought them both, the only shopping purchases of the trip.

"Will you have time to learn them before school begins?" Emilie asked. She was skeptical of her sister's actually making good use of the music.

"How odd, Emilie," Addie interjected. "You must have forgotten how happy you felt when we were able to play at Cousin Jane's. When we get home, we can uncover the piano and try these pieces. With no music, life becomes very dull, you must admit. Besides, now that you are out of school, you can play almost any time."

"No doubt the piano will need tuning," Emilie stated. "I do not enjoy a tinny sound."

Addie puzzled over her sister's testy tone, and she concluded Emilie rather envied her for going back to school, where time did not lie fallow. "What will you do while I am at Miss Clarke's?" Addie asked her directly.

Emilie paused, looking into the window of a flower shop where a tired bouquet of pink roses cried out for water. "Well, I will continue French lessons with Miss Boutilier. There is the wedding to plan for and attend in October. I can seek out my school friends if they are still in the city, the misses Morand and Anna Howell. But," she faltered, "I shall miss the way school orders each day."

Addie knew she too would feel as Emilie did were it not for school. The uncertainty evoked by Father's plans for a farm clouded the picture the girls imagined for the future. She had heard him talking with Ma since they returned to the city. Would they leave 309 Broadway now that he had purchased property in Morrisania? Was their present home redecorated to sell? No matter. She fingered the crisp paper of the pieces of music she bought and quickened her step for the final block of their trip.

Once they crossed Broadway, avoiding the wagons, omnibuses, and crowds of vendors who shouted inducements to buy, they arrived at the home they knew best. Tilda let them in, saying Ma and the "babies," as she called both little girls, were resting. Addie thought better of trying out her new music. Instead, she and Emilie lifted the sturdy, woven Osnaburg covering that protected the lovely instrument. Addie brought rags, and carefully, with a wet cloth, wiped the summer's accumulation of dust from the keys of the familiar, square Nunns and Clark piano.

Emilie acquired some of her sister's enthusiasm, and conspiratorially she closed the sliding doors between the two sections of the parlor. "Let's try quietly to play the four-hands piece. Just sight-read it, using the soft pedal," she whispered.

Addie agreed, and they sat down side by side, slowly making sense of the rhythm and harmonies of the waltz. Emilie, older and with more years of studying piano, took the florid *primo* part while her younger sister supplied the *secondo*. Although, as Emilie predicted, the piano needed a tuning, they both enjoyed themselves just the same. They did not notice when Cousin Henry unobtrusively slid open the pocket doors, entered the room, and sat down directly behind them. He clapped at the conclusion of the piece. Startled, both girls turned around.

"Where did you come from?" Emilie asked.

"The waltz is new from Meyer's, not worthy of applause yet," Addie put in. "We couldn't resist sight-reading it." She rose from the piano bench and closed the sliding doors Henry had left open.

"I've come to invite you both to Bloomfield for a few days. Can you spare the time before school, Addie? Mary and Elizabeth would be glad to have you."

Addie remembered the open invitation her aunt Mary Seymour had extended to her in July. Bloomfield, New Jersey, was not too far afield, she thought, and Father could not have many objections to their going, since school would not begin for three weeks.

"That would be delightful," Emilie responded, with an alacrity that revealed to Addie how at loose ends her sister was without the school routine and seeing her friends regularly.

"You mentioned in your letter that Madame Grisi was coming to New York," Addie said. "I should like very much to hear her sing."

"Ah yes, she is coming very soon, and you must accompany me to hear her."

"I do not care very much for opera," Emilie admitted, "but I expect Madame Grisi can make it exciting. Remember when Jenny Lind came from Sweden? She sang like a bird."

"Yes," Henry recalled, "and she sought out your father, don't you remember, and asked to see the printing press factory?"

CHAPTER TWENTY-FOUR

"I was only thirteen," Addie remarked. "Father has retold the story enough times that I feel I was there that day, but I wasn't. She strolled through the press works, enthralled by the steam engines and the skill of Father's men, who doffed their hats and bowed to her and hoped for a song."

"Then it's settled," Henry concluded suddenly, rising to his feet. "You both will be coming to Bloomfield. Is this Friday too soon?"

They both looked questioningly at each other, and then the Hoe girls agreed they would check with their parents.

"I'll come back later to confirm your coming." With that, Henry opened the doors and slipped out. He would no doubt head for Broome Street and his tasks at the Hoe factory. If he needed to hurry, he would catch an omnibus.

The ease with which the family could communicate in the city, with brothers Richard, Robert, and Peter Hoe living close to one another, made for a tight-knit family always aware of the needs and health of one another. While Bloomfield was across the Hudson River, it was less than a day's travel away, which meant that Aunt Mary Hoe Seymour's branch of the family was easily accessible, too, as was Aunt Emmeline Hoe Ely's family in Brooklyn.

The warmth and freedom of her family life, which Addie had always taken for granted, she saw, was not often possible for black families. Even the successful Mr. Jennings had to struggle to buy his relatives out of slavery. It was a cruel institution indeed.

CHAPTER TWENTY-FIVE

Hidden in the woods at the edge of the Delaware River, a family of four breathed a sigh of relief after a long day's travel on foot. The father opened the only bag they carried, extracted the last of their provisions—hunks of dry corn bread—and doled them out. His mother, a Negro woman with graying hair bound in a fraying scarf, smiled wearily when her son offered her food first, yet she refused it. "Give it to the little ones."

Reluctantly, the father followed her bidding and divided the meager fare between his daughter and son.

"Who knows when we can eat again, Grandma?" the little girl muttered before she began to gnaw on the stale bread. She handed her grandmother's portion back to her father, who paused and then wolfed it down.

"It doesn't matter, honey. I's not hungry," she said.

As soon as they had eaten, they rose from the clearing among the sheltering oaks and traveled on. The father and two children paused when they reached the edge of the thoroughfare leading to Philadelphia, while the grandmother slowly made her way a distance behind them. Summoning strength, the first three dashed across the road, seeking the path that resumed in the undergrowth.

Just then, as the father and children disappeared, a small trap rounded a corner and pulled to a halt barely a hundred feet away from the weary grandmother. Beauregard Wise, spying the old woman in the gathering darkness, shook the reins of the horse and before the woman could step across the highway, he was upon her. He wheezed, "Halt!" Then he hoisted his heavy frame to the ground beside the weary, frightened woman.

Without a thought for her condition or her advanced age, Wise set about to question her. "Are you not the mother of one Jabez and belong to one Willard Hartlow of Virginia?" He had studied the classified listings carefully in recent weeks and made note of slaves on the loose.

The old woman, too worn out to deny where she came from, admitted who she was. She prayed that her son and grandchildren would keep going without her.

The grasping Wise, gleeful that his regular perusal of the newspaper had paid off, took hold of one of her emaciated arms and ushered her rudely onto the trap. Now he would hasten south and collect his bounty. If he berated the woman enough, he thought, noting her weakened condition, she would no doubt tell where her son and the children were headed.

She collapsed onto the seat of the trap, grateful that her steps north were over. Well, the slave catchers they had dreaded throughout all the legs of their journey had not caught Jabez and the children yet. Her hunger and fatigue, plus the motion of the trap, put her to sleep.

When Wise pulled up at his hotel, he turned to rouse the woman, only to find that she had no pulse and was no more than a pile of dirty rags and fragile bones. He angrily considered how he could still obtain some balance of cash for at least locating her. He would write to her owner immediately and be on the lookout for Jabez, who could not be far away.

As the year approached the autumnal equinox, violent thunder storms wracked the skies and streets of the city. During one especially disturbing event, Addie sat watching the wide expanse of Broadway from her bedroom window. Lightning illuminated the empty street and ink-black sky with spectacular flashes of steel blue and white followed by reverberations that shook the house. She wondered if the lightning might strike the tall buildings further up the street. The rain began in sheets, pelting the windows and making it impossible to make out anything below.

The oak front door slammed in the hallway below. She wondered who could be out in this weather. Sister Emilie lay on the bed sleeping, wrapped in the coverlet, which was her way of enduring the storm. Addie made her way to the landing, and from down the stairs she could hear her father greeting someone in his hearty, welcoming manner.

Curious to know who was coming out in the midst of the storm, Addie descended to the hall just as Father and the visitor entered the front parlor. Still unable to divine who the guest might be, she stood outside the door to listen.

"Can I get you some brandy, Charles?" Father offered. Which Charles? she wondered.

"No, thank you, Richard." The gruff voice, Addie knew immediately, was that of Charles Stewart, Joe's father.

"Are you sure? You must be soaked."

"There's nothing that won't dry once I get home."

"It's good to see you again. How long has it been?"

"A couple of months, at least."

"How is Ann? Joe has been here a good deal."

"Ann is doing very well, thank you. She had her nervous troubles in the summer, but appears to be much better. How are your girls?"

"I'm happy to say at the moment they are chipper. My wife is well. The little ones prospered in South Salem, and the older girls managed to enjoy themselves and stay in good health. Addie has another year at Miss Clarke's. Emilie is nineteen, and she is a fine young woman for an eligible man to pursue. If you want to know, Joe tended to spend time with Addie when he joined us in the country—walks, and conversation on the porch, that sort of thing."

Addie's face began to feel hot as she stood outside the door.

"Ah, Joe has many interests. I did not realize that Addie was one of them. He travels a good deal, keeps occupied at the store, and, what with racing my filly, I am relieved but surprised to hear he has time for a girl."

"Addie will be eighteen this month."

The implication of her father's statement was not lost upon her. A girl was to fasten onto a man when she reached eighteen. Even if she did have strong feelings for Joe, she knew theirs was a complicated blend of shared empathy for the plight of slaves and honest, mutual pleasure in one another's company. If Mr. Stewart were to urge Joe to pursue her, Addie knew there would be a resistance from Joe that his father might not understand, straightforward fellow that he was.

Addie had stopped listening and sat in one of the new hall chairs, trying to make sense of her relationship with Joe. Descending the stairs, Emilie yawned when she found her, "Is the storm over? Why are you sitting in the hall?"

Addie stood, just as Father called out, "Emilie, come see who's here."

When both girls entered the parlor, Mr. Stewart enveloped each of them in an embrace. Hale and blustery, he always held them closer and longer than an uncle might. Addie felt sheepish for having listened in on their conversation, and she hoped that her blushing would not betray her. As Mr. Stewart returned to his armchair, the girls sat down demurely on the sofa and each took up her sewing. Outside, the worst of the storm was over, and the sound of rain in the downspouts and the splashing of conveyances in the street replaced the preceding violent thunder and lightning.

Father and Mr. Stewart discussed the printing presses and complications of fine-tuning the cutting devices for newsprint. Addie regarded Mr. Stewart in profile. Although a more imposing man than Joe, they each shared the same strong jaw, handsome hairline, and considerate manner.

"How is Retta?" Addie ventured to ask. "I hope she and her brothers and sisters are well."

"We enjoyed our stay at Cream Ridge very much," Emilie added.

"And we hope you both will come see us again," the older gentleman said. Noting a welcome ray of sunshine passing through the western window making a bright stripe on the carpet, he rose to leave. "Thank you, Richard, for providing a port in the storm. Ladies, it has been a pleasure to see you, lovely as ever."

CHAPTER TWENTY-FIVE

Father walked with him into the foyer and helped him into his coat.

"Joe tells me the billiard room you refurbished is very fine. I hope he is not wearing out his welcome with you."

"Hardly. He is never a bother. He is an exemplary guest. Please give Mrs. Stewart our kind wishes." As Mr. Stewart left, the door closing heavily behind him, Father rejoined his daughters in the parlor and took up *The Lamplighter*, which they had recommended to him. It was a tale of a pathetic orphan and a novel that they had found touching.

The morning that the Hoe girls left for Bloomfield to visit their aunt's, New York City put on a new face. The rainy spell had ended, followed by chilly nights and clear, sunny days. The streets were full of hawkers, travelers with bags, newsboys, businessmen in top hats, ragged beggars, women of questionable repute, policemen with night sticks, tinkers and their hand carts, workmen with lunch pails, whole families newly arrived from a steamship and holding all their worldly possessions in a bag and gazing about in wonder, drovers, gentlemen and ladies hustling about in a barouche or light carriage, and omnibuses drawn by huge cart horses.

Hugging their baby sisters and parents goodbye, Addie and Emilie departed from home accompanied by Henry Seymour. They awaited the car that would take them to the ferry in order to cross the Hudson River and thence, by a carriage sent by their uncle, Reverend Seymour, to Bloomfield. Cousin Henry was in high spirits. On the ferry, he insisted that the girls come to the railing to watch the cormorants diving for fish and so that he could point out the different boats coming and going on the glistening river.

"Will the boys have returned to the academy?" Emilie wanted to know, as they looked upon the teeming harbor. She referred to the students attending Bloomfield Academy, of which Reverend Seymour was the headmaster.

"I should think not," Henry replied. "Classes do not resume until October, very like Miss Clarke's."

"Is the course of study very different?" Addie wanted to know.

"I should expect they do not have time for diversions which you may enjoy in the city during the term. However, some of the boys find time for wrestling together, which seems to be a favorite sport, along with riding. There are several clubs to join. When I attended, under my father's thumb, I enjoyed the Athenian Club."

"What was that?"

"We dressed in classical costume and recited memorized passages from Greek and Latin 'lit-tra-ture.' Afterward, there were refreshments, usually cake provided by my mother. There is a public speaking contest toward the end of the year, when one receives a topic and must produce an extemporaneous speech."

"Oh, that would be the death of me!" Emilie commented.

Addie considered the demands placed upon her at school, and she knew Miss Clarke's curriculum, although it required her to apply herself at mathematics and that it involved acquiring knowledge of French, allowed greater freedom. They were not expected, after all, to prepare for the seminary. She knew women were teachers, but certainly none became preachers.

"Does one study French and drawing, as we do, at the Academy?" Addie asked.

"One might, on one's own time. History, geography, rhetoric, Bible, Latin, and Greek—and, oh yes, mathematics. That is the basic curriculum I studied."

Addie realized her father, a man of only limited schooling, while he valued education highly and urged her and her sister to pursue their academics vigorously, likely never would have devised his Lightning Printing Press had he himself spent his young life at an academy. As a boy, he entered the press factory his father owned and perforce took over all practical aspects of it early. His father, a carpenter who built presses, came from England and met his wife Rachel while he was building a bridge in Cross River with her father, Matthew Smith. Even though Richard March Hoe had achieved success that allowed his daughters to learn what he never had, he was content to see them become accomplished pianists and speakers of French. He delighted in his days in the factory, improving the machines he built and obtaining new patents for his ever-evolving invention, all the while aiding his employees in improving their minds.

Reverend Ebenezer Seymour, animated, gangly, and tall, greeted them at the door of the Seymour home, one of the imposing edifices on a tree-lined street with spacious lawns in Bloomfield. A Presbyterian minister for many years, he left off preaching to start an academy. Mary Hoe Seymour, his wife, the eldest of the Hoe sisters, stood in the doorway behind the Reverend along with Edward, Henry's brother, who was about to depart for Yale College. She cordially invited them to join them for dinner, as they were soon to sit down.

Aunt Mary showed them where to deposit their satchels. "How good to see you. Summer sunshine has given you both excellent color," she noted. Then she explained that daughters Mary and Elizabeth were taking books to a neighbor and would return momentarily. After removing bonnets and finding their accommodations, the Hoe girls joined the family in the spacious formal dining room. The large number of place settings confused Addie at first, until the Reverend explained that several new students would join them, first-year boys exploring the school in advance of the term. In addition to the family of Seymours and visiting cousins, four young gentlemen arrived to share a meal. Addie wondered if Aunt Mary entertained all such prospective students when they were considering attending the school.

A servant brought a huge roast of beef to the table. While Uncle Ebenezer carved, he made a running commentary about the school, what the young men should expect, and what the school would expect from them. Addie and Emilie exchanged smiles across the table with their cousins and looked forward to conversations with Edward, Mary and Elizabeth, their contemporaries. The younger children; Robert, eleven, and George, nine; wriggled in their chairs, doubtless having heard their father's introduction to Bloomfield Academy not a few times before. Henry gave them each a cautionary frown.

After the Reverend said the grace, he began to pass around heaping bowls of potatoes and beans. "What are your interests, boys?" the Reverend asked the visitors.

The guests looked at one another nervously, each hoping that another boy would take the lead. Finally, the smallest fellow, with an unruly cowlick, ventured an answer. "I carve wooden objects, sir, when I'm not working for my father, sir."

"What sorts of objects?"

"Animals. Human figures. Filigree for boxes. Whatever the wood leads me to make."

"I don't expect there will be much time for that at the school, but it is good that you have a hobby." He seemed satisfied with the young man's response. The servant came around the table and refilled glasses for the thirsty boys. By the end of dinner, each potential student had answered one of the headmaster's questions.

Aunt Mary left the table and returned with a tureen of custard that she ladled into bowls. She said nothing throughout the meal and only passed the bowls around. This formal ritual, with the Reverend interviewing the guests while the family sat mute, created a spectacle that explained a good deal to Addie about Henry's ambivalence toward academic life. Meals in the Hoe girls' household were rarely quiet, with Father exchanging news with Ma and all the family and guests expected to converse, even little sister Annie.

At the conclusion of the meal, Reverend Seymour turned to his own children as well as Addie and Emilie and announced, "You may be excused, children. Mary, thank you for preparing dinner." The four young visitors to the school, taking his cue, noisily pushed back their chairs, and in unison they thanked Mrs. Seymour, who merely nodded and smiled.

"Now we will visit the school building. I will then show you gentlemen the grounds. Also, I want you to view a collection of rare stones. That is my hobby, you see." The boys trooped out behind Reverend Seymour.

CHAPTER TWENTY-SIX

Breathing a sigh of relief the remaining members of the Seymour family gathered around Addie and Emilie after they had cleared the table. They wanted to hear about their relatives' summer adventures. When Robert and George heard their sisters asking about the wedding in which Addie and Emilie were to have supporting roles, the young boys skipped off to play. Aunt Mary and her daughters, who rarely traveled outside of Bloomfield, listened with enjoyment to descriptions of peach orchards in Delaware, boating off Setauket, and hiking Mount Waccabuc. The Hoe girls inquired about Edward's imminent enrollment at Yale, what he would study, and when he would come home again.

"He did well on the entrance examinations. He expects to study literature and languages," Elizabeth said. It was clear the family was proud of his prospects. While Henry listened attentively, Addie could see that he was not in the least envious of his academically inclined younger brother.

"Edward will make a name for himself at Yale, and I hope he will find time to write me a letter once in a while." Henry turned to Edward, who shyly smiled, not particularly pleased that all eyes were on him.

"I'll try not to forget" was his terse response. Handsome and intense, Edward bore a physical resemblance to his uncle Richard as a young man, with piercing blue eyes and a shock of unruly dark hair. Yet it was Henry whose kind and sunny disposition best resembled his uncle's.

At length, Reverend Seymour returned to the house. The four young applicants to the academy had mounted their horses and gone their separate ways to towns in the surrounding region. Weary, he sank into his armchair in the parlor, where the ladies sat in a circle chatting over their sewing. Addie observed the parson, gray about the temples, as he tried to stay awake over the newspaper Henry had brought him from the city. Clearly, the effort to entertain students was all-consuming, requiring his ceaseless, undivided attention. The rocks he collects, she thought, provide a welcome relief, as they are much quieter and easier to control than teenage boys.

Henry entered the room and sat next to Addie. When he saw his father less than engaged in reading, he delicately freed the newspaper from his hands as it drooped in his lap. He then asked if the women would like to hear news from the city, to which they nodded in agreement. There were articles about the lessening of the cholera epidemic. He read a report of a lurid murder, but omitted the paragraph which graphically described the mangled body of the victim. His sisters urged him to find something pleasant to read. Riffling through the pages, he sought out the society news and gave a dramatic reading of an article describing a grand wedding officiated by Dr. Tyng.

"Don't you think, eminent man that he is, Dr. Tyng would be wasted on a wedding?" his mother asked Henry when he had finished.

"What do you mean, Mother?" Elizabeth asked.

"He is a great preacher and a wedding would give far too little occasion for his eloquence."

"No," Henry ventured, "I disagree. He makes his fame increase and his virtue expand when he performs a simple ceremony." He folded the newspaper and placed it next to his dozing father.

Suddenly the Reverend awoke and, sensing he had missed something, he erupted, "What? Who?" and straightened his lank body.

Henry, smiling, answered wryly, "You might have missed something, Father."

"I slipped off for a moment, that's all, young man. When you have the responsibilities I have, you'll understand."

Addie saw the bristly relationship that existed between father and son. She kept her eyes fixed upon the embroidery she was adding to a collar.

Adopting a serious tone, Henry continued, "Father, I have been following closely the difficulty Uncle Richard has been having with cutting the paper once it has been printed by the Lightning Press."

"And so?" His father eyed him suspiciously.

"And so, I think a factory that made precision shears, to be installed on the press, could be a success. Uncle agrees. Of course, I'd need capital to start such a venture."

"And where do you propose to find it? Your mother and I do not have that kind of wealth, you ought to know."

"Oh, I'm not asking for support. I only thought you might like to hear what I've been considering. Work in the factory office isn't all I do. Seeing the ways to improve the presses means I'm in the shop, too."

"What about improving your mind?"

Henry seemed at a loss for words. Addie had heard enough. Not wanting to anger her uncle, yet unable to bear seeing Henry's aims diminished in her presence, she spoke up. "Henry accompanies us to hear all the great speakers and preachers in the city. There are, as you know, churches all about, and we take in as many sermons as we can. Also, he and we attend musical presentations of very high quality."

Henry colored to hear his cousin take his part. His mother and sisters left off sewing to see how Reverend Seymour would react. He only cleared his throat, seeming to ignore her, and regarded Henry. "I leave it to you, Henry, to forge ahead with any scheme you may have. But remember I have neither the cleverness nor the pocket to assist you."

"Thank you for hearing me out," Henry spoke, with no irony. He was on his own. Edward would have tuition for Yale; as for Henry's enterprises, he alone would have to figure out how to accomplish them. He sat silent, eyes downcast.

Emilie and Addie had no brothers for whom the question of a profession was an issue. Henry was as close to a brother as anyone they knew could be. While the scene pained them, it was inevitable that Henry would challenge his father and, with his three uncles' guidance, find his own road. Addie believed in Henry's abilities, so different from Edward's and his father's.

Elizabeth, who was fourteen and tired of the tension in the parlor, remembered that both of her cousins played the piano. Although her father forbade dancing, he was not averse to singing and piano music. "Might we sing awhile?" she asked, directing her question to her father, who had picked up his newspaper again. He nodded, and her mother, grateful for a change of subject, agreed.

Standing up for Henry was not without consequences. Her cousins Mary and Elizabeth both treated Addie warily, and Aunt Mary, she observed, although stolid and commanding with her own daughters, approached Addie and Emilie with deference. Later that day, she asked their opinion about the cloth for a dress that she planned to make for the opening of school. When there was a question about the best way to starch crinoline, Aunt Mary inquired as to the length of time to soak the fabric. In these encounters the girls answered forthrightly.

However, when she asked how Addie might address a bereaved parent of a student who had died of cholera, her niece was perplexed. "Dear Aunt, I cannot pretend to have the experience that you have had with such human problems. I do not know what one should say."

Her aunt smiled as though satisfied that her niece did not speak arrogantly or attempt to lecture her outside her realm of knowledge. It puzzled Addie to think Aunt Mary would suspect her of selfish pride, but she vowed she would henceforth weigh her words very carefully while staying in Bloomfield.

"What do *you* read?" Reverend Seymour asked Emilie and Addie one evening as they sewed with the Seymour girls.

"Oh no!" Addie thought, pricking her index finger with a needle. She pressed the tip with her opposing thumb, determined not to avoid answering. "Lately we have read *Katherine Ashton*, Miss Sewell's novel, and we enjoyed *Oliver Twist* by Charles Dickens very much."

"What did you absorb from reading such fiction?" he continued in his intimidating manner. Although he scanned the newspapers, she surmised,

CHAPTER TWENTY-SIX

he likely preferred the Bible and theological works to the exclusion of other forms of printed matter.

"While Miss Sewell's book describes very thoroughly life in an English girls' school, its prose cannot compare with the delightful stories and fluid style of Dickens."

"What moral do you draw from them?"

"That families are good, while orphans depend upon the quality of human social progress to survive and succeed in life."

A silence followed her remarks. Emilie caught Addie's eye. She gave her younger sister a slight nod before returning to her seam. Since there was no more interrogation, at least not that day, Reverend Seymour must have been satisfied.

The trees lining the neighborhood streets had become muted, no longer the vivid green of summer, as the Seymour children walked to church on Sunday morning with their visitors, whose stay would end the following day. The elder Seymours planned to attend prayer meeting that evening and therefore did not come with them. Henry, as the oldest son, escorted the family under trees already losing leaves that blew about. Happy to be returning to his work in the city, his spirits lifted. Edward had already departed for New Haven.

Addie wondered what the younger sisters thought of remaining in Bloomfield. "Will you attend school, Mary?" she asked.

"Why no, I am quite content now that I have completed lessons at the dame school nearby. We attend Father's Bible school at the church."

When they entered the Presbyterian church and approached the pew where the Seymours generally sat, a man was already sitting in it, and judging from the reaction of Henry and his siblings as they glanced in puzzlement at one another, his presence was unusual. The man's dark head of hair and seemingly short stature were vaguely familiar, Addie sensed. As he looked up and hastened to slide toward the inmost corner of the pew, she knew that he was indeed Beauregard Wise, the slave hunter. Due to his bulk taking up a good portion of the pew, Addie and Emilie were forced to file into the pew behind the Seymours, which meant she sat directly in back of the scurrilous Wise. She hoped he did not recognize her.

Knowing that Joe Stewart and Henry Seymour were often together in the city, Addie felt uncomfortable. When Henry gave the swarthy fellow a sidelong glance, Wise leered back with a self-satisfied smirk.

The sermon concerned the story of Nathan and the Ewe Lamb, King David's arrogance in sending Uriah the Hittite into battle to cover his sins with Bathsheba, and how we all need the Lord's forgiveness as much as

David when we exploit others as he did. Addie saw the connection so easy to make with slavery and the exploitation of Negro people. Did it register with Beauregard Wise? Would he change his ways? She suspected that he was calculating who might have news of slaves concealed in the vicinity. He eyed the congregation. Peering about, he rarely raised his eyes to the pulpit.

After the pastor's benediction, the congregation rose to depart. Henry and Beauregard Wise stood and exchanged words, but due to the buzz of conversation among the parishioners and the piping strains of the postlude from the melodeon, Addie could not hear what they said. She and Emilie emerged from the pew and joined the rest of the family, who were greeting the pastor.

At length, Henry caught up with them in the vestibule. Addie longed to know what the two men said, but waited to find out, hoping she might not have to ask. Henry was quiet, unfortunately. Beauregard Wise was nowhere to be seen. Very possibly, he departed from the rear of the church. Addie pondered how not to seem overly interested in him, but Elizabeth made the inquiry for her. "Henry, who was that ugly man sitting next to you? He looked like the fat spider that frightened Miss Muffet away."

"Yes, and he took up most of the pew," complained young George. "Robert and me were squashed."

"Robert and I," Mary corrected him. "Henry, who was that man?"

"He's someone I've seen at times on the cars, and he wanted to know if anyone around here has Negro servants."

"What did you tell him?" Mary asked.

"That I did not know, since I work in the city, and that the girl who helps our mother is white."

"What became of him? He did not leave with the congregation," Elizabeth said, and looked over her shoulder to see if he might be following them. But Wise had vanished.

"I met him in Delaware City," Addie admitted. "He attended a party when we were staying with Joe's sister in July." She said no more, not wanting to explain all she knew about the slave catcher, especially with the younger children likely to alarm their parents.

After the children had given a detailed account of the sermon at the demand of their father, and they had satisfied his religious questions for the day, they fled to change into everyday clothing. Henry and Addie repaired to the library. As she regarded the neatly shelved tomes stretching to the ceiling, Henry searched for the newspaper he had brought from New York the previous Friday. Addie debated resuming talk of the fellow who had appeared in church.

"Did the man you sat beside in church tell you his name?" She attempted to sound casual.

"No, but Joe has told me to beware of men like him. They are likely to be slave catchers, mercenary types who will go to any lengths for cash from slave owners."

"At the party in Delaware City, he introduced himself to me as Beauregard Wise."

"I wonder if that is his real name," Henry conjectured. "Did you dance with him?"

Addie blushed. "Yes," she confessed. "I hope he did not see me today. I would just as soon not renew that acquaintance."

After Sunday dinner, Reverend Seymour gave his two young sons permission to toss the new baseball Henry had brought them. Although a stern educator, he believed that exercise made boys healthier and more tractable, so, for a fraction of the late afternoon, they were excused to play in the front yard.

Not five minutes later, they burst into the parlor. "That man we saw in church just rode by," George reported.

"What man?" their father asked.

"The fat man who sat in our pew," Robert explained. "He rode a horse and stared at us as he went by."

Addie and Henry looked at one another. "Which way was he going?" Henry asked.

"Toward the depot," George answered. Addie felt a chill, although there was no perceptible draft in the room.

"What is all this, Henry?" the Reverend wanted to know. "Boys, you may go back outside."

"His name is Beauregard Wise, and I met him in Delaware City." Addie spoke up, but said no more than necessary.

Without any hesitation, Henry broke in. "He is a slave catcher, Father. He inquired if I knew who had Negro help around here."

"Well, he's gone now. Let's have no more fear of this stranger. He probably has heard that Negro boys are sheltered in schools like ours."

"Is that true?" Emilie asked.

"Not yet in my school," the Reverend scowled, reflecting an ambivalence about the role educators could play in abolition. "Quakers have no qualms about housing and teaching escaped slaves." Then he halted, as though putting blinders on, and took up the Biblical tract he had been reading when interrupted by his sons.

CHAPTER TWENTY-SEVEN

As the Hoe girls and Henry rode the cars from Bloomfield to the ferry the next day, Emilie reminded Addie her imminent birthday would require celebrating. Turning eighteen was a milestone of a sort, when a young woman became a full-fledged member of society. At least, so thought most of the people Addie and Emilie knew.

"There must be a party," Emilie went on. "Let's think about whom we shall invite. Cousins Robbie and Theodore, and, of course, you, Henry, must come; Emmie Ely, the Condits, Annie Westervelt, Miss Bigelow—if she'll deign to join us—and what about Miss Clarke?"

"Why not?" Henry replied. "She would not object to seeing us dance. Perhaps she'll join in."

"And Richmond and Nicholas Bowen, if they are in town," Emilie continued.

"And Joe," Addie added. "I hope that Ma and the babies are not indisposed. We must be sure Ma and Father have no objections to a party."

When finally the three young people descended from the omnibus outside 309 Broadway, they were pleased to find Grandma and Grandpa Gilbert and Uncle Thomas down from South Salem, conversing with Ma in the front room. After hasty greetings, Henry excused himself from the assemblage. Addie and Emilie bid him goodbye as he departed for R. Hoe and Company.

"How good to see you both!" Grandma exclaimed after initial embraces all around.

"What brings you to the city, Grandma?" Addie asked. "Grandpa, you look very well."

"Thomas had to secure tickets for their honeymoon. You have not forgotten the wedding, have you?"

"Of course not. Our collars are finished for our gowns."

Thomas, seated in a corner, was handsome and seemed stiffly dignified in his waistcoat, shirt and tie—uncustomary clothing for him.

"There is another reason I came along." Grandma crossed the room to Addie and presented her with a cardboard box. "Happy birthday, my dear."

Opening the package, Addie smiled to find a jolly calico apron edged with red ribbon and having two good-sized pockets, a happy reminder of the summer's cooking lessons. "Grandma, what a wonderful surprise, and did you make this yourself?"

CHAPTER TWENTY-SEVEN

"Of course, now you can cook anytime and anywhere. Have you made a pie for your father since coming home?"

"No, but I will soon, and I will wear your smock. Thank you."

Thomas stood and reminded his parents, "Come, Father, Mother; we really must be heading home." He appeared uncomfortable in the Hoes' grand, newly-decorated parlor.

"I suppose you are right. We have seen Joe. You have your and Mary's tickets, and we have delivered my granddaughter's gift." Addie realized how great a task Grandma had accomplished to induce her menfolk to come into the city.

"We shall see you in South Salem in a fortnight," Emilie reassured them.

"Thank you for stopping by," Ma added, as she helped the elder Gilberts into cape and tippet and gave Thomas his slouch hat. "I shall give your best wishes to Thirza."

Addie reflected on Grandma's remark, "We have seen Joe." Did she mean they had met at the Hoe brownstone? Had they found him at A. T. Stewart's store? At his boarding house? What could it mean?

"Was Joe here earlier?" she asked Ma once she and Emilie had taken their baggage and bonnets upstairs and returned to the parlor.

"No, he was not here," Ma replied. "We spent much of their visit talking of Aunt Thirza."

"What about her? Is she unwell?"

"Very. She may have cholera. Two doctors have been to see her. Laura is exhausted from taking care of her. They may hire a woman to come nurse her. We have been *very* worried."

Both girls listened with anxious faces, imagining their younger cousin Laura caring for someone mortally ill. The idea of Addie's grand birthday party evaporated when they considered Aunt Thirza's condition.

Spirits dampened, Addie and Emilie set about to dust and sweep. They began with their room and proceeded downstairs to the parlor. Due to the crisis, even Ellen, their family servant, had been called to assist at Uncle Robert's next door, where the pall of sickness held normalcy at bay.

"I hope Uncle Robert and the rest of the family escape whatever ails Aunt Thirza," Emilie commented as they dusted the piano in the back parlor. "Perhaps it would cheer Robbie and Theodore to come here on your birthday."

"We must see how Aunt is doing later in the week," Addie said, moving a lamp while Emilie cleaned beneath it. When they had made a dent in the accumulated dust downstairs, they retreated to their room. There were letters for them to write: a joint thank-you to the Seymours and, for Addie, a long overdue reply to Retta Stewart's letter of the previous month.

A hubbub in the nursery interrupted the quiet when little sisters Annie and Mary wakened from their afternoon naps. Annie burst in upon her older sisters, who were delighted to see her. Seated at the desk, Addie lifted her into her lap, drew the alphabet for her, and helped her trace the letters with her fingers. Emilie went through her satchel to find the rag doll cousin Mary Seymour had made, which, with its purple yarn hair, delighted Annie very much.

Presently, Ma entered, carrying baby Mary, whose sniffling made the older girls uncomfortable. They exchanged worried glances. Ma anticipated their question. "Perhaps it is her teething. She is due for more teeth to erupt soon." She somewhat allayed their worst fear, that Thirza's malady might spread to their house.

Addie looked over her little sister's curls to the crowds in the street below, wondering how they or anyone living in the burgeoning city could avoid disease when it struck. She was thankful for the family's relatively good health thus far.

By the week's end, Aunt Thirza began to improve. She would be weak for a long time, Dr. Coyle told Uncle Robert, yet it amazed him that she had the great resilience to survive the worst of it.

There was not time to prepare for Addie's birthday by inviting a large number of guests, yet Emilie easily prevailed upon Theodore and Robbie to come, and Emmie Ely, who came by on Thursday, agreed to join them for the small gathering the following evening. Tilda baked a spice cake, and when Joe came by to play a game of billiards with Father, Emilie also invited him to come. He volunteered to bring ice cream and to remind Henry about the occasion.

With short notice for the party, gifts for Addie were modest—Theodore's daguerreotype, a new pen from Robbie, a bureau scarf Emmie Ely had embroidered—except for Ma's and Father's present, a fine Kashmir shawl of a soft tan shade. Henry promised to bring her Dickens's *The Old Curiosity Shop* as soon as the bookseller could place it on the shelf. Addie opened each gift with great pleasure and was much moved by the thoughtfulness of her family. Joe had brought a can of peach ice cream kept cold in a bucket of ice lent him by the ice cream shop. Much touched by his efforts, she expected no other gift.

"*Eighteen*! Are you keeping up with your journal?" Theodore asked, reminding her that it was he who had urged her to keep one.

"As a matter of fact, I *am*," Addie answered.

"Years from now, your great-grandchildren will read about your life and marvel at your adventures," quipped Robbie.

"Rather tame reading matter, I fear," Addie responded dryly. Her journal entries, written just before she retired for the night, were brief catalogues of her days, hardly soul-searching revelations.

"How about making some music?" her father suggested while Addie arranged her gifts tidily on the sofa and Emilie folded the wrappings.

CHAPTER TWENTY-SEVEN

Emilie played a Stephen Foster tune on the piano until the cook, Tilda, appeared at the door with the cake, and everyone sang Addie a happy birthday. After refreshments and more singing, Robbie and Theodore disappeared for billiards with father upstairs. Emilie went upstairs to their room to show Cousin Emmie the dresses she and Addie would wear to the wedding in October. While Ma and Ellen put the little girls to bed, Joe, Henry, and Addie sat in the parlor conversing.

Henry took the opportunity to tell Joe about the slave catcher who appeared at the church service the previous Sunday. Addie told him it was Beauregard Wise. Joe, who had been lounging comfortably in a wingchair, his legs stretched before him, immediately sat at attention.

He frowned. "You mean he was in Bloomfield?"

"Yes, my younger brothers watched him ride by later that afternoon in the direction of the depot," Henry explained.

"That could mean he is here in the city. The encouraging fact is we know him. He is so singular in appearance that it would be impossible not to recognize him."

"Do you know who it is he's representing?" Addie asked. "Who has sent him north?"

"No, but I shall ask Mr. Jennings tomorrow if any of his acquaintances or his kin are aware of Wise."

Henry seemed to know of Joe's interest in slave catchers, but Addie was not sure if he was aware that Joe actually transported slaves en route to freedom.

Not allowing talk of Wise to dominate the evening, however, Addie began in a different vein. "Dear Henry, you need not buy me another novel. Your family entertained Emilie and me most kindly. That was gift enough."

"I debated whether Tennyson's poems might make a more inspired and inspiring gift, but I know how Dickens amuses you." He rose from his chair and, stifling a yawn, said, "If you don't mind, I will leave now. It's been a long day, but a delightful evening. Good night."

CHAPTER TWENTY-EIGHT

When they had seen Henry to the door, Joe and Addie returned to the sofa. There were many questions she wanted to ask him, yet they sat quietly side by side, and he took her hand in his. The voices from upstairs rose and fell as the billiard players assessed their shots or the cousins and their uncle shared some joke.

Joe brought from his vest pocket a small box and placed it in Addie's hand.

"Oh Joe, what can this be?" she inquired in surprise, regarding his expectant face.

"Open it, if you please," he urged.

She removed the lid to find a cameo locket on a gold chain. "It's lovely!" She raised her eyes to his. Then, observing a tiny hinge on one side of the locket, she carefully inserted a thumbnail and, opening it, found a daguerreotype of Joe himself, a somber likeness of him in miniature. Very moved, she leaned into his arms. They kissed, either for an instant or an eternity, suspended in time, forgetful of the Hoe household and any sounds within it.

When at last they drew apart, Joe spoke, still holding her hand. "I want you to remember me no matter what happens in the future. You are very dear to me."

"As are you to me."

"You know, I can never be sure where my steps will take me."

"I do understand, and I fear for you. You know that."

He looked into her eyes. "You realize I cannot give up until somehow the last slave has found freedom."

"I truly do understand." She nodded and drew the chain of the locket around her neck. Reaching behind her, Joe pushed her hair aside and fastened the clasp.

"By the way, will Miss Jennings agree to meet me sometime?"

"The best way to do that is to visit her church."

"But, with only Negroes attending, would *I*, would *we* be welcome?"

"The greater hurdle would be the policemen outside, who watch to see that white people and black 'keep to their own kind,' as they see it."

"If I wore a cape with a hood, could I be disguised enough to enter? Would the Negroes be disturbed?"

CHAPTER TWENTY-EIGHT

"We'll try next Sunday, if I can find out the time of the service from her father. Later in the week I'll stop by his shop." They sat staring into the fireplace a long time, their faces illuminated by the dying coals.

Addie bid him farewell reluctantly, after a final embrace. Once Joe retrieved the ice cream bucket to be returned to the café down the street, he set forth, looking first north, then south, into the cool September night. She pulled the massive front door closed and, leaning against it, she closed her eyes and sighed.

Since cousin Emmie Ely was spending the night, she and Emilie were chatting animatedly when Addie came upstairs to their room. They noted right away the locket that Joe had given her. "What is that hanging below your collar?" Emilie asked. Addie placed her birthday gifts on the bureau and carefully unclasped the necklace. Her sister and cousin came to her side as she opened the locket. They had much to say, examining the tiny version of Joe.

"Doesn't that mean he fancies you?" asked Emmie asked, who often required a full explanation. "Are you plighted?"

There it was, that expectation again. How was Addie to convey that the remembrance showed affection, not an engagement? "Daguerreotypes are in vogue, and it is my birthday." Addie did not mean to prevaricate, but at the same time she was not ready to spill her feelings about Joe on the bedroom carpet.

"You won't get much of an answer from her," Emilie assured her cousin. "She gave me the same response when Joe walked her home one summer night in South Salem."

As her cousin Emmie was sleeping in her bed, Addie prepared to sleep on the small bed by the window. She closed her eyes, reliving the evening of her eighteenth birthday. She listened to her sister describe their part as maids of honor at Thomas's and Mary's wedding. Addie dared not dream that she and Joe might make plans of that nature. Instead, she decided to be content with the precious moments they could be in one another's company.

CHAPTER TWENTY-NINE

School resumed the following week. Miss Clarke's was two blocks south of 309 Broadway, an easy walk in good weather, or a brief ride if one met the omnibus, which was often an unpredictable mode of transportation. If Addie wanted to arrive early, she could ride with Father, but that meant asking him and her uncles to go out of their way in the carriage, since the factory was east on Broome Street. She preferred to walk, although now she would be alone.

The first three days of the new term were delightfully uneventful, although she missed her sister's company. Addie found Mr. Wheeldon, the English and history teacher, very learned and amiable. He replaced poor Mr. Williams, who had contracted cholera in the spring on a Friday and was dead by Sunday. Miss Clarke herself was again in charge of French and Latin, while mathematics fell into the hands of the formidable Mr. Armstrong, aged and stern.

Seeing her friends once again was a pleasure, and when they ate their lunch clustered together in the day room on the first floor of the high-ceilinged, drafty building, the girls exchanged reports of their vacation. Mary Condit, Maria Seabury, Anna Westervelt, and Addie all had plenty of chatter to fill up the hour they were allowed for the noon repast.

Wending her way home on Thursday through the numerous shoppers and pedestrians, and avoiding what might appear underfoot, Addie became aware that someone was following her. She glanced over her shoulder. To her right a bulky, short man in a top hat suddenly disappeared between an omnibus and a hansom cab awaiting customers. She stopped long enough to survey Broadway, but again, as in Bloomfield, he disappeared and the distinctive form of the slave catcher was nowhere to be seen. Why did he not speak? Did he consider her bait to snag Joe and the black people he transported? It would be plain to anyone observing their house at 309 Broadway closely that Joe Stewart came by often.

In fact, when she arrived at home, shaken and flushed from hurrying the final block, Joe Stewart was sitting with Emilie in the parlor. They greeted her with questions. Dropping her satchel of books in the hall, she removed her bonnet and wiped her forehead with her handkerchief.

"Is it very warm today?" Emilie asked. "Your face is as red as these roses," she said, pointing to a vase on the end table at her elbow.

Joe must have read Addie's confusion about where to begin. "How is your course of study?" He rose and waved her to the armchair he had occupied, where she endeavored to compose herself and breathe more calmly.

When Emilie left the parlor, thinking that Joe and her sister might appreciate privacy, he took a chair opposite Addie and awaited her story. As he listened, the intensity in his gaze reminded her that the passion he felt about abolition motivated him in every circumstance, whether among the stevedores in Delaware City or in a drawing room in Manhattan.

"A block after the school, I sensed there was someone directly behind me. Looking back, I saw, quite surely, Beauregard Wise. He veered off between two vehicles on Broadway—heavy and squat he was—in a top hat this time. Do you think he is aware of your coming here?"

"I did not think so, but since he is in the vicinity, he might well be spying from within some alley, the brigand. That is all he is." Joe spoke angrily. "He cannot ply a trade honestly and must stoop to capture human beings for profit."

"Should we warn Father?"

"No. I shall be careful to come in the evenings, which is not a difficulty now that days are shorter." His indignant frown gave way to a happier thought. "I came to tell you that Miss Jennings and her father hope you will attend the service on Sunday at two o'clock. May I accompany you if you are allowed?"

"Of course, we attend various services in addition to Reverend Seabury's, as you know."

"But do ask permission. I will come for you at one o'clock. And as for going to school, I suggest you ride the omnibus for a few days."

Addie was grateful for Joe's presence and for his direction at this ominous turn of events. He spared her the anxiety of keeping her recent experience to herself, and now she could look forward to the honor of meeting the brave Miss Jennings. At dinner she asked Father and Ma for permission to attend the church service with Joe on Sunday afternoon, to which they readily assented. She did not say where. Emilie and Ma planned to attend Grace Episcopal on Sunday morning.

In the meantime, Addie had studying to do, but first she was obliged to take care of Annie, while her sister and Ma shopped. Early on Saturday morning, Addie went to the attic to retrieve her winter cape and hang it on the back porch to air. Following her upstairs, little Annie wondered, "Is winter coming?"

"Soon enough," Addie answered, with the cape over her arm as they came down the stairs. "You have grown and will need many new clothes for winter—your own wool cape, hat and leggings, and maybe a muff to keep your hands warm."

"I shan't like those scratchy clothes one bit," little Annie said as she trundled downstairs holding Addie's other hand. Then they tiptoed into the nursery, where baby Mary was sleeping, and little Annie chose a few toys to play with in the parlor.

All the while, despite her best efforts, Addie's mind was occupied with the prospect of attending church with Joe on Sunday afternoon. As she draped the cape over the porch railing, she hoped the weather would be chilly the next day so that her winter cape would not appear outlandish. When she put Annie on her lap to sing her favorite nursery rhymes, Addie so confused the verses that more than once the three-year-old protested.

When Ma returned in the afternoon with Emilie, and it was time to face opening her geometry text, she stared blankly at the theorem Mr. Armstrong expected her to understand and master. To commit it to memory, she copied it out, but she suspected that even that method would not suffice. Geometry might not be her best subject for the year, she thought, and besides, her anticipation of the morrow made her less than logical.

Sunday dawned cloudy with a cold drizzle of rain. While Emilie worried about what the weather would do to the bonnet she planned to wear to the morning service, Addie fervently and cheerfully hoped that chilly conditions would continue, to justify her wearing winter clothing in the afternoon. At last, after enduring the hours of waiting and preparing for one o'clock, Addie heard Father greeting Joe. She secured her cape and hurried downstairs.

"Off to the North Pole?" Father said, noting her woolen garb. As she pulled on her kid gloves and adjusted her boots, she did her best to feign nonchalance.

"I did not know what sort of conveyance we might be taking," she answered lamely.

"No need to worry, I hired a cab," Joe said to reassure her father.

On the ride the few blocks to the First Colored Congregational Church at Sixth Street near the Bowery, Joe told her about Thomas Jennings and his efforts to abolish slavery, and he described some of the staunchest workers in the task.

"Mr. Jennings, Reverend Pennington, and Doctor Smith strive to aid escaped slaves and help the Negroes who have resided in New York for years. The influx of people from Europe makes it hard now for them to make a living. Jobs often go to white immigrants. Slave catchers and the threat of kidnapping and deportation to the South make life doubly difficult."

The cab came to a stop, and the driver called, "First Colored Congregational." Addie drew the cowl of her cape over her head and pulled it close around her before Joe helped her down. From the street, she looked up at the modest façade of the building with the name of the church above the front entrance. There were no policemen anywhere in sight. From inside came the strains of "Just as I Am," a hymn Addie had heard in the Baptist church when she attended with the Stewarts in Cream Ridge.

CHAPTER TWENTY-NINE

As they entered, she could see that the organ music came from a melodeon placed next to the pulpit. Sitting regally, with fine posture, Miss Jennings expertly commanded the instrument while pumping the bellows with her feet. She must leave each service much fatigued, Addie thought. The chords of the hymn connected smoothly, yet the melody was distinct and reverent.

Joe and Addie found a place to sit at the rear of the sanctuary in a pew occupied by only one elderly man, who moved over graciously to give them room. The church was full by the time Elizabeth Jennings had played the final chord. The pastor announced the scripture from *Isaiah* and read it clearly and persuasively. Throughout the service, the congregants punctuated prayers and the powerful points in the sermon with a vigorous "Amen" or "Hallelujah."

The closing hymn was one Addie had never heard at the churches she had attended. The words were not in a hymnal, but rather, a tall man with abundant graying hair, which she observed as more curly even than her father's, lined out the phrases. It began, "Amazing Grace! How sweet the sound that saved a wretch like me." Its mournful, soulful sound and words of redemption sung by the many strong voices around them wrung tears from the two visitors. Some of the women toward the front added their own overtones to the melody, embellishing it and claiming it as their own. The music was no recitation from habit but a kind of sad exultation, Addie thought, if there could be such a thing.

At the end of the service, the pastor, whose message was one to inspire resolution of heart and mind, and whose peroration was to lead life in the love of Christ and serve as His hands, walked with bowed head to the rear of the church to greet and embrace his parishioners. As they waited to approach Miss Jennings, Joe told her the pastor was Reverend W. C. Pennington, one of the famous men he had mentioned earlier, and one of whom she might have heard or read, who traveled widely preaching and fighting for abolition.

They waited while Miss Jennings was covering the melodeon with a piece of purple cloth. Most of the church members had left. The pair walked up the central aisle, and when she heard them approach, she turned and smiled. "Joe, how good to see you. My father said you might be attending here today."

"Addie, my friend, wanted to meet you. She suspected she might have seen you before, in Setauket."

"I did travel out to see a friend in June."

"And did you take a sail on the bay with musicians?" Addie asked expectantly.

She looked surprised. Addie pushed her cowl back, and Elizabeth studied her face. "Yes, indeed, I did. You and your sister came aboard, if I am correct. That was a delightful time, a sweet memory." She smiled and extended her hand, which Addie took, smiling in return.

She continued to finish straightening the organ cover over the melodeon.

"I sent her word at her grandparents' about your cruel treatment in July," Joe said.

Turning away from them, Miss Jennings quietly collected her music and placed it in a leather bag. In a resigned tone of voice, she said, "The lawyer, Mr. Arthur, who does not seem much older than you, Addie, is sure we can take on the Third Avenue Railroad Company. We have to wait and see."

Addie observed her proud stance, the beautiful stitching on the collar of her black silk dress, and sensed the authority with which she spoke. Here was a fine lady. Addie felt a resurgence of the anger that the *Tribune* story had caused in her when she read it. "Joe drew a sketch of you, and it was a very good likeness, I can see now. You play the organ very well. And the last hymn was very beautiful."

"Thank you. 'Amazing Grace' can pull at your heartstrings, can't it?" she commented and turned to leave by the side door. "It was good to meet you," she said as she departed.

Joe and Addie remained a moment, taking in the plain pine pews and the austerity of the empty church, as the door closed behind Miss Jennings. Pulling the cowl back over her head, Addie followed Joe to the vestibule and into the street. The congregation had dispersed quickly in the rain that was falling heavily. The cab waited for them, a good walk from the church. At Joe's call, the driver popped his head out of the door of his cab, where he had kept dry during the service. The horse hung its head in the drenching rain. When they had climbed into the cab, Addie said, "I am grateful to you for allowing me to witness the service and meet Elizabeth Jennings."

"You are entirely welcome. Our society is very divided, and the more we can commune together and talk, the less the division will matter. My only regret when I bid goodbye to the Negroes I have assisted is that I will not ever get to know them once they go north." His musings ended, Joe turned and wrapped his bare hand around her gloved one. The act bespoke a loneliness that Addie sensed was part and parcel of pursuing his cause. To help others meant sacrifice. Could she herself become as devoted to ending slavery as Joe?

"You keep me in the dark about your movements, and I understand why. But the closer we become, not knowing how and where you might be sometimes takes more faith to endure than I have."

His dark eyes as somber as she had ever seen them, he looked as though he were about to speak, but instead he enfolded her in his arms. The rhythm of the horse's hooves on the cobblestones and drumming of rain on the roof of the cab lulled them both into laying aside causes and worries. All too soon the ride ended with the well-soaked driver announcing 309 Broadway.

CHAPTER THIRTY

Accompanying Addie to her door, Joe saw her inside. Not wanting to detain the driver longer than necessary, he left immediately, even though Father asked him to stay for a game of billiards. The woolen winter cape hung heavily about Addie, and she hastened to remove it and her very wet boots.

"A miserable afternoon to be out," Father commented after she returned from hanging the cape to dry in the kitchen by the stove and went upstairs to change her shoes. He and Ma sat in the parlor, he with the *Tribune* in hand and she knitting Annie's woolen stockings.

"How was the church service, Addie?" Ma asked, bent over her knitting. "Which church did you attend?"

"First Colored Congregational on Sixth Street," Addie replied. The cat was out of the bag. The truth was out. Ma looked up and ceased her stitches, while Father glanced over the top of the newspaper at her. Neither spoke, and Addie sat down and picked up her sewing basket, searching for a stocking to mend.

"Who was the preacher?" Father asked, putting down the paper and turning his full attention on her.

"Reverend Pennington spoke today. I do not know if he regularly preaches there."

"Were there other white people attending?" Ma fixed her with a suspicious look.

"I do not know. We sat in the back. Oh Father, they sang the loveliest hymn, 'Amazing Grace'. Do you know it?"

Father exchanged a glance with her stepmother and answered, "No, I don't believe I do."

Addie rose and opened the doors to the back parlor. She sat down at the piano and slowly worked out the notes of the triadic, simple melody. "The words are very moving too, but since they weren't written down, I can't recite them." She then rejoined her parents.

Ma took up the inevitable cautionary response. "Addie, Joe comes and goes in the city as he pleases. I'm not surprised he takes you along, but don't make a habit of attending that church. There is ill feeling for Negroes among immigrants, and I should not want you in the midst of any of it. Do you see?"

"I understand that, but there was no danger. The pastor greeted us in friendly fashion, and I met Miss Jennings. She plays the melodeon wonderfully well."

"Ah, Thomas Jennings's daughter," Father joined in, recognizing the name. "She was assaulted for being on the wrong omnibus, as I recall. Hers is a difficult case. There was a rally at that church soon after the unfortunate event. She has a lawyer, Chester Arthur, a young fellow, working on her behalf."

Somehow Father's knowledge of the Jennings family and his recounting the story reassured Ma. She only exhaled a heavy, audible sigh and resumed knitting.

Addie inwardly sighed, too, in relief that there was no proscription of her experience or Joe. Meeting Elizabeth Jennings was not a sin. Her father viewed the dynamic forces in the world as working toward some better end just ahead. His tinkering with machines reflected his overall faith that men can create new and better systems, in the social order as well as in his factory. While not actively an abolitionist himself, he championed men of imagination and energy, and that included Thomas Jennings and, by association, his talented daughter.

The day before Uncle Thomas's and Mary Lawrence's wedding in October, Emilie and Adeline rode the omnibus to the depot and took the cars north to South Salem. Along the railway the leaves had changed to bright orange, yellow and red and made vivid contrast against the azure sky. The colorful sight filled both young women with awe at the natural beauty only a few miles from the city's dominant gray.

They had packed their gowns and all the finery they deemed correct for their roles as bridesmaids.

"Will Mary have a bouquet?" Emilie wondered. "Most flowers have gone by."

"Perhaps she dried some roses in the summer. Remember how she and her stepmother were making detailed plans in August?"

"No doubt. I hope the weather holds."

Grandpa and Peter met them at the train, the former to enjoy the autumn air and the latter to drive the carriage. Both of them were eager to see the two young women. "Peter, have you been behaving yourself?" Addie asked. The strapping farmhand seemed to have grown since the summer.

"Yes, ma'am, I have no choice. School is in session. Besides filling the drinking water pail every morning, I also have to keep the woodbox full in the schoolhouse."

Addie smiled in amusement. It was plain to see that whoever taught school knew how to manage boys with ideas. Grandpa, pleased to see his "blooming granddaughters," kept turning about to observe their much loved faces.

CHAPTER THIRTY

When they arrived at the Gilbert farmhouse, Grandma had tea waiting. She told the girls they were expected at the Lawrences' directly. She beamed at Thomas when he came in from the barn. Thomas had been checking with Peter to assure himself that the teenage boy was prepared to perform the chores while the couple would be away on their honeymoon.

"Are you ready for the wedding, Uncle?" Addie asked.

"Thomas has been quieter than usual the past few days," Grandma interjected while pouring the tea.

Her youngest son and her last child to marry spoke in his own defense. "There are many things to attend to if we are to leave South Salem. A marriage cannot be a lark." His serious attitude reawakened in Addie her immense respect for this uncle near her own age. In him there was not an ounce of frivolity or insincerity. "We ought to get on to Mary's before dark," he continued.

Addie and Emilie left immediately, neither unpacking their bags nor changing their clothes. The ride to Mary's was delightful with Thomas driving the wagon. He relaxed and spoke freely of the wedding.

"What do you expect of us tomorrow morning?" Emilie asked.

"We will go down early to the Lawrences' and dress for the service there. Reverend Lindley will be coming to the house by nine o'clock to lead us in the ceremony. I hope that Mrs. Lawrence is well. Mary fears that she might be ailing."

"What about flowers?" Addie was curious to know as they rode through the autumnal landscape. "What will her bouquet be?"

"Don't worry. Her father ordered hothouse flowers from New Jersey. They arrived by the cars yesterday."

Once they entered the Lawrences' large colonial house and greeted Mary and her father, it was clear something was amiss. Even more lovely than either of the Hoe girls remembered, Mary related that her stepmother was very ill. "It means we cannot have the many guests we invited. Father has sent my brother Edward around to the neighbors to relay the news. Only the family may attend."

Addie knew Thomas's brothers and their families had probably already arrived at the Gilbert's for the event, and Mary's brothers DeWitt, Cyrus, and Darius were due to come up soon from the city.

"The preparations have been made. No matter what, the wedding will happen," the elder Cyrus Lawrence assured the worried young people gathered around him. "My wife will likely be indisposed, I'm sorry to say. The doctor tells me her fever is high and her cough is deep-seated."

Mary's beautiful face, framed by her golden ringlets, was not marred by the turn of events. Rather she seemed buoyed by a kind of serenity, and when she looked at Thomas and his steady blue eyes met hers, there was only an expectant joy between them. Not only was she, but he too was radiant.

Addie woke very early the next morning, and as she had done in the summer, she dressed quickly and went downstairs to the kitchen. Her grandmother was putting the finishing touches on the wedding cake that Mary had allowed her to contribute to the celebration. It was a wide, single-layer fruitcake. As she gave it a glistening sugar glaze, she greeted Addie with her customary warmth.

"Can I help?" Addie offered.

"No, not at all, my girl is coming from next door to clean up once we leave for the wedding. Do sit down and have a biscuit."

"I'm so excited that I'm not hungry," Addie replied. "Grandma, I know it is silly to think about anything except the wedding, but I won't see you again until we come in November. Please tell me, did Joe ever tell you about the Underground Railroad?"

Grandma swept a strand of gray hair back into the bun on the back of her head, and paused, a spoon in her hand, eyes fixed upon her creation. "Go down in the cellar," she said cryptically, without looking across the table at Addie.

Hesitating, Addie made her way down the steep stairs into that dim space of crocks and cobwebs. In the far corner, under the brick arch that held the chimney, was a cot, and lying on it under one of Grandma's quilts was the sleeping form of a man. Next to the bed was a broken down pair of leather brogues and a rumpled canvas sack spilling its meager contents onto the rag rug which Grandma had no doubt laid over the dirt floor.

Addie felt like weeping. Here was the result of her hope that somehow there could be a way to assist Joe in his secret work, his vital passion. Here was evidence that her notion was a reality and the cellar had become a sanctuary.

Not wanting to wake the weary man, she crept past the pickles and the salt pork in brine, the barrel filled with carrots buried in sand, and the vinegar she helped make in August, to the stairs and, as silently as possible, returned to the kitchen. Grandma, noting her cheeks wet with tears, handed her a dish towel. Drying her eyes, Addie tried to think of something to say.

Grandma spoke instead. "We will not speak about it. This is our secret, yours, mine, Grandpa's, and Thomas's." The older woman spoke with a finality that told Addie if there were objections to hiding escaped slaves, they had been overcome and were replaced with a firm commitment to help them on their way north.

When Emilie was awake, Addie and she dressed for the wedding, donning their matching brown challis gowns, smoothing the new collars, fastening the buttons and putting on the new silk stockings and shoes Ma had bought them at A. T. Stewart's store. Addie drew the locket Joe had given her from its tiny box and fastened it around her neck. The night before, she had brushed Emilie's hair and pinned it tight, as her sister had done for her. Now they each combed out their ringlets into smooth curls.

Thomas drove them, well in advance of the rest of the family, to the Lawrences' to dress Mary. The house was quiet when they arrived. Her father was attending her still very sick stepmother, Mary told them after she greeted them at the door. As they silently followed her through the house, they glanced briefly at the gifts she and Thomas had received. Pretty dishes, linens, and silverware were displayed on the sideboard. She took them upstairs to her room. Hanging from the closet door was her wedding dress.

"Oh Mary, how magnificent!" whispered Emilie, in awe.

"And you made it yourself," her sister added, admiring the creamy satin gown with a scooping neckline, very different from the girls' dresses with their prim collars, and one which would show off Mary's graceful neck. The skirt was decorated with an abundance of paste pearls. They lifted the creation over Mary's head, careful not to step on the vast circumference of the skirt, fitting it delicately over her camisole, bloomers, and petticoat.

"It is good that you have two of us to dress you," Addie commented as they set about to button the fifty crocheted buttons in the back.

"Who crocheted the buttons?" Emilie asked.

"My stepmother, your grandmother, and I. Thank heavens your grandma offered, or we should not have finished in time."

After they carefully arranged Mary's golden hair and added a circlet of waxed flowers above them, the bride-to-be motioned to a box on the bed. Addie opened it to find a bouquet of white roses, arranged with asparagus fern and tied together with a creamy satin ribbon that matched the dress.

"How did you keep the flowers fresh, and did they arrive arranged for you?" Emilie marveled.

"Heavens no, we put them in water as soon as they were delivered from the depot, and I arose early to make the bouquet. My stepmother had planned to make it, but, as you know, she could not." All of a sudden Mary broke off, very near tears. She buried her face in her hands. Downcast, forgetful of herself, she worried for the stepmother to whom her father had been married only a few months and who was now dangerously ill. Both of her future nieces came to her side. They forced Mary to look at her lovely reflection in the small mirror over the bureau. Addie gave her a handkerchief.

"It is your wedding day in any case," Emilie reminded her. "You are as beautiful and worthy a bride as there can ever be."

"And Thomas is our beloved uncle and the most wonderful man you will ever meet," Addie put in, as all three young women gazed into the mirror together. Finally Mary smiled, much comforted by their presence and words.

Meanwhile Mary's brothers DeWitt and Cyrus were in their room helping dress the groom. Thomas had asked them to assist him, lest he appear a bumpkin rather than the worthy husband he aspired to be. Both brothers were acquainted with the world of commerce now and traveled widely, associated with notable men, and thus, in Thomas's eyes, were well-versed in fashion and appearances, which on most occasions he eschewed.

The family guests congregated downstairs. Reverend Lindley arrived punctually and took his place in the front parlor, where the furniture had been removed, requiring all to stand for the service. Mary delegated Addie to proceed downstairs and report whether it was time to descend to the parlor. Returning upstairs, Addie joined Emilie, carefully lifting the hem of Mary's dress while she made her way to the parlor.

Cyrus Lawrence motioned to the fiddler, Cal Withers, to begin playing a sweetly solemn processional as Mary, preceded by the two bridesmaids, walked at her father's side to the fireplace, in front of which stood the pastor, along with Thomas and her brothers.

Both Mary and Thomas were very cool and self-assured in the brief ceremony which followed, with no misspoken words or awkward silences. Mary handed Emilie her bouquet when Thomas placed the ring upon her finger. The room full of aunts, uncles, brothers, parents, and cousins—some babes in arms—remained quiet throughout. The couple embraced a blissfully long time at the end. Then, without hesitation, they passed smiling through the throng.

After the reception in the dining room, where Grandma assumed the ailing Mrs. Lawrence's place to serve the tea, and after the couple had cut the wedding cake and thanked everyone for coming, Mary and Thomas slipped out and departed in the Gilberts' carriage for the train.

In her vivacious and direct manner, Emilie found a way to attract young Cyrus Lawrence's attention and questioned him about his ventures. Addie kept occupied passing plates of cake and refilling tea cups. When she found herself idle, next to DeWitt, they stood awkwardly, he seeming to be shy and aloof. Taller than Cyrus, he wore a remote expression that she found off-putting. Hence, when her sister suggested the two gentlemen come visit them in New York City, Addie had mixed feelings.

As they packed their bridesmaid dresses at the Gilberts' and changed for the return trip to the city, Addie wondered if the sleeping man in the cellar was still there and whether he was awake. Whoever would take him further must transport him after dark.

She and Emilie gave both grandparents their warmest goodbyes and went on their way with Peter driving the wagon to the depot.

CHAPTER THIRTY-ONE

Once again at 309 Broadway, when the day already seemed to have lasted a very long time already, Emilie persuaded Cyrus and DeWitt Lawrence, who had come by, to stay for the evening. They were full of news of the sinking of the *Arctic*, a steamship returning from England with over three hundred passengers that had collided with another ship. All except the crew went down in the North Atlantic. Cyrus Lawrence said he knew some of the people who might very well have been among the dead. Reflections on this sorry event occupied the minds of the young people.

"To think, the crew commandeered the lifeboats for themselves," Cyrus expostulated, "while the women and children drowned."

Addie and Emilie were both chilled by the thought. When Father came home from a long day at the factory, they regaled him with the news.

"There will be grave legal repercussions," Father said as he sank wearily onto the sofa. "I wonder what kind of insurance the Collins Line buys to cover such a disaster."

"One will have to think twice about traveling to Europe," DeWitt Lawrence commented, his sole remark of the evening.

"I should say every step we take is a risk," Father said, eyeing the speaker carefully. "Our business takes us abroad, and one disaster cannot stop trade, you must agree?"

"Perhaps it will stem the tide of immigration," Cyrus conjectured, "once the news spreads in Europe."

The long day and morbid discussion made Addie yawn. Emilie, on the other hand, relished learning as much as possible about Cyrus Lawrence, and she said as much after the men left, citing an early morning departure for the South as their reason. Cyrus shook Emilie's and Addie's hands as he left, while DeWitt, a step behind him, only nodded.

"The bride was lovely," Addie concluded in her journal when at last the day was over.

Several days later, on a windy afternoon when the debris from the streets blew about along with the autumn leaves from the backyards and the occasional shade tree, Addie made her way home from school. No omnibus was in sight.

Upon reaching the final block, she exhaled in relief that no one was following her. She had obeyed Joe about riding rather than walking since his warning.

A piano teacher was coming for her first lesson with him, and she hurried, arriving at the front steps just as Mr. Boyle approached from the opposite direction. He was older than her father, wore pince-nez, and carried a satchel, presumably filled with music. Addie greeted him, introduced herself to him, and they entered the house together. After introducing him to Ma and Emilie, she showed him into the back parlor.

He sat down to try out the piano. Satisfied with the tuning and touch of the Nunns and Clark, he asked her to play something for him. She opened the volume of music Father had given her in the summer and played a waltz, not well, she felt. He responded by ordering her to pare her fingernails before the next lesson. As for her performance, he ignored it entirely and prescribed a regimen of scales, then drew a book of exercises from his bag. He had a high-pitched, nasal voice, and humorless expression and speech. "I will require one hour of practice each day, and I have a device with which you are to exercise each finger. I shall strongly suggest that your father buy it. I designed it myself."

He brought from his satchel a contraption into which she was to insert her hand, and with which, using a set of coiled springs, she was to stretch each finger. Addie shuddered at the prospect of using this device, but she did not object to Mr. Boyle's leaving it for Father's consideration.

Henry came by once the distasteful man had left, and Addie described her first lesson. Her cousin eyed the device suspiciously and, upon seeing how disheartening was the man's effect upon her, he put his own hand inside the device to test it. "Ouch!" he exclaimed after it tugged mercilessly on his index finger. "Where did your father find such a teacher?"

"It was Ma. She heard about him through a friend who hired him for her daughter's lessons."

"I have seen such things advertised in the *Sun*. It reeks of quackery, if you ask me."

"What shall I do?" Addie despaired, since she loved music and had looked forward to studying again.

"Come to the opera with me," Henry suggested, changing the subject and always capable of cheering her up. "Madame Grisi is performing tonight at Castle Garden."

Not entirely consoled, she agreed to join her cousin and vowed to entreat Father *not* to engage Mr. Boyle, no matter what the results of using the machine might be.

When Father returned home shortly after, he listened to Addie's description of the lesson and then, like Henry, experimented with Mr. Boyle's contraption. It elicited the same response, so he too concluded the man was not to be trusted. "There are many new and excellent purposes for machines," he said, extracting his sore finger and rubbing it gingerly, "but injuring the hands of young piano pupils is not one of them. I shall ask Mr. Nunns whom he might recommend to teach you, Addie. In the meantime, Ma must tell the friend who recommended Boyle to be wary of him and his methods."

The experience of the afternoon lesson behind her, Addie dressed for the opera after tea, and Henry came by to collect her. They walked to Castle Garden, where a vast and eager crowd of New Yorkers gathered to hear the Italian soprano Madame Grisi, whose advance notice of her American tour had appeared several times in the newspapers over the previous weeks.

Addie and Henry found their seats with excitement. The programme gave the soprano's full name, Julia Grisi, but since she was a byword in Europe, she was known everywhere simply as "Madame Grisi." Enormous in size and clad in a striped silk gown, she sang arias from her role as Elvira in Bellini's *I Puritani* and the leading role as Druid priestess Norma. Her voice was powerful and magnificent, even though it was plain that she was not young, probably in her forties and much older than Mario, with whom she sang duets. The *bel canto* passages rippled from her, sending shivers up Addie's spine and causing extended periods of applause and cries of "Brava! Brava!" from the audience.

During the intermission, Henry and Addie descended from their seats to mingle with the crowd in the atrium below. The conversation surrounding them was of Madame Grisi and her talent.

"Henry, sometimes we complain of the noise and overcrowding in the city, but where else in the country can we hear something as wonderful and uplifting as Madame Grisi's music?" Addie remarked.

"Or as amazing to see as Castle Garden, or the Crystal Palace?" Henry added.

"I do not understand the Italian, but the sometimes silly stories seem only a vehicle for the exquisite music, don't you think?"

"Yes, it seems preposterous that Puritans could be singing such music when we think of them as prim and proper, controlled by their creed. Imagine, English Puritans singing a story written by a Frenchman, with music by an Italian and performed in America!" Henry laughed at the thought.

"Nevertheless, it is altogether enjoyable."

"Enjoyment runs contrary to Puritan theology," Henry reminded her, "yet I will allow that Bellini could make music out of any story."

"Is he still living?" Addie asked, as they again found their seats.

"No, he died the year he wrote *I Puritani*, 1835, as I recall." The young pair fell silent as the orchestra began to play and they were mesmerized again by Madame Grisi's arias. Once the diva had sung her final high note, she was inundated with flowers thrown from the audience, and she reappeared for several curtsies.

Outside Castle Garden, located in the Battery, Henry and Addie sought an omnibus to take them north on Broadway. Taking her cousin's arm, Addie said, "Thank you for asking me to join you this evening. The music transported me far from Mr. Boyle and his fiendish device." They both laughed.

The crowd, likely more than two thousand in number, poured onto the promenade, everyone seeking a conveyance or departing on foot. The cousins finally found an omnibus in which not all seats were taken. In the dim light of the lamps alongside, they did not see that the omnibus was intended for Negroes. The conductor looked surprised to see them, but he accepted their nickels without a word.

Before reaching the block on Broadway where Addie lived, the vehicle halted. Entering the side door was the squat, unmistakable form of the slave-catcher Wise. He sank onto a bench heavily, three seats in front of Addie and Henry. His head swiveled like an owl's as he surveyed the passengers. Since there was no lamp within the omnibus, he could not see far. Recognizing him, Addie and Henry froze and remained silent. When a young Negro man rose to alert the driver that he wished to step down, Wise immediately stood and followed.

"Addie, that's the man Joe warned me about!" Henry whispered.

"What can we *do*?" Addie responded. "It is almost my stop."

"Let's follow him."

The omnibus swayed to a stop as the driver reined in the cart horses. The conductor stepped aside, giving the Negro man room to descend. Wise stepped off immediately behind him. Henry and Addie stood, waited a moment, and then followed the men to the street.

Illuminated by the street lamp, Wise seemed intent upon engaging the young man in conversation. The Negro, backing away, replied in a deep voice. All Addie could hear was muttering on the part of Beauregard Wise and "no, no, no" from the other man. Wise stepped close and fumbled in his pocket.

Alarmed, Henry left Addie and stepped out of the shadows. He approached the pair and spoke in a breezy and, Addie thought, very brave fashion. "Gentlemen, can you direct me to 309 Broadway?"

Caught off guard and believing he was unobserved and thus unimpeded in his pursuit, Wise turned to face Henry and sneered truculently, "What? I haven't any idea where that is."

In that instant, the young black man fled into the night. Wise swore an oath Addie was glad she could not hear.

Henry replied gallantly, "Most uncouth of you, sir, and in the presence of my female companion!"

CHAPTER THIRTY-ONE

Wise turned and lurched away into the shadows in the direction of Irving House.

Waiting until they could no longer hear his footsteps, Addie and Henry proceeded the short distance home. Had Henry forestalled another kidnapping of a Negro? It certainly appeared so, they both agreed, and it was proof that all their suspicions about the man Wise were grounded in fact. Moreover, his actions suggested that he was prepared to threaten the Negro fellow with something—a gun or knife, perhaps.

Cousin Henry said a hasty "Good night," and Addie urged him to take all caution returning to his boarding house. She did not know what he could do to fend off Wise if he encountered him again. Ellen, the maid, let her into the house, and, unnerved as she was, Addie crept quietly upstairs to bed.

CHAPTER THIRTY-TWO

Joe Stewart, whom the Hoe family had not seen for weeks, appeared the next day. He had with him a newspaper with the personal account of the *Arctic* disaster written or dictated by James Luce, the captain of the ill-fated ship. Addie, Emilie, Ma, and Father gathered in the parlor to listen while Joe read aloud Luce's story. The captain claimed to have tried to force his crew to take charge of the sinking ship and assist passengers, but, in fact, they mutinied and only sought to save themselves. Moreover, Luce himself went down as his ship went down, and on coming to the surface, he saved himself by climbing onto one of the floating paddlewheels.

When Joe finished reading the dramatic account, Father asked, "Do you believe Luce? It is unlikely the crew had time to mutiny. Wouldn't the confusion have destroyed all protocols?"

"If you mean 'every man for himself,' then the captain had no authority since fear had taken over completely."

"Were there lifeboats?"

"He implies the crew commandeered them."

"In that case, there will be a further legal *mêlée*, as many people said when the news first came by telegraph."

"It certainly appears the captain is not to be blamed," Ma commented. "He defends his honor understandably, but what do the other survivors say?"

"We shall not see the end of this debacle for years once the insurance companies and the lawyers for the lost victims plead their cases," Father concluded. "Now Addie, tell us about Madame Grisi."

There ensued her description of the enchanting evening at Castle Garden, yet without mention of the sobering encounter on the way home. She saved that for when she and Joe could be alone. While she and her sister sewed, Father and Joe discussed the politics of the Know Nothing party, and debated how the November election might go.

The lateness of Addie's return from the opera the previous evening began to wear on her. She excused herself, yawning, and despite wanting to spend time with Joe, she retired for a nap upstairs. Stretching out fully clad on the comforter, Addie slept what seemed a very long time and awoke disoriented after a peculiar dream. In it, she led her little sister Annie through a deserted building. She knew they must find a way out and that they were pursued

CHAPTER THIRTY-TWO

by some malevolent being. While the anxiety from the dream abated, she looked about the familiar bedroom and judged that from the dim light in the room, it was nearly dark. Had Joe left? She smoothed her gown, splashed water on her face, and rearranged her hair.

Downstairs the parlor was empty. Addie, disappointed, went to the kitchen. Bridget, the young parlor maid, sat in a corner near the range where she was bent over a journal and, startled to see Addie, exclaimed, "Oh Miss, what must you think, me reading and all?"

"What are you reading?" Addie asked.

"A serial in the *Weekly* by Mr. Thack'ry. My brother read it, and now that I can read, I can get lost in it. If I don't know a word, Jim helps me." She folded the well-worn *Harper's Weekly* quickly and put it in the pocket of her apron.

"Have no fear," Addie reassured her. "Serials are entertaining, and I too enjoy them very much. Where are my stepmother and my sisters?"

"They went out for ice cream, and Mr. Hoe went upstairs to play billiards. The kettle has been hot for ages. Shall I make you a cup of tea?"

"No thank you." She returned to the front hall and could see that Joe's hat and gloves lay on the table. In the parlor, she lit the lamps and found her sewing. As though she had summoned him, she heard Joe's light, even tread on the stairs. "Joe, is that you?" she called out.

He entered the doorway alone. "Addie, I guessed you might be ill. Nothing wrong, it seems."

"Oh no, I only needed rest. Last night was more exhausting than I realized. Please forgive my disappearance. Come, sit down."

"Your father and Theodore are playing another round of billiards." He joined her on the sofa. "I am glad to find you here."

"There was an encounter on the way home from the opera that you must know about. Henry and I, by accident, embarked on the Third Avenue omnibus reserved for Negroes. It was late, and we could not read the sign in the dark. The conductor made no complaint, we paid, and sat in the middle seats. Beauregard Wise got on soon after us." Joe flinched as she continued, "Seated well in front of us, he found his mark, a young black fellow, and followed him onto the street not far from our house. We too got off and hid away from the street lamp. It was obvious that he meant to capture the fellow. Henry distracted Wise long enough for the Negro to run away."

Joe listened intently to her story and gripped the arm of the sofa until she finished. "Did Wise take issue with Henry? Was he aware of you?"

"He snarled an oath, but he did not do more than walk away. I cannot tell if he knew who was with Henry, but he learned that there was a woman near to hear his foul words."

"To think, he is prowling and pursuing his activities near 309 Broadway. Is he seeking a particular quarry, or does he have other intentions? I am mystified. Twice he has shown himself in your neighborhood." Joe toyed with the handle of Addie's sewing basket, a troubled expression clouding his handsome features.

"It has been many days since last we met." Addie, relieved that he now knew the facts, turned to him, putting her mending aside and hoping he would return her gaze.

He leaned forward and rubbed his brow, deep in thought, then glanced her way. "You say you actually danced with the man in Delaware City?" He recalled her meeting Wise. Was he actually stalking Addie, using his slave-catching bounty to fund his designs? Joe did not want to arouse her fears as he considered that possibility. He finally faced her, and, placing on the floor the sewing basket that lay between them, he embraced her and inwardly resolved to confound the mysterious predator one way or another.

As the front door creaked open and her sisters and Ma returned from their excursion, Joe said, "I am glad you told me what happened. I think I will leave now." Rising to greet her family, he added, "Be careful, Addie."

Instead of departing by the front door, he said his farewell, donning his hat and gloves, and made his way to the back of the house, leaving by way of the servants' entrance. Once in the back alley, he assessed the ways in which someone might observe the Hoes' residence. A stalker would be unlikely to view the family's and, in particular, Addie's, comings and goings by any means except by watching the front entrance. He circled back to Broadway and made note of the alleys on either side of 309 and across the street's broad expanse to the possible alcoves that might serve as vantage points. Because it was Saturday, there was little foot traffic as dark descended. He walked warily and resolved to note any suspicious person or activity. Seeing none, he returned to his boarding house on Bleecker Street.

A message was waiting for him in the foyer relating that a shipment was to arrive in the morning. "Shipment," Joe knew, was code for the arrival of an escaped slave who needed to be hidden and delivered to the next safe depot. He ate supper with the other boarders and retired early to be ready for the morning's task.

CHAPTER THIRTY-THREE

Addie and Emilie played the piano after tea. The duet they had tried out before went badly at first, but when they adjusted the tempo and tried again, they played it tolerably well. Father and Cousin Theodore, who came down to join them, urged the girls to play something they might all sing together. Emilie took over the keys, and Father led the singing.

Addie returned to her sewing and her own thoughts. She was slightly flattered and amused that Joe saw a connection between her brief dance with Beauregard Wise in July and his presence in the city. It did not occur to her that she could be in danger personally. His motivation was to capture Negroes; that was plain.

"Shall we go to hear Doctor Muhlenberg at Grace Episcopal in the morning?" Ma asked the assembled family, as the singing of rounds drew to a close and she prepared to take Annie and the baby upstairs to bed.

"Excellent thought," Father agreed. "He will no doubt preach about the *Arctic* and include the families of those lost and the survivors in his prayers."

Well before five o'clock Sunday morning, Joe was on his way to the nearest livery stable to procure a wagon and cart horse. Dense fog that had gathered overnight obscured the streets, even though the oil lamps still burned. Broken bottles from revels of the previous night littered the streets, along with horse manure that would not be removed until hired men shoveled it away when the shops opened on Monday.

Once he had laid the tarpaulin he brought with him in the rear of the wagon, he shook the reins and proceeded south to the appointed slip. He searched until he found the small skiff wedged between two schooners. He waited until he saw movement on the boat and then whistled three short notes. The shape of an old man emerged from the mist as he clambered onto the pier. Joe jumped down from the wagon and assisted the fellow into the back, where he tugged the heavy canvas over himself. Wasting no time, they pulled away from the murky harbor and headed for Bleecker Street.

After dropping off the elderly Negro at the rooming house, along with the heavy tarpaulin, Joe returned the horse and wagon to the livery stable. When he returned, the gentleman waited in the dark doorway for Joe, who took him inside, and immediately they ascended to his rooms.

Once inside, Joe finally spoke. "You must be hungry. There are biscuits in the tin and water in the pitcher. I'll bring a better meal later." He pointed out a settee where the weary man might sleep. "This evening I will take you north to South Salem to a farm. How long have you been traveling?"

"A farm," the old fellow sighed. "Thank you, suh. I been travelin' for two weeks. I hope to find my wife and son in Canada."

"Take some rest now. You'll need it for the wagon ride. It won't be smooth."

Joe went out, leaving the man safely locked in his rooms. He wanted to find Henry, who boarded only a few blocks away, and hear his account of the story Addie had told him.

The city was waking up as he walked the short distance to Mrs. Albert's boarding house on Morton. Morning fog was rising, and early church bells chimed. Joe rarely attended services, since Sundays were days when he could spare time for transporting slaves. He looked over his shoulder occasionally, ever mindful of the danger of being followed. The Fugitive Slave Act had changed the nature of his efforts, even though New York was safer than Delaware.

As he entered Henry's residence, the tantalizing fragrance of sausage cooking reminded him how hungry he was. Other boarders had begun to come down to breakfast. He climbed the stairs and found Henry's rooms. Not receiving an immediate response to his knock, he waited a few moments and tried again. A groggy Henry Seymour came to the door at last, opened it a crack and, recognizing Joe, let him in.

"Sorry to disturb you early," Joe said, as he drew the door closed behind him. Henry pulled on a robe over his nightshirt and waved him to a chair. "I have a question or two about Friday night."

"Oh, you must mean our meeting with that fellow Wise. Addie did not tell you all about it?"

"She did describe the encounter very well. I wondered if she might have left anything out."

Henry ran his fingers through his tousled hair and rubbed the sleep out of his eyes. Then he launched into the details of riding the omnibus, watching Wise leave to trail the black man, and the unfolding scene that the cousins watched from the shadows. "It was when Wise fumbled in his pocket for the weapon, a knife or a small gun perhaps, that I came forward. Perhaps it was nothing, but I could not let him accost the young man."

"Did Wise recognize you or Addie?"

"I could not say, but I would guess he did not, at least not right away. He swore when the young man ran away."

Joe apologized to Henry for waking him early on a Sunday morning. Henry good-naturedly invited him to stay as his guest downstairs for breakfast. Joe politely refused and left, emerging warily onto the street and seeking

CHAPTER THIRTY-THREE

a café where he might purchase breakfast for himself and provisions for the sleeping runaway slave.

While he ate, he thought over what Henry had told him. Addie must not have known that Wise threatened the young man with a weapon of some sort. It was clear to Joe that Wise was prepared to use force rather than legal means to take his quarry.

Getting back to his lodgings, Joe knocked gently on the door and let himself in, not wanting to scare the weary old man, who was his responsibility. He laid the bread and packet of cheese and two still-warm boiled eggs on the bureau.

"Where am I?" the gentleman said with a start when he heard Joe moving around.

"Don't be afraid. I brought you something to eat." Rising to a sitting position on the settee, the former slave struggled to make sense of where he was.

Joe moved the food he had brought to a small table and pulled it near the old fellow who, after an interval, asked where he might relieve himself. Joe directed him downstairs. After he slowly made his way back upstairs, he and Joe sat together. Before he began to eat, the man clasped his hands. "Thank you, God, for this food and this friend. Amen."

Joe considered the meaning of Wise's possessing a weapon. It was not illegal, but it meant that he was not merely using the new law to apprehend Negroes. He was a threat to anyone, white or black, who might oppose him.

Seeing his guest eat his meal with gusto, Joe suddenly realized he himself was very tired. He needed to rest before the taxing ordeal of carrying this frail man twenty miles north to his next safe haven. "You had best stay here. Don't go out. I've got to sleep. When I wake up, we'll travel on. Is that clear?"

"Yes it is, and I'm grateful to sit awhile."

Joe retired to the other of his two rooms and slept.

At Grace Episcopal, the famous Reverend Tyng elected to preach on the grave subject of the *Arctic*. Addie and her family sat transfixed as he described the terrible accident at sea, the cries of the women and children as they disappeared beneath the waves while only a few men survived. So moving was his sermon that Addie, Emilie, and Ma wept. Father wiped his nose with his handkerchief. Following the homily, which was a plea for changing men's hearts, the final hymn caused many a voice to falter over the final stanza: "*Jesus, Deliverer,/ Come Thou to me:/ Soothe thou my voyaging/ Over life's sea:/ Thou, when the storm of death/ Roars, sweeping by,/ Whisper, o Truth of truth —/ 'Peace! It is I.'*"

Few smiles lit the faces of the congregation as they departed the sanctuary, for many attending knew someone lost in the disaster. The Revered Doctor Tyng's countenance and his greetings to the parishioners were brief and subdued as he stood by the door.

CHAPTER THIRTY-FOUR

In the mid-afternoon, Joe awoke fully dressed, stiff and disoriented, with the sun from the only window of the room illuminating the wall opposite. Putting his shoes on and tucking in his shirt, he picked up his hat and coat from the foot of the bed, prepared for the journey. He could hear his elderly charge walking about in the adjoining room. When he opened the door, he found the Negro peering intently at the sketches Joe had pinned to the wall.

"Who is the Negro lady here?" the old man asked.

"That's a drawing I made for a friend." Joe's efforts to show what Elizabeth Jennings looked like decorated one wall, the best of which he had sent Addie months before.

"She don't look like a slave. That fine hat, the clothes she wears."

"She teaches school and plays the organ at her church. She lives here in New York City." Then Joe went on to tell the old man all about her and her brave stance on the omnibus, and how a young lawyer was defending her. "We won't know if she'll win her case for months, but there's a good chance she might."

The old man stared in awe at her likeness. The two men shared the remaining half of a loaf of bread and waited until twilight for Joe to set out to hire the wagon.

Cousin Emmie Ely came by on Sunday and joined Emilie and Addie for conversation in the parlor, catching up on the latest gossip. Emmie described the latest happenings on their street in Brooklyn, where a drunken man decided to climb a flagpole in the square and then had to jump and be caught in a blanket, but was none the worse for it. She told of how she wanted to remove a grease spot from her white dimity night dress, and applied a bar of soap, only to find the lye in the soap was too strong and burned a hole through it.

The two Hoe girls listened and, with spirits still dampened by the morning's church service, try as they might, they had little success finding an amusing tale to contribute. At length, Addie thought to describe Madame Grisi, her lovely voice and her arrestingly large size. "Perhaps she was with child," Emmie responded. "I read that she and Mario have other children."

CHAPTER THIRTY-FOUR

"That would make her high notes all the more remarkable, beautiful as they were," Addie responded. She did not go into the other remarkable aspects of the evening spent with Henry. They sewed and chatted until Father returned from his customary Sunday afternoon walk.

"Hello, ladies." He greeted them as removed his muffler and hat. "Is it time for tea? It is cold outside, the wind is brisk, and fall is upon us. Does anyone of you know why a fat man in a top hat is sitting at the bottom of the stoop?"

"No, I can't imagine why, or who he is," Ma responded.

Addie excused herself. She went upstairs and looked down from the bedroom window at the front steps. Sure enough, seated boldly on the steps, was the unbearable Wise resembling a rotund black spider all dressed in black from his top hat and overcoat to his boots. She glanced only long enough to ascertain his identity and then stood back from the window out of sight. Addie was glad Joe was nowhere around and was not likely to come by for some time.

It was nearly midnight by the time Joe and his human cargo reached the Gilbert farm. The arduous journey took him north through the city to the ferry and on up the Boston Post Road to South Salem. He helped the arthritic old man to the ground and, as silently as possible, led him around the back of the house to the shed door. Luckily, the Gilberts did not have a dog that would bark and awaken the sleepers upstairs. Lighting a match, he led his Negro charge down the narrow stone steps to the chimney arch where, anticipating their arrival, Grandma Gilbert had left an apple pie for the wayfarers. Joe found the candlestick in the alcove, lit it, and showed the man the cot prepared for him.

After they ate a piece of the pie, Joe bid him farewell and Godspeed, and then returned to the wagon. Now it would be up to another conductor, from Connecticut, to help the Negro on his way north. Joe considered, as he took the reins and urged the carthorse forward, whether the old man would be able to reach safety and a new life. He hoped the man's health would match his faith and that he would find his family.

At Cross River, Joe halted long enough for the horse to drink. He himself splashed cold water on his face before the long wagon ride to the city. Chilly as the October night might be, it was clear, and stars sprinkled across the night sky made the journey not unpleasant. So far the delivery of one more slave to another milepost on the road to freedom had taken place flawlessly.

When Joe began to doze, he was glad the horse stepped ahead, unerringly following the country road to the ferry. Then Joe sang ballads to keep awake, causing the horse's ears to twitch. He recalled the story Richard Hoe had told of how his father, Robert Hoe, helped build the bridge at Cross River early in the century, not long after he had arrived in America. A good many wagons had crossed that bridge since then.

Joe's was the sole wagon to make passage on the ferry across the Bronx River. On the next leg of the journey through the countryside north of Manhattan, he encountered deer and a family of raccoons in his path. The stars began to disappear when he approached the city itself, and the smoke from factories and fog from the rivers, combined with the light from street lamps, served to obliterate his view of the greater universe.

Once he reached the rooming house, the horse and wagon safely in the care of the livery boy, he climbed the stairs wearily and collapsed for a few hours of sleep before his regular week of work began.

Impatient with the cat-and-mouse nature of Beauregard Wise popping into her life, Addie determined that the next time he came her way, or appeared near their house, she would confront him. The day he sat on their front steps Father had gone out to question him why he chose the stoop to rest his large frame, but the man had left.

The week began with Addie traveling with Father and Uncle Robert to school, and on the way home she chose to walk, ignoring Joe's warnings. The street was crowded with every sort of vehicle, hand carts with vendors selling their wares, omnibuses stopping and starting, horses and carriages speeding around the slower heavy wagons pulled by teams of huge, straining draft horses, as well as riders on horseback, and foot traffic, of course. Addie thought the odds were slim that any of the people in the teeming streets or walking beneath the awnings of the shops would take note of one eighteen-year-old girl. She drew her bonnet ties more tightly so that her face was well hidden, and, satchel in hand, she walked resolutely north.

Hawkers of fresh vegetables and fruit shouted as she walked by, "Fresh pears! Fresh pears!" At one corner a newsboy, barefoot despite the autumn bite in the air, shouted above the crowd, "Survivor of the *Arctic* disaster tells all!" and repeated the sensational reminder of the tragedy over and over.

Addie hurried on, reflecting on the fact that the very finery that she and other women wore was one reason why not one woman survived the boat's sinking. Were women the weaker sex, as many were wont to say? She hoped not. What would she do if Wise or anyone were to try to obstruct her way or hurt her? She banished the thought, still intent on walking by herself, no matter the consequences.

Halfway home, she heard footsteps on the cobblestones directly behind her as she crossed the street. She suddenly turned to find Henry before her.

CHAPTER THIRTY-FOUR

"Aha! Why is my cousin hurrying, pale as a ghost?"

"It is only a few blocks from the school."

"I know, and you look as though the devil were on your trail."

She stammered, "I...I..." She did not want to admit she expected to confront the slave-catcher. "I need to be home to help Ma with the girls."

Henry looked skeptical and, taking her satchel, he carried it the rest of the way to 309 Broadway. Once they were inside the safe, quiet confines of the Hoes' front hall, they met Ellen, who related that Ma and the little sisters were out for the ride they planned to take to see Mrs. Condit. Addie's excuse now appeared very thin and false, as Henry quickly pointed out to her.

"Oh, Henry, I did not mean to deceive you. I wanted to walk home, despite Joe's caution about avoiding Beauregard Wise—who followed me one day. And then on Sunday he appeared on the front steps. If I can confront him, perhaps I can find out what he is after, and why. *We* do not have Negro help! What reason can he have for following me and approaching *our* house?"

Henry paced across the parlor to the window facing the thoroughfare. He stared down at the passersby and then turned to Addie. "Isn't it time you faced your father with your worries?"

"I know Mr. Wise from a brief encounter at a most civilized party. If he will tell me what he wants, I can listen and decide what to tell Father."

"Let's not be foolhardy here. You and I know he has one purpose, to catch Negroes. The less you say to Wise, the better. You've seen how he behaves."

"I shall take your thoughts into consideration," she replied, and she thanked Henry for walking with her and offering his advice. He left, uncertain whether she would in fact take it.

CHAPTER THIRTY-FIVE

As more reports from survivors of the *Arctic* emblazoned the front pages of the newspapers, it became clear that women and children watched as men raced to the lifeboats. In the evenings, as Ma sewed on a basque for her stepdaughter, Addie read the accounts aloud, becoming angry at the terrible injustice when the men, even officers and crew, exploited the patience of the passengers. She looked up from the page she was reading.

"What would any of us have done?"

"Nothing different from those poor souls," Ma answered with resignation. "They no doubt trusted the men would find a way to save them."

After reading the eyewitness accounts of the disaster, Addie and Emilie both wondered if they themselves could ever dare travel abroad, as they had often imagined. The *Arctic* was the splendid steamship advertised as the finest of its kind, with a huge, elegant ladies' saloon, sumptuous meals and spacious staterooms. Father had traveled to England for the printing press business, and had enjoyed the speed and comfort of steamships. Would he continue to risk his life in business ventures by taking the Collins Line, of which the *Arctic* had been the queen, she wondered.

Just then Father came in, and he announced, "A new piano teacher, a Mister Lander, will be coming this Friday, Addie. Be ready at four o'clock. Mr. Boyle has his contraption, which I brought to the factory, and he met me there to retrieve it. He was huffy and demanded pay for his inconvenience, which I gave. I told him to seek a patent if his device has any worth at all. And I am afraid Mr. Boyle left boiling mad. Now, Addie, you can keep all your fingers for future piano study."

On the ensuing three days, Henry was waiting on the school steps when Addie emerged to walk home. She knew he was protecting her, but it made her feel hemmed in. The kind thing to do was his way. Nevertheless, she was also aware that his work for Hoe and Company took him elsewhere, and he would not always be outside to meet her when school was dismissed. On Friday, in fact, he was obliged to go to New Jersey, as he informed her the day before.

The weather turned rainy over the course of the next day. Mr. Armstrong, the geometry teacher, whose class Addie dreaded as she had never dreaded anything before in her life, loomed over her shoulder when she could not avoid smudging her drawing of an equilateral triangle. Only a few more minutes and the class would be over, she knew.

"Thought must precede action, Miss Hoe!" he thundered, striding on to view the papers of classmates in front of her. "Girls, you must not apply pen to paper until you have fully planned your drawing."

Looking out of the high windows, she could see that it would be a soggy walk home with no umbrella. The ugly paper sat before her. She would attempt to draw the figure again at home. Maria Seabury told her Mr. Armstrong had never taught girls before. Addie knew she was only flattering herself to think that that made a bit of difference. Mr. Armstrong cowed her, and that was certain.

Emerging from the school, Addie and her classmates shouted their good-byes over the sound of rain and thunder, and went their separate routes home. She hiked her skirts around her ankles, and hoped her bonnet would not be entirely ruined by the time she got home. A most welcome omnibus drew to a stop nearby, and she skipped over a puddle of rainwater and muck to come along side it. Disheveled and with sopping shoes, she searched her bag for a nickel. When at last she found one and had given it to the porter, she located a seat next to a proper-appearing gentleman who removed his umbrella from the seat and moved toward the window to accommodate her. "Nasty weather" was his only comment as he peered out the befogged window. She nodded and took a breath. The ride would only be a few blocks. She paid close attention to the passing signs and landmarks she knew well, the stationers' and Irving House.

Glancing to her right, she reacted with acute surprise to see Beauregard Wise in a seat next to the window opposite. He wore his top hat and black clothing and stared straight ahead. Should she pretend not to know him? Should she speak to him? She sat bewildered for a moment, and then took courage. "Why, Mr. Wise, I believe," she said across the aisle, "what brings you to New York City?"

Beauregard Wise grimaced and turned away, feigning not to recognize her.

"You must remember our meeting in Delaware City," she persisted, "at the Reybolds'?"

The gentleman next to her cleared his throat. He was no doubt mystified that a well-turned out young woman would pursue a connection with so questionable an acquaintance. She saw the imposing façade of the Irving House coming up, and gathering up her satchel, she abandoned any further remarks to Mr. Wise, and, chagrined at his deception, left the omnibus.

He chose to ignore me, Addie marveled, instead of acknowledging our meeting. He can't have forgotten, of course not. He followed me and occupied our stoop for a long time. What can he want? Her thoughts tumbled about like oranges tossed by a juggler, one idea never settling to rest before another erupted and took flight in her mind.

While the new piano teacher waited for Addie, Mr. Lander had taken the liberty to open the Nunns and Clark and play a Chopin *scherzo* in a minor key. As soon as she entered, its mournful, magnificent chords filled the house and reordered Addie's tumult of thoughts to a sense of calm. Leaving her satchel, soaked cape and bonnet in the foyer, she silently entered the back parlor and stood listening until the end of the piece.

"How beautiful!" she sighed, in awe of the music and Mr. Lander's ability to interpret Chopin, whose compositions she admired. When he turned, startled at her presence, she observed he was probably her father's age. He was very neatly dressed in a well-worn brown suit and had a carefully clipped mustache.

"Miss Adeline Hoe? I am Mr. Lander." He rose and shook her hand. "I hope you do not mind my trying out the instrument, which is very fine, I might add."

"Oh no, you must always play something when you come," she urged, genuinely charmed by his performance.

When she sat down on the piano bench, Mr. Lander inquired about her training, neither suggesting nor making a judgment about its quality. She played the last piece she had studied in the spring, a transcription for piano of a Rossini aria. After an assignment of exercises and assessment of her knowledge of the fundamentals of music, he suggested she review the Rossini for the following week. When he left at the end of the hour, she felt most encouraged and was pleased to know as fine a musician and as promising an instructor as Mr. Lander.

Ma's voice calling from the hall reminded her of the pile of wet belongings she had dropped in a heap, and she hastened to take care of them. Before she went upstairs with the sodden clothes, her stepmother asked her to watch Annie while she and the baby rested. It was good to put the ride on the omnibus behind her and otherwise occupy herself, she thought, while she and Annie walked together upstairs.

Hanging her clothing to dry and changing her shoes, Addie heard what her little half sister had done all day. "Ellen let me float apples in the dishpan and I made a lake on the kitchen floor. Ellen said that was about enough. Then Ma and I made a pretty skirt for my doll out of scraps from what she's making for you. Uh oh. I shouldn't have said it. It's a surprise." Addie smiled while Annie's cheerful monologue ran on. They descended to the parlor and sang songs at the piano until tea and it was time for Father to appear.

CHAPTER THIRTY-SIX

When there was a metallic rapping on the front door, it meant someone not from the family was arriving. Uncles Robert and Peter, or the cousins, knocked with their knuckles or cane, or entered by the back door. Hearing the four loud raps of the brass doorknocker, Addie and Annie hastened to find Joe Stewart on the doorstep. "Come in out of the rain," she said. A flood of relief nearly overcame Addie. He read her expression and sensed something was wrong. Little Annie stood between them and looked from Addie's face to Joe's.

Despite longing to understand the emotions that begged an explanation, Joe scooped little Annie up in his arms and strode into the front room. "So, let me guess," he addressed Addie, "Geometry is no better." He set Annie on the carpet next to her dolls.

"Well, that is true," she admitted. "I shall never be an architect or an engineer as Nicholas Bowen plans to be. My theorems and figures never suit Mr. Armstrong."

"But?" He knew that geometry was not what troubled her.

Little sister Annie, disappointed to have lost Addie's attention, skipped out of the room to find Tilda, who might let her climb the stepstool and help make scones for tea.

"Come sit down," she urged. Joe joined her on the sofa without a word. "I had an odd experience you should know about. On the omnibus, when I was coming home earlier, Beauregard Wise was sitting in a seat across the aisle. I spoke to him, and reminded him we had met in Delaware City. He pretended he did not know me at all, putting on a blank face and turning away."

"It sounds as though he doesn't want anyone connecting him with the South."

"What can he want of us?"

"Has he come here?"

"Not inside, but on Sunday he sat on the front steps for a considerable time."

Joe looked puzzled. He turned to the window and stared into the gathering darkness, where the street lamps were beginning to be lit. When Ellen entered the room to close the drapes, shutting out the sounds of the late afternoon traffic as the city left off work, Joe turned and, in low, measured tones, spoke directly to Addie, seated next to him. "I beg you not to address Wise again. If he has you, or anyone in your family, as his target, I do not know what trouble he might cause."

"But Joe, what interest can he have in us?"

"I do not have an answer." He took her hand, ignoring the interruption of the maid passing through. Addie flushed, partly from embarrassment and partly from an awareness of the depth of his feeling for her. She knew he was assuming the burden of her worries, but, consoling though that might be, she intuited that the real danger was not to her but to him. Wise would be crazy to cause the Hoes any trouble. Her father, benign and generous though he was, did not suffer fools timidly in his work place or in the city at large, and he would engage the services of a constable if Wise were to threaten him or his family in any way. No, it was Joe himself Wise was after.

"Be careful," Addie warned, as they heard the voices of Ma and baby Mary coming downstairs and Father's whistling as he slammed the front door.

"Am I ever *not* careful?" Joe asked. His handsome brown eyes with dark circles under them revealed the strain his double life inflicted upon him.

Father, pleased to see her and their young friend, entered holding Annie, who clung to his neck. "Addie, my dear, how are you? Joe Stewart, how about a game of billiards later on?"

When Joe left after tea and billiards with Father, Addie settled down at her desk to write a few lines to Retta Stewart, whom she had not seen since the summer. She dipped her pen in ink and was about to write the greeting when someone knocked on the bedroom door. "Come in," she called, not looking up.

Ellen, the parlor maid, opened the door a crack, and seeing that Addie was alone, entered and walked quickly to her side. "Miss Addie, I could not help overhearing your conversation with Mr. Stewart this afternoon."

Startled by the urgency in her voice, Addie turned around and found Ellen twisting the edges of her apron, clearly disturbed about something. "What is the matter, Ellen?"

"I heard you mention the man who was on the steps Sunday afternoon. Pardon me, Miss."

"Yes? What about him?"

"After dinner dishes were done that day, I was leaving, as I always do, going home for the rest of Sunday. As I came to the street from the back… and…" She faltered, very near a bout of tears.

"What happened then, Ellen?" Addie persisted, with a cold sense of foreboding.

"That ugly man I overheard you mention? He was waiting for me at the corner by Irving House."

CHAPTER THIRTY-SIX

"What did he say?"

"First, he addressed me all proper-like, 'Oh, ma'am, a moment if you please.' So I stopped to hear him out. He wanted me to accept an extra job, keeping an eye out for who comes and goes at your house. 'There'll be cash in it for you,' he said. I says to him, 'I don't know all the folks who come and go, and I don't care to find out.' Then his voice got mean, and he said he could make me work for him. I says, 'How?' and then he says, 'Wait and see.' Then he went away. I've been worried ever since."

"Has he come back?"

"No, not that I know about."

"I'm glad you warned me. I think he wants to know about Mr. Stewart. Whatever you do, don't tell him if and when Joe Stewart comes here."

Lest Addie think she would accept Wise's offer of money for spying on the Hoes, Ellen dropped the edges of her apron and, regaining her dignity, replied, "I won't speak to that man again."

"Thank you, Ellen, for telling me what happened. I am sorry you were accosted. I'll see what can be done to stop the man from ever coming back."

"I only wanted to let you know." Relieved to have unburdened herself of the frightful information, Ellen went back downstairs.

Saturday dawned a magnificent autumn morning, with blue sky and streets washed by the rain and a crisp west wind ruffling the awnings of the shops on Broadway. Addie dressed warmly, fastened her bonnet tight, and determined to go to the A. T. Stewart store. Might she find Joe there at the weekend? She was not certain. With Emilie spending the night at cousin Emmie Ely's in Brooklyn, and Ma calling on Aunt Thirza, still frail from her long illness, Addie set off alone for the biggest store in the city, only a few blocks away.

Once she passed through the great marble foyer, she found her way to the tailoring department, and when one of the tailors she recognized from her last visit to the store passed by, she spoke to him. "Hello, excuse me, can you tell me if Mr. Stewart—that is, *Joe* Stewart—is here?"

"I'm sorry, miss. He is not here on Saturdays. He is either traveling or at his residence."

She thanked the gentleman, whose accent she suspected was German. He then nodded politely and returned to one of the chambers where he made or altered suits, well out of sight of the elegantly dressed ladies and gentlemen shopping in the aisles.

Disappointed not to find Joe, Addie set out for Bleecker Street, where she knew he lived at a Mrs. Grogan's boarding house, although she had never visited there. She walked north on Broadway, and, spying an omnibus headed in that direction, she hastened her step to meet it when it stopped at the next corner. She knew she had seen the sign for Bleecker when she rode out of the city en route to South Salem, and from discussions with Joe, she knew he lived on the west side.

When seven street signs bore no inscriptions for Bleecker, she became uneasy and asked the porter how much farther it would be. He answered five more stops. It was then well past the middle of the morning. Had she taken on too much? When she was not back by noon, Ma and Emilie, if they were back home, would worry.

Finally, after what seemed a very long time, the porter announced "Bleecker Street." She descended and began to walk along a row of similar, large frame houses. Since it was a fine day, residents stood on the steps or strolled nearby. She chose her steps carefully on the sidewalk that had not been recently cleaned. Screwing up her courage, Addie stopped a man toting a sack of potatoes on his shoulder. "Sir, would you please direct me to Mrs. Grogan's rooming house."

He looked startled, and instead of replying, he pointed with his free hand to the next building. Thanking the man, she could not believe her good fortune to find her destination so easily.

Inside the front door, she was struck by the residual odor of cabbage, lingering evidence of supper the night before. From the empty foyer, she saw to her left in an adjoining room the broad, long dining table set for the next meal, where Joe must eat, she thought, and she pictured him among other boarders, passing the gravy. An older woman, stout, with graying hair gathered in a tight bun on top of her head and wearing a bib apron, entered to place a cruet on the table.

Addie passed into the dining room and asked straightaway what room Mister Joseph Stewart occupied.

The woman looked Addie up and down. "Mister Stewart lives in number 14 on the second floor."

Upon hearing the room number, Addie was delighted, after her search, to have found him at last, or so it seemed. Giving the woman her thanks, she smiled in relief, and the woman, perhaps Mrs. Grogan herself, smiled back not unkindly.

Addie climbed the well-worn wooden stairs and walked along the bare hallway. She took note of the numbers until she found his door. She knocked timidly at first, and waited. Not a sound. Removing her gloves, she rapped longer and louder. Still no response. A portly gentleman passed by her. He unlocked a door across the hall and entered.

Dressed in her warm cape, she began to perspire and loosened her bonnet. She sighed. Perhaps Joe was far away delivering a runaway slave. Or perhaps

CHAPTER THIRTY-SIX

he was ordering fabric in Philadelphia. Her face felt hot as she realized how impetuous she had been to think she would find him when she arrived unannounced. Why, he might be anywhere. At least she now knew where he lived and could picture him there.

Disappointed, she decided to give up and, putting her gloves back on, she turned to retreat along the stuffy hallway. When she reached the stairs, she heard her name.

"Addie!" No one except Joe could have said it. She wheeled about and, looking back, saw Joe's silhouette in light streaming from his door. "Addie, is that you?"

"Joe!" She answered, "Yes, I came to find you."

"Come back."

She returned to find him in a disheveled state in trousers and nightshirt without shoes or socks. He stood holding the door open and stepped back for her to enter. His hair, usually combed neatly with a precise part, tumbled over his eyebrows, and he brushed it aside. "To what do I owe the pleasure of this visit?"

CHAPTER THIRTY-SEVEN

Even though Addie had begun her journey with determination, once she had achieved her object, she was at a loss for words. Self-conscious and mute, she entered his sitting room and paused, observing the sketches of Miss Jennings on the walls, the only decorations in the room. She noted the sofa with blankets folded at one end, the bare table with two chairs and on the floor a worn flowered carpet. A door led to another room, presumably where he had been sleeping when she knocked.

At last she spoke. "I apologize to have arrived without a word of warning."

Joe took in the girl before him, in her dark brown tippet and matching bonnet, custom-made gown and kid gloves, her cheeks rosy, her sharp eyes roving about his quarters. "I sleep like a sluggard on Saturdays. Can you guess why?" He stretched and yawned.

"Because you lead a double life and it catches up with you?"

He laughed. "Partly. I must be up at three a.m. and off to the docks."

"Of course. I understand. I won't stay long."

"You have something to say. Come, give me your bonnet and gloves." She hesitantly loosened her bonnet and gave it to him along with her bag and gloves. "Please sit down. I am out of tea, but I can offer you water."

"I should like that very much." She watched as he poured from a pitcher near the door. He brought the glass to where she sat on the edge of the sofa.

He pulled a chair from the table and, sensing her shyness, sat facing her and waited for her to rest and tell why she had traveled alone to find him. The sunlight from the window behind her illumined her auburn curls, creating a rim of light about her face. "How did you track me down?"

She told of going to the store, what the tailor told her, of coming by omnibus, and about the man with the potatoes. He listened, waiting for the reason for her visit, content to hear her lively tale filling his usually lonely rooms. "I was especially relieved and delighted when Mrs. Grogan, if it was indeed she, told me you lived in room 14."

"So, you found me. Are you disillusioned by the truly plain nature of this place?" His hand swept around the room.

"I did not come here to sightsee." Her eyes suddenly serious, she bent toward him. "Joe, I am afraid for you. Beauregard Wise has been coming around. He accosted Ellen, and after he tried to bribe her, he threatened her if she didn't tell him who comes and goes at 309 Broadway."

"You think I am the man he's looking for?"

"It is you, and only you, who comes to our house regularly who is not in the family…and who is rescuing Negroes."

"I'll stay away, if that's what will stop him."

"I could not accept that."

They were both silent, eyes fixed upon one another. He reached out and took her hands in his. "It will do no good for me to seek him out," he said, pondering what to do. "The less he sees of me, the safer we all are. I have worried that Wise has designs on you…following you…appearing the night you attended the opera."

Addie shuddered as if to shake off that thought. Joe pursued the idea further. "You called him out of his guise of anonymity on the omnibus. Now that he has made you aware of him, I do not trust that he won't try extorting money from your father…" He stopped. "You're afraid for my sake, and now you'll fear for your father's. Enough of this talk."

Suddenly remembering the time, she glanced out the window. It must be past noon, and it was a long journey home. "It solved nothing, my coming to warn you. I've only made matters worse." She rose from the sofa and drew her tippet about her shoulders.

He too stood. "No, don't say or think that. There will be a way to proceed. Tell Ellen not to worry. May I walk you to the corner?"

"Thank you, but I will go alone. If I am followed, it won't do for us to be seen together."

He retrieved her bonnet and bag, and watched while she prepared to leave. Filled with longing and admiration for her brave effort on his behalf, he took her in his arms, breathing in the scent of fresh air about her. Even though it was mid-day and there were not roses or moonlight, the suspended sense that time stood still came over them both. Finally he stepped away and she, with a parting half smile, drew open the door and was gone.

Joe leaned against the closed door. He reviewed their conversation and hoped for her safe return home. He decided against having supper downstairs with the other boarders. No doubt some of them, having seen Addie arrive and depart, would have comments to make. He and Belle Grogan had an understanding about the Negroes who came and went. She was an abolitionist herself, and therefore made no complaint about his nocturnal movements or Negro guests. But a lovely, well-dressed, young white woman, appearing on a Saturday morning, would draw interest.

Although he was tired and ought to be sleeping, he took out his sketch pad and charcoal. From memory he drew Addie as she appeared tying her bonnet on, the curve of her cheek, her half smile just before she left, adding the halo that surrounded her face in the sunlight.

The rattling omnibus came to a stop, the horses hanging their heads while the passengers stepped off on their way in the breezy autumn afternoon. Addie would still have another two blocks to walk to reach home. During the slow ride south on Broadway, she decided not to concoct a lie about where she had been all day, but would say she went to A. T. Stewart's store, the truth, or at least part of it. Its marvelous attractions and huge size made it entirely possible for someone to spend an entire day there. She was very hungry as she stepped down, and she hoped there would be plenty to eat at teatime.

As the driver shook the reins and the omnibus jerked forward, she glanced up at the remaining passengers riding by. In the very back she glimpsed distinctly the face of her nemesis Wise, peering out at her. She tried not to yield to panic as she walked home, but the conclusion that her trip to find Joe had led Wise straight to him was unavoidable. How could I have been so foolish, she asked herself. Was he behind me every step of my journey, or was it just by chance that he was on the same omnibus?

Although he finally slept long and hard after eating supper at the café near his rooms, Joe awoke in the early morning his limbs heavy and stiff. Obtaining a horse and wagon was routine after the many times he had assisted a man, or several men, or a mother and child, or an elderly person, all Negroes, to a safe place and not always to the same refuge. Their gratitude and the knowledge that they were one step closer to freedom was his only reward for the solitary, often grueling task. He depended on the close-mouthed team of conductors, from the deep South to Canada, to assure safe passage for each escaping slave. Any breach in the trail of secrecy placed a Negro in grave danger.

Starting out for the docks that Sunday morning was no different from previous rescues, but Joe took extra precautions. He wore his darkest clothing and stopped frequently on the street to look about him, sometimes climbing down from the wagon and affecting to adjust the horse's harness. Nearing the harbor, he made a final stop, and as he was climbing up to take the reins, a sailor lurched from behind him and with slurred speech begged a ride to his ship.

"I can't take you to your ship, but I can drop you at the Battery," he replied. The sailor climbed up beside him. So inebriated was he that he promptly fell asleep, leaning precariously one way and then another as the wagon rattled over the cobblestones. Joe woke him upon reaching the Battery, and the man stumbled off into the darkness.

The damp of morning fog combining with the biting chill of autumn made Joe hunch his shoulders and pull his woolen coat about him while he awaited the signal from the boat. The horse neighed and shifted impatiently in his harness. As before, the small skiff carrying his latest cargo came into view, a dark shape wedging itself between two barges. Behind him, despite the sound of bells from ships in the harbor, he thought he heard a creak as though a board in the wharf, lacking a nail, gave as someone stepped upon it. He slid off the wagon seat and stood on the side nearest the dock, completely in shadow, out of the dim light from the single street lamp several yards away.

Listening for sounds on the dock as well as the signal from the skiff, he watched for the slightest movement. The horse whinnied, giving Joe another inkling that he was not alone. Was it a night watchman on his rounds, hired to protect the goods on one of the barges? He hoped it was that or nothing.

Then sneaking toward the rear of the wagon came a shape, crouching yet moving closer. The three telltale whistles that Joe knew would require his answering to show he was ready to receive the Negroes would come at any moment. Surely the figure at the other end of the wagon waited for the emergence of the slaves, too. Joe also crouched and crept to the opposite end of the wagon. He would have to whistle very soon, giving himself away when the signal came. Perhaps not seeing him seated in the wagon would warn the conductor in the boat that something was amiss, causing him to postpone the signal. In the meantime, he must act.

Still hidden, Joe waited until the person advanced to the edge of the dock near the skiff where it rocked in the motion of the tide, sloshing between the two barges. He approached the stealthy witness to the transfer due to take place very soon. In that instant Joe realized the stranger was stalking him. The man rounded the end of the wagon and lunged.

Short and heavy, Wise barreled toward Joe with his head down. What Joe could not see was the knife Wise held in his right hand. The blade slashed at Joe's sleeve. Unable to see his opponent, Joe flattened himself against the side of the wagon as his wily assailant regained his footing for a new thrust. Joe estimated the location of the squat figure well enough to grab him around the neck with his right arm and reach for the knife with his left. They struggled, and Wise, using his vast weight, pushed down the slighter man, which proved his undoing. With superior strength and physical condition, Joe twisted the blade upward, away from himself.

Beauregard Wise, in his frenzy to force Joe down, landed squarely upon his own blade. He uttered a guttural sound, a fatal rasp, and went limp.

Horrified to realize the man was no more and that someone could be so vile as to kill for the booty a slave might bring, Joe, with disgust, rolled the inert body off himself and slowly struggled to his knees. He alerted the silently swaying skiff he was still alive.

From the small boat two young men emerged, along with their Underground Railroad conductor, the Quaker Elihu from Philadelphia. The three jumped onto the dock. "Joe, are you hurt?" The two young Negroes and Elihu, who manned the skiff, stood around him as he stumbled to his feet.

"We have the dead body of a slave catcher here." Joe's voice came in broken phrases. "It was an accident. He attacked me with a knife. We struggled…I grabbed his wrist, and when he fell on top of me, he…landed on the blade…"

The Quaker Elihu turned to the two Negroes. "Can you help us drag the body onto the boat?"

Apprehensive, they nonetheless readily agreed. The four men each took one of Wise's limbs and, straining, heaved the obese body into the bow of the small skiff. Jumping back onto the boat, the Quaker pulled the awkward, lifeless form fully onto the deck and handed Joe his bilge bucket.

"What will you do with the body?" Joe asked, as Elihu Pierce fumbled about at the rear of the boat, covering Wise with a canvas.

"Take the bucket and dump water where the man fell. There's bound to be a pool of blood." Obeying in numb shock, Joe did as his friend told him, dipping seawater onto the dock. Although he could not see the blood, he knew it was there. "Now, toss me that rope, and get on your way. The man, rest his soul, got what he deserved."

Still shaken, Joe, like an automaton, assisted onto the wagon the young men, who were equally unnerved by what they had observed. The fellows, in their early twenties, silently vaulted into the bed of the wagon and pulled the tarpaulin on top of them as they had done on other legs of their journey.

The dawn would be not long in coming, Joe thought, as he climbed onto the seat and shook the reins, grateful to leave the scene of mortal combat. The thought of the body floating off to sea with Elihu weighed upon him as he drove north. What had always been for him a worthy cause, despite the danger in it, was tarnished. Were there accomplices lurking in the shipyard waiting to assault him? It seemed that Wise acted alone. From the time he had first seen him at the wharf in Delaware City, Joe suspected Wise was a loner, but was that truly the case? Was there a place where slave catchers met to compare their strategies for trapping Negroes? Joe's transporting slaves north made him secretive and solitary himself, rarely coming in contact with other conductors. He wanted to believe that Wise's selfish motives for getting the entire bounty for each slave would have caused him to act alone.

CHAPTER THIRTY-EIGHT

Addie and Emilie welcomed Mary and Thomas Gilbert, who came by for the first time since their wedding. Their new Aunt Mary, more beautiful than ever and Uncle Thomas his quiet, congenial self sat in the parlor with their shoulders touching. They seemed completely at ease with one another.

"Is Grandma well?" Addie wanted to know.

"She is as broody as a setting hen these days," Thomas replied. "She stays close to the house, no jaunts to Ridgefield or New Canaan lately. You ladies need to come shake her out of her housebound ways."

"Mrs. Gilbert is a wonderful mother-in-law," Mary added, not exactly disagreeing with Thomas but seeing Grandma as the welcome, kindly replacement for the ailing stepmother she left behind. "I am learning something new from her every time I enter the kitchen or sit down with her to sew."

"What is new here?" Thomas looked from one niece to the other.

"Addie has a new piano teacher, a Mr. Lander," Emilie informed him. "We both attended a fascinating lecture about oracles at the Mechanics Institute last week."

"What are 'oracles'?" Mary asked.

"They tell what might happen. They are fortune tellers of sorts."

"They sound like speculators to me," Thomas commented. "Did you girls learn who it is you will marry?" Clearly, he was finding marriage a worthy state, Addie thought.

Emilie laughed, "Oh no, the oracles we heard about were all from literature."

"Addie, play something for us on the piano," Mary urged.

Not having seen Joe for over ten days, Addie had devoted all of her spare time at home practicing the piano. There were scales and exercises and the aria from Rossini, which improved enough that Mr. Lander suggested she put it aside. He introduced a new piece, a Bach prelude in four sharps that demanded slow, even treatment for each hand. When immersed in the complex, flowing lines of Bach's music, she escaped thinking about whether Joe was safe or whether a slave catcher was watching their house. "I can play the piece I reviewed for my new teacher, but the Bach isn't ready for anyone to hear just yet," she told her aunt as she lifted the lid and sat at the piano.

The Romantic piece flowed smoothly, and when the arpeggios in the accompaniment climbed, near the end, and the passion of the melody soared above them, she sensed that though she did not know the lyrics to the original aria, she was a vessel for their meaning and, perhaps, their beauty.

Her uncle and aunt applauded as the echoes of the tumultuous final chord faded away. "That was wonderful," Mary and Thomas both exclaimed at once.

Constrained by the two phases of his life, Joe had little time to dwell upon the events on the dock. He delivered to his rooming house the two brothers, who spoke together in his rooms as they tried to make sense of the events that brought them to the crowded streets of a city so big it seemed to have no end. As Joe tried to settle into sleep himself in the next room, he could hear their voices sorting through their latest experiences. Weariness finally overtook them all.

Fortunately, the journey through the silent towns on the Post Road to South Salem was interrupted only occasionally by a dog barking as they passed by. As before, the Gilbert house was dark when the wagon drew to a stop. Joe led them into the cellar, where the two fellows were obliged to take turns sleeping on the single cot, while their driver made his way back to the city. The parting of the three men had been sober and brief as the young men wished Joe Godspeed.

The wagon, empty now, rattled as it lurched ahead on the rough gravel road. The horse's hoof beats continued their hypnotic rhythm. Joe, however, was not tempted to fall asleep, much as he trusted the horse to follow the Post Road south.

He had too much to think about. His killing a man weighed monstrously upon him. Would he keep it secret all his life? Could he do that? His family was a collection of gentle people. He did remember the tale of his grandfather, who fought in the revolution and dispatched a murderer. The details of that encounter long ago came back to him.

Grandfather John Stewart, as his father Charles told the story, set about to capture John Bacon, who had committed many crimes in the vicinity of the New Jersey coast. Joined by a troop including the brother of the murdered man, Captain Stewart entered a tavern, spied Bacon, and pointed his musket at him, only to have the murderer point and cock his own gun in return. Grandfather dropped his musket, tackled him, and they fought. Even after a bayonet was thrust into him, Bacon revived and, hurling away the table that Stewart used to barricade the door, the criminal attempted to escape, whereupon Stewart shot him dead. How many times, as Joe was growing up, had Father told the story to him and his brothers, who always listened raptly?

CHAPTER THIRTY-EIGHT

There was a detail from the story that took on new meaning for Joe. Prior to Captain John Stewart's part in dispatching Bacon, the Governor of New Jersey had offered a bounty of fifty pounds to whoever captured the criminal. Did John Stewart and his band of men divide up the bounty? Beauregard Wise was also a bounty hunter, and the Fugitive Slave Act legitimized his livelihood. If Wise's death came to light, Joe could be jailed and put in federal prison. He would not be considered the hero his grandfather was. At that thought, Joe grasped the reins so abruptly that the horse faltered, shaking him from his anxious reverie. His passion for abolishing slavery was real and virtuous, but could he face prison and perhaps execution for his act of self-defense if it were discovered? These ruminations occupied him before the horse and wagon drew up at the livery stable on Bleecker Street.

There was a trip to order suiting fabric in Philadelphia that he must take, Joe realized, as he shaved and dressed the next morning. Traveling would postpone his looking into who of Wise's connections might remain in New York. On the other hand, leaving the city would be safer. If Wise had had help in planning his attack, that person could call him a murderer.

When he returned late in the week, a new thought occurred to him. He wasted no time walking to Thomas Jennings's tailor shop. If anyone would know about the presence of slave catchers, it was Mr. Jennings, whose contacts were many and widespread in Manhattan.

Entering the shop on Maiden Lane, Joe admired the handsome topcoat on display near the door, and then he walked toward the back of the shop. He observed the proprietor, who conversed with a salesman, his satchel of notions spread upon the broad oak counter. "Seven spools of your button twist will be all I need this week, Si."

"Are you sure?"

"Yes, indeed, and thank you."

After extracting the thread and setting the spools on the counter, the salesman buckled his bag of wares. "I'll see you next Friday." He tipped his hat and left.

Mr. Jennings, no longer a young man, sat down wearily on a stool and turned to Joe. "What can I do for you, Mr. Stewart? It has been a long time since you and I had dealings."

Joe smiled briefly, stepped closer, and began speaking in almost a whisper. "Mr. Jennings, can you take a moment to talk with me?"

A look of consternation spread over the elderly Jennings's face. He looked behind Joe to see who might be standing nearby. Then, with a nod, he drew Joe behind the tall looking glass in which customers viewed themselves in their new or altered clothes. "What can I do for you?"

"Do you know of slave catchers around here, or in New York City in general?"

Hesitating as he weighed the words of someone reputed to be trustworthy but whom he knew only through the tailoring trade, Mr. Jennings stood up and avoided Joe's gaze. He toyed with the tape measure draped about his neck.

Joe understood his uneasiness. "All I want to know is if there is a place where slave hunters are likely to be found together."

"As far as I know, most of them work alone," Mr. Jennings finally answered. "They can never know how law officers are going to be. Some policemen are behind them, and some are against them when a slave hunter grabs a Negro off the street."

Somewhat reassured by the assessment of a seasoned abolitionist, Joe thanked him, but gave no hint of his reason for asking questions. As he was departing from the shop, Elizabeth Jennings entered, dressed for school teaching with her book bag on her arm.

"Mister Stewart," she said in surprise.

He removed his hat. "Miss Jennings, I hope you are well."

She glanced toward her father to divine from his face some explanation for Joe's visit to their shop. "Yes, I am very well," she replied. As Joe opened the door to leave, she added, "And I hope you and your friend Addie are well."

Addie had never swooned before. Many of the novels that she and Emilie read included the occasional swooning female. Perhaps it was fainting, or perhaps one became so emotionally wrought up that one simply collapsed. In any case, on the Saturday that Joe arrived at their house on Broadway after what had seemed to her an eternity, although it had been only two weeks, Addie felt a lightness in her head. Drawing in her breath, she sank into a chair. Emilie, who went to open the door when he knocked, welcomed their guest and, unaware of her sister's state, called to her to come greet him. When she did not immediately appear, Emilie and Joe entered the front parlor to find her pale and attempting to rise.

"Please don't get up," Joe said, his usual polite self.

Emilie came to her side. "Addie, you are ill. Have you had a chill? You came home with wet feet." Sure that a cup of tea would help, she left to find Ellen.

"Where have you been?" Addie asked, once her initial reaction had passed. He sat down in a chair opposite hers. "Have you been away?"

"Yes, part of the time. It has been a hectic stretch. How have you passed the last two weeks?"

CHAPTER THIRTY-EIGHT

"Sick with worry," she admitted. He was silent. "When I left you that Saturday and took the omnibus home, Beauregard Wise was riding in a seat behind me, and after I got off, and as the horses pulled away, I saw him staring down at me."

"You need not be afraid," he said calmly.

"What do you mean? Of course I'm afraid! But not for myself. You are in danger. I did not know how to reach you." No longer pale, Addie's face filled with color now that she could give vent to the feelings that plagued her.

Joe knew he must reassure her, but he was reluctant immediately to report all that had occurred. "You will never see Wise again," he interrupted her outburst to say.

"What do you mean?" she asked, perplexed.

"He has gone back down south."

Emilie and Ma conversing in the hall and Ellen entering with the tea tray put an end to their conversation. Nevertheless, Joe wanted to explain himself. "Let's go for a walk after tea. The fresh air will do you good," he suggested.

Impatient to hear what he would say, Addie drank her tea quickly. She revived to see him at last and only half listened to Ma's description of Annie's toe infection and Emilie's account of Grandma Ely's recent demise.

Once on Broadway Joe and Addie turned south and walked to the café where in the sunny days of May they enjoyed ice cream. Gone was the awning that had offered welcome shade, but the tables and chairs remained, evidence that the proprietor expected balmy Indian summer days might follow. They sat facing one another at one of the diminutive round tables. Strangers passing by glanced curiously at the couple, oblivious to everything except one another, despite stares and the brisk fall wind ruffling Addie's bonnet ties.

"How shall I begin?" Joe spoke, taking her gloved hands in his. "Not long after you saw Wise, I was due to meet two escaped young men at the docks. Your warning encouraged me to take extra precautions that morning. I kept on the lookout for anything out of the ordinary. I stopped often, and once at the pier listened hard for any unusual sound. The boat came to the mooring." He paused and swallowed.

Addie squeezed his hand. "Yes?" She was transfixed by the unfolding drama.

He continued, "I heard a creak in a plank nearby, the cart horse whinnied, and I slid down from the seat into the shadow of the wagon."

"Oh Joe, what was it?"

"He must have seen me arrive, Wise, that is. He attacked with a knife, missed on the first lunge, then, when he came at me a second time, I caught his right wrist, of the hand holding the blade. He pushed me down, and as we fell, he landed on the blade…and died."

"He is *dead*?" Addie uttered in amazement, aghast. For the second time that afternoon, she turned white. "What did you do then?"

"I know this is all a shock to you as it was to me. At first I was numb. The other conductor, on the skiff, took charge, and with the help of the two Negroes we put the huge body on the boat."

"What will become of Wise's body?"

"I don't know. The past two weeks since have not been easy."

Addie stared in awed silence and finally spoke. "Joe, I am as much that man's killer as you."

"Nonsense."

"Yes, if I had not gone to find you, I'd never have led that man to your boarding house. He would never have trailed you to the docks." Her mind raced with a fever of questions. "Will the authorities look for him?"

"That troubles me. But, Addie, the Underground Railroad and the slave hunters are locked in a kind of war, just beneath the surface here and in many other places north and south. I hated to think saving Negroes could result in violence, but now I know firsthand that it can."

"How can it end?" Addie's voice contained a despair that Joe had known his story would inspire. "I love you, Joe, and I cannot allow you to risk more of the dangers you have met and might meet again rescuing Negroes."

"I love you," he replied. "I always have, ever since the first time I saw you long ago, when your father brought you and Emilie to see us in Cream Ridge."

"Wasn't it pity you felt? There we were, orphans, and Father, full of sadness, not knowing what to do with us."

"No, I saw how you took to all of us, going out to ride Retta's pony, curls flying, and smiling enough to lift anyone's spirits. As for your coming to find me, if you hadn't, I would very likely be dead. Your warning set me listening and watching in a way I had not done before."

A flock of pigeons alit near the café where, in the warm months, they would have found crumbs. They pecked about fruitlessly and upon some unseen signal suddenly took flight. The increasingly chilly fall wind penetrated the intimate walls of their conversation. Saying no more, Joe pulled Addie to her feet, stepped around the table, and took her in his arms. They walked arm and arm for a long time in the diminishing afternoon light.

CHAPTER THIRTY-NINE

The gnawing, specific fear that had caused Addie's inability to concentrate over recent weeks was gone, but in its place a vague anxiety for Joe remained, tempered by knowing he loved her as she loved him. If he continued to live a life complicated by midnight trysts with skiffs and secret messages, how could they ever enjoy a settled life? She often recalled the circumstances of his deadly encounter. The tasks of home and school soothed her to some extent. What she now knew split her off from the simple occupations and interests of her sisters, even her older sister Emilie.

"What can that Cyrus Lawrence be doing that we never see him?" Emilie lamented, leaning over the dining table where she cut a width of linen cloth, carefully snipping the crisp fabric with which she planned to make a handkerchief.

Passing by en route to the piano to practice the Bach, Addie paused, recalling the handsome younger of the two Lawrence brothers. "Have you set your bonnet for him?"

Emilie stood up and tossed off her direct reply, "I wouldn't dare until he shows more interest in me."

"But you do fancy him, I suspect."

"Yes, we got on very well at Thomas's and Mary's wedding. And you, Addie?"

"What about me?"

"I mean, whom do you fancy?" Emilie returned to her careful incision of the cloth.

"If he ever were to settle, Joe would be my choice."

"What is to stop him? Horse racing? Selling for A. T. Stewart? Men settle down eventually."

"Some do, but do you think that is the rule?"

"I suppose not."

Annie entered and climbed onto a chair to see what Emilie was doing. When she heard the strains of the intricate, melancholy baroque melody on the piano, she hopped down and hurried to join her sister on the piano bench. Addie ignored her while slowly penciling in a better fingering on the page of music. When she had played the improved fingering with her right hand and still had not acknowledged Annie's presence, the little sister played several random notes in the bass. Addie turned finally to look into her face. "What is it, Annie?"

"Please play 'Ashgrove' for me, Addie, please?"

Called back from her careful attention to Bach, Addie replied, "Annie dear, I must finish practicing this piece, and then I will play you anything you like." Her three-year-old half-sister nodded solemnly, and, disappointed, she jumped down from the bench and returned to her mother's side in the front parlor.

Ma must have mentioned the episode to Father and attached significance to Addie's not setting Annie in her lap right away as she had usually done. Later that evening, he found his reserved second daughter gazing into the coal fire glowing in the grate, her hands resting in her lap and her sewing basket nowhere in sight.

"Addie, Ma tells me you were annoyed with your little sister." Seated across the room, he held a volume open before him, *The Lamplighter*, which he had been meaning to finish.

"That is not the case at all. I...I have been trying to learn the Bach. I put Annie off for only a few minutes."

"I understand. A tot takes time and patience. I do hope you continue to give her the kind attention that has always been your habit. Is there anything, or anyone new in your life? I fear I am too involved in the factory and the telegraph company these days."

Addie, again drawn to stare into the fire's mellow glow, asked, without looking up, "How did you and my mother meet?"

His eyes shifted to the observe fire's coals. "We were very young, and enjoyed dancing, and in the small village of South Salem it was not long before we knew we wanted to marry. She, like you and Emilie, had lovely dark eyes."

"Did you love her?" She did not want to open the wounds that mention of her mother's death might cause, but never having dared ask before, she wanted to know about their love, perhaps because she had declared hers to another.

He closed *The Lamplighter* and laid it on the table next to his wing chair. "Yes, I loved her very much, and I love her still. I am grateful that in time, and by God's grace, your stepmother came into my...our life. A heart can heal."

Addie listened to each of his words, and was grateful for the answer to the question she had longed to ask. When he finished, she turned and smiled, glad for the opportunity to contemplate his past, of which he spoke only rarely.

CHAPTER THIRTY-NINE

"Now Addie, I have been thinking for some time of asking you and Emilie for your help."

"Help? What can we do?"

"There are five of my journeymen who have little daughters. If I buy each of them a doll, will you make clothes for them?"

Addie was surprised at his request but nonetheless responded immediately, intrigued by the project and moved by her father's generosity. "Are the dolls to be Christmas gifts?"

"Yes, would there be time to complete them?"

"Of course, unless you expect each doll to have a vast wardrobe."

Charles Stewart always seemed to arrive in time for tea. He knew that Tilda and Ellen, overseen by Ma, put on an excellent spread. Besides good bread and butter and hot tea, he could expect Tilda's sponge cake, cheese from the farm in South Salem, and perhaps an apple or peach tart, depending on the time of year. The late afternoon sun glinted on Ma's sterling tea service and a host of fine china teacups and saucers.

Seated by the fire were the printer's daughters, a lovely sight to behold and another attraction for Richard March Hoe's old friend. Since it was a Saturday afternoon, Mr. Stewart happened to find the press builder at home, making plans for his farm at Hunt's Point and studying a set of architectural designs.

"Good afternoon, Richard," he said upon being announced and entering the family circle.

"Charles, a most pleasant surprise! And you're just in time for tea."

"Do sit down," Ma encouraged him, and together they pulled a comfortable chair near the assembled group, which included Emilie, Addie, Annie, baby Mary, and their parents.

"A bitter cold November day, Charles, is it not? I walked to the Bowery earlier and wished I had dressed for winter," Father remarked.

"What are those drawings?" Charles was always curious to learn what new enterprises or inventions Richard might have in mind.

"Come and see." He rose and displayed what he had been studying. Father described to him plans for developing the old farm he had recently bought north of the city near the Bronx River. "The farmhouse needs renovating, but once that is done we can live in it while a more sufficient home is built on the property."

"An estate, perhaps, like Tony and Ann Reybold's estate in Delaware City?"

"Something like that, perhaps, with stables for horses, and I envision a dairy with prime stock. I've always fancied Jerseys. Does Tony have livestock?"

"Indeed he does, but only enough to serve him and his family. Incidentally, did you hear that he and one of his brothers were asked to identify the body of a man that washed up near the Reybold wharf?"

Addie froze from assiduously sewing a tiny skirt for a doll and listened intently for what Mr. Stewart might say next.

"No, that sort of news is commonplace at the harbor in New York, I fear," Mr. Hoe remarked off-handedly, as he eyed the detailed drawings before him.

"The body was extremely bloated, Tony said, as though it had been in the water for some time. It was a horrible sight, made more terrible since the man was very fat to begin with."

"Was he white or black? A poor escaped Negro perhaps?"

"No, a white man, middle-aged."

"How did he meet his death?" Ma asked. "Could they tell?"

"Not drowning. The authorities suspected stabbing, and they are waiting for reports of such a man coming up missing. Tony said the corpse reminded him of a fellow who came uninvited to a party in the summer. Do you girls remember him?" He turned to the sisters seated on the sofa.

Addie gulped and swallowed. Before she could answer, Emilie blurted, "Why, Addie danced with a fat man, didn't you?"

Before she could even nod, Father interrupted the ghoulish, unsettling conversation. "Come look at these property lines, Charles. Do you think they are clear? Shouldn't I hire a new survey?"

For several weeks there were no meetings at the dock. When he visited Elihu Pierce at the Blue Anchor, Joe spoke briefly about his plan to abandon his missions for a while. He reported that Wise's body had washed up on the Delaware shore. The Quaker only nodded. Both men knew the outcome of future rescues of slaves depended on utter discretion at every juncture. Word had come to Elihu from other conductors farther south on the Underground Railway that the dead rogue had operated alone. Wise's brash arrival at the Reybolds' party and his invading the church service were evidence of his wanton nerviness and revealed he resorted to anything to attain his mercenary ends.

"I understand your uneasiness and sense of guilt. But, Joe, you acted in self-defense. I am your witness if anyone should point a finger at you. Always remember that."

The two men shook hands. Joe left the tavern somewhat reassured, but he knew if he were ever to be discovered as an abolitionist responsible for Wise's

CHAPTER THIRTY-NINE

death, his future happiness with Addie would never be possible. He had to hope that time and a greater justice would be on his side.

In the months that followed, Addie would wait for news that the body was linked to the name of Beauregard Wise, but it never came. She wondered if Mr. Stewart knew the truth of the matter and was only trying to learn what the Hoes knew of Joe's part in Wise's death. If Father was aware of what Joe did on Sundays and how he traveled to South Salem, he did not say.

Addie learned the Bach prelude and as she put the treble and bass together, she became aware of a harmony that underlay the contrapuntal parts much like her connection with Joe. She feared less and trusted more that his life was his and that she would love him for who he was no matter where his devotion to others led him. Her part, sewing a gift for small children, wove a quiet beauty into the lives of people her father respected and who were less fortunate than she and her family were. Wherever the cadence of Joe's and her lives led, she would weave her strain of their two voices as best she could into one of a resonant truth and wholesome love.

THE 1854 DIARY OF ADELINE ELIZABETH HOE

Adeline Elizabeth Hoe, in "sausage curls." *(© Peter E. Randall.)*

FOREWORD TO THE DIARY

Adeline Elizabeth Hoe was seventeen when she began her diary in May of 1854. That summer she would travel from New York City to Setauket, a lovely village on Long Island Sound. She then spent a couple of weeks traveling to the homes of friends in New Jersey and Delaware. For six weeks, she stayed with her birth mother's family in South Salem, New York, a provincial nineteenth-century town in Westchester County where nearly everyone seemed to be related to her as cousin or uncle or grandparent. She visited her aunts' homes in Cream Ridge, New Jersey, and in Brooklyn. She began and ended her writing within her father's center of operations, the Hoe family home on Broadway in Manhattan, near the R. Hoe & Company offices and printing press factory on Broome Street.

Beyond those facts and the everyday recounting of the muslins she sewed and ironed, and the comings and goings of her family, Addie's inner life is almost too subtle to fathom. She had constant dealings with her young cousins, around her age. She visited frequently with girls who must have been classmates. The trajectory of her life later, after she married DeWitt Clinton Lawrence in 1857, is hard to imagine when she was a teenager. There is evidence from an examination of the historical period that suggests that, at almost eighteen, she entered the "marriageable age" that would have her expecting to find a suitable partner for her social class in the three years before age twenty-one.

What was her social station? By 1854, Adeline's father Richard March Hoe had become very successful in the manufacture of printing presses. In 1847 he had invented and patented the "Lightning Printing Press," and by 1851 his type-revolving cylinder press was turning out 20,000 pages per hour of the *New York Sun* newspaper. The *Baltimore Sun*, *Philadelphia Ledger*, and *New York Times* were other early purchasers of Hoe's printing press. The fame of his machine caused an international revolution in the growth of the newspapers and book publishing, which went hand in hand with the developments in the paper industry. Thus Addie lived within the household of a well-to-do man of industrial success, which allowed her the freedom to travel and meet a wide swath of society at that time.

Paralleling his dedication to his business, R. M. Hoe was a devoted family man with two older daughters; Emilie, born in 1834, and Adeline, born in 1836; by his first wife, Lucy Gilbert of South Salem, New York, who died in 1841. In 1843, he remarried Mary Say Corbin of Philadelphia, whose father was a physician with roots in Virginia. With his second wife, just nineteen years older than Adeline, Hoe fathered four more daughters: Annie, born in 1852, Mary, born in 1854, and Fannie and Helen, who were both born after the time of the diary. His two younger brothers, Robert and Peter, who also ran the printing press company, had growing families and lived nearby; they all shared a carriage. Richard March Hoe was well-respected in his work and in the city, and he began a school for the apprentices in his shop. His elder daughters attended a school on Broadway and studied piano. The family employed servants, a common custom in those days. The girls' contemporaries, cousins and other associates of Addie's father, came and went to play billiards and enjoy music and conversation. Theirs was a middle class upbringing by the standards of the day. They did not attend college. Their expectations, one might conclude, were for marriage and keeping a home. If they desired college learning, Adeline does not express it. While they sewed, they read aloud to one another the novels of Charles Dickens, Elizabeth Missing Sewell, and James Fennimore Cooper, as well as periodicals of the day.

What mattered to Adeline? She loved music and dancing, played the piano, and enjoyed attending concerts with friends and cousins. There was a particular young man who appears a great deal in the diary. He was Joe Stewart, a friend of the family, approximately six years older than Addie. He entered the house on Broadway frequently and seems to have been a clerk in one of the local stores. He and Adeline enjoyed ice cream together. He produced a sketch and sent it to her when she was away in South Salem. Research tells us that he was the youngest son of Charles Stewart of Cream Ridge, New Jersey, whose family figured often in the diary, and that Joe was a clerk living unmarried in a boarding house in Philadelphia by 1870.

Another young man frequently mentioned is Henry Seymour, Adeline's first cousin and the son of her father's older sister Mary, who married Reverend Ebenezer Seymour, a Presbyterian minister and school principal. Henry accompanied her to various functions and was someone in whom she confided.

The diary and annotation divides naturally into six sections, or chapters, coinciding with the trips that Addie and her sister took over the course of the six months during which she wrote her journal. Her home at 309 Broadway, now the location of several law firms, was the starting point of the journeys upon which she embarked. Already by 1854, the growth of businesses and other public edifices in Manhattan was beginning to edge out the single-family brownstone and frame structures. There was residential movement north. For a limited time, Addie could easily enjoy the downtown features of shops and places of entertainment and cultural life.

There are several ways in which Adeline expresses herself that might perplex the reader. For instance, ice cream was a novelty, a new commercial product sold on the streets of New York in 1854. Just as we might capitalize M&M's, she will elevate the treat Ice Cream by capitalizing it. Although Noah Webster had presented his dictionary in 1828, there are proper names that Adeline, generally a careful writer, misspells, such as "Niagra" and "Deleware." We have retained her old-fashioned spellings of certain words, such as "staid" for "stayed," but we have used "Miss" throughout rather than "Mifs," which she occasionally employed.

In the course of studying her reflections and experiences, my husband and I marveled at Addie's spirit and calm self-possession amid what seems to us in our century a life which, despite the family's relative affluence and freedom of movement, was circumscribed by social obligation and fraught with illness.

May who she was shine through our transcription of her feathery handwriting and the notes we wrote illuminating her prose.

—Helen Taylor Davidson
Plainfield, New Hampshire
March 13, 2012

29.100.1344 View, New York, Looking South from Union Square, 1849. *(Courtesy of the Museum of the City of New York, Print Collection.)*

I

NEW YORK CITY
LATE MAY TO MID-JUNE

Friday May 26th, 1854 New York

I have just arrived at the conclusion that it would be quite an agreeable amusement to keep a journal, and with a little urging from Robby[1] and Theodore[2] have made up my mind to try it, at least for a week or more. I came downstairs about half past six and dusted the dining room and library, and fed Annie's[3] bird. I then practised [*sic*] one half an hour. We then breakfasted. Henry[4] had a chill in the night + a fever immediately afterwards, of course he feels very miserably. Theodore feels very weak, though he is improving. Emilie[5] and I went out to make calls today. We found only Anna Howell, Mary Miller, and Sarah Condit at home.[6] This afternoon there was an A/annular eclipse of the Sun. Emmie Ely[7] came unexpectedly to stay all night.

Father has had five gentlemen here playing billiards[8] and taking tea with him. Uncle Robert and Aunt Thirza[9] came from Salem today, this [thus?] house is in such confusion that they will sleep here tonight. Aunt Thirza says grandpa's[10] hand is very bad and the doctor thinks he will be obliged to extract the bone to the second joint, he has not been able to leave his room for five weeks, and Grandma has sprained her ankle.

Emilie intends going up tomorrow to try and cheer them up a little and I hope she will succeed. I intended writing a letter to Eddie Seymour[11] but feel too much fatigued.

N.Y. Saturday May 27th

Emilie brought Mary[12] into our room this morning before we were dressed. I was very much astonished to see her looking as she did; one side of her face was entirely red, and the other covered with large red blotches, they also extended over every portion of her body. Ma was up all night with her, and the dear little thing seems to be in great pain. Her arm looks very red in fact more of a crimson hue. The docter [*sic*] has not been here yet so that we cannot tell what is the cause of the terrible eruption, Ma is very much afraid there is something very wrong in the vaccination. Emmie Ely started to go home about an hour ago. Henry started for the office at the same time, he expects to go to Bloomfield[13] this afternoon. Emilie is quite undecided about whether to go to Salem or not. I want her to go for her own sake and Grandma's, but I shall be very lonesome without her. Theodore will be here however and he will enliven me some (I hope). It has been a very dull morning but I hope the afternoon will prove more agreeable to us all. Emmie talks a little of going to Niagra[14] [*sic*] with us, and I only hope nothing will prevent our taking that delightful trip. Emilie has a very bad sore throat and has concluded not to go to Salem. Theodore came in while we were at dinner radiant with joy, saying that he was going to Salem. I hope he will enjoy it as much as he anticipates. Joe Stewart[15] is going home this afternoon, and we shall be all alone tomorrow. The doctor came this afternoon and pronounced Mary's complaint the measles. Mrs. Bailey[16] has been here all day, but she went home tonight. I have been holding Mary a long time since dinner.

N.Y. Sunday May 28th

Ellen[17] brought Annie into our room this morning before we were awake, for us to keep her while she got the water for her bath. Annie seemed very cross, but we consoled her by showing her pictures. Mary seems much better this morning and I hope will continue to improve. I hope Annie will not have the measles very badly, if she does take them, and we feel almost sure she will. Emilie went to All Saints this morning and I staid home to take care of the baby. We went out and took a ride before dinner, as far as the Battery, Father, Ma, Annie and I. We enjoyed it very much, and when we returned we found Sereno[18] here. He staid to dinner and went to church with me at Dr Tyng's.[19]

N.Y. Monday May 29th 1854

We came downstairs about six o'clock and swept and dusted the parlor and dining room. Ma and I went out and did some shopping as we expect Mary Robbins[20] tomorrow. I have been sewing some and holding Mary the greater part of the afternoon. Joe Stewart came here this evening and is now playing billiards with Father. He said the girls sent a great deal of love, and could hardly wait for July to come.[21] Nothing has occurred of importance today. Henry did not come in, and therefore I suppose he has had another chill. I expect to awake and find it raining tomorrow.

N.Y. Tuesday May 30th 1854

My anticipations were realized about the weather, as it was raining hard when I awoke. Mary and Margaret[22] came this morning and have been sewing hard all day, they have finished my dresses, and are coming on Thursday to make Emilie's. Lizzie Angell[23] came unexpectedly to spend the day and stay all night with us. I went to school today to paint and had quite a pleasant time. Ma has been very unwell indeed, her lungs feel very much inflamed and the baby has been very fretful. Joe Stewart came in a little while ago. Father has not been home since breakfast as there is a meeting of the Telegraphic Company at the Irving House;[24] and Joe has gone after him for Ma wants to see him very badly. Richmond[25] came in about a half an hour ago and says that Eleanor[26] will be here tomorrow if possible. I received a letter from Henry, he has had another chill but hopes to be in the city on Thursday.

N.Y. Wednesday May 31st

Emilie had very hard work to arouse me this morning, I was so very sleepy. I went downstairs and swept and dusted the library and busied myself about the kitchen and dining room. Ma felt a little better this morning and will I hope continue to improve. Aunt Emmeline came over today and invited Emilie to go over and stay all night; and she concluded to go after dinner. Emilie had only been gone a few minutes when Eleanor came in. I was delighted to see her, she staid until six o'clock, and Lizzie went a short time after. I wish they both could have stayed all night. Lizzie has been reading to me a long while today and I enjoyed it very much indeed. Mr. Swain[27] came in a few moments ago and they are going up to play billiards. We received a letter from Thomas[28] which quite raised my spirits, as he said they should expect us there as soon as we could come. Joe Stewart has been here tonight but went away as soon as Mr. Swain came.

N.Y. Thursday June 1st

I arose very early this morning and dusted as usual. Mr. Swain came downstairs about eight o'clock, but we did not breakfast until nine so that Emilie returned from Brooklyn just after we had finished. Mary Robbins came and finished Emilie's dresses. Eleanor came up to find out where Miss Clark[29] lived and as I was going to school I walked down with her. When I came home I found Ma and Father talking about going to Niagra [sic] with us. I do hope they can go. About six o'clock Edward Seymour came and invited me to go to Jullien[30] and I was very happy to accept the invitation. We enjoyed the music exceedingly. It was twelve o'clock when I retired.

N.Y. Friday June 2nd

This morning I swept and dusted our room before breakfast. We then shook and sunned our winter dresses and put them up. We also took down the curtains and folded them and put them up. I have sewed very little today. Uncle Robert has received word from Salem that cousin Elizabeth[31] is worse and they are going up tomorrow morning. Uncle Peter and Aunt Hannah[32] came up while we were at tea and Richmond and Joe a short time after them. Father went to look for a wet nurse for Mary today and I believe has found one.

N.Y. Saturday June 3rd

I ironed some muslin this morning before and after breakfast. The wet nurse came, and Ma likes her appearance very much. Ma, Emilie Annie and Ellen road [sic] over to Williamsburgh to see Ellen's baby,[33] they seem to be very much impressed with the filth and nakedness of the children, Ma said they reminded her of "wild Indians." I remained at home and took charge of Mary, but as she slept most of the time, I had a very fine opportunity to sew which I improved. I took a bath after dinner and was just finished arranging my hair, when Annie Westervelt[34] called. It was the first time she has been here since November. After she had been gone a short time Miss Clark, Nellie, and Sarah Kenny called with little Lizzie Miller,[35] Annie had gone to the Park so they waited until she returned. Mary Richards[36] is to be married on

Thursday notwithstanding her ill health and I suppose all things considered it is the wisest plan. Uncle Robert and Aunt Thirza went to Salem this morning and Robert and Arthur[37] are here now. Joe came in and asked us to go and get some Ice Cream[38] and I think we will accept the invitation. We enjoyed the Ice Cream very much.

N.Y. Sunday June 4th

The first Sunday in the month and a delightful day. We went over to our church this morning, just as we were starting Uncle Peter, Aunt Hannah, Stephy and Charley[39] drove up. Stephy looks miserably. We saw Eleanor this morning, she looked beautiful. Joe came in while we were at dinner and he and father went out and took a walk. I went to Dr. Tyng's but found him closed, I suppose in consequence of the long service this morning.

N.Y. Monday June 5th

We went out early this morning to do some shopping and make some calls, we did not get back until 3:00 o'clock. We did a great deal of shopping, but only made two calls. We did not find the Apgars[40] at home, but we saw Mrs. Ely and Sophia. We have been very busy making Annie a black silk travelling sack, this afternoon. The baby's nurse Mary has come and I am very glad, she appears to be a very nice person. I intend writing a letter to Retta Stewart[41] this evening. I have written a letter to Mary Seymour also.

N.Y. Tuesday June 6th

Emilie and I began putting the books and ornaments away for the summer, we packed them in trunks up in the garret. It was quite hard work and we wrapped the stair rods up separately in the first flight. After dinner we went out riding with Ma, she bought one dress. We went in Uncle Robert's after we returned, they are progressing quite rapidly with the painting. Uncle Robert, Aunt Thirza and Theodore returned from Salem this morning. Joe came just before tea, he intended to have gone over to Mr. Bowens[42] but he was so long in starting that he concluded it was too late, and we all arranged to go there Thursday and he and father concluded the evening at the billiard table, as usual. Albert Angel and Nicholas Bowen came in about nine o'clock, they had been up to see Lizzie but had not found her at home. Emilie was just ready to retire to her couch for the night and I was obliged to entertain them and I fear I did not succeed at all.

N.Y. Wednesday June 7th

I came downstairs early and busied myself about the house, after breakfast we finished putting away the stair rods and the drapes from all parts of the house. We then collected the table cloths and napkins and Ma cleaned out the wardrobe. Peter[43] took down the shades and cornices and we dusted and wrapped them up carefully. Mary Dunn[44] went out to see her baby and seemed to be quite troubled about it. Joe Stewart brought a young friend of his to play billiards. Henry went to the Young Men's Christian Association,[45] but returned quite early. We intended to have made calls today but the weather has been so unpleasant (although it did not begin to rain until nearly dark) that we were obliged to remain at home.

N.Y. Thursday June 8th

A.M. The weather still continues unpleasant and I believe that it rained all night. We busied ourselves about the house until one o'clock and as it cleared off we went out and made the remainder of our calls. We went to Lydia Seabury's[46] first then up to Mary Marsh's then to see Virginia White, we did not get home until four. We then ate some dinner and went over to take tea and spend the evening with Eleanor. Henry and Joe came after us, it lightened quite vividly before we started but we thought it was only heat lightning, but it proved differently and before we were to the Bowery it began to rain. Henry had an umbrella and Emilie and I took it and they got wet. Just before we got into the cars it began to pour and it continued to rain until a little while after we reached home. We got our feet very wet but I believe nothing else. A trunk was in the hall, and upon inquiry we found Aunt Theo and Miss Peck[47] were here, they expect to go to Greenwich on Saturday, Aunt is not at all benefitted by going to Rochester.[48]

N.Y. Friday, June 9th

We breakfasted quite early, as Ma had arranged to send the carriage for Mr. Eigenbrodt[49] at nine o'clock for him to come to the house and baptize Mary. The dear little baby was very good and laughed instead of crying. Mr. Eigenbrodt intends sailing for Europe tomorrow. I hope it will improve his health. Eleanor was up here and after Mr. Eigenbrodt left, we went out with her. We walked down to the Limherr[50] where Emily had a breastpin made of her own hair for Miss Clarke, we then took a stage and rode down to Barclay St. to Joe Stewart's[51] store where we wished to purchase some parasols, but after taking all that trouble they told us he was not in, so we took a stage to Canal St., but Eleanor went up in an East Broadway stage. We then walked to Miller's[52] and from there home. Ma had been out with Miss Peck and Aunt Theodosia. Aunt Theo was very tired. Emily went to see Miss Clarke and take her the breastpin. Aunts Emmeline and Rachel came over to dinner; while we were dining the men from Roux[53] came to take the parlor furniture. I washed some muslins before tea. Joe came and said that he was in the store all the time. It was very provoking. Richmond came in the evening and he and Henry took us to get some Ice Cream.

New York Saturday, June 10th

I arose at 5 ½ o'clock and came down to see that breakfast was ready for Aunt Theo and Miss Peck, who went to Greenwich this morning. We have been very busy putting away tables, divans, bed-clothes+ so forth. Anna Bowen[54] came up and stayed to dinner. Henry, Joe and Father went up in the billiard-room, we had been in bed about a half an hour when I heard Annie cry very badly, we went in and found her suffering from colic. Father came down and took her, she cried for a long time and when she stopped Mary began.

New York Sunday, June 11th

We did not get downstairs until pretty late, and Father did not come down until after eleven. We did not go to church this morning, but Henry and Joe went with us to Dr. Seabury's[55] this afternoon. Ellen went over to see her little boy, and Father and all of us have been singing since tea.

New York Monday, June 12th[56]

We arose early and went to work as usual, by putting the articles away in the house. Mr. Dupuy and six or seven of his men came and went to work in the third story. They began by taking all the doors down. Mr. D'Orsay came this morning also to paint the billiard-room and there was quite a sufficiency of men about the house. Ma and Father started for Philadelphia at one o'clock, they expect to return on Wednesday morning. Mr. Berrion [Benion?][57] and some more men from the factory took some of the carpets and shook them this morning. Mr. Berrion and Anne Johnson's husband staid and took down our bed-stead and took it and several bureaus upstairs in the attic. About six o'clock we changed our dresses and Emilie went out to get a pair of shoes. I was very much astonished and pleased to find Emmie Ely here, upon going down into the parlor. She came to stay all night with us. Henry came in, in a little while, and we had tea. While we were eating, Joe came in. He and Henry intended to go out and get us some Ice Cream as we were too tired to go ourselves, but before they started Theodore came in and just as they were going Robby appeared. I got the saucers all ready, but before they came, Arthur came, then Richmond and last of all Sereno. Theodore was either afraid there would be a scarcity or that he was one too many so he went home just as Henry and Joe appeared. We sent some in to him and Aunt Thirza. Emilie amused the gentlemen by giving them a piece of tape to write the names of the keys on. I was very tired and entertained them by lying on the sofa and going to sleep. Before we came to bed we counted the silver and put it in a box for Henry to take downtown with him. The men had taken and we were obliged to make use of a taper to undress ourselves by, but it answered the purpose exceedingly well. We were all very tired and I believe slept soundly.

New York Tuesday, June 13th

We breakfasted about seven o'clock, and as Miller had neglected to send my shoes on Saturday I concluded to go after them, so I rode down in the stage with Henry and Emmie and left them at Canal St. In my hurry I came away with her parasol which I had been holding in my hand. When I came home I found Mr. Berrion here moving the furniture and taking up carpets. We have been very busy as usual. The house looks like distress. It is not at all pleasant and I am very much afraid that it will rain tomorrow. We shall both be very much disappointed if it does, as it was our intention to go to Maria Seabury's on that day and all our arrangements are made accordingly. I believe Emilie and I have at last finished putting away the furniture. The dining-room is entirely deserted, and last night we were obliged to bring chairs in from the kitchen. Joe came as usual after tea and Eleanor and Nicholas, we brought them up into our room where we have spent a very pleasant evening. We want Eleanor to go to Jersey with us, but I believe she considers it an impossibility.

II

Stony Brook, Long Island
June 14–June 21

New York Wednesday, June 14th

A.M. When I first awoke this morning I found it very pleasant, but now it is only half past six and the sky is covered with clouds.

Stony Brook. We started from home about nine o'clock and arrived here at three o'clock. We found Maria and her father[1] at the depot waiting for us. The sun was warm and it was quite dusty but we enjoyed the ride very much. After tea we went out to take a walk. Maria took us through a kind of woods and over a bridge and into all sorts of places. When we were returning we met Mr. Mount,[2] he resides here but we had not seen him before. When we returned home I played some on the piano and then we retired. There was quite a heavy thunder shower.

Stony Brook Thursday, June 15th

Arose at six o'clock and breakfasted at seven. After breakfast I wrote a letter to Ma and then sewed and played. A friend of Maria's Miss Nunns[3] came to spend the day and night. She lives about three miles from here at a place called Setauket, her father is the piano maker. After dinner Mrs. Wells, Maria's sister,[4] came up, we spent a very pleasant afternoon. Mr. Mount painted a beautiful white lily this morning. Before sunset we went down to the beach, there is a beautiful view of the Sound and the surrounding country, from a hill near the harbor. On returning home we found Miss Mount[5] here she is a very pleasant girl. I have enjoyed the day very much.

Stony Brook Friday, June 16th

This morning we went out and took a ride to the water. We also sewed in the morning and in the afternoon we went to see Mr. Nunns. Maria, Julia, Sarah Nunns, Mr. Mount, the two Mr. Seaburys, Emilie and myself.[6] Some impertinent person had taken Mr. Seabury's wagon away, and we went in one without springs, the distance is about three miles and we got a very pleasant shaking up. When we had been there a few moments Mr. and Mrs. Groesbeck and the Misses Morand[7] came, they are very quiet indeed and hardly spoke a word. Miss Ellen Nunns[8] is a very pleasant lady and plays finely on the piano. Ma Mount[9] played the violin for us to dance after tea and I enjoyed it very much indeed. After enjoying ourselves very much we came home and enjoyed a night's rest.

The Mount House by William Sydney Mount, 1854. *(Courtesy of the Long Island Museum of American Art, History & Carriages. Bequest of Ward Melville, 1977.)*

Stony Brook June 17th Saturday

We sewed some time after breakfast and then went over to Mr. Mount's studio. He is just finishing a picture of Daniel Webster, which I should think was a very correct portrait. We looked at some engravings and then we all started to go to a field a short distance from the house, where is a gravestone of a slave of Maria's great-grandmother.[10] It is made of brown stone with a violin carved upon it and an appropriate epitaph to signify that the negro in whose honor it was erected was a distinguished figure. It was nearly dinner-time when we returned. At four o'clock Mrs. Seabury, the two children, Mr. Mount, Mr. Edward Seabury,[11] Maria, Emilie and I went out to make two or three calls. We first went to Mr. Hamilton's[12] where we had a very pleasant call. Mrs. Hamilton is a remarkably intelligent person and a perfect lady. We then called at Mr. Groesbeck's which is the place adjoining Mr. Hamilton's. The place is delightfully situated with a beautiful view of the Sound, a fine lawn extends nearly to the beach. Mr. and Mrs. Groesbeck and the two Misses Morand were very pleasant and we enjoyed our visit very much. We called at a Mr. Dominick's but did not find his lady at home. I noticed a very curious weather vane on a house not far from here, it is a small steamboat with wheels, engine and flags and when the wind blew the wheels turned with great rapidity and the engine worked beautiful.[13] We took tea as soon as we returned and as I did not feel quite well I retired.

Stony Brook Sunday June 18th 1854

I felt quite refreshed this morning when I arose. We went to church, but the minister has gone away to recruit himself and a gentleman read the service and a sermon. After dinner we went out to take a walk, we took books with us and sat in the woods and read. Nothing has occurred of importance. It was quite cool when we came here, but I think the weather is gradually getting warmer and I am very glad it is.

The Bone Player by William Sydney Mount, 1856. *(Courtesy of the Museum of Fine Arts, Boston, © 2012.)*

Stony Brook Monday June 19th

Maria woke us up quite early to take a walk and I believe we went about two miles before breakfast. I should suppose we walk enough here to satisfy Ma. We sewed and read after breakfasting and Maria and I played a duett [sic] on the piano. We intended going to call on Carrie Strong[14] this afternoon, but Mrs. Seabury said we had better have an early tea at five o'clock and go at that time, but we were just going to start, when it began to sprinkle and we decided not to go, so we went out to walk with Miss Mount going with us. We walked down to the shore and on returning we heard some music and stopping to listen we discovered the performers were in a boat sailing on a pretty pond. Maria proposed getting in so we all stepped in and had a very pleasant sail with some very good music on two violins a bass viol and bones and excellent singing. They were relations of Maria's. The music sounded delightfully on the water and we enjoyed it exceedingly. Maria has a very sore toe, the day before we came she let a beam or post belonging to a bedstead fall upon it and she has been continually hitting against something, so that I have no doubt that the nail will come off as it has festered under it.

Stony Brook June 20th Tuesday

We arose about the usual time, after breakfast as we sat sewing Ellen and Sarah Nunns, Mrs. Walker and her little boy,[15] came to spend the day. In the evening Mr. and Mrs. John Nunns, the two Misses Mount[16] and brother came and spent the evening. We enjoyed it very much.

New York June 21st Wednesday

Maria intended waking us up very early to hear the birds sing once before we went away, but she did not wake early enough. After breakfast we talked and read until it was time for us to start. Edward drove us and Maria and Thomas Seabury rode over for company. Mr. Mount came down with us on some business. We enjoyed the ride very much indeed, but it would have been still more pleasant but for the dreary anticipation of coming home and finding the house in such a very disagreeable condition. About twelve o'clock, we bid farewell to our friends. When we were within twenty miles of Brooklyn, the cars were suddenly stopped. The passengers started out to see what was the matter and discovered that a cow had been run over and had thrown the locomotive off the track, we were obliged to wait about half an hour while they were replacing it. Mr. Mount left the seat in front of us for a moment and it was immediately taken by two Irishmen who had been drinking and it was anything but agreeable to have them so near us. Henry came in the cars before we reached the tunnel. He looked very pale and I knew in a moment that he had been shaking again. Mr. Mount saw us in a carriage and then said good bye. After reaching home we took a kind of lunch and lounged about until father came. In the evening Mr. O'Donal and Richmond[17] came but they did not stay an hour as we were very tired. We were very glad to be able to go to bed early. Henry wrote us a long letter and sent it yesterday. I was very sorry we did [not] receive it while we were at Stony Brook.

III

Cream Ridge, NJ, to Philadelphia and Delaware City June 22–July 12[1]

Thursday June 22nd New York

This morning when I awoke it was very cloudy, and about nine o'clock it began to rain. The country needs rain very much, it is so very dry and dusty. I went up to see the billiard-room it is almost finished and looks beautifully. I am sure Ma cannot help admiring it. We have been trying to keep busy today in order not to feel lonely. Emilie has been sewing very fast and I have been washing some collars and undersleeves for both of us. The bell rang about four this afternoon and Bridget said there was a young gentleman downstairs, who wished to see us. I went down and found Mr. Mount[2] there. We were very much delighted to see him, we took him through the house and he admired the style of it very much, also the painting of the billiard-room. I believe they expect to finish it to-morrow. It has continued to rain all day. Aunt Thirza and Cousin Laura came in for a moment, she sent us some Ice Cream which she had been making it tasted very nicely. Joe came in the evening as usual but he went away early and we retired.

Friday June 23rd New York

I arose about six o'clock this morning and found it still drizzling. We managed to keep busy all day by mending and folding our clothes. After dinner Miss Clarke came and staid till dark with us. In the evening Eleanor, Richmond and Sereno came up and spent the evening, we had no other place than the kitchen to take them but we had a very pleasant visit with them. I received the letter which Henry wrote me while I was at Stony Brook. It rained very hard when Eleanor went home, and about two o'clock I awoke and I think I never heard it rain harder or thunder more violently.

Cream Ridge Saturday June 24th

We arose this morning before five o'clock and found the sun shining beautifully. We got our breakfast and started from the house at six. We reached Hightstown at half past ten and found Mr. John Stewart[3] waiting for us. We arrived here about half past twelve.⁴ Miss Lottie Stewart was here from Deleware [sic], and a Miss Lottie Morgan, who boards there, she is a very pleasant girl indeed. We enjoyed ourselves very much talking and looking at each other. Joe expected Charlie to meet him, but he has not made his appearance. We retired early but did not get to sleep till midnight.

Cream Ridge Sunday June 25th

This morning Ben Cox brought Lottie over, she had been to Trenton with her grandma on Saturday to do some shopping. Retta, Miss Lottie, Lottie Morgan and I went to church to Allentown in the morning, it was rather too windy to be very pleasant. In the afternoon Lydia, Mrs. Stewart and Emily went to the Baptist church near.⁵ We spent a very pleasant day reading and talking.

Cream Ridge Monday June 26th

We breakfasted this morning about six. Miss Lottie Stewart and Lottie Morgan started for Deleware [sic] about 7 ½ o'clock, and Joe took Henry to Hightstown a few minutes after. It is the most beautiful morning we have had for a long time. We have been busy sewing and reading *The Last of the Mohicans* and have enjoyed ourselves very much. Ben Cox⁶ came and took some of us and Joe took Emilie to Egypt to see Miss Anne Fort⁷, daughter of the Ex-Governor, she is a very pleasant girl indeed and we spent a very pleasant evening. When we came home Joe found a letter from Charlie saying that he should not be able to come up before next Saturday.

Cream Ridge June 27th Tuesday

We breakfasted about six o'clock this morning. After breakfast I sat down in the dining-room while Retta ironed some few things. We read and sewed until dinner and after dinner we all took a nap. We read and sewed in the afternoon and after tea we all went out and took a walk and enjoyed it very much looking at the stars and the new moon. We retired early.

Cream Ridge June 28th Wednesday

We read and sewed all the morning and in the afternoon we went to call at Mr. Cox's, we then got some nice mulberries and some delicious ice water. We had just reached home when it began to thunder and lighten violently and in a few moments it poured. We packed up our clothes to go to Deleware [sic] before retiring.

Delaware June 29th Thursday

This morning we arose about the usual time and started for Bordentown about 7 ½ o'clock. We were obliged to wait there a half an hour for the cars, after going about a mile in them we took the steamboat 'Richard Stockton'⁸ to Philadelphia where we arrived at nearly one. We met Charlie as we were coming off the boat, he walked to the Major Reybold with us and waited there some time as the boat did not start until two o'clock. We reached Delaware City at five o'clock after a pleasant sail of three hours. Mr. Reybold was at the landing and we had a pleasant ride of about two hours to his house. We were very tired and I had a raging headache but felt quite refreshed after coming from the boat. The day has been beautiful, but it is quite cloudy now and damp. I received a paper from Henry with the death of Horace and it is a great shock.[9]

Delaware Friday June 30th

We had quite a thunder shower before we arose and it continued to look very unpleasant and cloudy until after dinner. I wrote a letter Henry and one to Arthur. Retta went out and took a ride on horseback, it began to rain and poured for a second after she started but she kept on and it stopped in a moment. Miss Fannie Martin[10] came down in a little carriage and Retta rode with her while Joe took Misses. Lottie Morgan and Stewart, Emilie and I down to Del. City to meet the boat. We had a very pleasant ride but it was rather too warm and the sun too hot to be pleasant to ride. On our return we stopped for a Miss Hamilton[11] who boards in the city and she came home with us and staid all night. After tea we went out to take a walk and when we returned Retta and I had a delightful dance. We received a letter [from] Ma, and a delightful one too, also one from Henry. I sat with little Maggie[12] in my arms a long while at the piano, she loves it as well as Annie and I think looks something like her, she is very sweet.

Delaware Saturday July 1st

I wrote a letter this morning directly after breakfast to Emmie Ely. Joe drove Lottie Morgan, Miss Hamilton, Retta, Emilie and me to Delaware City; Miss Hamilton and Lottie Morgan left us there and we went to the Summit Bridge which is over the Delaware and Chesapeake Canal,[13] it is about seven miles from Mr. Reybold's. We left the carriage at a tavern and walked over the bridge and went down on the bank which is very far below. The view was very beautiful. We returned to the carriage after getting some very refreshing lemonade. It was about dinner time when we returned. Joe went to Del. City after Lottie Morgan and Miss Hamilton, the former boards here and gives music lessons twice a week in Del. City. Miss Hamilton expects to stay until Monday morning. After tea we went out on the road to see Joe try a fast horse, which is going to run a race next week. Three young gentlemen came here this evening. I played some on the piano and Retta and I had a very pleasant dance which I enjoyed very much, notwithstanding I am as lame as an old woman.

Delaware Sunday July 2nd

A delightful morning we went to church to St. Georges, there were twelve of us started from here. It was quite warm. In the afternoon we, Miss Lottie, Emilie and I, went to Delaware City to the Episcopal church. It is a very pretty church. We had some company in the evening.

Delaware Monday July 3rd

This morning Miss Lottie was obliged to go to Philadelphia for a girl, and Miss Hamilton, Retta and I rode down to the boat with her. We drove very fast as we were rather late about starting and Joe had seen the boat starting from Salem. John Reybold saw us coming and got the captain to wait a minute and Miss Lottie ran on board. Retta and I went shopping and then we came home and enjoyed the ride very much indeed. Just before dinner, I was playing on the piano and who should come in but Charlie. We were very glad to see him. Miss Lottie came home this afternoon, bringing a girl with her. After tea I went with Joe to Mr. John Reybold's as we heard that our letters had been carried down there. I had a very pleasant ride, and we went very fast some of the time. When we came home we found some company here, and we (that is) Retta and I enjoyed a waltz.

Delaware Tuesday July 4th

Last night was the hottest night we have had this summer. Retta and I got up and sat by the window and tried to cool our bed, but it made no difference and we tossed about until we could keep awake no longer. It does not seem like the 'Fourth of July' today. Everyone is complaining of the heat this morning. Mr. John Reybold and some friends of his from the city called on us this morning. This evening we started about half past six to go to Mrs. King's[14] to spend the evening. We stopped at Mr. John Reybold's and made a short call and then went on to Mr. King's, we enjoyed the evening very much indeed. It was the warmest evening we had this summer, there was not a breath of air stirring but we managed to keep quite comfortable by fanning ourselves and walking on the piazzas.

Delaware Wednesday July 5th

It was excessively warm this morning and has remained so all day. After breakfast we all went to Del. City to call on Miss Polk, a niece of Mr. Reybold, she is very pleasant and we made a long call. As we were obliged to wait for Joe to go to the store for some articles, we thought he was gone a long while, and when he returned he said one of the wheels had come off and he was obliged to wait to get it on, it was very fortunate that we were not in the carriage or we might have been injured. It was hot when we came back. I believe the thermometer stood at 100. We had the most terrific thunder shower I ever saw. The lightening [sic] struck near Mr. Reybold's, and the fire destroyed a great deal of property. It had almost stopped raining when we started to go to Mr. Barney Reybold's to a party which was given for us. We enjoyed the party very much indeed as we came home we saw a light in the direction of Philadelphia and Mr. Reybold said there must be a large fire there.[15] We packed our clothes before retiring.

Cream Ridge Thursday July 6th

We started from Mr. Reybold's at seven o'clock and enjoyed the sail up to Philadelphia very much as we had a very pleasant breeze all the way. We reached the city at 10

½ o'clock and we were running through the streets until half past two looking for a servant for Mrs. Stewart, and at last Joe engaged one who met him down at the boat, just as they were drawing the plank away and therefore we had all our trouble for nothing. We reached Bordentown at six o'clock and did not get home until nearly nine. We were all thoroughly tired and stiff.

Cream Ridge Friday July 7th

We did not arise this morning as early as usual, and when we came down to breakfast everyone was complaining, one with a back ache, another with a pain in a shoulder and every variety of disagreeable sensation. We sat and lounged all day, we could not possibly cause ourselves to laugh except once! When Charlie began to teaze [sic] Retta and then we laughed for about half an hour. After tea we went nearby to Fillmore and enjoyed the walk very much indeed we then sat on the porch for some time and at last retired.

Cream Ridge July 8th Saturday

I have not felt very well all day, but I think I am quite restored to health thanks to the excellent care of Charlie, who took malicious pleasure in making me take my medicine. Henry wrote that he would come up here on Saturday afternoon and Charlie went to meet him at Hightstown.[16] They did not make their appearance at seven o'clock as Charlie had promised, and we walked down to Fillmore[17] to meet them, we all got in the carriage and rode up with them, except Charlie who was obliged to walk. We ate tea and after tea we sat in the hall and ate molasses candy and talked about nothing. Joe was sick and retired early. We had quite an adventure after going to our room. Henry brought me a letter from Arthur.

Cream Ridge Sunday July 9th

We did not breakfast quite so early as usual this morning and did not go to church as there was no morning service in the church here. We went however in the afternoon. Just before we went to church Mr. Rue[18] called but he did not stay long. Mrs. Stewart has been sick all the afternoon. Mr. Cox and Mr. [Emley?] called in the evening.

Cream Ridge Monday July 10th

Mrs. Stewart was very ill, she fainted twice and still continues sick. Henry went this morning in the stage to Bordentown. Everyone seems very much depressed in spirits, but I hope they will not long continue below par. I have not felt well all day but feel better now. The weather has been cloudy but it has not made out to rain. We went out and took a little walk and had a very pleasant time. Mr. Cox, Mr. Woodward and Mr. Morgan came and spent the evening, we enjoyed their visit very much. Mrs. Stewart does not improve very fast.

Cream Ridge Tuesday July 11th 1854

All cross, but Lydia, who is in a most perfect state of happiness and good nature. We have been picking over gooseberries and stringing beans, also lounging. Charlie went to Philadelphia this afternoon, we were all very sorry he could not stay till tomorrow. We all went out and took a ride after nine o'clock it was a beautiful evening. We stopped a moment at Mr. Taylor's and saw Emma. We were very tired when we retired.

Cream Ridge Wednesday July 12th

We arose at the usual time and after breakfast we sat and sewed while the girls ironed. Mrs. Taylor and Emma came up to call. Emma was on horseback and did not get off the horse and we stood out and talked with her about an hour. We then packed our trunk. N.Y. We took dinner and then started for Hightstown. Mr. John Stewart drove us, we reached N.Y. about seven o'clock. Joe saw Henry when we were a long way from the wharf. We were standing on the dock a moment speaking with Henry when we felt someone grasp our hand, and looking up we saw Charlie. I was never more astonished in my life. He and Joe rode up as far as the Irving House with us. They came up after tea and we all played billiards and we enjoyed the evening notwithstanding the gloominess of the house and our lonely feeling at leaving our friends. Father has gone to Philadelphia.

IV

SOUTH SALEM, NEW YORK
JULY 13–SEPTEMBER 5

Haying in South Salem, New York, 1850s. *(Courtesy of the New York State Archives, Education Department, Division of Visual Instruction: instructional lantern slides, circa 1856–1939. [A3045-78, Dn HuX1.])*

New York July 13th Thursday

We arose about six and after breakfast we busied ourselves about the house. We found there was a great deal to do. Charlie and Joe[1] came up about eleven and stayed a few moments. Aunt Thirza invited us there to dinner and we were very happy to be able to accept the invitation. Charlie and Joe came up about five o'clock and spent the remainder of the evening with us. Uncle Peter came up, he has just returned from the White Mountains. He has been absent two weeks. Julia, John, Hannah and Stephy[2] accompanied him. The boys all came in and Sereno Smith.[3] They all enjoyed a game of billiards. Before Charlie went, we all wrote a letter to the girls,[4] which I know they will be glad to receive. Charlie is going tomorrow morning at seven o'clock.

New York Friday July 14th

The most stormy morning I ever saw, it actually poured when we arose. Charlie will have a stormy morning for going to Philadelphia. P.M. Charlie and Joe both came up here this morning. Charlie did not wake in time to go, and it was so stormy that he said he should not have gone anyhow this morning, but he went this afternoon at two o'clock. I was very sorry that he could not stay till tomorrow when we expect to go to Salem. We went in Uncle Robert's to dinner and then Emilie went to see Miss Clarke[5] and Arthur[6] came home after me. I feel very lonesome.[7] James[8] started to drive to Salem with Uncle Robert's horses this morning and I am afraid he will be sick. Emilie has not heard from Maria Seabury and I begin to feel alarmed lest her toe is getting much worse. It has rained all day steadily, but I hope it will be clear tomorrow. I wrote a letter to Retta this afternoon and this evening we all wrote to Charlie. Henry asked Joe to go to Bloomfield with him and I believe he has accepted the invitation. We all feel very dull. Father arrived from Philadelphia about eleven o'clock.

New York July 15th Saturday

Father woke us up quite early and we lounged about all day, packing our clothes and arranging those that we wished to leave. Eddie Seymour came in at about two o'clock and took dinner with us, the examination takes place at Yale College on the 25th of this month.[9]

South Salem.

We left N.Y. at four o'clock with Father, Uncle Robert, Aunt Thirza and Arthur and reached Salem at half past eight. I should scarcely have known Mary, she is so very much improved and grown, but Annie looked very natural. We were very tired and retired soon after we got home. Grandma[10] and all of the family seemed to be very glad to see us. Annie knew us perfectly well.

South Salem July 16th Sunday

A very pleasant day. I have not been to church today on account of the boil on my nose. All attended except me. Father, Ma and Emilie came home at noon. Grandma came home about three o'clock, very tired. Thomas[11] went to prayer meeting in the evening.

South Salem Monday July 17th, 1854

Father left for the city at six o'clock. It was so warm last night that I could scarcely sleep. Emilie took a ride on horseback with Arthur. I have been washing and taking care of the children during the morning. I wrote to Henry and gave the letter to Mr. Keeler.[12] I starched my muslins and took care of Annie after dinner.

South Salem Tuesday July 18th 1854

I rose quite early and James drove Grandma, Ma and I down to New Canaan. We started about seven o'clock and stopped at Cousin Jane's,[13] she gave us some cherries to eat also to carry to Mrs. Lindsley.[14] We went to see Minerva[15] and found her very, very ill. I should have not have known her, and indeed I did not until I heard Ma call her by name. She is very thin and as white as a corpse, and I have no doubt that she has the consumption. From there we went to New Canaan village, on the road for a mile or more, we had a very fine view of the Sound[16] and as it was very clear the scenery was really exquisite, as there were a great number of vessels in sight. We made quite a number of purchases, and saw M. E. Pardee[17] who we suppose was purchasing her wedding dress. We then started for home which was about ten or eleven miles distant, after going three miles we stopped at Mr. Peter Smith's, who was a cousin of Grandma Hoe.[18] They seemed to be very glad to see us and gave us a very refreshing dinner. We stayed there until about four o'clock and then started again for home. We stopped at Mr. [Ferris'?] for a few minutes, Grandma went into the house but Ma and I went to the store (Mr. Ferris')[19] and waited for her. We stopped at the Post Office and I found three letters for us from Charlie and Joe and from Mary Seymour. I was delighted to receive them. We arrived home about six after a very tiresome but pleasant day. Thomas went to pay his usual call tonight.[20]

South Salem Wednesday July 19th 1854

I arose about five o'clock and found Ma quite miserable as she had been awake nearly all night, but she has been lying down during the day and feels better now.[21] Before I had breakfasted Robert came over for me to take a ride on horseback, so I ate my breakfast and Peter[22] brought the pony and I had a very pleasant ride. When I came home I ironed all my muslins and was very tired when I finished. Imogene has been to Mr. Gilbert Mead's [23] to get some cherries and returned with quite a good number. We all sewed in the afternoon. James started early in the morning to go see a niece of his, who lives about ten miles from here. It has been very warm indeed, and the heat seems to be increasing rather than diminishing.

South Salem Thursday July 20th 1854

I arose this morning about six and found myself so lame and stiff that I can scarcely move, the effects of riding on horseback. Everyone seems to be complaining. Emilie has the rheumatism and Ma is not at all well, and Peter complaining and I don't know how many others are half sick. We went to the post office where we found some newspapers and four letters. Emilie found one from Lizzie Wright[24] and one from Theodore and I received one from Henry. We then went to spend the afternoon with Aunt Mary that is to be.[25] We enjoyed our visit there very much.

South Salem Friday July 21st 1854

James went down to NY this morning and left the horse at Whitlockville[26] for father this afternoon. Uncle Robert, Aunt Thirza and Laura[27] came to call on us. Emilie and I made our first lemon pie this afternoon and it turned out to be quite delicious.

Mary and Cyrus Lawrence came to spend the evening, and Mary Bouton[28] came to call. Father came up about nine o'clock and we were all delighted to see him. We enjoyed the evening very much. Cyrus Lawrence[29] has just returned from the South and intends going back in October. Theodore came up with Father.

South Salem Saturday July 22nd 1854

Father and Ma did not arise very early this morning and we did not breakfast until nine. Theodore and Robert came over on Charley[30] and Arthur rode Locke, they invited us to take a ride with them. Emilie rode first. Theodore rode Tom, and Father [rode] Paul with Annie in front of him. They went to the store and seemed to enjoy the ride very much. Father did not go with me and Theodore rode Paul. We started off finally, although it was very warm, we went around by Lake Wacabuck[31] and passed Uncle Solomon's.[32] Just as we were about a quarter of a mile from there, Robbie whipped up to pass a load of hay, and went past quite briskly, and as Paul would not be beaten, he started off full galop [sic] and Kate after him. Theodore was just quieting Paul, when Kate came behind and they both started at full speed and although we pulled with all our might we could not stop them until we reined up at Uncle Solomon's gate. I felt quite frightened, my hat had come off and my hair had fallen down, and the perspiration was pouring off my face in streams. I made Robbie come home with me on Locke for I was afraid of Paul. Father laughed like everything at us, and Robbie called Theodore "John Gilpin,"[33] but I thought it was no laughing matter. I have received a letter from Emmie Ely to-day dated on the 8th of this month, it was sent to Cream Ridge, and we left there before it arrived. Grandma has been working very hard today and is completely worn out. It has very much the appearance of rain. Father and Ma started about six o'clock to take a horse back ride to see Uncle Robert. I believe they met with no adventure and enjoyed the ride very much, although it was quite damp and Ma was afraid of taking cold. We retired early.

South Salem Sunday July 23rd 1854

Emilie is twenty years old today and I have no doubt feels quite aged. We went to church this morning and returned to dinner, but went back in the afternoon. It began to thunder just before church was out and although we were in front of everyone it began to rain before we got quite home, but we did not get wet much at all. We read in the afternoon and retired about nine o'clock. Emilie wrote to Maria Seabury, Lizzie Wright and Eleanor.

South Salem Monday July 24th

Arose early and worked quite a good deal before breakfast. Ma went to New York with Father this morning, as she expects the dress-maker tomorrow. It is quite showery. We have been sewing nearly all day. The children have been quite fretful, because the weather has been such that they could not go out as usual. Peter went to the washerwoman's and Grandma went with him; he drove Kate, she behaved very well but was quite frisky.

South Salem Tuesday July 25th 1854

We have all been very busy, Grandma has been baking and I have tried to assist her. The babies have been very good indeed. Peter went to the post office but did not find any letters for Emilie. I received a letter from Henry, one from Mary, and a sketch from Joe, also a paper.[34] Thomas went to see Mary to-night and of course enjoyed the evening very much.

South Salem Wednesday July 26th

I have written three letters or rather notes today and sewed some. Father came up with Ma this evening, Ma has been quite sick, but is better now. Doctor Beales was sent for on Monday evening, but he sent word that he had had the cholera dreadfully,[35] but would come in the morning. He told her it would be very imprudent for her to stay in the city and begged her to come back as soon as possible. Ma brought me a letter from Retta[36] and one from Henry, both of which I was very glad to receive.

South Salem Thursday July 27th

I worked around the house early the morning, and then I gathered a number of dead leaves from the yard, making the grass look beautifully. Father went to New York after dinner and Thomas took us all over to cousin James' to tea. We spent a very pleasant afternoon. After we came home we rode down to see Mary L., and she and Edward went with us to Boutonville, we enjoyed the ride very much.

South Salem Friday July 28th

Arthur came over directly after breakfast for one of us to ride [with] him, and as Ma was going to Elizabeth's after our clothes, we rode behind them. We had quite a long ride of five miles, and we enjoyed it very much. This afternoon Peter drove Ellen and Imogene to a field on the mountain to pick whortleberries, they had a jolly time but did not get many berries. We have had a very pleasant time this afternoon reading *The Lamplighter*.[37] Lucy Howe came over and has played with Annie for a long while. Arthur came over just about tea time for Emilie to ride with him, they went about three miles.

South Salem Saturday July 29th

We have been very busy sewing all day. Nothing has occurred of importance. We have had a very heavy shower this morning. Thomas is not at all well and Grandpa is very sick. Emilie has the rheumatism. Henry arrived from N.Y. about half past eight, he seemed to be very glad to come and I am sure we were glad to see him. I did not retire until late.

South Salem Sunday July 30th

A very pleasant day. Grandpa is no better and Thomas and Emilie did not go to church as they were not well enough. Ma went in the morning. Mary Louisa[38] was not at church, her mother said she was a little under the weather. Peter went after the doctor this evening, but he could not tell what was the matter with Grandpa, but thought he had taken a heavy cold.

South Salem Monday July 31st

Grandpa was no better this morning and the doctor said that he had an attack of Bronchitis. Henry woke me up early this morning and I went and took a ride with him, the horses behaved very well and we enjoyed it very much. Henry started for N.Y. at half past seven o'clock. I wish he could have staid longer. Annie was quite unwell and seemed very languid. We have been sewing and reading all the afternoon. I wrote a letter to Henry.

South Salem Tuesday August 1st

I have been very busy starching and ironing muslins and so forth. This morning Robbie came over for one of us to ride, and as we were going to take the clothes to the woman, Emilie rode on horseback and Ma and I and the baby went in the carriage, we enjoyed the ride very much indeed. Thomas went to get his horse shod, he stopped to see Mary and found her better than she was on Sunday, his boil is very bad indeed. He scarcely has a moment free from pain. Thomas brought me a letter from Henry, he said that Emmie wanted to find a place here to board during the month of August and I hope we shall be able to secure one for her.

South Salem Wednesday August 2nd 1854

I arose early and found almost everyone had passed a sleepless night. Thomas did not go to bed until four o'clock, and Annie scarcely slept an hour at a time, Grandpa was worse and Grandma could not sleep. I have worked quite a good deal this morning. Ma and Emilie went out to find a place for Emmie and at last secured one at Mrs. John Bouton's. I wrote a letter to Henry. Emilie and I went to Cross River to take tea with Julia and Emeline Reynolds. We spent quite a pleasant afternoon.

South Salem Thursday August 3rd

I arose quite early and helped Grandma in the morning, and then sewed. After dinner Lydia came over and spent about an hour and Aunt Thirza and Uncle Robert called a moment. We spent quite a pleasant afternoon reading and sewing. Father came home about nine o'clock and brought Ma a letter from Aunt Annie,[39] me one from Henry, and Emilie one from Maria Seabury and Lyd Stewart. Henry sent some toys for Mary, and Miss Sewell's new work *Katherine Ashton*.[40] Annie is not at all well, indeed she has a dreadful cold and is really ill.

South Salem August 4th Friday

A stormy morning and I fear we shall not be able to go to Uncle Solomon's to spend the day as we intended doing. Annie is very pale and languid and coughs a great deal, but she rested better last night and we are hoping she will improve fast. Mary is very well indeed at present. P.M. We all went over as it cleared off very finely. Annie seemed to be some better, but we had been there about an hour when she began to feel worse, and appeared to be in so much pain that they thought it best to go home, and they all went except Grandma, Emilie and I. When we came home we found Annie in a raging fever and very ill. About half past nine we sent for the doctor, but he did not reach here until after eleven. He did not say what was the matter.

South South [sic] Saturday August 5th[41]

I arose early and immediately went to see how Annie was. I found them all asleep, Father had not undressed himself, and he and Ma and Ellen had been kept awake nearly all night. The boys all came over to ride with us, and Father and I went with them first. I enjoyed the ride very much indeed. Emilie went afterward with Theodore, he gave me a letter from Henry which I was very glad to receive. The doctor did not come until late in the afternoon, and he did not say she was any better, but I hope she is. I have been sewing nearly all the afternoon and helping Thomas clean the yard. Cousin Jane[42] made us a short call.

South Salem August 6th Sunday

I found that Annie had been quite sick all night but she seemed better in the morning. I staid with her a long time. Emilie and Thomas went to church in the morning. Emilie returned at noon, and Grandma and I went in the afternoon. We heard there was quite an accident here yesterday evening. Mary C. Bouton was riding with two young ladies, and the horse was going pretty fast, she became frightened and jumped out of the wagon and into a pile of stones. She was thrown headlong and stunned, so that when she was taken up some little time after she scarcely breathed. The two young ladies were not hurt much in comparison with her though they jumped also afterwards. I believe the doctor thinks she will recover though there is danger of a fever. Thomas and I went to church in the evening and Mary L. went with us. Annie has seemed a little better all day and I hope she will be well soon.

South Salem, August 7 Monday

I have been in the room with Annie all night and did not sleep very well. Father started for N.Y. this morning and we expect Emmie Ely to return with the carriage. P.M. Father left his horse at Whitlockville as he came up this evening and Emmie came over with Owen.[43] Emilie went with her to Mrs. Bouton's and she came over to see us after dinner and staid until nearly tea time. Arthur came over to ride with Peter,[44] they went over to Cross River, and when they returned Emmie got on the horse and took a short ride, she seemed to enjoy it very much. I walked home with her or nearly there. Father came up and brought some medicines for Annie, Mary, Ma, and Emilie and I trust they will all recover soon.

South Salem Tuesday August 8th

Emmie and Annie Ely went to take a ride with Father. Emmie rode Tom and they enjoyed their ride very much indeed. When they returned Father drove Ma Emmie and me to the washerwoman's. We stopped at the post office and I found a letter from Henry and one from Mary,[45] which I was very happy to receive. We left Emmie home. In the afternoon Emmie came over to go to Ridgefield with us. We started about six o'clock and went down to Mr. Lawrence's, and we got off from there about seven. Edward [Adary?] and Nelson Abbott[46] went with us. We spent a very pleasant evening with the Misses Keeler,[47] there were three young ladies there from N.Y. We enjoyed our ride exceedingly.

South Salem August 9th Wednesday

Father came into our room early as he was going to New York, and told us that Ma was very sick with a cold, and the baby sick also. The baby continued to grow worse and all day has lain in the cradle and moaned. We were very much worried about her. The doctor came about noon and said she was very sick but he hoped she would be better. We had invited company and we were very busy. Hannah Maria and Julia Lawrence[48] came in the afternoon and just before tea Julia Reynolds[49] came. The baby continued to grow worse all the afternoon and we asked Julia Reynolds to stop for the doctor on their way home. Edward Lawrence[50] came up and staid a few minutes, he said that their girl had scalded her hand, and Mary had been obliged to stay home and work. Freddie Howe[51] came over very late. The doctor came after they were all gone and pronounced the baby dangerously ill. The little darling lay with her eyes shut and breathed very hard sometimes moaning. I expected she would die before morning. I was very sorry that we had company as I am sure they did not enjoy themselves as though we had all been well. Annie is improving quite fast, and I hope she will be well soon.

South Salem Thursday August 10th

Grandma came in our room and said that the baby was decidedly better. I cannot describe my feelings, it was such a relief. The baby is not free from pain, but she looks brighter and will nurse now. Emmie came over early to see how the baby was. Emmie staid until after dinner and then we took old Kate and drove ourselves to the village we stopped at the post office where we found two letters for Emmie, and one from Eleanor[52] to me. I went to Mrs. Bouton's with Emmie, but as there was no one at home, we went up to her room and sat there some time, we then rode home, and Emilie jumped in with us and we left Emmie home. Matthew Smith spent the evening with us. Father came up in the evening and is not going down until Monday.

South Salem August 11th Friday

Emmie came over early and we worked until nearly dinner time and then Emilie went home with her, and then staid until evening. I took care of Annie in the afternoon and in the evening Mary and Edward came after us to go to prayer meeting. We stopped for Emmie and Emilie. We enjoyed the evening very much.

South Salem Saturday August 12th

We arose early and I assisted Grandma by preparing some apples for pies. Emmie came early. Uncle Robert and Aunt Thirza called in the morning and Arthur rode over on horseback. Father rode up to North Salem on Kate and did not return until after dinner. Emilie and Emmie and I drove old Kate to the post office and then to the store. We made a short call on Mary Louisa and then went to the washerwoman's to get our clothes. We stopped a moment at Uncle Solomon's but they were all away. We then drove Emmie home. The bird flew away, for which we are very sorry.[53]

South Salem Sunday August 13th

We arose about six and breakfasted. Father and Ma did not come down until nearly nine. Theodore came over and brought a letter for Emmie, also one for me, from Henry and basket of peaches for which we have to thank Henry. We went to church, the service was not as interesting as usual. We returned at noon and took Emmie with us, and brought her back in the afternoon. In the evening Edward and Mary called for us and we all went to prayer meeting. I sat directly under an open window and was very much annoyed by the insects, which being attracted by the light were continually crawling over me, otherwise I should have enjoyed it much.

South Salem Monday August 14th

A charming morning really enough to make one feel happy, the air is delightfully cool and a great contrast from yesterday which was very warm and oppressive. Father started at six o'clock this morning and John went with him. We busied ourselves working for Grandma in the morning. Emmie came over and we all went to spend the evening with Mary L, we found Miss Keeler there from Ridgefield, and Miss Rockwood from New York.[54] We spent a very pleasant evening.

South Salem August 15th Tuesday

I arose quite early and found it quite cloudy and very unpleasant. We sewed in the morning and in the afternoon, Emilie and Emmie went to Ridgefield. Miss Rockwood and Harriet Keeler went with them and Peter went to take care of them. They did not return until half past six and I went home with Emmie and staid all night with her. We enjoyed each other's society very much.

South Salem Wednesday August 16th 1854

We arose quite early and sewed and read *Oliver Twist* all morning, and ate pears and cake. After dinner Emmie walked home with me, we sewed and read *The Lamplighter* until nearly night and then I walked a short distance with Emmie.

South Salem Thursday August 17th

I arose early and felt quite badly, having been kept awake nearly all night with a bad sore throat. Arthur came over and I took a long ride with him. When I returned Emmie went around the block with him and I read *The Lamplighter* aloud. We expected quite a good deal of company in the evening, and as we were dressing Imogene rushed into our room exclaiming, "There is a carriage load from N.Y." We had our dresses scattered around the parlor and her news made quite a commotion, we tumbled our clothes on the bed in our room, and Emilie went out to see who the people were while Emmie and I finished dressing. We found that it was Uncle Peter, Aunt Hannah, Dick,[55] and Uncle Robert's family. They made a short call. In the evening only five came of all we had invited, Miss Rockwood, Harriet Keeler, and three others. I was truly provoked.

South Salem Friday August 18th

Emmie came over early and we concluded to drive ourselves to call on Aunt Hannah. We first drove Emmie home to dress, and then Emmie, Emilie + Annie and I went to Uncle Solomon's, we made a short call, and while there Ma and Peter rode over on horseback. After dinner we all went to Cousin Jane's to take tea. Emmie met us there and we spent a very pleasant afternoon. Thomas went to prayer meeting. Father brought Joe up with him. They arrived about eight o'clock. Mary ran a needle a long way in her hand and Father was obliged to take the pincers to draw it out.

South Salem Saturday August 19th

We arose early, and Emmie came over right after breakfast. After we had worked some Emmie, Emilie, Arthur, Joe, Thomas and I went over the mountain. The scenery was really beautiful and majestic, the road lay behind the mountain and between Lake Wacabuck and South Pond. I never saw such rocks. Emmie, Arthur and I walked a little way over the roughest part. After dinner we went down and sat in the grove and sewed and ate candy. Arty lost his watch key, we looked for it, but there are so many leaves on the ground that it was impossible to find it. Ma, Father, Annie and Artie went to the washerwoman's, they drove Kate as Paul was lame and Tom had been out all the morning. Emmie and Joe went on horseback to the post office, they rode Grandpa's horses. I received a letter from Henry in which he mentioned the death of Emmeline Mead,[56] and although I had never seen her, it was a great shock. We walked half way home with Emmie just before tea. We retired early.

South Salem Sunday 20th August

We arose early and went to church. Joe drove us home, and we left Emmie at home and called for her in the afternoon. Emilie did not go to church in the afternoon. After church we took a walk in the woods and down to the brook. Emilie and Thomas went in the evening. I received a note from Henry by Theodore. I answered his note and wrote a few lines to Retta. We did not retire until quite late.

South Salem Monday August 21st

Theodore came over early in the morning to see what arrangements Father had made about going to the depot, as Peter is sick and Paul lame. They concluded to go with Uncle Robert's conveyance and Peter drove them over to Uncle Solomon's. We sewed and read aloud some in *Katherine Ashton* Miss Sewell's new work. Emmie came over very early and Emilie went home with her before dinner. In the evening Edward Lawrence came up to take us riding, we called for Emmie and Emilie, also for Harriet Keeler and cousins and Miss Rockwood. We took quite a long ride and I should have enjoyed it exceedingly had it not been for a violent earache, which disturbed me very much during the night. Mr. and Mrs. Lindsley and Miss Rockwood called upon us this afternoon, we enjoyed their call very much, and were very sorry the girls were away. I felt quite lonesome upon retiring, but the pain in my ear and head were so violent that I could think of nothing else.

South Salem Tuesday August 22nd

The pain in my ear was better this morning, for which I was thankful, but my head ached badly. The weather is very warm. Just before dinner Ma and Annie and I went to the store, Ma called at Mr. Bouton's and left Annie there. When we returned we took Emmie, Emilie and Annie in, as it was a small waggon [*sic*] we were quite crowded but still it was for a short distance. In the afternoon Uncle Solomon's people came over and took tea. Just as we finished tea Ralph Howe[57] drove over to call a moment, with Jane, Hannah, and Miss [Underburgh?]. In the evening Edward Lawrence came up and spent an hour or so, he took Emmie home very kindly. I received a letter from Henry.

South Salem Wednesday August 23rd

We arose early as usual. Grandma went to Ridgefield to do some shopping, and Ma and the rest of us read *Katherine Ashton* aloud and sewed. Emilie rode Kate, and Peter drove Emmie and I over to Uncle Solomon's. We made a short call and took Arty for Emilie's escort, we then rode around the block, and Peter left Emmie and I at Mr. Bouton's, where I remained all night. We sat in Emmie's room and enjoyed ourselves very much together. I wrote a letter to Aunt Emeline for Emmie while she arranged my hair. Thomas called for us and Nelson Abbott[58] went with Emilie to spend the evening with Mrs. Keeler. Thomas left us there and went to call on Mary. We enjoyed the evening very much and all came home with Nelson Abbott.

South Salem Thursday August 24th

Emmie and I did not awake until nearly eight o'clock. When we went downstairs we found Mrs. Bouton waiting very patiently at the table for us. We read *Oliver Twist* and I wrote a letter to Eleanor. Ma and Peter rode over on horseback, and after dinner Peter came after us. He went to the post office. I received a letter from Mary which I prize very highly. We came home and then went to Mr. Howe's to take tea and spend the evening. We enjoyed it very much indeed.

South Salem Friday August 25th

We arose early and dusted some. Emmie came over early and we read *The Lamplighter* and *Katherine Ashton* and sewed. After dinner Mary Louisa and Miss Pratt[59] came up to call on us, and invited us to her grandma's to tea, but we did not accept the invitation. I wrote a letter to Mary Seymour and Emmie wrote to her mother. Ma, Grandma and the two nurses and babies went down to call on Aunt Sally, they remained until late and we began to eat our supper as we supposed they had taken tea there. To our surprise a few moments after they came in, it rained though only a little. It was sufficient to encourage one, as the weather has been so very dry lately. We read *The Lamplighter* aloud and I cut out some collars. Father came up about nine o'clock. Emmie staid all night with us and we had some fine times. The night was so dark that Father seemed to think it was rather dangerous to drive.

South Salem Saturday August 26th

We arose quite early, and breakfasted with Thomas. Before Father and Ma were ready for their breakfast, Uncle Robert and Robby came over, the latter for Emmie to ride with him. When Emmie returned Ma and Father went out, they took a long ride on the summit of the mountain, and did not return till two o'clock. Ma said the view was truly exquisite, and she thought almost equal to that from the Catskill Mountain House.[60] We sewed and read after dinner and were surprised and pleased by a slight thunder shower. When the shower had passed, Peter harnessed old Kate and Emilie, Emmie and I drove over to the washerwoman's, and from there to the store, where we found two letters to Emmie, and one to myself. Aunt Emeline wrote that she thought it best for Emmie to go to Harriet Brockway's[61] immediately but she might use her own judgment. She is very undecided and talks of going on Thursday, but I do not know what she will decide upon. We cannot seem to decide upon our plans. Father finished *The Lamplighter* this evening. Just before retiring we had a heavy shower and I think we may entertain hopes that the drought is at an end.[62]

South Salem Sunday August 27th

We did not arise as early as usual this morning, I am sorry to say. The weather was very unpleasant, and it looked so much like rain that we concluded not to go to church. Grandma, Thomas and Imogene went. When they returned Grandma said that she had heard that Minerva was dead. It seems very sudden although I had expected to hear the sad news before. Ma intends now going to N.Y. a week from tomorrow and we are expecting to follow her on the next Saturday.

South Salem Monday August 28th

Emmie came over very early and Father went away about six o'clock. We worked all the morning and read *Katherine Ashton*. We wrote some letters and dressed ourselves after dinner. Mrs. Green[63] and son, Mrs. Lawrence and Mary came up and took tea. Emmie was not dressed and Thomas took her over to change her dress. We spent a very pleasant afternoon and evening. Peter took Emmie home, and Emilie went with her and staid all night.

Thomas Cole (American, 1801-1848). *A View of the Two Lakes and Mountain House, Catskill Mountains, Morning,* 1844. Oil on canvas, 35 13/16 x 53 7/8 in. (91 x 136.9 cm). *(Courtesy of the Brooklyn Museum, Dick S. Ramsay Fund, 52.16.)*

South Salem Tuesday August 29th

I arose pretty early and assisted Grandma. Emilie and Emmie came over directly after breakfast. We then drove ourselves to Uncle Solomon's. We all went to the pond and had a delightful sail. Theodore and Robby rode. I got my feet and dress quite wet as the boat leaked, but they dried soon. We found dinner waiting at Uncle Solomon's for us, and after partaking of it we came home. Ma had packed all the things up, and seemed quite tired. Peter went to the depot after Father with a load of things. Grandma and Ma then started off to make a few calls. They went to see Lydia and Mrs. L. Howe. Lydia is very miserable having been poisoned very badly. Thomas has a boil, and he is very much afraid that he is getting a felon on his finger. Emmie staid all night. When it was nearly time for Father to come, we heard a carriage drive up. We went out to see who it was, and found Uncle Benajah and Aunt Fanny,[64] we were very glad to see them. Father came home a few minutes after. I received a letter from Henry and Retta and was perfectly happy. Annie cried very much.

South Salem Wednesday August 30th

I arose early and looked on while the people made themselves ready to start. Uncle Benajah went away before we were up. Ma, Father, nurses, and babies started for N.Y. about nine o'clock. We have felt quite lonely since, I could not bear to have them go away. I wrote a letter to Retta and one to Henry, and we assisted Grandma by cleaning the breakfast table. After dinner we all went to make some calls. Grandma, Emilie,

Emmie and I went to Mrs. Lindsley's while cousin Jane and Aunt Fannie went to see Lydia. We had a very pleasant call. Miss Rockwood was there. Directly after tea we went down to Mr. Lawrence's to spend the evening. Mr. Lawrence's family were all there, and we had some fine music. We left there early, and when we reached Mr. Bouton's Emmie wanted me to stay all night with her, and I suddenly concluded to. Sarah Anne came up and talked with us a long time. Emmie was quite sick.

Wilton Thursday August 31st

We arose early and soon after breakfast Thomas, Emilie, and Aunt Fannie called for us to go to Wilton. We stopped at Lydia's and Aunt Fannie saw her very young son, who came to town this morning. We arrived at Huldah[65] about eleven, after a very pleasant ride. We remained there until five and then went to Aunt Fannie's. We felt quite fatigued and as we had not slept well the night before, we retired very early. We had quite a funny time in the night.

South Salem Friday September 1st

We did not [rise] very early, and it was quite late when we breakfasted. We sewed a little and then we went to call on Aunt Sophia,[66] she came up with us and staid to dinner. I wrote a note to Cousin Mary Ann,[67] and she came over to see us. We had an early dinner and started directly after, as we wanted to reach Salem in time for the lecture. We found Grandma in church. Three children were baptized, we had a very good address. Emmie wrote a letter to her father, and I wrote one to Ma, one to Henry, and a note to Aunt Fannie. After tea we read aloud and cut apples for pies. Emilie is not at all well and is afraid of the Quinsy.[68] We spent a very pleasant evening. I received a letter from Henry.

South Salem September 2nd 1854 Saturday

We sewed all the morning and Emmie cracked some nuts. After dinner Bobby and Theodore came over and we spent a very pleasant afternoon. Frederick and Arthur came over about five. Aunt Sally sent her girl up to tell Grandma that she wanted her to come down immediately, as a lady had just arrived from the West, whom she should be delighted to see. Grandma went down in great haste and found Mrs. Townsend there.[69] It made Grandma quite happy. The boys staid until after tea. Peter drove Emmie and I to the post office and we left Emmie at home. I received a letter from Henry and some papers. I saw Cousin Jane on my way home, she said that Lydia was not so well. We retired early.

South Salem September 3rd Sunday

We all went to church. It was Communion Sabbath. There were four persons united with the church and one baptized. The service was so long that there was no church in the afternoon. We went to prayer meeting in the evening, Grandma and Imogene went up to see Lydia. Her baby died this morning, and Grandma said she looked almost like a corpse herself, she was very tired and there had been about fifty people there today.

South Salem Monday September 4th

We arose early and washed some muslins. Emmie came over early and we all went out to the barn to see Peter off. He had three horses and a dog to take down, but is going to stop at White Plains tonight. We sewed all the morning. Emmie went home soon after dinner. Mrs. Townsend came up to stay all night. Uncle Robert and Aunt Thirza rode over after ten, they said that the doctor had met Peter on the road to Poundridge. He had turned near Bedford and got on the wrong road. Edward and Mary came after us to go to Mrs. Bouton's. We found the Howes there, Matthew Smith and Miss Rockwood. We spent a pleasant evening, and had some delicious water melons [sic]. It was late when we reached home.

South Salem Tuesday September 5th

We arose early and after breakfast I ironed some muslins. I sewed all the morning. After dinner Grandma and I dressed, as we were invited to Mr. Gilbert Mead's to tea. Emilie did not feel well enough to go. We expected Emmie over to go with us, but she did not come and we went alone. The boys were there and the people from Uncle Solomon's. We enjoyed the visit very much. When we came home, we stopped a moment at Mr. Howe's. Emmie was at our house when we came back, she came a few moments after we left and expected to have gone with us. We expect to go to N.Y., but it has very much the appearance of rain, and in that case we shall be very much disappointed.

V

A Week in Bloomfield, New Jersey, Before Returning to New York City September 6–September 12

Bloomfield Wednesday September 6th

We arose early and found the sky beautifully clear. We started for Whitlockville at six and reached there after a very pleasant ride at half past seven. As the day advanced it began to grow very warm. We left Emmie in the cars at Seventeenth St. When we reached home, Father had only just finished his breakfast. We walked around and packed our clothes, and then I went out and shopped a little. The weather was intensely warm. Anna Bowen came up to know if we could come there to tea. Henry came up about two and at three we started for Bloomfield. I never suffered so much as I did then with the heat. We found Edward at Newark with the carriage. We enjoyed the ride here very much. Henry and Edward went out to take a steam ride, they did not return till twelve but they enjoyed it very much. We felt very tired.

Bloomfield Thursday September 7th

Mary and I passed a very uncomfortable night. The heat was so very oppressive that we could scarcely sleep. We had a slight thunder shower during the night. I have sewed all the morning, and after dinner also. Our valise was to be sent out by Express, but it did not arrive here until this evening, and we were obliged to suffocate in our traveling dresses all day. Three young ladies called this afternoon and Aunt Mary had company to tea. Lucy[2] came up in the afternoon. Mary and I took a walk this evening.

Bloomfield Friday September 8th

Mary was sick all night, consequently she did not feel very much refreshed this morning. Lizzie washed some muslin and we all sewed. Emilie wrote a letter to Theodore. Aunt Mary had some company to dinner. After dinner we all sewed, and

Edward, Emilie and Lizzie went out to take a ride. Lucy came in the afternoon for Emilie to go home with her and stay all night. After tea two young ladies called, Miss Bradbury and Miss Bigelow.[3] Ellie Bigelow Mary's particular friend has the most exquisitely lovely face I ever saw. When they had gone Mary, Eddy and I went out to take a ride, we stopped at Mr. Bradbury's for them to go with us, but they were not allowed. We enjoyed our ride very much. When we returned I played some and we retired.

Bloomfield Saturday September 9th 1854

We arose early, after breakfast Mary and I arranged some rooms and made the beds, also dusted the parlors. The wind is blowing violently. We went down and made some cake, and then dressed ourselves. The Misses Seabury and Oaks[4] called upon us, we had quite a pleasant chat with them. Henry and Joe came about dark. After they had eaten tea we all went to get some Ice Cream. Henry and Emilie stopped for Miss Bigelow but her aunt would not allow her to go. We met a young lady on our way, Miss Kelsey[5] whom we persuaded to accompany us. We enjoyed the ice cream and lemonade very much. On our way home we stopped at the church as there was a choir meeting held there that night. It was very different from what I expected to see. Two young ladies were in the pulpit and a few others in the gallery. We staid a few moments and Eddy and I started to go home, upon reaching the door we found it raining violently, we were not at all prepared for such weather, and Henry started home for umbrellas and rubbers. He came back directly and said "that the carriage would be at the door in a few moments for the ladies". Five of us crowded into the back seat and two in the front. We arrived at home safely and without getting much wet. Eddy then drove the carriage back after the other young ladies, for which favor he incurred their lasting obligations. We were very much fatigued.

Bloomfield Sunday September 10th 1854

Aunt Mary came into our room before we arose and said that Henry was very sick, the Ice Cream and Lemonade had disagreed with him. It rained all night and was pouring when we awoke. Our window had been opened all night, the rain had been pouring in, so that the carpet was soaking wet. We did not go to church as it was so very wet. Henry was in bed all day. After dinner we laid down on sofas and went to sleep. Mary and Lizzie and I went into the Bible Class and were very much interested.

Bloomfield Monday September 11th

Henry and Joe went immediately after breakfast. Mary and I arranged the parlors and study. We then went down to make some cake as we expected the choir to meet here. Aunt Mary made some Ice Cream. The oven was too hot and our cake was burned. Lizzie made some more after dinner and we tried over again, at last succeeding. We were very tired and went upstairs to rest. Emilie and Lizzie went to Newark with Edward to meet Henry. A number of young ladies[6] came and we enjoyed the evening very much. Emilie was not well enough to be in the room, she has a very sore finger. Eddy went home with Ellie Biglow.

Bloomfield Thursday September 12th 1854

We did not wake until after breakfast. We then dressed ourselves and Emilie, Mary and I made several beds. Uncle Seymour and Eddy started for N. Haven[7] this morning. We sewed this morning and about four this afternoon we all started for Aunt Rachel's. Emilie's finger keeps growing worse. We spent a pleasant afternoon and evening with Aunt Rachel. Lucy came home and staid all night with Emilie. Miss Biglow was invited there but did not go. Mary and Lucy stopped there a moment on our way home, but she had gone to church.

VI

Autumn in New York City

N.Y. Wednesday September 13th

We arose early and I began to pack our clothes. Emilie did not sleep any until early morning and feels very badly. We got our dinner about twelve and started about one for this city, where we arrived at three. The house is in great confusion. Father has been very sick, but is almost well now. We sent for Dr. Beales,[1] he said that Emilie had a felon, and he lanced it twice. This evening she had an attack of cholera morbus[2] besides, and was in a great deal of pain.

New York Thursday September 14th

I went directly after breakfast to see Miss Clarke, she looked very well and said she would certainly come see Emilie this afternoon. We have to take all our meals at Uncle Robert's as they are painting the kitchen. Eleanor came up about five and Miss Clarke a few moments after. Nicholas came after Eleanor but it was raining so very violently that he did not go home, and he staid until after twelve playing billiards.

N.Y. Friday September 15th

Eleanor went home before breakfast. Uncle Robert and Aunt Thirza, Laura, and Eddy have gone to Bloomfield. I believe Emilie's finger is a little better this morning, but she feels very weak. I worked around the house until dinner. Aunt Hannah and children came in while we were dining. Father started for Milford[3] about four. I arranged the sheet closet this afternoon. Just as I was dressing to go to the opera, Emmie Ely came in. We made her go with us. Henry gave up his seat to her and took a promenade ticket. We were perfectly delighted, I never heard such magnificent music in all my life. Grisi[4] is a beautiful woman. It was very late or rather very early when we retired.

N.Y. Saturday September 16th

I have been busy all day, and have not accomplished much. We went in Uncle Robert's and spent the evening. Henry brought me a letter and one from Thomas. When we came home Joe brought us some cream for which we were obliged.

N.Y. Sunday September 17th

When I awoke, I felt very uncomfortably being covered with a rash which burned and itched like fire, my hands and feet are very much swollen. They all think it is poison and I have been bathing in salt and water. Emilie, Emmi, and Henry went to Christ's Church this morning and Dr. Alexander's this afternoon.[5] Joe came and staid until tea time, and we went in Uncle Robert's and spent the evening. Henry came home before us to write a letter. We were very much surprised to find Richmond here when we came in. He did not remain long.

N.Y. Monday September 18th

When I arose, the rash was gone but in less than an hour it returned worse than before. Aunt Thirza advised me to send for the doctor as she did not know what to do for it. Emmie went home early with Henry. The doctor came and said it was a nettle rash. Mr. Boyle[6] made us a call this morning he was delighted with the house. I was sitting alone in the library when I heard a knock at the door. I opened it expecting to see one of the men who are around the house. A lady entered the room, a friend of Ma's whom we had never seen. It was Mrs. Edward Firth,[7] she inquired particularly after Ma and the baby. We have been working very hard all day. Sereno and Joe came this evening. Theodore wrote a letter to Lizzie Wright[8] for Emilie as her finger disables her. We all wrote a letter to the girls. Theodore staid so late that he got locked out and was obliged to remain all night with Henry.

N.Y. Tuesday September 19th

We arose early and have been very busy all day. Mr. D'Orsay's[9] men had quite a fight with their tongues this morning so that Emilie was obliged to speak to them. I think they progress very slowly. We are getting settled quite quickly now in the second story. Aunt Thirza is not at all well today. This evening we had a very good serenade, and present many thanks to the donor. Joe came, but we retired very early and Henry and Joe played one game of billiards.

N.Y. Thursday September 21st 1854 [NB: entry out of order, but see below.]

The men seemed to get on very slowly today. We have busied ourselves this morning preparing the rooms for Ma's return. Nicolas came up this morning and said we might expect them home about four o'clock, and they would like some dinner. They did not reach home until five, and were very tired as they started from Milford at seven and had not stopped until reaching home. The baby has on short clothes and looks very lovely. Ma made me a present of a beautiful pair of earrings, and Emilie a pair of bracelets. Mary Ely and Mr. Baxter[10] were over this evening.

N.Y. Wednesday September 20th

Nothing occurred worthy of remembrance.

N.Y. Friday September 22nd

Ma and the babies went in Uncle Robert's with us to see Aunt Thirza. She is very poorly. We have been employed in arranging drawers and unpacking trunks. In the afternoon I arranged the butler's pantry. Henry and I went to see Mary Robbins about our dress making. Richmond and Joe are both here. Theodore went to Salem after cousin Laura, Aunt Thirza is worse this evening, she has an attack of Dysentery.

N.Y. Saturday September 23rd

Aunt Thirza is no better this morning. I have been ripping, washing and ironing an old dress to be made over. Aunt Hannah and Stephy[11] came up this morning and Stephy spent the day here. Ma and I took a walk this afternoon to Cole's [Coles'?][12] in Broadway also to Christ Church.

Sunday Sept. 24th 1854 N.Y.

Father and Ma went with us to Christ Church to hear Mr. Halsey.[13] We liked his sermon very much, it was a funeral sermon for Bishop Wainwright.[14] Sereno came up after dinner and went to Dr. Seabury's[15] with us. In the [evening] Joe came and Father brought four gentlemen in, they did not [stay] long and we all retired early. Uncle Peter and Mr. Blossom[16] came up to see how Aunt Thirza was and found her very weak.

Monday September 25th N.Y.

My eighteenth birthday, a very memorable event certainly. Ma and I went out early and did not reach home until after one. We went to the office and were weighed. Ma weighed 120 ½, and I 127. Aunt Hannah and Charlie were up this morning. Aunt Thirza is very ill, and Uncle Robert requested Dr. Taylor to consult with Dr. Beals. The Kenneys[17] were here today and Emilie went to see Miss Clarke this afternoon. Aunt Hannah and Uncle Peter were up again this evening. I think it very strange that I do not hear from Retta, probably I am forgotten. Annie has had a crying time tonight.

N.Y. Tuesday September 26th

Annie does not feel well today. Aunt Thirza is still very ill, they have sent for Mrs. Ackerman[18] to come and nurse her as cousin Laura is most worn out. Drs. Beales and Taylor were there a long while this morning, and Dr. Beales saw Ma as he was going away. He told her that Aunt Thirza was very dangerously ill, and I do not think he thought she would live long. Henry and I went to Dean's[19] and got some Ice Cream, we brought some home with us, and enjoyed eating it very much. The doctors were there this evening and were giving her a new remedy, they did not consider her as well as she was this morning. Dr. Alexander was there this afternoon.

N.Y. Wednesday September 27th

Henry went to inquire after Aunt Thirza and returned with the joyful news that she was better. Ma and the babies went to spend a few days at Aunt Hannah's while the paint is so fresh. Emilie and I have been working hard all the morning. About four we started to go to Brooklyn, where we passed a very pleasant evening. Mr. Baxter was there. We stopped and got some Cream.

N.Y. Thursday Sept. 28th

We busied ourselves nearly all day about the house. Aunt Emmeline came over this afternoon to see how Aunt Thirza was, and we were happy to say that she continued to improve, though very slowly. Richmond and Joe are both here tonight.

N.Y. Friday September 29th

Mary Robbins came today and I have been very busy indeed sewing. Theodore and Henry went with us to Uncle Peter's after tea, and from there to Mrs. Bowen's, where we spent a very pleasant evening. We stopped and got some Cream.

N.Y. Saturday September 30th

We have been very busy indeed all day sweeping and arranging the rooms. Ma was up here today to see about the house. Theodore and Robby staid all night with us as Henry went up home. Joe came as usual.

N.Y. Sunday October 1st 1854

We did not arise until late as we were very tired from the work of yesterday. We went over to Uncle Peter's and from there to our church All Saints. Mr. Eigenbrodt[20] has not yet returned from Europe, but is expected in about a fortnight or more. There were a great number of persons there. We did not get [text reads "home," but the word is crossed out] from church until nearly two. Joe came over after dinner and we went home about four o'clock. Theodore came in and staid all night. It began to rain about dusk and I expect it will continue a long time. Uncle Robert came in and wanted Theodore to go with him after a nurse for Aunt Thirza as Mrs. Ackerman was compelled to leave.

N.Y. Monday October 2nd

The day has been beautiful. I went to school today for the first time this year. Emilie went with me to take a French lesson. I like M. Delaney [possibly "Delauny" or "Delanny"][21] very much. I came home early and studied my lessons. Ma and the babies came home about eleven. Lucy came in about four o'clock from Bloomfield, and intends going to Salem tomorrow. It was quite late when we retired, Lucy did not stay with us.

N.Y. Tuesday October 3rd

It was very unpleasant when we arose but did not rain until after I went to school. Lucy did not go because of the rain. I missed one in Astronomy to my sorrow. I have just begun to study Geometry. Lucy came in and staid all night with us.

N.Y. Wednesday October 4th 1854

It rained very hard this morning and Father took me to school in the little carriage. Lucy went this morning. Aunt Thirza is improving daily. Margaret Robbins came this morning and finished my basque,[22] Ma went out with me and bought the trimming, and I studied in the evening. I received a letter from Retta and one from Eddie.

N.Y. Thursday October 5th

Arty[23] walked with me to school this morning. I began painting today. We went this evening to Dodsworth's Opening.[24] Miss Clarke kindly gave us the tickets and we went with the Kennys. The music was perfectly delightful. Mr. Dodsworth and Mr. Aptomas played a duet, upon the cornet and flute. We enjoyed the evening was very agreeable [sic]. Mr. Godfrey[25] was here when we came home.

N.Y. Friday October 6th

Emilie went to school to take a French lesson this morning. I did not recite my Geometry well today. I studied all the afternoon and evening. Joe came and played billiards of course.

N.Y. Saturday October 7th 1854

Arose early and swept our room, and then made some cake. I then took a bath and sewed. After dinner we all went out and shopped. Julia Smith and Fannie Price[26] came up to see us. We have been talking and writing all the evening.

N.Y. Sunday October 8th 1854

We all went to Dr. Tyng's this morning, and could scarcely hear a word as we were seated very near the door. This afternoon Emilie and I went to Dr. Muhlenberg's but we were very late and the church was so crowded that we could not get seats, and we went to Dr. Seabury's. Uncle Joseph was here a few moments.

N.Y. Monday October 9th 1854

I went to school and came home as soon as I had recited my lessons. I covered some dress boards for Ma, and mended some clothes.

South Salem Tuesday October 10th 1854

Annie is two years old today. Emilie and I started for Salem about half past seven, Uncle Joseph met us in the cars. Thomas met us at the depot, and we had a very delightful ride home. Uncle John, Aunt Sarah, and two children were there also Uncle Benajab, Aunt Fannie and two children. Grandpa seems much better than when we were here in the summer. We have enjoyed the day much. This evening Thomas went with us to see Mary. Her mother is very sick therefore they cannot have any but the family there tomorrow. DeWitt, Cyrus and Darius are all up. We had great fun looking at Mary's things, and practising standing up. When we came home Aunt Martha and two children had arrived and her brother Mr. Crosby.

New York Wednesday October 11th

We arose about half past five as we were to go down and dress the bride. Thomas went down there to dress as he wished DeWitt and Cyrus to dress him. Emilie and I were bridesmaids, and DeWitt and Cyrus groomsmen.[27] Thomas and Mary were very cool and really behaved admirably. We started about half past nine for the car and had a delightful ride. We reached this city about one. Mary and Lizzie came in about four and Emmie Ely came about six. We have just heard of the loss of the *Arctic*.[28] It is heartrending.

DeWitt and Cyrus came and spent this evening with us, after a great deal of persuasion on our part. The bride looked lovely.

Loss of the U. S. M. Steam Ship Arctic. Lithograph by Nathaniel Currier, 1854. *(Courtesy of the Mariner's Museum, Newport News, Virginia.)*

Thursday October 12th

Arose early. Henry and Emilie went to the boat with Thomas and Mary, but for some reason it did not run and they were compelled to go to Albany in the cars, much to their sorrow. DeWitt and Cyrus had intended going with them, but business prevented and as they are going south soon,[29] I do not suppose we shall see them again very soon. We went out today and bought our bonnets and my cloak. I have been trying to study all the afternoon but have not succeeded.

Friday October 13th 1854

I went to school this morning and have been studying all day. We all went to the Opera very unexpectedly, thanks to Henry. I can hardly make up my mind whether I like Madame Grisi best in 'Norma' or 'I Puritani'. We were perfectly delighted. I never heard such music before.

Saturday October 14th

I arose early and began to arrange our room, Lizzie swept and I dusted it. Mary and I made some cake, and then we sewed. It has rained very hard all day and this evening we had a thunder shower. Joe came and brought an *Extra Sun* with the letter from Captain Luce.[30] Father was quite sick this afternoon.

Sunday October 15th N.Y.

We all went to Christ Church this morning, where we heard an excellent sermon. Mr. Halsey spoke very feelingly and beautifully of the Arctic. This afternoon Ma and Father went to Dr. Hawks,[31] and we went to Dr. Muhlenberg's. I do not know when the wind has blown harder. This evening we have been singing.

Monday October 16th 1854

I went to school today. Mr. Keyser[32] came and staid all night.

Tuesday October 17th

Nothing occurred of importance. Richmond and Joe were here. Ellen went today.

Wednesday October 18th

Passed a very disagreeable day in school as my Geometry was not recited perfectly. Emilie and Mary and Lizzie took Annie to get a daguerreotype for Ellen, but did not succeed in getting a very good one. Ma and Father went to Patterson to spend the day with Mrs. Godwin.[33] Emilie and Mary Lizzie and Laura went to Brooklyn in the afternoon. Henry Artie and I went in the evening. They had quite a little company. Mary and Lizzie did not return with us.

Thursday October 19th

This evening we went to call on Jane Lawrence and spent a delightful evening. Mr. Stewart was here and staid all night.

Friday October 20th

Lucy came down this afternoon, we went in Uncle Robert's and spent the evening. Mary and Lizzie came in about nine o'clock having been at Mrs. Ginochio's[34] all day. We spent a very pleasant evening. I believe Henry intends going to Cream Ridge tomorrow.

Saturday October 21st 1854

I swept our room and then washed and ironed five muslins. Lizzie helped me and Mary made some cake. I then went out with Ma and Annie. Mary and Lizzie and Lucy went over to Brooklyn directly dinner.

N.Y. Sunday October 22nd

We went to Dr. Hawkes for the first time since father bought a pew. Sereno came up and went to church with Emilie.

Monday October 23rd 1854

Laura and Uncle Robert went to school with me this morning. I found some of the girls standing on the sidewalk. They immediately told me that there would be no school as Mr. Williams was dead. He was taken with the cholera on Friday night and died on Saturday evening. I went home immediately and went with Father, Ma and the children down to Lawrences.[35] Ma went down to the boat with Father as he was going to Philadelphia. We staid there a long while. The baby was taken five times, and we got quite a good one. Annie would not stand or sit a moment and of course we could not get one of her. Laura's was excellent. Mary and Lizzie were here when we came back. They expect to go home tomorrow. Henry wrote a note that Aunt Hannah wanted us all to go over there to tea, as Aunt Mary was there, and she would come home with us. I expected Mr. Boyle and of course could not go to tea. Theodore came in after tea and I went with him. We spent a pleasant evening. Uncle Peter made us promise that we would all go to Lawrence's tomorrow and have a group taken for him. Henry had a delightful visit at Cream Ridge, and I have no doubt wished it were longer. I received a little note from Retta.

Tuesday October 24th 1854

I went to school this morning and Laura went with me. I came from school early and we went to have our daguerreotypes taken. Emilie and I each had one taken for the Stewarts, and a group for Uncle Peter, we were very tired when we got home.

Wednesday October 25t 1854

Mary and Lizzie went away early this morning, and we feel very lonesome. Emmie Ely came over and staid all night. Joe brought some candy and we enjoyed it very much. Father came home.

Thursday October 26th 1854

Emmie went away early this morning. This evening Eleanor and Richmond[36] came up, they staid until late.

Friday October 27th

Thomas sent word that they would have come home this evening at ten o'clock. We had some tea ready for them and waited until twelve o'clock. When we had been in bed an hour Father woke us up and said they were here. We got up and dressed a little and gave them some tea.

Saturday October 28th 1854

Thomas and Mary were very much refreshed. They had enjoyed their trip very much. We had a very pleasant morning together. They went to Salem at four o'clock, to our sorrow.

Sunday October 29th 1854

We all went to Dr. Hawks this morning and it was Communion Sunday. This afternoon we went but they merely had prayers. Joe and Theodore came in the evening. Ma received a letter from Mr. Wolbert[37] saying that little Frank was no more, after a sickness of scarcely a night he died on Thursday.

Monday Oct 30th 1854

Emmie Ely invited a little company this evening, and Emilie and I went over this afternoon and took our clothes in a carpet bag, notwithstanding the rain. There were only two ladies and one gentleman there but we enjoyed the evening very much. Henry came over and we staid all night.

Tuesday October 31st 1854

Nothing of importance occurred.

Wednesday Nov 1st 1854

Nothing particular.

Thursday Nov 2nd 1854

Grandma, Uncle John, Aunt Sarah came down. They have all had Chicken pox. Grandma told us of the death of Harriet Keeler.[38] I had not even heard that she was ill. She died of the Typhus Fever. Uncle Joseph came this evening after most of us had retired. They all went to see a balloon ascend in the afternoon.

Friday Nov 3rd 1854

I spent a very disagreeable day at school. Uncle John and family started for Virginia this afternoon.[39] Lucy and the boys came in and spent the evening. Lucy staid all night.

Saturday, Nov 4th

Ma and I went down to the store that Joe belongs at, and purchased a cartload of things. Lucy went home soon after we returned. We sewed some this afternoon.

Sunday Nov 5th

We went to church this afternoon and morning. Joe, Richmond and Nicholas were up this evening.

Monday Nov 6th

Margaret Robbins came today. I took my first music lesson this afternoon. One of Mr. Boyle's daughters has been sick.

Tuesday Nov 7th 1854

Sallie and Nellie Kenny, also the two Mr. Matthews spent the evening with us. We enjoyed it very much.

Wednesday Nov 8th

Emmie Ely came over and staid all night. Sereno came and the boys and spent the evening, we ate nuts and so forth. Peter in trouble.[40]

Thursday Nov 9th

I went to school this morning but felt so sick that I was obliged to come home at ten o'clock. I went to bed staid there until two and then began to feel better. Miss Stafford[41] called also Julia Smith and Fannie Price. Old Mr. Stewart came and took tea with us.

Friday Nov 10th

Emilie is sick today, and she wanted to see Lucy, so Robbie went over to Brooklyn after her and she is going to stay until Monday morning for which I am glad.

Saturday Nov 11th

I have been very busy today. I swept and dusted our room and hung some pictures, and then dusted the library. I have been sewing since. Aunt Emmeline sent Barbara[42] over here on an errand. Emilie is better today. Stormed all day.

Sunday Nov 12th

Very stormy and we have not been to church today. Lucy and I went to Uncle Robert's and staid some time.

Monday Nov 13th

When I returned from school we all went out to take a ride. In the evening Father and Ma went to call on Mrs. Ball.[43] I put Annie to sleep. Theodore came in.

Tuesday Nov 14th

Emilie went over to Mr. Bowen's to take tea, and Theodore, Henry and I went there to spend the evening. Anna Angel was there and Mr. Pierce, they played duetts [sic] delightfully on the flute and piano.

Wednesday Nov 15th

Henry went over to Brooklyn and called at Mr. Atwater's,[44] he was not at home, but Miss Atwater was, and Henry seemed to enjoy his call very much.

Thursday Nov 16th

Albert Angel, and Nicholas came up this evening.

Friday Nov 17th

Emmie Ely came over to stay all night, she got a great fright coming over. Theodore, Joe and Henry have been acting like young high school boys this evening.

Saturday Nov 18th

Emmie staid until four o'clock and Emilie went home with her. She fixed Emilie's bonnet for her beautifully.

Sunday Nov 19th

We have been to church, Henry staid in as I should have been lonesome. This evening, we went to Dr. Macauley's in 5th Avenue to hear Dr. Cox.[45] There was a great crowd and we could not hear a word.

Monday Nov 20th

Emilie came directly to school from Brooklyn.

Tuesday Nov 21st

Nothing of importance.

Wednesday Nov 22nd

Nothing worth noting.

Thursday Nov 23rd

Thanksgiving Day in Jersey. Henry went home. Mary Ely came over and staid all night. Cousin Mary Ann, Aunt Thirza and the boys all came in, we spent a pleasant evening.

Friday Nov 24th

It rained fast when I came from school and I got wet nearly to my knees. Henry came up and I wrote and studied all the evening.

Saturday November 25th 1854

We worked early in the morning and about one we went out to make calls we did not return home until after four. I went in Uncle Robert's.

Sunday Nov 26th

We went to church and did not get home until half past one, as it was Communion Sunday. This afternoon Julia and Ellis Price came and sat with us. Theodore and Arthur went over to Brooklyn to attend the funeral of Dr. Spence, he died on Friday. Richmond and Nicholas are up now, Father is talking politics with Richmond.

Monday Nov 27th

Uncle Peter and Aunt Hannah came up. Henry did not come up till later.

Wednesday Nov 29th [sic]

Ma, Father and Annie went to Philadelphia today. Lucy came over from Brooklyn Mr. and Mrs. Keyser and Mrs. [Divoo? Dinoo?][46] came to see Ma. They did not stay long.

Tuesday Nov 28th [sic]

We went to the Irving Literary Union.[47] Mary [Marven?] came and went with Henry and me. Emilie went with Miss Clarke. We were delighted.

Thursday Nov 30th

Thanksgiving Day. Henry went to New Haven early this morning. Theodore and Lucy went to church with us. We took a very good dinner in Uncle Robert's. We spent the evening there.

Friday December 1st

Henry came down from New Haven early. I washed muslins. I then went out to buy some dresses for the five dolls which Father is going to present to his young friends on Christmas.[48] Emmie Ely came over late in the afternoon. We went in Uncle Robert's to see Aunt Theodosia who has just arrived there.

Saturday Dec 2nd

We worked this morning. About twelve Nellie and Sallie Kenny and Augusta Williams came to help us dress the dolls. Miss Clarke came to tea. We succeeded in accomplishing quite an amount of sewing.

Sunday December 3rd

A very stormy day. Henry and Emilie and Emmie went to church this morning, but I had such a bad cold that I did not go. It has been raining and snowing alternately all day. It is raining hard now. Theodore came in and staid a few moments.

Monday December 4th

I went to school as usual. We received a letter from Ma saying they would come on Tuesday. Made a doll's skirt.

Tuesday December 5th

Went to school. We expected them home at two, but they did not arrive until four and then very tired out.

Wednesday December 6th

I received a letter from Mary Seymour. Sereno came up this evening.

Thursday Dec 7th

Nothing occurred of importance.

Friday Dec 8th

Henry brought word that Uncle Ely's mother was dead and the funeral is to be at two o'clock tomorrow. Mr. Stewart came in a few moments. Emilie received a letter from Lizzie Wright in which her sister wrote me a few lines, for which I am thankful and shall answer soon. I received a letter from Rett. Henry and I went to call on Mary Marvin and spent a pleasant evening.

Saturday Dec 9th

This morning I swept and dusted our room as usual. The parlors are at last arranged. Anne Wolbert[49] and I, went over to Brooklyn to the funeral. We stopped for Theodore. Mrs. Ely died suddenly. Theodore went for Lucy and we left her home as we returned. This evening they all came in and enjoyed a dance. Mrs. MaCready[50] was here yesterday.

Sunday Dec 10th

I went to church this morning and Emilie went this afternoon. Joe came in. No one has been here this evening. Annie has not been at all well, but we hope is getting better now.

Monday Dec 11th 1854

This evening we went down to the Mechanics Institute to hear Dr. Bethune lecture on Oracles,[51] but we were too late and obliged to come home as the seats were all taken.

Tuesday Dec 12th 1854

Emilie Ely came over and staid all night. The boys came in.

Wednesday Dec 13th 1854

Aunt Anna and children went to New Rochelle this afternoon.

Thursday Dec 14th 1854

Ma received a letter from Mrs. Godfrey saying that she would not be able to make us a visit until spring. We sat down and wrote a letter to Stewarts to come on next week. I hardly expect them but hope they will come. Annie is very sick tonight.

Friday Dec 15th 1854

The boys were all in this evening.

Saturday Dec 16th 1854

We were very busy indeed this morning. Mrs. James Hoe[52] and daughter Isabella also Mrs. Richard Hoe called,[53] Ma was not at home and I was very sorry. Aunt Anna and children also Caddie Wolbert came down from New Rochelle this morning, they have had a very pleasant visit there. The boys came in this evening and we had a pleasant dance.

Sunday Dec 17th 1854

We all went to church this morning, it began snowing about two o'clock, and now the ground is all white. Emilie went to church this afternoon. Annie is better now.

Monday Dec 18th

Cad[54] went away this morning. This evening we all went to Uncle Peter's where we met Emmie, Mary, Peter and Mr. Baxter. We enjoyed the few hours much. Eddie returned from New Haven today. He arrived at our house at eleven p.m.

Tuesday Dec 19th

Louise Johnson[55] and her brother called this evening. Father went to Boston.

Wednesday Dec 20th

Emilie went over to church.

Thursday Dec 21st

Henry, Theodore, and I went over to call on Lucy and Ellie Biglow. We had a pleasant time.

Friday Dec 22nd

The boys were in a few moments.

Saturday Dec 23rd

Ma and I went shopping for Aunt Emeline and then took our purchases over there. In the evening we all received our presents. Emilie and I, each a silk umbrella, a morocco [sic] travelling bag, a pearl paste monnaie, and a basket of French confectionery. Lucy came over with us from Brooklyn.

Sunday Dec 24th

It was very unpleasant, I was not well and therefore Emilie went to church alone.

Monday Christmas Dec 25th 1854

We were in Uncle Robert's most of the time Emmie Ely came over. We all enjoyed the day much.

Tuesday Dec 26th 1854

Emilie and Annie Wolbert went over to see Eleanor and the children, but did not find them at home. Ma and I went shopping. The boys Frank and Ira[56] came in, we had a dance this evening. I wrote a letter to the Stewarts I think it is very strange they have not sent us a line. Lucy went to Salem early.

Wednesday Dec 27th

I received a present of a very pretty basket from Uncle Peter.

Chapter I: Diary Endnotes

1. Robert Hoe III (1839–1909) is Addie's first cousin, three years her junior. Here, in the summer of 1854, he is about fifteen years old. Among his many other accomplishments as an adult, he will become renowned as a collector of rare books.
2. Theodore Hoe Mead (1837–1909) is one of five children adopted by Robert Hoe Jr. (1815–1884) and Thirza Mead Hoe upon the death of parents Enoch Milan Mead (d. 1850) and Elizabeth Hoe (Mudge) Mead. Theodore and siblings Frederick, Edward S., and Herbert Mead were raised along with Robert's and Thirza's three children: Arthur M., Robert III, and Laura Hoe. Theodore will become author of *Our Mother Tongue*, a charming and detailed monograph containing discussion of American vs. British speech and pronunciation, and *Horsemanship for Women*. We have, here, the first encounter with family surnames connected to publishing houses: in this greater family circle we have Meads, Dodds, and Harpers—all of them principal figures in the establishment of major publishers still in business today.
3. Adeline's half-sister Annie Corbin Hoe (1852–1887) was the oldest daughter of the three (surviving) girls born to Richard March Hoe and his second wife, Mary Say Corbin.
4. Henry is yet another first cousin, the son of Reverend Ebenezer Seymour and Mary Hoe Seymour, sister of Richard March Hoe. Reverend Ebenezer Seymour was a Presbyterian minister in Bloomfield, New Jersey, for many years, then one of the founders and first headmaster of the Bloomfield Institute, a preparatory school for local boys and girls.
5. Adeline's older sister Emilie Amelia Hoe (1834–1909). Adeline's and Emilie's mother, Lucy Gilbert Hoe, died in 1841. Their father, Richard March Hoe, remarried two years later. With his second wife, Mary Say Corbin Hoe, he had four more daughters. Annie was two years old here in 1854; Mary was an infant born just a little while before Adeline undertook her journal. Two more girls, Fanny and Helen, were born after this period of the journal. Helen died in infancy.
6. We are presently in the dark here. The "calls" were, presumably, social, but is there a possibility that they were charitable in nature?
7. The older daughter of Emmeline Hoe Ely and Giles Sill Ely. Her mother was Richard March Hoe's sister. So, the oft-referred to "Emmie Ely" is yet another of Adeline's first cousins. She lived in Brooklyn.
8. Like ice cream (see below, Note #38), "billiards" is, in 1854, both an old and new topic. "The Noble Game of Billiards" originated in northern Europe in the 15th century. By 1800, billiard equipment had improved because of the Industrial Revolution. Originally played outdoors on grass, much like croquet, the indoor game gained a green felt surface for the table when it moved indoors. The mace to shove the ball became a "cue" and the hoops disappeared. By 1823, the cue tip became leather, and chalk was used to create friction between cue and billiard

ball. By 1835, slate had become popular for the billiard table bed. Goodyear discovered how to vulcanize rubber in 1839. By 1845, rubber was being used to make billiard cushions on the sides of the table. By 1850, billiards had evolved to its present form. In America, the game was likely brought over by the Dutch and the English, and until the 1870s it was usually played on an eleven-to-twelve-foot table with a length/width ratio of two-to-one. Michael Phelan, who arrived from Ireland in 1850, wrote the first American book on the game, devising rules and standards of behavior. Richard March Hoe and his friends probably played American Four-Ball Billiards on a four-pocket table, using two white balls and two red. (For more information, see Mike Shamos's "A Brief History of the Noble Game of Billiards," which can be found on the *Billiards Digest* website.)

9 "Uncle Robert" is Robert Hoe II, as mentioned in note #1 above. His wife, "Aunt Thirza," is Thirza Mead Hoe.

10 Adeline refers here to her mother's parents, Josiah and Sally Hoyt Gilbert, who live in South Salem, New York.

11 Edward Seymour, younger brother of Henry Seymour. See Note #4. He will matriculate at Yale College in the fall.

12 Adeline's infant half-sister, born early in 1854 (d.1925). She will grow up and marry Joseph Henry Harper of Harper Publishers.

13 Bloomfield, New Jersey, is about a dozen miles west of the Hoes' home at 309 Broadway in Lower Manhattan. Cousin Henry, we may imagine, would either walk or take a horse-drawn tram car to the Hudson River, cross by ferry, and proceed to Bloomfield.

14 The Niagara Falls Suspension Bridge was the world's first working railway suspension bridge, and stood 2.5 miles downstream from Niagara Falls from 1855–1897. It spanned 825 feet. It is significant that by 1854 the bridge was nearly complete, and the lower deck of the two-level structure was open for pedestrian and carriage travel. John August Roebling successfully completed the project, which became the prototype for the bridge from Brooklyn to Manhattan he would later build.

15 Joe Stewart is clearly a close friend and business associate of Richard March Hoe. He appears frequently in Adeline's journal. He is, we think, the son of Charles Stewart, manufacturer of bar and sheet iron, owner of a factory in Cream Ridge, New Jersey.

16 Mrs. Bailey is elusive. She was probably a nurse, but perhaps she was the wife of a Franklin Bailey, who lived in New York City and sold several printing patents to R. Hoe & Co. (In January of 1858, Adeline will write, in a letter to Cousin Robert, "Tell your mother we called on Mrs. Bailey today and found her quite smart. She looks very thin but seems in good spirits and was very glad to see us. I was quite astonished to find that she remembered who we had married. I think she is a lovely old lady.")

17 Ellen seems to be one of the several hired servants. We imagine her to be the "Ellen" referred to in Adeline's June 3rd journal entry; if so, she is a young mother and lives across the East River in Williamsburgh, formerly a separate township but incorporated into Brooklyn in 1854.

Chapter I: Diary Endnotes   259

18 Sereno Smith, born 1836, was Adeline's contemporary. He was the son of Matthew Smith III, cousin of Richard March Hoe. The Smiths were, from the very beginning of the company, very much at the center of operations of R.Hoe & Co., especially on the accounting side of the business.

19 Dr. Stephen H. Tyng was, according to his contemporary and fellow New York City minister Theodore Ledyard Cuyler, "the most conspicuous minister in the city." He was rector of St. George's Episcopal Church on Stuyvestant Square, acknowledged leader of the "Low Church" wing of the episcopacy. He was so eloquent that Henry Ward Beecher is said to have wished never to proceed or follow him on the speaker's platform. He also apparently had a hot temper, and he was a ferocious, inexorable fund-raiser.

20 Mary Robbins is, we think, a seamstress. With "Margaret" she will spend tomorrow "sewing hard all day".

21 On June 29, there was to be an extended trip to Delaware by way of Philadelphia, with a week-long stay in Cream Ridge, New Jersey, on the way back to Manhattan. One of "the girls" who goes on that adventure may be Charlotte Stewart, sister of Joe Stewart; it seems clear that "Lottie" is a special pal of Adeline's, with whom Adeline rides, walks, talks, and dances.

22 See Note #20 above.

23 Lizzie Angell has, so far, eluded efforts to uncover her identity. We assume that she is related to Anna Angell, who appears in the journal November 14, and to Albert Angell, who appears November 16.

24 The full name is the Magnetic Telegraph Company. The meeting is held at the Washington Irving House, just off 3rd Avenue. (Irving never lived in it.). Richard March Hoe installed the first private telegraph wire in the city, in 1849, connecting his office to the printing plant. The early days of the telegraph were apparently pretty wild, with lawsuits and countersuits over patents, and controversies with Samuel F. B. Morse, whose first public telegraph demonstration was in 1838, and first commercial telegraph line was installed between Washington, D.C. and Baltimore in 1843.

25 Richmond Bowen is the son of Alfred S. Bowen, the general superintendent of R. Hoe & Co.

26 Eleanor is Richmond's sister.

27 William M. Swain, editor of the Philadelphia *Ledger* for twenty years, was an early customer of R. Hoe & Co. He installed one of the first of Richard March Hoe's Lightning Printing Presses, and they were close friends for many years.

28 Adeline's uncle, Thomas Gilbert, younger brother of Adeline's mother Lucy Gilbert, and husband of Mary Lawrence. Take a deep breath, and let's go on: Mary Lawrence Gilbert is the sister of Cyrus J. Lawrence and DeWitt Clinton Lawrence. Adeline's older sister Emilie will marry Cyrus J. Lawrence in 1856; Adeline will marry DeWitt Clinton Lawrence in 1857. Uncle Thomas Gilbert is a central character and general factotum later in Adeline's journal when, in August and September, Adeline and the family are staying in South Salem at what, in our day, we might call the family compound. Among Uncle Thomas's many other duties, he is the one who takes care of the horses and wagons. In fact, he "runs the farm;" and he will inherit it.

29 Miss Arabella Clarke (Adeline corrects the spelling in subsequent journal entries) was principal of the Female Department of the Mechanics School located on 4th Avenue. Founded in 1820 by the Society of Mechanics and Tradesmen, the school, which had provided solely technical training to young men, added moral instruction to its curriculum and welcomed young women. James Henry, the school's actuary, in 1853 proposed the establishment of diplomas and medals to be awarded to "good mothers." The five-story school building was located at the corner of Bowery and Division Streets. Women would study drawing, painting, and music. Adeline will study geometry as well. Women would have access to the Ladies' Reading Room. "Truth, Punctuality, Integrity, Industry and Perseverance" were to be valued in order to promote virtue among the city's youth. The Institute closed after 1856, but its 5,000-volume library became the nucleus for the Library of Cooper Union, which opened in 1859.

30 Louis Antoine Jullien (1812–1860) seems to have been the Lawrence Welk of his day. A portly and sartorially splendid French conductor and composer of light music, Jullien was perhaps most distinguished by his thirty-six middle names: his father, also a conductor, apparently ebullient over Jullien's birth, invited the thirty-six members of his orchestra to contribute their own first names at the christening. Antoine was, we assume, first in alphabetical order. Louis Antoine . . . Jullien chased success while fleeing from creditors, from France to England to Scotland to Ireland and finally, in 1850, to America, where "the monster Julien [sic] Concerts drew immense houses night after night" (Holice and Debbie, *Our Firemen: The History of the NY Fire Departments*. Ch.16, Pt.5). Adeline and Cousin Edward Seymour probably went down to hear Jullien's Orchestra perform its nearly 300th American concert in four years, at the Battery Park Concert Hall, which was the converted fort and which, but a year afterward, would be *re*converted, this time into an immigration station. Jullien, sad to say, ended his life six years later, in debt, insane, and in prison.

31 Elizabeth Mead Smith, born 1811 in Waccabuc, New York, married William Smith in 1845. Her parents were Solomon Mead and Eunice Gilbert.

32 Uncle Peter is Peter S. Hoe, the third and youngest of the Hoe brothers, born 1821, thus nine years younger than Adeline's father. His wife is Hannah Mead Smith Hoe.

33 The clues to Ellen's identity remain inconclusive, and Adeline's pronoun reference is a bit vague: we assume "they" includes only Ma and her sister Emilie, inasmuch as Annie is two years old and Ellen is mother of a child among children who are filthy, naked, and remind Ma of "wild Indians." We picture Ma taking her twenty-year-old daughter Emilie and her two-year-old daughter Annie, along with Ellen, the servant, to see Ellen's family in a poor section of Williamsburgh.

34 Annie Westervelt is the daughter of the mayor of New York, Jacob Aaron Westervelt, preeminent builder of sailing and steam ships. He was mayor from 1853–55. Annie is a year older than Emilie and three years older than Adeline. In a letter to Cousin Robert in 1858, Adeline reports that Anna Westervelt is engaged to Richmond Bowen.

35 Aside from the clear implication that "little Lizzie Miller" is a playmate of Annie Hoe's, and thus a child of about four, we are unable to find out who these ladies are.

36 Is this Adeline's delicate way of saying that the family servant Mary Richards is "in a family way"?

37 Arthur M. Hoe (1841–1865) is the second son of Robert Hoe Jr.

38 Like billiards, ice cream is both old subject and new topic of interest, conversation and consumption. The construction "ice cream" dates back at least into the 18th century, and no doubt frozen cream was as old as milking cows in cold climates. But it was not until 1843 that Nancy Johnson secured the first U.S. patent on a hand-cranked freezer. Eight years later, Jacob Fussell, of Baltimore, a milk wholesaler who bought milk from Pennsylvania farmers and found that he had a lot of useless cream spilled around, built an ice cream *factory* in 1851 in Pennsylvania. He moved it to Baltimore two years later. He was clearly onto a lucrative thing, and in the 1850s he opened factories in several other cities, thus introducing mass-produced ice cream into American commerce. Like Alexander T. Stewart with his department stores pitching clothing to the emerging women's market, and like the many daguerreotypists pitching photo-portraits, Fussell was capitalizing on emerging markets which targeted women and children. We note with interest that Adeline capitalizes "Ice Cream" throughout her journal.

39 "Stephy" is Stephen S. Hoe, son of uncle and aunt Peter and Hannah Hoe. He is six or seven years old here. Little brother "Charley" is probably about three. As an adult, Charley will become a "member" of R. Hoe & Co.

40 Nor did we find them, either at their home or our own.

41 Sarah Margaretta Stewart, born 1838, is the younger sister of Joe Stewart. She will marry Theodore Freling-huysen Clarke.

42 We are quite certain that Adeline intends the possessive case here, and that the reference is to Alfred S. Bowen, general superintendent of R. Hoe & Co. He will be dispatched during the Civil War to run the Hoe operation in Boston. His son Nicholas, mentioned in Adeline's next sentence, was born in 1832 and is either just graduated or very soon to graduate from West Point at this time of Adeline's journal. Nicholas will be an engineer in the Union Army during the Civil War. His reports are key documents in General George McClellan's tactics at the Battle of Antietam in September 1862 and in General Burnside's tactics later in December at the Battle of Fredericksburg. Nicholas's sisters Anna and Eleanor are close friends of Adeline's (see Notes #25 and 26, above, and #54, below).

43 Is Peter a servant? Or does Adeline refer here to her uncle Peter S. Hoe? The former seems likely, given Adeline's habit of using "aunt" or "uncle" before the name.

44 Mary Dunn may be the wet nurse whom Adeline's father went looking for on June 2.

45 The YMCA was established in New York City in 1852 by George H. Petrie, a young businessman who had traveled to England a year earlier and had been impressed by this new organization established there in 1844. About ten blocks north of the Hoe residence, on Stuyvestant Square, Petrie's YMCA chapter was the first in the city. At the time of Adeline's journal, there were about 200 official members.

46 Lydia Seabury is the second daughter of the Reverend Samuel Seabury and his wife Lydia Huntington Seabury (of the Huntington family that gives its name to the town on Long Island's north shore).

47 Aunt Theo is the tenth child and youngest daughter of Robert Hoe, i.e. sister of Richard March Hoe, Robert Hoe Jr., and Peter Hoe. She was born in 1823 and is, at this time of Adeline's journal, unmarried.

48 Is this a conclusion or a prediction? That is, *did* Aunt Theo go to Rochester to be "benefitted," or does she *plan* to go in the future? What benefit would there be in a trip to Rochester, New York? It happens that precisely during this period of Adeline's journal there was much publicity about the homeopathic "water-cure," especially the practice of the water-cure in Rochester "as among the first communities to have a water-cure and by 1851 could boast of two." In that year, a gentleman named Hatfield Halsted, who prefaced his name with the dubious title of "Doctor" and described himself as a "magnetic physician," established Hatfield Hall, an idyllic, comfortable, and expensive retreat where patients undergoing the water-cure could purchase "electric pills," galvanized plasters, and magnetic ether. They also could ingest or be sprayed by the "best" of spring water from the renowned sulfur springs nearby. He advertised cures for spinal curvature, scrofula, "female diseases," dyspepsia, liver complaint, diarrhea, pulmonary disease, and even sexual problems. Halsted's chief competition came from Lorenzo Fleming, who opened Fleming's Lake View Water-Cure in 1853, an elegant establishment with the additional draw of therapeutic horseback riding and a distinguished clientele including Horace Mann, Governor Seward (later Lincoln's Secretary of State), and Lewis Tappan (of Tappanzee Bridge fame). Sadly, in July of 1854, after a fire which burned down one wing, Fleming's Lake View was closed for good. At about the same time, Hatfield Halsted got run out of town. So, a month after this journal entry of Adeline's, Rochester ceased to be a destination point for those seeking the water-cure.

49 Reverend William E. Eigenbrodt (1813–1894), a prominent New York City Episcopalian minister.

50 Limherr & Co. was a jeweler located at 577 Broadway. That this was a high-end jewelry store is suggested by the fact that in 1853 a full sized tea and coffee set crafted by Limherr and "worked of human hair" was chosen to be included in the Crystal Palace jewelry exhibition. (See C. Jeanenne Bell, G.G., *Collectors' Encyclopedia of Hairwork Jewelry* [Collector Books: Paducah, Kentucky, 1998], 23–24.) The going rates for breast pins made of hair were advertised between four and twelve dollars. Multiply by 16 to get a sense of what the cost would be today.

51 We have puzzled, almost to the point of madness and incipient marital discord, about this reference. All other references to Joe Stewart suggest that he is not only a family friend but a business associate. And he is *not* related to the famous Alexander L. Stewart of Stewart's Department Store (which was just up Broadway from the Hoes' home). Is Adeline jesting a bit, i.e. calling Stewart's Department Store "Joe's store" because he shops there a lot and shares a surname with the store's owner?

52 See Note #35 above. We envision family friends named Miller: the mother named Mary and the daughter "little Lizzie Miller," a playmate of Annie Hoe.

53 Alexander Roux (1813–1886) emigrated to the United States from France as a young man, settled in New York City, and established a business as maker of elegant and expensive furniture. He expanded and became what we might today

call an interior decorator, and he eventually oversaw 120 employees. To have Roux "do over" your home was, in those days, an expensive proposition. The Astors were among his clients. If you have a piece of furniture designed and crafted by Alexander Roux, head for the *Antiques Roadshow* at a dead run.

54 See Note #42: Anna Bowen is the daughter of Alfred S. Bowen and the sister of Richmond and Nicholas Bowen.

55 Reverend Samuel Seabury, father of Lydia (Note #46 above).

56 We imagine that Messrs. Dupuy and D'Orsay are employees of Alexander Roux, perhaps fellow immigrants from France.

57 We imagine Mr. Berrion and Anne Johnson's husband are employees of R. Hoe & Co.

Chapter II: Diary Endnotes

1. See Note #46 in Chapter 1: Reverend Samuel Seabury is a Presbyterian minister living in New York City; his daughter is Lydia. Reverend Samuel's brother, Charles Saltonstall Seabury, is a piano maker living in Stony Brook, Long Island; his daughter is Maria.

2. William Sidney Mount (1807–1868) was a major 19th century landscape artist and portrait painter. He was the third of four brothers. Both older brothers were painters as well; and the younger brother, Robert, was a renowned instructor of music and dance.

3. Sarah Nunns was a daughter of Robert Nunns "the piano maker." Robert Nunns and his partner John Clark were famous for a fine, square piano. In 1853, some eighty employees, including members of the Steinway family, were producing about 300 instruments annually at the Nunns & Clark factory in Setauket, Long Island, the village next to Stony Brook. We think it may be a relative of John Clark for whom Emilie had the breast pin made by Limherr jewelers (see June 9 journal entry).

4. Mrs. Wells is Julia Ann Seabury Wells, age twenty-two. She is married to Charles Henry Wells. Sad to say, Julia died in March of 1857 at age twenty-five, and her husband died in 1862 at age thirty-two.

5. Nina Mount (1837–1920), niece of William Sidney Mount, daughter of Henry Smith Mount, who was a floral painter and was raised in Stony Brook in the Hawkins-Mount family homestead.

6. Maria is Maria Seabury. Julia is Julia Mount, niece of William Sidney Mount. Sarah Nunns is daughter of the piano maker. Mr. Mount is William Sidney Mount. The two Mr. Seaburys are the brothers Rev. Samuel Seabury and Charles Saltonstall Seabury.

7. Adeline spells the name with a *c*, but it seems likely that the name is "Groesbeek." Charles Edward Groesbeek married Margaret Louisa Morand in Setauket in 1838. Two or three generations later, Annah Morand became the first librarian in the Ellen L. Clark Library in Setauket, dedicated in 1892. Groesbeek, Morand, Seabury, Mount, Hawkins, Nunns, Clark—these families are clearly at the center of the society of this "tri-town" (Stony Brook, Setauket, Brookhaven) area here in the middle of the 19th century.

8. Ellen Nunns is the sister of Sarah.

9. We think that "Ma Mount" is the sister-in-law of William Sidney Mount, i.e. wife of Shepard Alonzo Mount.

10. In the Hawkins burial ground in Stony Brook is a gravestone for an African American whom the family held in high esteem. At the top of the brown marker is a violin carved in relief. Below is the epitaph authored by Micah Hawkins, uncle of William Sidney Mount. It begins with a two-line quotation from Alexander Pope:

> "ENTIRELY TONE-LESS/ Honor and shame from no condition rise/ Act well thy part, there all the honor lies/ ANTHONY HANNIBAL CLAPP/ Of African descent./ Born at Horseneck Conn. 14, July 1749/

Chapter II: Diary Endnotes 265

came to Setauket in 1779,/ Here sojourning until he died 12, Oct. 1816/ Anthony, though indigent, was most content./ Though of a race depis'd, deserv'd he much/ respect = in his deportment modest and polite./ Forever faithfully performing in life's drama/ the eccentrick part assign'd him by his Maker./ His philosophy agreed with his example to be/ happy Himself, and to make others so, being/ selfish, but in the coveting from his acquaintance/ an undivided approbation, which he was so/ Fortunate as to obtain and keep - - Upon the Violin, few play'd as Toney play'd,/ His artless music was a language universal,/ and in its Effect – most Irresistible! Ay, and/ was he not of Setauket's - dancing - Steps --/ a Physiognomist, indeed; he was./ Nor young nor old of either sex, stood on/ The Floor to jig-it, but he knew the gait./ Peculiar of their Hobby, and unasked,/ Plac'd best foot foremost for them, by his Fiddle/ This Emblematick Lachrimatory, and Cenotaphs, the/ grateful tribute of a few,/ of either sex who knew his worth."

(From *William Sidney Mount: Painter of American Life*, Deborah J. Johnson; with essays by Elizabeth Johns. . .[et al], The American Federation of the Arts, 1998, n. 87, p. 98.)

Deborah Johnson includes the note that "Anthony Clapp made a lasting impression on William Sidney Mount. In 1853 he wrote, 'In wandering about the Hills the other day I visited the burial ground on our farm, a place appropriated for the slaves (belonging to our family) years gone by – and was so much struck with the sublimity and originality of one of the monuments to a distinguished fiddler. . . . The violin is carved in the stone the bridge is down the bow & strings are slack – Tone has departed with Toney. . . I have sat by Anthony when I was a child – to hear him play his Jigs & Hornpipes – He was a Master in that way – and acted well his part.' William S. Mount to C. M. Cadey, November 24, 1853, MSB."

11 Mr. Edward Seabury is the brother of Charles Seabury, Maria's father.

12 Here Adeline begins a record of social calls, and, despite considerable effort, we are unable to get much further than to underscore the obvious: that the Hamiltons, along with the Dominicks, Strongs, and Walkers are old families in the Stony Brook/Setauket area. We suspect that the Hamiltons are related to the Culper Spy Ring from the Revolutionary War period; the Dominicks may be connected to the piano-making business, but however that may be, we note that three of the Dominick family are buried in the Caroline Episcopal Church Cemetary in Setauket: George G. Dominick, died 1876; Benjamin Floyd Dominick, died 1883; and Blanche E. Donimick, died 1883.

13 Steamboat weathervanes were being made in Rhode Island by William C. Manchester in 1858. If this is one of Manchester's, it is very valuable: one of them sold at auction for $313,000 in 2008.

14 Caroline Amelia Strong, born 1832, was the daughter of Judge Selah B. Strong, patron of painter William Sydney Mount.

15 See Note #12, above.

16 Julia, age 23, and Maria, age 21, were the daughters of Shepherd A. and Elizabeth Mount.

17 Richard Bowen; see Note #25, Chapter 1. We are unable to identify Mr. O'Donal.

Chapter III: Diary Endnotes

1. In the last week of June and first two weeks of July, Adeline and her sister Emilie journey south to New Jersey and Delaware. They travel from New York City and board the steamboat *Richard Stockton*, probably in New Brunswick, New Jersey, for the trip down the Delaware & Raritan Canal to Bordentown. There they are met by John Stewart, older brother of Joe, and proceed by horse-drawn carriage to the Stewart home in Cream Ridge, New Jersey. (Today, in good traffic, we would have a drive of an hour and a half down the New Jersey Turnpike.) After a week there, they again travel by steamboat, the *Major Reybold*, from Bordentown down to Philadelphia, and south along the Delaware River to Delaware City, where they spend a week with Anthony Reybold and his wife Ann *Stewart* Reybold (sister of Joe). After a week at the Reybolds', they return to Cream Ridge to stay with the Stewarts for five days before their return to New York City on the 13th of July.

    The "Major" after whom the steamboat is named is Major Philip Reybold, a very interesting man, one of the "Reybold Bros." who built and named the steamboat, which operated 1832–1885 and carried a cargo of up to 461 tons. Major Reybold himself had died in February 1854, at the age of seventy-one. The "Mr. Reybold" who meets Adeline and Emilie at Delaware City on June 29 is his son Anthony.

    Themes in Reybold family history are similar to those in the Hoe family. Philip Reybold was orphaned at ten, supported his mother and siblings by hauling and selling fish around Philadelphia (as did Benjamin Franklin). He entered the business world before he was twenty, bought land in Delaware City, raised Merino sheep, and became, as well, the premier grower of peaches in the country. He took on the task of construction supervisor for the Chesapeake and Delaware Canal. He built steamboats. He started a company to make bricks, becoming the largest supplier of bricks and mortar in the central Atlantic states. He also fathered thirteen children, of whom ten survived. He and his sons were powerful in business and politics throughout the mid-Atlantic. He was also said to be, by one awed admirer, "near seven feet tall."

    More than anything else, perhaps, what we continue to glimpse is a web of strong family friendships among titans of mid-19th century business and commerce: the Hoes supplying printing machinery and cutting tools, the Stewarts manufacturing iron parts necessary for that machinery, and the Reybolds in the forefront of developments in transportation.

2. Probably referring to William Shepherd Mount, sixteen at the time, son of Shepard Alonzo Mount, William Sidney Mount's older brother. On the other hand, it may be that Bridget, a servant in the Hoes' home, is a much older woman and that the "young" man is William Sidney Mount himself.

3. Older brother of Joe Stewart.

Chapter III: Diary Endnotes 267

4   It is helpful to look at a map here: just below Trenton, New Jersey, where the Delaware River makes a sweeping turn back southwest toward Philadelphia, there is a cluster of small towns and villages which Adeline mentions or implicitly refers to in this section of her journal: Cream Ridge, Bordentown, New Egypt, and Allentown:

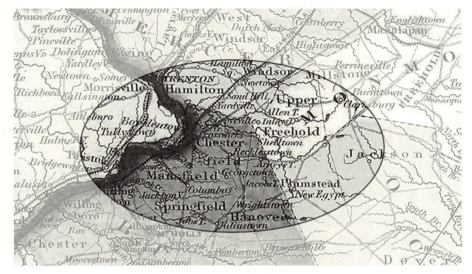

Map of New Jersey, 1856. *(Courtesy of the David Rumsey Map Collection, www.davidrumsey.com.)*

5   The Old Yellow Meeting House is "the Baptist Church near" mentioned in the diary:

The Old Yellow Meeting House in Cream Ridge, New Jersey. *(Courtesy of Frank L. Greenagel.)*

6   No more than a mile north of Cream Ridge is the Upper Freehold Township, where Brigadier General James Cox, American Revolutionary War veteran and member of the 11th U.S. House of Representatives, was born and lived. He and his wife Ann Potts had fourteen children; it seems reasonable to suppose that Ben Cox is among the Brigadier's grandchildren, although we have not yet been able to confirm this.

7   Anne is the daughter of George Franklin Fort (1809–1872): physician, judge, and Democratic Governor of New Jersey, 1851–1854.

8   The steamboat *Richard Stockton*, built in 1851, was one of the earliest of the new iron-hulled steamboats. It was 270 feet long from bow to stern, with a capacity of 630 tons. Its paddle wheels were twenty-two feet in diameter. Richard Stockton (1730–1781) was a signer of the Declaration of Independence, who died at age fifty-one from a variety of ailments contracted while imprisoned by the British during the Revolutionary War. His grandson, Robert F. Stockton, who resigned his naval commission in 1850 for a successful run for the United States Senate, resigned from the Senate in 1853 to become President of the Delaware & Raritan Canal Company. It seems reasonable to assume a connection between his political and financial trajectories.

DELAWARE RIVER STEAMBOAT RICHARD STOCKTON, 1851.

The Steam Vessel "Richard Stockton." Originally included in Samuel Ward Stanton's book *American Steam Vessels*, published 1895.

9   We are not at all certain about this reference, but consider it possible that Adeline refers here to the death of Horace Tuttle, who died at age twenty-nine on June 21, 1854.

10 We have not been able to establish who Miss Fannie Martin is.

11 Here, again, we are in the dark. It does seem that Adeline refers to contemporaries by first and surname, older women more formally. Perhaps Miss Hamilton is an older companion to the two young women, Fannie Martin and Lottie Morgan? It would be pleasing if we could establish a connection here to the "Mr. Hamilton" mentioned in Chapter 2 (see Chapter 2, Note #12), but we have been unable to do so.

12 We assume little Maggie is the daughter of Ann and Anthony Reybold; if she is about the same age as Adeline's half-sister, she is a toddler.

Chapter III: Diary Endnotes

13 The Summit Bridge to which Adeline refers was a long, covered wooden bridge that traversed the Delaware and Chesapeake Canal ninety feet above the bottom of the canal's channel. The Delaware and Chesapeake Canal was first proposed in the mid-17th century, but it was not completed and opened to the public until 1829. It cost nearly $2.5 million to build. Fourteen miles long, it traverses the narrow strip of land between Delaware City on the east end and the Black Creek branch of the Elk River on the west, in Maryland. The canal reduced the length of shipping routes between New York and New Jersey and the port of Baltimore by over 300 miles. Major Charles Reybold (see Notes #1 and #9, above) was a construction boss on the canal-building project.

14 Mr and Mrs King are neighbors.

15 Adeline is unaware of what she witnesses here. That afternoon in Philadelphia, during a play about the American Revolution, pyrotechnical devices, simulating gunfire, went awry, causing a huge conflagration which burned through the night and into the next day, destroying virtually an entire square block of the city, including the Philadelphia Museum of Art. The museum had been founded and built by Charles Wilson Peale, famous portrait painter (especially well known are his portraits of George Washington), inventor, naturalist, and friend and collaborator of Thomas Jefferson. "Peale's Museum" evolved into the Philadelphia Museum of Art. In 1838, Nathan Dunn, a merchant and philanthropist who had made his fortune in trade with China, added his extensive collection of Chinese art and built an addition to house it. When Dunn took his collection to England in 1841, the "Chinese Museum" became a storehouse for the out-of-fashion museum art and artifacts. Among items in storage was a famous contraption known as "The Mechanical Turk," invented and built in 1770 by the Austrian Wolfgang von Kempelen. "The Turk" was a nearly life-sized manikin which sat behind a small table on which sat a chess board, and the Turk purported to move chess pieces mechanically in response to opponents' moves. It scored victories all over Europe during a tour in 1781 (including one over Benjamin Franklin). Sold to Johann Nepomuk Maelzel, inventor of the metronome, it went on to defeat many more opponents, among them Napoleon. Maelzel brought the Turk to the United States in 1826. When he died thirteen years later, the Turk was purchased by John Kearsley Mitchell and donated to "Peale's Chinese Museum," where it languished in storage until meeting death by fire the evening of July 5, 1854, while Adeline watched, unknowing, from the carriage on the ride back to the Reybold home.

16 Hightstown is about ten miles north of Cream Ridge, and in the summer of 1854 it was the temporary end point on the Camden and Amboy Railroad (while new track was being laid to the south). It appears that Henry has been at work northeast in Elizabeth, New Jersey.

17 "Fillmore" is not now, and may in fact never officially have been, a separate village, but here, in 1854, it is known as a distinct geographical location, about a mile northeast of Cream Ridge. Originally called "Varmintown," presumably because of its especially numerous population of varmints, Fillmore was a cluster of no more than six homes, among which was a stone cottage and forge built originally by Abraham Lincoln's great-great-grandfather Mordecai Lincon [sic].

18 As with Mr. Emley and Messrs. Woodward and Morgan the next day, we are unable to establish who these men are. We conjecture that "Mr. Cox" is father of Ben Cox, referred to above.

Chapter IV: Diary Endnotes

1. Charles and Joseph Stewart of Cream Ridge, New Jersey.
2. Julia Smith, sister-in-law of Peter Hoe. We think John is her brother. Hannah is Aunt Hannah Mead Smith Hoe. Stephy is her son Stephen, then age seven.
3. Son of Richard March Hoe's partner Matthew Smith (died 1841). Sereno was born 1836, making him the same age as Adeline.
4. That is, the Stewart girls: Lottie, Retta, and Lydia.
5. See Chapter 1, Note #29. Miss Clarke appears regularly in Adeline's Journal. On June 9, "Emilie had a breastpin made for Miss Clarke." On June 23, "After dinner Miss Clarke came and staid till dark with us." In the two-day interval in New York City, July 13–15, between the trips to New Jersey, Delaware, and South Salem, New York, "We went to Uncle Robert's to dinner and then Emilie went to see Miss Clarke . . ." On September 14, Adeline goes "directly after breakfast to see Miss Clarke" and then Miss Clarke returns the call that evening. "Emilie went to see Miss Clarke this afternoon" on September 25. On October 5, "Miss Clarke kindly gave us tickets [to 'Dodsworth's opening]". On November 28, "Emilie went [to the Irving Literary Union] with Miss Clarke." And on December 2, "Miss Clarke came to tea." What may we surmise? First, it seems that the connection with Miss Clarke is primarily through sister Emilie. Second, she lives close by the Hoe family in New York City [she never appears in the Journal when Adeline is away from the city] and is a significant mentor and friend.
6. Uncle Robert's and Aunt Thirza's son; that is, Adeline's first cousin, age twelve or thirteen.
7. Adeline is, throughout the journal, so clearly resolute, uncomplaining, and disinclined to record (and, perhaps, even acknowledge) negative emotion, that it seems worthwhile to note the moments when she acknowledges loneliness. Here in this entry we note that she is in a large family group for dinner, but at Uncle Robert's, not her own home (which seems to have been under re-modeling all summer long). Then Emilie is off to see her Miss Clarke, and Adeline is alone in company with her very young cousin. We do not want to make overmuch of all this, but encourage readers to be alert to the contexts of her occasional recordings of loneliness.
8. Probably not the eight-year old, and youngest, (half) brother of Cyrus, DeWitt, and Mary Lawrence of South Salem, but, rather, a coachman/handyman (see July 18 journal entry below).
9. See Timothy Dwight, *Memories of Yale Life and Men 1854–1899*, especially page 14: "Candidates for admission to the Freshman Class are examined in Cicero's *Select Orations*, the whole of Virgil, Sallust, Jacobs', Colton's or Felton's *Greek Reader*, the first three books of Xenophon's *Anabasis*, Andrews and Stoddard's *Latin Grammar*, Goodrich's or Sophocles' *Greek Grammar*, Andrews' *Latin Exercises*, Arithmetic, English Grammar, and Geography; and hereafter, they will be examined also in the part of Day's *Algebra* preceding Quadratic Equations." The text goes on to promise

that the examination will be "strict and comprehensive." One-on-one interviews between candidates and professors would follow the written examinations.

10 Adeline's mother's mother, Sally Hoyt Gilbert, wife of Josiah.

11 Adeline's young uncle Thomas Gilbert (age twenty-five), who is courting Mary Lawrence and will marry her in October. We are amused by the ambiguity of "going to prayer meeting," which he does frequently. Perhaps the "prayers" are of a more this-worldly nature?

12 The Keeler family goes back a century in the history of the area, to the mid-1700s. The family owned a farm just over the border in Ridgefield, Connecticut, which became Keeler's Tavern (a museum open to the public now). Keelers farmed and manufactured boots and shoes. The "Mr. Keeler" to whom Adeline refers here is, among other things, postmaster.

13 Jane Hoyt Howe, niece of Sally Hoyt and Josiah Gilbert ("Grandma" and "Grandpa").

14 Julia West Lindsley, wife of Reverend Aaron Lindsley, pastor of the South Salem Presbyterian Church, 1852–68. In 1868, Reverend Lindsley answered a call to serve as pastor of First Presbyterian Church in Portland, Oregon. He later joined the faculty of the San Francisco Theological Seminary. He died in 1891 in an accident caused by a runaway horse.

15 We are not sure of her last name. It is possible that she is Minerva Lindsley, sister of the pastor, but it does not feel quite right given Adeline's formal reference to "Mrs. Lindsley" and the informality of referring to Minerva only by her first name. Adeline is right to be pessimistic about Minerva's condition, for news of Minerva's death is recorded in her journal entry of August 27.

16 This trip of a dozen miles or so is from South Salem down through Pound Ridge and into New Canaan, Connecticut, on what was then called the Old Post Road and is, in our time, Route 123. It ends at Long Island Sound. The New Canaan section is called Smith Ridge, and we think perhaps the name derives from the Smith family with whom Robert Hoe, Adeline's grandfather, went into partnership.

17 Mary E. Pardee, whose father is a local farmer.

18 Rachel Mead Smith Hoe (1782–1832), Adeline's grandmother.

19 Property maps of the area from the mid-1850s provide tantalizing glimpses of property owned by people named Ferris, but we are unable, so far, to locate exactly where this store was. If, as seems likely, it was adjacent to Keeler's post office, then it was on or just over the border into Ridgefield.

20 That is, his courtship call to Mary Lawrence.

21 Adeline is so frequently dismissive of her own illness—immediately following the report of an ailment with the recording of sustained work—that it is possible to overlook the extent to which illness stalks these people every day. In the seven-week period of her stay at the family compound in South Salem, Adeline records the illnesses or ailments suffered by *fourteen* different people, and *three* deaths. She specifically notes rheumatism, cholera, colds, bronchitis, sore throat, food poisoning, "Quinsy," infection, and boils, along with many references to fatigue, not feeling well, and so forth. We note that illness flares up at times when she also notes periods of intense hot weather, and we suspect that the water may not have been as pure as one would hope.

22 Peter, Imogene (who is mentioned two sentences later), and James (another two sentences later) are servants.

23 This is the first of several footnotes wherein we are speculating but not certain. We assume Gilbert Mead is a neighbor, farmer, and at least a distant relative. We have checked the burial records in the South Salem Presbyterian Church, and on that basis hazard a distinction between people who seem to belong inside the cluster of families who settled in the area, and those who are from "away."

24 See Note #22 above. The Wrights are a prominent South Salem area family. We assume, on the basis of the familiar nickname "Lizzie" for Elizabeth, that she is a contemporary and friend of Adeline's. Her later life will not be a happy one: she marries a gentleman named "Lightbody," who, in addition to providing the tongue-tripping rhyme in Elizabeth Wright Lightbody's married name, took ever more heavily to drink, and required from his wife the frequent report that he was, again, "ill."

25 Mary Lawrence, who will become "Aunt Mary" when she marries Thomas Gilbert in October.

26 A village three miles southwest of South Salem. The New York & Harlem Railroad had a station there in 1854.

27 Laura is Adeline's first cousin, daughter of Robert and Thirza, born in 1845.

28 The Boutons are frequent leaves on the Lawrence family tree, beginning in the 18th century. One was Hannah Bouton Lawrence, mother of Cyrus (who marries sister Emilie in 1856), DeWitt (who marries Adeline in 1857), and Mary Lawrence Gilbert. The Bouton family's property was a mile south of South Salem and called "Boutonville" on maps of the period.

29 In 1854, Cyrus J. Lawrence was in the process of establishing a mercantile business in New York City. He and his brother DeWitt would become, by 1858, brokers in shares of stock in companies drilling oil in Louisiana and probably other southern states. Their speculations evidently were profitable, and Cyrus established the Cyrus J. Lawrence brokerage. In 1988, Cyrus J. Lawrence, Inc. merged with Morgan Grenfell, Inc. See Edwin Charles Hill, *The Historical Register...Illus. w Portrait Plates*, New York, 1920, p. 20, wherein Cyrus is described as "able, upright, and sagacious, with a rare combination of courage and energy, with sound judgment and inflexible integrity."

30 Charley is the first of the five horses we now begin to get to know. The four others are Locke, Tom, Paul, and Kate.

31 Lake Waccabuc, first known as Long Pond:

Lake Waccabuc 1865 by Gunther Hartwick. *(Courtesy of the Mead Studwell Foundation. Photograph by Lynn Brockelman.)*

32 Solomon Mead, father of Aunt Thyrza.

33 *The Diverting History of John Gilpin, Showing How He Went Farther Than He Intended, And Came Home Safe Again*, by William Cowper (1731–1800). Cowper may be best known for his long poem *The Task*, or for his contributions to *The Olney Hymns*, but his very funny mock-heroic narrative about John Gilpin enjoyed great popularity. Poor old John Gilpin, a London linen draper, is informed by his wife that for their twentieth wedding anniversary, there will be a family trip to see the Bell at Edmonton, but inasmuch as the three Gilpin children plus Mrs. Gilpin's sister and her daughter will fill up the carriage, John will have to ride horseback—and carry the two jugs of liquor designated for the great occasion. The horse is unnerved by the clanking jugs slung over Gilpin's shoulders, and takes off on a trot, then a gallop, and overshoots the target of Edmonton by ten miles, finally coming to a halt. But on the return trip, the horse becomes nerved up again—somewhere along the way the jugs have shattered, the horse's flanks are covered with liquor and shards—and overshoots the target again. Many illustrators have had a good time with this tale, among them Randoph Caldecott:

Gilpin's Ride from *The Diverting History of John Gilpin*. This version of the 1782 poem by William Cowper was illustrated by Randolph Caldecott and published in 1878.

34 Henry Seymour, whose mother was Adeline's aunt Mary Hoe Seymour, and Joe Stewart. As we explore further, we surmise that Joe Stewart, while not related to the famous Alexander Stewart who founded the department store chain, does in fact oversee the manufacture of women's clothing. Perhaps the "sketch" is of woman's garment? The "paper" may well be an edition of Horace Greeley's *New York Tribune*, which had taken up, in the July 19 edition, the controversy over Elizabeth Jennings, a young black woman who, on her way to church, was thrown off a horse-drawn public rail car. Though injured, she got back on. She and her father, a black abolitionist and colleague of Frederic Douglass, sued the rail car company and won a settlement award of $225 the following January. The front-page headline in Greeley's *Tribune* for July 19 reads "Outrage Upon Colored Persons." Elizabeth Jennings is frequently referred to as the 19th century's Rosa Parks.

35 In the summer of 1854, cholera raged in London and New York City. Through the efforts of Mayor Westervelt and the New York City commissioners, a center for the treatment of cholera was set up on Franklin Street, where twelve new cases per day were being treated—this in addition to cases of cholera already being treated at the hospital on Mott Street in Manhattan and the hospital in Brooklyn. Also in 1854, in London, John Snow was exploring and promulgating the connection between dirty water and the virulent spread of cholera.

36 Margaretta Stewart, sister of Joe.

37 This was the first novel by the young American author Maria S. Cummins (1827–1866), of Salem, Massachusetts. It was published in Boston the previous March, sold 20,000 copies in twenty days, 65,000 copies in five months. It also sold 100,000 copies in Britain, and the novel was translated into several languages, including French, German, and Dutch. Its protagonist is the plucky and good-hearted orphan Gerty, to whom kindness is shown by "the lamplighter" Trueman Flint. Although Maria Cummins is no longer widely known or read, *The Lamplighter* was the second most widely read novel in 19th century America after *Uncle Tom's Cabin*.

38 As noted above, Mary Louisa, born in 1833, is younger sister of Cyrus J. and DeWitt Clinton Lawrence. She is engaged to Thomas Gilbert, Adeline's young uncle, and will be married two months hence, October 11, 1854.

39 Younger sister of Adeline's stepmother, Mary Say Corbin Hoe.

40 Elizabeth Missing Sewell was a highly regarded British novelist of the mid-century, and her novel *Katherine Ashton*, published early in 1854, was both very popular and thematically related to matters in the Hoe household. The protagonist is a young woman of the middle class who works in her father's bookstore. She struggles to reconcile the caste stratifications implicit in Episcopal doctrine and practice with the Biblical exhortations to "rise up" behaviorally and spiritually. She witnesses the sad outcome of her female friends' "marrying above their station," but, while apparently content with her work and lot in life, is unwilling to let the social *status quo* limit her imagination, intellectual growth, and good works. The words of one reviewer suggest why we have not bent heaven and earth to procure and read the novel: "We never read a work of this kind without feeling very glad that we are not the heroine, to be disciplined at the hand of the author." (*Athenaeum*, 1 July 1854, p. 312)

41 We noted above that during the seven weeks Adeline spent in South Salem she recorded eighteen instances of illness and three deaths. Might her error here, "South South" instead of "South Salem," be an indication of the anxieties these illnesses caused her? It does not seem in her nature to dwell on her deepest feelings or be deterred by them from carrying on her disciplined daily routines.

42 The first cousin, once removed, of Emilie and Adeline. Jane Hoyt Howe was probably approximately the age of Emilie's and Addie's mother, Lucy Gilbert Hoe, who died in 1841.

43 "Owen" eludes our efforts: perhaps he is the husband or son of Mrs. Bouton, with whom Emmie is staying? Or he might in fact be a horse. *Requiescat in pacem*.

44 Cousin Arthur and the farm hand, Peter.

45 Henry Seymour's sister.

46 The text of the journal is difficult to decipher clearly here. We assume these gentlemen are neighbors, but, so far, we have not been able to establish their identity in any detail.

47 As noted above, the Keeler family name peppers the history of Ridgefield, Connectiut, the town immediately east of South Salem. Keeler's Tavern has been in the town since the eighteenth century, and still is.

48 Hannah Maria Smith, daughter of Thomas and Sarah Smith. Julia Lawrence is, we think, a cousin of Cyrus and DeWitt Lawrence.

49 See Notes #22 and #23, above. We assume Julia Reynolds is of the Reynolds family, who date back into the 18th century in the history of the South Salem area.

50 Younger brother of DeWitt and Cyrus Lawrence. In 1857, when Addie marries DeWitt, he becomes her brother-in-law.

51 Son of Jane Hoyt Howe; that is, Addie's and Emilie's second cousin once removed.

52 Eleanor Bowen, daughter of the Manager of R Hoe Co. factory.

53 This is the bird mentioned in the first journal entry in May. "Annie's bird" must have made the journey with Adeline and Emilie to South Salem and spotted an opportunity to fly off to freedom.

54 We are unable to find out who this is.

55 Second son of Peter Hoe and Hannah Smith Hoe. He is four or five years old. He grew up to become one of the founders of the prestigious Grolier Club in New York City. He died in 1925.

56 We assume she is a member of the Mead family, whose forbears settled near the shore of Lake Waccabuc in the 18th Century.

57 Husband of Jane Hoyt Howe ("Cousin Jane").

58 The Abbotts; like the Meads, Reynolds, and Boutons; are a family whose roots drill deep into the history of South Salem. We imagine Nelson Abbott to be a contemporary of Emilie's and Addie's.

59 Miss Pratt has eluded us.

60 This is an elegant hotel built in 1824 overlooking the Hudson River Valley, in the heart of the landscape made famous by the Hudson River School of landscape painters—Durand, Cole, *et al*. Among its guests over the years were Presidents Grant, Arthur, and T. Roosevelt.

61 Harriet Brockway, like Miss Pratt in Note #57, Mrs. Green in Note #61, "Huldah" in Note #63, has eluded our efforts to track her down. We are hoping that this first printed record of Adeline's journal will find its way out among readers who can shed further light.

62 Adeline does not make over much of the drought, but the drought of 1854 was severe enough to warrant headlines and its own discrete place in meteorological history.

63 See Note #59, above. We have not been able to track down this reference.

64 Thomas's older brother and sister-in-law.

65 See Note #59, above.

66 By now one would think we could find out precisely where Aunt Sophia resides on the family tree, but she remains elusive.

67 As with Aunt Sophia, so too, we report in sad frustration, with Cousin Mary Ann.

68 Quinsy is a peritonsillar abscess associated with streptococcus infection; in our day we seem generally capable of checking the progress of strep throat soon enough to forestall the development of the abscess.

69 Of Mrs. Townsend, all we can say for sure is that she is one of "those Townsends" whose names come up frequently in the records of births, marriages, and deaths in the South Salem area.

Chapter V: Diary Endnotes

1. In 1854, Bloomfield was a town of about 5,000 people. Originally a northern section of Newark, it was incorporated separately in the 18th century. It was given the name "Bloomfield" in 1796, for Joseph Bloomfield, Revolutionary War general and, later, Governor of New Jersey. It was settled, apparently harmoniously, by both Dutch and English immigrants, and in the records of its history one finds both Dutch and British names in about equal measure. Two family names appear early on, the *Dodds* in the early 18th century, the *Meads* a little later. In the history of the Hoe family, there is record of marriage into both Dodd and Mead families. The Presbyterian church in Bloomfield is called "The Third Presbyterian Church" because it was the third in Newark, but it is the only one in the town of Bloomfield.

2. Very likely Lucy A. Dodd (1833–1912), friend of Emilie Hoe, who lived her entire life in Bloomfield.

3. "Miss Bradbury" is almost certainly the daughter of William Batchelder Bradbury (1816–1868). Bradbury was a vigorous promoter of choral music, well known for establishing youth choirs and choral training for children in New York City and then in Bloomfield, New Jersey. He also composed, annotated, and published hymn books. Among his well known hymns are "Sweet Hour of Prayer" and "Jesus Loves Me." The publisher of two of Bradbury's three volumes of hymns is Biglow&Main, located in Bloomfield. It is likely that "Miss Bigelow," the pulchritudinous "Ellie," is Biglow's daughter. There was at this time a bit of a tiff about the spelling of "Big[e]low," necessitating a tart letter from the family to the local newspaper reminding readers that there was *not* an *e* in "Biglow." Note Addie's correction of the spelling in her September 11th and 12th journal entries.

4. We've had Seaburys in Connecticut, Seaburys on Long Island, and now we have one here in Bloomfield. We have yet to sort out which branches are which on the family tree. Miss Oaks may well be the daughter of one of Bloomfield's foremost entrepreneurs; David Oakes (again the issue of yes-or-no on the silent *e*), manufacturer in Bloomfield of woolen goods, an early member—like Richard March Hoe—of the emergent Republican Party, and a vigorous abolitionist.

5. We have not been able to find more information about Miss Kelsey.

6. Bloomfield Academy was coeducational. It seems that the Seymour household was an especially busy place, with students of both sexes visiting frequently.

7. Edward Seymour, as noted earlier in Adeline's journal, is off to Yale "College."

Chapter VI: Diary Endnotes

1. A Doctor Albert Beals was a dentist and daguerreotypist operating at 156 Broadway in 1854. Since in the 19th century barbers, dentists and physicians shared tasks like pulling teeth, can it be Dr. Beals who lanced Emilie's painfully infected finger for her? Dr. Beals departed soon after, in 1855, for Virginia City, Nevada, where he set up a combined dentist's office and daguerrean gallery as well as involving himself in silver mining.

2. In the 19th century, the old name for late summer and fall diarrhea and vomiting, resulting in dehydration. As noted in Chapter 4, Note 35, John Snow, in 1854, was the first to identify the importance of contaminated water in causing cholera. There have been seven cholera pandemics in the last 200 years.

3. This is almost certainly Milford, Connecticut, although there are Milfords in New York, New Jersey, and Pennsylvania. Easily accessible by train, Milford had, in 1850, a population of 2,465. It was still recovering from the effects of a violent hurricane a decade earlier, which caused its ports, clogged with a build-up of silt in the hurricane, to be closed to shipping. Its foremost industries were the manufacturing of paper and of carriages and wagons, both of which, of course, were important concerns for Richard March Hoe and his brothers.

4. Addie is there on the third night of Julia Grisi's performing at Castle Garden. A dramatic soprano, with a two-octave range, Madame Grisi (1811–1899) came to America for a tour in 1854. Subsequently, on October 2nd, she sang with her partner, Signor Mario, at the Academy of Music, at East 14th and Irving Place. She was the first soprano to sing the role of Adalgisa in *Norma* by Bellini, in 1828; and in 1835 played the role of Norma in London. Madame Grisi formed an opera company with Mario de Candia. Her repertoire included roles from Mozart's operas as well as Bellini's. She did not always fare well with British and European critics, who found America's enthusiasm for her deliciously provincial, as suggested by this caustic observation in a British journal: "The attempts of American speculators to 'get up' enthusiasm for Madame Grisi and Signor Mario appear to have been lame, awkward, and not successful. Unable to trust to the talents they bring to the 'States', and to the vast and opulent audiences who are eager to listen and more eager to emulate European fashion in art . . . the New York journals have fitted up a mysterious inamorata, who pursues Senor Mario . . . The first ticket for Mario's first performance was knocked down by auction at an enormous price." (*The Athenaeum: Journal of Literature, Science and the Fine Arts For the Year 1854*, Part Two, p 1172. Published London, 1854.)

5. Here again, the Hoe family demonstrates the generalist nature of their Protestantism: Dr. Alexander is Rev. James Waddell Alexander (1804–1859), a notable Presbyterian minister and teacher.

6. Very likely inspecting the Hoes' recent renovations is Edward Boyle of the Bureau of Surveyors of the City of New York, an engineer. Building codes were

a particularly hot subject in New York in the 1850s and a central issue in the mayoral campaign of 1855.

7   Mrs. Edward Firth is, possibly, the wife of Edward Firth, whose family members were steel manufacturers in England. At this time Richard March Hoe was making an effort to acquire the most sturdy steel available for his presses and saw blades. Certain that British and European steel were superior to American steel, he had made, and would continue to make, frequent trips to England and the Continent.

8   We are confident that this "Lizzie Wright" is not the famous madam of the day, one of several rather jazzy proprietresses of unabashedly advertised houses of pleasure, e.g. Mrs. Hathaway's "fair Quakeresses," and Mrs. Everett's "beautiful señoritas." Ms. Wright advertised "French belles." There were many directories and guide books available for the carnally inclined. See *Gotham: A History of New York City to 1898* for further exciting details.

9   We assume that Mr. D'Orsay is head of the construction crew doing a major remodeling project in the Hoe home at 309 Broadway during the summer and fall of 1854. You will note that the names having to do with the renovation and remodeling have a French echo: D'Orsay, Roux, Dupuy. We do not want to make outrageous inferential leaps, but do note in the historical record an acceleration of French immigration to America in the years following the failed 1848 Revolution (20,000 in 1851) and the establishment of French-language newspapers in both New York City and Philadelphia.

10 Mr. Harvey Baxter, son of Timothy and Martha Baxter of Brooklyn, will, in 1855, marry Mary Ely (1833–1875), older sister of Emmie (born 1835) and daughter of Addie's Aunt Emmeline Hoe and Giles Ely.

11 Peter Hoe's wife Hannah and son Stephen.

12 Charles Coles, daguerrean and maker of morocco cases, located during the 1850s at 187 Broadway, very likely made the tiny, leather-bound case with brass clasp which holds the daguerreotypes of Adeline and Emilie, treasures which are, today, in the possession of Adeline's great-granddaughter Helen Taylor Davidson.

13 Reverend Charles Henry Halsey, DD (1810–1855), down from his parish in Sing Sing, Westchester County. There are a considerable number of church dignitaries in New York City this weekend (see Note #14 below).

14 On Saturday, special services of great length and with many church dignitaries present were held for the memorial service for Bishop Jonathan Mayhew Wainwright (1793–1854), one of the really significant figures in 19th century American church history. Dr. Wainwright was an extraordinary man: Doctor of Divinity degrees from both Union College and Harvard Divinity School, a Doctor of Civil Law from Oxford University, 599 published sermons, numerous scholarly publications (including three books of church music), not to mention being the father of fourteen children.

15 See Chapter 2, Note .#6: this is Maria Seabury's uncle, Rev. Samuel Seabury.

16 Henry E. Blossom is married to Peter Hoe's sister-in-law Mary Jane Smith. In 1850, he traveled to San Francisco from New York, leaving February 12 and arriving June 6. In 1859, he is a merchant at 133 Front Street in New York City. He died, at age 46, September 10, 1863.

17 We first met Sarah Kenney on June 3 (see Chapter 1, Note #35). Sad to say, we know little more here than we did then. Given Adeline's system of reference, wherein contemporaries and servants are referred to by their first names and members of the older generation by title and surname, we assume that the Kenneys are family friends.

18 Mrs. Ackerman remains a mystery to us. In our efforts to find her, we have learned a lot more about the history of nursing—education, licensing, hospitals—in NYC than we would ever have anticipated, but not what we hoped to discover about her.

19 A.E.Dean, Confectioner, 741 Broadway.

20 The Rev. William Eigenbrodt, who baptized Mary on June 9 (see Chapter 1 Note #49.)

21 Monsieur Jules Delaunay, teacher of modern and oriental languages, 130 9th St.

22 Now considered an item of *lingerie*, "basque" in Victorian fashion refers to a closely fitted bodice or jacket extending past the waist line over the hips. A basque might be worn over a hoop skirt in the early Victorian era. It was adopted as a fashion from Basque traditional dress, first by the French.

23 Cousin Arthur Hoe (1841–1865), son Uncle Robert and Aunt Thirza.

24 Mr. Allen Dodworth (1822–1896) was a musician well known in his time throughout America as conductor of the Dodworth Brass Band. He was an Englishman whose father emigrated from Sheffield when Allen was four years old, and founded the band which bore the family name. At 806-8 Broadway, near Union Square, Allen Dodworth built Dodworth Hall (or "Rooms" or "Saloon") in the early 1850s. It was for many years the principal concert hall for New York City. Between 1854 and 1855, the New York Philharmonic Society performed there four times. Mr. Dodworth, on the evening of October 5th, played the cornet, while Mr. Aptomas performed on the harp. Mr. Aptomas later published *A History of the Harp*.

25 It is very late at night, which would seem to rule out a professional call on Mr. Godfrey's part—and yet, as we have seen many times before, Richard March Hoe mixed business and socializing, often deep into the night. Was this "Mr. Godfrey" William A. Godfrey, the importer with an office at 34 Water Street, near the R. Hoe Co. factory? Perhaps. Or, he might have been Phineas Godfrey, an importer and seller of books—we know that RMH was a serious book collector, and he might have been equipping the library in the remodeling project underway. It's even possible, though less likely, we think, that "Mr. Godfrey" was the upholsterer whose establishment was on Carmine St. twenty blocks north and five blocks west of Broadway. All that said, we are not at all sure to whom Adeline refers here.

26 Julia Smith is sister of Peter Hoe's wife Hannah Smith Hoe and of Mary Jane Smith Blossom. Julia marries *Ellis* Price, Fanny's brother, in 1855; that is to say, Julia Smith is here at 309 Broadway in company with her soon-to-be sister-in-law. (As the project of annotating Adeline's journal moves toward its conclusion, we found ourselves becoming a little bit punchy, and we sympathize with dutiful readers of this text who might well, by now, be weary with the task of keeping Adeline's cast of characters clear in mind. Be consoled: "Fanny Price" is *not* the protagonist of Jane Austen's *Mansfield Park*.)

27 A proleptic tableau: Emilie will marry Cyrus Lawrence (1832–1909) two years hence, in October of 1856; Adeline will marry DeWitt Clinton Lawrence (1830–1897) two and a half years later, in April of 1857.

28 The steamship *S.S.Arctic*, one of four elegant ships built by the Collins Line in 1850, held the record for fastest Atlantic crossing, nine days and seventeen hours. On September 27, 1854, on a return voyage from Liverpool, it collided with the French ship *Vesta* off the coast of Canada and sank. In all, 350 people drowned, including *all* of the approximately 80 women and children. Among those killed were the eleven-year-old son of the Captain James Luce and family members of owner Edward Knight Collins. The six life boats on the *Arctic* would have been enough for all women and children aboard and most of the men passengers, but it was the *crew*, scrambling chaotically aboard the life boats, who survived. Thus the sinking of the *Arctic* was not only a tragedy but a scandal, and from this awful catastrophe derived legislation that would be applied a half century later in the aftermath of the sinking of the *Titanic*, April 15, 1912.

The *Titanic* was owned by the White Star Line, a subsidiary of the British company Oceanic Steam Navigation (OSN). OSN was, in turn, owned by a conglomerate called the International Mercantile Marine Co. (IMM), an *American* company whose primary owner was John Pierpont Morgan. You can envision, immediately, the emergent legal nightmare unfolding when the claims and lawsuits started to fly back and forth, a nightmare made even more awful by the fact that J. Bruce Ismay, president of the White Star Line, was British, that he was summoned to senate hearings in the United States, and was loathed by the American press, particularly the jingoistic William Randolph Hearst. It gets worse: British and American laws governing limited liability are very different. The worst case, for the White Star Line, would be a liability of over $90,000,000.

The lead lawyer for the White Star Line was Charles C. Burlingham, an admiralty lawyer and principal of the law firm Burlingham, Montgomery & Beecher. Burlingham was lawyer for three years in this case. Indefatigable, encyclopedic, and exuding calm when most were near apoplexy, he applied, amongst many others, a principle of law derived from the aftermath of the sinking of the *Arctic*: that the captain of the *Titanic* had in fact followed the procedures written subsequently into the law to avoid the kind of "loss of life due to negligence" that had occurred in the prior disaster. Against a potential liability of $90 million, the White Star Line paid $664,000, i.e. 4%.

Charles C. Burlingham was married to Adeline Hoe Lawrence's daughter Louisa, and in 1925 he became legal guardian of Adeline's grandsons Lawrence Hoe and Philip Longley Taylor and her granddaughter Rosamond Taylor.

29 DeWitt and Cyrus are, respectively, twenty-four and twenty-two years old here. They have already been "in business" for some time, possibly four or five years (neither went to college), and are at the outset of careers that will be multi-faceted and lucrative: variously described as bankers, stock brokers, speculators, they established offices in New York City but clearly traveled far and wide in this country and abroad. DeWitt was appointed to the Board of Appeals of the U.S. Patent Office in 1857. Cyrus established a stock brokerage in 1858 which eventually became the Cyrus J. Lawrence Co., a Wall Street firm which, through several manifestations and mergers, still exists today.

DeWitt seems to have been the more mercurial of the two. After Adeline's death in 1882, DeWitt married again, almost immediately, and when he died in 1897—in the Middletown, New York, Institute for the Insane—he left $50,000 to his second wife and child (stepchild?), and $20,000 to be divided equally among his five daughters with Adeline. Not a happy story. Cyrus seems to have been the more solid of the two brothers: patron of the Metropolitan Museum of Art, Museum of Natural History, American Archaeological Society, and member of the Grolier Club and Union League Club. He was also a knowledgeable and vigorous collector of art, whose highly prized originals included works of Mary Cassatt, whose stature he was one of the first to recognize. What DeWitt and Cyrus are specifically intending when "going south" is not clear, but we suspect commodities ventures in either oil or tobacco, or both. We know that by 1865 they were dealing in stocks and securities in the burgeoning mining and oil industries.

30 With his ship sinking, Captain James Luce of the *S.S.Arctic* stood atop a large wooden crate housing one of the paddle wheels of the steamer and made heroic, if futile, efforts to exhort his crew to behave in orderly fashion and attend to passengers. When the ship sank, he went below the surface but clung to the crate and after two *days* in the icy waters was rescued. He became a sympathetic figure to the press and public, and he toured the country in the months and years following, telling his story and making the case for legislation to ensure proper behavior by ships' crews in the event of disaster.

31 Rev. Frances Lister Hawks was an Episcopalian clergyman of generally high but sometimes questionable reputation: he ran up significant personal debts and had to be bailed out by his parishioners in the late 1840s. He had, as well, done service in the South, and would be later in New Orleans, returning to New York City after the Civil War.

32 Of Berrien & Keyser, Builders. It is likely that Berrien & Keyser were taking care of the systems work in the major remodeling project: furnace, water system, gas lines, etc.

33 Very likely the wife of A. H. Godwin, a successful businessman much involved with agriculture.

34 Wife, we believe, of a very high-end jewelry designer specializing in silver.

35 The reference is probably to Martin M. Lawrence, daguerreotypist, at 881 Broadway.

36 The Bowens. Richmond is son of R. Hoe & Co plant manager Alfred S. Bowen and brother of Nicholas Bowen, who becomes an engineer in the Civil War. See Chapter 1, Notes #25 and #26.

37 Frederick George Wolbert (1818–1901) married Anna Maria Corbin (1819–1885), sister of Mary Say Corbin Hoe, Adeline's step-mother. At this time they were living in New Rochelle. In the 1860s, he became clerk in the Court of Common Pleas in Philadelphia.

38 Of the Keeler family of Ridgefield and South Salem. See Chapter 4, Note #12.

39 Thomas Gilbert's older brother.

40 Is this Cousin Peter? The farm helper in South Salem? Whether the "trouble" concerns misbehavior or health we do not know.

41 Perhaps the daughter of silk-merchant Marshall B. Stafford, 241 Broadway.

42 We assume Barbara is a servant employed by Aunt Emmeline in Brooklyn.

43 The name occurs frequently in the history of R. Hoe & Co. Almost nine months

to the day from this entry, Richard March Hoe and Mary Say Corbin Hoe will welcome their next daughter, Fanny *Ball* Hoe into the world.

44 There are two possibilities here: James C. Atwater, a merchant with office and warehouse at 65 Broadway, home in Brooklyn, or Leonard D. Atwater, an importer with warehouse at 175 Broadway and also of Brooklyn.

45 We were hoping to confirm that the reference here is to Rev. Samuel H. Cox, famous Presbyterian minister of the 19th century, whose correspondence with Frederick Douglass was a topic of public interest and controversy, and whose opinion that Jesus was very likely a black man caused considerable stir. It would have been nice to locate a lecture by Rev. Cox at Macauley's 5th Avenue Theater, but our research has fallen short and we can only hope.

46 This is one of the few places in her journal where Adeline's handwriting is impossible to decipher. We are also unsure of "Marven" in the entry two days later. It does seem that what with one thing or the other—illnesses, a ferocious social activity, school, funerals—Adeline is making her entries hastily and without the level of detail she included in the summer. Perhaps she is weary of the chore of the daily record?

47 That is, to the Washington Irving Literary Union. See Chapter 1, Note #24.

48 While it might be possible to construe the five young friends as Richard March Hoe's five daughters, this seems a stretch. We imagine, rather, these are for children of RMH's colleagues at the company. This seems at least possible, given the record of RMH's enormous generosity to colleagues and employees and the progressive policies of the company toward all employees. When RMH died, thousands attended his funeral; not only was the church itself completely full, but so too were the grounds around it, and many people stood in the roads and walkways around the outside of the church property. It is also worth noting here that R. Hoe & Co employees never once joined the labor strikes that ripped often through New York City industry in the mid-to- late19th century.

49 Daughter of Frederic George Wolbert and Anna Maria *Corbin* Wolbert. See Note #37, above.

50 We have been unable thus far to pin down this reference.

51 Reverend George Washington Bethune (1805–1862) was a prominent Dutch Reform minister, writer of hymns, expert on Biblical texts, and an avid, if secretive, fisherman: he worked on five editions of Izaak Walton's *The Compleat Angler*, but did so under the pseudonym "The American Editor."

52 James C. Hoe was owner of a woodworking factory at 54-58 Gansevoort St. in what is now Greenwich Village. Isabella (1838–1894), his only daughter, went on to marry Howard Waldo, a manufacturer of and dealer in military goods.

53 Take a deep breath: the "Richard Hoe" here is a machinist who lives south on Broadway; he had a shop either within or adjacent to R. Hoe & Co. He is not "our" Richard March Hoe, i.e. "Father." If there is a family relationship, presumably distant, we are unable to delineate it authoritatively.

54 Caddie Wolbert, sister of Anna.

55 Daughter of Lawrence Johnson, of Philadelphia, who owned and operated a stereotyping plant in Philadelphia with which R. Hoe & Co. did a lot of business.

56 Frank and Ira are the sons of Rachel Hoe Dodd, Richard March Hoe's sister, and M. W. Dodd. Frank H. Dodd (1844–1916) graduated from Bloomfield Academy in 1860 and worked with his father in publishing. With Edward S. Mead he founded Dodd Mead & Co. in 1870. Ira (1842–1922) became Reverend Ira Seymour Dodd, having graduated from Yale in 1867. Among other pastorates, he served as pastor of Riverdale Presbyterian Church in New York City.

A SELECTED LIST OF SOURCES & WORKS CONSULTED

Bell, Jeanine. *Collector's Encyclopedia of Hairwork Jewelry*. Collector Books, 1998.

Bolton, Robert Jr. *History of the County of Westchester from Its First Settlement to the Present Time*. New York: Alexander S. Gould, 1848.

Burlingham, Michael John. *The Last Tiffany: A Biography of Dorothy Tiffany Burlingham*. New York: Atheneum, 1989.

Burrows, Edwin G. & Mike Wallace. *Gotham: A History of New York City To 1898*. New York & London: Oxford University Press, 1998.

Comparato, Frank E. *Chronicles of Genius & Folly: R Hoe & Company and the Printing Press as a Service to Democracy*. Culver City, California: Labyrinthos, 1979.

Frankenstein, Alfred. *Painter of Rural America: William Sidney Mount 1807–1868*. H. K. Press, 1968.

Hoe, Robert A., *A Short History of the Printing Press: And of the Improvements in Printing Machinery from the Time of Gutenberg up to the Present Day*. Printed and Published for Robert Hoe, New York: The Gilliss Press, 1902.

Johnson, Deborah J. et al. *William Sidney Mount: Painter of American Life*, American Federation of Arts, 1998.

Martin, George. *CCB: The Life and Century of Charles C. Burlingham*. New York: Hill & Wang, 2005.

McCullough, David. *The Great Bridge: The Epic Story of the Building Of the Brooklyn Bridge*. New York: Simon & Schuster, 1972.

Shonnard, Frederic and W.W. Spooner, *History of Westchester County New York From Its Earliest Settlement to the Year 1900*. New York: The Winthrop Press, 1900.

Thorn, John, ed., and Melanie Bower, *Picture Ed.*, *New York 400*. Philadelphia: Running Press Publishers, 2009.

Tucker, Stephen D. "History of R. Hoe & Co., 1834-1885," In *Proceedings of the American Antiquarian Society*, edited by Rollo Silver, 82 (1972): 351–453. Worcester, Massachusetts.

Ultan, Lloyd & Gary Hermalyn, *The Birth of the Bronx 1609-1900*. The Bronx County Historical Society, 2000.

ABOUT THE AUTHOR

Helen Taylor Davidson. *(© Peter E. Randall.)*

"History is living, something to be discovered and shared. There is a trust we feel when the past is in our care." So declares Helen Taylor Davidson, author of *Prelude*, and co-editor, with her husband Richard, of *The 1854 Diary of Adeline Elizabeth Hoe*. A lifelong music teacher, choral director, dramatist and writer, Davidson is the custodian of many heirlooms in a family whose American roots stem from the early 1600s. These include her ancestor's diary, which was transcribed and annotated through many years of research, and which became the inspiration for the novel, *Prelude*, covering those seminal transformations foreshadowing the horrors of the Civil War. The Davidsons live in Plainfield, New Hampshire, in the home where Helen was raised.

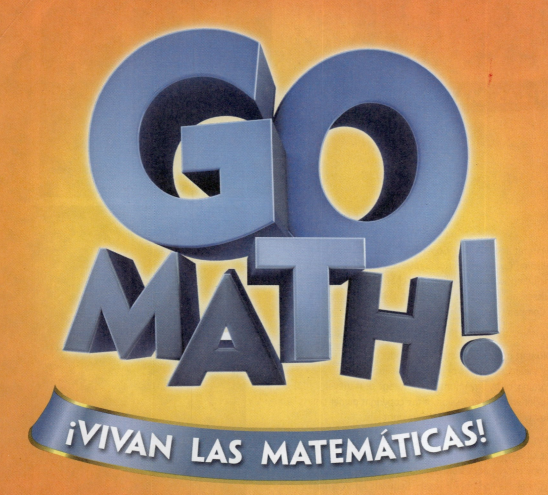

© Houghton Mifflin Harcourt Publishing Company • Cover Image Credits: (Goosander) ©Erich Kuchling/Westend61/Corbis; (Covered bridge, New Hampshire) ©eye35/Alamy Images

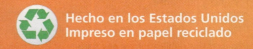

Hecho en los Estados Unidos
Impreso en papel reciclado

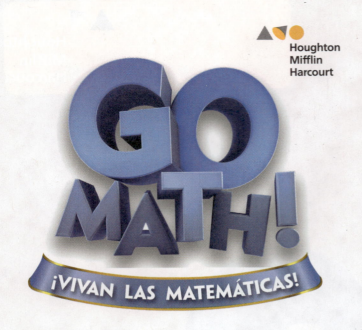

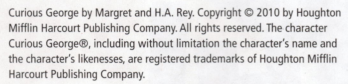

Curious George by Margret and H.A. Rey. Copyright © 2010 by Houghton Mifflin Harcourt Publishing Company. All rights reserved. The character Curious George®, including without limitation the character's name and the character's likenesses, are registered trademarks of Houghton Mifflin Harcourt Publishing Company.

Copyright © 2018 by Houghton Mifflin Harcourt Publishing Company

All rights reserved. No part of this work may be reproduced or transmitted in any form or by any means, electronic or mechanical, including photocopying or recording, or by any information storage or retrieval system, without the prior written permission of the copyright owner unless such copying is expressly permitted by federal copyright law.

Permission is hereby granted to individuals using the corresponding student's textbook or kit as the major vehicle for regular classroom instruction to photocopy entire pages from this publication in classroom quantities for instructional use and not for resale. Requests for information on other matters regarding duplication of this work should be addressed to Houghton Mifflin Harcourt Publishing Company, Attn: Intellectual Property Licensing, 9400 Southpark Center Loop, Orlando, Florida 32819-8647.

Printed in the U.S.A.

ISBN 978-1-328-99512-4

3 4 5 6 7 8 9 10 0877 24 23 22 21 20 19

4500746696   A B C D E F G

> If you have received these materials as examination copies free of charge, Houghton Mifflin Harcourt Publishing Company retains title to the materials and they may not be resold. Resale of examination copies is strictly prohibited.

> Possession of this publication in print format does not entitle users to convert this publication, or any portion of it, into electronic format.

Estimados estudiantes y familiares:

Bienvenidos a **Go Math! ¡Vivan las matemáticas!** para 2do. grado. En este estimulante programa de matemáticas, encontrarán actividades prácticas y problemas de la vida diaria que tendrán que resolver. Y lo mejor de todo es que podrán escribir sus ideas y respuestas directamente en el libro. El hecho de que puedan escribir y dibujar en las páginas, les ayudará a percibir más detalladamente lo que están aprendiendo y las matemáticas serán fáciles de entender.

También deseamos compartir con ustedes algo muy importante: se ha usado papel reciclado en la impresión de este libro. Queremos que sepan que al participar en el programa **Go Math! ¡Vivan las matemáticas!** ustedes estarán ayudando a proteger el medio ambiente.

Atentamente,
Los autores

Hecho en los Estados Unidos
Impreso en papel reciclado

GO MATH!
¡VIVAN LAS MATEMÁTICAS!

Autores

Juli K. Dixon, Ph.D.
Professor, Mathematics Education
University of Central Florida
Orlando, Florida

Edward B. Burger, Ph.D.
President, Southwestern University
Georgetown, Texas

Steven J. Leinwand
Principal Research Analyst
American Institutes for
 Research (AIR)
Washington, D.C.

Matthew R. Larson, Ph.D.
K-12 Curriculum Specialist for
 Mathematics
Lincoln Public Schools
Lincoln, Nebraska

Martha E. Sandoval-Martinez
Math Instructor
El Camino College
Torrance, California

Colaboradora

Rena Petrello
Professor, Mathematics
Moorpark College
Moorpark, California

Consultores de English Language Learners

Elizabeth Jiménez
CEO, GEMAS Consulting
Professional Expert on English
 Learner Education
Bilingual Education and
 Dual Language
Pomona, California

VOLUMEN I
Sentido numérico y valor posicional

La gran idea Ampliar la comprensión conceptual de las relaciones numéricas y el valor posicional.

 Ballenas 1

1 Conceptos numéricos 9

✓ **Muestra lo que sabes** 10
   Desarrollo del vocabulario 11
   Juego: Tres en línea 12
1 **Manos a la obra: Álgebra** • Números pares e impares . 13
2 **Álgebra** • Representar números pares 19
3 Comprender el valor posicional 25
4 Forma desarrollada 31
5 Diferentes maneras de escribir números 37
✓ **Revisión de la mitad del capítulo** 40
6 **Álgebra** • Diferentes maneras de mostrar números ... 43
7 **Resolución de problemas** • Decenas y unidades 49
8 Patrones de conteo hasta 100. 55
9 Patrones de conteo hasta el 1,000 61
✓ **Repaso y prueba del Capítulo 1** 67

¡Visítanos en Internet! Tus lecciones de matemáticas son interactivas. Usa iTools, Modelos matemáticos animados y el Glosario multimedia, entre otros.

Presentación del Capítulo 1

En este capítulo, explorarás y descubrirás las respuestas a las siguientes
Preguntas esenciales:

- ¿Cómo usas el valor posicional para hallar y describir los números de diferentes formas?
- ¿Cómo sabes el valor de un dígito?
- ¿De qué maneras se puede mostrar un número?
- ¿Cómo cuentas de 1 en 1, de 5 en 5, de 10 en 10 y de 100 en 100?

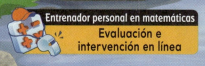

2 Números hasta el 1,000 71

En este capítulo, explorarás y descubrirás las respuestas a las siguientes **Preguntas esenciales**:
- ¿Cómo puedes usar el valor posicional para hacer un modelo, escribir y comparar números de 3 dígitos?
- ¿Cómo puedes usar bloques parar mostrar un números de 3 dígitos?
- ¿Cómo puedes escribir un número de 3 dígitos de maneras diferentes?
- ¿Cómo te puede ayudar el valor posicional a comparar números de...

Repaso de la lección y Repaso en espiral en cada lección

✓ **Muestra lo que sabes** 72
   Desarrollo del vocabulario 73
   Juego: Pesca de dígitos 74
1 Agrupar decenas en centenas 75
2 Explorar números de 3 dígitos 81
3 **Manos a la obra** • Hacer un modelo de números de 3 dígitos 87
4 Centenas, decenas y unidades 93
5 Valor posicional hasta el 1,000 99
6 Nombres de los números 105
7 Diferentes formas de los números 111
✓ **Revisión de la mitad del capítulo** 114
8 **Álgebra** • Diferentes maneras de mostrar números 117
9 Contar hacia adelante y hacia atrás de 10 en 10 y de 100 en 100 123
10 **Álgebra** • Patrones numéricos 129
11 **Resolución de problemas** • Comparar números 135
12 **Álgebra** • Comparar números 141
✓ **Repaso y prueba del Capítulo 2** 147

Suma y resta

La gran idea Desarrollar fluidez en la suma y la resta con números hasta 100. Resolver problemas de suma y resta con números hasta 1,000.

Librito de vocabulario Todo sobre los animales 151

3 Operaciones básicas y relaciones   159

✓ **Muestra lo que sabes** 160
   Desarrollo del vocabulario 161
   Juego: En busca de la oruga 162
1 Usar operaciones de dobles 163
2 Practicar operaciones de suma 169
3 Álgebra • Formar una decena para sumar 175
4 Álgebra • Sumar 3 sumandos 181
5 Álgebra • Relacionar la suma y la resta 187
6 Practicar operaciones de resta 193
✓ **Revisión de la mitad del capítulo** 196
7 Restar usando una decena 199
8 Álgebra • Hacer dibujos para representar problemas 205
9 Álgebra • Usar ecuaciones para representar problemas 211
10 Resolución de problemas • Grupos iguales 217
11 Álgebra • Suma repetida 223
✓ **Repaso y prueba del Capítulo 3** 229

¡Aprende en línea! Tus lecciones de matemáticas son interactivas. Usa iTools, Modelos matemáticos animados y el Glosario multimedia entre otros.

Presentación del Capítulo 3

En este capítulo, explorarás y descubrirás las respuestas a las siguientes
Preguntas esenciales:

- ¿Cómo puedes usar patrones y estrategias para hallar la suma y la diferencia de operaciones básicas?
- ¿Cuáles son las estrategias para recordar las operaciones de suma y de resta?
- ¿Cómo están relacionadas la suma y la resta?

Entrenador personal en matemáticas
Evaluación e intervención en línea

En este capítulo, explorarás y descubrirás las respuestas a las siguientes
Preguntas esenciales:
- ¿Cómo usas el valor posicional para sumar números de 2 dígitos y de qué formas se pueden sumar números de 2 dígitos?
- ¿Cómo formas una decena con un sumando para ayudarte a resolver un problema de suma?
- ¿Cómo anotas los pasos al sumar números de 2 dígitos?
- ¿De qué formas se pueden sumar 3 números o 4 números?

4 Suma de 2 dígitos — 233

✓ **Muestra lo que sabes**	234
Desarrollo del vocabulario	235
Juego: ¿Cuál es la suma?	236
1 Separar unidades para sumar	237
2 Hacer una compensación	243
3 Separar los sumandos en decenas y unidades	249
4 Reagrupar modelos para sumar	255
5 Hacer un modelo y anotar sumas de 2 dígitos	261
6 Suma de 2 dígitos	267
7 Practicar sumas de 2 dígitos	273
✓ **Revisión de la mitad del capítulo**	276
8 Reescribir sumas de 2 dígitos	279
9 **Resolución de problemas** • La suma	285
10 **Álgebra** • Escribir ecuaciones para representar la suma	291
11 **Álgebra** • Hallar la suma de 3 sumandos	297
12 **Álgebra** • Hallar la suma de 4 sumandos	303
✓ **Repaso y prueba del Capítulo 4**	309

Práctica y tarea

Repaso de la lección y Repaso en espiral en cada lección

5 Resta de 2 dígitos — 313

- ✓ **Muestra lo que sabes** 314
  - Desarrollo del vocabulario 315
  - Juego: Búsqueda de restas 316
- 1 *Álgebra* • Separar unidades para restar 317
- 2 *Álgebra* • Separar números para restar 323
- 3 Reagrupar modelos para restar 329
- 4 Hacer un modelo y anotar restas de 2 dígitos 335
- 5 Resta de 2 dígitos 341
- 6 Practicar la resta de 2 dígitos 347
- ✓ **Revisión de la mitad del capítulo** 350
- 7 Reescribir restas de 2 dígitos 353
- 8 Sumar para hallar diferencias 359
- 9 **Resolución de problemas** • La resta 365
- 10 *Álgebra* • Escribir ecuaciones para representar la resta 371
- 11 Resolver problemas de varios pasos 377
- ✓ **Repaso y prueba del Capítulo 5** 383

Presentación del Capítulo 5
En este capítulo, explorarás y descubrirás las respuestas a las siguientes **Preguntas esenciales**:
- ¿Cómo usas el valor posicional para restar números de 2 dígitos con o sin reagrupación?
- ¿Cómo puedes separar números para ayudarte a resolver un problema de resta?
- ¿Qué pasos usas para resolver problemas de resta de 2 dígitos?
- ¿De qué formas puedes hacer un modelo, mostrar y resolver problemas de resta?

6 Suma y resta de 3 dígitos — 387

- ✓ **Muestra lo que sabes** 388
  - Desarrollo del vocabulario 389
  - Juego: Baraja de 2 dígitos 390
- 1 Dibujar para representar la suma de 3 dígitos 391
- 2 Separar sumandos de 3 dígitos 397
- 3 Suma de 3 dígitos: Reagrupar unidades 403
- 4 Suma de 3 dígitos: Reagrupar decenas 409
- 5 Suma: Reagrupar unidades y decenas 415
- ✓ **Revisión de la mitad del capítulo** 418
- 6 **Resolución de problemas** • Resta de 3 dígitos 421
- 7 Resta de 3 dígitos: Reagrupar decenas 427
- 8 Resta de 3 dígitos: Reagrupar centenas 433
- 9 Resta: Reagrupar centenas y decenas 439
- 10 Reagrupar con ceros 445
- ✓ **Repaso y prueba del Capítulo 6** 451

Presentación del Capítulo 6
En este capítulo, explorarás y descubrirás las respuestas a las siguientes **Preguntas esenciales**:
- ¿Cuáles son algunas estrategias para sumar y restar números de 3 dígitos?
- ¿Cuáles son los pasos para hallar la suma en un problema de suma de 3 dígitos?
- ¿Cuáles son los pasos para hallar la diferencia en un problema de resta de 3 dígitos?
- ¿Cuándo necesitas reagrupar?

VOLUMEN 2
Medición y datos

La gran idea Usar unidades estándar de medidas y ampliar la comprensión conceptual de tiempo, datos y gráficas. Desarrollar la comprensión conceptual del dinero.

Librito de vocabulario Hacer una cometa 455

7 El dinero y la hora 463

- ✓ Muestra lo que sabes 464
- Desarrollo del vocabulario 465
- Juego: Conteo de 5 y de 10 466
- 1 Monedas de 10¢, monedas de 5¢ y monedas de 1¢ 467
- 2 Monedas de 25¢ 473
- 3 Contar monedas 479
- 4 **Manos a la obra** • Mostrar cantidades de dos maneras 485
- 5 Un dólar 491
- ✓ Revisión de la mitad del capítulo 494
- 6 Cantidades mayores que $1 497
- 7 **Resolución de problemas** • Dinero 503
- 8 La hora y la media hora 509
- 9 La hora cada 5 minutos 515
- 10 Práctica: Decir la hora 521
- 11 Uso de a. m. y p. m. 527
- ✓ Repaso y prueba del Capítulo 7 533

8 Longitud en unidades del sistema usual 537

- ✓ Muestra lo que sabes 538
- Desarrollo del vocabulario 539
- Juego: ¿Más corto o más largo? 540
- 1 **Manos a la obra** • Medir con modelos de pulgadas . . 541
- 2 **Manos a la obra** • Hacer y usar una regla 547
- 3 Estimar longitudes en pulgadas 553
- 4 **Manos a la obra** • Medir con una regla en pulgadas . . 559
- 5 **Resolución de problemas** • Sumar y restar en pulgadas 565
- ✓ Revisión de la mitad del capítulo 568
- 6 **Manos a la obra** • Medir en pulgadas y en pies . . 571
- 7 Estimar longitudes en pies 577
- 8 Elegir un instrumento 583
- 9 Mostrar datos de medida 589
- ✓ Repaso y prueba del Capítulo 8 595

¡Aprende en línea!
Tus lecciones de matemáticas son interactivas. Usa iTools, Modelos matemáticos animados y el Glosario multimedia entre otros.

En este capítulo, explorarás y descubrirás las respuestas a las siguientes **Preguntas esenciales**:

- ¿Cómo usas el valor de las monedas y los billetes para hallar el valor total de un grupo y cómo lees la hora que muestran los relojes analógicos y los relojes digitales?
- ¿Cuáles son los nombres y los valores de las diferentes monedas?
- ¿Cómo sabes la hora que muestra un reloj observando las manecillas del reloj?

En este capítulo, explorarás y descubrirás las respuestas a las siguientes **Preguntas esenciales**:

- ¿Cuáles son algunos métodos e instrumentos que se pueden usar para estimar y medir la longitud?
- ¿Qué instrumentos se pueden usar para medir la longitud y cómo los usas?
- ¿Qué unidades se pueden usar para medir la longitud y en qué se diferencian?
- ¿Cómo puedes estimar la longitud de un objeto?

9 Longitud en unidades métricas — 599

- ✓ **Muestra lo que sabes** **600**
- Desarrollo del vocabulario **601**
- Juegos: Estimar la longitud **602**
- 1 **Manos a la obra** • Medir con un modelo de un centímetro **603**
- 2 Estimar longitudes en centímetros **609**
- 3 **Manos a la obra** • Medir con una regla en centímetros **615**
- 4 **Resolución de problemas** • Sumar y restar longitudes **621**
- ✓ **Revisión de la mitad del capítulo** **624**
- 5 **Manos a la obra** • Centímetros y metros **627**
- 6 Estimar la longitud en metros **633**
- 7 **Manos a la obra** • Medir y comparar longitudes . . . **639**
- ✓ **Repaso y prueba del Capítulo 9** **645**

En este capítulo, explorarás y descubrirás las respuestas a las siguientes **Preguntas esenciales**:

- ¿Cuáles son algunos métodos e instrumentos que se pueden usar para estimar y medir la longitud en unidades métricas?
- ¿Qué instrumentos se pueden usar para medir la longitud en unidades métricas y cómo los usas?
- ¿Qué unidades métricas se pueden usar para medir la longitud y en qué se diferencian?
- Si conoces la longitud de un objeto, ¿cómo puedes estimar la longitud de otro objeto?

10 Datos — 649

- ✓ **Muestra lo que sabes** **650**
- Desarrollo del vocabulario **651**
- Juego: Formar decenas **652**
- 1 Reunir datos **653**
- 2 Leer pictografías **659**
- 3 Hacer pictografías **665**
- ✓ **Revisión de la mitad del capítulo** **668**
- 4 Leer gráficas de barras **671**
- 5 Hacer gráficas de barras **677**
- 6 **Resolución de problemas** • Mostrar datos **683**
- ✓ **Repaso y prueba del Capítulo 10** **689**

Práctica y tarea
Repaso de la lección y Repaso en espiral en cada lección

Presentación del Capítulo 10

En este capítulo, explorarás y descubrirás las respuestas a las siguientes **Preguntas esenciales**:

- ¿Cómo te ayudan las tablas de conteo, las pictografías y las gráficas de barras a resolver problemas?
- ¿Cómo se usan las marcas de conteo para anotar los datos de una encuesta?
- ¿Cómo se hace una pictografías?
- ¿Cómo sabes qué representan las barras de una gráfica de barras?

Geometría y fracciones

La gran idea Describir, analizar y dibujar figuras bidimensionales y tridimensionales. Desarrollar una comprensión conceptual de las fracciones.

Librito de vocabulario La labor de un agricultor............ 693

11 Geometría y conceptos de fracción 701

✓ **Muestra lo que sabes** 702
   Desarrollo del vocabulario 703
   Juego: Cuenta los lados 704
  1 Figuras tridimensionales 705
  2 Propiedades de las figuras tridimensionales 711
  3 Construir figuras tridimensionales 717
  4 Figuras bidimensionales. 723
  5 Ángulos de figuras bidimensionales 729
  6 Clasificar figuras bidimensionales 735
  7 **Manos a la obra** • División de rectángulos 741
✓ **Revisión de la mitad del capítulo** 744
  8 Partes iguales. 747
  9 Mostrar partes iguales de un entero 753
 10 Describir partes iguales 759
 11 **Resolución de problemas** • Partes iguales 765
✓ **Repaso y prueba del Capítulo 11** 771

Actividades de ciencia, tecnología,
ingeniería y matemáticas (STEM) .... STEM 1
Glosario ilustrado. H1
Índice H11

¡Aprende en línea!
Tus lecciones de matemáticas son interactivas. Usa iTools, Modelos matemáticos animados y el Glosario multimedia entre otros.

Resumen del Capítulo 11

En este capítulo, explorarás y descubrirás las respuestas a las siguientes
Preguntas esenciales:

- ¿Cuáles son algunas figuras bidimensionales y tridimensionales y cómo puedes mostrar las partes iguales de las figuras?
- ¿Cómo puedes describir algunas figuras bidimensionales y tridimensionales?
- ¿Cómo puedes describir figuras o partes iguales?

Entrenador personal en matemáticas
Evaluación e intervención en línea

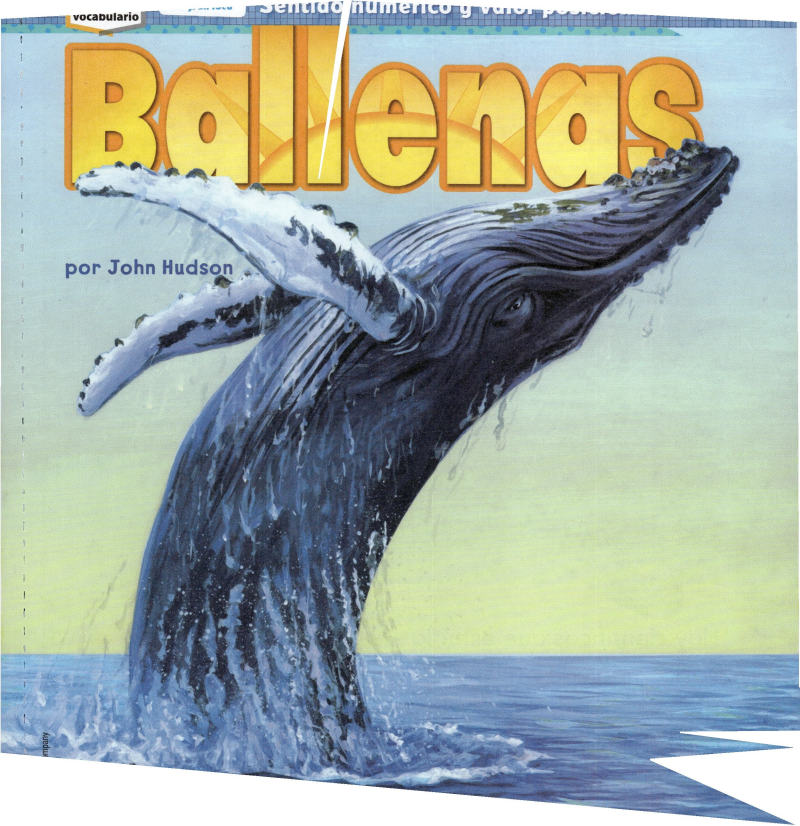

Ballenas

por John Hudson

Hay científicos que estudian las ballenas. Varios tipos de ballenas nadan por la costa oeste de los Estados Unidos de América. Un científico ve 8 ballenas azules. Las ballenas azules son los animales más grandes de la Tierra.

Estudios Sociales

¿En qué parte del mapa están los Estados Unidos de América?

El científico también ve 13 ballenas jorobadas. Las ballenas jorobadas cantan bajo el agua. ¿El científico vio más ballenas jorobadas o más ballenas azules?   más ballenas _____

¿En qué parte del mapa está el océano Pacífico?

Las ballenas también nadan por la costa este de Canadá y de los Estados Unidos de América. Las ballenas piloto nadan detrás de un líder, o *piloto*. Un científico ve un grupo de 29 ballenas piloto.

¿En qué parte del mapa está Canadá?

Las rorcuales comunes son nadadoras ágiles. Son las segundas ballenas más grandes del mundo. Un científico ve un grupo de 27 rorcuales comunes. ¿Cuántas decenas hay en el número 27?

_____ decenas

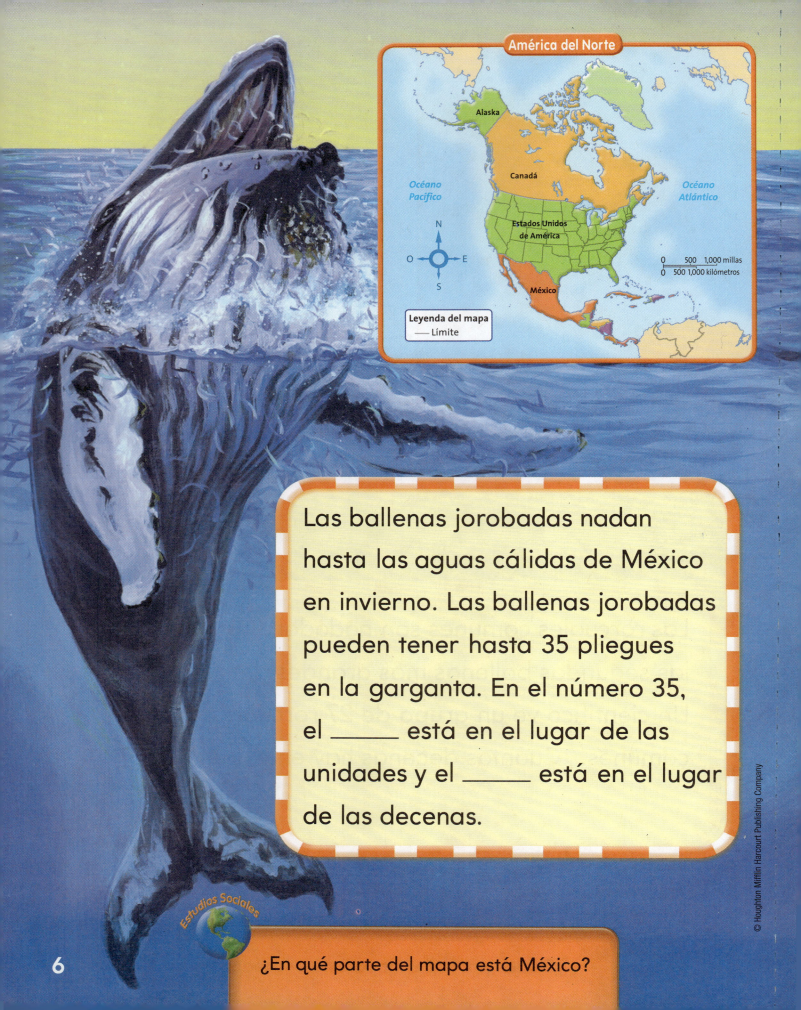

América del Norte

Las ballenas jorobadas nadan hasta las aguas cálidas de México en invierno. Las ballenas jorobadas pueden tener hasta 35 pliegues en la garganta. En el número 35, el _____ está en el lugar de las unidades y el _____ está en el lugar de las decenas.

¿En qué parte del mapa está México?

Nombre _____

Escribe sobre el cuento

Observa los dibujos. Dibuja y escribe tu propio cuento. Compara dos números en tu cuento.

Repaso del vocabulario

más   menos
decenas   mayor que
unidades   menor que

 **Matemáticas**

_____
_____
_____
_____
_____
_____

El tamaño de los números

La tabla muestra cuántas crías de ballena vieron los científicos.

Crías de ballena vistas	
Ballena	Número de ballenas
Jorobada	34
Azul	13
Rorcual común	27
Piloto	43

1. ¿Qué número de ballenas tiene un 4 en el lugar de las decenas?

   _____

2. ¿Cuántas decenas y unidades describen el número de crías de ballena azul que se vieron?

   _____ decena _____ unidades

3. Compara el número de crías de ballena jorobada y el número de crías de ballena piloto que se vieron. Escribe > o <.

   34 ◯ 43

4. Compara el número de crías de rorcual común y el número de crías de ballena azul que se vieron. Escribe > o <.

   27 ◯ 13

Escribe un cuento sobre un científico que observa animales marinos. Incluye números de 2 dígitos en tu cuento.

8

Nombre _____

✓ Muestra lo que sabes

Entrenador personal en matemáticas
Evaluación e intervención en línea

Representa números hasta el 20

Escribe el número que diga cuántos hay.

1. [ten-frame with 10 counters] [ten-frame with 3 counters] _____

2. [ten-frame with 10 counters] [ten-frame with 7 counters] _____

Usa una tabla con los números hasta el 100

Usa la tabla con los números hasta el 100.

3. Cuenta del 36 al 47. ¿Cuáles de los números de abajo dirás? Enciérralos en un círculo.

   42   31   48   39   37

1	2	3	4	5	6	7	8	9	10
11	12	13	14	15	16	17	18	19	20
21	22	23	24	25	26	27	28	29	30
31	32	33	34	35	36	37	38	39	40
41	42	43	44	45	46	47	48	49	50
51	52	53	54	55	56	57	58	59	60
61	62	63	64	65	66	67	68	69	70
71	72	73	74	75	76	77	78	79	80
81	82	83	84	85	86	87	88	89	90
91	92	93	94	95	96	97	98	99	100

Decenas

Escribe cuántas decenas hay. Escribe el número.

4. [4 tens rods]   ____ decenas   _____

5. [6 tens rods]   ____ decenas   _____

Esta página es para verificar la comprensión de destrezas importantes que se necesitan para tener éxito en el Capítulo 1.

Nombre _____

Desarrollo del vocabulario

Palabras de repaso
- unidades
- decenas
- contar hacia adelante
- contar hacia atrás

Visualízalo
Completa las casillas del organizador gráfico. Escribe oraciones sobre **unidades** y **decenas**.

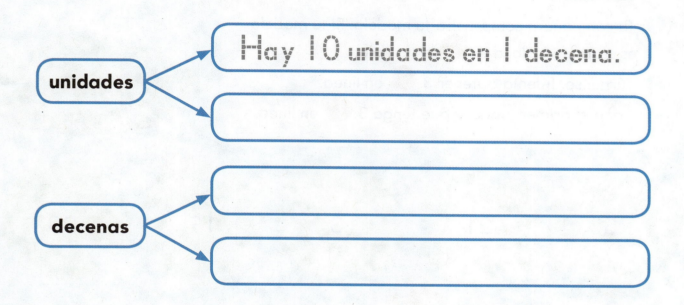

Hay 10 unidades en 1 decena.

Comprende el vocabulario

1. Comienza en el 1. **Cuenta hacia adelante** de uno en uno.

   1, ____, ____, ____, ____, ____

2. Comienza en el 8. **Cuenta hacia atrás** de uno en uno.

   8, ____, ____, ____, ____, ____

Capítulo 1 · Libro interactivo del estudiante · Glosario multimedia

once 11

Capítulo 1

Juego

Tres en línea

Materiales • 15 🔴 • 15 🟡 • ▬▬▬▬▬

Juega con un compañero.

1. Elige una hoja. Lee el número de la hoja. Usa ▬▬▬▬▬ para representar el número.
2. Tu compañero comprueba tu modelo. Si tu modelo es correcto, coloca tu 🔴 en la hoja.
3. Túrnense. Intenta obtener 3 🔴 en línea.
4. Gana el primer jugador que tenga 3 🔴 en línea.

5	21	13	19	20
25	15	7	8	12
11	9	14	16	24
22	23	17	18	10

12 doce

Vocabulario del Capítulo 1

decenas tens 18	**dígito** digit 21
dobles doubles 22	**es igual a** is equal to (=) 25
más plus (+) 34	**números impares** odd numbers 46
números pares even numbers 47	**unidades** ones 64

0, 1, 2, 3, 4, 5, 6, 7, 8 y 9 son **dígitos**.

10 unidades = 1 decena

2 más 1 es igual a 3
2 + 1 = 3

2 + 2 = 4

Los números impares muestran pares y una casilla sobrante.

2 más 1 es igual a 3
2 + 1 = 3

10 unidades = 1 decena

Los números pares muestran pares y ninguna casilla sobrante.

De visita con las palabras de ¡Vivan las matemáticas!

¡Vamos al mercado!

Recuadro de palabras
- decenas
- dígito
- dobles
- es igual a (=)
- más (+)
- números impares
- números pares
- unidades

Jugadores: 2 a 4

Materiales
- 1 🟥
- 1 🟦
- 1 🟩
- 1 🟨
- 1 🎲

Instrucciones

1. Coloca tu 🔲 en el círculo de SALIDA del mismo color.
2. Para sacar tu 🔲 de la SALIDA, debes lanzar un 6.
   - Si no sacas un 6, debes esperar hasta el siguiente turno.
   - Si sacas un 6, mueve tu 🔲 al siguiente círculo que tenga el mismo color que tu recorrido.
3. Una vez que tengas un 🔲 en el recorrido, lanza el 🎲 para jugar tu turno. Mueve tu 🔲 esa cantidad de veces.
4. Si caes en un espacio que tiene una pregunta, responde la pregunta. Si la respuesta no es correcta, retrocede 1 espacio.
5. Para alcanzar la META, debes mover tu 🔲 hacia adelante siguiendo el recorrido del mismo color del 🔲. El primer jugador que llegue a la META, es el ganador.

Capítulo 1 doce 12A

Juego

SALIDA

¿Qué número es igual a 12 + 7?

¿Qué dígito está en el lugar de las unidades en 19?

¿Cómo puedes usar dobles para sumar 4 y 5?

¿Cómo puedes saber que un número es par?

¿Qué dígito está en el lugar de las decenas en 45?

¿Cómo puedes saber que un número es impar?

SALIDA

¿Qué signo indica que un número es igual a otro?

¿Cuántas unidades hay en 24?

Juego

¿Qué significa más?

¿Qué números son pares? 32, 25, 13, 6

¿Qué significa + ?

¿Qué números son impares? 13, 34, 22, 47

¿Cómo puedes saber cuántas unidades hay en un número?

¿Cómo puedes saber cuántas decenas hay en un número?

SALIDA

¿Cómo puedes usar dobles para sumar 9 y 8?

¿Cuántas decenas hay en 37?

SALIDA

Capítulo 1 doce 12C

Diario

Escríbelo

Reflexiona

Elige una idea. Escribe acerca de la idea en el espacio de abajo.

- Explica dos cosas que sabes de los números pares y de los números impares.

- Escribe acerca de las diferentes maneras en que puedes mostrar 25.

- Di cómo contar en diferentes cantidades hasta 1,000.

_____
_____
_____
_____
_____
_____
_____
_____
_____

Nombre _____

Álgebra • Números pares e impares

Pregunta esencial ¿En qué se diferencian los números pares e impares?

Objetivo de aprendizaje Determinarás si un grupo, de hasta 20 objetos, tiene un número par o impar de elementos.

Usa 🟥 para mostrar cada número.

PARA EL MAESTRO • Lea el siguiente problema. Beca tiene 8 carros de juguete. ¿Puede ordenar sus carros en pares en un estante? Pida a los niños que coloquen pares de cubos verticalmente en los cuadros de diez. Continúe la actividad con los números 7 y 10.

Charla matemática PRÁCTICAS Y PROCESOS MATEMÁTICOS 6

Cuando formas pares con el 7 y con el 10, ¿en qué se diferencian estos modelos? **Explica.**

Capítulo 1   trece 13

Representa y dibuja

Cuenta cubos por cada número. Forma pares.
Los números **pares** muestran pares en que no sobran cubos.
Los números **impares** muestran pares con un cubo que sobra.

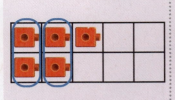 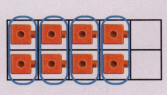 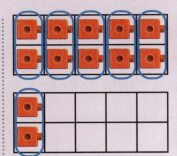 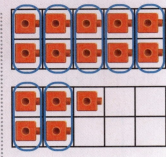

5 impar   8 par   12 _____   15 _____

Comparte y muestra

Usa los cubos. Cuenta el número de cubos.
Forma pares. Luego escribe **par** o **impar**.

1. 6 _____   2. 3 _____

3. 2 _____   4. 9 _____

5. 4 _____   6. 10 _____

7. 7 _____   8. 13 _____

9. 11 _____   10. 14 _____

14 catorce

Nombre _____

Por tu cuenta

Sombrea los cuadros de diez para mostrar el número.
Encierra en un círculo **par** o **impar**.

11. 17

par   impar

12. 16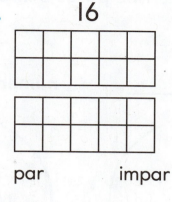

par   impar

13. 19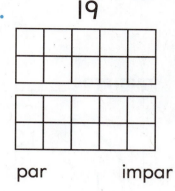

par   impar

14. Hay un número par de niños y un número impar de niñas en el salón de Lena. ¿Cuántos niños y niñas puede haber en su salón? Muestra tu trabajo.

_____

_____

15. **PRÁCTICAS Y PROCESOS MATEMÁTICOS 3**   **Da argumentos**

¿Qué dos números de la casilla son números pares?

_____ y _____

Explica cómo sabes que son números pares.

_____

_____

_____

Capítulo 1 • Lección 1

Resolución de problemas • Aplicaciones

Matemáticas

16. **PIENSA MÁS** Completa los espacios para describir los grupos de números. Escribe **pares** o **impares**.

números _____   números _____

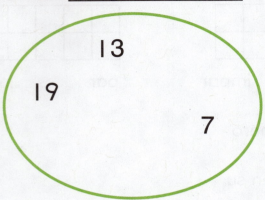   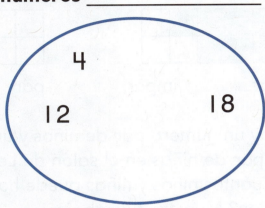

Escribe cada uno de los siguientes números dentro del círculo que corresponda.

5   6   10   11   24   25

17. **PIENSA MÁS** ¿Los cuadros de diez muestran un número par? Elige Sí o No.

   ○ Sí   ○ No

   ○ Sí   ○ No

 ACTIVIDAD PARA LA CASA • Pida a su niño que muestre un número, como el 9, con objetos pequeños y explique por qué el número es par o impar.

dieciséis

Nombre _____

Álgebra • Números pares e impares

Objetivo de aprendizaje Determinarás si un grupo, de hasta 20 objetos, tiene un número par o impar de elementos.

Sombrea algunos de los cuadros de diez para mostrar el número. Encierra en un círculo par o impar.

1. 15

   par   impar

2. 18

   par   impar

3. 11

   par   impar

Resolución de problemas · En el mundo

4. El Sr. Dell tiene un número impar de ovejas y un número par de vacas en su granja. Encierra en un círculo la opción que podría referirse a su granja.

   9 ovejas y 10 vacas

   10 ovejas y 11 vacas

   8 ovejas y 12 vacas

5. ESCRIBE Matemáticas Escribe dos números impares y dos números pares. Explica cómo sabes cuáles son números pares y cuáles son impares.

Capítulo 1   diecisiete 17

Repaso de la lección

1. Encierra en un círculo el número par.

   3
   4
   5
   9

2. Encierra en un círculo el número impar.

   2
   6
   7
   8

Repaso en espiral

3. Encierra en un círculo el número impar.

   10
   8
   3
   4

4. Encierra en un círculo el número par.

   7
   6
   5
   1

5. Encierra en un círculo el número par.

   9
   7
   5
   2

6. Encierra en un círculo el número impar.

   1
   4
   8
   10

Nombre _____

Álgebra • Representar números pares

Pregunta esencial ¿Por qué un número par puede mostrarse como la suma de dos sumandos iguales?

Objetivo de aprendizaje Mostrarás un número par como la suma de dos números iguales.

Escucha y dibuja

Forma pares con tus cubos. Haz un dibujo que muestre los cubos. Luego escribe los números que dices cuando cuentas para hallar el número de cubos.

_____   _____ cubos

 PARA EL MAESTRO • Dé a cada grupo pequeño de niños un conjunto de 10 a 15 cubos interconectables. Después de que los niños agrupen sus cubos en pares, pídales que hagan un dibujo de sus cubos y que escriban su secuencia de conteo para hallar el número total de cubos.

Charla matemática

Usa razonamiento
Explica cómo sabes si un número representado con cubos es un número par.

Capítulo 1   diecinueve **19**

Representa y dibuja

Un número par de cubos puede mostrarse como dos grupos iguales.

Puedes emparejar cada cubo del primer grupo con un cubo del segundo grupo.

$$6 = 3 + 3$$

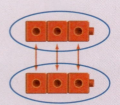

$$10 = 5 + 5$$

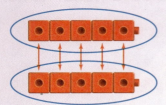

Comparte y muestra

¿Cuántos cubos hay en total? Completa el enunciado de suma para mostrar los grupos iguales.

1. ___ = ___ + ___

2. ___ = ___ + ___

3. ___ = ___ + ___

4. ___ = ___ + ___

Nombre _____

Por tu cuenta

Sombrea las casillas para mostrar dos grupos iguales por cada número. Completa el enunciado de suma para mostrar los grupos.

5. 10

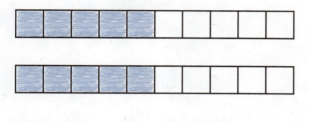

____ = ____ + ____

6. 16

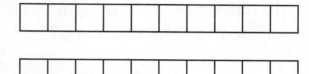

____ = ____ + ____

7. Elena y José tienen 18 tarjetas postales en total. Los dos tienen el mismo número de tarjetas postales. ¿Cuántas tarjetas postales tiene cada uno de ellos?

_____ tarjetas postales

PIENSA MÁS El número 7 es un número impar. Marc mostró el 7 con este enunciado de suma. Muestra estos números impares con enunciados de suma de la misma manera que Marc.

$7 = 3 + 3 + 1$

8. $5 = $ ____ + ____ + ____

9. $11 = $ ____ + ____ + ____

10. $9 = $ ____ + ____ + ____

11. $13 = $ ____ + ____ + ____

Capítulo 1 • Lección 2

Resolución de problemas • Aplicaciones

Resuelve. Escribe o dibuja para explicar.

12. **PRÁCTICAS Y PROCESOS MATEMÁTICOS 2** **Usa el razonamiento**
Jacob y Lucas tienen el mismo número de **caracoles**. Tienen 16 caracoles en total. ¿Cuántos caracoles tiene cada uno?

Jacob: _____ caracoles

Lucas: _____ caracoles

13. **PIENSA MÁS** Elige un número par entre el 10 y el 19. Haz un dibujo y luego escribe un enunciado para explicar por qué es un número par.

 ACTIVIDAD PARA LA CASA • Pida a su niño que explique lo que aprendió en esta lección.

Nombre _____

Álgebra • Representar números pares

Sombrea los cuadros para mostrar dos grupos iguales para cada número. Completa el enunciado de suma para mostrar los grupos.

Objetivo de aprendizaje Mostrarás un número par como la suma de dos números iguales.

1. 8

   ____ = ____ + ____

2. 18

   ____ = ____ + ____

3. 10

   ____ = ____ + ____

4. 14

   ____ = ____ + ____

5. 20

   ____ = ____ + ____

Resolución de problemas · En el mundo

Resuelve. Escribe o dibuja para explicar.

6. Los asientos de una camioneta están en pares. Hay 16 asientos. ¿Cuántos pares de asientos hay en total?

   ____ pares de asientos

7. ESCRIBE Matemáticas Haz un dibujo o escribe para mostrar que el número 18 es un número par.

Capítulo 1

veintitrés **23**

Repaso de la lección

1. Encierra en un círculo la suma que sea un número par.

   9 + 9 = 18
   9 + 8 = 17
   8 + 7 = 15
   6 + 5 = 11

2. Encierra en un círculo la suma que sea un número par.

   1 + 2 = 3
   3 + 3 = 6
   2 + 5 = 7
   4 + 7 = 11

Repaso en espiral

3. Encierra en un círculo el número par.

   7
   9
   10
   13

4. Encierra en un círculo el número impar.

   4
   11
   16
   20

5. Ray tiene un número impar de gatos. También tiene un número par de perros. Completa el enunciado.

   Ray tiene _____ gatos y _____ perros.

6. Encierra en un círculo la suma que sea un número par.

   2 + 3 = 5
   3 + 4 = 7
   4 + 4 = 8
   7 + 8 = 15

Nombre _____

Comprender el valor posicional

Pregunta esencial ¿Cómo sabes cuál es el valor de un dígito?

Objetivo de aprendizaje Usarás el valor posicional para describir los valores de los dígitos en números de 2 dígitos.

Escucha y dibuja · En el mundo

Escribe los números. Luego elige una manera de mostrar los números.

Decenas	Unidades

Decenas	Unidades

PARA EL MAESTRO • Lea el siguiente problema. Pida a los niños que escriban los números y que describan cómo eligieron representarlos. Gabriel colecciona tarjetas de béisbol. El número de tarjetas que tiene se escribe con un 2 y un 5. ¿Cuántas tarjetas puede tener?

Charla matemática — PRÁCTICAS Y PROCESOS MATEMÁTICOS 6

Explica por qué el valor del 5 es diferente en los dos números.

Capítulo 1   veinticinco **25**

Representa y dibuja

0, 1, 2, 3, 4, 5, 6, 7, 8 y 9 son **dígitos**. En un número de 2 dígitos, sabes cuál es el valor de un dígito por su posición.

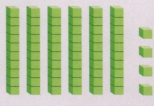

64

Decenas	Unidades
6	4

6 decenas 4 unidades

El dígito 6 está en el lugar de las decenas. Te dice que hay 6 decenas, o 60.

El dígito 4 está en el lugar de las unidades. Te dice que hay 4 unidades, o 4.

Comparte y muestra

Encierra en un círculo el valor del dígito rojo.

1. 2**6**

60   (6)

2. **5**8

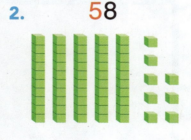

5   50

3. **4**0

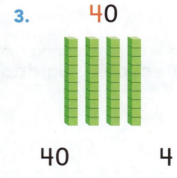

40   4

4. 7**3**

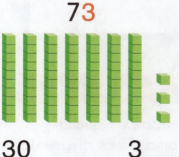

30   3

✓5. **2**4

2   20

✓6. 6**1**

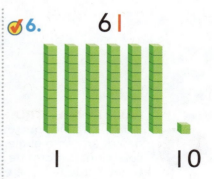

1   10

26 veintiséis

Nombre _____

Por tu cuenta

Encierra en un círculo el valor del dígito rojo.

7. 5**1**
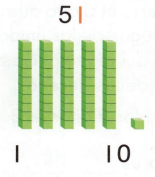
1   10

8. **4**9
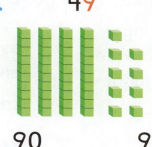
90   9

9. **7**0
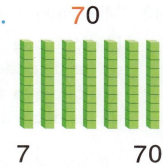
7   70

10. Phillip compró un rompecabezas. El número de piezas del rompecabezas tiene el dígito 6 en el lugar de las unidades y el dígito 3 en el lugar de las decenas. ¿Cuántas piezas tiene el rompecabezas de Phillip?

_____ piezas

11. Noah horneó unas tartas de manzana. El número de manzanas que usó tiene el dígito 1 en el lugar de las decenas y un número par menor que 5 en el lugar de las unidades. ¿Cuántas manzanas pudo usar Noah para hornear las tartas de manzana?

_____ manzanas

12. **PIENSA MÁS** Observa los dígitos de los números. Haz dibujos rápidos de los bloques que faltan.

47
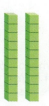

52

Capítulo 1 • Lección 3

veintisiete **27**

Resolución de problemas • Aplicaciones

Sigue las pistas y escribe el número de 2 dígitos.

13. Mi número tiene 8 decenas.

El dígito que está en el lugar de las unidades es mayor que el dígito que está en el lugar de las decenas.

Mi número es _____.

14. En mi número, el dígito que está en el lugar de las unidades es el doble del dígito que está en el lugar de las decenas.

La suma de los dígitos es 3.

Mi número es _____.

15. **PRÁCTICAS Y PROCESOS MATEMÁTICOS 1** **Busca sentido a los problemas**

En mi número, los dos dígitos son números pares.

El dígito que está en el lugar de las decenas es menor que el dígito que está en el lugar de las unidades. La suma de los dígitos es 6.

Mi número es _____.

16. **PIENSA MÁS** ¿Qué valor tiene el dígito 4 en el número 43?

ACTIVIDAD PARA LA CASA • Escriba el número 56. Pida a su niño que diga qué dígito está en el lugar de las decenas, qué dígito está en el lugar de las unidades y el valor de cada dígito.

Nombre _____

Comprender el valor posicional

Objetivo de aprendizaje Usarás el valor posicional para describir los valores de los dígitos en números de 2 dígitos.

Encierra en un círculo el valor del dígito subrayado.

1. 2<u>3</u>

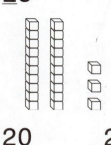

20   2

2. 4<u>8</u>

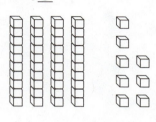

8   80

3. <u>1</u>8

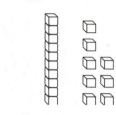

10   1

4. <u>4</u>3

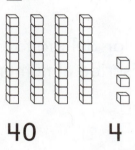

40   4

5. <u>5</u>4

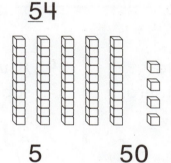

5   50

6. 6<u>5</u>

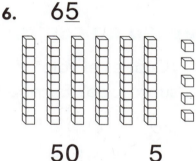

50   5

Resolución de problemas

Escribe el número de 2 dígitos que coincida con las pistas.

7. Mi número tiene un dígito de las decenas que es 8 más que el dígito de las unidades. El cero no es uno de mis dígitos.

Mi número es _____.

8. **ESCRIBE Matemáticas** Haz un dibujo rápido para mostrar el número 76. Describe el valor de cada dígito en este número.

Capítulo 1   veintinueve **29**

Repaso de la lección

1. ¿Cuál es el valor del dígito subrayado? Escribe el número.

   3<u>2</u>

   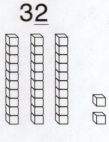

   _____

2. ¿Cuál es el valor del dígito subrayado? Escribe el número.

   <u>2</u>8

   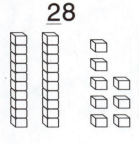

   _____

Repaso en espiral

3. ¿Cuál es el valor del dígito subrayado? Escribe el número.

   <u>5</u>3

   _____

4. ¿Cuál es el valor del dígito subrayado? Escribe el número.

   2<u>4</u>

   _____

5. ¿Es el número total de bolígrafos y de lápices un número par o impar? Escribe el número. Encierra en un círculo par o impar.

   2 bolígrafos + 3 lápices _____ en total

   par   impar

6. Encierra en un círculo la suma que sea un número par.

   5 + 2 = _____
   6 + 3 = _____
   7 + 4 = _____
   7 + 7 = _____

30 treinta

Nombre _____

Forma desarrollada

Pregunta esencial ¿Cómo se describe un número de 2 dígitos con decenas y unidades?

Objetivo de aprendizaje Describirás un número de 2 dígitos como decenas y unidades.

Usa ▭▭▭▭ ▪ para representar cada número.

Decenas	Unidades

PARA EL MAESTRO • Después de leer el siguiente problema, escriba 38 en el pizarrón. Pida a los niños que representen el número. Emmanuel colocó 38 adhesivos en su hoja. ¿Cómo pueden representar 38 con bloques? Continúe la actividad con 83 y 77.

Charla matemática

PRÁCTICAS Y PROCESOS MATEMÁTICOS 6

Explica cómo sabes la cantidad de decenas y de unidades que hay en el número 29.

Capítulo 1   treinta y uno **31**

Representa y dibuja

¿Qué significa 23?

Decenas	Unidades
I I	o o o

En el 23, el 2 tiene un valor de 2 decenas, o 20.
En el 23, el 3 tiene un valor de 3 unidades, o 3.

__2__ decenas __3__ unidades

__20__ + __3__

Comparte y muestra

Haz un dibujo rápido que muestre el número.
Describe el número de dos maneras.

1. 37

_____ decenas _____ unidades

_____ + _____

2. 54

_____ decenas _____ unidades

_____ + _____

3. 16

_____ decena _____ unidades

_____ + _____

4. 60

_____ decenas _____ unidades

_____ + _____

32 treinta y dos

Nombre _____

Por tu cuenta

Haz un dibujo rápido que muestre el número.
Describe el número de dos maneras.

5. 48

_____ decenas _____ unidades

_____ + _____

6. 31

_____ decenas _____ unidad

_____ + _____

7. Riley tiene unos dinosaurios de juguete. El número que tiene es uno menos que 50. Describe el número de dinosaurios de dos maneras.

_____

_____

Resuelve. Escribe o dibuja para explicar.

8. PIENSA MÁS Eric tiene 4 bolsas de 10 canicas y 6 canicas sueltas. ¿Cuántas canicas tiene Eric?

Matemáticas al instante

_____ canicas

Capítulo 1 • Lección 4   treinta y tres **33**

Resolución de problemas • Aplicaciones

PRÁCTICAS Y PROCESOS MATEMÁTICOS 6   **Haz conexiones**

Usa crayones. Sigue los pasos.

9. Comienza en el 51 y traza una línea verde hasta el 43.

10. Traza una línea azul desde el 43 hasta el 34.

11. Traza una línea roja desde el 34 hasta el 29.

12. Luego traza una línea amarilla desde el 29 hasta el 72.

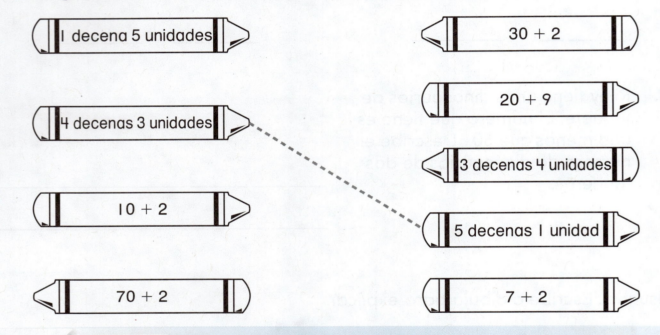

13. **PIENSA MÁS**   Haz un dibujo que muestre el número 26. Describe el número 26 de dos maneras.

_____ decenas _____ unidades

_____ + _____

ACTIVIDAD PARA LA CASA • Pida a su niño que escriba 89 como decenas más unidades. Luego pídale que escriba 25 como decenas más unidades.

Nombre _____

Forma desarrollada

Objetivo de aprendizaje Describirás un número de 2 dígitos como decenas y unidades.

Haz un dibujo rápido que muestre el número. Describe el número de dos maneras.

1. 68

   ____ decenas ____ unidades

   ____ + ____

2. 21

   ____ decenas ____ unidad

   ____ + ____

3. 70

   ____ decenas ____ unidades

   ____ + ____

4. 53

   ____ decenas ____ unidades

   ____ + ____

Resolución de problemas

5. Encierra en un círculo las maneras de escribir el número que muestra el modelo.

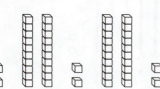

   4 decenas 6 unidades   40 + 6   64

   6 decenas 4 unidades   60 + 4   46

6. 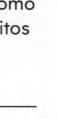 **Matemáticas** Explica cómo sabes los valores de los dígitos en el número 58.

   _____

   _____

Capítulo 1   treinta y cinco **35**

Repaso de la lección

1. Describe el número 92 en decenas y unidades.

   _____ decenas _____ unidades

2. Describe el número 45 en decenas y unidades.

   _____ decenas _____ unidades

Repaso en espiral

3. ¿Cuál es el valor del dígito subrayado? Escribe el número.

   4<u>9</u>

   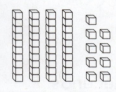

   _____

4. ¿Cuál es el valor del dígito subrayado? Escribe el número.

   3<u>4</u>

   _____

5. Describe el número 76 de otra manera.

   _____ decenas _____ unidades

6. Describe el número 52 de otra manera.

   _____ decenas _____ unidades

PRACTICA MÁS CON EL
Entrenador personal
en matemáticas

36 treinta y seis

Nombre _____

Diferentes maneras de escribir números

Pregunta esencial ¿De qué maneras diferentes se puede escribir un número de 2 dígitos?

Objetivo de aprendizaje Escribirás números de 2 dígitos en palabras, como decenas y unidades, como un número de 2 dígitos y como la suma de los valores de los dígitos de las decenas y las unidades.

Escucha y dibuja En el mundo

Escribe el número. Luego escríbelo como decenas y unidades.

_____ decenas _____ unidades

_____ + _____

_____ + _____

_____ decenas _____ unidades

PARA EL MAESTRO • Lea el siguiente problema. Taryn contó 53 libros en la mesa. ¿Cuántas decenas y unidades hay en 53? Continúe la actividad con los números 78, 35 y 40.

Charla matemática PRÁCTICAS Y PROCESOS MATEMÁTICOS

Analiza En el 44, ¿los dos dígitos tienen el mismo valor?

Capítulo 1   treinta y siete **37**

Representa y dibuja

Un número puede escribirse de diferentes maneras.

cincuenta y
nueve
5 decenas
9 unidades
50 + 9
59

unidades	números del 11 al 19	decenas
0 cero	11 once	10 diez
1 uno	12 doce	20 veinte
2 dos	13 trece	30 treinta
3 tres	14 catorce	40 cuarenta
4 cuatro	15 quince	50 cincuenta
5 cinco	16 dieciséis	60 sesenta
6 seis	17 diecisiete	70 setenta
7 siete	18 dieciocho	80 ochenta
8 ocho	19 diecinueve	90 noventa
9 nueve		

Comparte y muestra

Observa los ejemplos de arriba.
Luego, escribe el número de otra manera.

1. treinta y dos

   _____

2. 20 + 7

   _____

3. 63

   _____ decenas _____ unidades

4. noventa y cinco

   _____ + _____

5. 5 decenas 1 unidad

   _____

6. setenta y seis

   _____ + _____

7. veintiocho

   _____ decenas _____ unidades

8. 8 decenas 0 unidades

   _____

38 treinta y ocho

Nombre _____

Por tu cuenta

Escribe el número de otra manera.

9. 2 decenas 4 unidades

   _____

10. treinta

    _____ decenas _____ unidades

11. ochenta y cinco

    _____

12. 54

    _____ + _____

13. Luis tiene un número favorito. El número tiene el dígito 3 en el lugar de las unidades y el dígito 9 en el lugar de las decenas. ¿De qué otra manera se puede escribir este número?

    _____

14. El número de Daniel tiene un dígito mayor que 5 en el lugar de las unidades y un dígito menor que 5 en el lugar de las decenas. ¿Qué número puede ser el de Daniel?

    _____

PIENSA MÁS Completa los espacios en blanco para que el enunciado sea verdadero.

15. Sesenta y siete es lo mismo que _____ decenas _____ unidades.

16. 4 decenas _____ unidades es lo mismo que _____ + _____.

17. 20 + _____ es lo mismo que _____.

ACTIVIDAD PARA LA CASA • Escriba 20 + 6 en una hoja de papel. Pida a su niño que escriba el número de 2 dígitos. Repita con 4 decenas 9 unidades.

Capítulo 1 • Lección 5

Nombre _____

✓ Revisión de la mitad del capítulo

Conceptos y destrezas

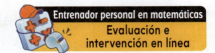
Entrenador personal en matemáticas
Evaluación e intervención en línea

Sombrea los cuadros de diez para mostrar el número. Encierra en un círculo **par** o **impar**.

1. 15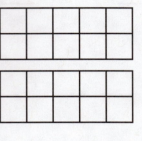

    par   impar

2. 18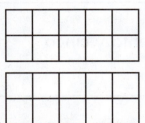

    par   impar

Haz un dibujo rápido que muestre el número.
Describe el número de dos maneras.

3. 35

    ____ decenas ____ unidades

    _____ + _____

4. 53

    ____ decenas ____ unidades

    _____ + _____

5. **PIENSA MÁS**   Escribe el número 42 de otra manera.

    _____

40   cuarenta

Nombre _____

Diferentes maneras de escribir números

Objetivo de aprendizaje Escribirás números de 2 dígitos en palabras, con decenas y unidades, como un número de 2 dígitos y como la suma de los valores de los dígitos de las decenas y las unidades.

Escribe el número de otra manera.

1. 32

   ____ decenas ____ unidades

2. cuarenta y uno

   _____

3. 9 decenas 5 unidades

   _____

4. 80 + 3

   _____

5. 57

   ____ decenas ____ unidades

6. setenta y dos

   ____ + ____

7. 60 + 4

   _____

8. 4 decenas 8 unidades

   _____

Resolución de problemas · En el mundo

9. Un número tiene el dígito 3 en el lugar de las unidades y el dígito 4 en el lugar de las decenas. ¿Cuál de estas es otra manera de escribir este número? Enciérrala en un círculo.

   3 + 4   40 + 3   30 + 4

10. ESCRIBE Matemáticas Escribe el número 63 de cuatro maneras diferentes.

Capítulo 1

Repaso de la lección

1. Escribe 3 decenas 9 unidades de otra manera.

   _____

2. Escribe el número dieciocho de otra manera.

   _____

Repaso en espiral

3. Escribe el número 47 en decenas y unidades.

   _____ decenas _____ unidades

4. Escribe el número 95 usando palabras.

   _____

5. ¿Cuál es el valor del dígito subrayado? Escribe el número.

   6<u>1</u>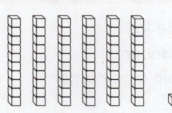

   _____

6. ¿Cuál es el valor del dígito subrayado? Escribe el número.

   <u>1</u>7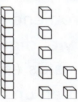

   _____

Nombre _____

Álgebra • Diferentes maneras de mostrar números

Pregunta esencial ¿Cómo puedes mostrar el valor de un número de diferentes maneras?

Objetivo de aprendizaje Mostrarás el valor de un número de 2 dígitos de diferentes maneras.

Usa ▭▭▭ ▪ para mostrar el número de maneras diferentes. Anota las decenas y las unidades.

_____ decenas _____ unidades

_____ decenas _____ unidades

_____ decenas _____ unidades

PARA EL MAESTRO • Lea el siguiente problema. Syed tiene 26 piedras. ¿De qué maneras diferentes se puede mostrar 26 con bloques? Pida a los niños que comiencen con 26 bloques de unidades. Luego, pídales que usen bloques de base diez y anoten el número de decenas y de unidades en cada uno de sus modelos.

Charla matemática
PRÁCTICAS Y PROCESOS MATEMÁTICOS

Describe cómo puedes usar la suma para escribir el número 26.

Capítulo 1 cuarenta y tres **43**

Representa y dibuja

Estas son algunas maneras de mostrar 32.

__3__ decenas   __2__ decenas   __1__ decena
__2__ unidades   __12__ unidades   __22__ unidades
__30__ + __2__   __20__ + __12__   __10__ + __22__

Comparte y muestra

Los bloques muestran los números de diferentes maneras. Describe los bloques de dos maneras.

1. 28

____ decenas
____ unidades
____ + ____

____ decena
____ unidades
____ + ____

____ decenas
____ unidades
____ + ____

2. 35

____ decenas
____ unidades
____ + ____

____ decenas
____ unidades
____ + ____

____ decenas
____ unidades
____ + ____

Nombre _____

Por tu cuenta

Los bloques muestran los números de diferentes maneras. Describe los bloques de dos maneras.

3. 43

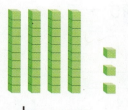      

____ decenas   ____ decenas   ____ decenas
____ unidades   ____ unidades   ____ unidades
____ + ____   ____ + ____   ____ + ____

4. Roderick tiene 7 cajas de 10 tarjetas y 4 tarjetas sueltas. ¿Cuántas tarjetas tiene Roderick?

_____ tarjetas

5. **PIENSA MÁS** Tengo 2 bolsas de 10 naranjas. También tengo 24 naranjas sueltas. ¿Cuántas naranjas tengo en total?

Tengo ____ naranjas.

Haz un dibujo rápido para mostrar el número.

Capítulo 1 • Lección 6

cuarenta y cinco **45**

Resolución de problemas • Aplicaciones

6. **PRÁCTICAS Y PROCESOS MATEMÁTICOS 6** **Haz conexiones** Completa los espacios en blanco para que cada enunciado sea verdadero.

   _____ decenas _____ unidades es igual a 90 + 3.

   2 decenas 18 unidades es igual a _____ + _____.

   5 decenas _____ unidades es igual a _____ + 17.

7. **MÁS AL DETALLE** Un número tiene el dígito 4 en el lugar de las unidades y el dígito 7 en el lugar de las decenas. ¿Cuál de estas es otra manera de escribir este número? Enciérralas en un círculo.

   40 + 7   70 + 4   setenta y cuatro

   4 decenas 34 unidades   4 + 7   4 decenas 7 unidades

8. **PIENSA MÁS** ¿Cuál de estas es otra manera de mostrar el número 42? Elige Sí o No en cada una.

	Sí	No
1 decena 42 unidades	○ Sí	○ No
30 + 12	○ Sí	○ No
2 decenas 22 unidades	○ Sí	○ No
3 decenas 2 unidades	○ Sí	○ No

ACTIVIDAD PARA LA CASA • Escriba el número 45. Pida a su niño que escriba o dibuje dos maneras de mostrar este número.

Nombre _____

Álgebra • Diferentes maneras de mostrar números

Objetivo de aprendizaje Mostrarás el valor de un número de 2 dígitos de diferentes maneras.

Los bloques muestran el número de diferentes maneras. Describe los bloques de dos maneras.

1. 24

___ decenas   ___ decena   ___ decenas
___ unidades   ___ unidades   ___ unidades
___ + ___   ___ + ___   ___ + ___

2. 36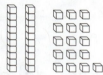

___ decenas   ___ decena   ___ decenas
___ unidades   ___ unidades   ___ unidades
___ + ___   ___ + ___   ___ + ___

Resolución de problemas En el mundo

3. Toni tiene estos bloques. Encierra en un círculo los bloques que podría usar para mostrar 34.

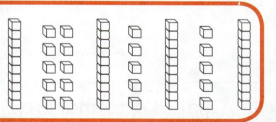

4. **ESCRIBE Matemáticas** Haz dibujos rápidos para mostrar el número 38 de tres maneras diferentes.

Capítulo 1   cuarenta y siete **47**

Repaso de la lección

1. ¿Qué número muestran los bloques? Escribe el número.

    2 decenas 13 unidades

    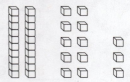

    _____

2. ¿Qué número muestran los bloques? Escribe el número.

    1 decena 16 unidades

    _____

Repaso en espiral

3. ¿Qué número muestran los bloques? Escribe el número.

    1 decena 17 unidades

    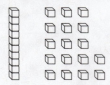

    _____

4. ¿Cuál es el valor del dígito subrayado? Escribe el número.

    2<u>9</u>

    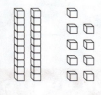

    _____

5. ¿Cuál es otra manera de escribir 9 decenas, 3 unidades? Escribe el número.

    _____

6. Describe el número 50 en decenas y unidades.

    _____ decenas _____ unidades

48 cuarenta y ocho

Nombre _____

Resolución de problemas • Decenas y unidades

Pregunta esencial ¿Por qué el hallar un patrón te sirve para hallar todas las maneras de mostrar un número con decenas y unidades?

Objetivo de aprendizaje Usarás la estrategia de *hallar un patrón* al hacer una lista para hallar todas las maneras de mostrar un número con decenas y unidades.

Gail tiene que comprar 32 lápices. Puede comprar los lápices sueltos o en cajas de 10 lápices. ¿De qué maneras puede Gail comprar 32 lápices?

Soluciona el problema

¿Qué debo hallar?

maneras en que puede comprar 32 lápices

¿Qué información debo usar?

Puede comprar lápices __sueltos__ o __cajas de 10__ lápices.

Muestra cómo resolver el problema.
Haz dibujos rápidos de 32. Completa la tabla.

Cajas de 10 lápices	Lápices sueltos
3	2
2	12
1	
0	

NOTA A LA FAMILIA • Su niño halló un patrón en las diferentes combinaciones de decenas y unidades. Usar un patrón ayuda a hacer una lista organizada.

Capítulo 1   cuarenta y nueve **49**

Haz otro problema

Halla un patrón para resolver.

- ¿Qué debo hallar?
- ¿Qué información debo usar?

1. Sara tiene 36 crayones. Los puede guardar en cajas de 10 crayones o como crayones sueltos. ¿Cuáles son todas las maneras en que Sara puede guardar los crayones?

Cajas de 10 crayones	Crayones sueltos
3	6

2. El Sr. Winter está guardando 48 sillas. Puede guardar las sillas en pilas de 10 o como sillas sueltas. ¿Cuáles son todas las maneras en que el Sr. Winter puede guardar las sillas?

Pilas de 10 sillas	Sillas sueltas
4	8

Charla matemática

PRÁCTICAS Y PROCESOS MATEMÁTICOS 7

Busca la estructura
Describe un patrón que puedes usar para escribir el número 32.

Nombre _____

Comparte y muestra

Halla un patrón para resolver.

3. Philip está colocando 25 marcadores en una bolsa. Puede colocar los marcadores en la bolsa en atados de 10 o sueltos. ¿Cuáles son todas las maneras en que Philip puede colocar los marcadores en la bolsa?

Atados de 10 marcadores	Marcadores sueltos

4. Los adhesivos se venden en paquetes de 10 adhesivos o sueltos. La señorita Allen quiere comprar 33 adhesivos. ¿Cuáles son todas las maneras en que puede comprar los adhesivos?

Paquetes de 10 adhesivos	Adhesivos sueltos

5. **PIENSA MÁS** Devin tenía 32 tarjetas de béisbol. Obtiene 7 tarjetas más. Las puede guardar en cajas de 10 tarjetas o sueltas. ¿Cuáles son todas las maneras en que Devin puede clasificar las tarjetas?

Cajas de 10 tarjetas	Tarjetas sueltas

Capítulo 1 • Lección 7

cincuenta y uno **51**

Por tu cuenta

Resuelve. Escribe o dibuja para explicar.

6. Busca la estructura

Luis puede guardar sus carritos de juguete en cajas de 10 carritos o sueltos. ¿De cuál de estas maneras puede guardar sus 24 carritos de juguete? Encierra en un círculo la respuesta.

| 4 cajas de 10 carritos y 2 carritos sueltos | 1 caja de 10 carritos y 24 carritos sueltos | 2 cajas de 10 carritos y 4 carritos sueltos |

7. PIENSA MÁS El Sr. Link necesita 30 vasos. Puede comprarlos en paquetes de 10 vasos o sueltos. ¿Cuáles son todas las maneras en que puede comprar los vasos? Halla un patrón para resolver.

Paquetes de 10 vasos	Vasos sueltos

Elige dos maneras de la tabla. Explica cómo estas dos maneras muestran el mismo número de vasos.

ACTIVIDAD PARA LA CASA • Pida a su niño que explique cómo resolvió uno de los problemas de esta página.

Nombre _____

Resolución de problemas • Decenas y unidades

Objetivo de aprendizaje Usarás la estrategia de *hallar un patrón* al hacer una lista para hallar todas las maneras de mostrar un número con decenas y unidades.

Halla un patrón para resolver.

1. Ann agrupa 38 piedras. Las puede colocar en grupos de 10 piedras o como piedras sueltas. ¿Cuáles son las maneras en que Ann puede agrupar las piedras?

Grupos de 10 piedras	Piedras sueltas

2. El Sr. Grant necesita 30 pedazos de fieltro. Puede comprarlos en paquetes de 10 o como pedazos sueltos. ¿Cuáles son las maneras en que el Sr. Grant puede comprar el fieltro?

Paquetes de 10 pedazos	Pedazos sueltos

3. **ESCRIBE Matemáticas** Elige uno de los problemas de arriba. Describe cómo organizaste las respuestas.

_____
_____
_____
_____
_____
_____

Capítulo 1   cincuenta y tres **53**

Repaso de la lección

1. La Srta. Chang empaqueta 38 manzanas. Las puede empaquetar en bolsas de 10 manzanas o como manzanas sueltas. Completa la tabla para mostrar otra manera en que la Srta. Chang puede empaquetar las manzanas.

Bolsas de 10 manzanas	Manzanas sueltas
2	18
1	28
0	38

Repaso en espiral

2. ¿Cuál es el valor del dígito subrayado? Escribe el número.

   5<u>4</u>

   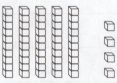

   _____

3. ¿Qué número muestran los bloques? Escribe el número.

   2 decenas 19 unidades

4. Escribe el número 62 en palabras.

   _____

5. ¿Qué número puede escribirse como 8 decenas, 6 unidades? Escribe el número.

Nombre _____

Patrones de conteo hasta 100

Pregunta esencial ¿Cómo se cuenta de 1 en 1, de 5 en 5 y de 10 en 10 con números menores que 100?

Objetivo de aprendizaje Contarás de 1 en 1, de 5 en 5 y de 10 en 10 con números hasta por lo menos 100.

Escucha y dibuja

Observa la tabla con los números hasta el 100.
Escribe los números que faltan.

1	2	3		5	6		8		10
11		13	14	15	16		18	19	20
	22	23	24		26	27	28	29	30
31	32		34	35	36		38	39	
41		43	44	45	46	47		49	50
51		53		55		57		59	60
	62		64	65	66	67	68		70
71	72	73	74		76		78	79	
81		83		85	86	87	88	89	90
	92		94	95	96		98		100

PARA EL MAESTRO • Pida a los niños que completen la tabla para revisar el conteo hasta 100.

Charla matemática

PRÁCTICAS Y PROCESOS MATEMÁTICOS

Describe algunas maneras diferentes de encontrar los números que faltan en la tabla.

Capítulo 1

Representa y dibuja

Puedes contar hacia adelante con diferentes cantidades.
Puedes comenzar a contar a partir de diferentes números.

Cuenta de uno en uno.

1, 2, 3, 4, __5__, __6__, ____, ____

29, 30, 31, 32, __33__, ____, ____, ____

Cuenta de cinco en cinco.

5, 10, 15, 20, ____, ____, ____, ____

50, 55, 60, 65, ____, ____, ____, ____

Comparte y muestra

Cuenta de uno en uno.

1. 15, 16, 17, ____, ____, ____, ____

Cuenta de cinco en cinco.

2. 15, 20, 25, ____, ____, ____, ____

3. 60, 65, ____, ____, ____, ____

Cuenta de diez en diez.

4. 10, 20, ____, ____, ____, ____

5. 30, 40, ____, ____, ____, ____

56   cincuenta y seis

Nombre _____

Por tu cuenta

Cuenta de uno en uno.

6. 77, 78, _____, _____, _____, _____, _____

Cuenta de cinco en cinco.

7. 35, 40, _____, _____, _____, _____, _____

Cuenta de diez en diez.

8. 20, 30, _____, _____, _____, _____, _____

9. Amber cuenta de cinco en cinco hasta 50. ¿Cuántos números dirá?

_____ números

10. PIENSA MÁS Dinesh cuenta de cinco en cinco hasta 100. Gwen cuenta de diez en diez hasta 100. ¿Quién dirá más números? Explica.

_____

_____

_____

_____

Matemáticas al instante

Capítulo 1 • Lección 8

Resolución de problemas • Aplicaciones   ESCRIBE Matemáticas

PRÁCTICAS Y PROCESOS MATEMÁTICOS 1 Analiza

11. Andy cuenta de uno en uno. Comienza en el 29 y se detiene en el 45. ¿Cuáles de los siguientes números dirá? Enciérralos en un círculo.

   31   20
       47   35
       46
   40   39

12. Camila cuenta de cinco en cinco. Comienza a contar en el 5 y se detiene en el 50. ¿Cuáles de los siguientes números dirá? Enciérralos en un círculo.

   55   25
       6   40
              18
   10   45

13. **PIENSA MÁS** Grace empieza en el número 40 y cuenta de tres maneras diferentes. Escribe para mostrar cómo cuenta.

Conteo de uno en uno. 40, ___, ___, ___, ___, ___, ___

Conteo de cinco en cinco. 40, ___, ___, ___, ___, ___, ___

Conteo de diez en diez. 40, ___, ___, ___, ___, ___, ___

ACTIVIDAD PARA LA CASA • Con su niño, practique el conteo de uno en uno hasta el 100, comenzando con números como el 58 o el 62.

Nombre _____

Patrones de conteo hasta 100

Objetivo de aprendizaje Contarás de 1 en 1, de 5 en 5 y de 10 en 10 con números hasta por lo menos 100.

Cuenta de uno en uno.

1. 58, 59, ___, ___, ___, ___, ___

Cuenta de cinco en cinco.

2. 45, 50, ___, ___, ___, ___, ___

3. 20, 25, ___, ___, ___, ___, ___

Cuenta de diez en diez.

4. 20, ___, ___, ___, ___, ___

Cuenta hacia atrás de uno en uno.

5. 87, 86, 85, ___, ___, ___

Resolución de problemas En el mundo

6. Tim cuenta los dedos de sus amigos de cinco en cinco. Cuenta seis manos. ¿Qué números dice?

   5, ___, ___, ___, ___, ___

7. **Matemáticas** Cuenta de uno en uno o de cinco en cinco. Escribe los primeros cinco números que contarías. Comienza en 15.

Repaso de la lección

1. Cuenta de cinco en cinco.

   70, ____, ____, ____, ____

2. Cuenta de diez en diez.

   60, ____, ____, ____, ____

Repaso en espiral

3. Cuenta hacia atrás de uno en uno.

   21, ____, ____, ____, ____

4. Un número tiene 2 decenas y 15 unidades. Escribe el número en palabras.

   _____

5. Describe el número 72 en decenas y unidades.

   ____ decenas ____ unidades

6. Halla la suma. ¿Es el total par o impar? Escribe par o impar.

   $9 + 9 =$ ____

   _____

Nombre _____

Patrones de conteo hasta el 1,000

Pregunta esencial ¿Cómo se cuenta de 1 en 1, de 5 en 5, de 10 en 10 y de 100 en 100 con números menores que 1,000?

Objetivo de aprendizaje Contarás de 1 en 1, de 5 en 5, de 10 en 10 y de 100 en 100 con números hasta por lo menos 1,000.

Escucha y dibuja

Escribe los números que faltan en la tabla.

401		403	404		406	407	408		410
411				415	416	417	418	419	
421	422	423	424	425		427	428	429	430
	432		434	435	436	437	438		
441	442	443	444		446	447		449	450
		454	455	456	457	458	459	460	
461	462						468	469	470
	472	473	474	475	476	477		479	480
481	482		484	485	486				490
	492	493		495	496	497	498		

PARA EL MAESTRO • Pida a los niños que completen la tabla para practicar el conteo con números de 3 dígitos.

Charla matemática

PRÁCTICAS Y PROCESOS MATEMÁTICOS 7

Busca la estructura ¿Cuáles patrones de conteo puedes usar para completar la tabla?

Capítulo 1   sesenta y uno **61**

Representa y dibuja

El conteo puede hacerse de diferentes maneras. Cuenta hacia adelante usando patrones.

Cuenta de cinco en cinco.

95, 100, 105, __110__, __115__, _____, _____

140, 145, 150, __155__, _____, _____, _____

Cuenta de diez en diez.

300, 310, 320, _____, _____, _____, _____

470, 480, 490, _____, _____, _____, _____

Comparte y muestra

Cuenta de cinco en cinco.

1. 745, 750, 755, _____, _____, _____, _____

Cuenta de diez en diez.

2. 520, 530, 540, _____, _____, _____, _____

3. 600, 610, _____, _____, _____, _____

Cuenta de cien en cien.

4. 100, 200, _____, _____, _____, _____

5. 300, 400, _____, _____, _____, _____

Nombre _____

Por tu cuenta

Cuenta de cinco en cinco.

6. 215, 220, 225, _____, _____, _____, _____

7. 905, 910, _____, _____, _____, _____

Cuenta de diez en diez.

8. 730, 740, 750, _____, _____, _____, _____

9. 160, 170, _____, _____, _____, _____

Cuenta de cien en cien.

10. 200, 300, _____, _____, _____, _____

11. **PIENSA MÁS** Martín empieza en 300 y cuenta de cinco en cinco hasta 420. ¿Cuáles son los últimos 6 números que dirá?

_____, _____, _____, _____, _____, _____

12. La feria del libro tiene 390 libros. Hay 5 cajas más con 10 libros en cada caja. Cuenta de diez en diez. ¿Cuántos libros hay en la feria del libro?

_____ libros

Capítulo 1 • Lección 9

Resolución de problemas • Aplicaciones

PRÁCTICAS Y PROCESOS MATEMÁTICOS 7 — Busca un patrón

13. Lisa cuenta de cinco en cinco. Comienza en el 120 y se detiene en el 175. ¿Cuáles de los siguientes números dirá? Enciérralos en un círculo.

170   151   135
155   200   180

14. George cuenta de diez en diez. Comienza en el 750 y se detiene en el 830. ¿Cuáles de los siguientes números dirá? Enciérralos en un círculo.

755   690   780
760   795   810

15. PIENSA MÁS Carl cuenta de cien en cien. ¿Cuáles de las siguientes maneras muestran cómo puede contar? Elige Sí o No para cada una.

	Sí	No
100, 110, 120, 130, 140	○	○
100, 200, 300, 400, 500	○	○
500, 600, 700, 800, 900	○	○
300, 305, 310, 315, 320	○	○

ACTIVIDAD PARA LA CASA • Con su niño, cuente de cinco en cinco desde el 150 hasta el 200.

Nombre _____

Patrones de conteo hasta el 1,000

Objetivo de aprendizaje Contarás de 1 en 1, de 5 en 5, de 10 en 10 y de 100 en 100 con números hasta por lo menos 1,000.

Cuenta de cinco en cinco.

1. 415, 420, _____, _____, _____, _____

2. 675, 680, _____, _____, _____, _____

Cuenta de diez en diez.

3. 210, 220, _____, _____, _____, _____

Cuenta de cien en cien.

4. 300, 400, _____, _____, _____, _____

Cuenta hacia atrás de uno en uno.

5. 953, 952, _____, _____, _____, _____

Resolución de problemas

6. Luisa tiene un frasco con 100 monedas de 1¢. Agrega grupos de 10 monedas al frasco. Agrega 5 grupos. ¿Qué números dice?

_____, _____, _____, _____, _____

7. **ESCRIBE Matemáticas** Cuenta desde 135 hasta 175. Escribe estos números y describe su patrón.

_____

Capítulo 1   sesenta y cinco **65**

Repaso de la lección

1. Cuenta de diez en diez.

160, ____, ____, ____, ____

2. Cuenta de cien en cien.

400, ____, ____, ____, ____

Repaso en espiral

3. Cuenta de cinco en cinco.

245, ____, ____, ____, ____

4. Cuenta hacia atrás de uno en uno.

71, ____, ____, ____, ____

5. Describe el número 45 de otra manera.

____ decenas ____ unidades

6. Describe 7 decenas 9 unidades de otra manera.

_____

Nombre _____

✓ Repaso y prueba del Capítulo 1

1. ¿Muestra el cuadro de diez un número par?
   Elige Sí o No.

      ○ Sí   ○ No

      ○ Sí   ○ No

2. Escribe un número par entre 7 y 16. Haz un dibujo y escribe un enunciado para explicar por qué es un número par.

   _____

   _____

3. ¿Cuál es el valor del dígito 5 en el número 75?

   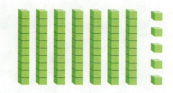 _____

Capítulo 1   sesenta y siete **67**

4. **MÁS AL DETALLE** Ted tiene un número par de marcadores amarillos y un número impar de marcadores verdes. Elige todos los grupos de marcadores que Ted podría tener.

   ○ 8 marcadores amarillos y 3 marcadores verdes

   ○ 3 marcadores amarillos y 6 marcadores verdes

   ○ 4 marcadores amarillos y 2 marcadores verdes

   ○ 6 marcadores amarillos y 7 marcadores verdes

5. Jeff empieza en 190 a contar de diez en diez. ¿Cuáles son los siguientes 6 números que dirá?

   190, _____, _____, _____, _____, _____, _____

6. Megan cuenta de uno en uno hasta 10. Luis cuenta de cinco en cinco hasta 20. ¿Quién dirá más números? Explica.

   _____

   _____

   _____

Nombre _____

7. Haz un dibujo para mostrar el número 43.

[ ]

Describe el número 43 de dos maneras.

[4] decenas   [4] unidades
[3]   [3]

_____ + _____

8. Yuly vive en Maple Road. Su dirección tiene el dígito 2 en el lugar de las unidades y el dígito 4 en el lugar de las decenas. ¿Cuál es la dirección de Yuly?

_____ Maple Road

9. ¿Muestran los números un conteo de cinco en cinco? Elige Sí o No.

76, 77, 78, 79, 80	○ Sí	○ No
20, 30, 40, 50, 60	○ Sí	○ No
70, 75, 80, 85, 90	○ Sí	○ No
35, 40, 45, 50, 55	○ Sí	○ No

Capítulo 1   sesenta y nueve **69**

10. **PIENSA MÁS+** La Sra. Payne necesita 35 cuadernos. Puede comprarlos en paquetes de 10 cuadernos o sueltos. ¿Cuáles son todas las maneras en que la Sra. Payne puede comprar los cuadernos? Halla un patrón para resolver.

Paquetes de 10 cuadernos	Cuadernos sueltos

Elige dos de las maneras de la tabla. Explica cómo estas dos maneras muestran el mismo número de cuadernos.

11. Ann tiene un número favorito. Tiene un dígito menor que 4 en el lugar de las decenas y un dígito mayor que 6 en el lugar de las unidades. ¿Cuáles podrían ser el número favorito de Ann? Elige Sí o No.

$30 + 9$	○ Sí	○ No
sesenta y siete	○ Sí	○ No
2 decenas 8 unidades	○ Sí	○ No

Escribe otro número que pueda ser el favorito de Ann. _____

Capítulo 2

Números hasta el 1,000

Piensa como matemático

La Casa Blanca tiene 412 puertas y 147 ventanas. Observa el dígito 1 en cada uno de estos números. ¿Cómo se compara el valor de estos dígitos?

Nombre _____

 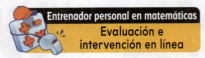

Identifica números hasta el 30

Escribe cuántos hay.

1.  _____ hojas

2. 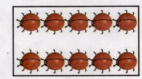 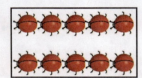  _____ insectos

Valor posicional: Números de 2 dígitos

Encierra en un círculo el valor del dígito rojo.

3. 4**7**   4. 8**4**   5. **6**5

   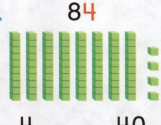   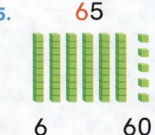

40   4   4   40   6   60

Compara números de 2 dígitos usando símbolos

Compara. Escribe >, <, o =.

6. 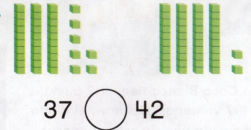   7.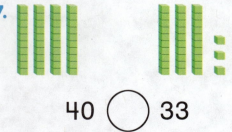

37 ◯ 42   40 ◯ 33

Esta página es para verificar la comprensión de destrezas importantes que se necesitan para tener éxito en el Capítulo 2.

Nombre _____

Desarrollo del vocabulario

Palabras de repaso
más
menos
dígitos
decenas
unidades

Visualízalo
Completa las casillas del organizador gráfico.
Escribe enunciados con **menos** y **más**.

menos → 9 bolígrafos es menos que 11 bolígrafos.

menos → _____

más → _____

más → _____

Comprende el vocabulario
Usa las palabras de repaso. Completa los enunciados.

1. 3 y 9 son _____ del número 39.

2. 7 está en el lugar de las _____ en el número 87.

3. 8 está en el lugar de las _____ en el número 87.

Capítulo 2

Juego
Pesca de dígitos

Materiales
- 12 🔴
- 12 🟡
- 1 🎲

Juega con un compañero.

1. Nombra un lugar para un dígito. Puedes decir **lugar de las decenas o lugar de las unidades**. Lanza el 🎲.

2. Empareja el número del 🎲 y el lugar que nombraste con un pez.

3. Pon una 🔴 en ese pez. Túrnense.

4. Empareja todos los peces. El jugador que tenga más 🔴 en el tablero gana.

56 12 14
23 46 25
32 53 65
61 41 34

Vocabulario del Capítulo 2

centena hundred 5	**comparar** compare 11
decenas tens 18	**dígito** digit 21
es igual a is equal to (=) 25	**es menor que (<)** is less than (<) 26
es menor que (>) is greater than (>) 27	**millar** thousand 38

Usa estos símbolos cuando **comparas:** >, <, =.

241 > 234

123 < 128

247 = 247

Hay 10 decenas en una **centena**.

0, 1, 2, 3, 4, 5, 6, 7, 8, y 9 son **dígitos**.

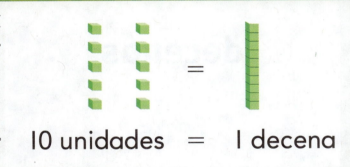

10 unidades = 1 decena

123 **es menor que** 128.

123 < 128

| 2 | más | 1 | es igual a | 3 |
| 2 | + | 1 | = | 3 |

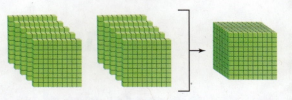

Hay 10 centenas en 1 **millar**.

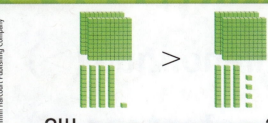

241 **es mayor que** 234.

241 > 234

De visita con las palabras de ¡Vivan las matemáticas!

Juego

Adivina la palabra

Recuadro de palabras
centena
comparar
decenas
dígito
es igual a (=)
es mayor que (>)
es menor que (<)
millar

Jugadores: 3 a 4

Materiales
- cronómetro

Instrucciones
1. Túrnense para jugar.
2. Elige una palabra de matemáticas, pero no la digas en voz alta.
3. Coloca el cronómetro en 1 minuto.
4. Da una palabra clave acerca de tu palabra. Da a cada jugador una oportunidad de adivinar la palabra.
5. Si nadie adivina correctamente, repite el Paso 4 con otra pista. Repite hasta que un jugador adivine la palabra o cuando el tiempo se acabe.
6. El primer jugador que adivine la palabra obtiene 1 punto. Si el jugador puede usar la palabra en una oración, obtiene 1 punto más. Luego a ese jugador le corresponde el siguiente turno.
7. El primer jugador en obtener 5 puntos, es el ganador.

Capítulo 2

Diario

Escríbelo

Reflexiona

Elige una idea. Escribe acerca de la idea en el espacio de abajo.

- Dibuja y escribe todas las diferentes maneras en que puedes mostrar el número 482. Usa otra hoja de papel para dibujar.
- Explica cómo se comparan dos números.
- Escribe oraciones que incluyan al menos dos de estos términos.

dígito   es igual a   centena   millar

Nombre _____

Agrupar decenas en centenas

Pregunta esencial ¿Cómo agrupas decenas en centenas?

Objetivo de aprendizaje Agruparás 10 decenas como una centena.

Escucha y dibuja · En el mundo

Encierra en un círculo grupos de decenas.
Cuenta los grupos de decenas.

PARA EL MAESTRO • Lea el siguiente problema y pida a los niños que agrupen bloques de unidades para resolver. Marco tiene 100 tarjetas. ¿Cuántos grupos de 10 tarjetas puede formar?

Charla matemática
PRÁCTICAS Y PROCESOS MATEMÁTICOS 6

Describe ¿Cuántas unidades hay en 3 decenas? ¿Cuántas unidades hay en 7 decenas? Explica.

Capítulo 2　　　　　　　　　　　　　　　setenta y cinco **75**

Representa y dibuja

10 decenas es lo mismo que 1 **centena**.

__10__ decenas

__1__ centena

__100__

Comparte y muestra

Escribe cuántas decenas hay. Encierra en un círculo grupos de 10 decenas. Escribe cuántas centenas hay. Escribe el número.

1.

__20__ decenas

_____ centenas

_____

2.

_____ decenas

_____ centenas

_____

3.

_____ decenas

_____ centenas

_____

4.

_____ decenas

_____ centenas

_____

Nombre _____

Por tu cuenta

Escribe cuántas decenas hay. Encierra en un círculo grupos de 10 decenas. Escribe cuántas centenas hay. Escribe el número.

5.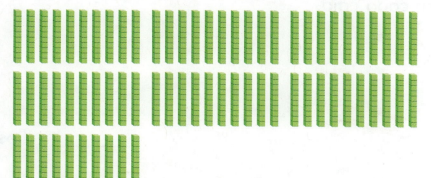

_____ decenas

_____ centenas

_____

6.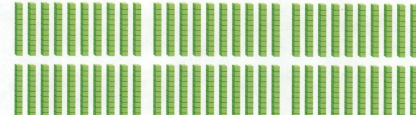

_____ decenas

_____ centenas

_____

7.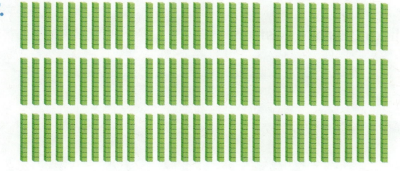

_____ decenas

_____ centenas

_____

8. **PIENSA MÁS** Wally tiene 400 tarjetas. ¿Cuántas pilas de 10 tarjetas puede hacer?

_____ pilas de 10 tarjetas

Resolución de problemas • Aplicaciones

Resuelve. Escribe o dibuja para explicar.

9. La Sra. Martin tiene 80 cajas de clips. Hay 10 clips en cada caja. ¿Cuántos clips tiene?

_____ clips

10. **PIENSA MÁS** Los lápices se venden en cajas de 10. El Sr. García necesita 100 lápices. Ya tiene 40 lápices. ¿Cuántas cajas de 10 lápices debe comprar?

_____ cajas de 10 lápices

Haz un dibujo para explicar tu respuesta.

ACTIVIDAD PARA LA CASA • Pida a su niño que haga un dibujo rápido de 20 decenas y luego le diga cuántas centenas hay.

Nombre _____

Agrupar decenas en centenas

Objetivo de aprendizaje Agruparás 10 decenas como una centena.

Escribe cuántas decenas hay. Encierra en un círculo grupos de 10 decenas. Escribe cuántas centenas hay. Escribe el número.

1. _____ decenas

   _____ centenas

   _____

2. _____ decenas

   _____ centenas

   _____

Resolución de problemas

Resuelve. Escribe o dibuja para explicar.

3. El granjero Gray tiene 30 macetas. Plantó 10 semillas en cada maceta. ¿Cuántas semillas plantó?

   _____ semillas

4. **ESCRIBE Matemáticas** Elena tiene 50 pilas de monedas de un centavo. En cada pila hay diez monedas. Explica cómo averiguar cuántas monedas de un centavo tiene Elena en total.

   _____
   _____
   _____
   _____

Capítulo 2

Repaso de la lección

1. Mai tiene 40 decenas. Escribe cuántas centenas hay. Escribe el número.

   _____

   _____

2. Hay 80 decenas. Escribe cuántas centenas hay. Escribe el número

   _____

   _____

Repaso en espiral

3. Escribe el número igual a 5 decenas y 13 unidades.

   _____

4. Cuenta de cinco en cinco.

   5, 10, 15

   ____, ____, ____, ____

5. Carlos tiene 58 lápices. ¿Cuál es el valor del dígito 5 en este número?

   _____

6. Encierra con un círculo la suma que sea un número par.

   $2 + 3 = 5$

   $4 + 4 = 8$

   $5 + 6 = 11$

   $8 + 7 = 15$

Nombre _____

Explorar números de 3 dígitos

Pregunta esencial ¿Cómo escribes un número de 3 dígitos para un grupo de decenas?

Objetivo de aprendizaje Escribirás un número de 3 dígitos representado por un grupo de decenas.

Encierra en un círculo grupos de bloques para mostrar centenas. Cuenta las centenas.

_____ centenas

_____ pajillas

PARA EL MAESTRO • Lea el siguiente problema y pida a los niños que encierren en un círculo grupos de bloques de decenas para resolver. La Sra. Rodríguez tiene 30 atados de pajillas. Hay 10 pajillas en cada atado. ¿Cuántas pajillas tiene la Sra. Rodríguez?

Analiza Describe cómo cambiaría el número de centenas si hubiera 10 atados de pajillas más.

Capítulo 2　　　　ochenta y uno **81**

Representa y dibuja

¿Qué número se muestra con 11 decenas?

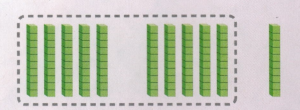

__11__ decenas

__1__ centena __1__ decena

__110__

En el número 110, hay un 1 en el lugar de las centenas y un 1 en el lugar de las decenas.

Comparte y muestra

Encierra en un círculo las decenas para formar 1 centena. Escribe el número de diferentes maneras.

1. ____ decenas

____ centena ____ decenas

____

2. ____ decenas

____ centena ____ decenas

____

3. ____ decenas

____ centena ____ decenas

____

Nombre _____

Por tu cuenta

Encierra en un círculo las decenas para formar 1 centena. Escribe el número de diferentes maneras.

4.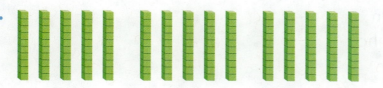

_____ decenas

_____ centena _____ decenas

_____

5.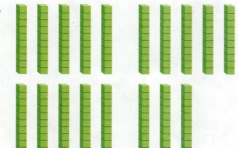

_____ decenas

_____ centena _____ decenas

_____

6. **MÁS AL DETALLE** Saúl tiene 130 tarjetas de béisbol. ¿Cuántas tarjetas más necesita para tener 200 tarjetas de béisbol en total?

_____ tarjetas de béisbol

7. **PIENSA MÁS** Kendra tiene 120 adhesivos. Completa una página con 10 adhesivos. ¿Cuántas páginas puede completar?

_____ páginas

Capítulo 2 • Lección 2

ochenta y tres **83**

Resolución de problemas • Aplicaciones

Resuelve. Escribe o dibuja para explicar.

8. **Analiza** Hay 16 cajas de galletas. Hay 10 galletas en cada caja. ¿Cuántas galletas hay en total?

   _____ galletas

9. Simón hace 8 torres de 10 bloques cada una. Ron hace 9 torres de 10 bloques cada una. ¿Cuántos bloques usaron?

   _____ bloques

10. Ed tiene 150 canicas. ¿Cuántas bolsas de 10 canicas necesita para tener 200 canicas en total?

    _____ bolsas de 10 canicas

ACTIVIDAD PARA LA CASA • Pida a su niño que dibuje 110 X en 11 grupos de 10 X.

Nombre _____

Explorar números de 3 dígitos

Objetivo de aprendizaje Escribirás un número de 3 dígitos representado por un grupo de decenas.

Encierra en un círculo las decenas para formar 1 centena. Escribe el número de diferentes maneras.

1.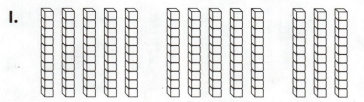

_____ decenas

_____ centena _____ decenas

_____

2.

_____ decenas

_____ centena _____ decenas

_____

Resolución de problemas

Resuelve. Escribe o dibuja para explicar.

3. Millie tiene una caja de 1 centena de cubos. También tiene una bolsa de 70 cubos. ¿Cuántos trenes de 10 cubos puede formar?

_____ trenes de 10 cubos

4. **ESCRIBE Matemáticas** Dibuja o escribe para explicar por qué 1 centena 4 decenas es la misma cantidad que 14 decenas.

_____
_____
_____

Capítulo 2 — ochenta y cinco **85**

Repaso de la lección

1. Encierra en un círculo decenas para formar 1 centena. Escribe el número de otra manera.

   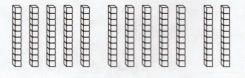

   _____ decenas

   _____ centena _____ decenas

   _____

2. Encierra en un círculo decenas para formar 1 centena. Escribe el número de otra manera.

   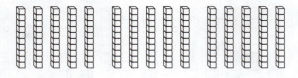

   _____ decenas

   _____ centena _____ decenas

   _____

Repaso en espiral

3. Encierra en un círculo el número impar.

   18   10

   9   4

4. Escribe el número que sea igual a 2 decenas 15 unidades.

   _____

5. Describe el número 78 de dos maneras diferentes.

   _____ decenas + _____ unidades

   _____ + _____

6. Escribe el número 55 de otra manera.

   _____

86   ochenta y seis

Nombre _____

Hacer un modelo de números de 3 dígitos

Pregunta esencial ¿Cómo muestras un número de 3 dígitos usando bloques?

Objetivo de aprendizaje Representarás un número de 3 dígitos con bloques.

Escucha y dibuja En el mundo — Manos a la obra

Usa . Dibuja para mostrar lo que hiciste.

PARA EL MAESTRO • Lea el siguiente problema. Jack tiene 12 bloques de decenas. ¿Cuántas centenas y decenas tiene Jack? Pida a los niños que muestren los bloques de Jack y luego hagan dibujos rápidos. Luego, pida a los niños que encierren en un círculo 10 decenas y resuelvan el problema.

Charla matemática — PRÁCTICAS Y PROCESOS MATEMÁTICOS

Si Jack tuviera 14 decenas, ¿cuántas centenas y decenas tendría? **Explica**

Capítulo 2

ochenta y siete **87**

Representa y dibuja

En el número 348, el 3 está en el lugar de las centenas, el 4 está en el lugar de las decenas y el 8 está en el lugar de las unidades.

Escribe la cantidad de centenas, decenas y unidades.	__3__ centenas + __4__ decenas + __8__ unidades
Muestra el número 348 con bloques.	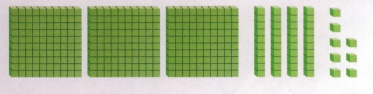
Haz un dibujo rápido.	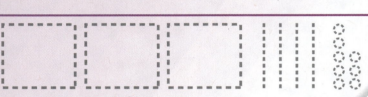

Comparte y muestra

Escribe cuántas centenas, decenas y unidades hay.

Muestra con . Luego haz un dibujo rápido.

 1. 234

___ centenas + ___ decenas +

___ unidades

 2. 156

___ centena + ___ decenas +

___ unidades

88 ochenta y ocho

Nombre _____

Por tu cuenta

Escribe cuántas centenas, decenas y unidades hay.

Muestra con . Luego haz un dibujo rápido.

3. 125

___ centena + ___ decenas + ___ unidades

4. 312

___ centenas + ___ decena + ___ unidades

5. 245

___ centenas + ___ decenas + ___ unidades

6. 103

___ centena + ___ decenas + ___ unidades

7. PIENSA MÁS Lexi necesita 144 cuentas. En una caja grande hay 100 cuentas. En una caja mediana hay 10 cuentas. En una caja pequeña hay 1 cuenta. Lexi tiene 1 caja grande y 4 cajas pequeñas. ¿Cuántas cajas medianas de cuentas necesita?

_____ cajas medianas

Resolución de problemas • Aplicaciones

ESCRIBE Matemáticas

8. **PIENSA MÁS** ¿En qué se parecen los números 342 y 324? ¿En qué se diferencian?

_____

_____

_____

Matemáticas al instante

PRÁCTICAS Y PROCESOS MATEMÁTICOS 4 Haz un modelo de matemáticas

Escribe el número que coincida con la pista.

9. Un modelo de mi número tiene 2 bloques de centenas, ningún bloque de decenas y 3 bloques de unidades.

Mi número es _____.

10. Un modelo de mi número tiene 3 bloques de centenas, 5 bloques de decenas y ningún bloque de unidades.

Mi número es _____.

11. **PIENSA MÁS** Hay 2 cajas de 100 lápices y algunos lápices sueltos sobre la mesa. Elige todos los números que muestran cuántos lápices puede haber en total.

○ 200
○ 106
○ 203
○ 207

ACTIVIDAD PARA LA CASA • Escriba el número 438. Pídale a su niño que le diga los valores de los dígitos de este número.

Nombre _____

Hacer un modelo de números de 3 dígitos

Objetivo de aprendizaje Representarás un número de 3 dígitos con bloques.

Escribe cuántas centenas, decenas y unidades hay.

Muestra con . Luego haz un dibujo rápido.

1. 118

Centenas	Decenas	Unidades

2. 246

Centenas	Decenas	Unidades

Resolución de problemas En el mundo

3. Escribe el número que coincida con las pistas.
   - Mi número tiene 2 centenas.
   - El dígito de las decenas tiene 9 más que el dígito de las unidades.

   Mi número es _____.

Centenas	Decenas	Unidades

4. **ESCRIBE Matemáticas** Escribe un número de 3 dígitos con los dígitos 2, 9, 4. Haz un dibujo rápido para mostrar el valor de tu número.

Capítulo 2

noventa y uno **91**

Repaso de la lección

1. ¿Qué número muestran estos bloques?

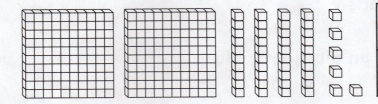

Centenas	Decenas	Unidades

_____

Repaso en espiral

2. Escribe el número que tenga el mismo valor que 28 decenas.

   _____

3. Describe el número 59 de dos maneras.

   ____ decenas ____ unidades

   ____ + ____

4. Encierra en un círculo el número impar.

   11   12

   18   20

5. Escribe el número que sea igual a 7 decenas y 3 unidades.

   _____

Centenas, decenas y unidades

Pregunta esencial ¿Cómo escribes el número de 3 dígitos que se muestra con un conjunto de bloques?

Objetivo de aprendizaje Escribirás el número de 3 dígitos representado por un conjunto de bloques.

Escucha y dibuja — En el mundo

Escribe el número de centenas, decenas y unidades. Luego haz un dibujo rápido.

Centenas	Decenas	Unidades

Centenas	Decenas	Unidades

PARA EL MAESTRO • Lea el siguiente problema a los niños. Sebastion tiene 243 bloques amarillos. ¿Cuántas centenas, decenas y unidades hay en este número? Repita con 423 bloques rojos.

Charla matemática — PRÁCTICAS Y PROCESOS MATEMÁTICOS

Describe en qué se parecen los dos números. **Describe** en qué se diferencian.

Capítulo 2 — noventa y tres **93**

Representa y dibuja

Escribe cuántas centenas, decenas y unidades hay en el modelo. ¿De qué dos maneras se puede escribir este número?

Centenas	Decenas	Unidades
2	4	7

247

200 + 40 + 7

Comparte y muestra

Escribe cuántas centenas, decenas y unidades hay en el modelo. Escribe el número de dos maneras.

1.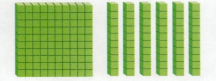

Centenas	Decenas	Unidades

_____

_____ + _____ + _____

2.

Centenas	Decenas	Unidades

_____

_____ + _____ + _____

3.

Centenas	Decenas	Unidades

_____

_____ + _____ + _____

Nombre _____

Por tu cuenta

Escribe cuántas centenas, decenas y unidades hay en el modelo. Escribe el número de dos maneras.

4.

Centenas	Decenas	Unidades

_____

_____ + _____ + _____

5.

Centenas	Decenas	Unidades

_____

_____ + _____ + _____

6.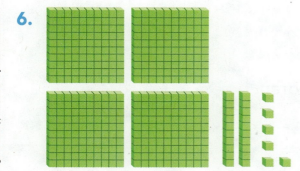

Centenas	Decenas	Unidades

_____

_____ + _____ + _____

Resuelve. Escribe o dibuja para explicar.

7. **PIENSA MÁS** Un modelo de mi número tiene 4 bloques de unidades, 5 bloques de decenas y 7 bloques de centenas. ¿Qué número soy?

Matemáticas al instante

_____

Capítulo 2 • Lección 4

noventa y cinco **95**

Resolución de problemas • Aplicaciones

8. **MÁS AL DETALLE** El dígito de las centenas de mi número es mayor que el dígito de las decenas. El dígito de las unidades es menor que el dígito de las decenas. ¿Cuál podría ser mi número? Escríbelo de dos maneras.

_____ + _____ + _____

_____

9. **PIENSA MÁS** Karen tiene estas bolsas de canicas. ¿Cuántas canicas tiene en total?

_____ canicas

Explica cómo utilizaste la imagen para hallar el número de canicas que tiene Karen.

_____

_____

_____

 ACTIVIDAD PARA LA CASA • Diga un número de 3 dígitos, como 546. Pida a su niño que haga un dibujo rápido de ese número.

Nombre _____

Centenas, decenas y unidades

Objetivo de aprendizaje Escribirás el número de 3 dígitos representado por un conjunto de bloques.

Escribe cuántas centenas, decenas y unidades hay en el modelo. Escribe el número de dos maneras.

1.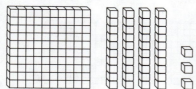

Centenas	Decenas	Unidades

_____

_____ + _____ + _____

2.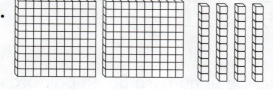

Centenas	Decenas	Unidades

_____

_____ + _____ + _____

Resolución de problemas

3. Escribe el número que responde el acertijo. Usa la tabla. Un modelo de mi número tiene 6 bloques de unidades, 2 bloques de centenas y 3 bloques de decenas. ¿Qué número soy?

Centenas	Decenas	Unidades

_____

4. **ESCRIBE Matemáticas** Escribe un número que tenga un cero en el lugar de las decenas. Haz un dibujo rápido de tu número.

Capítulo 2

Repaso de la lección

1. Escribe el número 254 como la suma de centenas, decenas y unidades.

   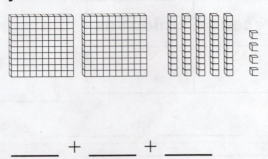

   ___ + ___ + ___

2. Escribe el número 307 como la suma de centenas, decenas y unidades.

   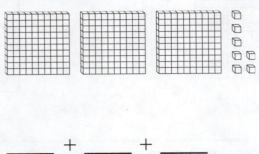

   ___ + ___ + ___

Repaso en espiral

3. Describe el número 83 de dos maneras.

   ___ decenas ___ unidades

   ___ + ___

4. Escribe el número 86 en palabras.

   _____

5. Escribe el número que tenga el mismo valor que 32 decenas.

   _____

6. Encierra en un círculo el número impar.

   2   6

   10   17

Nombre _____

Valor posicional hasta el 1,000

Pregunta esencial ¿Cómo sabes los valores de los dígitos de los números?

Objetivo de aprendizaje Usarás el valor posicional para describir los valores de los dígitos en números hasta el 1,000.

Escucha y dibuja En el mundo

Escribe los números. Luego haz dibujos rápidos.

_____ hojas de papel de colores

Centenas	Decenas	Unidades

_____ hojas de papel blanco

Centenas	Decenas	Unidades

PARA EL MAESTRO • Lea el siguiente problema. Hay 245 hojas de papel de colores en el gabinete de materiales. Hay 458 hojas de papel blanco junto a la mesa. Pida a los niños que escriban cada número y hagan dibujos rápidos para mostrar los números.

Charla matemática
PRÁCTICAS Y PROCESOS MATEMÁTICOS 1
Describe en qué se diferencian 5 decenas de 5 centenas.

Capítulo 2   noventa y nueve **99**

Representa y dibuja

El lugar de un dígito en un número indica su valor.

El 3 en el 327 tiene un valor de 3 centenas, o 300.

El 2 en el 327 tiene un valor de 2 decenas, o 20.

El 7 en el 327 tiene un valor de 7 unidades, o 7.

Hay 10 centenas en 1 **millar**.

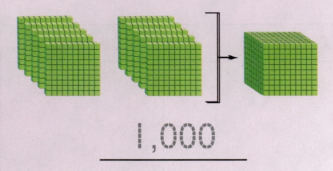

1,000

El 1 está en el lugar de los millares y tiene un valor de 1 millar.

Comparte y muestra

Encierra en un círculo el valor o el significado del dígito rojo.

1. 70**2**   2 unidades   2 decenas   2 centenas

2. 4**5**9   500   50   5

3. **3**62   3 centenas   3 decenas   3 unidades

Nombre _____

Por tu cuenta

Encierra en un círculo el valor o el significado del dígito rojo.

4. 5**4**9   400   40   4

5. 60**7**   7 unidades   7 decenas   7 centenas

6. **1**,000   1 unidad   1 centena   1 millar

7. **9**14   90   900   9,000

8. **PIENSA MÁS** El valor del dígito de las unidades en el número favorito de George es 2. El valor del dígito de las centenas es 600 y el valor del dígito de las decenas es 90. Escribe el número favorito de George. _____

9. **MÁS AL DETALLE** Escribe el número que coincida con las pistas.

- El valor de mi dígito de las centenas es 300.
- El valor de mi dígito de las decenas es 0.
- El valor de mi dígito de las unidades es un número par mayor que 7.

El número es _____.

Capítulo 2 • Lección 5   ciento uno **101**

Resolución de problemas • Aplicaciones

10. PIENSA MÁS Ty está haciendo un diagrama de Venn. ¿En qué parte del diagrama debe escribir los otros números?

Números con un 5 en el lugar de las decenas   Números con un 2 en el lugar de las centenas

152

| 152 |
| 215 |
| 454 |
| 257 |
| 352 |
| 205 |
| 250 |

11. PRÁCTICAS Y PROCESOS MATEMÁTICOS ③ Aplica Describe dónde se debe escribir 752 en el diagrama. Explica tu respuesta.

_____

_____

_____

12. PIENSA MÁS + Rellena los círculos que estén al lado de los números que tienen un 4 en el lugar de las decenas.

○ 764
○ 149
○ 437
○ 342

ACTIVIDAD PARA LA CASA • Pida a su niño que escriba números de 3 dígitos, como "un número que tenga 2 centenas" y "un número que tenga un 9 en el lugar de las unidades".

Nombre _____

Valor posicional hasta el 1,000

Objetivo de aprendizaje Usarás el valor posicional para describir los valores de los dígitos en números hasta el 1,000.

Encierra en un círculo el valor o el significado del dígito subrayado.

1. 3<u>3</u>7	3	30	300
2. 46<u>2</u>	200	20	2
3. <u>5</u>72	5	50	500
4. 56<u>7</u>	7 unidades	7 decenas	7 centenas
5. <u>4</u>62	4 centenas	4 unidades	4 decenas

Resolución de problemas

6. Escribe el número de 3 dígitos que responde el acertijo.
   - Tengo el mismo dígito en mis centenas y en mis unidades.
   - El valor del dígito de mis decenas es 50.
   - El valor del dígito de mis unidades es 4.   El número es _____.

7. ESCRIBE Matemáticas ¿Cuál es el valor del 5 en 756? Escribe y dibuja para mostrar lo que sabes.

_____

Capítulo 2   ciento tres **103**

Repaso de la lección

1. ¿Cuál es el valor del dígito subrayado?

   3̲15

   _____

2. ¿Cuál es el significado del dígito subrayado?

   6 4̲ 8

   ____ decenas

Repaso en espiral

3. ¿Qué número se puede escribir como 40 + 5?

   _____

4. ¿Qué número tiene el mismo valor que 14 decenas?

   _____

5. Escribe el número que se describe como 1 decena 16 unidades.

   _____

6. Encierra en un círculo el número par.

   7   16

   21   25

104 ciento cuatro

Nombre _____

Nombres de los números

Pregunta esencial ¿Cómo escribes números de 3 dígitos en palabras?

Objetivo de aprendizaje Escribirás números de 3 dígitos en palabras.

Escucha y dibuja

Escribe los números que faltan en la tabla. Luego halla y encierra en un círculo los números en palabras abajo.

	12	13		15	16	17	18	19	20
21	22	23	24	25	26	27	28		30
31	32	33	34		36	37	38	39	40
41	42	43	44	45		47	48	49	50
51		53	54	55	56	57	58	59	60

cuarenta y uno   noventa y dos   catorce

once   treinta y cinco   cuarenta y seis

cincuenta y tres   veintinueve   cincuenta y dos

Charla matemática

PRÁCTICAS Y PROCESOS MATEMÁTICOS 6

Explica Describe cómo escribir en palabras el número con un 5 en el lugar de las decenas y un 7 en el lugar de las unidades.

NOTA A LA FAMILIA • En esta actividad, su niño repasó los números menores que 100 en palabras.

Capítulo 2

ciento cinco **105**

Representa y dibuja

Puedes escribir números de 3 dígitos en palabras. Primero, observa el dígito de las centenas. Luego, observa el dígito de las decenas y el dígito de las unidades.

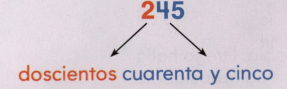

doscientos cuarenta y cinco

setecientos trece

Comparte y muestra

Escribe el número en palabras.

1. 506

   quinientos seis

2. 189

   _____

3. 328

   _____

Escribe el número.

4. cuatrocientos quince

   _____

5. doscientos noventa y uno

   _____

6. seiscientos tres

   _____

7. ochocientos cuarenta y siete

   _____

Nombre _____

Por tu cuenta

Escribe el número.

8. setecientos diecisiete _____

9. trescientos noventa _____

Escribe el número en palabras.

10. 568

_____

11. 321

_____

12. **MÁS AL DETALLE** Mi número de 3 dígitos tiene un 4 en el lugar de las centenas. Tiene un número en el lugar de las decenas mayor que el de las unidades. La suma de los dígitos es 6.

¿Cuál es mi número? _____

Escribe el número usando palabras. _____

13. **PIENSA MÁS** Alma cuenta doscientas sesenta y ocho hojas. ¿De qué otra manera se escribe este número? Encierra en un círculo la respuesta.

$2 + 6 + 8$

$200 + 60 + 8$

$2 + 60 + 8$

Capítulo 2 • Lección 6

Resolución de problemas • Aplicaciones

 **Relaciona símbolos y palabras**

Encierra en un círculo la respuesta de cada problema.

14. Derek cuenta ciento noventa carros. ¿De qué otra manera se escribe este número?

119

190

910

15. Beth contó trescientas cincuenta y seis pajillas. ¿De qué otra manera se escribe este número?

3 + 5 + 6

30 + 50 + 60

300 + 50 + 6

16. **PIENSA MÁS** Hay 537 sillas en la escuela. Escribe el número en palabras.

_____

Muestra el número de otras dos maneras diferentes.

Centenas	Decenas	Unidades

_____ + _____ + _____

 ACTIVIDAD PARA LA CASA • Pida a su niño que escriba el número 940 en palabras.

108 ciento ocho

Nombre _____

Nombres de los números

Objetivo de aprendizaje Escribirás números de 3 dígitos en palabras.

Escribe el número.

1. doscientos treinta y dos

   _____

2. quinientos cuarenta y cuatro

   _____

3. ciento cincuenta y ocho

   _____

4. novecientos cincuenta

   _____

5. cuatrocientos veinte

   _____

6. seiscientos setenta y ocho

   _____

Escribe el número en palabras.

7. 317

   _____

Resolución de problemas En el mundo

Encierra en un círculo la respuesta.

8. Seiscientos veintiséis niños asisten a la escuela Elm Street. ¿De qué otra manera se puede escribir este número?

    266   626   662

9. **Matemáticas** Escribe un número de 3 dígitos usando los dígitos 5, 9 y 2. Luego escribe tu número en palabras.

   _____

Capítulo 2

ciento nueve **109**

Repaso de la lección

1. Escribe el número 851 en palabras.

   _____

2. Escribe el número doscientos sesenta usando números.

   _____

Repaso en espiral

3. Escribe un número con el dígito 8 en el lugar de las decenas.

   _____

4. Escribe el número que se muestra con estos bloques.

   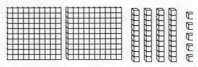

   _____

5. Cuenta de cinco en cinco.

   650, 655,

   ____, ____, ____

6. Sam tiene 128 canicas. ¿Cuántas centenas hay en este número?

   ____ centena

Nombre _____

Diferentes formas de los números

Pregunta esencial ¿Cuáles son tres maneras de escribir un número de 3 dígitos?

Objetivo de aprendizaje Escribirás un número de 3 dígitos con dígitos, palabras y la suma de los valores de los dígitos de las centenas, decenas y unidades.

Escucha y dibuja — En el mundo

Escribe el número. Escribe cuántas centenas, decenas y unidades tiene usando los dígitos.

[_____] ____ centenas ____ decenas ____ unidades

[_____] ____ centenas ____ decenas ____ unidades

[_____] ____ centenas ____ decenas ____ unidad

PARA EL MAESTRO • Lea el siguiente problema. Evan tiene 426 canicas. ¿Cuántas centenas, decenas y unidades hay en 426? Continúe la actividad con 204 y 341.

Charla matemática

PRÁCTICAS Y PROCESOS MATEMÁTICOS 6

¿Cuántas centenas hay en 368? **Explica.**

Capítulo 2   ciento once **111**

Representa y dibuja

Puedes usar un dibujo rápido para mostrar un número.
Puedes escribir un número de diferentes maneras.

quinientos treinta y seis

__5__ centenas __3__ decenas __6__ unidades

__500__ + __30__ + __6__

__536__

Comparte y muestra

Lee el número y haz un dibujo rápido.
Luego escribe el número de diferentes maneras.

1. cuatrocientos siete

   ____ centenas ____ decenas
   ____ unidades
   ____ + ____ + ____
   ____

2. trescientos veinticinco

   ____ centenas ____ decenas
   ____ unidades
   ____ + ____ + ____
   ____

3. doscientos cincuenta y tres

   ____ centenas ____ decenas
   ____ unidades
   ____ + ____ + ____
   ____

Nombre _____

Por tu cuenta

Lee el número y haz un dibujo rápido.
Luego escribe el número de diferentes maneras.

4. ciento setenta y dos

 ____ centena ____ decenas

 ____ unidades

 _____ + _____ + _____

 _____

5. trescientos cuarenta y seis

 ____ centenas ____ decenas

 ____ unidades

 _____ + _____ + _____

 _____

6. PIENSA MÁS Piensa en un número de 3 dígitos con un cero en el lugar de las unidades. Usa palabras para escribir ese número.

_____

7. PIENSA MÁS Ellen usó los siguientes bloques para mostrar 452. ¿Qué está mal? Tacha bloques y haz dibujos rápidos de los bloques que faltan.

 ACTIVIDAD PARA LA CASA • Pida a su niño que muestre el número 315 de tres maneras.

Nombre _____

✓ Revisión de la mitad del capítulo

Conceptos y destrezas

Encierra en un círculo decenas para formar 1 centena.
Escribe el número de diferentes maneras.

1.

   _____ decenas

   _____ centena _____ decenas

   _____

Escribe cuántas centenas, decenas y unidades hay en el modelo. Escribe el número de dos maneras.

2.

Centenas	Decenas	Unidades

_____

_____ + _____ + _____

Encierra en un círculo el valor o el significado del dígito rojo.

3. 5 28   5   50   500

4. 67 4   4 unidades   4 decenas   4 centenas

5. **PIENSA MÁS** Escribe el número seiscientos cuarenta y cinco de otra manera.

   _____

114 ciento catorce   Capítulo 2

Nombre _____

Diferentes formas de los números

Objetivo de aprendizaje Escribirás un número de 3 dígitos con dígitos, palabras y la suma de los valores de los dígitos de las centenas, decenas y unidades.

Lee el número y haz un dibujo rápido.
Luego escribe el número de diferentes maneras.

1. doscientos cincuenta y uno ____ centenas ____ decenas ____ unidad

   _____ + _____ + _____

   _____

2. trescientos doce ____ centenas ____ decena ____ unidades

   _____ + _____ + _____

   _____

Resolución de problemas

Escribe el número de otra manera.

3. 200 + 30 + 7

   _____

4. 895

   _____

5. **ESCRIBE Matemáticas** Haz un dibujo rápido de 3 centenas, 5 decenas y 7 unidades. ¿Qué número muestra tu dibujo rápido? Escríbelo de tres maneras diferentes.

Capítulo 2   ciento quince **115**

Repaso de la lección

1. Escribe el número 392 en centenas, decenas y unidades

    ____ centenas ____ decenas

    ____ unidades

2. ¿De qué otra manera se puede escribir el número 271?

    ____ centenas ____ decenas

    ____ unidad

Repaso en espiral

3. ¿Cuál es el valor del dígito subrayado?

    5̲6

    _____

4. ¿Qué número muestran estos bloques?

    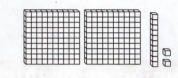

    _____

5. ¿De qué otra manera se puede escribir el número 75?

    ____ + ____

6. ¿Qué número puede escribirse como 60 + 3?

116 ciento dieciséis

Nombre _____

Álgebra • Diferentes maneras de mostrar números

Pregunta esencial ¿Cómo puedes usar bloques o dibujos rápidos para mostrar el valor de un número de diferentes maneras?

Objetivo de aprendizaje Usarás bloques o dibujos rápidos para mostrar el valor de un número de diferentes maneras.

Escucha y dibuja — En el mundo

Haz dibujos rápidos para resolver.
Escribe cuántas decenas y unidades hay.

_____ decenas _____ unidades

_____ decenas _____ unidades

PARA EL MAESTRO • Lea a los niños este problema. La Sra. Peabody tiene 35 libros en un carrito para llevar a los salones de clases. Puede usar cajas que contienen 10 libros cada una y también puede poner libros sueltos en el carrito. ¿De qué dos maneras puede poner los libros en el carrito?

PRÁCTICAS Y PROCESOS MATEMÁTICOS 4

Representa Describe cómo hallaste diferentes maneras de mostrar 35 libros.

Capítulo 2 — ciento diecisiete **117**

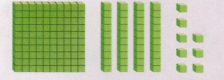

Representa y dibuja

Estas son dos maneras de mostrar 148.

Centenas	Decenas	Unidades
1	4	8

Centenas	Decenas	Unidades
0	14	8

Comparte y muestra

Usa dibujos rápidos para mostrar el número de una manera diferente. Escribe dos maneras de mostrar cuántas centenas, decenas y unidades hay.

1. 213

Centenas	Decenas	Unidades

Centenas	Decenas	Unidades

2. 132

Centenas	Decenas	Unidades

Centenas	Decenas	Unidades

ciento dieciocho

Nombre _____

Por tu cuenta

Usa dibujos rápidos para mostrar el número de una manera diferente. Escribe dos maneras para mostrar cuántas centenas, decenas y unidades hay.

3. 144

Centenas	Decenas	Unidades

Centenas	Decenas	Unidades

4. 204

Centenas	Decenas	Unidades

Centenas	Decenas	Unidades

5. PRÁCTICAS Y PROCESOS MATEMÁTICOS 3 **Argumenta**

Sue dijo que 200 + 20 + 23 es igual a 200 + 30 + 3. ¿Es correcto? Explica.

_____

_____

_____

Capítulo 2 • Lección 8

ciento diecinueve 119

Resolución de problemas • Aplicaciones

Las canicas se venden en cajas, en bolsas o sueltas. Cada caja contiene 10 bolsas de canicas. Cada bolsa contiene 10 canicas.

6. **PIENSA MÁS** Haz dibujos que muestren dos maneras de comprar 324 canicas.

Usa la información anterior sobre las canicas.

7. **PIENSA MÁS** Solo hay una caja de canicas en la tienda. Hay muchas bolsas de canicas y canicas sueltas. Haz un dibujo que muestre una manera de comprar 312 canicas.

¿Cuántas cajas, bolsas y canicas sueltas mostraste?

_____

_____

 ACTIVIDAD PARA LA CASA • Escriba el número 156. Pida a su niño que haga dibujos rápidos de dos maneras de mostrar este número.

Álgebra • Diferentes maneras de mostrar números

Objetivo de aprendizaje Usarás bloques o dibujos rápidos para mostrar el valor de un número de diferentes maneras.

Escribe cuántas centenas, decenas y unidades hay en el modelo.

1. 135

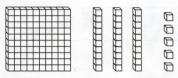

Centenas	Decenas	Unidades

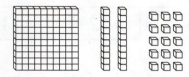

Centenas	Decenas	Unidades

Resolución de problemas • En el mundo

Los marcadores se venden en cajas, paquetes o como marcadores sueltos. Cada caja tiene 10 paquetes. Cada paquete tiene 10 marcadores.

2. Haz dibujos que muestren dos maneras de comprar 276 marcadores.

3. **ESCRIBE Matemáticas** Haz dibujos rápidos para mostrar el número 326.

Capítulo 2   ciento veintiuno **121**

Repaso de la lección

1. Escribe el número que se puede mostrar con este número de centenas, decenas y unidades.

Centenas	Decenas	Unidades
1	2	18

_____

2. Escribe el número que se puede mostrar con este número de centenas, decenas y unidades.

Centenas	Decenas	Unidades
2	15	6

_____

Repaso en espiral

3. ¿Qué número puede escribirse como 6 decenas, 2 unidades?

_____

4. ¿Qué número puede escribirse como 30 + 2?

_____

5. Escribe el número 584 en palabras.

_____

6. Escribe el número 29 en palabras.

_____

Nombre _____

Contar hacia adelante y hacia atrás de 10 en 10 y de 100 en 100

Pregunta esencial ¿Cómo usas el valor posicional para hallar 10 más, 10 menos, 100 más o 100 menos que un número de 3 dígitos?

Objetivo de aprendizaje Hallarás 10 más, 10 menos, 100 más o 100 menos que un número de 3 dígitos.

Escucha y dibuja — En el mundo

Haz dibujos rápidos de los números.

Niñas

Centenas	Decenas	Unidades

Niños

Centenas	Decenas	Unidades

PARA EL MAESTRO • Diga a los niños que hay 342 niñas en la escuela Central. Pida a los niños que hagan dibujos rápidos de 342. Luego dígales que hay 352 niños en la escuela. Pídales que hagan dibujos rápidos de 352.

Charla matemática — PRÁCTICAS Y PROCESOS MATEMÁTICOS

Describe en qué se diferencian los dos números.

Capítulo 2   ciento veintitrés **123**

Representa y dibuja

Puedes mostrar 10 menos o 10 más que un número cambiando el dígito en el lugar de las decenas.

10 menos que 264

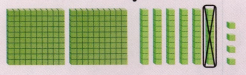

Centenas	Decenas	Unidades
2	5	4

10 más que 264

Centenas	Decenas	Unidades
2	7	4

Puedes mostrar 100 menos o 100 más que un número cambiando el dígito en el lugar de las centenas.

100 menos que 264

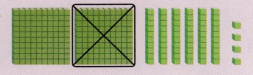

Centenas	Decenas	Unidades
1	6	4

100 más que 264

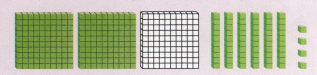

Centenas	Decenas	Unidades
3	6	4

Comparte y muestra

Escribe el número.

1. 10 más que 648

   _____

2. 100 menos que 513

   _____

3. 100 más que 329

   _____

4. 10 menos que 827

   _____

124 ciento veinticuatro

Nombre _____

Por tu cuenta

Escribe el número.

5. 10 más que 471

_____

6. 10 menos que 143

_____

7. 100 más que 555

_____

8. 100 menos que 757

_____

9. 100 más que 900

_____

10. 10 menos que 689

_____

11. 100 menos que 712

_____

12. 10 menos que 254

_____

13. **PIENSA MÁS** Kyla escribió el siguiente acertijo. Completa los espacios en blanco para que el enunciado sea correcto.

_____ es 10 menos que 948 y 10 más que _____.

14. **PIENSA MÁS** Rick tiene 10 crayones más que Lori. Lori tiene 136 crayones. Tom tiene 10 crayones menos que Rick. ¿Cuántos crayones tiene cada niño?

Rick: _____ crayones

Tom: _____ crayones

Lori: _____ crayones

Capítulo 2 • Lección 9

Resolución de problemas • Aplicaciones

 **Analiza las relaciones**

15. El libro de Juan tiene 248 páginas. Esto es 10 páginas más que el libro de Kevin. ¿Cuántas páginas tiene el libro de Kevin?

_____ páginas

16. Hay 217 dibujos en el libro de Tina. Hay 100 dibujos menos en el libro de Mark. ¿Cuántos dibujos hay en el libro de Mark?

_____ dibujos

17. **MÁS AL DETALLE** Usa las pistas para responder la pregunta.

- Shawn cuenta 213 carros.
- María cuenta 100 carros menos que Shawn.
- Jayden cuenta 10 carros más que María.

¿Cuántos carros cuenta Jayden? _____ carros

18. **PIENSA MÁS** Raúl tiene 235 adhesivos. Gabby tiene 100 adhesivos más que Raúl. Thomas tiene 10 adhesivos menos que Gabby. Escribe el número de adhesivos que tiene cada niño.

_____ Raúl   _____ Gabby   _____ Thomas

 ACTIVIDAD PARA LA CASA • Escriba el número 596. Pida a su niño que mencione el número que tiene 100 más que 596.

Nombre _____

Contar hacia adelante y hacia atrás de 10 en 10 y de 100 en 100

Objetivo de aprendizaje Hallarás 10 más, 10 menos, 100 más o 100 menos que un número de 3 dígitos.

Escribe el número.

1. 10 más que 451

   _____

2. 10 menos que 770

   _____

3. 100 más que 367

   _____

4. 100 menos que 895

   _____

5. 10 menos que 812

   _____

6. 100 más que 543

   _____

7. 10 más que 218

   _____

8. 100 más que 379

   _____

Resolución de problemas

Resuelve. Escribe o dibuja la explicación.

9. Sarah tiene 128 adhesivos.
   Alex tiene 10 adhesivos menos que Sarah.
   ¿Cuántos adhesivos tiene Alex?

   _____ adhesivos

10. **ESCRIBE Matemáticas** Elige cualquier número de 3 dígitos. Describe cómo hallar el número que es 10 más.

    _____

Capítulo 2   ciento veintisiete **127**

Repaso de la lección

1. Escribe el número que tiene 10 menos que 526.

   _____

2. Escribe el número que tiene 100 más que 487.

   _____

Repaso en espiral

3. Escribe otra manera de describir 14 decenas.

   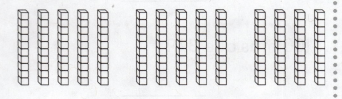

   ____ centena ____ decenas

4. ¿Cuál es el valor del dígito subrayado?

   5$\underline{8}$7

   _____

5. ¿Qué número puede escribirse como 30 + 5?

   _____

6. ¿Qué número puede escribirse como 9 decenas y 1 unidad?

   _____

Nombre _____

Álgebra • Patrones numéricos

Pregunta esencial ¿Cómo te ayuda el valor posicional a identificar y ampliar los patrones de conteo?

Objetivo de aprendizaje Usarás el valor posicional para identificar los números siguientes en un patrón de conteo.

Escucha y dibuja En el mundo

Sombrea los números del patrón de conteo.

801	802	803	804	805	806	807	808	809	810
811	812	813	814	815	816	817	818	819	820
821	822	823	824	825	826	827	828	829	830
831	832	833	834	835	836	837	838	839	840
841	842	843	844	845	846	847	848	849	850
851	852	853	854	855	856	857	858	859	860
861	862	863	864	865	866	867	868	869	870
871	872	873	874	875	876	877	878	879	880
881	882	883	884	885	886	887	888	889	890
891	892	893	894	895	896	897	898	899	900

PARA EL MAESTRO • Lea el siguiente problema y comente cómo pueden resolverlo los niños usando un patrón de conteo. En la panadería Flor se vendieron 823 pastelillos por la mañana. Por la tarde se vendieron cuatro paquetes de 10 pastelillos. ¿Cuántos pastelillos se vendieron en total?

Charla matemática

PRÁCTICAS Y PROCESOS MATEMÁTICOS 7

Busca la estructura
¿Qué número sigue en el patrón de conteo que ves? Explica.

Capítulo 2   ciento veintinueve **129**

Representa y dibuja

Observa los dígitos de los números. ¿Qué dos números son consecutivos en el patrón de conteo?

114, 214, 314, 414, ▪, ▪

El dígito de las _____ cambia de a uno por vez.

Los dos números siguientes son _____ y _____.

Comparte y muestra

Observa los dígitos para hallar los dos números siguientes.

1. 137, 147, 157, 167, ▪, ▪

   Los dos números siguientes son _____ y _____.

2. 245, 345, 445, 545, ▪, ▪

   Los dos números siguientes son _____ y _____.

3. 421, 431, 441, 451, ▪, ▪

   Los dos números siguientes son _____ y _____.

4. 389, 489, 589, 689, ▪, ▪

   Los dos números siguientes son _____ y _____.

Nombre _____

Por tu cuenta

Observa los dígitos para hallar los dos números siguientes.

5. 193, 293, 393, 493, ▪, ▪

   Los dos números siguientes son _____ y _____.

6. 484, 494, 504, 514, ▪, ▪

   Los dos números siguientes son _____ y _____.

7. 500, 600, 700, 800, ▪, ▪

   Los dos números siguientes son _____ y _____.

8. 655, 665, 675, 685, ▪, ▪

   Los dos números siguientes son _____ y _____.

9. **PIENSA MÁS** Mark leyó 203 páginas. Laney leyó 100 páginas más que Mark. Gavin leyó 10 páginas menos que Laney. ¿Cuántas páginas leyó Gavin?

   _____ páginas

Resolución de problemas • Aplicaciones

Resuelve.

10. **MÁS AL DETALLE** Había 135 botones en un frasco. Después de que Robin puso más botones en el frasco, había 175 botones. ¿Cuántos grupos de 10 botones colocó en el frasco?

   _____ grupos de 10 botones.

   Explica cómo resolviste el problema.

   _____

   _____

   _____

11. **PIENSA MÁS** Escribe el siguiente número de cada patrón de conteo.

   162, 262, 362, 462, _____

   347, 357, 367, 377, _____

   609, 619, 629, 639, _____

 ACTIVIDAD PARA LA CASA • Con su niño, túrnense para escribir patrones numéricos en los que cuenten hacia adelante de diez en diez o de cien en cien.

Nombre_____

Álgebra • Patrones numéricos

Objetivo de aprendizaje Usarás el valor posicional para identificar los números siguientes en un patrón de conteo.

Observa los dígitos para hallar los dos números siguientes.

1. 232, 242, 252, 262, ☐, ☐

   Los dos números siguientes son _____ y _____.

2. 185, 285, 385, 485, ☐, ☐

   Los dos números siguientes son _____ y _____.

3. 428, 528, 628, 728, ☐, ☐

   Los dos números siguientes son _____ y _____.

4. 654, 664, 674, 684, ☐, ☐

   Los dos números siguientes son _____ y _____.

Resolución de problemas · En el mundo

5. ¿Qué números faltan en el patrón?

   431, 441, 451, 461, , 481, 491, ☐

   Los números que faltan son _____ y _____.

6. **ESCRIBE Matemáticas** ¿Cómo sabes cuando un patrón muestra contar hacia adelante de diez en diez?

_____

_____

Capítulo 2

Repaso de la lección

1. ¿Qué número sigue en este patrón?

   453, 463, 473, 483, _____

2. ¿Qué número sigue en este patrón?

   295, 395, 495, 595, _____

Repaso en espiral

3. Escribe el número setecientos cincuenta y uno usando dígitos.

   _____

4. ¿Cuál es el valor del dígito subrayado?

   1̲95

   _____

5. ¿Cuál es otra manera de escribir 56?

   ____ decenas ____ unidades

6. Escribe el número 43 en decenas y unidades.

   ____ decenas ____ unidades

Nombre _____

Resolución de problemas • Comparar números

Pregunta esencial ¿Cómo puedes hacer un modelo para resolver un problema de comparación de números?

Objetivo de aprendizaje Usarás bloques y la estrategia de *hacer un modelo* para mostrar los valores de los dígitos de los números al resolver problemas de comparación de números.

Los niños compraron 217 envases de leche chocolateada y 188 envases de leche común. ¿Compraron más envases de leche chocolateada o de leche común?

Soluciona el problema

¿Qué debo hallar?

Si los niños compraron ___más___

envases de leche común

o de leche chocolateada

¿Qué información debo usar?

_____ envases de leche chocolateada

_____ envases de leche común

Muestra cómo resolver el problema.
Haz un modelo de los números. Haz dibujos rápidos de tus modelos.

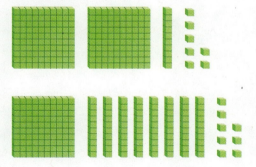

Los niños compraron más envases de leche _____.

NOTA A LA FAMILIA • Su niño usó bloques de base diez para representar los números del problema. Estos modelos se usaron como una herramienta para comparar números y resolver el problema.

Capítulo 2   ciento treinta y cinco **135**

Haz otro problema

Haz un modelo de los números. Haz dibujos rápidos que muestren cómo resolviste el problema.

- ¿Qué debo hallar?
- ¿Qué información debo usar?

1. En el zoológico hay 137 aves y 142 reptiles. ¿Hay más aves o más reptiles en el zoológico?

   más _____

2. El libro de Tom tiene 105 páginas. El libro de Delia tiene 109 páginas. ¿Qué libro tiene menos páginas?

   el libro de _____

Charla matemática

Compara Explica qué hiciste para resolver el segundo problema.

PRÁCTICAS Y PROCESOS MATEMÁTICOS 3

Nombre _____

Comparte y muestra

Haz un modelo de los números. Haz dibujos rápidos que muestren cómo resolviste el problema.

3. El rompecabezas de Mary tiene 164 piezas. El rompecabezas de Jake tiene 180 piezas. ¿Qué rompecabezas tiene más piezas?

el rompecabezas de _____

4. Hay 246 personas en el partido. Hay 251 personas en el museo. ¿En qué lugar hay menos personas?

en el _____

5. Hay 131 crayones en una caja. Hay 128 crayones en una bolsa. ¿Hay más crayones en la caja o en la bolsa?

en la _____

6. Hay 308 libros en el primer salón. Hay 273 libros en el segundo salón. ¿En qué salón hay menos libros?

en el _____ salón

Resolución de problemas • Aplicaciones

7. **PIENSA MÁS** Hay 748 niños en la escuela de Dan. Hay 651 niños en la escuela de Karen. Hay 763 niños en la escuela de Jason. ¿Qué escuela tiene más de 759 niños?

   la escuela de _____

8. **PRÁCTICAS Y PROCESOS MATEMÁTICOS** **Analiza** Hay 136 crayones en una caja. Usa los dígitos 4, 1 y 2 para escribir un número mayor que 136.

   _____

9. **PIENSA MÁS** Becky tiene 134 sellos. Sara tiene 129 sellos. ¿Quién tiene más sellos?

   _____

   Sara compra 10 sellos más. ¿Quién tiene más sellos ahora?

   _____

   Haz dibujos rápidos para mostrar los sellos que Becky y Sara tienen ahora.

 ACTIVIDAD PARA LA CASA • Pida a su niño que explique cómo resolvió uno de los problemas de esta página.

Nombre _____

Resolución de problemas • Comparar números

Objetivo de aprendizaje Usarás bloques y la estrategia de *hacer un modelo* para mostrar los valores de los dígitos de los números al resolver problemas de comparación de números.

Haz un modelo de los números. Haz dibujos rápidos que muestren cómo resolviste el problema.

1. Lauryn tiene 128 canicas. Kristin tiene 118 canicas. ¿Quién tiene más canicas?

2. Nick tiene 189 tarjetas de colección. Kyle tiene 198 tarjetas de colección. ¿Quién tiene menos tarjetas?

3. Un piano tiene 36 teclas negras y 52 teclas blancas. ¿Hay más teclas negras o más teclas blancas en un piano?

4. **ESCRIBE Matemáticas** Haz un dibujo para mostrar cómo puedes usar modelos para comparar 345 y 391.

Capítulo 2   ciento treinta y nueve **139**

Repaso de la lección

1. Gina tiene 245 adhesivos. Encierra en un círculo el número que sea menor que 245.

   285   254
   245   239

2. El libro de Carl tiene 176 páginas. Encierra en un círculo el número que sea mayor que 176.

   203   174
   168   139

Repaso en espiral

3. Escribe 63 como una suma de decenas y unidades.

   _____ + _____

4. Escribe 58 en decenas y unidades.

   _____ decenas

   _____ unidades

5. El Sr. Ford viajó 483 millas en su carro. ¿Cuántas centenas hay en este número?

   _____

6. Escribe 20 en palabras.

   _____

Nombre _____

Álgebra • Comparar números

Pregunta esencial ¿Cómo se comparan los números de 3 dígitos?

Objetivo de aprendizaje Usarás el valor posicional para comparar dos números de 3 dígitos con los símbolos >, = y <.

Escucha y dibuja — En el mundo

Haz dibujos rápidos para resolver el problema.

Había más _____ en el parque.

PARA EL MAESTRO • Lea el siguiente problema y pida a los niños que hagan dibujos rápidos para comparar los números. Había 125 mariposas y 132 aves en el parque. ¿Había más mariposas o más aves en el parque?

Explica cómo comparaste los números.

Capítulo 2 — ciento cuarenta y uno **141**

Representa y dibuja

Utiliza el valor posicional para **comparar** números. Comienza por observar los dígitos de mayor valor posicional.

> **> es mayor que**
> **< es menor que**
> **= es igual a**

Centenas	Decenas	Unidades
4	8	3
5	7	0

4 centenas < 5 centenas

483 < 570

Centenas	Decenas	Unidades
3	5	2
3	4	6

Las centenas son iguales.
5 decenas > 4 decenas

352 > 346

Comparte y muestra

Compara los números. Escribe >, <, o =.

1.

Centenas	Decenas	Unidades
2	3	9
1	7	9

239 ◯ 179

2.

Centenas	Decenas	Unidades
4	3	5
4	3	7

435 ◯ 437

 3.   764
   674

764 ◯ 674

 4.   519
   572

519 ◯ 572

142 ciento cuarenta y dos

Nombre _____

Por tu cuenta

Compara los números. Escribe >, <, o =.

5. 378
504

378 ◯ 504

6. 821
821

821 ◯ 821

7. 560
439

560 ◯ 439

8. 934
943

934 ◯ 943

PIENSA MÁS Escribe el número de 3 dígitos y compara los números. Usa >, < o =.

9. 400 + 70 + 5
400 + 70 + 5

_____ ◯ _____

10. 700 + 30 + 6
600 + 80 + 7

_____ ◯ _____

PRÁCTICAS Y PROCESOS MATEMÁTICOS 2 **Usa razonamiento** Escribe un número de 3 dígitos en la casilla para que la comparación sea verdadera.

11. 526 < ☐

12. 319 > ☐

13. ☐ > 782

14. ☐ < 131

Capítulo 2 • Lección 12

ciento cuarenta y tres **143**

Resolución de problemas • Aplicaciones

Resuelve. Escribe o dibuja para explicar.

15. **PIENSA MÁS** La Sra. York tiene 300 adhesivos rojos, 50 adhesivos azules y 8 adhesivos verdes. El Sr. Reed tiene 372 adhesivos. ¿Quién tiene más adhesivos?

_____

16. **PRÁCTICAS Y PROCESOS MATEMÁTICOS** **Analiza** Jasmine tiene unas tarjetas con números. Utiliza los dígitos de estas tarjetas para formar dos números de 3 dígitos. Usa cada dígito solo una vez. Compara los números.

   1   2   5
   6   3   8

_____ ◯ _____

17. **PIENSA MÁS +** ¿Es verdadera la comparación? Elige Sí o No.

	Sí	No
453 > 354	○	○
253 < 164	○	○
391 > 417	○	○
490 < 528	○	○

 ACTIVIDAD PARA LA CASA • Pida a su niño que explique cómo comparar los números 281 y 157.

Nombre _____

Álgebra • Comparar números

Objetivo de aprendizaje Usarás el valor posicional para comparar dos números de 3 dígitos con los símbolos >, = y <.

Compara los números. Escribe >, < o =.

1. 489
   605

   489 ◯ 605

2. 719
   719

   719 ◯ 719

3. 370
   248

   370 ◯ 248

4. 645
   654

   645 ◯ 654

5. 205
   250

   205 ◯ 250

6. 813
   781

   813 ◯ 781

Resolución de problemas · En el mundo

Resuelve. Escribe o dibuja para explicar.

7. Toby tiene 178 monedas de 1¢.
   Berta tiene 190 monedas de 1¢.
   ¿Quién tiene más monedas de 1¢?

   _____ tiene más monedas de 1¢.

8. **ESCRIBE Matemáticas** Explica cómo comparar 645 y 738 es diferente a comparar 645 y 649.

   _____
   _____

Capítulo 2   ciento cuarenta y cinco **145**

Repaso de la lección

1. Escribe >, <, o = para comparar.

    315 ◯ 351

2. Escribe >, <, o = para comparar.

    401 ◯ 399

Repaso en espiral

3. ¿Qué número tiene el mismo valor que 50 decenas?

    _____

4. Escribe un número que tenga un 8 en el lugar de las centenas.

    _____

5. Ned cuenta de cinco en cinco. Comienza en el 80. ¿Qué número debería decir después?

    _____

6. El Sr. Dean tiene un número par de gatos y un número impar de perros. Muestra cuántos perros y gatos puede tener.

    6 gatos y _____ perros

Nombre _____

 Repaso y prueba del Capítulo 2

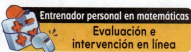

1.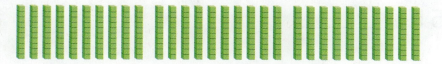

   ¿Las siguientes opciones muestran una manera de representar los bloques? Elige Sí o No.

3 centenas	○ Sí	○ No
30 unidades	○ Sí	○ No
30 centenas	○ Sí	○ No
30 decenas	○ Sí	○ No

2. Robin tiene 180 adhesivos. ¿Cuántas páginas de 10 adhesivos necesita para tener 200 adhesivos en total?

   _____ páginas de adhesivos

3. Sanjo tiene 348 canicas. Harry tiene 100 canicas menos que Sanjo. Ari tiene 10 canicas más que Harry. Escribe el número de canicas que tiene cada niño.

   _____   _____   _____
   Sanjo   Ari   Harry

Capítulo 2   ciento cuarenta y siete **147**

4. Escribe el siguiente número de cada patrón de conteo.

214, 314, 414, 514, _____

123, 133, 143, 153, _____

5. **PIENSA MÁS** ¿Es verdadera la comparación? Elige Sí o No.

787 < 769	○ Sí	○ No
405 > 399	○ Sí	○ No
396 > 402	○ Sí	○ No
128 < 131	○ Sí	○ No

6. **MÁS AL DETALLE** Cody piensa en el número 627. Escríbelo en palabras.

_____

Muestra el número de Cody de otras dos maneras.

Centenas	Decenas	Unidades

_____ + _____ + _____

Nombre _____

7. Matty necesita 200 botones. Amy le da 13 bolsas con 10 botones en cada una. ¿Cuántos botones necesita ahora?

_____ botones

8. Hay 4 cajas de 100 hojas de papel y varias hojas sueltas en el gabinete de materiales. Elige todos los números que muestren cuántas hojas de papel puede haber en total.

- ○ 348
- ○ 324
- ○ 406
- ○ 411

9. Los bloques se venden en cajas, en bolsas o sueltos. Cada caja contiene 10 bolsas. Cada bolsa contiene 10 bloques. Tara necesita 216 bloques. Haz un dibujo para mostrar una manera de comprar 216 bloques.

¿Cuántas cajas, bolsas y bloques sueltos mostraste?

_____

_____

Capítulo 2   ciento cuarenta y nueve **149**

10. Daniel y Hannah coleccionan carros de juguete. Daniel tiene 132 carros y Hannah tiene 138 carros. ¿Quién tiene más carros? _____

Daniel recibe 10 carros más y Hannah recibe 3 carros más. ¿Quién tiene más carros ahora? _____

Haz dibujos rápidos para mostrar cuántos carros tienen Daniel y Hannah ahora.

Carros de Daniel	Carros de Hannah

11. Elige todos los números que tienen el dígito 2 en el lugar de las decenas.

    ○ 721
    ○ 142
    ○ 425
    ○ 239

12. Ann tiene 239 caracoles. Escribe el número en palabras.

_____

150 ciento cincuenta

Librito de vocabulario

La gran idea: **Suma y resta**

Todo sobre los animales

por John Hudson

LA GRAN IDEA Desarrollar fluidez en la suma y la resta con números hasta el 100. Resolver problemas de suma y resta con números hasta el 1,000.

La jirafa es el animal terrestre más alto del mundo. Las jirafas adultas miden de 13 a 17 pies de altura. Las jirafas recién nacidas miden unos 6 pies de altura.

Un grupo de 5 jirafas bebe agua en un abrevadero. Otro grupo de 5 jirafas come hojas de un árbol. ¿Cuántas jirafas hay en total?

_____ jirafas

Ciencias
¿Cómo cuidan las jirafas a sus crías?

El avestruz es el ave más grande del mundo. Los avestruces no pueden volar, pero pueden correr rápido. ¡Los huevos de avestruz pesan unas 3 libras cada uno! Varias avestruces ponen huevos en un nido compartido.

Hay 6 huevos en un nido. Luego ponen 5 huevos más en ese nido. ¿Cuántos huevos hay en el nido ahora?

_____ huevos

¿Cómo cuidan los avestruces a sus crías?

Los canguros saltan con las dos patas traseras para moverse rápido. Cuando se mueven lentamente, usan las cuatro patas.

Los canguros grises occidentales viven en grupos llamados manadas. En una manada hay 8 canguros. Luego se unen 4 canguros más a la manada. ¿Cuántos canguros tiene la manada en total?

_____ canguros

¿Cómo cuidan los canguros a sus crías?

A los jabalíes les gusta comer raíces. Cavan con sus fuertes hocicos. Los jabalíes pueden medir hasta 6 pies de largo.

Los jabalíes viven en grupos llamados piaras. En una piara hay 14 jabalíes. Si hay 7 jabalíes comiendo, ¿cuántos jabalíes no están comiendo?

_____ jabalíes

¿Cómo cuidan los jabalíes a sus crías?

Los alces son el tipo de ciervo más grande. Los machos tienen cuernos que miden de 5 a 6 pies de ancho. Los alces saben trotar y galopar. ¡También son buenos nadadores!

Un guardabosques vio 7 alces por la mañana y 6 alces por la tarde. ¿Cuántos alces vio el guardabosques ese día?

_____ alces

¿Cómo cuidan los alces a sus crías?

Nombre _____

Escribe sobre el cuento

Elige un tipo de animal. Haz un dibujo y escribe tu propio cuento sobre ese tipo de animal. Haz sumas en tu cuento.

Repaso del vocabulario
suma   en total

jirafa   avestruz   canguro

ESCRIBE Matemáticas

_____
_____
_____
_____

¿Cuántos huevos hay?

Dibuja más huevos de avestruz en cada nido. Escribe un enunciado de suma debajo de cada nido para mostrar cuántos huevos hay en cada nido ahora.

_____   _____

 Elige otro animal del cuento.
Escribe otro cuento que tenga suma.

Capítulo 3

Operaciones básicas y relaciones

Piensa como matemático

El pez loro vive cerca de los arrecifes de coral en aguas oceánicas tropicales. Desprende con sus dientes afilados el alimento del coral.

Imagina que hay 10 peces loro comiendo en el coral. 3 peces se van nadando. ¿Cuántos peces están aún comiendo?

Nombre _____

✓ Muestra lo que sabes

Entrenador personal en matemáticas
Evaluación e intervención en línea

Usa símbolos para sumar

Usa el dibujo. Usa + e = para completar el enunciado de suma.

1.    3 ◯ 1 ◯ 4

2.    2 ◯ 3 ◯ 5

Sumas hasta el 10

Escribe la suma.

3. 4   4. 5   5. 2   6. 6   7. 9
   +3   +0   +7   +2   +1

Dobles y dobles más uno

Escribe el enunciado de suma.

8.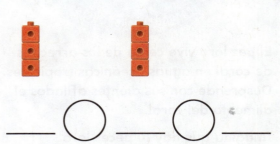

___ ◯ ___ ◯ ___

9.

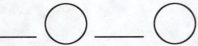

___ ◯ ___ ◯ ___

Esta página es para verificar la comprensión de destrezas importantes que se necesitan para tener éxito en el Capítulo 3.

Nombre _____

Desarrollo del vocabulario

Palabras de repaso
suma
resta
más
menos
igual
contar hacia adelante
contar hacia atrás

Visualízalo
Clasifica las palabras de repaso en el organizador gráfico.

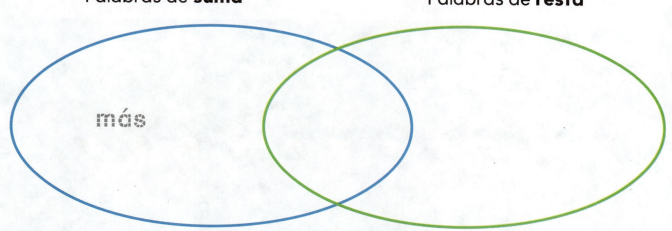

Palabras de **suma** — más

Palabras de **resta**

Comprende el vocabulario

1. Encierra en un círculo el enunciado de **suma**.
   $3 + 6 = 9$ $9 - 6 = 3$

2. Encierra en un círculo el enunciado de **resta**.
   $8 + 2 = 10$ $10 - 2 = 8$

3. Encierra en un círculo la operación de **contar hacia adelante**.
   $5 - 1 = 4$ $4 + 1 = 5$

4. Encierra en un círculo la operación de **contar hacia atrás**.
   $8 - 2 = 6$ $6 + 2 = 8$

Capítulo 3 · Libro interactivo del estudiante · Glosario multimedia   ciento sesenta y uno **161**

Capítulo 3

Juego: En busca de la oruga

Materiales

- 1
- 1
- 1

Juega con un compañero.

1. Coloca el cubo en la SALIDA.
2. Lanza el y muévete esa cantidad de espacios.
3. Di la suma o la diferencia. Tu compañero revisa tu respuesta.
4. Túrnense. El primer jugador que alcanza la LLEGADA gana.

LLEGADA

$7 + 3$ $3 - 1$ $3 + 4$ $6 - 0$ $5 + 2$

$2 + 4$

$1 + 6$ $4 - 1$ $3 + 0$ $6 - 3$ $5 - 2$

$5 - 5$

$7 - 4$ $3 + 5$ $0 + 4$ $7 - 5$ $2 + 3$ $5 - 3$

SALIDA

$4 + 4$ $6 - 1$ $2 + 2$ $5 + 3$ $8 - 2$

162 ciento sesenta y dos

Vocabulario del Capítulo 3

decenas	**diferencia**
tens	difference
18	20

dígito	**es igual a**
digit	is equal to (=)
21	25

números impares	**números pares**
odd numbers	even numbers
46	47

suma	**sumandos**
sum	addends
59	60

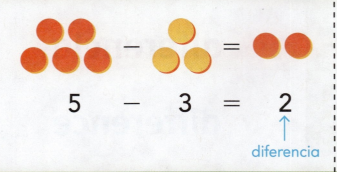

5 − 3 = 2
↑
diferencia

10 unidades = 1 decena

2 más 1 es igual a 3
2 + 1 = 3

0, 1, 2, 3, 4, 5, 6, 7, 8, y 9 son **dígitos**.

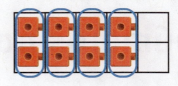

Los números pares muestran pares sin cubos que sobren.

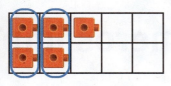

Los números impares muestran pares con un cubo de sobra.

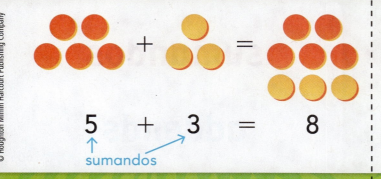

5 + 3 = 8
↑   ↑
sumandos

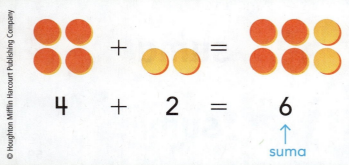

4 + 2 = 6
↑
suma

De visita con las palabras de ¡Vivan las matemáticas!

Juego

¡Vamos al arrecife de coral!

Jugadores: 2

Materiales
- 1 🟥
- 1 🟦
- 1 🎲

Recuadro de palabras
decena
diferencia
dígito
es igual a (=)
números impares
números pares
suma
sumandos

Instrucciones

1. Cada jugador elige un 🟦 y lo coloca en la SALIDA.
2. Lanza el 🎲 para jugar tu turno. Mueve el 🟦 esa cantidad de espacio alrededor del recorrido hacia la derecha.
3. Si caes en estos cuadrados:

   Espacio blanco Di el significado de la palabra de matemáticas o úsala en una oración. Si es correcto, salta hacia el siguiente espacio con esa palabra.

   Espacio verde Sigue las instrucciones del espacio. Si no hay instrucciones, te quedas en el mismo lugar.
4. El primer jugador que llega a la META, es el ganador.

Capítulo 3   ciento sesenta y dos 162A

Juego

INSTRUCCIONES

1. Cada jugador elige un  y lo coloca en la SALIDA.
2. Lanza el 🎲 para jugar tu turno. Mueve el 🔲 esa cantidad de espacios alrededor del recorrido hacia la derecha.
3. Si caes en estos cuadrados:
   Espacio blanco Di el significado de la palabra de matemática o úsala en una oración. Si es correcto, salta hacia el siguiente espacio que tenga esa palabra.
   Espacio verde Sigue las instrucciones del espacio. Si no hay instrucciones, te quedas en el mismo lugar.
4. El primer jugador que llega a la META, es el ganador.

MATERIALES

META — suma — números pares — números impares — sumandos

suma — sumandos — **Retrocede** — diferencia — decenas

números pares — números impares — dígito — es igual a —

dígito — números — números pares — suma — sumandos

es igual a — decenas — **Retrocede** — sumandos — suma

SALIDA — decenas — es igual a — dígito — números impares

162B ciento sesenta y dos

Diario

Escríbelo

Reflexiona

Elige una idea. Escribe acerca de la idea en el espacio de abajo.

- Piensa en lo que hiciste en la clase de matemáticas de hoy.
  Completa esta oración:

  Aprendí que _____.

- Escribe tu propio problema para que uses la suma. Luego pide a un compañero que resuelva el problema.

- Usa las palabras *sumandos* y *suma* para explicar cómo se resuelve este problema:

  12 + 23 = _____.

Nombre _____

Lección 3.1

Usar operaciones de dobles

Pregunta esencial ¿Cómo puedes usar operaciones de dobles para hallar la suma de operaciones de dobles cercanas?

Objetivo de aprendizaje Usarás operaciones de dobles para hallar la suma de otras operaciones.

Escucha y dibuja

Haz un dibujo para mostrar el problema. Luego escribe un enunciado de suma para el problema.

_____ carritos

PARA EL MAESTRO • Lea el siguiente problema y pida a los niños que hagan un dibujo del problema. Nathan tiene 6 carritos. Alisha le regala 6 carritos más. ¿Cuántos carritos tiene Nathan ahora? Después de que los niños escriban el enunciado de suma, pídales que mencionen otras operaciones de dobles que conozcan.

Charla matemática PRÁCTICAS Y PROCESOS MATEMÁTICOS 4

Representa Explica por qué decimos que $4 + 4 = 8$ es una operación de dobles.

Capítulo 3 ciento sesenta y tres **163**

Representa y dibuja

Puedes usar operaciones de dobles para hallar las sumas de otras operaciones.

$3 + 4 = ?$	$7 + 6 = ?$
↓	↓
$3 + 3 + 1 = ?$	$7 + 7 - 1 = ?$
$3 + 3 = 6$	$7 + 7 = 14$
$6 + 1 = 7$	$14 - 1 = 13$
Por lo tanto, $3 + 4 =$ _____.	Por lo tanto, $7 + 6 =$ _____.

Comparte y muestra

Escribe una operación de dobles que te sirva para hallar la suma. Escribe la suma.

1. $2 + 3 =$ _____

   ____ + ____ = ____

2. $4 + 5 =$ _____

   ____ + ____ = ____

3. $4 + 3 =$ _____

   ____ + ____ = ____

4. $6 + 7 =$ _____

   ____ + ____ = ____

5. $5 + 6 =$ _____

   ____ + ____ = ____

6. $8 + 7 =$ _____

   ____ + ____ = ____

Nombre _____

Por tu cuenta

Escribe una operación de dobles que te sirva para hallar la suma. Escribe la suma.

7. 5 + 4 = _____

____ + ____ = ____

8. 6 + 5 = _____

____ + ____ = ____

9. 6 + 7 = _____

____ + ____ = ____

10. 7 + 8 = _____

____ + ____ = ____

11. 8 + 9 = _____

____ + ____ = ____

12. 5 + 6 = _____

____ + ____ = ____

13. 7 + 6 = _____

____ + ____ = ____

14. 9 + 8 = _____

____ + ____ = ____

15. PIENSA MÁS El Sr. Norris escribió una operación de dobles. Tiene una suma mayor que 6. Los números que sumó son menores que 6. ¿Qué operación pudo haber escrito?

_____

Capítulo 3 • Lección 1

PRÁCTICAS Y PROCESOS MATEMÁTICOS • COMUNICAR • PERSEVERAR • CONSTRUIR ARGUMENTOS

Resolución de problemas • Aplicaciones  Matemáticas

Resuelve. Escribe o dibuja para explicar.

16. **PRÁCTICAS Y PROCESOS MATEMÁTICOS** **Analiza** Andrea tiene 8 botones rojos y 9 botones azules. ¿Cuántos botones tiene Andrea?

_____ botones

17. **MÁS AL DETALLE** Henry ve 3 conejos. Callie ve el doble de ese número de conejos. ¿Cuántos conejos más ve Callie que Henry?

_____ conejos más

18. **PIENSA MÁS** ¿Podrías usar la operación de dobles para hallar la suma de 4 + 5? Elige Sí o No.

4 + 4 = 8	○ Sí	○ No
5 + 5 = 10	○ Sí	○ No
9 + 9 = 18	○ Sí	○ No

 ACTIVIDAD PARA LA CASA • Pida a su niño que escriba tres operaciones de dobles con sumas menores que 17.

166 ciento sesenta y seis

Nombre _____

Usar operaciones de dobles

**Práctica y tarea
Lección 3.1**

Objetivo de aprendizaje Usarás operaciones de dobles para hallar la suma de otras operaciones.

Escribe una operación de dobles que puedas usar para hallar la suma. Escribe la suma.

1. $2 + 3 = $ ___

   ___ + ___ = ___

2. $7 + 6 = $ ___

   ___ + ___ = ___

3. $3 + 4 = $ ___

   ___ + ___ = ___

4. $8 + 9 = $ ___

   ___ + ___ = ___

Resolución de problemas · En el mundo

Resuelve. Escribe o dibuja la explicación.

5. Hay 4 hormigas en un tronco. Luego 5 hormigas trepan al tronco. ¿Cuántas hormigas hay en el tronco ahora?

   ____ hormigas

6. **Matemáticas** Dibuja o escribe para mostrar dos formas de usar operaciones de dobles para hallar 6 + 7.

   _____
   _____

Capítulo 3 · ciento sesenta y siete **167**

Repaso de la lección

1. Escribe una operación de dobles que puedas usar para hallar la suma. Escribe la suma.

    4 + 3 = ___

    ___ + ___ = ___

2. Escribe una operación de dobles que puedas usar para hallar la suma. Escribe la suma.

    6 + 7 = ___

    ___ + ___ = ___

Repaso en espiral

3. En la escuela de Lía hay 451 niños. ¿Qué número es mayor que 451?

    ___

4. ¿Qué número muestran estos bloques?

    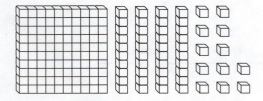

5. Escribe un número con el dígito 8 en el lugar de las decenas.

    ___

6. Encierra en un círculo la suma que es un número par.

    2 + 3 = 5
    3 + 4 = 7
    4 + 5 = 9
    6 + 6 = 12

Nombre _____

Practicar operaciones de suma

Pregunta esencial ¿De qué maneras se pueden recordar las sumas?

Lección 3.2

Objetivo de aprendizaje Usarás propiedades y estrategias matemáticas de cálculo mental para sumar y restar con fluidez números menores que 20.

Escucha y dibuja En el mundo

Haz dibujos para mostrar los problemas.

_____

_____

PARA EL MAESTRO • Lea los dos problemas siguientes. Pida a los niños que hagan un dibujo y que escriban un enunciado numérico para cada uno. El lunes, Tony vio 3 perros y 6 gatos. ¿Cuántos animales vio? El martes, Tony vio 6 perros y 3 gatos. ¿Cuántos animales vio?

PRÁCTICAS Y PROCESOS MATEMÁTICOS

Analiza Explica en qué se parecen los dos problemas. Explica en qué se diferencian.

Capítulo 3 ciento sesenta y nueve **169**

Representa y dibuja

Estas son maneras de recordar operaciones.

Puedes contar hacia adelante 1, 2 o 3.

6 + 1 = __7__
6 + 2 = __8__
6 + 3 = __9__

*Cambiar el orden de los **sumandos** no cambia la suma.*

__8__ = 2 + 6
__8__ = 6 + 2

Comparte y muestra

Escribe las sumas.

1. 4 + 4 = ___
   4 + 5 = ___

2. 5 + 0 = ___
   2 + 0 = ___

3. 3 + 8 = ___
   8 + 3 = ___

4. ___ = 5 + 5
   ___ = 5 + 4

5. 5 + 7 = ___
   7 + 5 = ___

6. ___ = 7 + 7
   ___ = 7 + 8

7. ___ = 3 + 7
   ___ = 7 + 3

8. 9 + 3 = ___
   3 + 9 = ___

9. ___ = 6 + 6
   ___ = 6 + 5

Nombre _____

Por tu cuenta

Escribe las sumas.

10. $7 + 1 = $ ___

    $1 + 7 = $ ___

11. ___ $= 4 + 0$

    ___ $= 9 + 0$

12. $5 + 5 = $ ___

    $5 + 4 = $ ___

13. $8 + 2 = $ ___

    $2 + 8 = $ ___

14. $3 + 3 = $ ___

    $3 + 4 = $ ___

15. $7 + 8 = $ ___

    $8 + 7 = $ ___

16. ___ $= 4 + 1$

    ___ $= 1 + 4$

17. $0 + 7 = $ ___

    $0 + 6 = $ ___

18. $8 + 8 = $ ___

    $8 + 9 = $ ___

19. $5 + 3 = $ ___

    $3 + 5 = $ ___

20. ___ $= 9 + 9$

    ___ $= 9 + 8$

21. $6 + 7 = $ ___

    $7 + 6 = $ ___

22. **PIENSA MÁS** Sam pintó 3 cuadros. Ellie pintó el doble que ese número de cuadros. ¿Cuántos cuadros pintaron en total?

_____ cuadros

Capítulo 3 • Lección 2

PRÁCTICAS Y PROCESOS MATEMÁTICOS ANALIZAR • BUSCAR ESTRUCTURAS • PRECISIÓN

Resolución de problemas • Aplicaciones

Resuelve. Escribe o dibuja para explicar.

23. **MÁS AL DETALLE** Chloe hace 8 dibujos. Reggie hace 1 dibujo más que Chloe. ¿Cuántos dibujos hacen en total?

_____ dibujos

24. **PRÁCTICAS Y PROCESOS MATEMÁTICOS** **Analiza** Joanne hizo 9 tazones de arcilla la semana pasada. Hizo el mismo número de tazones esta semana. ¿Cuántos tazones de arcilla hizo en las dos semanas?

_____ tazones de arcilla

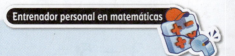

25. **PIENSA MÁS** Hay 9 pasas en el tazón. Devon coloca 8 pasas más. Completa el enunciado de suma para hallar cuántas pasas hay en el tazón ahora.

_____ + _____ = _____

_____ uvas pasas

ACTIVIDAD PARA LA CASA • Pida a su niño que escriba varias operaciones de suma que conozca.

Nombre _____

**Práctica y tarea
Lección 3.2**

Practicar operaciones de suma

Objetivo de aprendizaje Usarás propiedades y estrategias matemáticas de cálculo mental para sumar y restar con fluidez números menores que 20.

Escribe las sumas.

1. $9 + 1 = $ ___
   $1 + 9 = $ ___

2. $7 + 6 = $ ___
   $6 + 7 = $ ___

3. $8 + 0 = $ ___
   $5 + 0 = $ ___

4. ___ $= 7 + 9$
   ___ $= 9 + 7$

5. $4 + 4 = $ ___
   $4 + 5 = $ ___

6. $9 + 9 = $ ___
   $9 + 8 = $ ___

7. $8 + 8 = $ ___
   $8 + 7 = $ ___

8. $2 + 2 = $ ___
   $2 + 3 = $ ___

9. ___ $= 6 + 3$
   ___ $= 3 + 6$

10. $6 + 6 = $ ___
    $6 + 7 = $ ___

11. ___ $= 0 + 7$
    ___ $= 0 + 9$

12. $5 + 5 = $ ___
    $5 + 6 = $ ___

Resolución de problemas En el mundo

Resuelve. Escribe o dibuja para explicar.

13. Jason tiene 7 rompecabezas. Quincy tiene el mismo número de rompecabezas que Jason. ¿Cuántos rompecabezas tienen los dos?

    ____ rompecabezas

14. **ESCRIBE Matemáticas** Escribe o dibuja para explicar una forma de hallar las sumas: $6 + 7$, $8 + 4$, $2 + 9$.

    _____

Capítulo 3

Repaso de la lección

1. ¿Cuál es la suma?

   $8 + 7 =$ ___

2. ¿Cuál es la suma?

   $2 + 9 =$ ___

Repaso en espiral

3. Escribe otra manera de describir 43.

   ___ + ___

4. Escribe el número que es 100 más que 276.

   _____

5. Cuenta de diez en diez.

   20, 30, 40, ___, ___, ___

6. Escribe <, >, o = para comparar.

   127 ___ 142

174 ciento setenta y cuatro

Nombre _____

Álgebra • Formar una decena para sumar

Lección 3.3

Pregunta esencial ¿Cómo se usa la estrategia de formar una decena para hallar la suma?

Objetivo de aprendizaje Usarás la estrategia de *formar una decena* para hallar sumas.

Escucha y dibuja — En el mundo

Escribe la operación debajo del cuadro de diez cuando escuches el problema que coincida con el modelo.

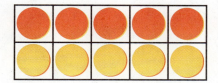
_____

_____

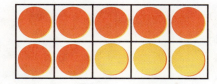
_____

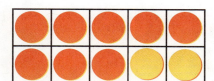
_____

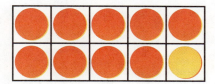
_____

PARA EL MAESTRO • Lea el siguiente problema. Hay 6 perros grandes y 4 perros pequeños. ¿Cuántos perros hay en total? Pida a los niños que hallen el cuadro de diez que represente el problema y escriban el enunciado de suma. Repita el problema con cada operación de suma que representan los otros cuadros de diez.

Charla matemática

PRÁCTICAS Y PROCESOS MATEMÁTICOS 7

Buscar estructuras
Describe el patrón que ves en estas operaciones para formar una decena.

Capítulo 3

ciento setenta y cinco **175**

Representa y dibuja

7 + 5 = ?

Debes sumar 3 y 7 para formar una decena. Separa 5 en 3 y 2.

7 + 5
7 + 3 + 2
10 + 2 = __12__

Por lo tanto, 7 + 5 = _____.

Comparte y muestra

Muestra cómo formar una decena para hallar la suma. Escribe la suma.

1. 8 + 3 = _____
   2 1
   10 + ____ = ____

2. 2 + 9 = _____
   1 1
   10 + ____ = ____

3. 8 + 5 = _____
   10 + ____ = ____

4. 4 + 7 = _____
   10 + ____ = ____

5. 3 + 9 = _____
   10 + ____ = ____

6. 7 + 6 = _____
   10 + ____ = ____

Nombre _____

Por tu cuenta

Muestra cómo formar una decena para hallar la suma. Escribe la suma.

7. 4 + 9 = ____
    3 1
    10 + ____ = ____

8. 9 + 8 = ____
    1 7
    10 + ____ = ____

9. 8 + 6 = ____

    10 + ____ = ____

10. 5 + 9 = ____

    10 + ____ = ____

11. 7 + 9 = ____

    10 + ____ = ____

12. 8 + 4 = ____

    10 + ____ = ____

13. **MÁS AL DETALLE** Álex está pensando en una operación de dobles. Tiene una suma mayor que la suma de 7 + 7 pero menor que la suma de 8 + 9. ¿En qué operación está pensando Álex?

    ____ + ____ = ____

14. **PIENSA MÁS** Hay 5 abejas en una colmena. ¿Cuántas abejas más tienen que entrar en la colmena para que haya 14 en total?

    ____ abejas más

Capítulo 3 • Lección 3   ciento setenta y siete **177**

Resolución de problemas • Aplicaciones

Resuelve. Escribe o dibuja para explicar.

15. Analiza Hay 9 bicicletas grandes en la tienda. Hay 6 bicicletas pequeñas en la tienda. ¿Cuántas bicicletas hay en la tienda?

_____ bicicletas

16. Max está pensando en una operación de dobles. Tiene una suma mayor que la suma de 6 + 4 pero menor que la suma de 8 + 5. ¿En qué operación está pensando Max?

_____ + _____ = _____

17. Natasha tiene 8 caracoles. Luego encuentra 5 caracoles más. Haz un dibujo para mostrar cómo hallar el total de caracoles que tiene.

¿Cuántos caracoles tiene ahora? _____ caracoles

ACTIVIDAD PARA LA CASA • Pida a su niño que diga pares de números que tengan una suma de 10. Luego pídale que escriba los enunciados de suma.

Nombre _____

**Práctica y tarea
Lección 3.3**

Álgebra • Formar una decena para sumar

Objetivo de aprendizaje Usarás la estrategia de *formar una decena* para hallar sumas.

Muestra cómo formar una decena para hallar la suma. Escribe la suma.

1. $9 + 7 =$ ___

    $10 +$ ___ $=$ ___

2. $8 + 5 =$ ___

    $10 +$ ___ $=$ ___

3. $8 + 6 =$ ___

    $10 +$ ___ $=$ ___

4. $3 + 9 =$ ___

    $10 +$ ___ $=$ ___

5. $8 + 7 =$ ___

    $10 +$ ___ $=$ ___

6. $6 + 5 =$ ___

    $10 +$ ___ $=$ ___

Resolución de problemas · En el mundo

Resuelve. Escribe o dibuja para explicar.

7. Hay 9 niños en el autobús. Luego suben 8 niños más al autobús. ¿Cuántos niños hay en el autobús ahora?

    ___ niños

8. **ESCRIBE Matemáticas** Describe cómo puedes usar la estrategia de formar una decena para hallar la suma de 7 + 9.

Capítulo 3

ciento setenta y nueve **179**

Repaso de la lección

1. Encierra en un círculo la operación que tenga la misma suma que 8 + 7.

   10 + 3
   10 + 4
   10 + 5
   10 + 6

2. Escribe una operación que tenga la misma suma que 7 + 5.

   ___ + ___

Repaso en espiral

3. Escribe el número que se muestra como 200 + 10 + 7.

   ___

4. Encierra en un círculo el número impar.

   2   4   6   7

5. ¿Cuál es el valor del dígito subrayado?

   6<u>5</u>

   ___

6. ¿Cuál es otra manera de escribir el número 47?

   ___ decenas ___ unidades

Nombre _____

Álgebra • Sumar 3 sumandos

Pregunta esencial ¿Cómo sumas tres números?

Lección 3.4

Objetivo de aprendizaje Usarás las propiedades de la suma para sumar tres números.

Escucha y dibuja

Escribe la suma de cada par de sumandos.

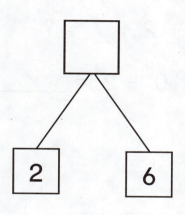
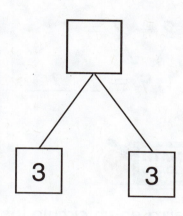
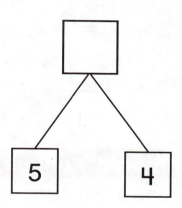

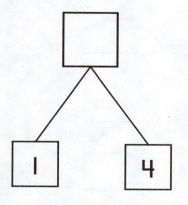
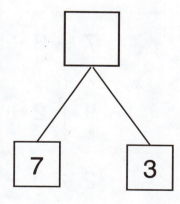
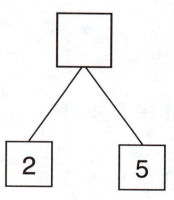

PARA EL MAESTRO • Después de que los niños anoten la suma de cada par de sumandos, pídales que compartan sus resultados y comenten las estrategias que usaron.

PRÁCTICAS Y PROCESOS MATEMÁTICOS

Describe cómo hallaste la suma de 5 y 4.

Capítulo 3

ciento ochenta y uno **181**

Representa y dibuja

Puedes agrupar números de diferentes maneras para sumar.

Elige dos sumandos.
Busca operaciones que conozcas.

Cambiar la manera en que los números están agrupados no cambia la suma.

3 + 2 + 7 = ?
5 + 7 = __12__

3 + 2 + 7 = ?
3 + 9 = _____

3 + 2 + 7 = ?
10 + 2 = _____

Comparte y muestra

Resuelve de dos maneras. Encierra en un círculo los dos sumandos que sumas primero.

1. 1 + 8 + 2 = _____   1 + 8 + 2 = _____

2. 7 + 3 + 3 = _____   7 + 3 + 3 = _____

3. 4 + 2 + 4 = _____   4 + 2 + 4 = _____

4. 2 + 8 + 2 = _____   2 + 8 + 2 = _____

5. 3   3
    2   2
  + 6   + 6

6. 7   7
    0   0
  + 2   + 2

182 ciento ochenta y dos

Nombre _____

Por tu cuenta

Resuelve de dos maneras. Encierra en un círculo los dos sumandos que sumas primero.

7. $4 + 1 + 6 =$ _____ $4 + 1 + 6 =$ _____

8. $4 + 3 + 3 =$ _____ $4 + 3 + 3 =$ _____

9. $1 + 5 + 3 =$ _____ $1 + 5 + 3 =$ _____

10. $6 + 4 + 4 =$ _____ $6 + 4 + 4 =$ _____

11. $5 + 5 + 5 =$ _____ $5 + 5 + 5 =$ _____

12. $7 + 0 + 6 =$ _____ $7 + 0 + 6 =$ _____

13.   5   5
      3   3
    + 4   + 4

14.   4   4
      2   2
    + 5   + 5

PRÁCTICAS Y PROCESOS MATEMÁTICOS 7 Busca una estructura

Escribe el sumando que falta.

15.   5
      5
    + ☐
    ―――
     14

16.   4
      ☐
    + 4
    ―――
     12

17.   3
      ☐
    + 7
    ―――
     11

18.   5
      3
    + ☐
    ―――
     13

Capítulo 3 • Lección 4

PRÁCTICAS Y PROCESOS MATEMÁTICOS   COMUNICAR • PERSEVERAR • CONSTRUIR ARGUMENTOS

Resolución de problemas • Aplicaciones En el mundo

ESCRIBE Matemáticas

Elige una manera de resolver.
Escribe o dibuja para explicar.

19. **PIENSA MÁS** Nick, Alex y Sophia comen 15 pasas en total. Nick y Alex comen 4 pasas cada uno. ¿Cuántas pasas come Sophia?

_____ pasas

20. **PRÁCTICAS Y PROCESOS MATEMÁTICOS 1** **Analiza**
Hay 5 uvas verdes y 4 uvas rojas en un tazón. Eli pone 4 uvas más en el tazón. ¿Cuántas uvas hay en el tazón ahora?

_____ uvas

21. **PIENSA MÁS** La Sra. Moore compró 4 manzanas pequeñas, 6 manzanas medianas y 3 manzanas grandes. ¿Cuántas manzanas compró?

_____ manzanas

ACTIVIDAD PARA LA CASA • Pida a su niño que describa dos maneras de sumar 3, 6 y 2.

184   ciento ochenta y cuatro

Nombre _____

Álgebra • Sumar 3 sumandos

**Práctica y tarea
Lección 3.4**

Objetivo de aprendizaje Usarás las propiedades de la suma para sumar tres números.

Resuelve de dos maneras. Encierra en un círculo los dos sumandos que sumas primero.

1. $2 + 3 + 7 =$ ___　　　　$2 + 3 + 7 =$ ___

2. $5 + 3 + 3 =$ ___　　　　$5 + 3 + 3 =$ ___

3. $4 + 5 + 4 =$ ___　　　　$4 + 5 + 4 =$ ___

4.　　5　　　　　5
　　　4　　　　　4
　　+ 5　　　　+ 5

5.　　6　　　　　6
　　　3　　　　　3
　　+ 4　　　　+ 4

Resolución de problemas

Elige una manera de resolver. Escribe o dibuja para explicar.

6. Amber tiene 2 crayones rojos, 5 crayones azules y 4 crayones amarillos. ¿Cuántos crayones tiene en total?

_____ crayones

7. ESCRIBE Matemáticas Escribe o dibuja para explicar dos formas de hallar la suma de $3 + 4 + 5$.

_____

Capítulo 3　　　　　　　　　　　　ciento ochenta y cinco **185**

Repaso de la lección

1. ¿Cuál es la suma de 2 + 4 + 6?

   _____

2. ¿Cuál es la suma de 5 + 4 + 2?

   _____

Repaso en espiral

3. Escribe >, < o = para comparar.

   688 ____ 648

4. ¿Qué número puede escribirse como 4 decenas, 2 unidades?

   _____

5. ¿Qué número tiene el mismo valor que 50 decenas?

   _____

6. ¿Cuál es el siguiente número del patrón?

   420, 520, 620, 720, _____

Álgebra • Relacionar la suma y la resta

Lección 3.5

Pregunta esencial ¿Cómo se relacionan la suma y la resta?

Objetivo de aprendizaje Usarás una operación de suma para hallar la diferencia en una operación de resta relacionada.

Escucha y dibuja En el mundo

Completa el modelo de barras para mostrar el problema.

| 8 | 7 |

_____

_____ pelotas de fútbol

| _____ | 7 |

15

_____ pelotas de fútbol

PARA EL MAESTRO • Lea los siguientes problemas. Pida a los niños que completen el modelo de barras de cada uno. El equipo de fútbol tiene 8 pelotas rojas y 7 pelotas amarillas. ¿Cuántas pelotas de fútbol tiene el equipo? El equipo de fútbol tiene 15 pelotas en el vestuario. Los niños sacaron las 7 pelotas amarillas para el campo. ¿Cuántas pelotas de fútbol quedan adentro?

PRÁCTICAS Y PROCESOS MATEMÁTICOS 6

Explica en qué se parecen y en qué se diferencian los modelos de barras.

Capítulo 3

ciento ochenta y siete **187**

Representa y dibuja

Puedes usar operaciones de suma para recordar **diferencias**. Las operaciones relacionadas tienen las mismas partes y el mismo entero.

Piensa en los sumandos de una operación de suma para hallar la diferencia en una operación de resta relacionada.

6	7

13

6 + 7 = 13

___	7

13

13 − 7 = ___

Comparte y muestra

Escribe la suma y la diferencia de las operaciones relacionadas.

1. 5 + 4 = ___
   9 − 4 = ___

2. 2 + 7 = ___
   9 − 2 = ___

3. 3 + 8 = ___
   11 − 8 = ___

4. 5 + 8 = ___
   13 − 5 = ___

5. ___ = 1 + 8
   ___ = 9 − 1

6. 9 + 9 = ___
   18 − 9 = ___

7. ___ = 8 + 7
   ___ = 15 − 8

8. 4 + 7 = ___
   11 − 7 = ___

9. 7 + 5 = ___
   12 − 7 = ___

Nombre _____

Por tu cuenta

Escribe la suma y la diferencia de las operaciones relacionadas.

10. $4 + 3 = \_\_\_$
    $7 - 3 = \_\_\_$

11. $2 + 6 = \_\_\_$
    $8 - 6 = \_\_\_$

12. $6 + 4 = \_\_\_$
    $10 - 6 = \_\_\_$

13. $7 + 3 = \_\_\_$
    $10 - 7 = \_\_\_$

14. $8 + 6 = \_\_\_$
    $14 - 6 = \_\_\_$

15. $\_\_\_ = 3 + 9$
    $\_\_\_ = 12 - 9$

16. $6 + 5 = \_\_\_$
    $11 - 5 = \_\_\_$

17. $7 + 7 = \_\_\_$
    $14 - 7 = \_\_\_$

18. $9 + 6 = \_\_\_$
    $15 - 9 = \_\_\_$

19. $5 + 9 = \_\_\_$
    $14 - 9 = \_\_\_$

20. $\_\_\_ = 4 + 8$
    $\_\_\_ = 12 - 4$

21. $9 + 7 = \_\_\_$
    $16 - 7 = \_\_\_$

PRÁCTICAS Y PROCESOS MATEMÁTICOS 6 Haz conexiones

Escribe una operación de resta relacionada para cada operación de suma.

22. $7 + 8 = 15$

    _____

23. $5 + 7 = 12$

    _____

24. $6 + 7 = 13$

    _____

25. $9 + 8 = 17$

    _____

Capítulo 3 • Lección 5   ciento ochenta y nueve **189**

PRÁCTICAS Y PROCESOS MATEMÁTICOS • ANALIZAR • BUSCAR ESTRUCTURAS • PRECISIÓN

Resolución de problemas • Aplicaciones

 ESCRIBE Matemáticas

Resuelve. Escribe o dibuja para explicar.

26. Trevor tiene 7 cometas. Pam tiene 4 cometas. ¿Cuántas cometas más que Pam tiene Trevor?

_____ cometas más

27. **PIENSA MÁS** El Sr. Sims tiene una bolsa de 7 peras y otra bolsa de 6 peras. Su familia come 5 peras. ¿Cuántas peras quedan?

_____ peras

28. **PIENSA MÁS** Elin cuenta 7 gansos en el agua y otros en la orilla. Hay 16 gansos en total. Haz un dibujo para mostrar los dos grupos de gansos.

Escribe un enunciado numérico que te ayude a hallar cuántos gansos hay en total en la orilla.

_____

¿Cuántos gansos hay en la orilla? _____ gansos

 ACTIVIDAD PARA LA CASA • Pida a su niño que le diga algunas operaciones de resta que conozca bien.

Nombre _____

Práctica y tarea
Lección 3.5

Álgebra • Relacionar la suma y la resta

Objetivo de aprendizaje Usarás una operación de suma para hallar la diferencia en una operación de resta relacionada.

Escribe la suma y la diferencia de las operaciones relacionadas.

1. $9 + 6 =$ ___
   $15 - 6 =$ ___

2. $8 + 5 =$ ___
   $13 - 5 =$ ___

3. $9 + 9 =$ ___
   $18 - 9 =$ ___

4. $7 + 3 =$ ___
   $10 - 3 =$ ___

5. $7 + 5 =$ ___
   $12 - 5 =$ ___

6. $6 + 8 =$ ___
   $14 - 6 =$ ___

7. $6 + 7 =$ ___
   $13 - 6 =$ ___

8. $8 + 8 =$ ___
   $16 - 8 =$ ___

9. $6 + 4 =$ ___
   $10 - 4 =$ ___

Resolución de problemas

Resuelve. Escribe o dibuja para explicar.

10. Hay 13 niños en el autobús. Luego bajan 5 niños del autobús. ¿Cuántos niños hay en el autobús ahora?

    ____ niños

11. ESCRIBE Matemáticas Escribe una operación de resta relacionada para $9 + 3 = 12$. Explica qué relación hay entre las dos operaciones.

_____

Repaso de la lección

1. Escribe una operación de suma relacionada para $15 - 6 = 9$.

   ___ + ___ = ___

2. Escribe una operación de resta relacionada para $5 + 7 = 12$.

   ___ − ___ = ___

Repaso en espiral

3. ¿Cuál es otra manera de escribir 4 centenas?

   ___

4. ¿Cuál es el siguiente número del patrón?

   515, 615, 715, 815, ___

5. ¿Qué número tiene 10 más que 237?

   ___

6. Escribe el número 110 en centenas y decenas.

   ___ + ___

Nombre _____

Practicar operaciones de resta

Pregunta esencial ¿De qué maneras se pueden recordar las diferencias?

Lección 3.6

Objetivo de aprendizaje Hallarás las diferencias al usar una operación de suma relacionada o contar hacia atrás de 1 en 1, de 2 en 2 o de 3 en 3.

 Escucha y dibuja En el mundo

Usa el modelo de Gina para responder la pregunta.

Modelo de Gina

_____   _____

PARA EL MAESTRO • Diga a los niños que Gina puso 4 fichas cuadradas de colores dentro del círculo y luego puso 3 fichas cuadradas de colores fuera del círculo. Luego pregunte: ¿Qué operación de suma podría escribirse para el modelo de Gina? Repita con problemas para las tres operaciones que están relacionadas con esta operación de suma.

 Charla matemática

PRÁCTICAS Y PROCESOS MATEMÁTICOS 3

Compara estrategias
Explica cómo se relacionan las diferentes operaciones del modelo de Gina.

Capítulo 3   ciento noventa y tres **193**

Representa y dibuja

Estas son algunas maneras de hallar diferencias.

Puedes contar hacia atrás de 1 en 1, de 2 en 2 o de 3 en 3.

7 − 2 = ___

Comienza con 7. Di 6, 5.

9 − 3 = ___

Comienza con 9. Di 8, 7, 6.

Puedes pensar en el sumando que falta para restar.

8 − 5 = $5 + 3 = 8$

Por lo tanto, 8 − 5 = ___.

Comparte y muestra

Escribe la diferencia.

1. 6 − 4 = ___
2. 10 − 7 = ___
3. ___ = 5 − 2
4. 14 − 6 = ___
5. ___ = 8 − 4
6. 11 − 3 = ___
7. ___ = 7 − 5
8. 10 − 4 = ___
9. 5 − 0 = ___
10. 13 − 9 = ___
11. 9 − 3 = ___
12. ___ = 7 − 6
13. 12 − 3 = ___
14. 6 − 3 = ___
15. 9 − 5 = ___
16. 10 − 6 = ___
17. ___ = 8 − 3
18. 13 − 5 = ___

Nombre _____

Por tu cuenta

Escribe la diferencia.

19. $11 - 2 = $ ___
20. $9 - 7 = $ ___
21. ___ $= 7 - 4$

22. $12 - 5 = $ ___
23. $8 - 6 = $ ___
24. ___ $= 7 - 0$

25. ___ $= 10 - 5$
26. $15 - 8 = $ ___
27. $13 - 7 = $ ___

28. $10 - 8 = $ ___
29. $8 - 5 = $ ___
30. ___ $= 9 - 6$

31. ___ $= 9 - 4$
32. $11 - 8 = $ ___
33. $12 - 7 = $ ___

34. **PIENSA MÁS**

Escribe las diferencias. Luego escribe la siguiente operación del patrón.

$10 - 1 = $ ___
$8 - 1 = $ ___
$6 - 1 = $ ___
$4 - 1 = $ ___

_____

$12 - 9 = $ ___
$13 - 9 = $ ___
$14 - 9 = $ ___
$15 - 9 = $ ___

_____

$18 - 9 = $ ___
$17 - 8 = $ ___
$16 - 7 = $ ___
$15 - 6 = $ ___

_____

ACTIVIDAD PARA LA CASA • Practique en voz alta las operaciones de resta de esta lección con su niño.

Capítulo 3 • Lección 6

Nombre _____

✓ Revisión de la mitad del capítulo

Conceptos y destrezas

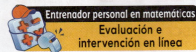

Escribe la suma.

1. 3 + 6 = ____
2. 8 + 0 = ____
3. 7 + 7 = ____

4. 9 + 4 = ____
5. ____ = 5 + 6
6. 2 + 8 = ____

7. 3 + 7 + 2 = ____
8. 4 + 4 + 6 = ____

Muestra cómo formar una decena para hallar la suma.
Escribe la suma.

9. 9 + 7 = ____

10. 6 + 8 = ____

10 + ____ = ____

10 + ____ = ____

Escribe la suma y la diferencia de las operaciones relacionadas.

11. 5 + 4 = ____
    9 − 4 = ____

12. 3 + 9 = ____
    12 − 9 = ____

13. 8 + 7 = ____
    15 − 8 = ____

14. **PIENSA MÁS** Lily tiene 6 carritos de juguete y Yong tiene 5 carritos de juguete. ¿Cuántos carritos de juguete tienen en total?

____ carritos de juguete

196 ciento noventa y seis

Nombre _____

Practicar operaciones de resta

Práctica y tarea
Lección 3.6

Objetivo de aprendizaje Hallarás las diferencias al usar una operación de suma relacionada o contar hacia atrás de 1 en 1, de 2 en 2 o de 3 en 3.

Escribe la diferencia.

1. $15 - 9 =$ ___
2. $13 - 8 =$ ___
3. ___ $- 13 = 5$

4. $14 - 7 =$ ___
5. $10 - 8 =$ ___
6. $12 - 7 =$ ___

7. ___ $- 10 = 7$
8. $16 - 7 =$ ___
9. $8 - 4 =$ ___

10. $11 - 5 =$ ___
11. $13 - 6 =$ ___
12. ___ $- 12 = 9$

13. $16 - 9 =$ ___
14. ___ $- 11 = 9$
15. $12 - 8 =$ ___

Resolución de problemas

Resuelve. Escribe o dibuja para explicar.

16. El maestro Li tiene 16 lápices. Les da 9 lápices a algunos estudiantes. ¿Cuántos lápices tiene el maestro Li ahora?

    ___ lápices

17. **ESCRIBE Matemáticas** Escribe o dibuja para explicar dos formas distintas de hallar la diferencia de $12 - 3$.

Repaso de la lección

1. Escribe la diferencia.

    13 − 6 = ___

2. Escribe la diferencia.

    12 − 3 = ___

Repaso en espiral

3. ¿Cuál es el valor del dígito subrayado?

    6<u>2</u>5

    ___

4. Cuenta de cinco en cinco.

    405, ___, ___, ___

5. Devin tiene 39 bloques. ¿Cuál es el valor del dígito 9 en este número?

    ___

6. ¿Qué número tiene el mismo valor que 20 decenas?

    ___

Nombre _____

Lección 3.7

Restar usando una decena

Pregunta esencial ¿Por qué es más fácil hallar diferencias si se obtiene 10 en una resta?

Objetivo de aprendizaje Hallarás la diferencia en una recta numérica al obtener 10 y luego usar una operación de decenas.

Escucha y dibuja En el mundo

Encierra en un círculo la cantidad que restas en cada problema.

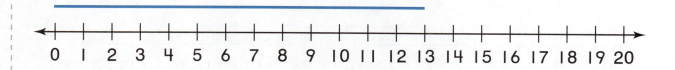

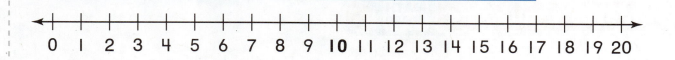

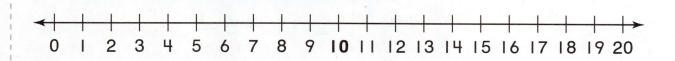

PARA EL MAESTRO • Lea el siguiente problema. Deveron tiene 13 crayones. Le da 3 crayones a Tyler. ¿Cuántos crayones tiene Deveron ahora? Pida a los niños que encierren en un círculo la parte del segmento de recta azul que muestre lo que se resta del entero. Repita la actividad con dos problemas más.

Busca estructuras
Describe un patrón de los tres problemas y sus respuestas.

PRÁCTICAS Y PROCESOS MATEMÁTICOS 7

Capítulo 3

ciento noventa y nueve **199**

Representa y dibuja

Puedes restar por pasos para hacer una operación con decenas.

14 − 6 = ?
     4 2

Resta por pasos:
14 − 4 = 10
10 − 2 = 8

− 2   − 4

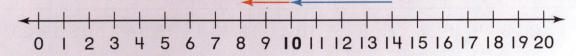

Por lo tanto, 14 − 6 = __8__.

Comparte y muestra

Muestra la operación con decenas que hiciste. Escribe la diferencia.

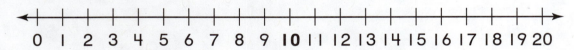

1. 12 − 5 = ____
    2 3

10 − ____ = ____

2. 11 − 6 = ____
    1 5

10 − ____ = ____

3. 15 − 7 = ____

10 − ____ = ____

4. 13 − 7 = ____

10 − ____ = ____

Nombre _____

Por tu cuenta

Muestra la operación con decenas que hiciste. Escribe la diferencia.

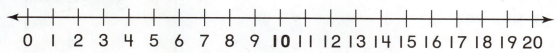

5. 13 − 5 = ____
   3 2
   10 − ____ = ____

6. 15 − 6 = ____
   5 1
   10 − ____ = ____

7. 12 − 8 = ____

   10 − ____ = ____

8. 14 − 8 = ____

   10 − ____ = ____

9. PIENSA MÁS Chris tenía 15 adhesivos. Dio a Ann y Suzy el mismo número de adhesivos. Ahora Chris tiene 7 adhesivos. ¿Cuántos adhesivos dio a cada niña?

____ adhesivos

Resuelve. Escribe o dibuja para explicar.

10. PIENSA MÁS Beth tiene una caja de 16 crayones. Le da 3 crayones a Jake y 7 crayones a Wendy. ¿Cuántos crayones tiene Beth ahora?

____ crayones

Capítulo 3 • Lección 7   doscientos uno **201**

Resolución de problemas • Aplicaciones

MÁS AL DETALLE Escribe enunciados numéricos que tienen tanto suma como resta. Usa cada opción solo una vez.

Opciones:
~~9 − 2~~
~~3 + 4~~
1 + 4
14 − 6
5 + 4
15 − 6
10 − 5
4 + 4

11. $9 - 2 = 3 + 4$
    $\quad\; 7 \;\; = \;\; 7$

12. _____ = _____

13. _____ = _____

14. _____ = _____

15. **PIENSA MÁS** ¿Tiene el enunciado numérico la misma diferencia que $15 - 7 = \blacksquare$? Elige Sí o No.

	Sí	No
$10 - 6 = \blacksquare$	○	○
$10 - 2 = \blacksquare$	○	○
$10 - 4 = \blacksquare$	○	○

ACTIVIDAD PARA LA CASA • Pida a su niño que diga pares de números que tengan una diferencia de 10. Luego pídale que escriba los enunciados numéricos.

Nombre _____

Restar usando una decena

**Práctica y tarea
Lección 3.7**

Objetivo de aprendizaje Hallarás la diferencia en una recta numérica al obtener 10 y luego usar una operación de decenas.

Muestra la operación con decenas que usaste. Escribe la diferencia.

1. 14 − 6 = ___

   10 − ___ = ___

2. 12 − 7 = ___

   10 − ___ = ___

3. 13 − 7 = ___

   10 − ___ = ___

4. 15 − 8 = ___

   10 − ___ = ___

Resolución de problemas

Resuelve. Escribe o dibuja la explicación.

5. Carl leyó 15 páginas el lunes en la noche y 9 páginas el martes en la noche. ¿Cuántas páginas más leyó el lunes en la noche que el martes en la noche?

   ___ páginas más

6. **ESCRIBE Matemáticas** Describe cómo usar una operación con decenas para hallar la diferencia de 15−8.

   _____

Capítulo 3   doscientos tres **203**

Repaso de la lección

1. Muestra la operación de decenas que usaste.
   Escribe la diferencia.

   $12 - 6 =$ ___
   $10 - 4 =$ ___

2. Muestra la operación de decenas que usaste.
   Escribe la diferencia.

   $13 - 8 =$ ___
   $10 - 5 =$ ___

Repaso en espiral

3. Escribe una operación de resta relacionada para $7 + 3 = 10$.

   _____

4. Joe tiene 8 camioncitos. Carmen tiene 1 camioncito más que Joe. ¿Cuántos camioncitos tienen los dos en total?

   ____

5. Hay 276 personas en el avión. Escribe un número que sea mayor que 276.

   ____

6. Escribe >, < o = para comparar.

   537 ____ 375

Nombre _____

Álgebra • Hacer dibujos para representar problemas

Lección 3.8

Pregunta esencial ¿Cómo se usan los modelos de barras para mostrar problemas de suma y de resta?

Objetivo de aprendizaje Usarás dibujos y enunciados numéricos para representar y resolver problemas de suma y resta.

Escucha y dibuja En el mundo

Completa el modelo de barras para mostrar el problema.
Completa el enunciado numérico para resolver.

_____ + _____ = _____   _____ monedas de 1¢

_____ − _____ = _____   _____ monedas de 1¢

PARA EL MAESTRO • Lea cada problema y pida a los niños que completen los modelos de barras. Hailey tiene 5 monedas de 1¢ en el bolsillo y 7 monedas de 1¢ en la cartera. ¿Cuántas monedas de 1¢ tiene en total? Blake tiene 12 monedas de 1¢ en su alcancía. Le da 5 monedas de 1¢ a su hermana. ¿Cuántas monedas de 1¢ tiene ahora?

Charla matemática

PRÁCTICAS Y PROCESOS MATEMÁTICOS 6

Explica en qué se parecen y en qué se diferencian los problemas.

Capítulo 3

Representa y dibuja

Puedes usar modelos de barras para mostrar problemas.

Ben come 14 galletas. Ron come 6 galletas. ¿Cuántas galletas más que Ron come Ben?

14 − 6 = 8

_____ galletas más

Suzy tenía 14 galletas. Le dio 6 galletas a Grace. ¿Cuántas galletas tiene Suzy ahora?

_____

_____ galletas

Comparte y muestra

Completa el modelo de barras. Luego escribe un enunciado numérico para resolver.

1. El Sr. James compró 15 rosquillas simples y 9 rosquillas con pasas. ¿Cuántas rosquillas simples más que rosquillas con pasas compró?

_____

_____ rosquillas simples más

206 doscientos seis

Nombre _____

Por tu cuenta

Completa el modelo de barras. Luego escribe un enunciado numérico para resolver.

2. Cole tiene 5 libros sobre perros y 6 libros sobre gatos. ¿Cuántos libros tiene Cole?

| 5 | 6 |

_____

_____ libros

3. **PIENSA MÁS** Anne tiene 16 clips azules y 9 clips rojos. ¿Cuántos clips azules más que clips rojos tiene?

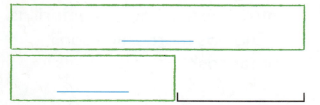

_____

_____ clips azules más

4. **MÁS AL DETALLE** Completa los espacios en blanco. Luego rotula el modelo de barras y resuelve. La señorita Gore tenía 18 lápices.
Le dio ____ lápices a Erin.
¿Cuántos lápices tiene la señorita Gore ahora?

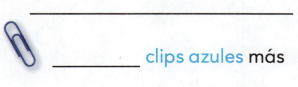

_____ lápices

Capítulo 3 • Lección 8   doscientos siete **207**

PRÁCTICAS Y PROCESOS MATEMÁTICOS • COMUNICAR • PERSEVERAR • CONSTRUIR ARGUMENTOS

Resolución de problemas • Aplicaciones

Usa la información de la tabla para resolver. Escribe o dibuja para explicar.

Flores que recogió Jenna	
Flores	Número
rosas	6
tulipanes	8
margaritas	11

5. Jenna pone todas las rosas y los tulipanes en un florero. ¿Cuántas flores puso en el florero?

   _____ flores

6. **PIENSA MÁS** Cuatro de las margaritas son blancas. Las otras margaritas son amarillas. ¿Cuántas margaritas son amarillas?

   _____ margaritas amarillas

7. **PIENSA MÁS** Rita cuenta 4 ranas en la hierba y otras en el agua. Hay 10 ranas en total. ¿Cuántas ranas hay en el agua? Haz un dibujo y escribe un enunciado numérico para resolver.

   _____

   _____ ranas están en el agua.

 ACTIVIDAD PARA LA CASA • Pida a su niño que describa lo que aprendió en esta lección.

**Práctica y tarea
Lección 3.8**

Álgebra • Hacer dibujos para representar problemas

Objetivo de aprendizaje Usarás dibujos y enunciados numéricos para representar y resolver problemas de suma y resta.

Completa el modelo de barras. Luego escribe un enunciado numérico para resolver.

1. Adam tiene 12 camioncitos. Le regala 4 camioncitos a Ed. ¿Cuántos camioncitos tiene Adam ahora?

   _____

   _____ camioncitos

2. La abuela tiene 14 rosas rojas y 7 rosas rosadas. ¿Cuántas rosas rojas más que rosas rosadas tiene?

   _____

   _____ rosas rojas más

3. ESCRIBE Matemáticas Explica cómo usaste el modelo de barras para resolver el problema del Ejercicio 2.

Capítulo 3

doscientos nueve 209

Repaso de la lección

1. Completa el modelo de barras. Luego resuelve. Abby tiene 16 uvas. Jason tiene 9 uvas. ¿Cuántas uvas más que Jason tiene Abby?

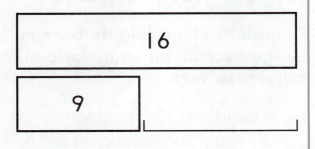

_____ uvas más

Repaso en espiral

2. Escribe una operación de resta que tenga la misma diferencia que 16 − 7.

   _____

3. ¿Cuál es la diferencia?

   $18 - 9 =$ _____

4. ¿Cuál es otra manera de escribir 300 + 20 + 5?

   _____

5. ¿Cuál es el valor del dígito subrayado?

   2$\underline{8}$

   _____

Nombre _____

Álgebra • Usar ecuaciones para representar problemas

Pregunta esencial ¿Cómo se usan los enunciados numéricos para mostrar situaciones de suma y resta?

Lección 3.9

Objetivo de aprendizaje Escribirás enunciados numéricos con un símbolo para el número que falta al representar problemas de suma y resta.

Escucha y dibuja En el mundo

Escribe un problema que pueda resolverse con este modelo de barras.

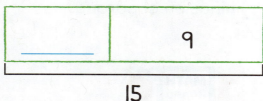

_____
_____
_____
_____
_____

PARA EL MAESTRO • Comente con los niños cómo puede usarse este modelo de barras para representar una situación de suma o resta.

Charla matemática

PRÁCTICAS Y PROCESOS MATEMÁTICOS 2

¿Deberías sumar o restar para resolver tu problema? **Explica.**

Capítulo 3

doscientos once **211**

Representa y dibuja

Un problema puede representarse con un enunciado numérico.

Había varias niñas y 4 niños en el parque. Había 9 niños y niñas en total. ¿Cuántas niñas había en el parque?

 $+ 4 = 9$

Piensa: $5 + 4 = 9$

> El ▢ es un marcador de posición para el número que falta.

Por lo tanto, había __5__ niñas en el parque.

Comparte y muestra

Escribe un enunciado numérico para el problema. Usa un ▢ para el número que falta. Luego resuelve.

1. Había 14 hormigas en la acera. Luego 6 hormigas se fueron al césped. ¿Cuántas hormigas quedaron en la acera?

   _____

   _____ hormigas

2. Había 7 perros grandes y 4 perros pequeños en el parque. ¿Cuántos perros había en el parque?

   _____

   _____ perros

Nombre _____

Por tu cuenta

Escribe un enunciado numérico para el problema.
Usa un ▢ para el número que falta. Luego resuelve.

3. Un grupo de niños estaba volando 13 cometas. Algunas cometas se guardaron. Luego los niños estaban volando 7 cometas. ¿Cuántas cometas se guardaron?

_____

_____ cometas

4. Hay 18 niños en el campo. 9 de los niños están jugando fútbol. ¿Cuántos niños no están jugando fútbol?

_____

_____ niños

5. PRÁCTICAS Y PROCESOS MATEMÁTICOS ② **Usa razonamiento**
Mathew encontró 9 bellotas. Greg encontró 6 bellotas. ¿Cuántas bellotas encontraron ambos niños?

_____

_____ bellotas

6. PIENSA MÁS Había algunos patos en un estanque. Llegaron cuatro patos más. Entonces había 12 patos en el estanque. ¿Cuántos patos había en el estanque al comienzo?

_____

_____ patos

Capítulo 3 • Lección 9

PRÁCTICAS Y PROCESOS MATEMÁTICOS • ANALIZAR • BUSCAR ESTRUCTURAS • PRECISIÓN

Resolución de problemas • Aplicaciones

Lee el problema. Escribe o dibuja para mostrar cómo resolviste los problemas.

> En el campamento hay 5 niños jugando y 4 niños haciendo manualidades. Hay otros 5 niños merendando.

7. ¿Cuántos niños hay en el campamento en total?

_____ niños

8. **MÁS AL DETALLE** Imagina que llegan 7 niños más al campamento y se unen a los niños que están jugando. ¿Cuántos niños más hay jugando que niños que no están jugando?

_____ niños más

9. **PIENSA MÁS** Ashley tenía 9 crayones. Le dio 4 crayones a su hermano. ¿Cuántos crayones tiene Ashley ahora? Escribe un enunciado numérico para el problema. Usa un ▢ para el número que falta. Luego resuelve.

_____

Ashley tiene _____ crayones ahora.

 ACTIVIDAD PARA LA CASA • Pida a su niño que explique cómo resolvió uno de los problemas de esta página.

214 doscientos catorce

Nombre _____

Álgebra • Usar ecuaciones para representar problemas

**Práctica y tarea
Lección 3.9**

Objetivo de aprendizaje Escribirás enunciados numéricos con un símbolo para el número que falta al representar problemas de suma y resta.

Escribe un enunciado numérico para el problema. Usa ■ para el número que falta. Luego resuelve.

1. Había 15 manzanas en un tazón. Dany usó algunas manzanas para hacer un pastel. Ahora hay 7 manzanas en el tazón. ¿Cuántas manzanas usó Dany para hacer el pastel?

   _____

   _____ manzanas

2. Amy tiene 16 bolsas de regalo. Llena 8 bolsas de regalo con silbatos. ¿Cuántas bolsas de regalo no tienen silbatos?

   _____

   _____ bolsas de regalo

Resolución de problemas · En el mundo

Escribe o haz un dibujo que muestre cómo resolviste el problema.

3. Tony tiene 7 cubos azules y 6 cubos rojos. ¿Cuántos cubos tiene en total?

   _____ cubos

4. ESCRIBE Matemáticas Escribe un problema para el enunciado de suma 7 + = 9. Resuelve el problema.

   _____

   _____

   _____

Capítulo 3   doscientos quince **215**

Repaso de la lección

1. Fred peló 9 zanahorias. Nancy peló 6 zanahorias. ¿Cuántas zanahorias menos que Fred peló Nancy?

   _____ zanahorias menos

2. Omar tiene 8 canicas. Joy tiene 7 canicas. ¿Cuántas canicas tienen en total?

   _____ canicas

Repaso en espiral

3. ¿Cuál es la suma?

   $8 + 8 =$ _____

4. ¿Cuál es la suma?

   $5 + 4 + 3 =$ _____

5. ¿Qué número tiene el mismo valor que 1 centena, 7 decenas?

   _____

6. ¿Cuál es otra manera de escribir el número 358?

   _____ centenas _____ decenas _____ unidades

Nombre _____

Resolución de problemas • Grupos iguales

RESOLUCIÓN DE PROBLEMAS
Lección 3.10

Pregunta esencial ¿Cómo ayuda la representación cuando se resuelve un problema de grupos iguales?

Objetivo de aprendizaje Usarás fichas, el conteo salteado y la estrategia de *representar* para hallar el número total de objetos distribuidos en grupos iguales.

Theo pone sus adhesivos en 5 hileras. Hay 3 adhesivos en cada hilera. ¿Cuántos adhesivos tiene Theo?

Soluciona el problema

¿Qué debo hallar?

cuántos adhesivos
tiene Theo

¿Qué información debo usar?

5 hileras de adhesivos

3 adhesivos en cada hilera

Muestra cómo resolver el problema.

_____ adhesivos

NOTA A LA FAMILIA: Su niño representó el problema con fichas. Las fichas son una herramienta concreta que ayuda a los niños a representar el problema.

Capítulo 3   doscientos diecisiete **217**

Haz otro problema

Representa el problema.
Haz un dibujo que muestre lo que hiciste.

- ¿Qué debo hallar?
- ¿Qué información debo usar?

1. María pone sus postales en 4 hileras.
   Hay 3 postales en cada hilera.
   ¿Cuántas postales tiene María?   _____ postales

2. Jamal pone 4 juguetes en cada caja.
   ¿Cuántos juguetes pondrá en 4 cajas?   _____ juguetes

Charla matemática

PRÁCTICAS Y PROCESOS MATEMÁTICOS 7

Explica cómo te ayudó la representación y el conteo salteado a resolver el segundo problema.

218 doscientos dieciocho

Nombre _____

Comparte y muestra

Representa el problema.
Haz un dibujo que muestre lo que hiciste.

3. El Sr. Fulton pone 3 bananas en cada bandeja. ¿Cuántas bananas hay en 4 bandejas?

_____ bananas

4. Hay 3 hileras de manzanas. Hay 5 manzanas en cada hilera. ¿Cuántas manzanas hay en total?

_____ manzanas

5. PIENSA MÁS Hay 4 platos. Dexter pone 2 uvas en cada plato. Luego pone 2 uvas en 6 platos más. ¿Cuántas uvas pone en los platos en total?

_____ uvas

Capítulo 3 • Lección 10   doscientos diecinueve **219**

Resolución de problemas • Aplicaciones

6. Haz conexiones

Ángela representó un problema con estas fichas.

Escribe un problema de grupos iguales que Ángela podría haber representado con estas fichas.

_____

_____

_____

7. PIENSA MÁS Max y 4 amigos toman prestados unos libros de la biblioteca. Cada persona toma 3 libros. Haz un dibujo que muestre los grupos de libros.

¿Cuántos libros tomaron prestados en total?

_____ libros

ACTIVIDAD PARA LA CASA • Pida a su niño que explique cómo resolvió uno de los problemas de esta lección.

220 doscientos veinte

Práctica y tarea
Lección 3.10

Resolución de problemas • Grupos iguales

Objetivo de aprendizaje Usarás fichas, el conteo salteado y la estrategia de *representar* para hallar el número total de objetos distribuidos en grupos iguales.

Haz una representación del problema.
Haz un dibujo que muestre lo que hiciste.

1. El Sr. Anderson tiene 4 platos de galletas. Hay 5 galletas en cada plato. ¿Cuántas galletas hay en total?

   _____ galletas

2. La Sra. Trane pone algunos adhesivos en 3 hileras. Hay 2 adhesivos en cada hilera. ¿Cuántos adhesivos tiene la Sra. Trane?

   _____ adhesivos

3. **ESCRIBE Matemáticas** Dibuja 3 hileras con 2 fichas en cada hilera. Escribe un problema que se pueda representar usando esas fichas.

   _____

   _____

Capítulo 3

doscientos veintiuno **221**

Repaso de la lección

1. Jaime pone 3 naranjas en cada bandeja. ¿Cuántas naranjas hay en 5 bandejas?

    _____ naranjas

2. Maurice tiene 4 hileras de juguetes de 4 juguetes cada una. ¿Cuántos juguetes tiene en total?

    _____ juguetes

Repaso en espiral

3. Jack tiene 12 lápices y 7 bolígrafos. ¿Cuántos lápices más que bolígrafos tiene?

    _____ lápices

4. Laura tiene 9 manzanas. Jon tiene 6 manzanas. ¿Cuántas manzanas tienen los dos?

    _____ manzanas

5. Encierra en un círculo el número par.

    1   3   5   8

6. ¿Cuál es la suma?

    $7 + 9 =$ _____

Nombre _____

Álgebra • Suma repetida

Pregunta esencial ¿Cómo puedes escribir un enunciado de suma para problemas de grupos iguales?

Lección 3.11

Objetivo de aprendizaje Usarás un enunciado de suma para representar el número total de objetos distribuidos en grupos iguales.

Escucha y dibuja En el mundo

Usa fichas para representar el problema. Luego haz un dibujo de tu modelo.

PARA EL MAESTRO • Lea el siguiente problema y pida a los niños que primero hagan un modelo del problema con fichas y después hagan un dibujo de su modelo. Clayton tiene 3 hileras de tarjetas. Hay 5 tarjetas en cada hilera. ¿Cuántas tarjetas tiene Clayton?

Describe cómo hallaste el número total de fichas de tu modelo.

Capítulo 3   doscientos veintitrés **223**

Representa y dibuja

Si tienes grupos iguales, puedes sumar para hallar la cantidad total.

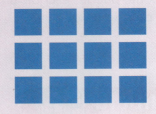

3 hileras de 4

Escribe: __4__ + __4__ + __4__ = ____

____ en total

Comparte y muestra

Halla el número de figuras de cada hilera. Completa el enunciado de suma para hallar el total.

1.

3 hileras de ____

___ + ___ + ___ = ___

2.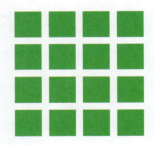

4 hileras de ____

__ + __ + __ + __ = ___

3.

5 hileras de ____

___ + ___ + ___ + ___ + ___ = ___

224 doscientos veinticuatro

Nombre _____

Por tu cuenta

Halla el número de figuras de cada hilera.
Completa el enunciado de suma para hallar el total.

4.

2 hileras de _____

___ + ___ = ___

5.

3 hileras de _____

___ + ___ + ___ = ___

6.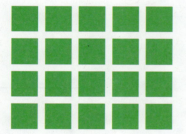

4 hileras de _____

__ + __ + __ + __ = ___

7.

4 hileras de _____

__ + __ + __ + __ = ___

8.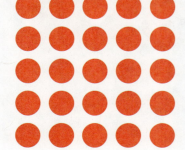

5 hileras de _____

___ + ___ + ___ + ___ + ___ = ___

Capítulo 3 • Lección 11   doscientos veinticinco **225**

PRÁCTICAS Y PROCESOS MATEMÁTICOS • COMUNICAR • PERSEVERAR • CONSTRUIR ARGUMENTOS

Resolución de problemas • Aplicaciones

Resuelve. Escribe o dibuja para explicar.

9. **PIENSA MÁS** Hay 6 fotos en la pared. Hay 2 fotos en cada hilera. ¿Cuántas hileras de fotos hay?

_____ hileras

10. **MÁS AL DETALLE** La Sra. Chen pone 5 hileras de 2 sillas y 2 hileras de 3 sillas. ¿Cuántas sillas usa la Sra. Chen?

_____ sillas

11. **PIENSA MÁS** Halla el número de fichas de cada hilera. Completa el enunciado numérico para hallar el número total de fichas.

___ + ___ + ___ = ___

_____ fichas

 ACTIVIDAD PARA LA CASA • Pida a su niño que haga 2 hileras con 4 objetos pequeños en cada una. Luego pida a su niño que halle el número total de objetos.

Nombre _____

**Práctica y tarea
Lección 3.11**

Álgebra • Suma repetida

Halla el número de figuras de cada hilera. Completa el enunciado de suma para hallar el total.

Objetivo de aprendizaje Usarás un enunciado de suma para representar el número total de objetos distribuidos en grupos iguales.

1.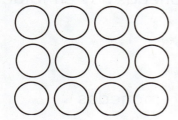

   3 hileras de ____

   ___ + ___ + ___ = ___

2.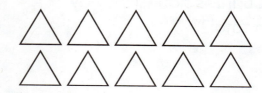

   2 hileras de ____

   ___ + ___ = ___

Resolución de problemas

Resuelve. Escribe o dibuja la explicación.

3. Un salón de clases tiene 3 hileras de pupitres. Hay 5 pupitres en cada hilera. ¿Cuántos pupitres hay en total?

   ____ pupitres

4. ✏️ **ESCRIBE** ▸ **Matemáticas** Explica cómo se escribe un enunciado de suma para un dibujo de 4 hileras con 3 objetos en cada una.

   _____

Capítulo 3   doscientos veintisiete **227**

Repaso de la lección

1. Un álbum tiene 4 páginas. Hay 2 adhesivos en cada página. ¿Cuántos adhesivos hay en total?

    _____ adhesivos

2. Ben forma 5 hileras de monedas. Coloca 3 monedas en cada hilera. ¿Cuántas monedas hay en total?

    _____ monedas

Repaso en espiral

3. Hay 5 manzanas y 4 naranjas. ¿Cuántas frutas hay?

    _____ frutas

4. Cuenta de diez en diez.

    40, _____, _____, _____, _____

5. Escribe el número 260 de otra manera.

6. Escribe una operación que tenga la misma suma que 7 + 5.

228 doscientos veintiocho

Nombre _____

✓ Repaso y prueba del Capítulo 3

1. Erin pone 3 latas pequeñas, 4 latas medianas y 5 latas grandes en un estante. ¿Cuántas latas pone en el estante?

   _____ latas

2. Rellena el círculo que está al lado de todas las operaciones de dobles que podrías usar para hallar la suma de 3 + 2.

   ○ 2 + 2
   ○ 5 + 5
   ○ 3 + 3
   ○ 1 + 1

3. ¿Tiene el enunciado numérico la misma diferencia que 14 − 6 = ▇?
   Elige Sí o No.

10 − 1 = ▇	○ Sí	○ No
10 − 2 = ▇	○ Sí	○ No
10 − 3 = ▇	○ Sí	○ No
10 − 4 = ▇	○ Sí	○ No

Capítulo 3   Opciones de evaluación Prueba del capítulo   doscientos veintinueve · **229**

4. El Sr. Brown vendió 5 mochilas rojas y 8 mochilas azules. Escribe el enunciado numérico. Muestra cómo puedes formar una decena para hallar la suma. Escribe la suma.

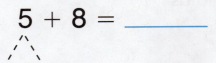

5 + 8 = _____

10 + _____ = _____

5. Halla el número de figuras de cada hilera.

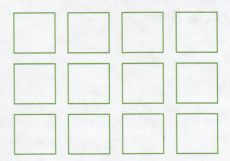

3 hileras de _____

Completa el enunciado de suma para hallar el total.

_____ + _____ + _____ = _____

6. Tania y 3 amigos colocaron piedras sobre la mesa. Cada persona colocó 2 piedras sobre la mesa. Haz un dibujo que muestre los grupos de piedras.

¿Cuántas piedras pusieron sobre la mesa?

_____ piedras

Nombre _____

7. **PIENSA MÁS** Lily ve 15 perritos marrones y 8 perritos blancos en la tienda de animales. ¿Cuántos perritos marrones más que perritos blancos vio? Haz un dibujo y escribe un enunciado numérico para resolver.

_____

_____ perritos marrones más

8. Mark cuenta 6 patos en un estanque y algunos patos en el césped. Hay 14 patos en total. Haz un dibujo que muestre los dos grupos de patos.

Escribe un enunciado numérico que te ayude a hallar cuántos patos hay en el césped.

_____ + _____ = _____

¿Cuántos patos hay en el césped? _____ patos

9. Hay 8 duraznos en una canasta. La Sra. Dalton pone 7 duraznos más en la canasta. Completa el enunciado de suma para hallar cuántos duraznos hay en la canasta ahora.

_____ + _____ = _____

_____ duraznos

Capítulo 3

10. **MÁS AL DETALLE** Usa los números de las fichas cuadradas para escribir las diferencias.
Luego escribe la operación que sigue en el patrón.

| 4 | 5 | 6 | 7 |

12 − 6 = _____   11 − 6 = _____
12 − 7 = _____   12 − 6 = _____
12 − 8 = _____   13 − 6 = _____

_____   _____

11. José quería compartir 18 fresas con su hermano a partes iguales. Haz un dibujo para mostrar cómo puede compartir José las fresas.

¿Cuántas fresas recibirá José?

_____ fresas

12. Hank tiene 13 uvas. Le da 5 uvas a su hermana. ¿Cuántas uvas tiene Hank ahora? Escribe un enunciado numérico para el problema. Usa un ▨ para el número que falta. Luego resuelve.

_____

_____ uvas

232 doscientos treinta y dos

Capítulo 4
Suma de 2 dígitos

Aprendo más con Jorge el Curioso

Las teclas de un piano moderno están hechas de madera o plástico. Un piano moderno tiene 36 teclas negras y 52 teclas blancas. ¿Cuántas teclas tiene en total?

Nombre _____

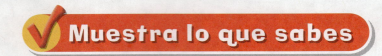 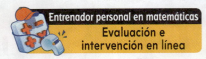

Patrones de suma

Suma 2. Completa cada enunciado de suma.

1. 1 + __2__ = __3__

2. 2 + ___ = ___

3. 3 + ___ = ___

4. 4 + ___ = ___

5. 5 + ___ = ___

6. 6 + ___ = ___

Operaciones de suma

Escribe la suma.

7. 7
   +3

8. 8
   +8

9. 6
   +7

10. 4
   +4

11. 9
   +5

12. 8
   +7

Decenas y unidades

Escribe cuántas decenas y unidades hay en cada número.

13. 43

____ decenas ____ unidades

14. 68

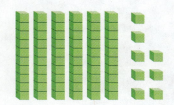

____ decenas ____ unidades

Esta página es para verificar la comprensión de destrezas importantes que se necesitan para tener éxito en el Capítulo 4.

Nombre _____

Desarrollo del vocabulario

Palabras de repaso
suma
sumando
dígito
decenas
unidades

Visualízalo
Completa el organizador gráfico con las palabras de repaso.

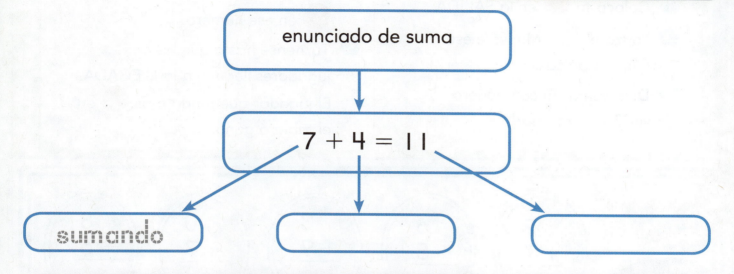

Comprende el vocabulario

1. Escribe un número que tenga el **dígito** 3 en el lugar de las **decenas**. _____

2. Escribe un número que tenga el **dígito** 5 en el lugar de las **unidades**. _____

3. Escribe un número que tenga el mismo dígito en el lugar de las **decenas** que en el lugar de las **unidades**. _____

4. Escribe un número que tenga **dígitos** que sumen una **suma** de 8. _____

Capítulo 4

Juego
¿Cuál es la suma?

Materiales
- 12 🔴
- 12 🟡
- 1 🎲

Juega con un compañero.

1. Coloca tu 🔴 en la SALIDA.
2. Lanza el 🎲. Muévete ese número de casillas.
3. Di la suma. Tu compañero verifica tu resultado.
4. Si tu resultado es correcto, halla ese número en el centro del tablero. Coloca una de tus 🔴 en ese número.
5. Túrnense hasta que los dos jugadores lleguen a la LLEGADA. El jugador que tenga más 🔴 en el tablero gana.

SALIDA

LLEGADA

| 2+7 | 6+5 | 3+9 | 0+7 | 8+6 |

7	18	9	11	15
13	6	17	8	10
16	4	12	14	5

9+8   6+2
1+4   8+7

| 5+8 | 9+9 | 7+9 | 2+2 | 4+6 | 5+1 |

Vocabulario del Capítulo 4

centena hundred 5	**columna** column 10
decenas tens 18	**dígito** digit 21
es igual a is equal to (=) 25	**reagrupar** regroup 55
suma sum 59	**unidades** ones 64

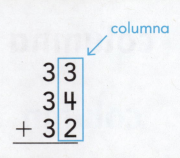

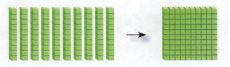

Hay 10 decenas en 1 **centena**.

0, 1, 2, 3, 4, 5, 6, 7, 8, y 9 son **dígitos**.

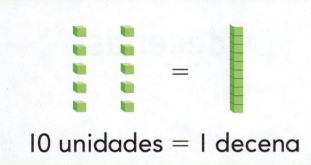

10 unidades = 1 decena

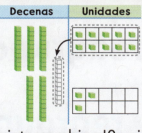

Puedes intercambiar 10 unidades por 1 decena para **reagrupar**.

2 más 1 es igual a 3
2 + 1 = 3

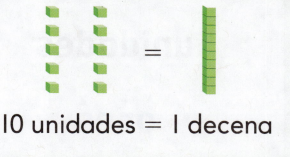

10 unidades = 1 decena

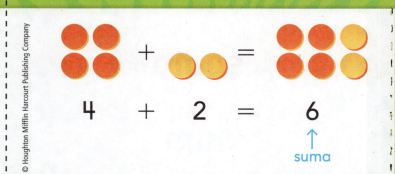

4 + 2 = 6

De visita con las palabras de ¡Vivan las matemáticas!

Juego

Concentración

Recuadro de palabras
centena
columna
decena
dígito
es igual a (=)
reagrupar
suma
unidades

Jugadores: 2 a 3

Materiales
- un juego de tarjetas de palabras

Instrucciones
1. Coloquen las tarjetas boca abajo en hileras. Túrnense para jugar.
2. Elige dos tarjetas. Colócalas boca arriba.
   - Si las tarjetas coinciden, te quedas con el par y juegas un turno más.
   - Si las tarjetas no coinciden, colócalas boca abajo de nuevo.
3. El juego termina cuando todas las tarjetas están emparejadas. Los jugadores cuentan sus pares. El jugador con la mayor cantidad de pares es el ganador.

Capítulo 4 · doscientos treinta y seis 236A

Escríbelo

Reflexiona

Elige una idea. Escribe acerca de la idea en el espacio de abajo.

- Explica de qué manera los dibujos rápidos te ayudan a sumar números de 2 dígitos.
- Di todas las maneras diferentes en que puedes sumar números de 2 dígitos.
- Escribe tres cosas que sabes acerca de reagrupar.

Nombre _____

Separar unidades para sumar

Lección 4.1

Pregunta esencial ¿Por qué es más fácil sumar un número si lo separamos?

Objetivo de aprendizaje Sumarás dos números al separar las unidades para formar una decena.

Usa ▭▭▭▭▭ ▪. Haz un dibujo para mostrar lo que hiciste.

 PARA EL MAESTRO • Lea el siguiente problema. Pida a los niños que lo resuelvan usando bloques. Griffin leyó 27 libros sobre animales y 6 libros sobre el espacio. ¿Cuántos libros leyó?

 PRÁCTICAS Y PROCESOS MATEMÁTICOS 6

Describe lo que hiciste con los bloques.

Capítulo 4 — doscientos treinta y siete **237**

Representa y dibuja

Separa las unidades para formar una decena.
Usa esto como una manera de sumar.

27 + 8 = _?_

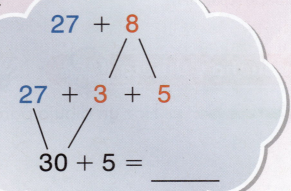

27 + 8 = _____

Comparte y muestra

Haz dibujos rápidos. Separa las unidades para formar una decena. Luego suma y escribe la suma.

1. 15 + 7 = _____

2. 26 + 5 = _____

3. 37 + 8 = _____

4. 28 + 6 = _____

Nombre _____

Por tu cuenta

Separa las unidades para formar una decena. Luego suma y escribe la suma.

5. 23 + 9 = _____

6. 48 + 5 = _____

7. 18 + 5 = _____

8. 33 + 9 = _____

9. 27 + 6 = _____

10. 49 + 4 = _____

11. **MÁS AL DETALLE** Alex pone en una sala 32 mesas pequeñas y 9 mesas grandes. Luego pone otras 9 mesas grandes al lado de la pared. ¿Cuántas mesas pone Alex?

_____ mesas

12. **PIENSA MÁS** Bruce ve 29 robles y 4 arces en el parque. Luego ve el doble de pinos que de arces. ¿Cuántos árboles ve Bruce?

_____ árboles

Capítulo 4 • Lección 1

PRÁCTICAS Y PROCESOS MATEMÁTICOS ANALIZAR • BUSCAR ESTRUCTURAS • PRECISIÓN

Resolución de problemas • Aplicaciones

Resuelve. Escribe o dibuja para explicar.

13. **MÁS AL DETALLE** Megan tiene 38 fotos de animales, 5 fotos de personas y 3 fotos de insectos. ¿Cuántas fotos tiene?

_____ fotos

14. **PRÁCTICAS Y PROCESOS MATEMÁTICOS** **Analiza**
Jamal tiene una caja con 22 carritos de juguete. Coloca otros 9 carritos de juguete en la caja. Luego saca 3 carritos de juguete de la caja. ¿Cuántos carritos de juguete quedan en la caja ahora?

_____ carritos de juguete

15. **PIENSA MÁS** Dan tiene 16 lápices. Quentin le da 5 lápices más. Elige todas las formas que puedes usar para hallar el número de lápices que tiene Dan en total.

○ $16 + 5$

○ $16 + 4 + 1$

○ $16 - 5$

ACTIVIDAD PARA LA CASA • Diga un número de 0 a 9. Pida a su niño que diga un número para sumarlo al suyo y obtener una suma de 10.

240 doscientos cuarenta

Nombre _____

Práctica y tarea
Lección 4.1

Separar unidades para sumar

Objetivo de aprendizaje Sumarás dos números al separar las unidades para formar una decena.

Separa las unidades para formar una decena.
Luego suma y escribe la suma.

1. $62 + 9 =$ ____
2. $27 + 7 =$ ____
3. $28 + 5 =$ ____
4. $17 + 8 =$ ____
5. $57 + 6 =$ ____
6. $23 + 9 =$ ____
7. $39 + 7 =$ ____
8. $26 + 5 =$ ____
9. $13 + 8 =$ ____
10. $18 + 7 =$ ____

Resolución de problemas

Resuelve. Escribe o dibuja para explicar.

11. Jimmy tiene 18 avioncitos. Su madre le trajo 7 avioncitos más. ¿Cuántos avioncitos tiene ahora?

____ avioncitos

12. ESCRIBE Matemáticas Explica cómo hallarías la suma de $46 + 7$.

_____

_____

Capítulo 4   doscientos cuarenta y uno **241**

Repaso de la lección

1. ¿Cuál es la suma?

   26 + 7 = _____

2. ¿Cuál es la suma?

   15 + 8 = _____

Repaso en espiral

3. Hanna tiene 4 cuentas azules y 8 cuentas rojas. ¿Cuántas cuentas tiene Hanna?

   4 + 8 = _____ cuentas

4. Rick tiene 4 adhesivos. Luego gana 2 más. ¿Cuántos adhesivos tiene Rick ahora?

   4 + 2 = _____ adhesivos

5. ¿Cuál es la suma?

   4 + 5 + 4 = _____

6. Escribe 281 usando centenas, decenas y unidades.

   _____ centenas _____ decenas

   _____ unidades

Nombre _____

Lección **4.2**

Hacer una compensación

Pregunta esencial ¿Cómo puedes convertir un sumando en una decena para resolver un problema de suma?

Objetivo de aprendizaje Convertirás un sumando en un número de decenas para ayudar a resolver un problema de suma.

Escucha y dibuja En el mundo

Haz dibujos rápidos para mostrar los problemas.

PARA EL MAESTRO • Pida a los niños que hagan dibujos rápidos para resolver este problema. Kara tiene 47 adhesivos. Compra 20 adhesivos más. ¿Cuántos adhesivos tiene ahora? Repita lo mismo con este problema. Tyrone tiene 30 adhesivos y compra 52 más. ¿Cuántos adhesivos tiene ahora?

Analiza cómo hallaste la cantidad de adhesivos que tiene Tyrone.

Capítulo 4

doscientos cuarenta y tres **243**

Representa y dibuja

Saca unidades de un sumando para que el otro sumando sea el siguiente número de decenas.

$25 + 48 = ?$

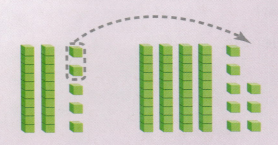

> La suma es más fácil cuando uno de los sumandos es un número de decenas.

$\underline{23} + \underline{50} = \underline{}$

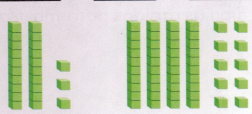

Comparte y muestra

Muestra cómo hacer que un sumando sea el siguiente número de decenas. Completa el nuevo enunciado de suma.

1. $37 + 25 = ?$

$\underline{40} + \underline{} = \underline{}$

2. $27 + 46 = ?$

$\underline{} + \underline{} = \underline{}$

3. $14 + 29 = ?$

$\underline{} + \underline{} = \underline{}$

Nombre _____

Por tu cuenta

Muestra cómo hacer que un sumando sea el siguiente número de decenas. Completa el nuevo enunciado de suma.

4. $18 + 13 = ?$

____ + ____ = ____

5. $24 + 18 = ?$

____ + ____ = ____

6. **MÁS AL DETALLE** Luis encuentra 44 caracoles. Wayne encuentra 39 caracoles. ¿Cuántos caracoles necesitan si quieren tener 90 caracoles en total?

_____ caracoles

Resuelve. Escribe o haz un dibujo para explicar.

7. **PIENSA MÁS** Zach encuentra 38 ramas. Kelly encuentra 27 ramas. ¿Cuántas ramas más necesitan los dos niños si quieren conseguir 70 ramas en total?

_____ ramas más

Capítulo 4 • Lección 2   doscientos cuarenta y cinco **245**

Resolución de problemas • Aplicaciones

Resuelve. Escribe o dibuja para explicar.

8. **Haz conexiones** La tabla muestra las hojas que recogió Philip. Quiere tener una colección de 52 hojas de solo dos colores. ¿Qué dos colores de hojas debe usar?

Hojas recogidas	
Color	Número
verde	27
marrón	29
amarillo	25

_____ y _____

9. **Piensa más** Ava tiene 39 hojas de papel blanco. Tiene 22 hojas de papel verde. Haz un dibujo y escribe para explicar cómo hallar el número de hojas de papel que tiene Ava.

Ava tiene _____ hojas de papel.

ACTIVIDAD PARA LA CASA • Pida a su niño que elija un problema de esta página y explique cómo resolverlo de otra manera.

Nombre _____

Hacer una compensación

Práctica y tarea
Lección 4.2

Objetivo de aprendizaje Convertirás un sumando en un número de decenas para ayudar a resolver un problema de suma.

Muestra cómo hacer que un sumando sea el siguiente número de decenas. Completa el nuevo enunciado de suma.

1. $15 + 37 = ?$  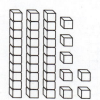 ___ + ___ = ___

2. $22 + 49 = ?$ 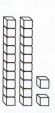 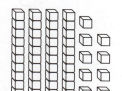 ___ + ___ = ___

3. $38 + 26 = ?$ ___ + ___ = ___

Resolución de problemas

Resuelve. Escribe o dibuja para explicar.

4. El roble de la escuela medía 34 pies de alto. Luego creció 18 pies más. ¿Cuánto mide el roble ahora?

   _____ pies de alto

5. **ESCRIBE Matemáticas** Explica por qué harías de uno de los sumandos una decena para resolver un problema de suma.

   _____
   _____

Capítulo 4   doscientos cuarenta y siete **247**

Repaso de la lección

1. ¿Cuál es la suma?

   18 + 25 = ___

   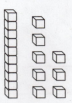 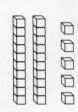

2. ¿Cuál es la suma?

   27 + 24 = ___

    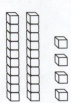

Repaso en espiral

3. Encierra en un círculo el número par.

   27   14   11   5

4. Andrew ve 4 peces. Kim ve el doble de ese número de peces. ¿Cuántos peces ve Kim?

   ___ peces

5. ¿Cuál es la operación de resta relacionada para 7 + 6 = 13?

   _____

6. ¿Cuál es la suma?

   2 + 8 = ___

Lección 4.3

Nombre _____

Separar los sumandos en decenas y unidades

Pregunta esencial ¿Cómo separas sumandos para sumar decenas y después sumar unidades?

Objetivo de aprendizaje Separarás sumandos en decenas y unidades para sumar números menores que 100.

Escucha y dibuja

Escribe el número. Luego escribe el número como decenas más unidades.

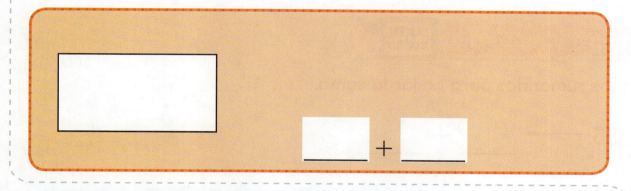

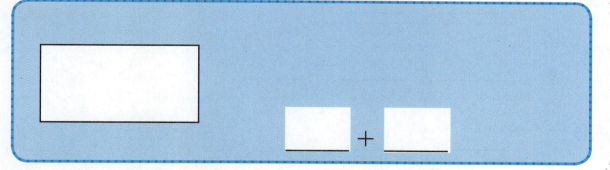

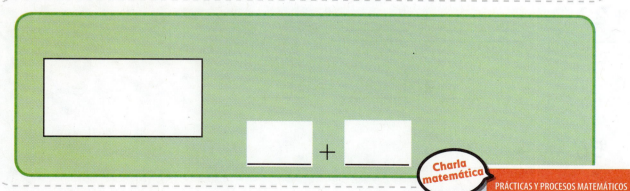

PARA EL MAESTRO • Dirija la atención de los niños a la casilla anaranjada. Pida a los niños que escriban 25 dentro del rectángulo grande. Luego pida a los niños que escriban 25 como decenas más unidades. Repita la actividad con 36 y 42.

Charla matemática

PRÁCTICAS Y PROCESOS MATEMÁTICOS

¿Cuál es el valor del 6 en el número 63? **Explica** cómo lo sabes.

Capítulo 4   doscientos cuarenta y nueve **249**

Representa y dibuja

Separa los sumandos en decenas y unidades.
Suma las decenas y suma las unidades.
Luego halla la suma.

```
 27  →   20 + 7
+48  →   40 + 8
         ―――――――
         60 + 15 = ___
```

$60 + 15$

$10 \quad 5$

$70 + 5 = $ ___

Comparte y muestra

Separa los sumandos para hallar la suma.

1. $\quad 35 \longrightarrow \underline{\quad} + \underline{\quad}$

    $+54 \longrightarrow \underline{\quad} + \underline{\quad}$

    $\underline{\quad} + \underline{\quad} = \underline{\quad}$

2. $\quad 43 \longrightarrow \underline{\quad} + \underline{\quad}$

    $+29 \longrightarrow \underline{\quad} + \underline{\quad}$

    $\underline{\quad} + \underline{\quad} = \underline{\quad}$

3. $\quad 56 \longrightarrow \underline{\quad} + \underline{\quad}$

    $+38 \longrightarrow \underline{\quad} + \underline{\quad}$

    $\underline{\quad} + \underline{\quad} = \underline{\quad}$

Nombre _____

Por tu cuenta

Separa los sumandos para hallar la suma.

4. 14 ⟶ ___ + ___

   +23 ⟶ ___ + ___

   ___ + ___ = ___

5. 37 ⟶ ___ + ___

   +45 ⟶ ___ + ___

   ___ + ___ = ___

6. **MÁS AL DETALLE** Chris leyó 15 páginas de su libro. Tony leyó 4 páginas más que Chris. ¿Cuántas páginas leyeron Chris y Tony?

_____ páginas

7. **PIENSA MÁS** Julie leyó 18 páginas de su libro en la mañana. Leyó el mismo número de páginas en la tarde. ¿Cuántas páginas leyó en total?

_____ páginas

Capítulo 4 • Lección 3

PRÁCTICAS Y PROCESOS MATEMÁTICOS • COMUNICAR • PERSEVERAR • CONSTRUIR ARGUMENTOS

Resolución de problemas • Aplicaciones

Escribe o dibuja para explicar.

8. PRÁCTICAS Y PROCESOS MATEMÁTICOS ❶ Comprende los problemas Christopher tiene 35 tarjetas de béisbol. El resto son tarjetas de básquetbol. Tiene 58 tarjetas en total. ¿Cuántas tarjetas de básquetbol tiene?

_____ tarjetas de básquetbol

9. PRÁCTICAS Y PROCESOS MATEMÁTICOS ❶ Evalúa Tomás tiene 17 lápices. Compra 26 lápices más. ¿Cuántos lápices tiene ahora?

_____ lápices

10. PIENSA MÁS + Sasha usó 38 adhesivos rojos y 22 adhesivos azules. Muestra cómo puedes separar los sumandos para hallar cuántos adhesivos usó Sasha.

$$38 \longrightarrow \underline{} + \underline{}$$

$$+22 \longrightarrow \underline{} + \underline{}$$

$$\underline{} + \underline{} = \underline{} \text{ adhesivos}$$

 ACTIVIDAD PARA LA CASA • Escriba 32 + 48 en una hoja de papel. Pida a su niño que separe los números y halle la suma.

252 doscientos cincuenta y dos

Nombre _____

Práctica y tarea
Lección 4.3

Separar los sumandos en decenas y unidades

Objetivo de aprendizaje Separarás sumandos en decenas y unidades para sumar números menores que 100.

Separa los sumandos para hallar la suma.

1. $\begin{array}{r} 18 \\ +21 \end{array}$ → ___ + ___
    ___ + ___
    ___ + ___ = ___

2. $\begin{array}{r} 33 \\ +49 \end{array}$ → ___ + ___
    ___ + ___
    ___ + ___ = ___

Resolución de problemas En el mundo

Elige una manera de resolver.
Escribe o dibuja para explicar.

3. Christopher tiene 28 tarjetas de béisbol.
   Justin tiene 18 tarjetas de béisbol.
   ¿Cuántas tarjetas de béisbol tienen
   los dos en total?   _____ tarjetas de béisbol

4. ESCRIBE Matemáticas Explica cómo separar los sumandos para hallar la suma de 25 + 16.

   _____

   _____

Capítulo 4   doscientos cincuenta y tres **253**

Repaso de la lección

1. ¿Cuál es la suma?

    27
    + 12
    ____

2. ¿Cuál es la suma?

    17
    + 35
    ____

Repaso en espiral

3. ¿Cuál es el valor del dígito subrayado?

    2<u>5</u>

    _____

4. ¿Qué número tiene el mismo valor que 12 decenas?

    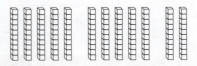

    _____

5. Ally tiene 7 cubos interconectables. Greg tiene 4 cubos interconectables. ¿Cuántos cubos interconectables tienen los dos?

    _____ cubos

6. Juan pintó un cuadro de un árbol. Primero pintó 15 hojas. Luego pintó 23 hojas más. ¿Cuántas hojas pintó?

    _____ hojas

Nombre _____

Reagrupar modelos para sumar

Lección 4.4

Pregunta esencial ¿Cuándo reagrupas en la suma?

Objetivo de aprendizaje Representarás la suma hasta 100 con la reagrupación para hallar sumas.

Escucha y dibuja — En el mundo — Manos a la obra

Usa para representar el problema.
Haz dibujos rápidos para mostrar lo que hiciste.

Decenas	Unidades

 PARA EL MAESTRO • Lea el siguiente problema. Brandon tiene 24 libros. Su amigo Mario tiene 8 libros. ¿Cuántos libros tienen los dos?

Charla matemática

PRÁCTICAS Y PROCESOS MATEMÁTICOS 5

Usa herramientas Describe cómo formaste la decena en tu modelo.

Capítulo 4

doscientos cincuenta y cinco **255**

Representa y dibuja

Suma 37 y 25.

Paso 1 Observa las unidades. ¿Puedes formar una decena?

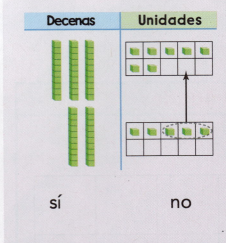

sí   no

Paso 2 Si puedes formar una decena, reagrupa.

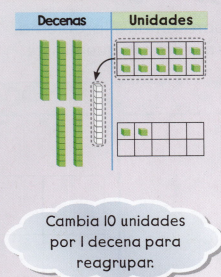

Cambia 10 unidades por 1 decena para reagrupar.

Paso 3 Escribe la cantidad de decenas y unidades. Escribe la suma.

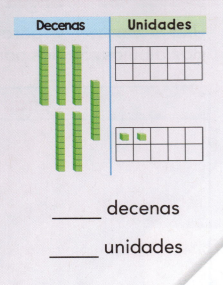

____ decenas

____ unidades

____

Comparte y muestra

Haz un dibujo que muestre la reagrupación. Escribe cuántas decenas y unidades hay en la suma. Escribe la suma.

1. Suma 47 y 15.

____ decenas

____ unidades

2. Suma 48 y 8.

____ decenas

____ unidades

3. Suma 26 y 38.

____ decenas

____ unidades

256 doscientos cincuenta y seis

Nombre _____

Por tu cuenta

Haz un dibujo que muestre si reagrupas. Escribe cuántas decenas y unidades hay en la suma. Escribe la suma.

4. Suma 79 y 6.

Decenas	Unidades

____ decenas
____ unidades
____

5. Suma 18 y 64.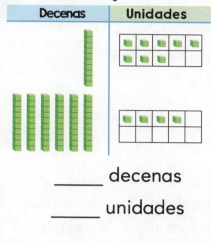

____ decenas
____ unidades
____

6. Suma 23 y 39.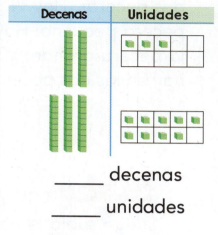

____ decenas
____ unidades
____

7. Suma 54 y 25.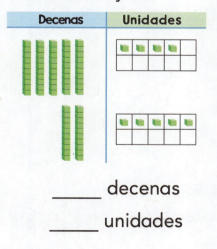

____ decenas
____ unidades
____

8. Suma 33 y 7.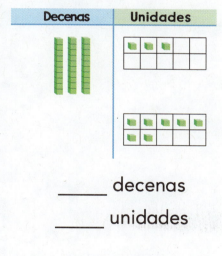

____ decenas
____ unidades
____

9. Suma 27 y 68.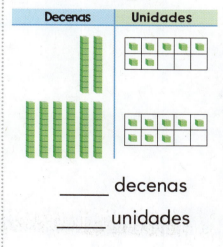

____ decenas
____ unidades
____

10. **PIENSA MÁS** Kara tiene 25 muñecos y 12 libros. Jorge tiene 8 muñecos más que Kara. ¿Cuántos muñecos tiene Jorge?

____ muñecos

Capítulo 4 • Lección 4

PRÁCTICAS Y PROCESOS MATEMÁTICOS • ANALIZAR • BUSCAR ESTRUCTURAS • PRECISIÓN

Resolución de problemas • Aplicaciones

Escribe o dibuja para explicar.

11. **PRÁCTICAS Y PROCESOS MATEMÁTICOS ❶ Comprende los problemas** La Sra. Sanders tiene dos peceras. Hay 14 peces en la pecera pequeña. Hay 27 peces en la pecera grande. ¿Cuántos peces hay en las dos peceras?

_____ peces

12. **PIENSA MÁS** Charlie subió 69 escalones. Luego subió 18 escalones más. Muestra dos formas diferentes para hallar cuántos escalones subió Charlie.

Charlie subió _____ escalones.

 ACTIVIDAD PARA LA CASA • Pida a su niño que escriba un problema con números de 2 dígitos sobre la suma de dos grupos de sellos.

258 doscientos cincuenta y ocho

Nombre _____

Reagrupar modelos para sumar

**Práctica y tarea
Lección 4.4**

Dibuja para mostrar cómo reagrupar. Escribe cuántas decenas y unidades hay en la suma. Escribe la suma.

Objetivo de aprendizaje Representarás la suma hasta 100 con la reagrupación para hallar sumas.

1. Suma 63 y 9.

   ____ decenas
   ____ unidades
   ____

2. Suma 25 y 58.

   ____ decenas
   ____ unidades
   ____

3. Suma 58 y 18.

   ____ decenas
   ____ unidades
   ____

4. Suma 64 y 26.

   ____ decenas
   ____ unidades
   ____

5. Suma 17 y 77.

   ____ decenas
   ____ unidades
   ____

6. Suma 16 y 39.

   ____ decenas
   ____ unidades
   ____

Resolución de problemas

Elige una manera de resolver. Escribe o dibuja para explicar.

7. Cathy tiene 43 hojas en su colección. Jane tiene 38 hojas. ¿Cuántas hojas tienen las dos niñas?   ____ hojas

8. **ESCRIBE Matemáticas** Supón que vas a sumar 43 y 28. ¿Tienes que reagrupar? Explica.

_____

Capítulo 4   doscientos cincuenta y nueve **259**

Repaso de la lección

1. Suma 27 y 48. ¿Cuál es la suma?

Decenas	Unidades

   _____

Repaso en espiral

2. ¿Cuál es la suma?

   7 + 7 = _____

3. Encierra en un círculo el número impar.

   6   12   21   22

4. ¿Cuál es la suma?

   39 + 46 = _____

5. ¿Cuál es la suma?

   5 + 3 + 4 = _____

Nombre _____

Hacer un modelo y anotar sumas de 2 dígitos

Lección 4.5

Pregunta esencial ¿Cómo anotas la suma de 2 dígitos?

Objetivo de aprendizaje Anotarás las sumas para modelos de suma hasta 100.

Escucha y dibuja En el mundo

Usa  para representar el problema.
Haz dibujos rápidos para mostrar lo que hiciste.

Decenas	Unidades

PARA EL MAESTRO • Lea el siguiente problema. La clase del Sr. Riley recogió 54 latas para la colecta de alimentos. La clase de la Srta. Bright recogió 35 latas. ¿Cuántas latas recogieron las dos clases?

 Charla matemática

PRÁCTICAS Y PROCESOS MATEMÁTICOS 6

Haz conexiones ¿Cambiaste bloques en tu modelo? Explica por qué.

Capítulo 4   doscientos sesenta y uno **261**

Representa y dibuja

Traza sobre los dibujos rápidos de los pasos.

Paso 1 Haz un modelo de 37 + 26. ¿Hay 10 unidades para reagrupar?

Paso 2 Escribe la decena reagrupada. Escribe cuántas unidades hay en el lugar de las unidades ahora.

Paso 3 ¿Cuántas decenas hay? Escribe cuántas decenas hay en el lugar de las decenas.

Comparte y muestra

Haz dibujos rápidos como ayuda para resolver. Escribe la suma.

1.

2.

262 doscientos sesenta y dos

Nombre _____

Por tu cuenta

Haz dibujos rápidos como ayuda para resolver.
Escribe la suma.

3.
Decenas	Unidades
☐	
3	4
+	9

Decenas	Unidades

4.
Decenas	Unidades
☐	
2	7
+ 2	4

Decenas	Unidades

5.
Decenas	Unidades
☐	
3	5
+ 2	3

Decenas	Unidades

6.
Decenas	Unidades
☐	
5	9
+	6

Decenas	Unidades

7. **PIENSA MÁS** Tim tiene 36 adhesivos. Margo tiene 44 adhesivos. ¿Cuántos adhesivos más necesitan para tener 100 en total?

_____ adhesivos más

8. **MÁS AL DETALLE** Un panadero quiere vender 100 panes. De momento ha vendido 48 de maíz y 42 integrales. ¿Cuántos panes más tiene que vender el panadero?

_____ panes más

Capítulo 4 • Lección 5

doscientos sesenta y tres **263**

Resolución de problemas • Aplicaciones

Escribe o dibuja para explicar.

9. Comprende los problemas

Chris y Bianca obtuvieron 80 puntos en total en el concurso de deletreo. Cada niño obtuvo más de 20 puntos. ¿Cuántos puntos podría haber obtenido cada niño?

Chris: _____ puntos

Bianca: _____ puntos

10. PIENSA MÁS

Don construyó una torre con 24 bloques. Construyó otra torre con 18 bloques. ¿Cuántos bloques usó para las dos torres? Haz dibujos rápidos para resolver. Escribe la suma.

Decenas	Unidades

_____ bloques

¿Reagrupaste para hallar la respuesta? Explica.

_____

_____

_____

ACTIVIDAD PARA LA CASA • Escriba dos números de 2 dígitos y pregunte a su niño si reagruparía para hallar la suma.

Práctica y tarea
Lección 4.5

Nombre _____

Hacer un modelo y anotar sumas de 2 dígitos

Objetivo de aprendizaje Anotarás las sumas para modelos de suma hasta 100.

Haz dibujos rápidos como ayuda para resolver. Escribe la suma.

1. | Decenas | Unidades |
    |---|---|
    | 3 | 8 |
    | +1 | 7 |

Decenas	Unidades

2. | Decenas | Unidades |
    |---|---|
    | 5 | 8 |
    | +2 | 6 |

Decenas	Unidades

3. | Decenas | Unidades |
    |---|---|
    | 4 | 2 |
    | +3 | 7 |

Decenas	Unidades

4. | Decenas | Unidades |
    |---|---|
    | 5 | 3 |
    | +3 | 8 |

Decenas	Unidades

Resolución de problemas En el mundo

Elige una manera de resolver. Escribe o dibuja para explicar.

5. Había 37 niños en el parque el sábado y 25 niños en el parque el domingo. ¿Cuántos niños había en el parque esos dos días?

   _____ niños

6. **ESCRIBE Matemáticas** Explica por qué debes anotar un 1 en la columna de las decenas cuando tienes que reagrupar en un problema de suma.

_____

_____

Capítulo 4   doscientos sesenta y cinco **265**

Repaso de la lección

1. ¿Cuál es la suma?

Decenas	Unidades
☐	
3	4
+ 2	8

2. ¿Cuál es la suma?

Decenas	Unidades
☐	
4	3
+ 2	7

Repaso en espiral

3. Adam reunió 14 monedas de 1¢ la primera semana y 9 monedas de 1¢ la segunda semana. ¿Cuántas monedas de 1¢ más reunió la primera semana que la segunda semana?

   14 − 9 = _____ monedas

4. ¿Cuál es la suma?

   3 + 7 + 9 = _____

5. Janet tiene 5 canicas. Encuentra el doble de ese número de canicas en su bolso de arte. ¿Cuántas canicas tiene Janet ahora?

   5 + ___ = _____ canicas

6. ¿Cuál es la diferencia?

   13 − 5 = _____

Nombre _____

Suma de 2 dígitos

Lección 4.6

Pregunta esencial ¿Cómo anotas los pasos cuando sumas números de 2 dígitos?

Objetivo de aprendizaje Anotarás los pasos para sumar números menores que 100.

 Escucha y dibuja En el mundo

Haz dibujos rápidos para representar cada problema.

Decenas	Unidades

Decenas	Unidades

PARA EL MAESTRO • Lea el siguiente problema y pida a los niños que hagan dibujos rápidos para resolverlo. Jason anotó 35 puntos en un juego y 47 puntos en otro juego. ¿Cuántos puntos anotó Jason? Repita la actividad con este problema. Patty anotó 18 puntos. Luego anotó 21 puntos. ¿Cuántos puntos anotó en total?

Charla matemática PRÁCTICAS Y PROCESOS MATEMÁTICOS

Analiza relaciones
Explica cuándo tienes que reagrupar unidades.

Capítulo 4

doscientos sesenta y siete **267**

Representa y dibuja

Suma 59 y 24.

Paso 1 Suma las unidades.

$9 + 4 = 13$

Paso 2 Reagrupa; 13 unidades es lo mismo que 1 decena y 3 unidades.

Paso 3 Suma las decenas.

$1 + 5 + 2 = 8$

Decenas	Unidades
5	9
+ 2	4
	3

Resultado: 83

Comparte y muestra

Reagrupa si es necesario. Escribe la suma.

1.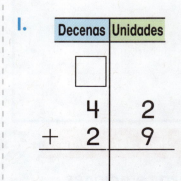
Decenas	Unidades
4	2
+ 2	9

2.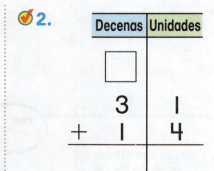
Decenas	Unidades
3	1
+ 1	4

3.
Decenas	Unidades
2	7
+ 4	5

268 doscientos sesenta y ocho

Nombre _____

Por tu cuenta

Reagrupa si es necesario. Escribe la suma.

4.
Decenas	Unidades
☐	
4	8
+	7

5.
Decenas	Unidades
☐	
3	5
+ 4	2

6.
Decenas	Unidades
☐	
7	3
+ 2	0

7.
3	3
+ 2	7

8.
5	2
+	5

9.
3	6
+ 5	8

10.
6	4
+ 2	5

11.
3	5
+ 3	8

12.
3	8
+ 5	2

Resuelve. Haz un dibujo o escribe para explicar.

13. 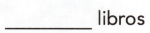 Jin tiene 31 libros sobre gatos y 19 libros sobre perros. Le regala 5 libros a su hermana. ¿Cuántos libros tiene Jin ahora?

_____ libros

PRÁCTICAS Y PROCESOS MATEMÁTICOS • COMUNICAR • PERSEVERAR • CONSTRUIR ARGUMENTOS

Resolución de problemas • Aplicaciones

14. **MÁS AL DETALLE** Abby sumó de otra manera. Halla la suma como Abby.

```
  35
+ 48
  13
+ 70
  83
```

```
  57
+ 29
─────
```

15. **PRÁCTICAS Y PROCESOS MATEMÁTICOS 3** **Verifica el razonamiento de los demás**
Explica por qué la manera de sumar de Abby funciona.

_____

_____

_____

16. **PIENSA MÁS** Melissa vio 14 leones marinos y 29 focas. ¿Cuántos animales vio? Escribe un enunciado numérico para hallar el número total de animales que vio.

_____

Explica cómo muestra el problema el enunciado numérico.

_____

_____

 ACTIVIDAD PARA LA CASA • Pida a su niño que muestre dos maneras de sumar 45 y 38.

270 doscientos setenta

Nombre _____

Suma de 2 dígitos

**Práctica y tarea
Lección 4.6**

Objetivo de aprendizaje Anotarás los pasos para sumar números menores que 100.

Reagrupa si es necesario. Escribe la suma.

1.
```
  4 7
+ 2 5
```

2.
```
  3 3
+ 1 8
```

3.
```
  2 8
+ 6 4
```

4.
```
  1 3
+ 6 5
```

5.
```
  1 7
+ 2 6
```

6.
```
  3 6
+ 5 3
```

7.
```
  5 8
+ 2 5
```

8.
```
  3 7
+ 4 9
```

Resolución de problemas

Resuelve. Escribe o dibuja para explicar.

9. Ángela dibujó 16 flores en un papel esta mañana. Dibujó 25 flores más en la tarde. ¿Cuántas flores dibujó en total?

_____ flores

10. **ESCRIBE Matemáticas** ¿Qué diferencia hay entre el Ejercicio 5 y el Ejercicio 6? Explica.

_____
_____

Capítulo 4   doscientos setenta y uno **271**

Repaso de la lección

1. ¿Cuál es la suma?

   ```
     2 | 1
   + 3 | 7
   ─────
   ```

2. ¿Cuál es la suma?

   ```
     3 | 8
   + 5 | 2
   ─────
   ```

Repaso en espiral

3. ¿Cuál es el siguiente número del patrón de conteo?

   103, 203, 303, 403, ____

4. Rita contó 13 burbujas. Ben contó 5 burbujas. ¿Cuántas burbujas menos que Rita contó Ben?

   13 − 5 = ____ burbujas

5. ¿Qué número es 100 más que 265?

   ____

6. Escribe 42 como una suma de decenas y unidades.

   ____ + ____

Nombre _____

Practicar sumas de 2 dígitos

Lección 4.7

Pregunta esencial ¿Cómo anotas los pasos cuando sumas números de 2 dígitos?

Objetivo de aprendizaje Practicarás la suma de 2 dígitos con y sin reagrupación.

Escucha y dibuja En el mundo

Elige una manera de resolver el problema.
Escribe o haz un dibujo para mostrar lo que hiciste.

PARA EL MAESTRO • Lea el siguiente problema. En la carrera corrieron 45 niños y 63 niñas. ¿Cuántos niños corrieron en la carrera?

Charla matemática

PRÁCTICAS Y PROCESOS MATEMÁTICOS 6

Explica por qué elegiste esa manera de resolver el problema.

Capítulo 4

doscientos setenta y tres **273**

Representa y dibuja

La Sra. Meyers vendió 47 refrigerios antes del juego. Luego vendió 85 refrigerios durante el juego. ¿Cuántos refrigerios vendió en total?

Paso 1 Suma las unidades.

$7 + 5 = 12$

Reagrupa 12 unidades como 1 decena, 2 unidades.

```
  1
  4 7
+ 8 5
-----
    2
```

Paso 2 Suma las decenas.

$1 + 4 + 8 = 13$

```
  1
  4 7
+ 8 5
-----
    2
```

Paso 3 13 decenas pueden reagruparse como 1 centena 3 decenas. Escribe el dígito de las centenas y el dígito de las decenas en la suma.

```
  1
  4 7
+ 8 5
-----
1 3 2
```

Comparte y muestra

Escribe la suma.

1.
```
  3 8
+ 9 4
-----
```

2.
```
  4 5
+ 5 2
-----
```

3.
```
  8 3
+ 7 6
-----
```

4.
```
  5 6
+ 3 5
-----
```

✓5.
```
  6 3
+ 5 1
-----
```

✓6.
```
  7 4
+ 4 9
-----
```

274 doscientos setenta y cuatro

Nombre _____

Por tu cuenta

Escribe la suma.

7.
    52
+ 37

8.
    88
+ 21

9.
    74
+ 67

10.
    93
+ 54

11.
    92
+ 78

12.
    56
+ 16

13.
    31
+ 45

14.
    43
+ 72

15. **PIENSA MÁS** Sin hallar la suma, encierra en un círculo los pares de sumandos cuya suma sea mayor que 100.

    Explica cómo decidiste qué pares encerrar en un círculo.

    73   54
    18   71

    47   36
    62   59

_____

_____

_____

_____

ACTIVIDAD PARA LA CASA • Diga a su niño dos números de 2 dígitos. Pídale que escriba los números y halle la suma.

Capítulo 4 • Lección 7   doscientos setenta y cinco **275**

Nombre _____

 Revisión de la mitad del capítulo

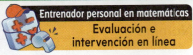

Conceptos y destrezas

Separa unidades para formar una decena.
Luego suma y escribe la suma.

1. $37 + 8 = $ _____
2. $55 + 7 = $ _____

Separa los sumandos para hallar la suma.

3. $27 \rightarrow$ _____ + _____

   $+36 \rightarrow$ _____ + _____

   _____ + _____ = _____

Escribe la suma.

4. 2 8
   + 5 7
   _____

5. 6 7
   + 3 1
   _____

6. 7 1
   + 1 9
   _____

7. **PIENSA MÁS** Julia reunió 25 latas para reciclar. Dan reunió 14 latas. ¿Cuántas latas reunieron en total?

   _____ latas

276 doscientos setenta y seis

Nombre _____

Practicar sumas de 2 dígitos

**Práctica y tarea
Lección 4.7**

Objetivo de aprendizaje Practicarás la suma de 2 dígitos con y sin reagrupación.

Escribe la suma.

1.
```
   58
 + 17
 ----
```

2.
```
   44
 + 86
 ----
```

3.
```
   36
 + 13
 ----
```

4.
```
   49
 + 72
 ----
```

5.
```
   58
 + 87
 ----
```

6.
```
   32
 + 59
 ----
```

Resolución de problemas

Resuelve. Escribe o dibuja para explicar.

7. Hay 45 libros en el estante.
   Hay 37 libros sobre la mesa.
   ¿Cuántos libros hay en el estante y sobre la mesa en total?

   _____ libros

8. ESCRIBE Matemáticas Describe cómo debes reagrupar para hallar la suma de 64 + 43.

   _____

   _____

Repaso de la lección

1. ¿Cuál es la suma?

    $$\begin{array}{r} 56 \\ + 35 \\ \hline \end{array}$$

2. ¿Cuál es la suma?

    $$\begin{array}{r} 74 \\ + 15 \\ \hline \end{array}$$

Repaso en espiral

3. ¿Cuál es el valor del dígito subrayado?

    5̲26

    _____

4. El maestro Stevens quiere colocar 17 libros en el estante. Colocó 8 libros en el estante. ¿Cuántos libros más tiene que colocar en el estante?

    17 − 8 = _____ libros

5. ¿Cuál es la diferencia?

    11 − 6 = _____

6. Escribe 83 como una suma de decenas y unidades.

    _____ + _____

278 doscientos setenta y ocho

Nombre _____

Reescribir sumas de 2 dígitos

Pregunta esencial ¿Qué dos maneras diferentes hay para escribir problemas de suma?

Lección 4.8

Objetivo de aprendizaje Reescribirás problemas de suma hasta 100 de manera diferente.

Escucha y dibuja — En el mundo

Escribe los números de cada problema de suma.

+ _____

+ _____

+ _____

+ _____

PARA EL MAESTRO • Lea el siguiente problema y pida a los niños que escriban los sumandos en formato vertical. La familia de Juan condujo 32 millas hasta la casa de su abuela. Después condujeron 14 millas hasta la casa de su tía. ¿Cuántas millas condujeron? Repita con tres problemas más.

Charla matemática — PRÁCTICAS Y PROCESOS MATEMÁTICOS 7

Busca estructuras Explica por qué es importante alinear los dígitos de estos sumandos en columnas.

Capítulo 4 · doscientos setenta y nueve **279**

Representa y dibuja

Suma. 28 + 45 = ?

Paso 1 Escribe el dígito de las decenas de 28 en la columna de las decenas.

Escribe el dígito de las unidades en la columna de las unidades.

```
  2 8
+ 4 5
-----
```

Repite con 45.

Paso 2 Suma las unidades. Reagrupa si lo necesitas. Suma las decenas.

```
  2 8
+ 4 5
-----
```

Comparte y muestra

Reescribe el problema de suma. Luego suma.

1. 25 + 8

   +_____

2. 37 + 10

   +_____

3. 25 + 45

   +_____

4. 38 + 29

   +_____

5. 20 + 45

   +_____

6. 63 + 9

   +_____

✓ 7. 15 + 36

   +_____

✓ 8. 74 + 18

   +_____

280 doscientos ochenta

Nombre _____

Por tu cuenta

Reescribe el problema de suma. Luego suma.

9. 27 + 54

10. 34 + 30

11. 26 + 17

12. 48 + 38

13. 50 + 32

14. 61 + 38

15. 37 + 43

16. 79 + 17

17. 45 + 40

18. 21 + 52

19. 17 + 76

20. 68 + 29

21. **PIENSA MÁS** ¿En cuál de los problemas anteriores pudiste hallar la suma sin reescribirlo? Explica.

_____

_____

_____

Capítulo 4 • Lección 8

PRÁCTICAS Y PROCESOS MATEMÁTICOS • ANALIZAR • BUSCAR ESTRUCTURAS • PRECISIÓN

Resolución de problemas • Aplicaciones

Usa la tabla. Escribe o haz un dibujo para mostrar cómo resolviste los problemas.

Puntos anotados esta temporada	
Jugador	Número de puntos
Anna	26
Lou	37
Becky	23
Kevin	19

22. **Analiza relaciones** ¿Qué dos jugadores anotaron 56 puntos en total? Suma para comprobar tu respuesta.

_____ y _____

23. **PIENSA MÁS** Shawn dice que puede hallar la suma de 20 + 63 sin reescribirlo. Explica cómo hallar la suma con cálculo mental.

_____
_____
_____
_____

ACTIVIDAD PARA LA CASA • Pida a su niño que escriba y resuelva otro problema usando la tabla de arriba.

Nombre _____

Práctica y tarea
Lección 4.8

Reescribir sumas de 2 dígitos

Reescribe los números. Luego suma.

Objetivo de aprendizaje Reescribirás problemas de suma hasta 100 de manera diferente.

1. 27 + 19

   +_____

2. 36 + 23

   +_____

3. 31 + 29

   +_____

4. 48 + 23

   +_____

5. 53 + 12

   +_____

6. 69 + 13

   +_____

7. 24 + 38

   +_____

8. 46 + 37

   +_____

Resolución de problemas

Usa la tabla. Muestra cómo resolviste el problema.

9. ¿Cuántas páginas leyeron Sasha y Kara en total?

   _____ páginas

Páginas leídas esta semana	
Niño	Número de páginas
Sasha	62
Kara	29
Juan	50

10. ESCRIBE Matemáticas Explica qué puede pasar si alineas los dígitos incorrectamente al reescribir los problemas de suma.

_____
_____
_____

Capítulo 4

doscientos ochenta y tres **283**

Repaso de la lección

1. ¿Cuál es la suma de 39 + 17?

   $+\underline{}$

2. ¿Cuál es la suma de 28 + 16?

   $+\underline{}$

Repaso en espiral

3. ¿Qué número es otra manera de escribir 60 + 4?

   ____

4. En el salón de clases hay 4 escritorios por hilera. Hay 5 hileras. ¿Cuántos escritorios hay en el salón de clases?

   ____ escritorios

5. Una ardilla recolectó 17 bellotas. Luego la ardilla recolectó 31 bellotas. ¿Cuántas bellotas recolectó la ardilla en total?

   ____ bellotas

6. ¿Qué número puede escribirse como 3 centenas, 7 decenas, 5 unidades?

   ____

Nombre _____

Resolución de problemas • La suma

RESOLUCIÓN DE PROBLEMAS
Lección 4.9

Pregunta esencial ¿Cómo ayuda dibujar un diagrama cuando resuelves problemas?

Objetivo de aprendizaje Usarás la estrategia de *dibujar un diagrama* de modelos de barras para resolver problemas de suma hasta 100.

Kendra tenía 13 crayones. Su papá le regaló algunos más. Entonces tenía 19 crayones. ¿Cuántos crayones le regaló a Kendra su papá?

Soluciona el problema

¿Qué debo hallar?

cuántos crayones
_____
le regaló a Kendra su papá

¿Qué información debo usar?

Tenía _____ crayones.

Después de que él le regaló algunos

más, ella tenía _____ crayones.

Muestra cómo resolver el problema.

| 13 | ____ |

19

13 + ▨ = 19

Hay 19 crayones en total.

_____ crayones

NOTA A LA FAMILIA: • Su niño usó un modelo de barras y un enunciado numérico para representar el problema. Esto ayuda a mostrar la cantidad que falta para resolver el problema.

Capítulo 4   doscientos ochenta y cinco **285**

Haz otro problema

Rotula el modelo de barras. Escribe un enunciado numérico con un ▇ en el lugar del número que falta. Resuelve.

- ¿Qué debo hallar?
- ¿Qué información debo usar?

1. El Sr. Kane tiene 24 bolígrafos rojos. Compra 19 bolígrafos azules. ¿Cuántos bolígrafos tiene ahora?

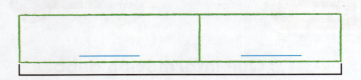

_____   _____ bolígrafos

2. Hannah tiene 10 lápices. Jim y Hannah tienen 17 lápices en total. ¿Cuántos lápices tiene Jim?

_____   _____ lápices

Charla matemática PRÁCTICAS Y PROCESOS MATEMÁTICOS

Explica cómo sabes si una cantidad es una parte o el entero de un problema.

286 doscientos ochenta y seis

Nombre _____

Comparte y muestra

Rotula el modelo de barras. Escribe un enunciado numérico con un ▢ en el lugar del número que falta. Resuelve.

3. Aimee y Matthew atrapan 17 grillos en total. Aimee atrapa 9 grillos. ¿Cuántos grillos atrapa Matthew?

_____ grillos

_____

4. Percy cuenta 16 saltamontes en el parque. Luego cuenta otros 15 saltamontes en casa. ¿Cuántos saltamontes cuenta en total?

_____ saltamontes

_____

5. PIENSA MÁS Hay tres grupos de búhos. Hay 17 búhos en cada uno de los dos primeros grupos. En total hay 47 búhos. ¿Cuántos búhos hay en el tercer grupo?

_____ búhos

Capítulo 4 • Lección 9

| PRÁCTICAS Y PROCESOS MATEMÁTICOS | REPRESENTAR • RAZONAR • ENTENDER |

Por tu cuenta Matemáticas

Escribe o dibuja para explicar.

6. Hay 37 clips en una caja y 24 clips sobre la mesa. ¿Cuántos clips hay en total?

_____ clips

7. **Comprende los problemas**
Jeff tiene 19 tarjetas postales y dos bolígrafos. Compra 20 tarjetas postales más. ¿Cuántas postales tiene ahora?

_____ tarjetas postales

8. **MÁS AL DETALLE** En una granja hay 41 gallinas. Hay 13 gallinas en cada uno de los 2 gallineros del corral. El resto de gallinas está afuera. ¿Cuántas gallinas hay afuera?

_____ gallinas

9. **PIENSA MÁS** Hay 23 libros en una caja. Hay 29 libros en un estante. ¿Cuántos libros hay en total?

_____ libros

 ACTIVIDAD PARA LA CASA • Pida a su niño que explique cómo resolver uno de los problemas de arriba.

Nombre _____

Resolución de problemas • Suma

**Práctica y tarea
Lección 4.9**

Objetivo de aprendizaje Usarás la estrategia de *dibujar un diagrama* de modelos de barras para resolver problemas de suma hasta 100.

Rotula el modelo de barras. Escribe un enunciado numérico con un ▪ en lugar del número que falta. Resuelve.

1. Jacob cuenta 37 hormigas en la acera y 11 hormigas en el césped. ¿Cuántas hormigas cuenta Jacob?

    _____ hormigas

2. Hay 14 abejas en la colmena y 17 abejas en el jardín. ¿Cuántas abejas hay en total?

    _____ abejas

3. ✏️ **Matemáticas** Describe cómo rotulaste el modelo de barras y escribiste el enunciado numérico para resolver el Ejercicio 2.

Capítulo 4

doscientos ochenta y nueve **289**

Repaso de la lección

1. Sean y Abby tienen 23 marcadores entre los dos. Abby tiene 14 marcadores. ¿Cuántos marcadores tiene Sean?

   _____

2. La maestra James tiene 22 estudiantes en su clase. El maestro Williams tiene 24 estudiantes en su clase. ¿Cuántos estudiantes hay en las dos clases?

   _____

Repaso en espiral

3. ¿Cuál es la diferencia?

   $15 - 9 =$ _____

4. ¿Cuál es la suma?

   $7 + 5 =$ _____

5. Jan tiene 10 bloques. Le regala 9 bloques a Tim. ¿Cuántos bloques tiene Jan ahora?

   $14 - 9 =$ _____ bloques

6. ¿Cuál es el siguiente número del patrón de conteo?

   29, 39, 49, 59, _____

Nombre _____

Álgebra • Escribir ecuaciones para representar la suma

Lección 4.10

Pregunta esencial ¿Cómo escribes un enunciado numérico para representar un problema?

Objetivo de aprendizaje Mostrarás un problema de suma al escribir un enunciado numérico con un símbolo en el lugar del número que falta.

Escucha y dibuja — En el mundo

Haz un dibujo para mostrar cómo hallaste la respuesta.

PARA EL MAESTRO • Lea el siguiente problema y pida a los niños que elijan su propio método para resolverlo. Hay 15 niños en el autobús. Luego 9 niños más suben al autobús. ¿Cuántos niños hay en el autobús ahora?

Charla matemática

PRÁCTICAS Y PROCESOS MATEMÁTICOS 5

Comunica Explica cómo hallaste el número de niños que había en el autobús.

Capítulo 4

doscientos noventa y uno **291**

Representa y dibuja

Puedes escribir un enunciado numérico para mostrar un problema.

Sandy tiene 16 lápices. Nancy tiene 13 lápices. ¿Cuántos lápices tienen en total?

16 + 13 =

PIENSA:
   16 lápices
 + 13 lápices
   29 lápices

Tienen _____ lápices en total.

Comparte y muestra

Escribe un enunciado numérico para el problema. Usa un ■ en el lugar del número que falta. Luego resuelve.

1. Carl ve 25 melones en la tienda. Hay 15 pequeños y el resto son grandes. ¿Cuántos melones son grandes?

    _____

   _____ melones

2. El jueves fueron 83 personas al cine. Había 53 niños y el resto eran adultos. ¿Cuántos adultos había en el cine?

   _____

   _____ adultos

292 doscientos noventa y dos

Nombre _____

Por tu cuenta

Escribe un enunciado numérico para el problema. Usa un ▪ en el lugar de los números que faltan. Luego resuelve.

3. Jake tenía algunos sellos. Luego compró 20 sellos más. Ahora tiene 56 sellos. ¿Cuántos sellos tenía Jake al comienzo?

_____   _____ sellos

4. PIENSA MÁS La clase de Braden fue al parque. Vieron 26 robles y 14 arces. También vieron 13 cardenales y 35 azulejos. Compara el número de árboles y el número de aves que vio la clase.

_____ ◯ _____

Matemáticas al instante

5. PRÁCTICAS Y PROCESOS MATEMÁTICOS 6 **Explica** Amy necesita aproximadamente 70 clips. Sin sumar, encierra en un círculo 2 cajas que se aproximarían a la cantidad que necesita Amy.

| 70 clips | 81 clips | 54 clips |
| 19 clips | 35 clips | 32 clips |

Explica por qué las elegiste.

_____
_____
_____

Capítulo 4 • Lección 10   doscientos noventa y tres **293**

Resolución de problemas • Aplicaciones

6. Comprende los problemas
El Sr. Walton horneó 24 panes la semana pasada. Horneó 28 panes esta semana. ¿Cuántos panes horneó en las dos semanas?

_____ panes

7. PIENSA MÁS Denise vio estas bolsas de naranjas en la tienda.

Denise compró 26 naranjas. ¿Qué dos bolsas de naranjas compró?
Escribe o haz un dibujo para mostrar cómo resolviste el problema.

Explica cómo hallaste los números que suman un total de 26.

_____
_____
_____

ACTIVIDAD PARA LA CASA • Pida a su niño que explique cómo escribe un enunciado numérico que represente un problema.

Nombre _____

**Práctica y tarea
Lección 4.10**

Álgebra • Escribir ecuaciones para representar la suma

Objetivo de aprendizaje Mostrarás un problema de suma al escribir un enunciado numérico con un símbolo en el lugar del número que falta.

Escribe un enunciado numérico para el problema. Usa un en lugar del número que falta. Luego resuelve.

1. Emily y sus amigos fueron al parque. Vieron 15 petirrojos y 9 azulejos. ¿Cuántas aves vieron?

   _____   _____ aves

2. Joe tiene 13 peces en una pecera. Tiene 8 peces en otra pecera. ¿Cuántos peces tiene Joe?

   _____   _____ peces

Resolución de problemas · En el mundo

Resuelve.

3. Hay 21 estudiantes en la clase de Kathleen. 12 de ellos son mujeres. ¿Cuántos varones hay en la clase de Kathleen?

   _____ varones

4. **ESCRIBE Matemáticas** Explica por qué decidiste escribir ese enunciado numérico para el Ejercicio 1.

   _____
   _____
   _____
   _____

Capítulo 4

Repaso de la lección

1. Clara tiene 14 bloques. Jasmine tiene 6 bloques. ¿Cuántos bloques tienen en total?

    14 + 6 = _____ bloques

2. Matt encontró 16 bellotas en el parque. Trevor encontró 18 bellotas. ¿Cuántas bellotas encontraron los dos?

    16 + 18 = _____ bellotas

Repaso en espiral

3. Leanne contó 19 hormigas. Gregory contó 6. ¿Cuántas hormigas más que Gregory contó Leanne?

    19 − 6 = _____ hormigas

4. ¿Cuál es la suma?

    4 + 3 + 6 = _____

5. La maestra Santos colocó caracoles en 4 hileras. Colocó 6 caracoles en cada hilera. ¿Cuántos caracoles hay en total?

    _____ caracoles

6. Encierra en un círculo el número par.

    9   14   17   21

296 doscientos noventa y seis

Nombre _____

Álgebra • Hallar la suma de 3 sumandos

Lección 4.11

Pregunta esencial ¿De qué maneras se pueden sumar 3 números?

Objetivo de aprendizaje Sumarás tres números de 2 dígitos hasta 1,000.

Escucha y dibuja En el mundo

Haz un dibujo para mostrar cada problema.

PARA EL MAESTRO • Lea el siguiente problema y pida a los niños que hagan un dibujo para mostrarlo. El Sr. Kim compró 5 globos azules, 4 globos rojos y 5 globos amarillos. ¿Cuántos globos compró el Sr. Kim? Repita con otro problema.

Charla matemática PRÁCTICAS Y PROCESOS MATEMÁTICOS

¿Qué números sumaste primero en el primer problema? **Explica** por qué.

Capítulo 4 — doscientos noventa y siete **297**

Representa y dibuja

Hay distintas maneras de sumar tres números.

¿Cómo puedes sumar 23, 41 y 17?

Piensa en distintas maneras de elegir dígitos de la **columna** de las unidades para sumar primero.

Primero puedes formar una decena. Luego suma el otro dígito de las unidades. Luego suma las decenas.

```
  2 3
  4 1
+ 1 7
```
$3 + 7 = 10$
$10 + 1 = 11$

Suma de arriba abajo. Primero suma los dos dígitos de la parte superior de la columna de las unidades, luego suma el siguiente dígito. Luego suma las decenas.

```
  2 3
  4 1
+ 1 7
```
$3 + 1 = 4$
$4 + 7 = 11$

Comparte y muestra

Suma.

1.
```
   33
   34
 + 32
```

2.
```
   47
   21
 +  7
```

3.
```
   65
   13
 + 15
```

4.
```
   58
   27
 + 22
```

5.
```
   12
   22
 + 36
```

6.
```
   10
   42
 + 36
```

7.
```
   31
   21
 + 16
```

8.
```
   30
   29
 + 48
```

298 doscientos noventa y ocho

Nombre _____

Por tu cuenta

Suma.

9.   22
       27
     +18

10.   26
       31
     +19

11.   24
       11
     +53

12.   33
       43
     + 4

13.   40
       17
     +32

14.   25
       25
     +25

15.   19
       65
     +24

16.   73
        4
     +16

17. **MÁS AL DETALLE** La Sra. Carson está preparando comida para una fiesta. Hace 20 sándwiches de jamón, 34 sándwiches de pavo y 38 sándwiches de atún. ¿Cuántos sándwiches prepara para la fiesta?

_____ sándwiches

18. **PIENSA MÁS** Sofía tenía 44 canicas. Compró 24 canicas más. Luego John le regaló 35 canicas. ¿Cuántas canicas tiene Sofía ahora?

_____ canicas

Capítulo 4 • Lección 11   doscientos noventa y nueve **299**

PRÁCTICAS Y PROCESOS MATEMÁTICOS • ANALIZAR • BUSCAR ESTRUCTURAS • PRECISIÓN

Resolución de problemas • Aplicaciones

Resuelve. Escribe o dibuja para explicar.

19. **Evalúa** La Sra. Shaw tiene 23 cuadernos rojos, 15 cuadernos azules y 27 cuadernos verdes. ¿Cuántos cuadernos tiene en total?

_____ cuadernos

20. **Haz un modelo de matemáticas** Escribe un problema que pueda resolverse con este enunciado numérico.

12 + 28 + ■ = 53

_____
_____
_____
_____

21. **PIENSA MÁS** El Sr. Samson dio a sus estudiantes 31 lápices amarillos, 27 lápices rojos y 25 lápices azules. ¿Cuántos lápices dio en total a sus estudiantes?

_____ lápices

ACTIVIDAD PARA LA CASA • Pida a su niño que muestre dos formas de sumar 17, 13 y 24.

300 trescientos

Nombre _____

**Práctica y tarea
Lección 4.11**

Álgebra • Hallar la suma de 3 sumandos

Objetivo de aprendizaje Sumarás tres números de 2 dígitos hasta 1,000.

Suma.

1.
```
  2 3
  2 0
+ 2 5
```

2.
```
  1 5
  2 2
+ 3 8
```

3.
```
  1 3
  5 2
+ 3 4
```

4.
```
  2 7
  4 0
+ 1 9
```

5.
```
  3 1
  4 5
+ 2 4
```

6.
```
  3 4
  1 1
+ 2 8
```

7.
```
  4 2
  3 6
+ 1 1
```

8.
```
  1 8
  2 2
+ 3 4
```

9.
```
  5 3
  1 9
+ 2 5
```

Resolución de problemas

Resuelve. Escribe o dibuja la explicación.

10. Liam tiene 24 lápices amarillos, 15 lápices rojos y 9 lápices azules. ¿Cuántos lápices tiene en total?

_____ lápices

11. ESCRIBE Matemáticas Describe cómo hallarías la suma de 24, 36 y 13.

Capítulo 4   trescientos uno **301**

Repaso de la lección

1. ¿Cuál es la suma?

    $$\begin{array}{r} 22 \\ 31 \\ +\ 16 \\ \hline \end{array}$$

2. ¿Cuál es la suma?

    $$\begin{array}{r} 17 \\ 26 \\ +\ 30 \\ \hline \end{array}$$

Repaso en espiral

3. ¿Qué número es 10 más que 127?

    _____

4. El teléfono del Sr. Howard tiene 4 hileras de teclas. Hay 3 teclas en cada hilera. ¿Cuántas teclas tiene el teléfono del Sr. Howard?

    _____ teclas

5. Bob lanzó 8 herraduras. Liz lanzó 9 herraduras. ¿Cuántas herraduras lanzaron los dos?

    8 + 9 = _____ herraduras

6. ¿Qué número se puede escribir como 3 centenas 1 decena 5 unidades?

    _____

Nombre _____

Álgebra • Hallar la suma de 4 sumandos

Lección 4.12

Pregunta esencial ¿De qué maneras se pueden sumar 4 números?

Objetivo de aprendizaje Sumarás cuatro números de 2 dígitos hasta 1,000.

Escucha y dibuja En el mundo

Muestra cómo resolviste cada problema.

PARA EL MAESTRO • Lea este problema y pida a los niños que elijan una manera de resolverlo. Shelly cuenta 16 hormigas en su granja de hormigas. Pedro cuenta 22 hormigas en su granja. Tara cuenta 14 hormigas en su granja. ¿Cuántas hormigas cuentan los 3 niños? Repita con otro problema.

Charla matemática

PRÁCTICAS Y PROCESOS MATEMÁTICOS 6

Describe cómo hallaste la respuesta del primer problema.

Capítulo 4 — trescientos tres **303**

Representa y dibuja

Los dígitos de una columna se pueden sumar de más de una manera. Suma las unidades primero. Luego suma las decenas.

Halla una suma que conozcas. Luego súmale a esta suma.

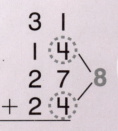

PIENSA: 8 + 1 = 9, luego súmale 7. La suma de las unidades es 16 unidades.

Suma pares de dígitos primero. Luego suma estas sumas.

PIENSA: 5 + 11 = 16, por lo tanto, hay 16 unidades en total.

Comparte y muestra

Suma.

1. 23
    11
    22
    +31

2. 30
    15
    3
    +25

3. 13
    26
    54
    +12

4. 27
    2
    23
    +13

5. 45
    14
    35
    +51

6. 32
    21
    15
    +30

Nombre _____

Por tu cuenta

Suma.

7. 36
    12
    21
  + 26

8. 14
    23
    20
  + 11

9. 22
    13
    15
  + 27

10. 45
    12
    41
  + 22

11. 59
    31
    51
  + 73

12. 34
    10
    31
  + 22

13. **MÁS AL DETALLE** Unas amigas necesitan 100 lazos para hacer un proyecto. Sara lleva 12 lazos, Ángela lleva 50 lazos y Nora lleva 34 lazos. ¿Cuántos lazos más necesitarán?

_____ lazos más

Resuelve. Dibuja o escribe para explicar.

14. **PIENSA MÁS** Laney sumó cuatro números que suman un total de 128. Derramó jugo sobre un número. ¿Qué número es?

22 + 43 + ⬤ + 30 = 128

_____

Matemáticas al instante

Capítulo 4 • Lección 12   trescientos cinco **305**

Resolución de problemas • Aplicaciones

Usa la tabla.
Escribe o haz un dibujo para mostrar cómo resolviste los problemas.

Caracoles recolectados en la playa	
Niño	Número de caracoles
Katie	34
Paúl	15
Noah	26
Laura	21

15. **Evalúa** ¿Cuántos caracoles recolectaron en total los cuatro niños en la playa?

_____ caracoles

16. ¿Qué dos niños recolectaron más caracoles en la playa: Katie y Paúl o Noah y Laura?

_____

17. **PIENSA MÁS** Había 24 cuentas rojas, 31 cuentas azules y 8 cuentas verdes en un frasco. Luego Emma puso 16 cuentas en el frasco. Escribe un enunciado numérico que muestre el número de cuentas que hay ahora en el frasco.

_____

ACTIVIDAD PARA LA CASA • Pida a su niño que explique qué aprendió en esta lección.

Nombre _____

Álgebra • Hallar la suma de 4 sumandos

**Práctica y tarea
Lección 4.12**

Objetivo de aprendizaje Sumarás cuatro números de 2 dígitos hasta 1,000.

Suma.

1.
```
  1 8
  3 2
  2 3
+   3
```

2.
```
  4 5
  3 1
  2 9
+ 7 2
```

3.
```
  2 4
  6 2
  7 0
+ 3 3
```

4.
```
  8 3
  3 2
  6 1
+ 2 2
```

5.
```
  3 7
  1 5
  3 1
+ 1 2
```

6.
```
  2 1
  1 3
  9 6
+ 1 8
```

Resolución de problemas

Resuelve. Muestra cómo resolviste el problema.

7. Kinza corre 16 minutos el lunes, 13 minutos el martes, 9 minutos el miércoles y 20 minutos el jueves. ¿Cuántos minutos corre Kinza en total?

_____ minutos

8. ESCRIBE Matemáticas Describe dos estrategias diferentes que podrías usar para sumar 16 + 35 + 24 + 14.

Capítulo 4   trescientos siete **307**

Repaso de la lección

1. ¿Cuál es la suma?

$$\begin{array}{r}12\\33\\56\\+32\\\hline\end{array}$$

2. ¿Cuál es la suma?

$$\begin{array}{r}41\\74\\43\\+20\\\hline\end{array}$$

Repaso en espiral

3. Laura tiene 6 margaritas. Luego encuentra 7 margaritas más. ¿Cuántas margaritas tiene ahora?

    6 + 7 = _____ margaritas

4. ¿Cuál es la suma?

$$\begin{array}{r}52\\+27\\\hline\end{array}$$

5. Alan tiene 25 tarjetas de colección. Compra 8 más. ¿Cuántas tarjetas tiene ahora?

    25 + 8 = _____ tarjetas

6. Jen vio 13 conejillos de Indias y 18 jerbos en la tienda de mascotas. ¿Cuántas mascotas vio?

    13 + 18 = _____ mascotas

Repaso y prueba del Capítulo 4

1. Beth horneó 24 pastelitos de zanahoria. Luego horneó 18 pastelitos de manzana. ¿Cuántos pastelitos horneó?

   Rotula el modelo de barra. Escribe un enunciado numérico con un ▢ en el lugar del número que falta. Resuelve.

   _____   _____ pastelitos

2. Carlos tiene 23 llaves rojas, 36 llaves azules y 44 llaves verdes. ¿Cuántas llaves tiene?

   Carlos tiene | 67 | llaves.
   | 80 |
   | 103 |

3. Mike ve 17 carritos azules y 25 carritos verdes en la tienda de juguetes. ¿Cuántos carritos ve?

   ○ 17 + 25   ○ 25 − 17   ○ 25 + 17   ○ 17 + 17

   Mike ve _____ carritos.

   Describe cómo resolviste el problema.

   _____

   _____

Capítulo 4   trescientos nueve **309**

4. Jerry tiene 53 lápices en un cajón. Tiene 27 lápices en otro cajón.

   Escribe o haz un dibujo que explique cómo hallar el número de lápices que hay en los dos cajones.

   Jerry tiene _____ lápices.

5. **PIENSA MÁS** Lauren ve 14 aves. Su amigo ve 7 aves. ¿Cuántas aves ven Lauren y su amigo? Haz dibujos rápidos para resolver. Escribe la suma.

Decenas	Unidades

   _____ aves

   ¿Reagrupaste para hallar la respuesta? Explica.

6. Matt dice que puede hallar la suma de 45 + 50 sin reescribirla. Explica cómo puedes resolver este problema con un cálculo mental.

Nombre _____

7. Ling ve estos tres carteles en el teatro.

| Sección A | Sección B | Sección C |
| 35 asientos | 43 asientos | 17 asientos |

¿Qué dos secciones tienen 78 asientos?
Explica por qué las elegiste.

_____

_____

8. Leah puso 21 canicas blancas, 31 canicas negras y 7 canicas azules en una bolsa. Luego, su hermana agregó 19 canicas amarillas.

Escribe un enunciado numérico para mostrar el número de canicas que hay en la bolsa.

_____

9. Nicole hizo un collar. Usó 13 cuentas rojas y 26 cuentas azules. Muestra cómo puedes separar los sumandos para hallar el número de cuentas que usó Nicole.

$$13 \longrightarrow \underline{} + \underline{}$$

$$+\ 26 \longrightarrow \underline{} + \underline{}$$

$$\underline{} + \underline{} = \underline{}$$

Capítulo 4   trescientos once **311**

10. **MÁS AL DETALLE** Sin hallar las sumas, ¿tiene el par de sumandos una suma mayor que 100?
Elige Sí o No.

51 + 92   ○ Sí   ○ No

42 + 27   ○ Sí   ○ No

82 + 33   ○ Sí   ○ No

62 + 14   ○ Sí   ○ No

Explica cómo decidiste qué pares suman un total mayor que 100.

_____

_____

_____

11. Leslie encuentra 24 clips en su mesa. Encuentra 8 clips más en su caja de los lápices. Elige todas las formas que puedes usar para hallar cuántos clips tiene Leslie en total.

○ 24 + 8
○ 24 − 8
○ 24 + 6 + 2

12. El Sr. O'Brien visitó un faro. Subió 26 escalones. Luego subió 64 escalones más hasta llegar arriba. ¿Cuántos escalones subió en el faro?

_____ escalones

Capítulo 5
Resta de 2 dígitos

Hay cientos de tipos de libélulas. Si hay 52 libélulas en un jardín y 10 se van volando, ¿cuántas libélulas quedan? ¿Cuántas quedan si se van volando 10 más?

Capítulo 5   trescientos trece 313

Nombre _____

✓ Muestra lo que sabes

Patrones de resta

Resta 2. Completa cada enunciado de resta.

1. 7 − _2_ = _5_
2. 6 − ___ = ___
3. 5 − ___ = ___
4. 4 − ___ = ___
5. 3 − ___ = ___
6. 2 − ___ = ___

Operaciones de resta

Escribe la diferencia.

7. 8 − 5
8. 14 − 6
9. 9 − 6
10. 16 − 7
11. 12 − 6
12. 10 − 8

Decenas y unidades

Escribe cuántas decenas y unidades hay en cada modelo.

13. 54

____ decenas ____ unidades

14. 45

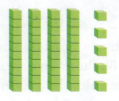

____ decenas ____ unidades

Esta página es para verificar la comprensión de destrezas importantes que se necesitan para tener éxito en el Capítulo 5.

Nombre _____

Desarrollo del vocabulario

Palabras de repaso
diferencia
reagrupar
decenas
unidades
dígito

Visualízalo
Completa las casillas del organizador gráfico.

diferencia

Descríbelo.
_____
_____

Ejemplos
10 − 4 = 6
_____

No son ejemplos
4 + 6 = 10
_____

Comprende el vocabulario
Dibuja una línea para completar el enunciado.

1. Un **dígito** puede ser •   • que 2 **decenas**.

2. Puedes **reagrupar** •   • 0, 1, 2, 3, 4, 5, 6, 7, 8 o 9.

3. 20 **unidades** son lo mismo •   • para cambiar 10 unidades por 1 decena.

- Libro interactivo del estudiant
- Glosario multimedia

Capítulo 5   trescientos quince **315**

Capítulo 5

Juego: Búsqueda de restas

Materiales
- 3 conjuntos de tarjetas con números 4-9
- 18 🔴

Juega con un compañero.

1. Baraja todas las tarjetas. Colócalas boca abajo en una pila.
2. Toma una tarjeta. Halla un cuadrado con un problema de resta que tenga este número como diferencia. Tu compañero comprueba tu respuesta.
3. Si estás en lo cierto, coloca una 🔴 en ese cuadrado. Si no hay coincidencia, pasa tu turno.
4. Túrnense. El primer jugador que tenga 🔴 en todos los cuadrados es el ganador.

Jugador 1

12 − 5	9 − 2	10 − 5
16 − 7	13 − 7	17 − 9
7 − 3	11 − 5	18 − 9

Jugador 2

8 − 3	15 − 7	11 − 6
17 − 8	9 − 3	16 − 8
13 − 9	6 − 2	14 − 7

Vocabulario del Capítulo 5

columna	decenas
column	tens
10	18

diferencia	dígito
difference	digit
20	21

es igual a	reagrupar
is equal to (=)	regroup
25	55

sumandos	unidades
addends	ones
60	64

10 unidades = 1 decena

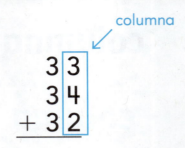

columna

0, 1, 2, 3, 4, 5, 6, 7, 8, y 9 son **dígitos**.

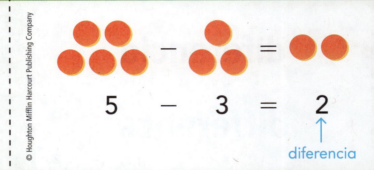

5 − 3 = 2

diferencia

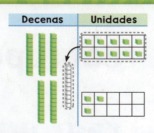

Puedes cambiar 10 unidades por 1 decena para **reagrupar**.

2 más 1 es igual a 3
2 + 1 = 3

10 unidades = 1 decena

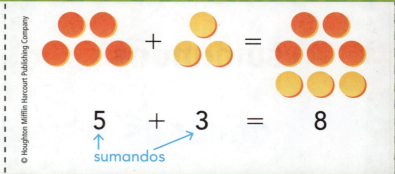

5 + 3 = 8

sumandos

De visita con las palabras de ¡Vivan las matemáticas!

¡BINGO!

Jugadores: 3 a 6

Materiales
- 1 juego de tarjetas de palabras
- 1 tablero de Bingo para cada jugador
- fichas de juego

Instrucciones
1. El encargado del juego elige una tarjeta de palabras y lee la palabra. Luego el encargado del juego coloca la tarjeta de palabras en una segunda pila.
2. Los jugadores colocan una ficha sobre la palabra cada vez que la encuentren en sus tableros de Bingo.
3. Se repiten los pasos 1 y 2 hasta que un jugador marque 5 casillas ya sea en línea vertical, horizontal u oblicua y grite "¡Bingo!"
4. Comprueben las respuestas. Pidan al jugador que dijo "¡Bingo!" que lea las palabras en voz alta mientras el encargado del juego comprueba las tarjetas de palabras de la segunda pila.

Recuadro de palabras
- columna
- decena
- diferencia
- dígito
- es igual a (=)
- reagrupar
- sumando
- unidades

Diario

Escríbelo

Reflexiona

Elige una idea. Escribe acerca de la idea en el espacio de abajo.

- Explica de qué manera los dibujos rápidos te ayudan a sumar números de 2 dígitos.
- Di todas las diferentes maneras en que puedes sumar números de 2 dígitos.
- Escribe sobre alguna ocasión en que ayudaste a explicar algo a un compañero. ¿Qué no entendía tu compañero? ¿Qué hiciste para ayudarlo?

Nombre _____

Lección **5.1**

Álgebra • Separar unidades para restar

Pregunta esencial ¿Cómo separar un número hace que sea más fácil restar?

Objetivo de aprendizaje Separarás unidades para que sea más fácil restar.

Escucha y dibuja

Escribe dos sumandos para cada total.

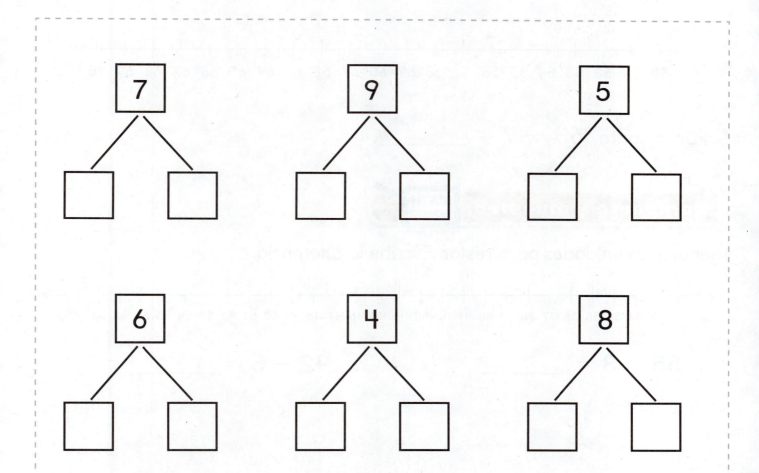

PARA EL MAESTRO • Después de que los niños anoten sumandos para cada suma, comente con la clase las diferentes operaciones que los niños representaron en sus hojas.

Charla matemática

PRÁCTICAS Y PROCESOS MATEMÁTICOS **6**

Describe cómo elegiste sumandos para cada suma.

Capítulo 5

trescientos diecisiete **317**

Representa y dibuja

Separa las unidades. Resta en dos pasos.

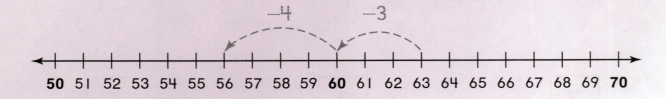

Comienza en 63. Resta 3 para llegar a 60. Luego resta 4 más.

Por lo tanto, 63 − 7 = _____.

Comparte y muestra

Separa las unidades para restar. Escribe la diferencia.

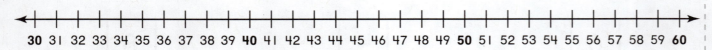

1. 55 − 8 = _____
   5   3

2. 42 − 5 = _____
   2   3

3. 41 − 9 = _____

4. 53 − 6 = _____

5. 44 − 7 = _____

6. 52 − 8 = _____

318   trescientos dieciocho

Nombre _____

Por tu cuenta

Separa las unidades para restar. Escribe la diferencia.

7. 75 − 7 = _____

8. 86 − 8 = _____

9. 82 − 5 = _____

10. 83 − 7 = _____

11. 72 − 7 = _____

12. 76 − 9 = _____

13. 85 − 8 = _____

14. 71 − 6 = _____

15. **PIENSA MÁS** Cheryl trajo 27 rosquillas para la venta de platos hechos al horno. Mike trajo 24 rosquillas. Vendieron todas menos 9. ¿Cuántas rosquillas vendieron?

_____ rosquillas

16. **PRÁCTICAS Y PROCESOS MATEMÁTICOS** **Analiza** Lexi tiene 8 crayones menos que Ken. Ken tiene 45 crayones. ¿Cuántos crayones tiene Lexi?

_____ crayones

Capítulo 5 • Lección 1

| PRÁCTICAS Y PROCESOS MATEMÁTICOS | COMUNICAR • PERSEVERAR • CONSTRUIR ARGUMENTOS |

Resolución de problemas • Aplicaciones

Escribe o dibuja para explicar.

17. Cheryl construyó un trencito con 27 vagones. Luego agregó 18 vagones más. ¿Cuántos vagones tiene el trencito ahora?

_____ vagones

18. **Analiza** Samuel tenía 46 canicas. Dio algunas canicas a un amigo y le quedan 9 canicas. ¿Cuántas canicas dio Samuel a su amigo?

_____ canicas

19. **PIENSA MÁS** Matthew tenía 73 bloques. Dio 8 bloques a su hermana. ¿Cuántos bloques tiene Matthew ahora?

Escribe o haz un dibujo para mostrar cómo resolver el problema.

Matthew tiene _____ bloques ahora.

 ACTIVIDAD PARA LA CASA • Pida a su niño que describa cómo hallar 34 − 6.

Nombre _____

Álgebra • Separar unidades para restar

Práctica y tarea
Lección 5.1

Objetivo de aprendizaje Separarás unidades para que sea más fácil restar.

Separa las unidades para restar.
Escribe la diferencia.

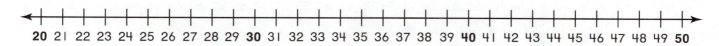

1. $36 - 7 =$ _____
2. $35 - 8 =$ _____
3. $37 - 9 =$ _____
4. $41 - 6 =$ _____
5. $44 - 5 =$ _____
6. $33 - 7 =$ _____
7. $32 - 4 =$ _____
8. $31 - 6 =$ _____

Resolución de problemas

Elige una manera de resolver. Escribe o dibuja la explicación.

9. Beth tiene 44 canicas. Le regala 9 canicas a su hermano. ¿Cuántas canicas tiene Beth ahora?

_____ canicas

10.  **Matemáticas** Dibuja una recta numérica y muestra cómo hallar la diferencia entre $24 - 6$ usando el método de separar de esta lección.

Capítulo 5   trescientos veintiuno **321**

Repaso de la lección

1. ¿Cuál es la diferencia?

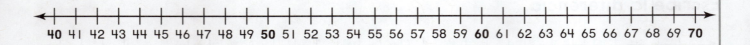

$58 - 9 = $ ___

Repaso en espiral

2. ¿Cuál es la diferencia?

   $14 - 6 = $ ___

3. ¿Cuál es la suma?

   $3 + 6 + 2 = $ ___

4. ¿Cuál es la suma?

   $64 + 7 = $ ___

5. ¿Cuál es la suma?

   $56 + 18 = $ ___

Nombre _____

Álgebra • Separar números para restar

Pregunta esencial ¿Por qué es más fácil restar si separamos un número?

Lección 5.2

Objetivo de aprendizaje Separarás un número de 2 dígitos para restarlo de otro número de 2 dígitos.

Escucha y dibuja En el mundo

Dibuja saltos en la recta numérica para mostrar cómo separar el número para restar.

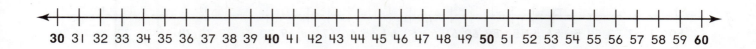

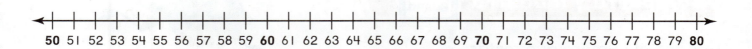

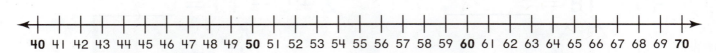

PARA EL MAESTRO • Lea el siguiente problema. Pida a los niños que dibujen saltos en la recta numérica para resolver. La Sra. Hill tenía 45 pinceles. Dio 9 pinceles a los estudiantes de su clase de arte. ¿Cuántos pinceles tiene la Sra. Hill ahora? Repita el mismo problema con 72 – 7 y 53 – 6.

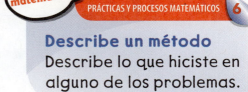

Describe un método
Describe lo que hiciste en alguno de los problemas.

Capítulo 5 — trescientos veintitrés **323**

Representa y dibuja

Separa el número que restas en decenas y unidades.

Resta 10.
Luego, resta 2 para llegar a 60.
Luego resta 5 más.

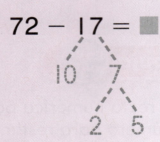

10 + 2 + 5 = 17

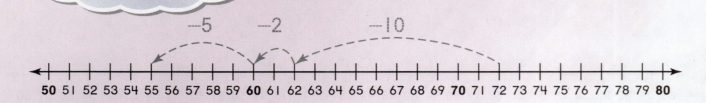

Por lo tanto, 72 − 17 = _____.

Comparte y muestra

Separa el número que restas.
Escribe la diferencia.

1. 43 − 18 = _____

2. 45 − 14 = _____

3. 46 − 17 = _____

4. 44 − 16 = _____

324 trescientos veinticuatro

Nombre _____

Por tu cuenta

Separa el número que restas.
Escribe la diferencia.

```
← 40 41 42 43 44 45 46 47 48 49 50 51 52 53 54 55 56 57 58 59 60 61 62 63 64 65 66 67 68 69 70 →
```

5. 57 − 15 = _____

6. 63 − 17 = _____

7. 68 − 19 = _____

8. 61 − 18 = _____

9. **PIENSA MÁS** Jane tiene 53 juguetes en una caja. Saca algunos. Ahora quedan 36 juguetes en la caja. ¿Cuántos juguetes sacó Jane de la caja?

_____ juguetes

10. **MÁS AL DETALLE** Observa los pasos de Tom para resolver un problema. Resuelve este problema de la misma manera.

42 − 15 = ?

Tom
35 − 18 = ?

35 − 10 = 25
25 − 5 = 20
20 − 3 = ⑰

Capítulo 5 • Lección 2

trescientos veinticinco

PRÁCTICAS Y PROCESOS MATEMÁTICOS • ANALIZAR • BUSCAR ESTRUCTURAS • PRECISIÓN

Resolución de problemas • Aplicaciones

11. Hay 38 personas en la biblioteca. Luego entran a la biblioteca 33 personas más. ¿Cuántas personas hay en la biblioteca ahora?

_____ personas

12. **PRÁCTICAS Y PROCESOS MATEMÁTICOS 1** **Analiza** Alex tiene 24 juguetes en un baúl. Saca algunos juguetes del baúl. Luego hay 16 juguetes en el baúl. ¿Cuántos juguetes sacó del baúl?

_____ juguetes

13. **PIENSA MÁS** Gail tiene dos pilas de papeles. Hay 32 papeles en la primera pila. Hay 19 papeles en la segunda pila. ¿Cuántos papeles más hay en la primera pila que en la segunda pila?

Escribe o haz un dibujo para explicar cómo resolviste el problema.

_____ papeles más

ACTIVIDAD PARA LA CASA • Pida a su niño que escriba un problema de resta que tenga números de 2 dígitos.

Nombre _____

Álgebra • Separar números para restar

Práctica y tarea
Lección 5.2

Objetivo de aprendizaje Separarás un número de 2 dígitos para restarlo de otro número de 2 dígitos.

Separa el número que restas.
Escribe la diferencia.

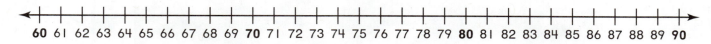

1. $81 - 14 = $ _____

2. $84 - 16 = $ _____

3. $77 - 14 = $ _____

4. $83 - 19 = $ _____

5. $81 - 17 = $ _____

6. $88 - 13 = $ _____

7. $84 - 19 = $ _____

8. $86 - 18 = $ _____

Resolución de problemas En el mundo

Resuelve. Escribe o dibuja la explicación.

9. El Sr. Pearce compró 43 plantas. Le dio 14 plantas a su hermana. ¿Cuántas plantas tiene el Sr. Pearce ahora?

_____ plantas

10. **ESCRIBE Matemáticas** Dibuja una recta numérica y muestra cómo hallar la diferencia entre 36 – 17. Usa el método de separar de esta lección.

Capítulo 5   trescientos veintisiete **327**

Repaso de la lección

1. ¿Cuál es la diferencia?

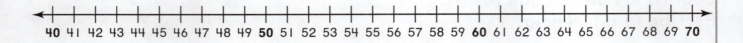

$$63 - 19 = \underline{}$$

Repaso en espiral

2. ¿Cuál es la suma?

$$\begin{array}{r} 14 \\ + \, 23 \\ \hline \end{array}$$

3. ¿Cuál es la suma?

$$8 + 7 = \underline{}$$

4. Escribe una operación de resta relacionada para $6 + 8 = 14$.

    _____

5. John tiene 7 cometas. Annie tiene 4 cometas ¿Cuántas cometas tienen en total?

    ____ cometas

Nombre _____

Reagrupar modelos para restar

Pregunta esencial ¿Cuándo reagrupas en la resta?

Lección 5.3

Objetivo de aprendizaje Representarás una resta con números hasta 100 con reagrupación.

Escucha y dibuja En el mundo — Manos a la obra

Usa para representar el problema.
Haz dibujos rápidos para mostrar tu modelo.

Decenas	Unidades

 PARA EL MAESTRO • Lea el siguiente problema. Michelle contó 21 mariposas en su jardín. Luego 7 mariposas se fueron volando. ¿Cuántas mariposas quedaron en el jardín?

Describe por qué cambiaste un bloque de decenas por 10 bloques de unidades.

Capítulo 5 — trescientos veintinueve **329**

Representa y dibuja

¿Cómo restas 26 de 53?

Paso 1 Muestra 53. ¿Hay unidades suficientes para restar 6?

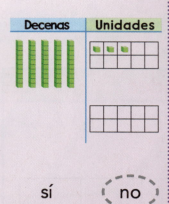

sí   no

Paso 2 Si no hay suficientes unidades, reagrupa 1 decena como 10 unidades.

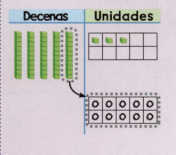

Paso 3 Resta 6 unidades de 13 unidades.

Paso 4 Resta las decenas. Escribe las decenas y las unidades. Escribe la diferencia.

____ decenas

____ unidades

____

Comparte y muestra

Dibuja para mostrar la reagrupación. Escribe la diferencia de dos maneras. Escribe las decenas y las unidades. Escribe el número.

1. Resta 13 de 41.

____ decenas

____ unidades

____

2. Resta 9 de 48.

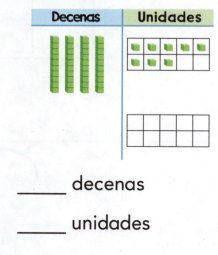

____ decenas

____ unidades

____

3. Resta 28 de 52.

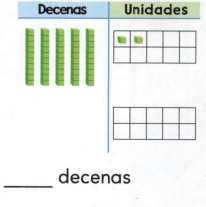

____ decenas

____ unidades

____

330 trescientos treinta

Nombre _____

Por tu cuenta

Dibuja para mostrar la reagrupación. Escribe la diferencia de dos maneras. Escribe las decenas y las unidades. Escribe el número.

4. Resta 8 de 23.

Decenas	Unidades

_____ decena

_____ unidades

_____

5. Resta 36 de 45.

Decenas	Unidades

_____ decenas

_____ unidades

_____

6. Resta 6 de 43.

Decenas	Unidades

_____ decenas

_____ unidades

_____

7. Resta 39 de 67.

Decenas	Unidades

_____ decenas

_____ unidades

_____

8. Resta 21 de 50.

Decenas	Unidades

_____ decenas

_____ unidades

_____

9. Resta 29 de 56.

Decenas	Unidades

_____ decenas

_____ unidades

_____

10. **MÁS AL DETALLE** Dibuja para hallar qué número se restó de 53.

Resta _____ de 53.

__3__ decenas __4__ unidades

__34__

Decenas	Unidades

Capítulo 5 • Lección 3   trescientos treinta y uno **331**

PRÁCTICAS Y PROCESOS MATEMÁTICOS   REPRESENTAR • RAZONAR • ENTENDER

Resolución de problemas • Aplicaciones

Escribe o dibuja para explicar.

11. **PIENSA MÁS** Billy tiene 18 canicas menos que Sara. Sara tiene 34 canicas. ¿Cuántas canicas tiene Billy?

_____ canicas

12. **PIENSA MÁS +** Había 67 animales de juguete en la tienda. El vendedor vendió 19 animales de juguete. ¿Cuántos animales de juguete hay en la tienda ahora?

Haz un dibujo para mostrar cómo hallaste la respuesta.

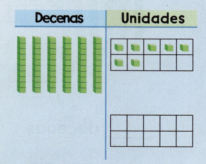

_____ animales de juguete

Describe cómo resolviste el problema.

_____

_____

_____

ACTIVIDAD PARA LA CASA • Pida a su niño que escriba un problema de resta y luego explique cómo resolverlo.

Nombre _____

Reagrupar modelos para restar

**Práctica y tarea
Lección 5.3**

Objetivo de aprendizaje Representarás una resta con números hasta 100 con reagrupación.

Dibuja para mostrar la reagrupación. Escribe la diferencia de dos maneras. Escribe las decenas y las unidades. Escribe el número.

1. Resta 9 de 35.

   ____ decenas ____ unidades

   _____

2. Resta 14 de 52.

   ____ decenas ____ unidades

   _____

Resolución de problemas

Elige una manera de resolver. Escribe o dibuja la explicación.

3. El Sr. Ortega hizo 51 galletas. Regaló 14 galletas. ¿Cuántas galletas tiene ahora?

   _____ galletas

4. ESCRIBE Matemáticas Haz un dibujo rápido para 37. Haz un dibujo para mostrar cómo restarías 19 de 37. Escribe para explicar lo que hiciste.

Repaso de la lección

1. Resta 9 de 36. ¿Cuál es la diferencia?

Decenas	Unidades

_____

2. Resta 28 de 45. ¿Cuál es la diferencia?

Decenas	Unidades

_____

Repaso en espiral

3. ¿Cuál es la diferencia?

$$51 - 8 = \_\_\_$$

40 41 42 43 44 45 46 47 48 49 **50** 51 52 53 54 55 56 57 58 59 **60**

4. ¿Cuál es la suma?

$$38 + 35 = \_\_\_$$

5. ¿Cuál es la suma?

```
   63
   18
 + 9
 ____
```

Lección 5.4

Nombre _____

Hacer un modelo y anotar restas de 2 dígitos

Pregunta esencial ¿Cómo anotas restas de 2 dígitos?

Objetivo de aprendizaje Representarás y anotarás restas de números hasta 100.

Escucha y dibuja En el mundo Manos a la obra

Usa 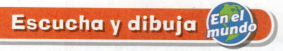 para representar el problema. Haz dibujos rápidos para mostrar tu modelo.

Decenas	Unidades

PARA EL MAESTRO • Lea el siguiente problema. El Sr. Kelly hizo 47 pastelitos. Sus estudiantes comieron 23 de los pastelitos. ¿Cuántos pastelitos no se comieron?

Charla matemática PRÁCTICAS Y PROCESOS MATEMÁTICOS 6

Explica un método
¿Cambiaste bloques en tu modelo? Explica por qué.

Capítulo 5 · trescientos treinta y cinco **335**

Representa y dibuja

Traza sobre los dibujos rápidos de los pasos.

Resta.   56
        −19

Paso 1 Muestra 56. ¿Hay suficientes unidades para restar 9?

Paso 2 Si no hay suficientes unidades, reagrupa 1 decena como 10 unidades.

Paso 3 Resta las unidades.
$16 - 9 = 7$

Paso 4 Resta las decenas.
$4 - 1 = 3$

Comparte y muestra

Haz un dibujo rápido para resolver. Escribe la diferencia.

1. Decenas Unidades
       4   7
    − 1   5

2. Decenas Unidades
       3   2
    − 1   8

336 trescientos treinta y seis

Nombre _____

Por tu cuenta

Haz un dibujo rápido para resolver. Escribe la diferencia.

3. | Decenas | Unidades |
    |---------|----------|
    | ☐ | ☐ |
    | 3 | 5 |
    | − 2 | 9 |

Decenas	Unidades

4. | Decenas | Unidades |
    |---------|----------|
    | ☐ | ☐ |
    | 2 | 8 |
    | − | 5 |

Decenas	Unidades

5. | Decenas | Unidades |
    |---------|----------|
    | ☐ | ☐ |
    | 5 | 3 |
    | − 2 | 6 |

Decenas	Unidades

6. | Decenas | Unidades |
    |---------|----------|
    | ☐ | ☐ |
    | 3 | 2 |
    | − 1 | 3 |

Decenas	Unidades

7. **MÁS AL DETALLE** Hay 16 petirrojos en los árboles. Llegan 24 más. Luego 28 petirrojos se van volando. ¿Cuánto petirrojos quedan en los árboles?

_____ petirrojos

Capítulo 5 • Lección 4

PRÁCTICAS Y PROCESOS MATEMÁTICOS   COMUNICAR • PERSEVERAR • CONSTRUIR ARGUMENTOS

Resolución de problemas • Aplicaciones

8. **PIENSA MÁS** El rompecabezas de Claire tiene 85 piezas. Ha usado 46 piezas hasta ahora. ¿Cuántas piezas de rompecabezas no se han usado aún?

_____ piezas de rompecabezas

9. **PRÁCTICAS Y PROCESOS MATEMÁTICOS** **Analiza** Había algunas personas en el parque. 24 personas se fueron a casa. Quedaron 19 personas en el parque. ¿Cuántas personas había en el parque antes?

_____ personas

10. **PIENSA MÁS** El Sr. Sims tiene una caja de 44 gomas de borrar. Da 18 gomas de borrar a sus estudiantes. ¿Cuántas gomas de borrar tiene el Sr. Sims ahora?

Muestra cómo resolviste el problema.

_____ gomas de borrar

 ACTIVIDAD PARA LA CASA • Escriba 73 – 28 en una hoja de papel. Pregunte a su niño si reagruparía para hallar la diferencia.

338 trescientos treinta y ocho

Nombre _____

Hacer un modelo y anotar restas de 2 dígitos

**Práctica y tarea
Lección 5.4**

Objetivo de aprendizaje Representarás y anotarás restas de números hasta 100.

Haz un dibujo rápido para resolver. Escribe la diferencia.

1.

Decenas	Unidades
☐	☐
4	3
−1	7

Decenas	Unidades

2.

Decenas	Unidades
☐	☐
3	8
−2	9

Decenas	Unidades

Resolución de problemas

Resuelve. Escribe o dibuja la explicación.

3. Kendall tiene 63 adhesivos. Su hermana tiene 57 adhesivos. ¿Cuántos adhesivos más que su hermana tiene Kendall?

_____ adhesivos más

4. **ESCRIBE Matemáticas** Haz un dibujo rápido para mostrar el número 24. Luego haz un dibujo rápido para mostrar 24 después de reagrupar una decena como diez unidades. Explica cómo es que ambos dibujos muestran el mismo número, 24.

_____
_____
_____

Capítulo 5   trescientos treinta y nueve **339**

Repaso de la lección

1. ¿Cuál es la diferencia?

Decenas	Unidades
☐	☐
4	7
− 1	8

2. ¿Cuál es la diferencia?

Decenas	Unidades
☐	☐
3	3
− 2	9

Repaso en espiral

3. ¿Cuál es la diferencia?

10 − 6 = _____

4. ¿Cuál es la suma?

16 + 49 = _____

5. ¿Cuál es la suma?

28 + 8 = _____

6. ¿Cuál es la diferencia?

52 − 6 = _____

340 trescientos cuarenta

Nombre _____

Resta de 2 dígitos

Lección 5.5

Pregunta esencial ¿Cómo anotas los pasos cuando restas números de 2 dígitos?

Objetivo de aprendizaje Anotarás los pasos para restar números menores que 100.

 Escucha y dibuja En el mundo

Haz un dibujo rápido para representar cada problema.

Decenas	Unidades

Decenas	Unidades

PARA EL MAESTRO • Lea el siguiente problema. Devin tenía 36 robots de juguete en su estante. Trasladó 12 de sus robots a su armario. ¿Cuántos robots hay en el estante ahora? Repita la actividad con este problema: Devin tenía 54 carritos. Dio 9 carritos a su hermano. ¿Cuántos carritos tiene Devin ahora?

Charla matemática PRÁCTICAS Y PROCESOS MATEMÁTICOS 2

Usa el razonamiento
Explica por qué funciona la reagrupación.

Capítulo 5

trescientos cuarenta y uno **341**

Representa y dibuja

Resta.   42
        −15

Paso 1 ¿Hay suficientes unidades para restar 5?

Decenas	Unidades
||||	∘∘

Decenas	Unidades
☐	☐
4	2
− 1	5

Paso 2 Reagrupa 1 decena como 10 unidades.

Decenas	Unidades
||||	∘∘∘∘∘ ∘∘∘∘∘ ∘∘

Decenas	Unidades
3	12
4̸	2̸
− 1	5

Paso 3 Resta las unidades.

$12 - 5 = 7$

Decenas	Unidades
||||	∘∘∘∘∘ ∘∘∘∘∘ ∘∘

Decenas	Unidades
3	12
4̸	2̸
− 1	5
	7

Paso 4 Resta las decenas.

$3 - 1 = 2$

Decenas	Unidades
||X|	∘∘∘∘∘ ∘∘∘∘∘ ∘∘

Decenas	Unidades
3	12
4̸	2̸
− 1	5
2	7

Comparte y muestra

Reagrupa si lo necesitas. Escribe la diferencia.

1.
Decenas	Unidades
☐	☐
3	1
− 1	4

✓ 2.
Decenas	Unidades
☐	☐
5	6
− 2	1

✓ 3.
Decenas	Unidades
☐	☐
7	2
− 3	5

Nombre _____

Por tu cuenta

Reagrupa si lo necesitas. Escribe la diferencia.

4.
Decenas	Unidades
☐	☐
2	3
− 1	4

5.
Decenas	Unidades
☐	☐
8	7
− 5	7

6.
Decenas	Unidades
☐	☐
3	4
− 1	8

7.
Decenas	Unidades
☐	☐
6	1
− 1	3

8.
```
  4 | 5
− 1 | 8
```

9.
```
  5 | 2
− 3 | 6
```

10.
```
  3 | 2
− 1 | 3
```

11.
```
  7 | 5
− 4 | 3
```

12.
```
  5 | 6
− 2 | 7
```

13.
```
  9 | 4
− 2 | 9
```

14.
```
  8 | 7
− 3 | 9
```

15.
```
  8 | 3
− 4 | 6
```

16. **PIENSA MÁS** Spencer escribió 5 cuentos menos que Katie. Spencer escribió 18 cuentos. ¿Cuántos cuentos escribió Katie?

_____ cuentos

Capítulo 5 • Lección 5

PRÁCTICAS Y PROCESOS MATEMÁTICOS • ANALIZAR • BUSCAR ESTRUCTURAS • PRECISIÓN

Resolución de problemas • Aplicaciones

17. **PRÁCTICAS Y PROCESOS MATEMÁTICOS 6** Explica un método

Encierra en un círculo los problemas que podrías resolver con un cálculo mental.

54 − 10 = ___   63 − 27 = ___   93 − 20 = ___

39 − 2 = ___   41 − 18 = ___   82 − 26 = ___

Explica cuándo usas el cálculo mental.

_____

_____

_____

18. **PIENSA MÁS +** Hay 34 pollos en el gallinero. Si 6 pollos salen al jardín, ¿cuántos pollos quedarán aún en el gallinero?

Encierra en un círculo el número de la casilla válido para que el enunciado sea verdadero.

Quedan | 8 / 18 / 28 | pollos en el gallinero.

ACTIVIDAD PARA LA CASA • Pida a su niño que escriba un problema de resta de 2 dígitos en que no se necesite reagrupar. Pida a su niño que explique por qué eligió esos números.

Resta de 2 dígitos

**Práctica y tarea
Lección 5.5**

Objetivo de aprendizaje Anotarás los pasos para restar números menores que 100.

Reagrupa si lo necesitas.
Escribe la diferencia.

	Decenas	Unidades
1.	4	7
	− 2	8

	Decenas	Unidades
2.	3	3
	− 1	8

	Decenas	Unidades
3.	2	8
	− 1	4

	Decenas	Unidades
4.	6	6
	− 1	9

5.
```
  7 | 7
− 2 | 6
```

6.
```
  5 | 8
− 3 | 4
```

7.
```
  5 | 2
− 2 | 5
```

8.
```
  8 | 7
− 4 | 9
```

Resolución de problemas

Resuelve. Escribe o dibuja para explicar.

9. La Sra. Paul compró 32 gomas de borrar. Les dio 19 gomas de borrar a los estudiantes. ¿Cuántas gomas de borrar le quedan?

_____ gomas de borrar

10. **ESCRIBE Matemáticas** Escribe algunos enunciados sobre las maneras diferentes de mostrar la resta para un problema como 32 − 15.

_____

_____

Repaso de la lección

1. ¿Cuál es la diferencia?

$$\begin{array}{r} 4\,|\,8 \\ -\,3\,|\,9 \\ \hline \end{array}$$

2. ¿Cuál es la diferencia?

$$\begin{array}{r} 8\,|\,4 \\ -\,6\,|\,6 \\ \hline \end{array}$$

Repaso en espiral

3. ¿Cuál es la diferencia?

Decenas	Unidades
☐	☐
3	2
− 1	9

4. Escribe una operación de suma que tenga la misma suma que 8 + 7.

10 + ____

5. Van 27 niños y 23 niñas de excursión al museo. ¿Cuántos niños van de excursión al museo en total?

____ niños

6. Hay 17 bayas en la canasta. Luego alguien se come 9 bayas. ¿Cuántas bayas hay ahora?

____ bayas

Practicar la resta de 2 dígitos

Lección 5.6

Pregunta esencial ¿Cómo anotas los pasos cuando restas números de 2 dígitos?

Objetivo de aprendizaje Practicarás la resta de 2 dígitos con y sin reagrupación.

Elige una manera de resolver el problema. Dibuja o escribe para mostrar lo que hiciste.

 PARA EL MAESTRO • Lea el siguiente problema y pida a los niños que elijan su propio método para resolverlo. Hay 74 libros en el salón de clases del Sr. Barron. 19 de los libros son sobre las computadoras. ¿Cuántos libros no son sobre las computadoras?

 Describe una manera diferente en que podrías haber resuelto el problema.

Capítulo 5   trescientos cuarenta y siete **347**

Representa y dibuja

Carmen tenía 50 tarjetas de juego. Luego dio 16 tarjetas de juego a Theo. ¿Cuántas tarjetas de juego tiene Carmen ahora?

Paso 1 Observa las unidades. No hay suficientes unidades para restar 6 de 0. Por lo tanto, reagrupa.

```
  4 10
  5̶ 0̶
-  1 6
```

Paso 2 Resta las unidades.

$10 - 6 = 4$

```
  4 10
  5̶ 0̶
-  1 6
        4
```

Paso 3 Resta las decenas.

$4 - 1 = 3$

```
  4 10
  5̶ 0̶
-  1 6
     3 4
```

Comparte y muestra

Escribe la diferencia.

1.
```
   3 8
 - 1 9
```

2.
```
   6 5
 - 3 2
```

3.
```
   5 0
 - 1 2
```

4.
```
   2 3
 -   4
```

☑ 5.
```
   7 0
 - 3 8
```

☑ 6.
```
   5 2
 - 1 7
```

348 trescientos cuarenta y ocho

Nombre _____

Por tu cuenta

Escribe la diferencia.

7.
   4 1
 − 2 4

8.
   5 8
 − 1 6

9.
   6 0
 − 1 3

10.
   5 2
 − 4 7

11.
   7 2
 − 4 6

12.
   3 7
 −   6

13.
   7 4
 − 4 6

14.
   9 0
 − 1 8

15. **MÁS AL DETALLE** Escribe los números que faltan en los problemas de resta. Se muestra la reagrupación para cada problema.

   6 15   7 13
  _ _ _   _ _ _
 −   −
   ___   ___
   4 7   2 5

16. **PIENSA MÁS** Adam saca 38 piedras de una caja. Quedan 23 piedras en la caja. ¿Cuántas piedras había en la caja al comienzo?

____ piedras

ACTIVIDAD PARA LA CASA • Pida a su niño que le muestre una manera de hallar 80 − 34.

Nombre _____

 # Revisión de la mitad del capítulo

Conceptos y destrezas

Separa el número que restas. Usa la recta numérica como ayuda. Escribe la diferencia.

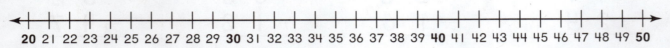

1. 34 − 8 = _____

2. 45 − 17 = _____

Haz un dibujo rápido para resolver. Escribe la diferencia.

3.
Decenas	Unidades
4	2
− 2	9

Decenas	Unidades

4.
Decenas	Unidades
5	4
− 2	3

Decenas	Unidades

Escribe la diferencia.

5.
```
  7 8
− 4 3
-----
```

6.
```
  6 0
− 2 6
-----
```

7.
```
  8 5
− 3 7
-----
```

8. **PIENSA MÁS** Marissa tenía 51 dinosaurios de juguete. Dio 14 dinosaurios de juguete a su hermano. ¿Cuántos dinosaurios de juguete tiene ahora?

_____ dinosaurios de juguete

350 trescientos cincuenta

Nombre _____

Práctica y tarea
Lección 5.6

Practicar la resta de 2 dígitos

Objetivo de aprendizaje Practicarás la resta de 2 dígitos con y sin reagrupación.

Escribe la diferencia.

1.
```
   5 0
 - 1 8
```

2.
```
   4 3
 - 1 7
```

3.
```
   7 5
 - 1 8
```

4.
```
   2 2
 -   6
```

5.
```
   6 0
 - 3 5
```

6.
```
   4 2
 - 3 4
```

Resolución de problemas

Resuelve. Escribe o dibuja la explicación.

7. Julie tiene 42 hojas de papel. Le da 17 hojas a Kari. ¿Cuántas hojas de papel tiene Julie ahora?

_____ hojas de papel

8. **ESCRIBE Matemáticas** Dibuja y escribe para explicar en qué se diferencian estos dos problemas:
35 − 15 = _____ y
43 − 26 = _____.

Capítulo 5   trescientos cincuenta y uno **351**

Repaso de la lección

1. ¿Cuál es la diferencia?

$$\begin{array}{r} 73 \\ -\ 47 \\ \hline \end{array}$$

2. ¿Cuál es la diferencia?

$$\begin{array}{r} 54 \\ -\ 13 \\ \hline \end{array}$$

Repaso en espiral

3. ¿Cuál es la suma?

9 + 9 = ___

4. ¿Cuál es la diferencia?

14 − 7 = ___

5. ¿Cuál es la suma?

36 + 25 = ___

6. ¿Cuál es la suma?

7 + 2 + 3 = ___

Nombre _____

Reescribir restas de 2 dígitos

Lección 5.7

Pregunta esencial ¿Cuáles son dos maneras diferentes de escribir problemas de restas?

Objetivo de aprendizaje Reescribirás de manera diferente problemas de resta de números menores que 100.

Escribe los números de cada problema de resta.

— _____	— _____
— _____	— _____

PRÁCTICAS Y PROCESOS MATEMÁTICOS 6

Explica por qué es importante alinear los dígitos de los números en columnas.

PARA EL MAESTRO • Lea el siguiente problema. Pida a los niños que escriban los números en formato vertical. Había 45 niños en una fiesta. Luego 23 niños se fueron a casa. ¿Cuántos niños quedaron aún en la fiesta? Repita con tres problemas más.

Capítulo 5 trescientos cincuenta y tres **353**

Representa y dibuja

¿Cuánto es 81 − 36?
Reescribe el problema de resta.
Luego halla la diferencia.

Paso 1 Para 81, escribe el dígito de las decenas en la columna de las decenas.

Escribe el dígito de las unidades en la columna de las unidades.

```
  8 1
− 3 6
_____
```

Repite con 36.

Paso 2 Observa las unidades. Reagrupa si lo necesitas.

Resta las unidades.
Resta las decenas.

```
  7 11
  8 1
− 3 6
_____
```

Comparte y muestra

Reescribe el problema de resta. Luego halla la diferencia.

1. 37 − 4
2. 48 − 24
3. 85 − 37
4. 63 − 19

5. 62 − 37
6. 51 − 27
7. 76 − 3
8. 95 − 48

Nombre _____

Por tu cuenta

Reescribe el problema de resta. Luego halla la diferencia.

9. 49 − 8

10. 85 − 47

11. 63 − 23

12. 51 − 23

13. 60 − 15

14. 94 − 58

15. 47 − 20

16. 35 − 9

17. 78 − 10

18. 54 − 38

19. 92 − 39

20. 87 − 28

21. **PIENSA MÁS** ¿En cuáles de los problemas anteriores pudiste hallar la diferencia sin reescribirlos? Explica.

_____
_____
_____

Capítulo 5 • Lección 7   trescientos cincuenta y cinco **355**

PRÁCTICAS Y PROCESOS MATEMÁTICOS • REPRESENTAR • RAZONAR • ENTENDER

Resolución de problemas • Aplicaciones

Lee sobre la excursión de la clase. Luego responde las preguntas.

> La clase de Pablo fue al museo de arte. Vieron 26 pinturas hechas por niños. Vieron 53 pinturas hechas por adultos. También vieron 18 esculturas y 31 fotografías.

22. ¿Cuántas pinturas más fueron hechas por adultos que por niños?

_____ pinturas más

23. MÁS AL DETALLE ¿Cuántas pinturas más que esculturas vieron?

_____ pinturas más

24. PIENSA MÁS Tom hizo 23 dibujos el año pasado. Beth hizo 14 dibujos. ¿Cuántos dibujos más hizo Tom que Beth?

Rellena el círculo que está al lado de todas las formas de mostrar el problema.

○   23
   − 14

○   23
   + 14

○ 23 − 14

○ 23 + 14

_____ dibujos más

 ACTIVIDAD PARA LA CASA • Pida a su niño que escriba y resuelva un problema de resta sobre una excursión en familia.

356 trescientos cincuenta y seis

Nombre _____

Reescribir restas de 2 dígitos

**Práctica y tarea
Lección 5.7**

Objetivo de aprendizaje Reescribirás de manera diferente problemas de resta de números menores que 100.

Reescribe el problema de resta.
Luego halla la diferencia.

1. 35 − 19

2. 47 − 23

3. 55 − 28

Resolución de problemas

Resuelve. Escribe o dibuja la explicación.

4. Jimmy fue a la juguetería. Vio 23 trenes de madera y 41 trenes de plástico. ¿Cuántos trenes de plástico más vio que trenes de madera?

_____ trenes de plástico más

5. **ESCRIBE Matemáticas** ¿Es más fácil restar cuando los números están escritos arriba y abajo de otros? Explica tu respuesta.

_____
_____
_____
_____

Capítulo 5 · trescientos cincuenta y siete **357**

Repaso de la lección

1. ¿Cuál es la diferencia entre 43 − 17?

2. ¿Cuál es la diferencia entre 50 − 16?

Repaso en espiral

3. ¿Cuál es la suma?

   $$\begin{array}{r} 29 \\ 4 \\ 25 \\ +\ 16 \\ \hline \end{array}$$

4. ¿Cuál es la suma de 41 + 19?

5. Escribe una operación de suma que tenga la misma suma que 5 + 9.

   10 + ____

6. ¿Cuál es la diferencia?

   45 − 13 = ____

Nombre _____

Sumar para hallar diferencias

Pregunta esencial ¿Cómo puedes usar la suma para resolver problemas de resta?

Lección 5.8

Objetivo de aprendizaje Usarás la suma para resolver problemas de resta.

Haz dibujos para mostrar el problema.
Luego escribe un enunciado numérico para tu dibujo.

_____   _____ marcadores

Ahora haz dibujos para mostrar la siguiente parte del problema. Escribe un enunciado numérico para tu dibujo.

_____   _____ marcadores

 PARA EL MAESTRO • Pida a los niños que hagan dibujos para representar este problema. Sophie tenía 25 marcadores. Dio 3 marcadores a Josh. ¿Cuántos marcadores tiene Sophie ahora? Luego pregunte a los niños: ¿Cuántos marcadores tendría Sophie si Josh le devolviera 3 marcadores?

 PRÁCTICAS Y PROCESOS MATEMÁTICOS

Describe lo que sucede cuando vuelves a sumar el número que restaste.

Capítulo 5   trescientos cincuenta y nueve **359**

Representa y dibuja

Cuenta de menor a mayor desde el número que restas para hallar la diferencia.

$$45 - 38 = \boxed{}$$

Comienza en 38. Cuenta de menor a mayor hasta 40.

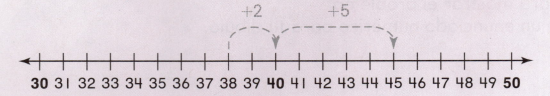

Luego cuenta de menor a mayor 5 más hasta 45.

$2 + 5 = 7$

Por lo tanto, $45 - 38 = $ _____.

Comparte y muestra

Usa la recta numérica. Cuenta de menor a mayor para hallar la diferencia.

1. $36 - 27 = $ _____

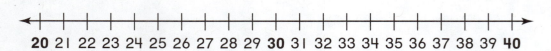

2. $56 - 49 = $ _____

3. $64 - 58 = $ _____

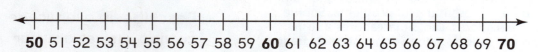

Nombre _____

Por tu cuenta

Usa la recta numérica. Cuenta de menor a mayor para hallar la diferencia.

4. 33 − 28 = _____

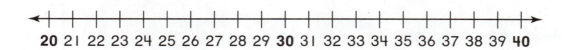

5. 45 − 37 = _____

6. 58 − 49 = _____

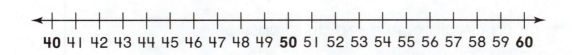

7. **PIENSA MÁS** Había 55 libros sobre la mesa. Sandra recogió algunos libros. Ahora quedan 49 libros sobre la mesa. ¿Cuántos libros recogió Sandra?

_____ libros

Capítulo 5 • Lección 8 trescientos sesenta y uno **361**

PRÁCTICAS Y PROCESOS MATEMÁTICOS • COMUNICAR • PERSEVERAR • CONSTRUIR ARGUMENTOS

Resolución de problemas • Aplicaciones

Resuelve. Puedes usar la recta numérica como ayuda.

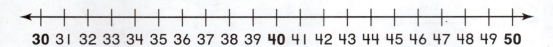

8. Hay 46 piezas de juego en una caja. Adam saca 38 piezas de juego de la caja. ¿Cuántas piezas de juego quedan en la caja?

_____ piezas de juego

9. **PIENSA MÁS** Rachel tenía 27 palitos planos. Luego dio 19 palitos planos a Theo. ¿Cuántos palitos planos tiene Rachel ahora?

Encierra en un círculo el número de la casilla válido para que el enunciado sea verdadero.

Rachel tiene | 6 / 7 / 8 | palitos planos ahora.

Explica cómo puedes usar la suma para resolver el problema.

_____

_____

 ACTIVIDAD PARA LA CASA • Pida a su niño que describa cómo usó una recta numérica para resolver un problema de esta lección.

Nombre _____

Sumar para hallar diferencias

**Práctica y tarea
Lección 5.8**

Objetivo de aprendizaje Usarás la suma para resolver problemas de resta.

Usa la recta numérica. Cuenta de menor a mayor para hallar la diferencia.

1. 36 − 29 = ___

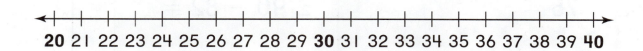

2. 43 − 38 = ___

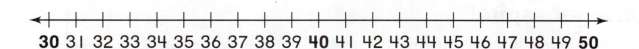

Resolución de problemas

Resuelve. La recta numérica te sirve para resolver.

50 51 52 53 54 55 56 57 58 59 **60** 61 62 63 64 65 66 67 68 69 **70**

3. Jill tiene 63 tarjetas. Usa 57 tarjetas en un proyecto. ¿Cuántas tarjetas tiene Jill ahora?

_____ tarjetas

4. **ESCRIBE Matemáticas** Explica cómo se puede usar una recta numérica para hallar la diferencia entre 34 − 28.

_____
_____

Capítulo 5   trescientos sesenta y tres **363**

Repaso de la lección

Usa la recta numérica. Cuenta de menor a mayor para hallar la diferencia.

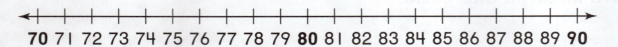

1. 82 − 75 = ____

2. 90 − 82 = ____

Repaso en espiral

3. Jordan tiene 41 carritos en casa. Lleva 24 carritos a la escuela. ¿Cuántos carritos dejó en casa?

   ____ carritos

4. Pam tiene 15 peces. Tiene 9 peces dorados y el resto son peces tropicales. ¿Cuántos peces son peces tropicales?

   ____ peces tropicales

5. ¿Cuál es la suma?

   $$\begin{array}{r} 3\,5 \\ +\,1\,9 \\ \hline \end{array}$$

6. Hay 5 lápices en cada mesa. Hay 3 mesas. ¿Cuántos lápices hay en total?

   ____ lápices

364 trescientos sesenta y cuatro

Nombre _____

Resolución de problemas •
La resta

Pregunta esencial ¿Cómo puede ayudar el dibujo de un diagrama cuando se resuelven problemas de resta?

RESOLUCIÓN DE PROBLEMAS
Lección 5.9

Objetivo de aprendizaje Usarás la estrategia de *dibujar un diagrama* de modelos de barras para resolver problemas de resta de números menores que 100.

Jane y su mamá hicieron 33 títeres para la feria de artesanías. Vendieron 14 títeres. ¿Cuántos títeres les quedan?

Soluciona el problema

¿Qué debo hallar?

_____cuántos títeres_____
les quedan

¿Qué información debo usar?

Hicieron _____ títeres.

Vendieron _____ títeres.

Muestra cómo resolver el problema.

33 − 14 = ■

_____ títeres

NOTA A LA FAMILIA • Su niño usó un modelo de barras y un enunciado numérico para representar el problema. El uso de un modelo de barras muestra lo que se sabe y lo que se necesita para resolver el problema.

Capítulo 5

Haz otro problema

Rotula el modelo de barras. Escribe un enunciado numérico con un ■ en el lugar del número que falta. Resuelve.

- ¿Qué debo hallar?
- ¿Qué información debo usar?

1. Carlette tenía una caja de 46 palitos planos. Usó 28 palitos planos para hacer un velero. ¿Cuántos palitos planos no se usaron?

_____   _____ palitos planos

2. La clase de Rob hizo 31 tazones de arcilla. La clase de Sarah hizo 15 tazones de arcilla. ¿Cuántos tazones de arcilla más hizo la clase de Rob que la clase de Sarah?

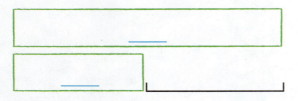

_____   _____ tazones de arcilla más

Charla matemática   PRÁCTICAS Y PROCESOS MATEMÁTICOS

Explica cómo sabes que el Ejercicio 1 es un problema de quitar.

366 trescientos sesenta y seis

Nombre _____

Comparte y muestra

Rotula el modelo de barras. Escribe un enunciado numérico con un ■ en el lugar del número que falta. Resuelve.

3. El Sr. Hayes hace 32 marcos de madera. Regala 15 marcos. ¿Cuántos marcos le quedan?

_____ marcos

4. Wesley tiene 21 cintas en una caja. Tiene 15 cintas en la pared. ¿Cuántas cintas más tiene en la caja que en la pared?

_____ cintas más

5. PIENSA MÁS Jennifer escribió 9 poemas en la escuela y 11 poemas en casa. Escribió 5 poemas más que Nell. ¿Cuántos poemas escribió Nell?

_____ poemas

PRÁCTICAS Y PROCESOS MATEMÁTICOS ANALIZAR • BUSCAR ESTRUCTURAS • PRECISIÓN

Por tu cuenta ESCRIBE Matemáticas

6. **MÁS AL DETALLE** Hay 70 niños. 28 niños están caminando y 16 están en un pícnic. El resto de los niños están jugando fútbol. ¿Cuántos niños están jugando fútbol?

Dibuja un modelo de barras para el problema. Describe cómo muestra tu dibujo el problema. Luego resuelve el problema.

_____

_____

_____

7. **PIENSA MÁS** Hay 48 galletas en una bolsa. Los niños comen 25 galletas. ¿Cuántas galletas quedan en la bolsa?

Encierra en un círculo el modelo de barras que puede usarse para resolver el problema.

25	23		48	25		73	48
----	----		----	----		----	----
48		73		25

Escribe un enunciado numérico con un ▪ en el lugar del número que falta. Resuelve.

_____

_____ galletas

ACTIVIDAD PARA LA CASA • Pida a su niño que explique cómo resolvió uno de los problemas de esta página.

Nombre _____

Resolución de problemas •
La resta

**Práctica y tarea
Lección 5.9**

Objetivo de aprendizaje Usarás la estrategia de *dibujar un diagrama* de modelos de barras para resolver problemas de resta de números menores que 100.

Rotula el modelo de barras. Escribe un enunciado numérico con un ▪ en lugar del número que falta. Resuelve.

1. Megan recogió 34 flores. Algunas flores son amarillas y 18 flores son rosadas. ¿Cuántas flores amarillas recogió?

   _____ flores amarillas

2. Alex tenía 45 carritos. Puso 26 carritos en una caja. ¿Cuántos carritos no están en la caja?

   _____ carritos

3. ESCRIBE Matemáticas Explica cómo un modelo de barras se puede usar para mostrar un problema de resta.

_____
_____
_____
_____

Capítulo 5   trescientos sesenta y nueve **369**

Repaso de la lección

1. Había 39 calabazas en la tienda. Luego se vendieron 17 calabazas. ¿Cuántas calabazas quedan en la tienda?

_____ calabazas

2. Había 48 hormigas en una colina. Luego se fueron 13 hormigas. ¿Cuántas hormigas quedaron en la colina?

_____ hormigas

Repaso en espiral

3. Ashley tenía 26 marcadores. Su amiga le dio 17 marcadores más. ¿Cuántos marcadores tiene Ashley ahora?

_____ marcadores

4. ¿Cuál es la suma?

$$\begin{array}{r} 46 \\ +\ 24 \\ \hline \end{array}$$

5. Escribe una operación de resta que tenga la misma diferencia entre 15 − 7.

10 − _____

6. ¿Cuál es la suma?

34 + 5 = _____

Nombre _____

Álgebra • Escribir ecuaciones para representar la resta

Lección 5.10

Pregunta esencial ¿Cómo escribes un enunciado numérico para representar un problema?

Objetivo de aprendizaje Mostrarás un problema de resta al escribir un enunciado numérico con un símbolo para el número que falta.

Escucha y dibuja En el mundo

Dibuja para mostrar el problema. Escribe un enunciado numérico. Luego resuelve.

_____

PARA EL MAESTRO • Lea este problema a los niños. Franco tiene 53 crayones. Da algunos crayones a Courtney. Ahora Franco tiene 38 crayones. ¿Cuántos crayones dio Franco a Courtney?

Charla matemática PRÁCTICAS Y PROCESOS MATEMÁTICOS 4

Describe cómo muestra tu dibujo el problema.

Capítulo 5   trescientos setenta y uno **371**

Representa y dibuja

Puedes escribir un enunciado numérico para mostrar un problema.

Liza tiene 65 tarjetas postales. Da 24 tarjetas postales a Wesley. ¿Cuántas tarjetas postales tiene Liza ahora?

65 − 24 = ▨

PIENSA:
65 tarjetas postales
−24 tarjetas postales
41 tarjetas postales

Liza tiene _____ tarjetas postales ahora.

Comparte y muestra

Escribe un enunciado numérico para el problema. Usa un ▨ en el lugar del número que falta. Luego resuelve.

1. Había 32 aves en los árboles. Luego se fueron volando 18 aves. ¿Cuántas aves hay en los árboles ahora?

_____   _____ aves

2. Carla leyó 43 páginas de su libro. Joe leyó 32 páginas de su libro. ¿Cuántas páginas más leyó Carla que Joe?

_____   _____ páginas más

Nombre _____

Por tu cuenta

Escribe un enunciado numérico para el problema.
Usa un ▢ en el lugar del número que falta. Luego resuelve.

3. Había 40 hormigas en una roca. Algunas hormigas se desplazaron al césped. Ahora hay 26 hormigas en la roca. ¿Cuántas hormigas se desplazaron al césped?

_____   _____ hormigas

4. **PIENSA MÁS** Keisha tenía una bolsa de cintas. Sacó 29 cintas de la bolsa. Luego quedaron 17 cintas en la bolsa. ¿Cuántas cintas había en la bolsa al comienzo?

_____   _____ cintas

5. **MÁS AL DETALLE** Hay 50 abejas en una colmena. Algunas abejas se van volando. Si quedan menos de 20 abejas en la colmena, ¿cuántas abejas pueden haberse ido volando?

Usa la resta para comprobar tu respuesta.

_____ abejas

Capítulo 5 • Lección 10   trescientos setenta y tres **373**

Resolución de problemas • Aplicaciones

6. **PRÁCTICAS Y PROCESOS MATEMÁTICOS 6** **Haz conexiones**
Brendan hizo esta recta numérica para hallar una diferencia. ¿Qué restaba de 100? Explica tu respuesta.

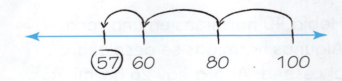

_____

_____

_____

7. **PIENSA MÁS** Hay 52 dibujos en la pared. De estos, 37 son de felinos salvajes y el resto son de aves. ¿Cuántos dibujos son de aves?

Usa los números y los símbolos de las fichas cuadradas para completar el enunciado numérico del problema.

| 15 | 25 | 37 | 52 | − | + | = |

_____ aves

ACTIVIDAD PARA LA CASA • Pida a su niño que explique cómo resolvió un problema de esta lección.

Nombre _____

Álgebra • Escribir ecuaciones para representar la resta

**Práctica y tarea
Lección 5.10**

Objetivo de aprendizaje Mostrarás un problema de resta al escribir un enunciado numérico con un símbolo para el número que falta.

Escribe un enunciado numérico para el problema. Usa una ▬ en lugar del número que falta. Luego resuelve.

1. 29 niños fueron a la escuela en bicicleta. Después algunos de los niños se fueron a casa y 8 niños se quedaron en la escuela. ¿Cuántos niños fueron a casa en bicicleta?

   _____

   _____ niños

Resolución de problemas · En el mundo

Resuelve. Escribe o dibuja la explicación.

2. Había 21 niños en la biblioteca. Después de que 7 niños se fueron de la biblioteca, ¿cuántos niños se quedaron en la biblioteca?

   _____ niños

3. **Matemáticas** Describe maneras diferentes en las que puedes mostrar un problema. Usa uno de los problemas de esta lección como ejemplo.

   _____
   _____
   _____
   _____

Repaso de la lección

1. Cindy tenía 42 cuentas. Usó algunas cuentas para una pulsera. Le quedan 14 cuentas. ¿Cuántas cuentas usó para la pulsera?

   _____ cuentas

2. Jake tenía 36 tarjetas de béisbol. Le dio 17 tarjetas a su hermana. ¿Cuántas tarjetas de béisbol tiene Jake ahora?

   _____ tarjetas

Repaso en espiral

3. ¿Cuál es la suma?

   $6 + 7 = $ _____

4. ¿Cuál es la diferencia?

   $16 - 9 = $ _____

5. ¿Cuál es la diferencia?

   $$\begin{array}{r} 4\,6 \\ -\,3\,9 \\ \hline \end{array}$$

6. Escribe una operación de suma que tenga la misma suma que $6 + 8$.

   $10 + $ _____

376 trescientos setenta y seis

Nombre _____

Resolver problemas de varios pasos

Pregunta esencial ¿Cómo decides qué pasos seguir para resolver un problema?

Lección 5.11

Objetivo de aprendizaje Decidirás qué pasos seguir para resolver un problema.

Escucha y dibuja En el mundo

Rotula el modelo de barras para mostrar cada problema. Luego resuelve.

PARA EL MAESTRO • Lea este primer problema a los niños. Cassie tiene 32 hojas de papel. Da 9 hojas de papel a Jeff. ¿Cuántas hojas de papel tiene Cassie ahora? Después de que los niños resuelvan, lea este segundo problema. Cassie hace 18 dibujos. Jeff hace 16 dibujos. ¿Cuántos dibujos hacen en total?

Charla matemática

PRÁCTICAS Y PROCESOS MATEMÁTICOS 1

Describe en qué se diferencian los dos modelos de barras.

Capítulo 5   trescientos setenta y siete **377**

Representa y dibuja

Los modelos de barras te ayudan a saber lo que debes hacer para resolver un problema.

Ali tiene 27 sellos. Matt tiene 38 sellos. ¿Cuántos sellos más necesitan para tener 91 sellos en total?

| 27 | 38 |

_____

Tienen _____ sellos en total.

| _____ | _____ |

91

Necesitan _____ sellos más.

Primero, halla cuántos sellos tienen ahora.

Luego, halla cuántos sellos más necesitan.

Comparte y muestra

Completa los modelos de barras con los pasos que sigues para resolver el problema.

PIENSA: ¿Qué debes hallar primero?

1. Jen tiene 93 cuentas. Ana tiene 46 cuentas rojas y 29 cuentas azules. ¿Cuántas cuentas más tiene Jen que Ana?

_____ cuentas más

378 trescientos setenta y ocho

Nombre _____

Por tu cuenta

Completa los modelos de barras con los pasos que sigues para resolver el problema.

2. Max tiene 35 tarjetas de colección. Compra otras 22 tarjetas. Luego da 14 tarjetas a Rudy. ¿Cuántas tarjetas tiene Max ahora?

_____ tarjetas

3. Drew tiene 32 carritos. Cambia 7 de esos carritos por otros 11 carritos. ¿Cuántos carritos tiene Drew ahora?

_____ carritos

4. Marta y Debbie tienen 17 cintas cada una. Compran 1 paquete que contiene 8 cintas. ¿Cuántas cintas tienen ahora en total?

_____ cintas

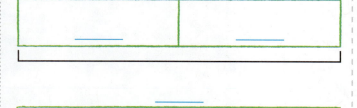

PRÁCTICAS Y PROCESOS MATEMÁTICOS COMUNICAR • PERSEVERAR • CONSTRUIR ARGUMENTOS

Resolución de problemas • Aplicaciones

5. **PIENSA MÁS** Shelby tenía 32 piedras. Halla otras 33 piedras en el parque y da 28 piedras a George. ¿Cuántas piedras tiene ahora?

_____ piedras

6. **MÁS AL DETALLE** Benjamín halla 31 piñas en el parque. Juntas, Jenna y Ellen hallan el mismo número de piñas que Benjamín. ¿Cuántas piñas puede haber hallado cada niña?

Jenna: _____ piñas

Ellen: _____ piñas

7. **PIENSA MÁS** Tanya halla 22 hojas. Maurice halla 5 hojas más que Tanya. ¿Cuántas hojas encuentran en total?

Haz un dibujo o escribe para mostrar cómo resuelves el problema.

_____ hojas

 ACTIVIDAD PARA LA CASA • Pida a su niño que explique cómo resolvería el Ejercicio 6 si el número 31 se cambiara por 42.

Resolver problemas de varios pasos

**Práctica y tarea
Lección 5.11**

Objetivo de aprendizaje Decidirás qué pasos seguir para resolver un problema.

Completa los modelos de barras con los pasos que sigues para resolver el problema.

1. Greg tiene 60 bloques. Su hermana le da 17 bloques más. Usa 38 bloques para hacer una torre. ¿Cuántos bloques no usó en la torre?

   _____ bloques

Resolución de problemas

Resuelve. Escribe o dibuja la explicación.

2. Ava tiene 25 libros. Regala 7 libros. Luego Tom le da 12 libros. ¿Cuántos libros tiene Ava ahora?

   _____ libros

3. **ESCRIBE Matemáticas** Elige uno de los problemas de esta página. Describe cómo decidiste qué pasos tenías que seguir para resolver el problema.

Repaso de la lección

1. Sara tiene 18 crayones. Max tiene 19 crayones. ¿Cuántos crayones más necesitan para tener 50 crayones en total?

   _____ crayones

2. Jon tiene 12 monedas de 1¢. Lucy tiene 17 monedas de 1¢. ¿Cuántas monedas de 1¢ más necesitan para tener 75 monedas de 1¢ en total?

   _____ monedas

Repaso en espiral

3. ¿Cuál es la diferencia?

   $58 - 13 =$ _____

   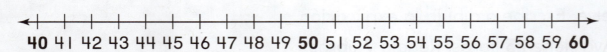

4. ¿Cuál es la suma?

   ```
     4 7
   + 1 5
   ```

5. Hay 26 tarjetas en una caja. Bryan toma 12 tarjetas. ¿Cuántas tarjetas quedan en la caja?

   _____ tarjetas

Nombre _____

✓ Repaso y prueba del Capítulo 5

1. ¿Necesitas reagrupar para restar? Elige Sí o No.

   65 − 23   ○ Sí   ○ No

   50 − 14   ○ Sí   ○ No

   37 − 19   ○ Sí   ○ No

   77 − 60   ○ Sí   ○ No

2. Usa la recta numérica. Cuenta de menor a mayor para hallar la diferencia.

   52 − 48 = _____

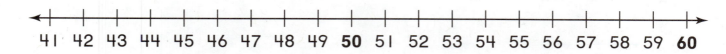

3. Ed tiene 28 bloques. Sue tiene 34 bloques. ¿Quién tiene más bloques? ¿Cuántos más? Rotula el modelo de barras. Resuelve.

   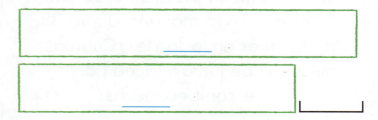

   Encierra en un círculo la palabra y el número de cada casilla para que el enunciado sea verdadero.

Ed		6	
Sue	tiene	16	bloques más.
		52	

Capítulo 5   trescientos ochenta y tres **383**

Separa el número que restas. Escribe la diferencia.

4. $42 - 8 = $ _____

5. $53 - 16 = $ _____

---

6. ¿Cuánto es $33 - 19$? Usa los números de las fichas cuadradas para reescribir el problema de resta. Luego halla la diferencia.

   | 14 | 19 | 33 | 52 |

   _____
   − _____
   _____

---

7. **MÁS AL DETALLE** El rompecabezas de Jacob tiene 84 piezas. Jacob junta 27 piezas en la mañana. Junta 38 piezas más en la tarde. ¿Cuántas piezas debe juntar Jacob para terminar el rompecabezas?

   Completa los modelos de barras con los pasos que sigues para resolver el problema.

   _____ piezas más

Nombre _____

Reagrupa si es necesario. Escribe la diferencia.

8.
Decenas	Unidades
☐	☐
5	5
− 2	8

9.
Decenas	Unidades
☐	☐
3	2
− 1	2

10. Halla la diferencia.

$$90 - 62 = \boxed{}$$

Rellena el círculo que hay al lado de un número de cada columna para mostrar la diferencia.

Decenas	Unidades
○ 2	○ 1
○ 3	○ 2
○ 5	○ 8

11. Hay 22 niños en el parque. Cinco niños están en los columpios. El resto de los niños están jugando a la pelota. ¿Cuántos niños están jugando a la pelota?

○ 13   ○ 23   ○ 17   ○ 27

Capítulo 5   trescientos ochenta y cinco **385**

12. **PIENSA MÁS** Resta 27 de 43. Haz un dibujo para mostrar la reagrupación. Rellena el círculo al lado de todas las formas de escribir la diferencia.
    ○ 1 decena 6 unidades
    ○ 66
    ○ 6 decenas 1 unidad
    ○ 16

13. Jill colecciona sellos. Su álbum de sellos tiene espacio para 64 sellos. Necesita 18 sellos más para llenar el álbum. ¿Cuántos sellos tiene Jill ahora? Escribe un enunciado numérico para el problema.

    Usa un ■ en el lugar del número que falta. Luego resuelve.

    _____

    Jill tiene _____ sellos.

14. Haz un dibujo rápido para resolver. Escribe la diferencia.

    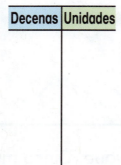

Decenas	Unidades
☐	☐
6	2
− 2	5

Decenas	Unidades

    Explica qué hiciste para hallar la diferencia.

    _____
    _____

386 trescientos ochenta y seis

Capítulo 6
Suma y resta de 3 dígitos

Las mariposas monarca se posan juntas durante la migración.

Si cuentas 83 mariposas en un árbol y 72 en otro, ¿cuántas mariposas contaste en total?

Nombre _____

 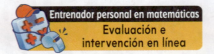

Haz un modelo de la resta de decenas

Escribe la diferencia.

1.

   5 decenas — 3 decenas
   = ____ decenas
   50 — 30 = ____

2.

   7 decenas — 2 decenas
   = ____ decenas
   70 — 20 = ____

Suma de 2 dígitos

Escribe la suma.

3. 54
   + 25

4. 35
   + 18

5. 82
   + 67

6. 29
   + 81

Centenas, decenas y unidades

Escribe las centenas, las decenas y las unidades que se muestran. Escribe el número. (2.NBT.A.1)

7.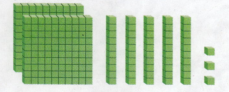

Centenas	Decenas	Unidades

_____

8.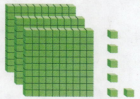

Centenas	Decenas	Unidades

Esta página es para verificar la comprensión de destrezas importantes que se necesitan para tener éxito en el Capítulo 6.

Nombre _____

Desarrollo del vocabulario

Palabras de repaso
reagrupar
suma
diferencia
centenas

Visualízalo
Escribe ejemplos de maneras de reagrupar para completar el organizador gráfico.

```
            reagrupar
           /        \
 Nombro 13 unidades
 como 1 decena y
 3 unidades.
```

Comprende el vocabulario

1. Escribe un número que tenga un dígito de **centenas** que sea mayor que su dígito de decenas. _____

2. Escribe un enunciado de suma que tenga una **suma** de 20. _____

3. Escribe un enunciado de resta que tenga una **diferencia** de 10. _____

Capítulo 6 — Juego: Baraja de 2 dígitos

Materiales
- tarjetas con números del 10 al 50
- 15
- 15

Juega con un compañero.

1. Baraja las tarjetas con números. Colócalas boca abajo en una pila.
2. Toma dos tarjetas. Di la suma de los dos números.
3. Tu compañero comprueba tu suma.
4. Si tu suma es correcto, coloca una ficha sobre un botón. Si reagrupaste para resolver, coloca una ficha sobre otro botón.
5. Túrnense. Cubran todos los botones. El jugador que tenga más fichas en el tablero gana.
6. Repitan el juego, diciendo la diferencia entre los dos números en cada turno.

Vocabulario del Capítulo 6

centena hundred 5	**columna** column 10
diferencia difference 20	**dígito** digit 21
es igual a is equal to (=) 25	**reagrupar** regroup 55
suma sum 59	**sumandos** addends 60

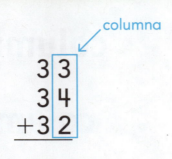
← columna

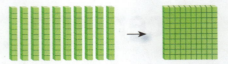

Hay 10 decenas en 1 **centena**.

0, 1, 2, 3, 4, 5, 6, 7, 8 y 9 son dígitos.

5 − 3 = 2
↑ diferencia

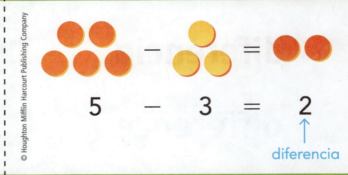

Puedes cambiar 10 unidades por 1 decena y **reagrupar**.

2 más 1 es igual a 3
2 + 1 = 3

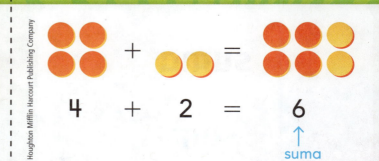

5 + 3 = 8
↑ ↑
sumandos

4 + 2 = 6
↑ suma

De visita con las palabras de ¡Vivan las matemáticas!

¡Dibújalo!

Jugadores: 3 a 4

Materiales
- cronómetro
- bloc de dibujo

Instrucciones
1. Túrnense para jugar.
2. Elige una palabra de matemáticas del Recuadro de palabras. No digas la palabra.
3. Fijen el cronómetro en 1 minuto.
4. Hagan dibujos y números para dar pistas de la palabra de matemáticas.
5. El primer jugador que adivina la palabra obtiene 1 punto. Si usa la palabra en una oración, obtiene 1 punto más. El jugador obtiene el siguiente turno.
6. El primer jugador que obtiene 5 puntos es el ganador.

Recuadro de palabras
- centena
- columna
- diferencia
- dígito
- es igual a
- reagrupar
- suma
- sumandos

Escríbelo

Reflexiona
Elige una idea. Escribe acerca de la idea en el espacio de abajo.

- Di cómo resolver este problema.

  $42 - 25 =$ _____

- Escribe un párrafo en que uses al menos **tres** de estas palabras.

  sumandos   dígito   suma   centena   reagrupar

- Explica algo que sabes acerca de reagrupar.

Nombre _____

Dibujar para representar la suma de 3 dígitos

Lección 6.1

Pregunta esencial ¿Cómo haces dibujos rápidos para mostrar la suma de números de 3 dígitos?

Objetivo de aprendizaje Harás dibujos rápidos para mostrar la suma de números menores que 1,000.

Escucha y dibuja

Haz dibujos rápidos para representar problema. Luego resuelve.

Decenas	Unidades
	_____ páginas

 PARA EL MAESTRO • Lea este problema a los niños. Manuel leyó 45 páginas de un libro. Luego leyó 31 páginas más. ¿Cuántas páginas leyó Manuel? Pida a los niños que hagan dibujos rápidos para resolver el problema.

 PRÁCTICAS Y PROCESOS MATEMÁTICOS 5

Usa herramientas Explica cómo tus dibujos rápidos muestran el problema.

Capítulo 6 — trescientos noventa y uno **391**

Representa y dibuja

Suma 234 y 141.

Centenas	Decenas	Unidades

____3____ centenas ____7____ decenas

____5____ unidades

____375____

Comparte y muestra

Haz dibujos rápidos. Escribe cuántas centenas, decenas y unidades hay en total. Escribe el número.

1. Suma 125 y 344.

Centenas	Decenas	Unidades

_____ centenas _____ decenas

_____ unidades

_____

2. Suma 307 y 251.

Centenas	Decenas	Unidades

_____ centenas _____ decenas

_____ unidades

_____

392   trescientos noventa y dos

Nombre _____

Por tu cuenta

Haz dibujos rápidos. Escribe cuántas centenas, decenas y unidades hay en total. Escribe el número.

3. Suma 231 y 218.

Centenas	Decenas	Unidades

____ centenas ____ decenas

____ unidades

____

4. Suma 232 y 150.

Centenas	Decenas	Unidades

____ centenas ____ decenas

____ unidades

____

5. **PIENSA MÁS** Usa los dibujos rápidos para hallar los dos números que se sumaron. Luego escribe cuántas centenas, decenas y unidades hay en total. Escribe el número.

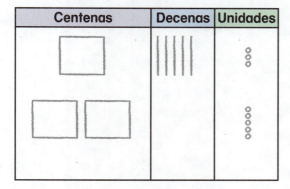

Suma _____ y _____.

____ centenas ____ decenas

____ unidades

____

Capítulo 6 • Lección 1   trescientos noventa y tres **393**

PRÁCTICAS Y PROCESOS MATEMÁTICOS • ANALIZAR • BUSCAR ESTRUCTURAS • PRECISIÓN

Resolución de problemas • Aplicaciones

6. **PRÁCTICAS Y PROCESOS MATEMÁTICOS 2** **Representa un problema**

Hay 125 poemas en el libro de Carrie y 143 poemas en el libro de Angie. ¿Cuántos poemas hay en los dos libros en total?

Haz un dibujo rápido para resolver.

_____ poemas

7. **PIENSA MÁS +** Rhys quiere sumar 456 y 131.

Ayuda a Rhys a resolver este problema. Haz dibujos rápidos. Escribe cuántas centenas, decenas y unidades hay en total. Escribe el número.

Centenas	Decenas	Unidades

_____ centenas _____ decenas _____ unidades

_____

ACTIVIDAD PARA LA CASA • Escriba 145 + 122. Pida a su niño que explique cómo puede hacer dibujos rápidos para hallar la suma.

Práctica y tarea
Lección 6.1

Nombre _____

Dibujar para representar la suma de 3 dígitos

Objetivo de aprendizaje Harás dibujos rápidos para mostrar la suma de números menores que 1,000.

Haz dibujos rápidos. Escribe cuántas centenas, decenas y unidades hay en total. Escribe el número.

1. Suma 142 y 215.

Centenas	Decenas	Unidades

____ centenas ____ decenas

____ unidades

____

Resolución de problemas

Resuelve. Escribe o dibuja para explicar.

2. Un granjero vendió 324 limones y 255 limas. ¿Cuántas frutas vendió el granjero en total?

_____ frutas

3. **ESCRIBE Matemáticas** Haz dibujos rápidos y escribe para explicar cómo sumarías 342 y 416.

_____

_____

_____

Capítulo 6   trescientos noventa y cinco **395**

Repaso de la lección

1. La Sra. Carol vendió 346 boletos para niños y 253 boletos para adultos. ¿Cuántos boletos vendió la Sra. Carol en total?

   _____ boletos

2. El Sr. Harris contó 227 guijarros grises y 341 guijarros blancos. ¿Cuántos guijarros contó el Sr. Harris?

   _____ guijarros

Repaso en espiral

3. Pat tiene 3 hileras de caracoles. Hay 4 caracoles en cada hilera. ¿Cuántos caracoles tiene Pat en total?

   _____ caracoles

4. Kara contó 32 bolígrafos rojos, 25 bolígrafos azules, 7 bolígrafos negros y 24 bolígrafos verdes. ¿Cuántos bolígrafos contó Kara en total?

   _____ bolígrafos

5. Kai tenía 46 bloques. Le dio 39 bloques a su hermana. ¿Cuántos bloques le quedan a Kai?

   46 − 39 = _____ bloques

6. Una tienda tiene 55 carteles a la venta. Tiene 34 carteles de deportes. El resto son de animales. ¿Cuántos carteles son de animales?

   _____ carteles

Lección 6.2

Nombre _____

Separar sumandos de 3 dígitos

Pregunta esencial ¿Cómo separas sumandos para sumar centenas, decenas y luego unidades?

Objetivo de aprendizaje Separarás sumandos para hallar sumas de números menores que 1,000.

Escucha y dibuja

Escribe el número. Haz un dibujo rápido del número. Luego escribe el número de diferentes maneras.

_____

____ centenas ____ decenas ____ unidades

_____ + _____ + _____

_____

____ centenas ____ decenas ____ unidades

_____ + _____ + _____

PARA EL MAESTRO • Pida a los niños que escriban 258 en el espacio en blanco de la esquina izquierda de la primera casilla. Pida a los niños que hagan un dibujo rápido de este número y luego completen las otras dos formas del número. Repita la actividad con 325.

Charla matemática
PRÁCTICAS Y PROCESOS MATEMÁTICOS 6

Haz conexiones ¿Qué número puede escribirse como 400 + 20 + 9?

Capítulo 6

trescientos noventa y siete **397**

Representa y dibuja

Separa los sumandos en centenas, decenas y unidades.
Suma las centenas, las decenas y las unidades.
Luego halla la suma.

```
 538   ⟶   500 + 30 + 8
+216   ⟶   200 + 10 + 6
           ─────────────
           700 + ___ + ___ = _____
```

Comparte y muestra

Separa los sumandos para hallar la suma.

1. 321   ⟶   ____ + ____ + ____
   +457   ⟶   ____ + ____ + ____

              ____ + ____ + ____ = ____

2. 744   ⟶   ____ + ____ + ____
   +162   ⟶   ____ + ____ + ____

              ____ + ____ + ____ = ____

3. 254   ⟶   ____ + ____ + ____
   +536   ⟶   ____ + ____ + ____

              ____ + ____ + ____ = ____

Nombre _____

Por tu cuenta

Separa los sumandos para hallar la suma.

4. 374 ⟶ ____ + ____ + ____
   +518 ⟶ ____ + ____ + ____

   ____ + ____ + ____ = ____

5. 425 ⟶ ____ + ____ + ____
   +232 ⟶ ____ + ____ + ____

   ____ + ____ + ____ = ____

6. 849 ⟶ ____ + ____ + ____
   +123 ⟶ ____ + ____ + ____

   ____ + ____ + ____ = ____

7. **PIENSA MÁS** El Sr. Jones tiene muchas hojas de papel. Tiene 158 hojas de papel azul, 100 hojas de papel rojo y 231 hojas de papel verde. ¿Cuántas hojas de papel tiene en total?

   ____ hojas de papel

Capítulo 6 • Lección 2   trescientos noventa y nueve **399**

PRÁCTICAS Y PROCESOS MATEMÁTICOS • REPRESENTAR • RAZONAR • ENTENDER

Resolución de problemas • Aplicaciones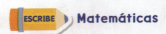

8. **MÁS AL DETALLE** Wesley sumó de otra manera.

```
   327
 + 468
 -----
   700      7 centenas
    80      8 decenas
 +  15     15 unidades
 -----
   795
```

Usa la manera de Wesley para hallar la suma.

```
   539
 + 247
```

9. **PIENSA MÁS** Hay 376 niños en una escuela. Hay 316 niños en otra escuela. ¿Cuántos niños hay en las dos escuelas?

```
   376    →    300 + 70 + 6
 + 316    →    300 + 10 + 6
```

Selecciona un número de cada columna para resolver el problema.

Centenas	Decenas	Unidades
○ 2	○ 4	○ 2
○ 4	○ 8	○ 3
○ 6	○ 9	○ 6

ACTIVIDAD PARA LA CASA • Escriba 347 + 215. Pida a su niño que separe los números y luego halle la suma.

Nombre _____

Separar sumandos de 3 dígitos

Práctica y tarea
Lección 6.2

Objetivo de aprendizaje Separarás sumandos para hallar sumas de números menores que 1,000.

Separa los sumandos para hallar la suma.

1. 518 → ____ + ____ + ____
   +221 → ____ + ____ + ____
   ____ + ____ + ____ = ____

2. 438 → ____ + ____ + ____
   +142 → ____ + ____ + ____
   ____ + ____ + ____ = ____

Resolución de problemas

Resuelve. Escribe o dibuja para explicar.

3. Hay 126 crayones en un balde. Un maestro pone 144 crayones más en el balde. ¿Cuántos crayones hay en el balde ahora?

_____ crayones

4. **ESCRIBE Matemáticas** Haz dibujos rápidos y escribe para explicar cómo separar sumandos para hallar la suma de 324 + 231.

Capítulo 6

Repaso de la lección

1. ¿Cuál es la suma?

    $$\begin{array}{r}218\\+\ 145\\\hline\end{array}$$

2. ¿Cuál es la suma?

    $$\begin{array}{r}664\\+\ 223\\\hline\end{array}$$

Repaso en espiral

3. Ang recogió 19 bayas y Barry recogió 21 bayas. ¿Cuántas bayas recogieron en total?

    19 + 21 = _____ bayas

4. Escribe una operación de resta relacionada para 9 + 6 = 15

    _____

5. Hay 25 peces dorados y 33 peces betas. ¿Cuántos peces hay en total?

    25 + 33 = _____ peces

6. Resta 16 de 41. Haz un dibujo para mostrar la reagrupación. ¿Cuál es la diferencia?

Decenas	Unidades
|||||	□

    _____

Nombre _____

Suma de 3 dígitos: Reagrupar unidades

Lección 6.3

Objetivo de aprendizaje Reagruparás unidades para sumar números menores que 1,000.

Pregunta esencial ¿Cuándo reagrupas unidades en la suma?

Usa [bloques] para hacer un modelo del problema. Haz dibujos rápidos para mostrar lo que hiciste.

Centenas	Decenas	Unidades

PARA EL MAESTRO • Lea el siguiente problema y pida a los niños que hagan un modelo de él con bloques. Había 213 personas en el espectáculo del viernes y 156 personas en el espectáculo del sábado. ¿Cuántas personas hubo en el espectáculo en las dos noches? Pida a los niños que hagan dibujos rápidos para mostrar cómo resolvieron el problema.

Charla matemática

PRÁCTICAS Y PROCESOS MATEMÁTICOS 6

Describe cómo hiciste un modelo del problema.

Capítulo 6   cuatrocientos tres **403**

Representa y dibuja

Suma las unidades.
6 + 7 = 13

Reagrupa 13 unidades como 1 decena y 3 unidades.

Centenas	Decenas	Unidades
	1	
2	4	6
+ 1	1	7
		3

Suma las decenas.
1 + 4 + 1 = 6

Centenas	Decenas	Unidades
	1	
2	4	6
+ 1	1	7
	6	3

Suma las centenas.
2 + 1 = 3

Centenas	Decenas	Unidades
	1	
2	4	6
+ 1	1	7
3	6	3

Comparte y muestra

Escribe la suma.

1.

Centenas	Decenas	Unidades
3	2	8
+ 1	3	4

2.

Centenas	Decenas	Unidades
4	4	5
+	2	3

404 cuatrocientos cuatro

Nombre _____

Por tu cuenta

Escribe la suma.

3.
Centenas	Decenas	Unidades
	☐	
5	2	6
+ 1	0	3

4.
Centenas	Decenas	Unidades
	☐	
3	4	8
+ 1	1	9

5.
Centenas	Decenas	Unidades
	☐	
6	2	8
+ 3	4	7

6.
Centenas	Decenas	Unidades
	☐	
2	3	5
+ 2	5	7

7.
Centenas	Decenas	Unidades
	☐	
5	6	2
+ 3	2	9

8.
Centenas	Decenas	Unidades
	☐	
1	4	7
+ 1	2	5

9. **PIENSA MÁS** El jueves, el zoológico recibió 326 visitantes. El viernes, el zoológico recibió 200 visitantes más que el jueves. ¿Cuántos visitantes recibió el zoológico los dos días en total?

_____ visitantes

Capítulo 6 • Lección 3   cuatrocientos cinco **405**

PRÁCTICAS Y PROCESOS MATEMÁTICOS • COMUNICAR • PERSEVERAR • CONSTRUIR ARGUMENTOS

Resolución de problemas • Aplicaciones

Resuelve. Escribe o dibuja para explicar.

10. **Representa con matemáticas** La tienda de regalos está a 140 pasos de la entrada del zoológico. La parada del tren está a 235 pasos de la tienda de regalos. ¿Cuántos pasos hay en total?

_____ pasos

11. **PIENSA MÁS** La clase de Katina usó 249 adornos para decorar su tablero de anuncios. La clase de Gunter usó 318 adornos. ¿Cuántos adornos usaron las dos clases en total?

_____ adornos

¿Tuviste que reagrupar para resolver? Explica.

 ACTIVIDAD PARA LA CASA • Pida a su niño que explique por qué solo reagrupó en algunos de los problemas de la lección.

Nombre _____

Suma de 3 dígitos: Reagrupar unidades

**Práctica y tarea
Lección 6.3**

Objetivo de aprendizaje Reagruparás unidades para sumar números menores que 1,000.

Escribe la suma.

1.
Centenas	Decenas	Unidades
	☐	
1	4	8
+2	3	4

2.
Centenas	Decenas	Unidades
	☐	
3	2	1
+3	1	8

3.
Centenas	Decenas	Unidades
	☐	
4	1	4
+1	7	9

4.
Centenas	Decenas	Unidades
	☐	
6	0	2
+2	5	8

Resolución de problemas · En el mundo

Resuelve. Escribe o dibuja para explicar.

5. Hay 258 margaritas amarillas y 135 margaritas blancas en el jardín. ¿Cuántas margaritas hay en el jardín en total? _____ margaritas

6. **ESCRIBE Matemáticas** Halla la suma de 136 + 212. ¿Reagrupaste? Explica por qué sí o por qué no.

_____

Capítulo 6   cuatrocientos siete **407**

Repaso de la lección

1. ¿Cuál es la suma?

Centenas	Decenas	Unidades
	☐	
4	3	5
+ 1	4	6

2. ¿Cuál es la suma?

Centenas	Decenas	Unidades
	☐	
4	3	6
+ 3	0	6

Repaso en espiral

3. ¿Cuál es la diferencia?

   $9 - 4 =$ _____

4. ¿Cuál es la suma?

   $$\begin{array}{r} 82 \\ + 59 \\ \hline \end{array}$$

5. ¿Cuál es la suma?

   $26 + 7 =$ _____

6. Suma 243 y 132. ¿Cuántas centenas, decenas y unidades hay en total?

   _____ centenas _____ decenas

   _____ unidades

Nombre _____

Suma de 3 dígitos: Reagrupar decenas

Lección 6.4

Pregunta esencial ¿Cuándo reagrupas decenas en la suma?

Objetivo de aprendizaje Reagruparás decenas para sumar números menores que 1,000.

Escucha y dibuja En el mundo · Manos a la obra

Usa  para hacer un modelo del problema. Haz dibujos rápidos para mostrar lo que hiciste.

Centenas	Decenas	Unidades

Charla matemática — PRÁCTICAS Y PROCESOS MATEMÁTICOS 6

PARA EL MAESTRO • Lea el siguiente problema y pida a los niños que usen bloques para hacer un modelo del problema. El lunes visitaron el zoológico 253 niños. El martes visitaron el zoológico 324 niños. ¿Cuántos niños visitaron el zoológico esos dos días? Pida a los niños que hagan dibujos rápidos para mostrar cómo resolvieron el problema.

Explica cómo muestran tus dibujos rápidos lo que sucedió en el problema.

Capítulo 6 cuatrocientos nueve **409**

Representa y dibuja

Suma las unidades.

2 + 5 = 7

	Centenas	Decenas	Unidades
	☐	☐	
	1	4	2
+	2	8	5
			7

Suma las decenas.

4 + 8 = 12

Reagrupa 12 decenas como 1 centena y 2 decenas.

	Centenas	Decenas	Unidades
	☐	☐	
	1	4	2
+	2	8	5
		2	7

Suma las centenas.

1 + 1 + 2 = 4

	Centenas	Decenas	Unidades
	1	☐	
	1	4	2
+	2	8	5
	4	2	7

Comparte y muestra

Escribe la suma.

1.

	Centenas	Decenas	Unidades
	☐	☐	
	3	4	7
+	2	9	1

2.

	Centenas	Decenas	Unidades
	☐	☐	
	1	6	5
+	3	5	4

3.

	Centenas	Decenas	Unidades
	☐	☐	
	5	3	8
+	1	4	0

410 cuatrocientos diez

Nombre _____

Por tu cuenta

Escribe la suma.

4.
Centenas	Decenas	Unidades
☐	☐	
1	5	6
+	4	2

5.
Centenas	Decenas	Unidades
☐	☐	
7	6	4
+ 1	5	3

6.
Centenas	Decenas	Unidades
☐	☐	
3	7	2
+ 1	8	5

7.
```
  2 2 4
+ 1 5 7
-------
```

8.
```
  3 1 4
+ 4 3 5
-------
```

9.
```
  7 5 3
+ 1 5 2
-------
```

10. **MÁS AL DETALLE** En un juego de bolos Jack anotó 116 puntos y 124 puntos. Hal anotó 128 puntos y 134 puntos. ¿Quién anotó más puntos? ¿Cuántos puntos más se anotaron?

_____ _____ puntos más

PRÁCTICAS Y PROCESOS MATEMÁTICOS 6 **Presta atención a la precisión**
Reescribe los números. Luego suma.

11. 760 + 178

$+$ _____

12. 216 + 346

$+$ _____

13. 423 + 285

$+$ _____

Capítulo 6 • Lección 4

cuatrocientos once **411**

PRÁCTICAS Y PROCESOS MATEMÁTICOS • ANALIZAR • BUSCAR ESTRUCTURAS • PRECISIÓN

Resolución de problemas • Aplicaciones

14. **PIENSA MÁS** Estas listas muestran las frutas que se vendieron. ¿Cuántas frutas vendió el Sr. Olson?

    Sr. Olson
    257 manzanas
    281 ciruelas

    Sr. Luis
    314 peras
    229 duraznos

    _____ frutas

15. **MÁS AL DETALLE** ¿Quién vendió más frutas?

    _____

    ¿Cuántas más?

    _____ frutas más

16. **PIENSA MÁS** En el teatro del parque de la ciudad, asistieron 152 personas a la representación de la mañana. Otras 167 personas fueron a la representación por la tarde.

    ¿Cuántas personas en total vieron las dos representaciones? _____ personas

    Rellena el círculo al lado de cada enunciado verdadero acerca de la forma de resolver el problema.

    ○ Debes reagrupar las decenas como 1 decena y 9 unidades.

    ○ Debes reagrupar las decenas como 1 centena y 1 decena.

    ○ Debes sumar 2 unidades + 7 unidades.

    ○ Debes sumar 1 centena + 1 centena + 1 centena.

ACTIVIDAD PARA LA CASA • Pida a su niño que elija una nueva combinación de frutas de esta página y halle el número total de frutas de los dos tipos.

Suma de 3 dígitos: Reagrupar decenas

**Práctica y tarea
Lección 6.4**

Objetivo de aprendizaje Reagruparás decenas para sumar números menores que 1,000.

Escribe la suma.

1. | Centenas | Decenas | Unidades |
    |---|---|---|
    | ☐ | ☐ | |
    | 1 | 8 | 7 |
    | +2 | 3 | 2 |

2. | Centenas | Decenas | Unidades |
    |---|---|---|
    | ☐ | ☐ | |
    | 3 | 2 | 2 |
    | +3 | 5 | 6 |

3. | Centenas | Decenas | Unidades |
    |---|---|---|
    | ☐ | ☐ | |
    | 2 | 8 | 5 |
    | +5 | 3 | 1 |

4. | | | |
    |---|---|---|
    | 4 | 4 | 5 |
    | + | 3 | 4 |

5. | | | |
    |---|---|---|
    | 6 | 2 | 0 |
    | +2 | 8 | 8 |

6. | | | |
    |---|---|---|
    | 5 | 5 | 7 |
    | +1 | 8 | 0 |

Resolución de problemas

Resuelve. Escribe o dibuja para explicar.

7. Hay 142 carritos azules y 293 carritos rojos en la juguetería. ¿Cuántos carritos hay en total?

   _____ carritos

8. **ESCRIBE Matemáticas** Halla la suma de 362 + 265. ¿Reagrupaste? Explica por qué o por qué no.

_____

_____

Capítulo 6

cuatrocientos trece **413**

Repaso de la lección

1. ¿Cuál es la suma?

    472
    + 255
    -----

2. Annika tiene 144 monedas de 1¢ y Yahola tiene 284 monedas de 1¢ ¿Cuántas monedas de 1¢ tienen en total?

    144
    + 284

Repaso en espiral

3. ¿Cuál es la suma?

    56
    + 38
    ----

4. ¿Cuál es la suma?

    326
    + 139
    -----

5. Francis tiene 8 carritos, luego su hermano le da otros 9 carritos más. ¿Cuántos carritos tiene Francis ahora?

    8 + 9 = _____ carritos

6. ¿Cuál es la diferencia?

    82
    − 34

Nombre _____

Suma: Reagrupar unidades y decenas

Lección 6.5

Pregunta esencial ¿Cómo sabes cuándo reagrupar en la suma?

Objetivo de aprendizaje Reagruparás unidades y decenas para sumar números menores que 1,000.

Escucha y dibuja — En el mundo

Usa el cálculo mental. Escribe la suma para cada problema.

```
   40          200          70          500
+  20       + 700        + 30        + 300
____        _____        ____        _____
```

10 + 30 + 40 = _____

100 + 400 + 200 = _____

10 + 50 + 40 = _____

600 + 300 = _____

PARA EL MAESTRO • Anime a los niños a resolver estos problemas de suma con rapidez. Es posible que primero deba comentar los problemas con los niños, indicándoles que cada uno consiste en sumar decenas o sumar centenas.

Analiza ¿Te resultaron algunos de los problemas más fáciles de resolver que otros? Explica.

PRÁCTICAS Y PROCESOS MATEMÁTICOS 1

Capítulo 6

cuatrocientos quince **415**

Representa y dibuja

A veces reagruparás más de una vez en los problemas de suma.

```
  1 1
  2 5 9
+ 4 7 6
-------
  7 3 5
```

9 unidades + 6 unidades = 15 unidades, o 1 decena y 5 unidades

1 decena + 5 decenas + 7 decenas = 13 decenas o 1 centena y 3 decenas

1 centena + 2 centenas + 4 centenas = 7 centenas

PIENSA:
¿Hay 10 o más unidades?
¿Hay 10 o más decenas?

Comparte y muestra

Escribe la suma.

1.
```
  1 8 4
+ 3 2 9
-------
```

2.
```
  5 4 6
+ 2 7 8
-------
```

3.
```
  3 2 7
+ 3 5 3
-------
```

4.
```
  2 3 4
+ 1 5 2
-------
```

☑ 5.
```
  3 7 5
+ 2 7 2
-------
```

☑ 6.
```
  1 8 9
+ 6 2 3
-------
```

Nombre _____

Por tu cuenta

Escribe la suma.

7.
```
  5 7 4
+ 2 8 1
-------
```

8.
```
  4 1 6
+ 4 8 3
-------
```

9.
```
  3 4 6
+ 5 9 7
-------
```

10.
```
  3 6 5
+ 2 8 3
-------
```

11.
```
  6 4 7
+ 1 0 9
-------
```

12.
```
  5 4 6
+ 3 5 6
-------
```

13.
```
  3 4 8
+ 6 3 1
-------
```

14.
```
  4 5 5
+ 1 3 9
-------
```

15.
```
  5 6 3
+ 2 4 5
-------
```

16. **PIENSA MÁS** Miko escribió estos problemas. ¿Qué dígitos faltan?

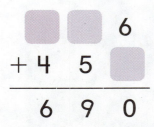

```
  ☐ ☐ 6
+   4 5 ☐
---------
    6 9 0
```

```
    6 ☐ 7
+   2 3 ☐
---------
  ☐     6 2
```

Matemáticas al instante

ACTIVIDAD PARA LA CASA • Pida a su niño que explique cómo resolver 236 + 484.

Capítulo 6 • Lección 5

Nombre _____

 # Revisión de la mitad del capítulo

Conceptos y destrezas

Entrenador personal en matemáticas
Evaluación e intervención en línea

Separa los sumandos para hallar la suma.

1. 567 → ____ + ____ + ____
   +324 → ____ + ____ + ____

   ____ + ____ + ____ = ____

Escribe la suma.

2.
```
  2 4 8
+ 3 4 6
-------
```

3.
```
  6 3 7
+ 2 6 4
-------
```

4.
```
  3 9 1
+ 5 3 7
-------
```

5. **PIENSA MÁS** Hay 148 dólares de arena pequeños y 119 dólares de arena grandes en la playa. ¿Cuántos dólares de arena hay en total en la playa?

_____ dólares de arena

418 cuatrocientos dieciocho

Nombre _____

Suma: Reagrupar unidades y decenas

**Práctica y tarea
Lección 6.5**

Objetivo de aprendizaje Reagruparás unidades y decenas para sumar números menores que 1,000.

Escribe la suma.

1.
```
  547
+ 435
```

2.
```
  367
+ 284
```

3.
```
  485
+ 456
```

4.
```
  187
+ 306
```

5.
```
  647
+ 128
```

6.
```
  523
+ 174
```

Resolución de problemas · En el mundo

Resuelve. Escribe o dibuja para explicar.

7. Saúl y Luisa anotaron 167 puntos cada uno en un juego de computadora. ¿Cuántos puntos anotaron en total?

_____ puntos

8. ESCRIBE Matemáticas Escribe la suma para 275 más 249 y halla la suma. Luego haz dibujos rápidos para comprobar tu trabajo.

Capítulo 6 cuatrocientos diecinueve **419**

Repaso de la lección

1. ¿Cuál es la suma?

   $$\begin{array}{r} 348 \\ +\ 272 \\ \hline \end{array}$$

2. ¿Cuál es la suma?

   $$\begin{array}{r} 123 \\ +\ 217 \\ \hline \end{array}$$

Repaso en espiral

3. Escribe una operación de suma que tenga el mismo total que 9 + 4.

   10 + ____

4. ¿Cuál es la suma?

   $$\begin{array}{r} 32 \\ 15 \\ +\ 46 \\ \hline \end{array}$$

5. Suma 29 y 35. Dibuja para mostrar la reagrupación. ¿Cuál es la suma?

Decenas	Unidades

   ____

6. Tom tenía 25 pretzels. Regaló 12 pretzels. ¿Cuántos pretzels le quedan a Tom?

   25 − 12 = ____ pretzels

Nombre _____

Resolución de problemas • Resta de 3 dígitos

RESOLUCIÓN DE PROBLEMAS
Lección 6.6

Pregunta esencial ¿Cómo puede ayudar un modelo cuando se resuelven problemas de resta?

Objetivo de aprendizaje Usarás bloques y la estrategia de *hacer un modelo* para resolver problemas de resta de números menores que 1,000.

Había 436 personas en la exhibición de arte. De ellas, 219 se fueron a casa. ¿Cuántas personas se quedaron en la exhibición de arte?

¿Qué debo hallar?

cuántas personas
se quedaron en la exhibición de arte

¿Qué información debo usar?

Había _____ personas en la exhibición de arte.

Luego, _____ personas se fueron a casa.

Muestra cómo resolver el problema.

Haz un modelo. Luego haz un dibujo rápido de tu modelo.

_____ personas

NOTA A LA FAMILIA • Su niño hizo un modelo y un dibujo rápido para representar y resolver un problema de resta.

Capítulo 6   cuatrocientos veintiuno **421**

Haz otro problema

Haz un modelo para resolver. Luego haz un dibujo rápido de tu modelo.

- ¿Qué debo hallar?
- ¿Qué información debo usar?

1. Hay 532 obras de arte en la exhibición. De ellas, 319 obras de arte son pinturas. ¿Cuántas obras de arte no son pinturas?

    _____ obras de arte

2. 245 niños van al evento de pintar caras. De ellos, 114 son niños. ¿Cuántas son niñas?

    _____ niñas

Charla matemática

Explica cómo resolviste el primer problema de esta página.

Nombre _____

Comparte y muestra

Haz un modelo para resolver. Luego haz un dibujo rápido de tu modelo.

✓ 3. Había 237 libros en la mesa. La señorita Jackson quitó 126 libros de la mesa. ¿Cuántos libros quedaron en la mesa?

_____ libros

✓ 4. Había 232 tarjetas postales en la mesa. Los niños usaron 118 tarjetas postales. ¿Cuántas tarjetas postales no se usaron?

_____ tarjetas postales

5. **PIENSA MÁS** En la mañana, 164 niños y 31 adultos vieron la película. En la tarde, 125 niños vieron la película. ¿Cuántos niños menos vieron la película en la tarde que en la mañana?

_____ niños menos

Capítulo 6 • Lección 6

PRÁCTICAS Y PROCESOS MATEMÁTICOS REPRESENTAR • RAZONAR • ENTENDER

Por tu cuenta

PRÁCTICAS Y PROCESOS MATEMÁTICOS ① Comprende los problemas

6. Había algunas uvas en un tazón. Los amigos de Clancy comieron 24 uvas. Quedaron 175 uvas en el tazón. ¿Cuántas uvas había antes en el tazón?

_____ uvas

7. **PIENSA MÁS** En la escuela de Gregory, hay 547 niños y niñas. Hay 246 niños. ¿Cuántas niñas hay?

Haz un dibujo rápido para resolver.

Encierra en un círculo el número válido para que el enunciado sea verdadero.

Hay 201
     301   niñas.
     793

ACTIVIDAD PARA LA CASA • Pida a su niño que elija un problema de esta lección y lo resuelva de otra manera.

424 cuatrocientos veinticuatro

Resolución de problemas • Resta de 3 dígitos

Práctica y tarea
Lección 6.6

Objetivo de aprendizaje Usarás bloques y la estrategia de *hacer un modelo* para resolver problemas de resta de números menores que 1,000.

Haz un modelo para resolver. Luego haz un dibujo rápido de tu modelo.

1. El sábado fueron 770 personas al puesto de bocadillos. El domingo fueron 628 personas. ¿Cuántas personas más fueron al puesto de bocadillos el sábado que el domingo?

    _____ personas más

2. Había 395 vasos de helado de limón en el puesto de bocadillos. Se vendieron 177 vasos de helado de limón. ¿Cuántos vasos de helado de limón quedan en el puesto?

    _____ vasos

3. Había 576 botellas de agua en el puesto de bocadillos. Se vendieron 469 botellas de agua. ¿Cuántas botellas de agua hay en el puesto ahora?

    _____ botellas

4. **ESCRIBE Matemáticas** Haz dibujos rápidos para mostrar cómo restar 314 de 546.

Capítulo 6

Repaso de la lección

1. Hay 278 libros de matemáticas y ciencias. De ellos, 128 son libros de matemáticas. ¿Cuántos libros de ciencias hay?

   _____ libros

2. Un libro tiene 176 páginas. El Sr. Roberts leyó 119 páginas. ¿Cuántas páginas le quedan por leer?

   _____ páginas

Repaso en espiral

3. ¿Cuál es la suma?

   $1 + 6 + 2 =$ _____

4. ¿Cuál es la diferencia?

   $54 - 8 =$ _____

5. ¿Cuál es la suma?

   $$\begin{array}{r} 356 \\ +\ 174 \\ \hline \end{array}$$

6. ¿Cuál es la suma?

   $$\begin{array}{r} 22 \\ +\ 16 \\ \hline \end{array}$$

Resta de 3 dígitos: Reagrupar decenas

Lección 6.7

Pregunta esencial ¿Cuándo reagrupas decenas en la resta?

Objetivo de aprendizaje Reagruparás decenas para restar números menores que 1,000.

Usa [bloques] para hacer un modelo del problema.
Haz un dibujo rápido para mostrar lo que hiciste.

Centenas	Decenas	Unidades

PARA EL MAESTRO • Lea el siguiente problema y pida a los niños que usen bloques para hacer un modelo del problema. 473 personas fueron al partido de fútbol americano. Al final del partido todavía quedaban 146 personas. ¿Cuántas personas se fueron antes de que terminara el partido? Pida a los niños que hagan dibujos rápidos de su modelo.

Charla matemática
PRÁCTICAS Y PROCESOS MATEMÁTICOS

Describe qué hacer cuando no hay suficientes unidades de donde restar.

Capítulo 6   cuatrocientos veintisiete **427**

Representa y dibuja

354 − 137 = ?

¿Hay suficientes unidades para restar 7?

sí   (no)

Reagrupa 1 decena como 10 unidades.

Centenas	Decenas	Unidades
	4	14
3	5̸	4̸
− 1	3	7

Ahora hay suficientes unidades.

Resta las unidades.

14 − 7 = 7

Centenas	Decenas	Unidades
	4	14
3	5̸	4̸
− 1	3	7
		7

Resta las decenas.

4 − 3 = 1

Resta las centenas.

3 − 1 = 2

Centenas	Decenas	Unidades
	4	14
3	5̸	4̸
− 1	3	7
2	1	7

Comparte y muestra

Resuelve. Escribe la diferencia.

1.
Centenas	Decenas	Unidades
	☐	☐
4	3	1
− 3	2	6

2.
Centenas	Decenas	Unidades
	☐	☐
6	5	8
− 2	3	7

Nombre _____

Por tu cuenta

Resuelve. Escribe la diferencia.

3.
Centenas	Decenas	Unidades
	☐	☐
7	2	8
−1	0	7

4.
Centenas	Decenas	Unidades
	☐	☐
4	5	2
−2	1	6

5.
Centenas	Decenas	Unidades
	☐	☐
9	6	5
−2	3	8

6.
Centenas	Decenas	Unidades
	☐	☐
4	8	9
−1	4	9

7. **MÁS AL DETALLE** Una librería tiene 148 libros sobre personas y 136 libros sobre lugares. Se vendieron algunos libros. Ahora quedan 137 libros. ¿Cuántos libros se vendieron?

_____ libros

8. **PIENSA MÁS** Había 287 libros de música y 134 libros de ciencias en la tienda. Después de vender algunos libros, quedan 159 libros. ¿Cuántos libros se vendieron?

_____ libros

Capítulo 6 • Lección 7

PRÁCTICAS Y PROCESOS MATEMÁTICOS • COMUNICAR • PERSEVERAR • CONSTRUIR ARGUMENTOS

Resolución de problemas • Aplicaciones

 **Comprende los problemas**

Resuelve. Dibuja o escribe para explicar.

9. Hay 235 silbatos y 42 campanas en la tienda. Ryan cuenta 128 silbatos en el estante. ¿Cuántos silbatos no están en el estante?

_____ silbatos

10. El Dr. Jackson tenía 326 sellos.

Vende 107 sellos. ¿Cuántos sellos le quedan ahora?

_____ sellos

¿Harías las siguientes acciones para resolver el problema? Elige Sí o No.

Restar 107 de 326.	○ Sí	○ No
Reagrupar 1 decena como 10 unidades.	○ Sí	○ No
Reagrupar las centenas.	○ Sí	○ No
Restar 7 unidades de 16 unidades.	○ Sí	○ No
Sumar 26 + 10.	○ Sí	○ No

 ACTIVIDAD PARA LA CASA • Pida a su niño que explique por qué reagrupó solo en algunos problemas de esta lección.

Nombre _____

Resta de 3 dígitos: Reagrupar decenas

**Práctica y tarea
Lección 6.7**

Objetivo de aprendizaje Reagruparás decenas para restar números menores que 1,000.

Resuelve. Escribe la diferencia.

1.

Centenas	Decenas	Unidades
	☐	☐
7	7	4
− 2	3	6

2.

Centenas	Decenas	Unidades
	☐	☐
5	5	1
− 1	1	3

3.

Centenas	Decenas	Unidades
	☐	☐
4	8	9
− 2	7	3

4.

Centenas	Decenas	Unidades
	☐	☐
7	7	2
− 2	5	4

Resolución de problemas · En el mundo

Resuelve. Escribe o dibuja para explicar.

5. Había 985 lápices. Se vendieron algunos lápices. Luego quedaron 559 lápices. ¿Cuántos lápices se vendieron? _____ lápices

6. ESCRIBE Matemáticas   Elige uno de los ejercicios de arriba. Haz dibujos rápidos para comprobar tu trabajo.

Capítulo 6   cuatrocientos treinta y uno **431**

Repaso de la lección

1. ¿Cuál es la diferencia?

    $$\begin{array}{r} 346 \\ -127 \\ \hline \end{array}$$

2. ¿Cuál es la diferencia?

    $$\begin{array}{r} 568 \\ -226 \\ \hline \end{array}$$

Repaso en espiral

3. ¿Cuál es la diferencia?

    $45 - 7 =$ ____

4. Leroy tiene 11 cubos. Jane tiene 15 cubos. ¿Cuántos cubos tienen en total?

    ____ cubos

5. Mila pone 5 flores en cada florero. ¿Cuántas flores pondrá en 3 floreros?

    ____ flores

6. El Sr. Hill tiene 471 lápices. Reparte 164 lápices. ¿Cuántos lápices le quedan?

    ____ lápices

Resta de 3 dígitos: Reagrupar centenas

Lección 6.8

Pregunta esencial ¿Cuándo reagrupas centenas en la resta?

Objetivo de aprendizaje Reagruparás centenas para restar números menores que 1,000.

Escucha y dibuja En el mundo

Haz dibujos rápidos para mostrar el problema.

Centenas	Decenas	Unidades

PARA EL MAESTRO • Lea el siguiente problema y pida a los niños que hagan un modelo de él con dibujos rápidos. El club de lectura tiene 349 libros. De ellos, 173 libros tratan sobre los animales. ¿Cuántos libros no tratan sobre los animales?

Charla matemática

PRÁCTICAS Y PROCESOS MATEMÁTICOS 1

Describe qué hacer cuando no hay suficientes decenas de donde restar.

Capítulo 6 · cuatrocientos treinta y tres **433**

Representa y dibuja

428 − 153 = ?

Resta las unidades.
8 − 3 = 5

Centenas	Decenas	Unidades
4	2	8
− 1	5	3
		5

Centenas	Decenas	Unidades
☐ ☐ ☐ ☐	‖	ooo⊗

No hay suficientes decenas de donde restar.

Reagrupa 1 centena.
4 centenas y 2 decenas ahora son 3 centenas y 12 decenas.

Centenas	Decenas	Unidades
3	12	
4	2	8
− 1	5	3
		5

Centenas	Decenas	Unidades
☐ ☐ ☐ ☐	‖‖‖‖‖ ‖‖	ooooo

Resta las decenas.
12 − 5 = 7

Resta las centenas.
3 − 1 = 2

Centenas	Decenas	Unidades
3	12	
4̸	2	8
− 1	5	3
2	7	5

Centenas	Decenas	Unidades
☐ ☒ ☒	‖‖‖‖ ‖‖	ooooo

Comparte y muestra

Resuelve. Escribe la diferencia.

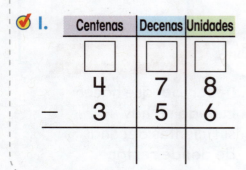

1.
Centenas	Decenas	Unidades
☐	☐	☐
4	7	8
− 3	5	6

2.
Centenas	Decenas	Unidades
☐	☐	☐
8	1	4
− 2	6	3

Nombre _____

Por tu cuenta

Resuelve. Escribe la diferencia.

3.
Centenas	Decenas	Unidades
☐	☐	☐
6	2	9
− 4	8	2

4.
Centenas	Decenas	Unidades
☐	☐	☐
9	3	6
− 1	7	3

5.
```
  4 | 3 | 5
−   | 9 | 2
```

6.
```
  3 | 8 | 7
−   | 4 | 7
```

7.
```
  5 8 8
− 4 5 0
```

8.
```
  3 4 5
− 2 6 3
```

PRÁCTICAS Y PROCESOS MATEMÁTICOS 3 — Da argumentos

9. Elige uno de los ejercicios anteriores. Describe la resta que hiciste. Asegúrate de hablar de los valores de los dígitos en los números.

_____

_____

_____

_____

Capítulo 6 • Lección 8   cuatrocientos treinta y cinco **435**

PRÁCTICAS Y PROCESOS MATEMÁTICOS • ANALIZAR • BUSCAR ESTRUCTURAS • PRECISIÓN

Resolución de problemas • Aplicaciones

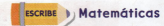

10. **PIENSA MÁS** Sam hizo dos torres. Usó 139 bloques para la primera torre. Usó 276 bloques en total. ¿Para qué torre usó más bloques? _____

Explica cómo resolviste el problema.

_____

_____

11. **PIENSA MÁS** Estos son los puntos que obtuvo cada clase en un juego de matemáticas.

- **Sra. Rose** 444 puntos
- **Sr. Chang** 429 puntos
- **Sr. Pagano** 293 puntos

¿Cuántos puntos más obtuvo la clase del Sr. Chang que la clase del Sr. Pagano? Haz un dibujo y explica cómo hallaste la respuesta.

_____ puntos más

ACTIVIDAD PARA LA CASA • Pida a su niño que explique cómo hallar la diferencia de 745 − 341.

Nombre _____

Resta de 3 dígitos: Reagrupar centenas

**Práctica y tarea
Lección 6.8**

Objetivo de aprendizaje Reagruparás centenas para restar números menores que 1,000.

Resuelve. Escribe la diferencia.

1.

Centenas	Decenas	Unidades
☐	☐	☐
7	2	7
− 2	5	6

2.

Centenas	Decenas	Unidades
☐	☐	☐
9	6	7
− 1	5	3

3.

6	3	9
− 4	7	2

4.

4	4	8
− 3	6	3

Resolución de problemas

Resuelve. Escribe o dibuja la explicación.

5. Había 537 personas en el desfile. De esas personas, 254 tocaban un instrumento. ¿Cuántas personas no tocaban un instrumento? _____ personas

6. **ESCRIBE Matemáticas** Escribe el problema de resta para 838 − 462. Halla la diferencia. Luego haz dibujos rápidos para comprobar tu diferencia.

Capítulo 6   cuatrocientos treinta y siete **437**

Repaso de la lección

1. ¿Cuál es la diferencia?

    538
    − 135

2. ¿Cuál es la diferencia?

    218
    − 126

Repaso en espiral

3. ¿Cuál es la diferencia?

    52 − 15 = ____

4. Wallace tiene 8 crayones y Alma tiene 7. ¿Cuántos crayones tienen en total?

    8 + 7 = ____ crayones

5. ¿Cuál es la suma?

    47
    + 26

6. En febrero, la clase de la maestra Lin leyó 392 libros. La clase del maestro Hook leyó 173 libros. ¿Cuántos libros más leyó la clase de la maestra Lin?

    392
    − 173
    ____ libros

Nombre _____

Resta: Reagrupar centenas y decenas

Lección 6.9

Objetivo de aprendizaje Reagruparás centenas y decenas para restar números menores que 1,000.

Pregunta esencial ¿Cómo sabes cuándo debes reagrupar en la resta?

Escucha y dibuja En el mundo

Usa el cálculo mental. Escribe la diferencia para cada problema.

```
   50          600          80          900
 − 20        − 400        − 30        − 300
 ____        _____        ____        _____
```

90 − 40 = _____

700 − 500 = _____

70 − 60 = _____

800 − 300 = _____

PARA EL MAESTRO • Anime a los niños a resolver estos problemas de resta con rapidez. Es posible que primero deba comentar los problemas con los niños, indicándoles que cada uno consiste en restar decenas o restar centenas.

Charla matemática PRÁCTICAS Y PROCESOS MATEMÁTICOS 6

¿Te resultaron algunos de los problemas más fáciles de resolver? **Explica.**

Capítulo 6   cuatrocientos treinta y nueve **439**

Representa y dibuja

A veces reagruparás más de una vez en los problemas de resta.

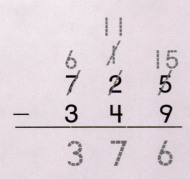

Reagrupa 2 decenas y 5 unidades como 1 decena y 15 unidades. Resta las unidades.

Reagrupa 7 centenas y 1 decena como 6 centenas y 11 decenas. Resta las decenas.

Resta las centenas.

Comparte y muestra

Resuelve. Escribe la diferencia.

1.
```
  4 2 1
- 1 3 8
```

2.
```
  2 7 4
- 1 8 2
```

3.
```
  5 4 6
- 2 6 7
```

4.
```
  8 5 9
-   5 7
```

✓5.
```
  7 4 7
- 1 5 9
```

✓6.
```
  9 3 8
- 3 7 0
```

Nombre _____

Por tu cuenta

Resuelve. Escribe la diferencia.

7.
```
  3 4 2
-  1 3 8
```

8.
```
  4 6 3
-  2 8 1
```

9.
```
  8 5 5
-  4 9 7
```

10.
```
  6 5 7
-  3 8 4
```

11.
```
  5 2 1
-  1 4 6
```

12.
```
  7 5 8
-  5 3 7
```

13.
```
  5 4 2
-  1 6 8
```

14.
```
  8 2 3
-  6 7 3
```

15.
```
  9 4 7
-  5 7 9
```

16. **PIENSA MÁS** Alex escribió estos problemas. ¿Qué números faltan?

```
    4 15
  9 ▢ ▢
-  6 2 8
  3 2 7
```

```
   7 13
  ▢ ▢ 7
-  1 5 ▢
  6 8 1
```

Capítulo 6 • Lección 9   cuatrocientos cuarenta y uno **441**

Resolución de problemas • Aplicaciones

17. **MÁS AL DETALLE** Esta es la manera en que Walter halló la diferencia de 617 − 350.

350 ⎬ + 50
400
     ⎬ + 200
600
     ⎬ + 17
617

267

Halla la diferencia de 843 − 270 con la manera de Walter.

18. **PRÁCTICAS Y PROCESOS MATEMÁTICOS** **Analiza** Hay 471 niños en la escuela de Caleb. De ellos, 256 van a la escuela en autobús.

¿Cuántos niños no van a la escuela en autobús?

_____ niños

19. **PIENSA MÁS** La Sra. Herrell tenía 427 piñas. Dio 249 piñas a sus niños.

¿Cuántas piñas le quedan?

_____ piñas

ACTIVIDAD PARA LA CASA • Pida a su niño que halle la diferencia al restar 182 de 477.

Nombre _____

Resta: Reagrupar centenas y decenas

Práctica y tarea
Lección 6.9

Objetivo de aprendizaje Reagruparás centenas y decenas para restar números menores que 1,000.

Resuelve. Escribe la diferencia.

1.
    8 1 6
− 3 4 5

2.
    9 3 2
− 1 6 3

3.
    7 9 6
− 4 6 8

Resolución de problemas

Resuelve.

4. El libro para colorear de Mila tiene 432 páginas. Ya coloreó 178 páginas. ¿Cuántas páginas del libro le faltan por colorear?

_____ páginas

5. **ESCRIBE Matemáticas** Haz dibujos rápidos para mostrar cómo restar 546 de 735.

Capítulo 6   cuatrocientos cuarenta y tres **443**

Repaso de la lección

1. ¿Cuál es la diferencia?

    $$\begin{array}{r} 349 \\ -\ 187 \\ \hline \end{array}$$

2. ¿Cuál es la diferencia?

    $$\begin{array}{r} 336 \\ -\ 178 \\ \hline \end{array}$$

Repaso en espiral

3. ¿Cuál es la suma?

    $$\begin{array}{r} 246 \\ +\ 533 \\ \hline \end{array}$$

4. ¿Cuál es la diferencia?

    $$\begin{array}{r} 38 \\ -\ 14 \\ \hline \end{array}$$

5. ¿Cuál es la diferencia?

    $17 - 9 =$ _____

6. Lisa tiene 15 margaritas. Regala 7 margaritas. Luego encuentra 3 margaritas más. ¿Cuántas margaritas tiene Lisa ahora?

    _____ margaritas

Nombre _____

Reagrupar con ceros

Pregunta esencial ¿Cómo reagrupas cuando hay ceros en el número con que comienzas?

Lección 6.10

Objetivo de aprendizaje Hallarás la diferencia en números de 3 dígitos cuando hay ceros en el número con que comienzas.

Escucha y dibuja En el mundo

Escribe o haz un dibujo para mostrar cómo resolviste el problema.

PARA EL MAESTRO • Lea el siguiente problema y pida a los niños que lo resuelvan. El Sr. Sánchez hizo 403 galletas. Vendió 159 galletas. ¿Cuántas galletas le quedan al Sr. Sánchez ahora? Anime a los niños a comentar y mostrar diferentes maneras de resolver el problema.

PRÁCTICAS Y PROCESOS MATEMÁTICOS

Describe otra manera en que podrías resolver el problema.

Capítulo 6   cuatrocientos cuarenta y cinco **445**

Representa y dibuja

La Srta. Dean tiene un libro de 504 páginas. Hasta ahora ha leído 178 páginas. ¿Cuántas páginas más le quedan por leer?

$$\begin{array}{r} 5\ 0\ 4 \\ -\ 1\ 7\ 8 \\ \hline \end{array}$$

Paso 1 No hay suficientes unidades de donde restar.

Como hay 0 decenas, reagrupa 5 centenas como 4 centenas y 10 decenas.

$$\begin{array}{r} {}^{4}\ {}^{10} \\ \cancel{5}\ \cancel{0}\ 4 \\ -\ 1\ 7\ 8 \\ \hline \end{array}$$

Paso 2 Luego reagrupa 10 decenas y 4 unidades como 9 decenas y 14 unidades.

Ahora hay suficientes unidades de donde restar.

$14 - 8 = 6$

$$\begin{array}{r} {}^{9} \\ {}^{4}\ \cancel{10}\ {}^{14} \\ \cancel{5}\ \cancel{0}\ \cancel{4} \\ -\ 1\ 7\ 8 \\ \hline 6 \end{array}$$

Paso 3 Resta las decenas.

$9 - 7 = 2$

Resta las centenas.

$4 - 1 = 3$

$$\begin{array}{r} {}^{9} \\ {}^{4}\ \cancel{10}\ {}^{14} \\ \cancel{5}\ \cancel{0}\ \cancel{4} \\ -\ 1\ 7\ 8 \\ \hline 3\ 2\ 6 \end{array}$$

Comparte y muestra

Resuelve. Escribe la diferencia.

 1.

$$\begin{array}{r} 3\ 0\ 8 \\ -\ 2\ 5\ 9 \\ \hline \end{array}$$

 2.

$$\begin{array}{r} 7\ 5\ 5 \\ -\ 4\ 3\ 8 \\ \hline \end{array}$$

 3.

$$\begin{array}{r} 8\ 0\ 1 \\ -\ 3\ 7\ 5 \\ \hline \end{array}$$

Nombre _____

Por tu cuenta

Resuelve. Escribe la diferencia.

4.
```
  5 6 3
- 1 8 2
```

5.
```
  9 0 4
- 5 6 8
```

6.
```
  7 0 5
- 2 3 1
```

7.
```
  6 0 3
- 3 2 8
```

8.
```
  4 4 2
- 2 3 8
```

9.
```
  9 0 1
- 6 7 5
```

10.
```
  7 0 2
- 4 2 6
```

11.
```
  6 8 4
- 2 1 9
```

12.
```
  4 7 9
- 1 3 7
```

13. **PIENSA MÁS** Miguel tiene 125 tarjetas de béisbol más que Chad. Miguel tiene 405 tarjetas de béisbol. ¿Cuántas tarjetas de béisbol tiene Chad?

_____ tarjetas de béisbol

PRÁCTICAS Y PROCESOS MATEMÁTICOS • COMUNICAR • PERSEVERAR • CONSTRUIR ARGUMENTOS

Resolución de problemas • Aplicaciones

14. **PRÁCTICAS Y PROCESOS MATEMÁTICOS** **Analiza** Claire tiene 250 monedas de 1¢. Algunas están en una caja y otras en su alcancía. Hay más de 100 monedas de 1¢ en cada lugar. ¿Cuántas monedas de 1¢ puede haber en cada lugar?

_____ monedas de 1¢ en una caja

_____ monedas de 1¢ en su alcancía

Explica cómo resolviste el problema.

_____
_____
_____

15. **PIENSA MÁS** Hay 404 personas en el partido de béisbol. 273 son fanáticos del equipo azul. El resto son fanáticos del equipo rojo. ¿Cuántos fanáticos hay del equipo rojo?

¿Describe el enunciado cómo resolver el problema?
Elige Sí o No.

	Sí	No
Reagrupar 1 decena como 14 unidades.	○	○
Reagrupar 1 centena como 10 decenas.	○	○
Restar 3 unidades de 4 unidades.	○	○
Restar 2 centenas de 4 centenas.	○	○

Hay _____ fanáticos del equipo rojo.

 ACTIVIDAD PARA LA CASA • Pida a su niño que explique cómo resolvió uno de los problemas de esta lección.

Nombre _____

Reagrupar con ceros

Práctica y tarea
Lección 6.10

Objetivo de aprendizaje Hallarás la diferencia en números de 3 dígitos cuando hay ceros en el número con que comienzas.

Resuelve. Escribe la diferencia.

1.
```
  8 0 6
- 3 4 5
```

2.
```
  9 0 2
- 7 8 3
```

3.
```
  7 9 4
- 2 6 8
```

4.
```
  6 8 7
- 1 4 4
```

5.
```
  5 0 5
- 1 6 7
```

6.
```
  3 0 7
- 1 5 4
```

Resolución de problemas

Resuelve.

7. Hay 303 estudiantes.
   Hay 147 niñas.
   ¿Cuántos niños hay?

   _____ niños

8. 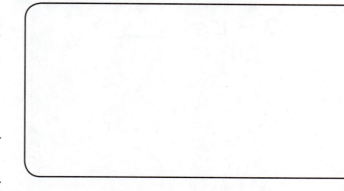 **Matemáticas** Escribe el siguiente problema de resta: 604 − 357. Describe cómo restarás para hallar la diferencia.

   _____

   _____

Capítulo 6   cuatrocientos cuarenta y nueve   **449**

Repaso de la lección

1. ¿Cuál es la diferencia?

$$\begin{array}{r} 301 \\ -187 \\ \hline \end{array}$$

2. ¿Cuál es la diferencia?

$$\begin{array}{r} 406 \\ -268 \\ \hline \end{array}$$

Repaso en espiral

3. ¿Cuál es la suma?

$$\begin{array}{r} 35 \\ +79 \\ \hline \end{array}$$

4. Hay 555 estudiantes en la escuela primaria Roosevelt y 282 estudiantes en la escuela primaria Jefferson. ¿Cuántos estudiantes hay en las dos escuelas en total?

$$\begin{array}{r} 555 \\ +282 \\ \hline \end{array}$$

_____ estudiantes

5. ¿Cuál es la diferencia?

$10 - 2 =$ _____

6. La meta de Gabriel es leer 43 libros este año. Hasta el momento leyó 11 libros. ¿Cuántos libros le quedan por leer hasta alcanzar su meta?

$$\begin{array}{r} 43 \\ -11 \\ \hline \end{array}$$

_____ libros

Nombre _____

✓ Repaso y prueba del Capítulo 6

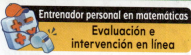

1. El Sr. Kent tenía 948 palitos planos. Su clase de arte usó 356 palitos planos. ¿Cuántos palitos planos le quedan al Sr. Kent ahora?

   _____ palitos planos

2. En la biblioteca hay 668 libros y revistas. Hay 565 libros en la biblioteca. ¿Cuántas revistas hay?

   Encierra en un círculo el número válido para que el enunciado sea verdadero.

   Hay | 13 / 103 / 1,233 | revistas.

3. Hay 176 niñas y 241 niños en la escuela. ¿Cuántos niños y niñas hay en total en la escuela?

   $$\begin{array}{r} 176 \\ +241 \end{array} \longrightarrow \begin{array}{r} 100+70+6 \\ 200+40+1 \end{array}$$

   Selecciona un número de cada columna para resolver el problema.

Centenas	Decenas	Unidades
○ 2	○ 1	○ 3
○ 3	○ 3	○ 5
○ 4	○ 4	○ 7

Capítulo 6   Opciones de evaluación Prueba del capítulo   cuatrocientos cincuenta y uno **451**

4. **PIENSA MÁS +** Anna quiere sumar 246 y 132.

   Ayuda a Anna a resolver este problema. Haz dibujos rápidos. Escribe cuántas centenas, decenas y unidades hay en total. Escribe el número.

Centenas	Decenas	Unidades

   _____ centenas _____ decenas

   _____ unidades

   _____

5. La Sra. Preston tenía 513 hojas. Dio 274 hojas a sus estudiantes. ¿Cuántas hojas le quedan? Haz un dibujo para mostrar cómo hallaste la respuesta.

   _____ hojas

6. Un agricultor tiene 112 pacanas y 97 nogales. ¿Cuántas pacanas más que nogales tiene el agricultor?

   Rellena el círculo al lado de todos los enunciados que describen lo que harías.

   ○ Reagruparía las centenas.

   ○ Sumaría 12 + 97.

   ○ Restaría 7 unidades de 12 unidades.

   ○ Reagruparía las decenas.

Nombre _____

7. Amy tiene 408 cuentas. Da 322 cuentas a su hermana. ¿Cuántas cuentas tiene Amy ahora?

¿Describe el enunciado cómo hallar la respuesta?
Elige Sí o No.

Reagrupar 1 decena como 18 unidades.	○ Sí	○ No
Reagrupar 1 centena como 10 decenas.	○ Sí	○ No
Restar 2 decenas de 10 decenas.	○ Sí	○ No

Amy tiene _____ cuentas.

8. MÁS AL DETALLE Raúl usó este método para hallar la suma de 427 + 316.

```
   427
 + 316
  ----
   700
    30
 +  13
  ----
   743
```

Usa el método de Raúl para hallar la suma.

```
   229
 + 313
```

Describe cómo resuelve Raúl los problemas de suma.

_____

_____

Capítulo 6　　　　　　　　　　　　cuatrocientos cincuenta y tres **453**

9. Sally obtiene 381 puntos en un juego. Ty obtiene 262 puntos.
¿Cuántos puntos más obtiene Sally que Ty?

○ 121   ○ 643   ○ 129   ○ 119

10. Usa los números de las fichas cuadradas para resolver el problema.

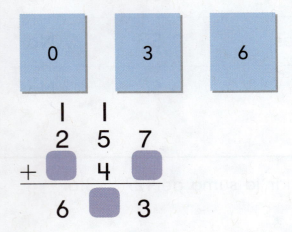

Describe cómo resolviste el problema.

_____

_____

_____

_____

_____

Glosario ilustrado

a. m. A.M.

Las horas después de medianoche y antes del mediodía se escriben con **a. m.**
Las 11:00 a. m. es una hora de la mañana.

ángulo angle

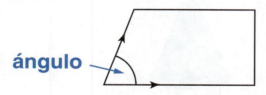

arista edge

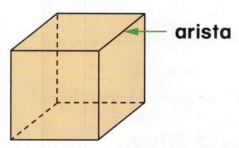

Una **arista** se forma cuando dos caras de una figura tridimensional se unen.

cara face

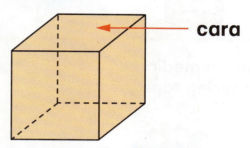

Cada superficie plana de este cubo es una **cara**.

centena hundred

Hay 10 decenas en 1 **centena**.

centímetro centimeter

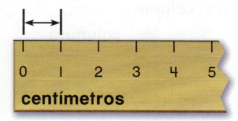

H1

cilindro cylinder

cinta de medir measuring tape

clave key

Número de partidos de fútbol							
Marzo	⚽	⚽	⚽	⚽			
Abril	⚽	⚽	⚽	⚽	⚽		
Mayo	⚽	⚽	⚽	⚽	⚽	⚽	
Junio	⚽	⚽	⚽	⚽	⚽	⚽	⚽

Clave: Cada ⚽ representa 1 partido.

La **clave** indica la cantidad que representa cada dibujo.

columna column

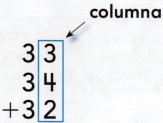

comparar compare

Compare la longitud del lápiz y el crayón.

El lápiz es más largo que el crayón.
El crayón es más corto que el lápiz.

cono cone

cuadrilátero quadrilateral

Una figura bidimensional con 4 lados es un **cuadrilátero**.

cuarta parte de quarter of

Una **cuarta parte de** la figura es verde.

H2

cuarto de fourth of

Un **cuarto de** la figura es verde.

cuartos fourths

Esta figura tiene 4 partes iguales. Estas partes iguales se llaman **cuartos**.

cubo cube

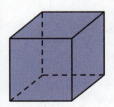

datos data

Comida favorita	
Comida	Conteo
pizza	IIII
sándwich	IIII I
ensalada	III
pasta	IIII

La información de esta tabla se llama **datos**.

decena ten

10 unidades = 1 decena

diagrama de puntos line plot

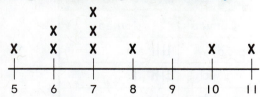

Longitud de los pinceles en pulgadas

diferencia difference

9 − 2 = 7
         ↑
     diferencia

H3

dígito digit

0, 1, 2, 3, 4, 5, 6, 7, 8 y 9 son **dígitos**.

---

dobles doubles

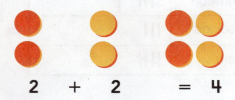

2 + 2 = 4

---

dólar dollar

Un **dólar** tiene el valor de 100 centavos.

---

encuesta survey

Comida favorita	
Comida	Conteo
pizza	IIII
sándwich	HHT I
ensalada	III
pasta	HHT

La **encuesta** es una serie de datos reunidos a partir de las respuestas a una pregunta.

---

es igual a (=) is equal to

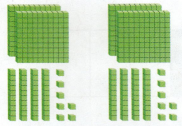

247 **es igual a** 247.

247 = 247

---

es mayor que (>) is greater than

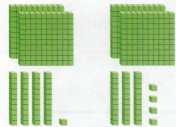

241 **es mayor que** 234.

241 > 234

---

es menor que (<) is less than

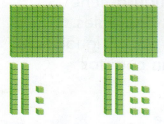

123 **es menor que** 128.

123 < 128

esfera sphere

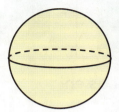

---

estimación estimate

Una **estimación** es una cantidad que indica aproximadamente cuántos hay.

---

gráfica de barras bar graph

---

hexágono hexagon

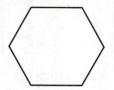

El **hexágono** es una figura bidimensional de 6 lados.

---

hora hour

Hay 60 minutos en 1 **hora**.

---

impar odd

1, 3, 5, 7, 9, 11, . . .

números impares

---

lado side

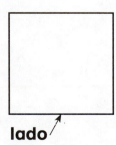

Esta figura tiene 4 **lados**.

H5

más (+) plus

2   más   1   es igual a   3
2   +   1   =   3

medianoche midnight

La **medianoche** es a las 12:00 de la noche.

mediodía noon

El **mediodía** es a las 12:00 del día.

metro meter

1 **metro** tiene la misma longitud que 100 centímetros.

millar thousand

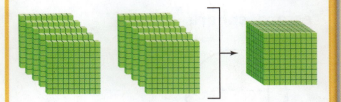

Hay 10 centenas en 1 **millar**.

minuto minute

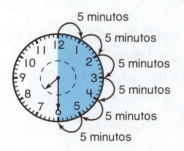

En media hora hay 30 **minutos**.

mitad de half of

La **mitad de** la figura es verde.

mitades halves

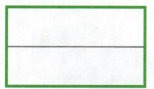

Esta figura tiene 2 partes iguales.
Estas partes iguales se llaman **mitades**.

moneda de 1¢ penny

Esta moneda vale un centavo o **1¢**.

moneda de 5¢ nickel

Esta moneda vale cinco centavos o **5¢**.

moneda de 10¢ dime

Esta moneda vale diez centavos o **10¢**.

moneda de 25¢ quarter

Esta moneda vale veinticinco centavos o **25¢**.

p. m. P.M.

Las horas después del mediodía y antes de la medianoche se escriben con **p. m.**
Las 11:00 p. m. es una hora de la noche.

par even

2, 4, 6, 8, 10, . . .

números pares

pentágono pentagon

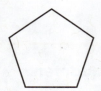

El **pentágono** es una figura bidimensional de 5 lados.

pictografía picture graph

Número de partidos de fútbol							
Marzo	⚽	⚽	⚽	⚽			
Abril	⚽	⚽	⚽				
Mayo	⚽	⚽	⚽	⚽	⚽	⚽	
Junio	⚽	⚽	⚽	⚽	⚽	⚽	⚽

Clave: Cada ⚽ representa 1 partido.

pie foot

1 **pie** tiene la misma longitud que 12 pulgadas.

prisma rectangular rectangular prism

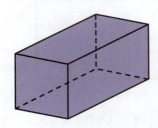

pulgada inch

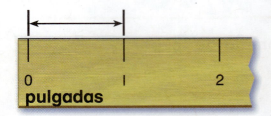

punto decimal decimal point

$1.00
↑
punto decimal

reagrupar regroup

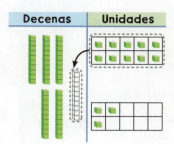

Puedes cambiar 10 unidades por 1 decena para **reagrupar**.

---

regla de 1 yarda yardstick

La **regla de 1 yarda** es un instrumento de medida que muestra 3 pies.

---

símbolo de centavo cent sign

53¢
↑
símbolo de centavo

---

símbolo de dólar dollar sign

$1.00
↑
símbolo de dólar

---

suma sum

9 + 6 = 15
↗
suma

---

sumando addend

5 + 8 = 13
↑ ↑
sumandos

H9

un tercio de third of

Un tercio de la figura es verde.

unidades ones

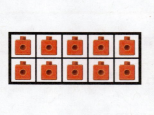

10 unidades = 1 decena

tercios thirds

Esta figura tiene 3 partes iguales.
Estas partes iguales se llaman **tercios**.

vértice vertex

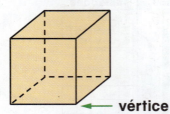
← vértice

El punto de una esquina de una figura tridimensional es un **vértice**.

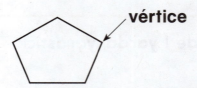
→ vértice

Esta figura tiene 5 **vértices**.

y cuarto quarter past

15 minutos después de las 8:00.
8 **y cuarto**.

Índice

A

a. m., 527–530
Actividad para la casa, 16, 22, 28, 34, 39, 46, 52, 58, 64, 78, 84, 90, 96, 102, 108, 113, 120, 126, 132, 138, 144, 166, 172, 178, 184, 190, 195, 202, 208, 214, 220, 226, 240, 246, 252, 258, 264, 270, 275, 282, 288, 294, 300, 306, 320, 326, 332, 338, 344, 349, 356, 362, 368, 374, 380, 394, 400, 406, 412, 417, 424, 430, 436, 442, 328, 470, 476, 482, 488, 493, 500, 506, 512, 518, 524, 530, 544, 550, 556, 562, 574, 580, 586, 592, 606, 612, 618, 630, 636, 642, 656, 662, 667, 674, 680, 686, 708, 714, 720, 726, 732, 738, 743, 750, 756, 762, 768
Actividad para la casa. Ver Participación de la familia;
Actividades
Actividad para la casa, 16, 22, 28, 34, 39, 46, 52, 58, 64, 78, 84, 90, 96, 102, 108, 113, 120, 126, 132, 138, 144, 166, 172, 178, 184, 190, 195, 202, 208, 214, 220, 226, 240, 246, 252, 258, 264, 270, 275, 282, 288, 294, 300, 306, 320, 326, 332, 338, 344, 349, 356, 362, 368, 374, 380, 394, 400, 406, 412, 417, 424, 430, 436, 442, 448, 470, 476, 482, 488, 493, 500, 506, 512, 518, 524, 530, 544, 550, 556, 562, 567, 574, 592, 606, 612, 618, 630, 636, 642, 656, 662, 667, 674, 680, 686, 708, 714, 720, 726, 732, 738, 743, 750, 756, 762, 768
Juegos. Ver Juegos
Manos a la obra Actividades: 13, 19, 31, 43, 87, 237, 255, 329, 335, 403, 409, 427, 467, 473, 479, 485, 541, 547, 553, 571, 583, 589, 603, 609, 615, 627, 639, 653, 665, 671, 723, 729, 735, 741, 747

Algoritmos
alternativos, 237–240, 243–246, 249–252, 317–320, 323–326, 397–400
estándares, 261–264, 267–270, 273–275, 279–282, 335–338, 341–344, 347–349, 353–356, 403–406, 409–412, 415–417, 421–424, 427–430, 433–436
Analiza, 319, 326, 338, 448, 470, 719
Ángulos
definición, 730
en figuras bidimensionales, 729–732, 735–738
Aplica, 586, 655
Argumenta, 15, 119, 435
Aristas, 712–714

B

Busca estructuras, 52, 183, 720

C

Caras
de figuras tridimensionales, 711–714
definición, 712
Centenas
agrupar decenas en, 75–78
definición, 76
patrones de conteo con, 61–64, 123–126, 130–132
valor posicional, 75–78, 81–84, 87–90, 93–96, 99–102, 105–108, 111–113, 117–120, 141–144
Centímetros, 603–606, 609–612, 615–618, 621–624, 627–630
Charla matemática
Charla matemática aparece en cada lección de la Edición para el estudiante. Algunos ejemplos son: 13, 163, 341, 553, 659, 735
Cilindros, 705–708, 711, 717

Índice **H11**

Círculos, 705, 711

Clave, uso en una pictografía, 659–662, 665-**667**, 671

Compara
  definición, 142
  números, 135–138, 141–144
  números usando símbolos 141–144

Comparte y muestra
  Comparte y muestra aparece en cada lección de la Edición para el estudiante. Algunos ejemplos son: 14, 170, 330, 542, 654, 736

Comunica ideas matemáticas. *Ver* Charla matemática

Conos, 705–708, 711

Contar
  cuenta hacia adelante y cuenta hacia atrás de 10 en 10, 123–126
  cuenta hacia adelante y cuenta hacia atrás de 100 en 100, 123–126
  de 1 en 1, 55–58, 61, 468
  de 5 en 5, 55–58, 61–64, 468
  de 10 en 10, 55–58, 61–64, 129–132, 468
  de 100 en 100, 61–64, 129–132
  monedas para hallar el valor total, 467–470, 473–476, 479–482, 485–488, 493, 497–499

Contar salteado *Ver* Contar

Cuadrados, 711–714, 723–726, 735–738

Cuadriláteros, 723–726, 730–732, 735–738, 741–743

Cuartos, 747–750, 753–756, 759–762, 765-768

Cubos
  caras, aristas y vértices, 711–714
  construir prismas rectangulares a partir de, 718–720
  identifica y describe, 705–708, 717

Datos
  diagramas de puntos, 589–592, 686
  encuestas, 653–656

gráficas de barras
  definición, 672
  hacer, 677–680, 683–686
  leer, 671–674
  usar para resolver problemas, 671–674, 677–680, 683–686
pictografías
  cómo hacer, 665–667
  cómo usar para resolver problemas, 659–662, 665–667, 671
  definición, 660
  leer, 659–662
tablas de conteo, 653–656, 659, 666–667

Desarrollo del vocabulario, 11, 73, 161, 235, 315, 389, 465, 539, 601, 651, 703

Describir/Explicar un método, 344

Diagramas de puntos, 589–592, 686

Diagramas de Venn, 102, 161

Dibujos rápidos, 27, 32–33, 49, 87–90, 93, 99, 112–113, 117, 123, 135–137, 141, 238, 243, 255–258, 261–264, 267, 309–310, 329, 335–338, 341, 391–394 397, 403, 409, 415, 427, 433

Dígitos
  definición, 26
  valores de, 25–28, 31–34, 37–39, 87–90, 93–96, 99–102, 111–113, 123–126, 279–282, 353–356

Dinero
  contar colecciones, 467–470, 473–476, 479–482
  dólar, 491–493, 497–500, 503–506
  equivalencias, 485–488, 491–493
  monedas de 1¢, 467–470, 473–476, 479–482, 485-488, 492–493, 497–500
  monedas de 5¢, 467–470, 473–476, 479–482, 485–488, 491–493, 497–500, 503–506
  monedas de 10¢, 467–470, 473–476, 479–482, 485–488, 491–493, 497–500, 503–506
  monedas de 25¢, 473–476, 479–482, 485–488, 492–493, 497–500
  símbolo de centavo, 467–470, 473–476, 479–482, 485–488, 491, 497
  símbolo de dólar, 492–493, 497–500, 503–506

División de figuras, 741–743, 747–750, 753–756, 759–762, 765–768

Dólar, 491–493, 497–500, 503–506

En el mundo
  Escucha y dibuja, 25, 31, 37, 43, 75, 81, 87, 93, 99, 111, 117, 123, 129, 141, 163, 169, 175, 187, 193, 199, 205, 211, 223, 237, 243, 255, 261, 267, 273, 279, 291, 297, 303, 323, 329, 335, 341, 347, 353, 359, 371, 377, 391, 403, 409, 415, 427, 433, 439, 445, 467, 473, 479, 485, 491, 497, 509, 515, 521, 527, 541, 547, 553, 559, 571, 583, 589, 603, 609, 615, 627, 633, 639, 659, 671, 677, 705, 717
  Resolución de problemas, 22, 34, 46, 49, 58, 64, 78, 84, 96, 102, 108, 120, 126, 132, 97, 144, 166, 172, 178, 184, 190, 208, 214, 226, 240, 246, 252, 258, 264, 270, 282, 294, 300, 306, 320, 326, 332, 338, 344, 356, 362, 374, 380, 394, 400, 406, 412, 430, 436, 442, 448, 470, 476, 482, 488, 500, 512, 518, 524, 392, 544, 550, 556, 562, 574, 580, 586, 592, 606, 612, 618, 630, 636, 642, 656, 662, 674, 680, 686, 708, 714, 720, 726, 732, 756

Soluciona el problema, 49, 135, 217, 285, 365, 421, 503, 565, 621, 683, 765

Encuestas, 653–656

Entiende los problemas, 28, 252, 258, 264, 288, 294, 424, 430, 488, 506

Entrenador personal en matemáticas, 10, 22, 52, 72, 102, 144, 160, 172, 214, 234, 252, 264, 314, 332, 344, 388, 394, 430, 436, 464, 500, 538, 544, 586, 642, 650, 680, 686, 702, 720, 750

Escribe matemáticas, 16, 22, 28, 34, 46, 58, 64, 78, 84, 90, 96, 102, 108, 120, 126, 132, 138, 144, 157, 166, 172, 178, 184, 190, 202, 208, 214, 220, 226, 240, 246, 252, 258, 264, 270, 275, 282, 288, 294, 300, 306, 320, 326, 332, 338, 344, 356, 362, 368, 374, 380, 394, 400, 406, 412, 424, 430, 436, 442, 448, 461, 470, 476, 482, 488, 500, 506, 512, 518, 524, 530, 544, 550, 556, 562, 574, 580, 586, 592, 606, 612, 618, 630, 636, 642, 656, 662, 674, 680, 686, 708, 714, 726, 732, 738, 756, 762, 768

Escucha y dibuja
  Escucha y dibuja aparece en la mayoría de las lecciones de la Edición para el estudiante. Algunos ejemplos son: 25, 49, 391, 415, 671, 753
  Problemas, 1–8, 151–158, 455–462, 693–700

Esferas, 705–711, 711, 717

Estimación
  longitud en centímetros, 609–612
  longitud en metros, 633–636
  longitud en pies, 577–580
  longitud en pulgadas, 553–556

Estrategia de *halla un patrón*, 49–52

Estrategia de *haz un diagrama*, 285–288, 365–368, 565–567, 621–623, 765–768

Estrategia de *haz un modelo*, 135–138, 421–424

Estrategia de *separar*
  resta, 317–320, 323–326
  suma, 176–177, 237–240, 249–252, 397–400

Estrategia de *representar*, 217–220, 503–506

Estrategias para resolver problemas
  busca un patrón, 49–52
  haz un diagrama, 285–288, 365–368, 565–567, 621–623, 765–768
  haz un modelo, 135–138, 421–424
  haz una gráfica, 683–686
  Representa, 217–220, 503–506

Evaluación
  Muestra lo que sabes, 10, 72, 160, 234, 314, 388, 464, 538, 600, 650, 702
  Repaso y prueba del capítulo, 67–70, 147–150, 229–232, 309–312, 383–386, 451–454, 533–536, 595–598, 645–648, 689–692, 771–774

Revisión de la mitad del capítulo, 40, 114, 196, 276, 350, 418, 494, 568, 624, 668, 744

Evaluar, 300, 306

Explicar, 524, 550, 574, 674

F

Figuras
　bidimensionales
　　ángulos, 729–732, 736–738
　　atributos, 723–726, 729–732, 735–738
　　divide en partes iguales, 741–743, 747–750, 753–756, 759–762, 765–768
　　identifica y describe 723–726
　tridimensionales
　　atributos, 711–714
　　construye, 717–720
　　identifica y describe, 705–708

Fluidez
　suma y resta hasta 20, 163–166, 169–172, 175–178, 181–184, 187–190, 193–195, 199–202, 205–208, 211–214
　suma y resta hasta 100, 237–240, 243–246, 249–252, 255–258, 261–264, 267–270, 273–275, 279–282, 297–300, 303–306, 317–320, 323–326, 329–332, 335–338, 341–344, 347–349, 353–356, 359–362

Forma desarrollada, 31–34, 37–40, 43–46, 93–96, 111–113

Forma escrita, 38–39, 105–108, 111–113

Forma escrita de los números, 37–39, 105–108, 111–113

Fracciones, bases,
　partes iguales de un todo, 747–750, 753–756, 759–762, 765–768

G

Glosario, H1–H10

Gráficas de barras,
　cómo usar para resolver problemas, 671–674, 677–680, 683–686
　definición, 672
　hacer, 677–680, 683–686
　leer, 671–674

Gráficas y tablas
　diagramas de puntos, 589–592
　gráficas de barras
　　definición, 672
　　hacer, 677–680, 683–686
　　leer, 671–674
　　usar para resolver problemas, 671–674, 677–680, 683–686
　pictografía
　　definición, 660
　　hacer, 665–667
　　leer, 659–662
　　usar para resolver problemas, 659–662, 665–667, 671
　tablas de conteo, 653–656, 659, 666–667

Grupos iguales, 20–22, 217–220, 223–226

H

Hacer conexiones, 34, 46, 189, 220, 246, 374, 476, 512, 708, 714, 738, 750

Haz otro problema, 50, 136, 218, 286, 366, 422, 504, 566, 622, 684, 766

Hexágonos, 723–726, 730–731

J

Juegos
　Baraja de dos dígitos, 390
　Búsqueda de restas, 316
　Conteo de 5 y de 10, 466
　¿Cuál es la suma?, 236
　Cuenta los lados, 704
　En busca de la oruga, 162
　Estimar la longitud, 602
　Formar decenas, 652
　¿Más corto o más largo?, 540
　Pesca de dígitos, 74
　Tres en línea 12

Lados, 723–726, 637–732, 735–738

Longitud
cómo elegir herramientas para medir, 583–586
comparación, 639–642
datos presentados en diagramas de puntos, 589–592, 686
en metros, 627–630, 633–636
en pies, 571–574, 577–580
en pulgadas, 541–544, 547–550, 553, 559–562, 565–567, 571–574
estimación, 553–556, 577–580, 609–612, 633–636
relación inversa entre el tamaño de las unidades y el número de unidades necesarias para medir, 571–574, 627–630
sumar y restar, 565–567, 621–623

Manos a la obra, actividades. *Ver* Actividades

Manos a la obra, lecciones, 13–16, 87–90, 485–488, 541–544, 547–550, 559–562, 571–574, 603–606, 615–618, 627–630, 639–642, 741–743

Más al detalle, 46, 96, 101, 126, 132, 166, 172, 178, 202, 207, 214, 226, 240, 270, 288, 306, 325, 331, 349, 356, 368, 373, 380, 400, 412, 442, 482, 500, 530, 629, 655, 662, 667, 673, 680, 686, 713, 714, 720, 725, 756, 768

Matemáticas al instante, 16, 21, 27, 33, 39, 45, 51, 63, 77, 83, 95, 120, 125, 144, 165, 166, 171, 177, 184, 190, 195, 201, 207, 213, 219, 226, 239, 245, 251, 257, 258, 263, 269, 275, 281, 287, 293, 299, 305, 319, 325, 332, 338, 343, 349, 355, 361, 367, 373, 380, 393, 399, 405, 412, 417, 303, 423, 429, 436, 441, 447, 448, 327, 469, 470, 475, 487, 493, 499, 505, 511, 518, 524, 529, 391, 544, 550, 555, 562, 567, 574, 580, 586, 592, 606, 612, 618, 623, 630, 636, 641, 642, 656, 661, 667, 673, 679, 685, 686, 707, 713, 719, 726, 731, 737, 743, 749, 750, 756, 762, 767

Materiales y objetos manipulativos
bloques de base diez, 31, 43, 87–90, 135–138, 237, 255, 261, 335, 403, 409, 421–424, 427
bloques de patrones, 735, 747
cinta métrica, 584–586
cubos de una unidad 603–606, 615, 717–720
cubos interconectables, 13–14, 19, 653, 665
dinero de juguete, 467, 473, 479, 485–488, 503–506
fichas cuadradas de colores, 541–543, 548, 741–743
fichas cuadradas de dos colores, 217–220, 223
regla de 1 yarda, 584–585
reglas en centímetros, 615–618, 628–630, 639–642
reglas en pulgadas, 560–562, 572–574, 577–580, 584–585, 589–592

Medianoche, 528

Medición. *Ver* Longitud

Mediodía, 528, 530

Metros, 627–630, 633–636

Millares, 99–102

Minutos, 510–512, 515–518, 521–524

Mitades, 747–750, 753–756, 759–762, 765–768

Modelos de barras
problemas de resta, 205–208, 365–368, 377–380
problemas de suma, 187–188, 205–208, 285–288, 291, 377–380
problemas de varios pasos, 377–380

Monedas
contar colecciones, 467–470, 479–482, 485–488
monedas de 1¢, 467–470, 473–476, 479–482, 485–488, 491–493, 497–500, 503–506
monedas de 5¢, 467–470, 473–476, 479–482, 485–488, 491–493, 497–500, 503–506

Índice **H15**

monedas de 10¢, 467–470, 473–476, 479–482, 485–488, 491–493, 497–498, 503–506

monedas de 25¢, 473–476, 479–482, 485–488, 492–493, 497–500

signo de centavo (¢), 468–470, 473–476, 479–482, 485–488, 491, 497

Muestra lo que sabes, 10, 72, 160, 234, 314, 388, 464, 538, 600, 650, 702

Números
clasifica como pares o impares, 13–16
comparar, 135–138, 141–144
diferentes formas de, 111–113
diferentes maneras de escribir, 37–40, 105–108, 117–120
en patrones, 49–52, 55–58, 61–64, 129–132, 195
forma desarrollada, 31–34, 37–39, 93–96, 111–113
representar de distintas maneras, 43–46, 117–120
valor posicional y, 25–28, 81–84, 87–90, 93–96, 99–102, 105–108, 111–113, 117–120, 123–126

Números de dos dígitos
componer y descomponer, 43–46, 49–52
distintas maneras de representar, 31–34, 37–39, 43–46, 49–52
forma desarrollada, 31–34
forma escrita, 37–39
patrones de conteo, 55–58
resta, 317–320, 323–326, 329–332, 335–338, 341–344, 347–349, 353–356, 359–362, 365–368, 371–374, 377–380
suma, 237–240, 243–246, 249–252, 255–258, 261–264, 267–270, 273–275, 279–282, 285–288, 291–294, 297–300, 303–306
valor posicional, 25–28, 31–34, 37–40, 43–46

Números de tres dígitos
comparar, 135–138, 141–144
componer y descomponer, 117–120

diferentes formas, 111–113
forma desarrollada, 93–96, 111–113
forma escrita, 105–108, 111–113
patrones de conteo, 61–64, 123–126, 129–132
representar con dibujos rápidos, 87–90, 93, 99, 117, 123, 391–394, 397, 403, 409, 415, 421–424, 427, 433, 439
resta, 421–424, 427–430, 433–436, 439–442, 445–448
suma, 391–394, 397–400, 403–406, 409–412, 415–417
valor posicional, 81–84, 87–90, 93–96, 99–102, 111–113, 123–126, 141–144

Números impares, 13–16, 19, 21

Números pares
como suma de dos sumandos iguales, 19–22
definición, 14
representar y clasificar, 13–16

Operaciones básicas, 163–166, 169–172, 175–178, 181–184, 187–190, 193–195, 199–202, 205–208, 211–214

Operaciones con dobles y casi dobles, 163–166

Orden de sumandos, 169–172, 181–184, 297–300, 303–306

Organizadores gráficos, 11, 73, 161, 235, 315, 389, 465, 539, 601, 651, 703

p. m., 527–530

Para el maestro
En la mayoría de las lecciones de la Edición para el estudiante. Algunos ejemplos son: 13, 37, 359, 409, 633, 705

Partes iguales de un todo, 747–750, 753–756, 759–762, 765–768

Participación de la familia
Actividad para la casa, 16, 22, 28, 34, 39, 46, 52, 58, 64, 78, 84, 90, 96, 102, 108, 113, 120, 126, 132, 138, 144, 166, 172, 178, 184, 190, 195, 202, 208, 214, 220, 226, 240, 246, 252, 258, 264, 270, 275, 282, 288, 294, 300, 306, 320, 326, 332, 338, 344, 349, 356, 362, 368, 374, 380, 394, 400, 406, 412, 417, 304, 424, 430, 436, 442, 448, 328, 470, 476, 482, 488, 493, 500, 506, 512, 518, 524, 530, 392, 544, 550, 556, 562, 574, 580, 586, 592, 606, 612, 618, 630, 636, 642, 656, 662, 667, 674, 680, 686, 708, 714, 720, 726, 732, 738, 743, 750, 756, 762, 768

Patrones de conteo
hasta 100, 55–58
hasta 1,000, 61–64, 128–132

Patrones numéricos, 49–52, 55–58, 61–64, 129–132, 195

Pentágonos, 724–726, 730–732, 736, 738

Pictografía, 660
cómo hacer, 665–667
leer, 659–662
usar para resolver problemas, 659–662, 665–667, 671

Piensa como matemático, 9, 71, 159, 233, 313, 387, 463, 537, 599, 649, 701

Piensa más, 16, 21, 22, 27, 28, 33, 34, 39, 40, 45, 46, 51, 52, 57, 58, 63, 64, 77, 78, 83, 84, 90, 95, 96, 102, 107, 108, 113, 120, 125, 126, 131, 132, 138, 144, 165, 166, 171, 172, 177, 178, 184, 190, 195, 201, 202, 207, 213, 214, 219, 220, 226, 239, 240, 245, 246, 251, 257, 258, 263, 264, 269, 270, 275, 276, 281, 282, 287, 288, 293, 294, 299, 300, 305, 306, 319, 320, 325, 326, 332, 338, 343, 344, 349, 350, 355, 356, 361, 362, 367, 368, 373, 374, 380, 393, 394, 399, 400, 405, 406, 412, 417, 423, 424, 429, 430, 436, 441, 442, 327, 328, 469, 470, 475, 476, 482, 487, 488, 493, 499, 500, 505, 506, 511, 512, 518, 524, 529, 530, 544, 550, 555, 556, 562, 567, 574, 580, 586, 592, 606, 612, 618, 623, 630, 636, 641, 642, 656, 661, 662, 667, 673, 674, 679, 680, 685, 686, 707, 708, 713, 714, 719, 720, 726, 731, 732, 737, 738, 743, 744, 749, 750, 756, 762, 767, 768

Piensa más +, 22, 52, 102, 144, 172, 1256, 252, 264, 332, 344, 394, 430, 500, 530, 544, 586, 606, 642, 680, 686, 720, 750

Pies, 571–574, 577–580

Pon atención a la precisión, 411

Por tu cuenta
Por tu cuenta aparece en cada lección de la Edición para el estudiante. Algunos ejemplos son: 15, 183, 349, 549, 673, 737

Prácticas matemáticas
MP1 Entienden problemas y perseveran en resolverlos 49, 193, 205, 211, 217, 273, 285, 291, 365, 371, 377, 421, 503, 565, 621, 659, 665, 671, 683, 765

MP2 Razonan de manera abstracta y cuantitativa 135, 187, 211, 285, 291, 365, 371, 377, 389, 565, 621, 639, 659, 671

MP3 Construyen argumentos viables y critican el razonamiento de otros 13, 19, 55, 117, 267, 347, 371, 677, 683

MP4 Realizan modelos matemáticos 31, 49, 87, 135, 205, 211, 223, 237, 243, 261, 285, 291, 335, 365, 371, 377, 421, 479, 485, 491, 497, 503, 565, 589, 621, 639, 653, 665, 677, 683, 717, 723, 729, 735, 759, 765

MP5 Utilizan estratégicamente las herramientas adecuadas 199, 217, 255, 317, 323, 329, 359, 391, 541, 547, 559, 571, 583, 589, 603, 615, 627, 711, 741, 753

MP6 Ponen atención a la precisión 25, 37, 43, 75, 99, 117, 141, 181, 223, 237, 243, 249, 267, 279, 297, 303, 341, 353, 391, 397, 403, 409, 415, 427, 439, 445, 467, 473, 509, 517, 521, 527, 389, 541, 547, 553, 559, 571, 577, 589, 603, 609, 615, 627,

Índice **H17**

633, 654, 659, 665, 671, 677, 705, 711, 729, 735, 747, 753, 759, 765

MP7 Buscan y utilizan estructuras 3, 19, 43, 49, 55, 61, 75, 81, 87, 93, 99, 105, 111, 117, 123, 129, 163, 169, 175, 187, 217, 255, 261, 273, 279, 329, 347, 353, 467, 473, 491, 497, 503, 527, 389, 553, 571, 577, 609, 627, 633, 723, 729

MP8 Buscan y expresan regularidad en razonamientos repetitivos 19, 43, 75, 81, 93, 141, 169, 175, 181, 187, 199, 249, 267, 297, 303, 317, 323, 341, 359, 397, 403, 409, 415, 301, 427, 433, 439, 445, 479, 485, 509, 515, 521, 541, 583, 603, 741, 747

Pregunta esencial
Pregunta esencial aparece en cada lección de la Edición para el estudiante. Algunos ejemplos son: 13, 181, 329, 553, 671, 711

Preparación para la prueba
Repaso y prueba del capítulo, 67–70, 147–150, 229–232, 309–312, 383–386, 451–454, 533–536, 595–598, 645–648, 689–692, 771–774
Revisión de la mitad del capítulo, 40, 114, 196, 276, 350, 418, 494, 568, 624, 668, 744

Prismas rectangulares
caras, aristas y vértices, 711–714
identificar y describir, 705–708, 717

Problemas, 1–8, 151–158, 455–461, 693–700; *Ver* Resolución de problemas, Tipos de problemas

Problemas de varios pasos, 126, 131, 184, 190, 214, 288, 293, 319, 377–380, 405, 412, 436, 679, 680

Propiedades de la suma,
agrupar sumandos de distintas maneras, 181–184, 297–300, 303–306
sumar cero, 170–171
sumar en cualquier orden, 169–172

Pulgadas, 541–543, 547–550, 553–556, 559–562, 565–567, 571–574, 589–592

Punto decimal
en cantidades de dinero, 492–493, 498–500, 503–506

Reagrupar,
en una resta, 329–332, 335–338, 341–344, 347–349, 353–356, 427–430, 433–436, 439–442, 445–448
en una suma, 255–258, 261–264, 267–270, 273–275, 280–282, 297–300, 303–306, 403–406, 409–412, 415–417

Recta numérica, 199–201, 318–319, 323–325, 360–362, 374, 565–567, 621–623

Rectángulos, 729, 731, 736–738
dividen en filas y columnas, 741–743
partes iguales de, 748–750, 753–756, 759–762, 765–768

Regla de una yarda, 583–586

Relación inversa
entre el tamaño de las unidades y el número de unidades necesarias para medir, 571–574, 627–630
entre suma y resta, 187–190, 194

Relojes, 509–512, 515–518, 521–524, 527–530

Relojes analógicos, 509–512, 515–518, 521–524, 527–530

Relojes digitales, 510–512, 516–518, 521–524, 527–530

Repaso y prueba del capítulo, 67–70, 147–150, 229–232, 309–312, 383–386, 451–454, 533–536, 595–598, 645–648, 689–692, 771–774

Representa y dibuja
Representa y dibuja aparece en la mayoría de las lecciones de la Edición para el estudiante. Algunos ejemplos son: 14, 164, 342, 542, 660, 736

Resolución de problemas
　　Lecciones, 49–52, 135–138, 217–220, 285–288, 365–368, 421–424, 503–506, 565–568, 621–624, 683–686, 765–768
　　Problemas de varios pasos, 126, 131, 184, 190, 214, 288, 293, 319, 377–380, 405, 412, 436, 679, 680
　　Resolución de problemas en el mundo, 22, 34, 46, 49, 58, 64, 78, 84, 96, 102, 108, 120, 126, 132, 135, 144, 166, 172, 178, 184, 208, 214, 226, 240, 246, 252, 258, 264, 270, 282, 294, 300, 306, 320, 326, 332, 338, 344, 356, 362, 374, 380, 394, 400, 406, 412, 304, 430, 436, 442, 448, 328, 470, 476, 482, 488, 500, 512, 518, 524, 530, 392, 544, 550, 556, 562, 574, 580, 586, 592, 606, 612, 618, 630, 636, 642, 656, 662, 674, 680, 686, 708, 714, 720, 726, 732, 756
　　Resuelve el problema, 49, 135, 217, 285, 365, 421, 503, 565, 621, 683, 765

Ver también Tipos de problemas, problemas

Resta
　　escribe ecuaciones para representar problemas, 205–208, 211–214, 359, 365–368, 371–374
　　estrategia de separar, 317–320, 323–326
　　números de dos dígitos, 317–320, 323–326, 329–332, 335–338, 341–344, 347–349, 353–356, 359–362, 365–368, 371–374, 377–380
　　números de tres dígitos, 421–424, 427–430, 433–436, 439–442, 445–448
　　operaciones básicas, 187–190, 193–195, 199–202, 205–208, 211–214
　　reagrupar centenas, 433–436
　　reagrupar centenas y decenas, 439–442
　　reagrupar con ceros, 445–448
　　reagrupar decenas, 427–430

　　relacionar con la suma, 187–190
　　representada con modelos de barras, 87–188, 205–207, 211, 365–368, 377–380
　　usar la recta numérica, 199–202, 318–320, 323–326, 359–362
　　usar modelos y dibujos rápidos, 329–332, 335–338, 341, 421–424, 427, 433, 439

Ver también Resolución de problemas; Tipos de problemas, problemas

Revisión de la mitad del capítulo, 40, 114, 196, 276, 350, 418, 494, 568, 624, 668, 744

Símbolo de centavo, 468–470, 473–476, 479–482, 485–488, 491, 497

Símbolo de dólar, 492–493, 497–500, 503–506

Soluciona el problema, 49, 135, 217, 285, 365, 421, 503, 565, 621, 683, 765

Suma
　　de grupos iguales, 217–220, 223–226
　　escribir ecuaciones para representar problemas, 205–208, 211–214, 285–288, 291–294
　　estrategias de operaciones básicas
　　　forma una decena, 175–178, 182–184
　　　operaciones con dobles y casi dobles, 163–166
　　　usa operaciones relacionadas, 187–190
　　números de dos dígitos, 237–240, 243–246, 249–252, 255–258, 261–264, 267–270, 273–275, 279–282, 285–288, 291–294, 297–300, 303–306
　　hallar sumas de 3 números de dos dígitos, 297–300
　　hallar sumas de 4 números de dos dígitos, 303–306
　　separar sumandos para sumar, 237–240, 249–252

Índice **H19**

números de tres dígitos, 391–394, 397–400, 403–406, 409–412, 415–417
reagrupar, 403–406, 409–412, 415–417
separar para sumar, 397–400
operaciones básicas, 163–166, 169–172, 175–178, 181–184, 187–190, 211–214
para hallar diferencias, 187–189, 359–362
reagrupar en, 255–258, 261–264, 267–270, 273–275, 280–282, 297–300, 303–306, 403–406, 409–412, 415–417
relación con la resta, 187–190, 359–362
representada con modelos de barras, 187–188, 205–208, 285–288, 377–380
separar sumandos para sumar, 176–177, 237–240, 249–252, 397–400
sumar tres sumandos de 1 dígito, 181–184
usar la compensación, 243–246
usar modelos y dibujos rápidos, 237–238, 243, 255–258, 261–264, 267, 329, 335–338, 341, 391–394, 397, 403, 409, 419, 421, 427

Sumandos
definición, 170
desconocidos, 183, 194, 212–214, 232, 285–287, 292–293, 300, 305, 309, 371–373, 622–623, 648
orden de, 169–172, 181–184, 297–300, 303–306
que faltan, Ver Sumandos, desconocidos
separar para sumar, 176–177, 237–240, 249–252, 397–400
suma 3 de dos dígitos, 297–300
suma 3 de un dígito, 181–184
suma 4 de dos dígitos, 303–306

Tabla con los números hasta el 100, 10, 55
Tablas de conteo, 653–656, 659, 666–667

Tercios, 747–750, 753–756, 759–762, 561–768
Tiempo
a. m. y p. m., 527–530
decir la hora, 509–512, 515–518, 521–524, 527–530
mediodía y medianoche, 528
relojes
analógicos, 509–512, 515–518, 521–524, 527–530
digitales, 510–512, 516–518, 521–523, 527–529
Tipos de problemas, para problemas
Compara
Diferencia desconocida, 190, 206–208, 214, 231, 232, 326, 338, 356, 366–367, 372, 384–386, 412, 423, 439, 648, 654–656, 659–662, 672, 674, 680
Lo más desconocido, 343, 642
Lo menos desconocido, 319, 332, 367, 447, 612
Juntar/Separar
Los dos sumandos desconocidos, 246, 264, 282, 311, 380, 448, 606, 662, 768
Suma desconocida, 152, 156, 166, 169, 172, 175, 178, 184, 187, 190, 193, 196, 205, 207–208, 212–214, 230, 233, 237, 240, 246, 252, 255, 258, 261, 264, 267, 273–274, 276, 282, 287–288, 292–294, 297, 300, 303, 306, 310–312, 326, 356, 377, 379, 385, 387, 394, 400, 403, 406, 409, 412, 415, 418, 434–436, 452, 566–567, 595, 598, 622, 636, 655–656, 661–662, 671–674, 677, 680, 692
Sumando desconocido, 155, 184, 208, 212–213, 232, 252, 286–287, 292, 332, 347, 367, 374, 385–386, 422, 430, 433, 442, 448, 692
Quitar
Cambio desconocido, 187, 213, 320, 326, 371, 373, 427, 430
Inicio desconocido, 338, 373, 424
Resultado desconocido, 159, 187, 190, 199, 205–207, 212, 229, 313, 320, 323, 329, 332, 335, 338,

341, 344, 348, 350, 353, 359, 362, 365, 367–368, 372, 379, 384–386, 394, 421, 423–424, 430, 433, 436, 445–446, 453, 565–567, 621–623, 642

Suma
Cambio desconocido, 285, 378
Inicio desconocido, 213, 293
Resultado desconocido, 153, 154, 163, 172, 178, 184, 214, 230, 237, 243, 252, 264, 270, 279, 286–288, 291, 300, 306, 310, 320, 326, 359, 368, 377, 379–380, 391, 623, 674

Triángulos, 723–726, 729–732, 735–738, 551–750, 753

Unidades de medida. Ver Longitud
Usa diagramas, 726, 732, 768
Usa el razonamiento, 22, 143, 213, 327, 544
Usa gráficas, 661
Usa modelos, 470, 517

Valor posicional,
comparar números usando, 141–144
en estimación, 141–144
números de 2-dígitos, 25–28, 31–34, 37–39, 43–46
números de 3-dígitos, 75–78, 81–84, 87–90, 93–96, 99–102, 105–108, 111–113, 117–120, 123–126
y patrones de conteo, 123–126, 129–132

Verifica el razonamiento de otros, 270
Vértice/Vértices, 711–714, 723–726
Vocabulario
Desarrollo del vocabulario, 11, 73, 161, 235, 315, 389, 465, 539, 601, 651, 703
Juego de vocabulario, 12A, 74A, 162A, 236A, 316A, 390A, 466A, 540A, 602A, 652A, 704A
Repaso del vocabulario, 11, 73, 157, 161, 235, 315, 389, 461, 465, 539, 601, 651, 703
Tarjetas de vocabulario del capítulo, Al inicio de cada capítulo.